GOTHIC

SCIENCE FICTION

SHORT STORIES

ANTHOLOGY OF NEW & CLASSIC TALES

Foreword by Andy Sawyer

FLAME TREE PUBLISHING

FANTASY

This is a FLAME TREE Book

Publisher & Creative Director: Nick Wells
Project Editor: Laura Bulbeck
Editorial Board: Frances Bodiam, Josie Mitchell, Gillian Whitaker

With special thanks to Amanda Crook, Kaiti Porter

Publisher's Note: Due to the historical nature of the text, we're aware that there may be some language used which has the potential to cause offence to the modern reader. However, wishing overall to preserve the integrity of the text, rather than imposing contemporary sensibilities, we have left it unaltered.

FLAME TREE PUBLISHING
6 Melbray Mews, Fulham,
London SW6 3NS, United Kingdom
www.flametreepublishing.com

First published 2015

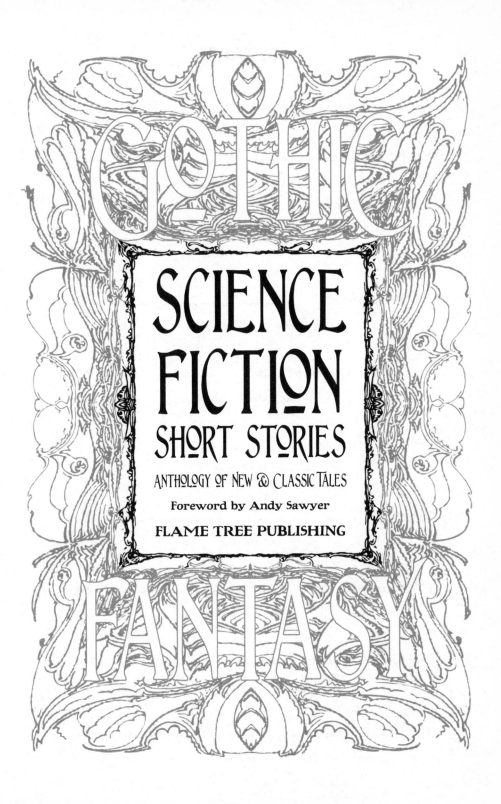

GOTHIC

SCIENCE FICTION

SHORT STORIES

ANTHOLOGY OF NEW & CLASSIC TALES

Foreword by Andy Sawyer

FLAME TREE PUBLISHING

FANTASY

Contents

Foreword:
Science Fiction Short Stories

THE WRITER AND CRITIC DAMON KNIGHT once remarked that 'science fiction is ... what we point to when we say it.' One of the interesting things about science fiction (SF) is watching the way it crystallises in the hands of people we don't really think of as SF writers, such as Mark Twain, whose 'Captain Stormfield's Visit to Heaven' (1907) ends as a satirical fantasy about religion but begins as a glorious prefiguration of what we now call Steampunk; or E.M. Forster, whose dystopian tale 'The Machine Stops' (1909) is an answer to the rigorously planned future which H.G. Wells agitated for in his political writings. There is clearly another echo of Wells in Jack London's 'The Shadow and the Flash' (1903), which reflects *The Invisible Man*, published in 1897; though London has not one but *two* 'invisible men', each with their rival theories about how to achieve invisibility.

Forster may have warned us against too close a trust in the future, but Jules Verne (or rather, his son Michel, who drew upon his father's unpublished speculations) stands wide-eyed in wonder at the marvels available at the push of a button in the 29th century, although he cannot resist a sly dig at contemporary newspaper tycoons and imperial rivalries. One of SF's roots is certainly an obsession with the mystery of understanding the world, but while Verne anticipates the future, H. Rider Haggard, better known for 'lost race' romances such as *She* (1887), speculated about history, identity, and the transmigration of souls. 'Smith and the Pharoahs' (1921) shows an ordinary clerk finding his links to the mysterious world of ancient Egypt. In contrast, the detection in Arthur B. Reeve's 'The Invisible Ray' (1912) centres upon new discoveries about the nature of matter, particularly the spectrum of 'rays', vibrations and radioactivity. Edwin A. Abbott's *Flatland* (published in 1884, it is both an amusing social satire *and* one of the great explorations of the idea of 'other dimensions'), and Edward Payne Mitchell's 'The Tachypomp' (1874) draw upon the paradoxes thrown up by mathematics. Mitchell's version of a *very* old story (the lover set an impossible task to win a fair lady's hand) shows science fiction forming even as we read it. Arthur Conan Doyle's irascible Professor Challenger is one of the great scientist-heroes of the early years of SF, but defeats the inventor of 'The Disintegration Machine' (1929) through a trick made more amusing by its slapstick simplicity. Edgar Wallace, once an immensely popular thriller writer, wrote what we would now call SF on numerous occasions, including the original script for *King Kong* (1933). His 'Planetoid 127' (1926) shares with Ray Cummings' 'Phantoms of Reality' (1930) the idea of a world almost identical to ours but separated by 'dimension' or time.

Could the different treatment of these two stories be explained by the fact that the more action-packed version by Cummings appeared in one of the American 'pulp' magazines, now dedicated to a named, specialist genre called 'science fiction' and aimed at an unsophisticated market seeking for thrills? There are thrills aplenty in Philip Francis Nowlan's *Armageddon 2419 AD* (1928), with its colourful gadgetry and gung-ho Americans resisting invasion. The pulps were the natural home for authors such as Stanley G. Weinbaum, H. Beam Piper, and Henry Kuttner whose work brought an increasing sophistication to the field. Weinbaum's title 'The Worlds of If' (1935) could almost be a definition of SF, and its version of the parallel-world tale comes with an engaging, silly narrator. H. Beam Piper's time-shift story offers its hero (and his war-torn world) a second chance, while Kuttner's harried scriptwriter is offered multiple personalities by a time-travelling robot. Once more, futures and parallel worlds add a distorted reflection to the foibles and obsessions of the present.

These stories form a fascinating background to a vein of writing which, after over a century, still shows no sign of wearing out. The new writers here respond enthusiastically to SF's visions of new frontiers, technologies and futures – here's to another century and more of SF!

Andy Sawyer, 2015

Publisher's Note

THIS COLLECTION of Gothic Fantasy stories is part of a new anthology series, which includes sumptuous hardcover editions on Horror, Ghosts and Science Fiction. Each one carries a potent mix of classic tales and new fiction, forming a path from the origins of the gothic in the early 1800s, with the dystopian horror of Mary Shelley's 'The Mortal Immortal' to the chill of M.R. James's classic ghost stories, and the fine stories of the many modern writers featured in our new series. We have tried to mix some renowned classic stories (Edgar Allan Poe's 'The Black Cat'), with the less familiar (E.M. Forster's 'The Machine Stops'), and a healthy dose of previously unpublished modern stories from the best of those writing today.

Our 2015 call for new submissions was met by a tidal wave of entries, so the final selection was made to provide a wide and challenging range of tales for the discerning reader. Our editorial board of six members read each entry carefully, and it was difficult to turn down so many good stories, but inevitably those which made the final cut were deemed to be the best for our purpose, and we're delighted to publish them here.

GOTHIC

SCIENCE FICTION

SHORT STORIES

ANTHOLOGY OF NEW & CLASSIC TALES

Foreword by Andy Sawyer

FLAME TREE PUBLISHING

FANTASY

Flatland

Edwin A. Abbott

Part I: This World

Section 1: Of the Nature of Flatland

I CALL our world Flatland, not because we call it so, but to make its nature clearer to you, my happy readers, who are privileged to live in Space.

Imagine a vast sheet of paper on which straight Lines, Triangles, Squares, Pentagons, Hexagons, and other figures, instead of remaining fixed in their places, move freely about, on or in the surface, but without the power of rising above or sinking below it, very much like shadows – only hard with luminous edges – and you will then have a pretty correct notion of my country and countrymen. Alas, a few years ago, I should have said "my universe:" but now my mind has been opened to higher views of things.

In such a country, you will perceive at once that it is impossible that there should be anything of what you call a "solid" kind; but I dare say you will suppose that we could at least distinguish by sight the Triangles, Squares, and other figures, moving about as I have described them. On the contrary, we could see nothing of the kind, not at least so as to distinguish one figure from another. Nothing was visible, nor could be visible, to us, except Straight Lines; and the necessity of this I will speedily demonstrate.

Place a penny on the middle of one of your tables in Space; and leaning over it, look down upon it. It will appear a circle.

But now, drawing back to the edge of the table, gradually lower your eye (thus bringing yourself more and more into the condition of the inhabitants of Flatland), and you will find the penny becoming more and more oval to your view, and at last when you have placed your eye exactly on the edge of the table (so that you are, as it were, actually a Flatlander) the penny will then have ceased to appear oval at all, and will have become, so far as you can see, a straight line.

The same thing would happen if you were to treat in the same way a Triangle, or a Square, or any other figure cut out from pasteboard. As soon as you look at it with your eye on the edge of the table, you will find that it ceases to appear to you as a figure, and that it becomes in appearance a straight line. Take for example an equilateral Triangle – who represents with us a Tradesman of the respectable class. Figure 1 represents the Tradesman as you would see him while you were bending over him from above; figures 2 and 3 represent the Tradesman, as you would see him if your eye were close to the level, or all but on the level of the table; and if your eye were quite on the level of the table (and that is how we see him in Flatland) you would see nothing but a straight line.

When I was in Spaceland I heard that your sailors have very similar experiences while they traverse your seas and discern some distant island or coast lying on the horizon. The far-off land may have bays, forelands, angles in and out to any number and extent; yet at a distance you see none of these (unless indeed your sun shines bright upon them revealing the projections and retirements by means of light and shade), nothing but a grey unbroken line upon the water.

Well, that is just what we see when one of our triangular or other acquaintances comes towards us in Flatland. As there is neither sun with us, nor any light of such a kind as to make shadows, we have none of the helps to the sight that you have in Spaceland. If our friend comes closer to us we see his line becomes larger; if he leaves us it becomes smaller; but still he looks like a straight line; be he a Triangle, Square, Pentagon, Hexagon, Circle, what you will – a straight Line he looks and nothing else.

You may perhaps ask how under these disadvantageous circumstances we are able to distinguish our friends from one another: but the answer to this very natural question will be more fitly and easily given when I come to describe the inhabitants of Flatland. For the present let me defer this subject, and say a word or two about the climate and houses in our country.

Section 2: Of the Climate and Houses in Flatland

AS WITH YOU, so also with us, there are four points of the compass: North, South, East, and West.

There being no sun nor other heavenly bodies, it is impossible for us to determine the North in the usual way; but we have a method of our own. By a Law of Nature with us, there is a constant attraction to the South; and, although in temperate climates this is very slight – so that even a Woman in reasonable health can journey several furlongs northward without much difficulty – yet the hampering effort of the southward attraction is quite sufficient to serve as a compass in most parts of our earth. Moreover, the rain (which falls at stated intervals) coming always from the North, is an additional assistance; and in the towns we have the guidance of the houses, which of course have their side-walls running for the most part North and South, so that the roofs may keep off the rain from the North. In the country, where there are no houses, the trunks of the trees serve as some sort of guide. Altogether, we have not so much difficulty as might be expected in determining our bearings.

Yet in our more temperate regions, in which the southward attraction is hardly felt, walking sometimes in a perfectly desolate plain where there have been no houses nor trees to guide me, I have been occasionally compelled to remain stationary for hours together, waiting till the rain came before continuing my journey. On the weak and aged, and especially on delicate Females, the force of attraction tells much more heavily than on the robust of the Male Sex, so that it is a point of breeding, if you meet a Lady on the street, always to give her the North side of the way – by no means an easy thing to do always at short notice when you are in rude health and in a climate where it is difficult to tell your North from your South.

Windows there are none in our houses: for the light comes to us alike in our homes and out of them, by day and by night, equally at all times and in all places, whence we know not. It was in old days, with our learned men, an interesting and oft-investigate question, "What is the origin of light?" and the solution of it has been repeatedly attempted, with no other result than to crowd our lunatic asylums with the would-be solvers. Hence, after fruitless attempts to suppress such investigations indirectly by making them liable to a heavy tax, the Legislature, in comparatively recent times, absolutely prohibited them. I – alas, I alone in Flatland – know now only too well the true solution of this mysterious problem; but my knowledge cannot be made intelligible to a single one of my countrymen; and I am mocked at – I, the sole possessor of the truths of Space and of the theory of the introduction of Light from the world of three Dimensions – as if I were the maddest of the mad! But a truce to these painful digressions: let me return to our homes.

The most common form for the construction of a house is five-sided or pentagonal, as in the annexed figure. The two Northern sides RO, OF, constitute the roof, and for the most part have no doors; on the East is a small door for the Women; on the West a much larger one for the Men; the South side or floor is usually doorless.

Square and triangular houses are not allowed, and for this reason. The angles of a Square (and still more those of an equilateral Triangle,) being much more pointed than those of a Pentagon, and the lines of inanimate objects (such as houses) being dimmer than the lines of Men and Women, it follows that there is no little danger lest the points of a square of triangular house residence might do serious injury to an inconsiderate or perhaps absentminded traveller suddenly running against them: and therefore, as early as the eleventh century of our era, triangular houses were universally forbidden by Law, the only exceptions being fortifications, powder-magazines, barracks, and other state buildings, which is not desirable that the general public should approach without circumspection.

At this period, square houses were still everywhere permitted, though discouraged by a special tax. But, about three centuries afterwards, the Law decided that in all towns containing a population above ten thousand, the angle of a Pentagon was the smallest house-angle that could be allowed consistently with the public safety. The good sense of the community has seconded the efforts of the Legislature; and now, even in the country, the pentagonal construction has superseded every other. It is only now and then in some very remote and backward agricultural district that an antiquarian may still discover a square house.

Section 3: Concerning the Inhabitants of Flatland

THE GREATEST LENGTH or breadth of a full grown inhabitant of Flatland may be estimated at about eleven of your inches. Twelve inches may be regarded as a maximum.

Our Women are Straight Lines.

Our Soldiers and Lowest Class of Workmen are Triangles with two equal sides, each about eleven inches long, and a base or third side so short (often not exceeding half an inch) that they form at their vertices a very sharp and formidable angle. Indeed when their bases are of the most degraded type (not more than the eighth part of an inch in size), they can hardly be distinguished from Straight lines or Women; so extremely pointed are their vertices. With us, as with you, these Triangles are distinguished from others by being called Isosceles; and by this name I shall refer to them in the following pages.

Our Middle Class consists of Equilateral or Equal-Sided Triangles.

Our Professional Men and Gentlemen are Squares (to which class I myself belong) and Five-Sided Figures or Pentagons.

Next above these come the Nobility, of whom there are several degrees, beginning at Six-Sided Figures, or Hexagons, and from thence rising in the number of their sides till they receive the honourable title of Polygonal, or many-Sided. Finally when the number of the sides becomes so numerous, and the sides themselves so small, that the figure cannot be distinguished from a circle, he is included in the Circular or Priestly order; and this is the highest class of all.

It is a Law of Nature with us that a male child shall have one more side than his father, so that each generation shall rise (as a rule) one step in the scale of development and nobility. Thus the son of a Square is a Pentagon; the son of a Pentagon, a Hexagon; and so on.

But this rule applies not always to the Tradesman, and still less often to the Soldiers, and to the Workmen; who indeed can hardly be said to deserve the name of human Figures, since they have not all their sides equal. With them therefore the Law of Nature does not hold; and the son of an Isosceles (i.e. a Triangle with two sides equal) remains Isosceles still. Nevertheless, all hope is not such out, even from the Isosceles, that his posterity may ultimately rise above his degraded condition. For, after a long series of military successes, or diligent and skillful labours, it is generally found that the more intelligent among the Artisan and Soldier classes manifest a slight increase of their third side or base, and a shrinkage of the two other sides. Intermarriages (arranged by the Priests) between the sons and daughters of these more intellectual members of the lower classes generally result in an offspring approximating still more to the type of the Equal-Sided Triangle.

Rarely – in proportion to the vast numbers of Isosceles births – is a genuine and certifiable Equal-Sided Triangle produced from Isosceles parents **(footnote 1)**. Such a birth requires, as its antecedents, not only a series of carefully arranged intermarriages, but also a long-continued exercise of frugality and self-control on the part of the would-be ancestors of the coming Equilateral, and a patient, systematic, and continuous development of the Isosceles intellect through many generations.

The birth of a True Equilateral Triangle from Isosceles parents is the subject of rejoicing in our country for many furlongs round. After a strict examination conducted by the Sanitary and Social Board, the infant, if certified as Regular, is with solemn ceremonial admitted into the class of Equilaterals. He is then immediately taken from his proud yet sorrowing parents and adopted by some childless Equilateral, who is bound by oath never to permit the child henceforth to enter his former home or so much as to look upon his relations again, for fear lest the freshly developed organism may, by force of unconscious imitation, fall back again into his hereditary level.

The occasional emergence of an Equilateral from the ranks of his serf-born ancestors is welcomed, not only by the poor serfs themselves, as a gleam of light and hope shed upon the monotonous squalor of their existence, but also by the Aristocracy at large; for all the higher classes are well aware that these rare phenomena, while they do little or nothing to vulgarize their own privileges, serve as almost useful barrier against revolution from below.

Had the acute-angled rabble been all, without exception, absolutely destitute of hope and of ambition, they might have found leaders in some of their many seditious outbreaks, so able as to render their superior numbers and strength too much even for the wisdom of the Circles. But a wise ordinance of Nature has decreed that in proportion as the working-classes increase in intelligence, knowledge, and all virtue, in that same proportion their acute angle (which makes them physically terrible) shall increase also and approximate to their comparatively harmless angle of the Equilateral Triangle. Thus, in the most brutal and formidable off the soldier class – creatures almost on a level with women in their lack of intelligence – it is found that, as they wax in the mental ability necessary to employ their tremendous penetrating power to advantage, so do they wane in the power of penetration itself.

How admirable is the Law of Compensation! And how perfect a proof of the natural fitness and, I may almost say, the divine origin of the aristocratic constitution of the States of Flatland! By a judicious use of this Law of Nature, the Polygons and Circles are almost always able to stifle sedition in its very cradle, taking advantage of the irrepressible and boundless hopefulness of the human mind. Art also comes to the aid of Law and Order. It is generally found possible – by a little artificial compression or expansion on the part of the State physicians – to make some of the more intelligent leaders of a rebellion perfectly Regular, and to admit them at once into the privileged classes; a much larger number, who are still below the standard, allured by the prospect of being ultimately ennobled, are induced to enter the State Hospitals, where they are kept in honourable confinement for life; one or two alone of the most obstinate, foolish, and hopelessly irregular are led to execution.

Then the wretched rabble of the Isosceles, planless and leaderless, are either transfixed without resistance by the small body of their brethren whom the Chief Circle keeps in pay for emergencies of this kind; or else more often, by means of jealousies and suspicious skillfully fomented among them by the Circular party, they are stirred to mutual warfare, and perish by one another's angles. No less than one hundred and twenty rebellions are recorded in our annals, besides minor outbreaks numbered at two hundred and thirty-five; and they have all ended thus.

Footnote 1. "What need of a certificate?" a Spaceland critic may ask: "Is not the procreation of a Square Son a certificate from Nature herself, proving the Equal-sidedness of the Father?" I reply that no Lady of any position will mary an uncertified Triangle. Square offspring has sometimes resulted from a slightly Irregular Triangle; but in almost every such case the Irregularity of the first generation is visited on the third; which either fails to attain the Pentagonal rank, or relapses to the Triangular.

Section 4: Concerning the Women

IF OUR highly pointed Triangles of the Soldier class are formidable, it may be readily inferred that far more formidable are our Women. For, if a Soldier is a wedge, a Woman is a needle; being, so to speak, ALL point, at least at the two extremities. Add to this the power of making herself practically invisible at will, and you will perceive that a Female, in Flatland, is a creature by no means to be trifled with.

But here, perhaps, some of my younger Readers may ask HOW a woman in Flatland can make herself invisible. This ought, I think, to be apparent without any explanation. However, a few words will make it clear to the most unreflecting.

Place a needle on the table. Then, with your eye on the level of the table, look at it sideways, and you see the whole length of it; but look at it end-ways, and you see nothing but a point, it has become practically invisible. Just so is it with one of our Women. When her side is turned towards us, we see her as a straight line; when the end containing her eye or mouth – for with us these two organs are identical – is the part that meets our eye, then we see nothing but a highly lustrous point; but when the back is presented to our view, then – being only sub-lustrous, and, indeed, almost as dim as an inanimate object – her hinder extremity serves her as a kind of Invisible Cap.

The dangers to which we are exposed from our Women must now be manifest to the meanest capacity of Spaceland. If even the angle of a respectable Triangle in the middle class is not without its dangers; if to run against a Working Man involves a gash; if collision with an Officer of the military class necessitates a serious wound; if a mere touch from the vertex of a Private Soldier brings with it danger of death; – what can it be to run against a woman, except absolute and immediate destruction? And when a Woman is invisible, or visible only as a dim sub-lustrous point, how difficult must it be, even for the most cautious, always to avoid collision!

Many are the enactments made at different times in the different States of Flatland, in order to minimize this peril; and in the Southern and less temperate climates, where the force of gravitation is greater, and human beings more liable to casual and involuntary motions, the Laws concerning Women are naturally much more stringent. But a general view of the Code may be obtained from the following summary:

1. Every house shall have one entrance on the Eastern side, for the use of Females only; by which all females shall enter "in a becoming and respectful manner" and not by the Men's or Western door.
2. No Female shall walk in any public place without continually keeping up her Peace-cry, under penalty of death.
3. Any Female, duly certified to be suffering from St. Vitus's Dance, fits, chronic cold accompanied by violent sneezing, or any disease necessitating involuntary motions, shall be instantly destroyed.

In some of the States there is an additional Law forbidding Females, under penalty of death, from walking or standing in any public place without moving their backs constantly from right to left so as to indicate their presence to those behind them; other oblige a Woman, when travelling, to be followed by one of her sons, or servants, or by her husband; others confine Women altogether in their houses except during the religious festivals. But it has been found by the wisest of our Circles or Statesmen that the multiplication of restrictions on Females tends not only to the debilitation and diminution of the race, but also to the increase of domestic murders to such an extent that a State loses more than it gains by a too prohibitive Code.

For whenever the temper of the Women is thus exasperated by confinement at home or hampering regulations abroad, they are apt to vent their spleen upon their husbands and children; and in the less temperate climates the whole male population of a village has been sometimes destroyed in one or two hours of a simultaneous female outbreak. Hence the Three Laws, mentioned above, suffice for the better regulated States, and may be accepted as a rough exemplification of our Female Code.

After all, our principal safeguard is found, not in Legislature, but in the interests of the Women themselves. For, although they can inflict instantaneous death by a retrograde movement, yet unless they can at once disengage their stinging extremity from the struggling body of their victim, their own frail bodies are liable to be shattered.

The power of Fashion is also on our side. I pointed out that in some less civilized States no female is suffered to stand in any public place without swaying her back from right to left. This practice has been universal among ladies of any pretensions to breeding in all well-governed States, as far back as the memory of Figures can reach. It is considered a disgrace to any state that legislation should have to enforce what ought to be, and is in every respectable female, a natural instinct. The rhythmical and, if I may so say, well-modulated undulation of the back in our ladies of Circular rank is envied and imitated by the wife of a common Equilateral, who can achieve nothing beyond a mere monotonous swing, like the ticking of a pendulum; and the regular tick of the Equilateral is no less admired and copied by the wife of the progressive and aspiring Isosceles, in the females of whose family no "back-motion" of any kind has become as yet a necessity of life. Hence, in every family of position and consideration, "back motion" is as prevalent as time itself; and the husbands and sons in these households enjoy immunity at least from invisible attacks.

Not that it must be for a moment supposed that our Women are destitute of affection. But unfortunately the passion of the moment predominates, in the Frail Sex, over every other consideration. This is, of course, a necessity arising from their unfortunate conformation. For as they have no pretensions to an angle, being inferior in this respect to the very lowest of the Isosceles, they are consequently wholly devoid of brainpower, and have neither reflection, judgment nor forethought, and hardly any memory. Hence, in their fits of fury, they remember no claims and recognize no distinctions. I have actually known a case where a Woman has exterminated her whole household, and half an hour afterwards, when her rage was over and the fragments swept away, has asked what has become of her husband and children.

Obviously then a Woman is not to be irritated as long as she is in a position where she can turn round. When you have them in their apartments – which are constructed with a view to denying them that power – you can say and do what you like; for they are then wholly impotent for mischief, and will not remember a few minutes hence the incident for which they may be at this moment threatening you with death, nor the promises which you may have found it necessary to make in order to pacify their fury.

On the whole we got on pretty smoothly in our domestic relations, except in the lower strata of the Military Classes. There the want of tact and discretion on the part of the husbands produces at times indescribable disasters. Relying too much on the offensive weapons of their acute angles instead of the defensive organs of good sense and seasonable simulations, these reckless creatures too often neglect the prescribed construction of the women's apartments, or irritate their wives by ill-advised expressions out of doors, which they refuse immediately to retract. Moreover a blunt and stolid regard for literal truth indisposes them to make those lavish promises by which the more judicious Circle can in a moment pacify his consort. The result is massacre; not, however, without its advantages, as it eliminates the more brutal and troublesome of the Isosceles; and by many of our Circles the destructiveness of the Thinner Sex is regarded as one among many providential arrangements for suppressing redundant population, and nipping Revolution in the bud.

Yet even in our best regulated and most approximately Circular families I cannot say that the ideal of family life is so high as with you in Spaceland. There is peace, in so far as the absence of slaughter may be called by that name, but there is necessarily little harmony of tastes or pursuits; and the cautious wisdom of the Circles has ensured safety at the cost of domestic comfort. In every Circular or Polygonal household it has been a habit from time immemorial – and now has become a kind of instinct among the women of our higher classes – that the mothers and daughters should constantly keep their eyes and mouths towards their husband and his male friends; and for a lady in a family of distinction to turn her back upon her husband would be regarded as a kind of portent, involving loss of status. But, as I shall soon shew, this custom, though it has the advantage of safety, is not without disadvantages.

In the house of the Working Man or respectable Tradesman – where the wife is allowed to turn her back upon her husband, while pursuing her household avocations – there are at least intervals of quiet, when the wife is neither seen nor heard, except for the humming sound of the continuous Peace-cry; but in the homes of the upper classes there is too often no peace. There the voluble mouth and bright penetrating eye are ever directed toward the Master of the household; and light itself is not more persistent than the stream of Feminine discourse. The tact and skill which suffice to avert a Woman's sting are unequal to the task of stopping a Woman's mouth; and as the wife has absolutely nothing to say, and absolutely no constraint of wit, sense, or conscience to prevent her from saying it, not a few cynics have been found to aver that they prefer the danger of the death-dealing but inaudible sting to the safe sonorousness of a Woman's other end.

To my readers in Spaceland the condition of our Women may seen truly deplorable, and so indeed it is. A Male of the lowest type of the Isosceles may look forward to some improvement of his angle, and to the ultimate elevation of the whole of his degraded caste; but no Woman can entertain such hopes for her sex. "Once a Woman, always a Woman" is a Decree of Nature; and the very Laws of Evolution seem suspended in her disfavour. Yet at least we can admire the wise Prearrangement which has ordained that, as they have no hopes, so they shall have no memory to recall, and no forethought to anticipate, the miseries and humiliations which are at once a necessity of their existence and the basis of the constitution of Flatland.

Section 5: Of Our Methods of Recognizing One Another

YOU, WHO ARE blessed with shade as well as light, you, who are gifted with two eyes, endowed with a knowledge of perspective, and charmed with the enjoyment of various colours, you, who can actually see an angle, and contemplate the complete circumference of a Circle in the happy region of the Three Dimensions – how shall I make it clear to you the extreme difficulty which we in Flatland experience in recognizing one another's configuration?

Recall what I told you above. All beings in Flatland, animate and inanimate, no matter what their form, present to our view the same, or nearly the same, appearance, viz. that of a straight Line. How then can one be distinguished from another, where all appear the same?

The answer is threefold. The first means of recognition is the sense of hearing; which with us is far more highly developed than with you, and which enables us not only to distinguish by the voice of our personal friends, but even to discriminate between different classes, at least so far as concerns the three lowest orders, the Equilateral, the Square, and the Pentagon – for the Isosceles I take no account. But as we ascend the social scale, the process of discriminating and being discriminated by hearing increases in difficulty, partly because voices are assimilated, partly because the faculty of voice-discrimination is a plebeian virtue not much developed among the Aristocracy. And wherever there is any danger of imposture we cannot trust to this method. Amongst our lowest orders, the vocal organs are developed to a degree more than correspondent with those of hearing, so that an Isosceles can easily feign the voice of a Polygon, and, with some training, that of a Circle himself. A second method is therefore more commonly resorted to.

Feeling is, among our Women and lower classes – about our upper classes I shall speak presently – the principal test of recognition, at all events between strangers, and when the question is, not as to the individual, but as to the class. What therefore "introduction" is among the higher classes in Spaceland, that the process of "feeling" is with us. "Permit me to ask you to feel and be felt by my friend Mr So-and-so" – is still, among the more old-fashioned of our country gentlemen in districts remote from towns, the customary formula for a Flatland introduction. But in the towns, and among men of business, the words "be felt by" are omitted and the sentence is abbreviated to, "Let me ask you to feel Mr So-and-so"; although it is assumed, of course, that the "feeling" is to be reciprocal. Among our still more modern and dashing young gentlemen – who are extremely averse to superfluous effort and supremely indifferent to the purity of their native language – the formula is still further curtailed by the use of "to feel" in a technical sense, meaning, "to recommend-for-the-purposes-of-feeling-and-being-felt"; and at this moment the "slang" of polite or fast society in the upper classes sanctions such a barbarism as "Mr Smith, permit me to feel Mr Jones."

Let not my Reader however suppose that "feeling" is with us the tedious process that it would be with you, or that we find it necessary to feel right round all the sides of every individual before we determine the class to which he belongs. Long practice and training, begun in the schools and continued in the experience of daily life, enable us to discriminate at once by the sense of touch, between the angles of an equal-sided Triangle, Square, and Pentagon; and I need not say that the brainless vertex of an acute-angled Isosceles is obvious to the dullest touch. It is therefore not necessary, as a rule, to do more than feel a single angle of an individual; and this, once ascertained, tells us the class of the person whom we are addressing, unless indeed he belongs to the higher sections of the nobility. There the difficulty is much greater. Even a Master of Arts in our University of Wentbridge has been known to confuse a ten-sided with a twelve-sided Polygon; and there is hardly a Doctor of Science in or out of that famous University who could pretend to decide promptly and unhesitatingly between a twenty-sided and a twenty-four sided member of the Aristocracy.

Those of my readers who recall the extracts I gave above from the Legislative code concerning Women, will readily perceive that the process of introduction by contact requires some care and discretion. Otherwise the angles might inflict on the unwary Feeling irreparable injury. It is essential for the safety of the Feeler that the Felt should stand perfectly still. A start, a fidgety shifting of the position, yes, even a violent sneeze, has been known before now to prove fatal to the incautious, and to nip in the bud many a promising friendship. Especially is this true among the lower classes of the Triangles. With them, the eye is situated so far from their vertex that they can scarcely take cognizance of what goes on at that extremity of their frame. They are, moreover, of a rough coarse nature, not sensitive to the delicate touch of the highly organized Polygon. What wonder then if an involuntary toss of the head has ere now deprived the State of a valuable life!

I have heard that my excellent Grandfather – one of the least irregular of his unhappy Isosceles class, who indeed obtained, shortly before his decease, four out of seven votes from the Sanitary and Social Board for passing him into the class of the Equal-sided – often deplored, with a tear in his venerable eye, a miscarriage of this kind, which had occurred to his great-great-great-Grandfather, a respectable Working Man with an angle or brain of 59 degrees 30 minutes. According to his account, my unfortunately Ancestor, being afflicted with rheumatism, and in the act of being felt by a Polygon, by one sudden start accidentally transfixed the Great Man through the diagonal and thereby, partly in consequence of his long imprisonment and degradation, and partly because of the moral shock which pervaded the whole of my Ancestor's relations, threw back our family a degree and a half in their ascent towards better things. The result was that in the next generation the family brain was registered at only 58 degrees, and not till the lapse of five generations was the lost ground recovered, the full 60 degrees attained, and the Ascent from the Isosceles finally achieved. And all this series of calamities from one little accident in the process of Feeling.

As this point I think I hear some of my better educated readers exclaim, "How could you in Flatland know anything about angles and degrees, or minutes? We see an angle, because we, in the region of Space, can see two straight lines inclined to one another; but you, who can see nothing but on straight line at a time, or at all events only a number of bits of straight lines all in one straight line – how can you ever discern an angle, and much less register angles of different sizes?"

I answer that though we cannot see angles, we can infer them, and this with great precision. Our sense of touch, stimulated by necessity, and developed by long training, enables us to distinguish angles far more accurately than your sense of sight, when unaided by a rule or measure of angles. Nor must I omit to explain that we have great natural helps. It is with us a Law of Nature that the brain of the Isosceles class shall begin at half a degree, or thirty minutes, and shall increase (if it increases at all) by half a degree in every generation until the goal of 60 degrees is reached, when the condition of serfdom is quitted, and the freeman enters the class of Regulars.

Consequently, Nature herself supplies us with an ascending scale or Alphabet of angles for half a degree up to 60 degrees, Specimen of which are placed in every Elementary School throughout the land. Owing to occasional retrogressions, to still more frequent moral and intellectual stagnation, and to the extraordinary fecundity of the Criminal and Vagabond classes, there is always a vast superfluity of individuals of the half degree and single degree class, and a fair abundance of Specimens up to 10 degrees. These are absolutely destitute of civil rights; and a great number of them, not having even intelligence enough for the purposes of warfare, are devoted by the States to the service of education. Fettered immovably so as to remove all possibility of danger, they are placed in the classrooms of our Infant Schools, and there they are utilized by the Board of Education for the purpose of imparting to the offspring of the Middle Classes the tact and intelligence which these wretched creatures themselves are utterly devoid.

In some States the Specimens are occasionally fed and suffered to exist for several years; but in the more temperate and better regulated regions, it is found in the long run more advantageous for the educational interests of the young, to dispense with food, and to renew the Specimens every month – which is about the average duration of the foodless existence of the Criminal class. In the cheaper schools, what is gained by the longer existence of the Specimen is lost, partly in the expenditure for food, and partly in the diminished accuracy of the angles, which are impaired after a few weeks of constant "feeling." Nor must we forget to add, in enumerating the advantages of the more expensive system, that it tends, though slightly yet perceptibly, to the diminution of the redundant Isosceles population – an object which every statesman in Flatland constantly keeps in view. On the whole therefore – although I am not ignorant that, in many popularly elected School Boards, there is a reaction in favour of "the cheap system" as it is called – I am myself disposed to think that this is one of the many cases in which expense is the truest economy.

But I must not allow questions of School Board politics to divert me from my subject. Enough has been said, I trust, to shew that Recognition by Feeling is not so tedious or indecisive a process as might have been supposed; and it is obviously more trustworthy than Recognition by hearing. Still there remains, as has been pointed out above, the objection that this method is not without danger. For this reason many in the Middle and Lower classes, and all without exception in the Polygonal and Circular orders, prefer a third method, the description of which shall be reserved for the next section.

Section 6: Of Recognition by Sight

I AM ABOUT TO APPEAR very inconsistent. In the previous sections I have said that all figures in Flatland present the appearance of a straight line; and it was added or implied, that it is consequently impossible to distinguish by the visual organ between individuals of different classes: yet now I am about to explain to my Spaceland critics how we are able to recognize one another by the sense of sight.

If however the Reader will take the trouble to refer to the passage in which Recognition by Feeling is stated to be universal, he will find this qualification – "among the lower classes." It is only among the higher classes and in our more temperate climates that Sight Recognition is practised.

That this power exists in any regions and for any classes is the result of Fog; which prevails during the greater part of the year in all parts save the torrid zones. That which is with you in Spaceland an unmixed evil, blotting out the landscape, depressing the spirits, and enfeebling the health, is by us recognized as a blessing scarcely inferior to air itself, and as the Nurse of arts and Parent of sciences. But let me explain my meaning, without further eulogies on this beneficent Element.

If Fog were non-existent, all lines would appear equally and indistinguishably clear; and this is actually the case in those unhappy countries in which the atmosphere is perfectly dry and transparent. But wherever there is a rich supply of Fog, objects that are at a distance, say of three feet, are appreciably dimmer than those at the distance of two feet eleven inches; and the result is that by careful and constant experimental observation of comparative dimness and clearness, we are enabled to infer with great exactness the configuration of the object observed.

An instance will do more than a volume of generalities to make my meaning clear.

Suppose I see two individuals approaching whose rank I wish to ascertain. They are, we will suppose, a Merchant and a Physician, or in other words, an Equilateral Triangle and a Pentagon; how am I to distinguish them?

It will be obvious, to every child in Spaceland who has touched the threshold of Geometrical Studies, that, if I can bring my eye so that its glance may bisect an angle (A) of the approaching stranger, my view will lie as it were evenly between the two sides that are next to me (viz. CA and AB), so that I shall contemplate the two impartially, and both will appear of the same size.

Now in the case of (1) the Merchant, what shall I see? I shall see a straight line DAE, in which the middle point (A) will be very bright because it is nearest to me; but on either side the line will shade away rapidly to dimness, because the sides AC and AB recede rapidly into the fog and what appear to me as the Merchant's extremities, viz. D and E, will be very dim indeed.

On the other hand in the case of (2) the Physician, though I shall here also see a line (D'A'E') with a bright centre (A'), yet it will shade away less rapidly to dimness, because the sides (A'C', A'B') recede less rapidly into the fog: and what appear to me the Physician's extremities, viz. D' and E', will not be not so dim as the extremities of the Merchant.

The Reader will probably understand from these two instances how – after a very long training supplemented by constant experience – it is possible for the well-educated classes among us to discriminate with fair accuracy between the middle and lowest orders, by the sense of sight. If my Spaceland Patrons have grasped this general conception, so far as to conceive the possibility of it and not to reject my account as altogether incredible – I shall have attained all I can reasonably expect. Were I to attempt further details I should only perplex. Yet for the sake of the young and inexperienced, who may perchance infer – from the two simple instances I have given above, of the manner in which I should recognize my Father and my Sons – that Recognition by sight is an easy affair, it may be needful to point out that in actual life most of the problems of Sight Recognition are far more subtle and complex.

If for example, when my Father, the Triangle, approaches me, he happens to present his side to me instead of his angle, then, until I have asked him to rotate, or until I have edged my eye around him, I am for the moment doubtful whether he may not be a Straight Line, or, in other words, a Woman. Again, when I am in the company of one of my two hexagonal Grandsons, contemplating one of his sides (AB) full front, it will be evident from the accompanying diagram that I shall see one whole line (AB) in comparative brightness (shading off hardly at all at the ends) and two smaller lines (CA and BD) dim throughout and shading away into greater dimness towards the extremities C and D.

But I must not give way to the temptation of enlarging on these topics. The meanest mathematician in Spaceland will readily believe me when I assert that the problems of life, which present themselves to the well-educated – when they are themselves in motion, rotating, advancing or retreating, and at the same time attempting to discriminate by the sense of sight between a number of Polygons of high rank moving in different directions, as for example in a ball-room or conversazione – must be of a nature to task the angularity of the most intellectual, and amply justify the rich endowments of the Learned Professors of Geometry, both Static and Kinetic, in the illustrious University of Wentbridge, where the Science and Art of Sight Recognition are regularly taught to large classes of the elite of the States.

It is only a few of the scions of our noblest and wealthiest houses, who are able to give the time and money necessary for the thorough prosecution of this noble and valuable Art. Even to me, a Mathematician of no mean standing, and the Grandfather of two most hopeful and perfectly regular Hexagons, to find myself in the midst of a crowd of rotating Polygons of the higher classes, is occasionally very perplexing. And of course to a common Tradesman, or Serf, such a sight is almost as unintelligible as it would be to you, my Reader, were you suddenly transported to my country.

In such a crowd you could see on all sides of you nothing but a Line, apparently straight, but of which the parts would vary irregularly and perpetually in brightness or dimness. Even if you had completed your third year in the Pentagonal and Hexagonal classes in the University, and were perfect in the theory of the subject, you would still find there was need of many years of experience, before you could move in a fashionable crowd without jostling against your betters, whom it is against etiquette to ask to "feel," and who, by their superior culture and breeding, know all about your movements, while you know very little or nothing about theirs. In a word, to comport oneself with perfect propriety in Polygonal society, one ought to be a Polygon oneself. Such at least is the painful teaching of my experience.

It is astonishing how much the Art – or I may almost call it instinct – of Sight Recognition is developed by the habitual practice of it and by the avoidance of the custom of "Feeling." Just as, with you, the deaf and dumb, if once allowed to gesticulate and to use the hand-alphabet, will never acquire the more difficult but far more valuable art of lip-speech and lip-reading, so it is with us as regards "Seeing" and "Feeling." None who in early life resort to "Feeling" will ever learn "Seeing" in perfection.

For this reason, among our Higher Classes, "Feeling" is discouraged or absolutely forbidden. From the cradle their children, instead of going to the Public Elementary schools (where the art of Feeling is taught), are sent to higher Seminaries of an exclusive character; and at our illustrious University, to "feel" is regarded as a most serious fault, involving Rustication for the first offence, and Expulsion for the second.

But among the lower classes the art of Sight Recognition is regarded as an unattainable luxury. A common Tradesman cannot afford to let his son spend a third of his life in abstract studies. The children of the poor are therefore allowed to "feel" from their earliest years, and they gain thereby a precocity and an early vivacity which contrast at first most favourably with the inert, undeveloped, and listless behaviour of the half-instructed youths of the Polygonal class; but when the latter have at last completed their University course, and are prepared to put their theory into practice, the change that comes over them may almost be described as a new birth, and in every art, science, and social pursuit they rapidly overtake and distance their Triangular competitors.

Only a few of the Polygonal Class fail to pass the Final Test or Leaving Examination at the University. The condition of the unsuccessful minority is truly pitiable. Rejected from the higher class, they are also despised by the lower. They have neither the matured and systematically trained powers of the Polygonal Bachelors and Masters of Arts, nor yet the native precocity and mercurial versatility of the youthful Tradesman. The professions, the public services, are closed against them, and though in most States they are not actually debarred from marriage, yet they have the greatest difficulty in forming suitable alliances, as experience shews that the offspring of such unfortunate and ill-endowed parents is generally itself unfortunate, if not positively Irregular.

It is from these specimens of the refuse of our Nobility that the great Tumults and Seditions of past ages have generally derived their leaders; and so great is the mischief thence arising that an increasing minority of our more progressive Statesmen are of opinion that true mercy would dictate their entire suppression, by enacting that all who fail to pass the Final Examination of the University should be either imprisoned for life, or extinguished by a painless death.

But I find myself digressing into the subject of Irregularities, a matter of such vital interest that it demands a separate section.

Section 7: Concerning Irregular Figures

THROUGHOUT THE previous pages I have been assuming – what perhaps should have been laid down at the beginning as a distinct and fundamental proposition – that every human being in Flatland is a Regular Figure, that is to say of regular construction. By this I mean that a Woman must not only be a line, but a straight line; that an Artisan or Soldier must have two of his sides equal; that Tradesmen must have three sides equal; Lawyers (of which class I am a humble member), four sides equal, and, generally, that in every Polygon, all the sides must be equal.

The sizes of the sides would of course depend upon the age of the individual. A Female at birth would be about an inch long, while a tall adult Woman might extend to a foot. As to the Males of every class, it may be roughly said that the length of an adult's size, when added together, is two feet or a little more. But the size of our sides is not under consideration. I am speaking of the equality of sides, and it does not need much reflection to see that the whole of the social life in Flatland rests upon the fundamental fact that Nature wills all Figures to have their sides equal.

If our sides were unequal our angles might be unequal. Instead of its being sufficient to feel, or estimate by sight, a single angle in order to determine the form of an individual, it would be necessary to ascertain each angle by the experiment of Feeling. But life would be too short for such a tedious groping. The whole science and art of Sight Recognition would at once perish; Feeling, so far as it is an art, would not long survive; intercourse would become perilous or impossible; there would be an end to all confidence, all forethought; no one would be safe in making the most simple social arrangements; in a word, civilization might relapse into barbarism.

Am I going too fast to carry my Readers with me to these obvious conclusions? Surely a moment's reflection, and a single instance from common life, must convince every one that our social system is based upon Regularity, or Equality of Angles. You meet, for example, two or three Tradesmen in the street, whom you recognize at once to be Tradesman by a glance at their angles and rapidly bedimmed sides, and you ask them to step into your house to lunch. This you do at present with perfect confidence, because everyone knows to an inch or two the area occupied by an adult Triangle: but imagine that your Tradesman drags behind his regular and respectable vertex, a parallelogram of twelve or thirteen inches in diagonal: what are you to do with such a monster sticking fast in your house door?

But I am insulting the intelligence of my Readers by accumulating details which must be patent to everyone who enjoys the advantages of a Residence in Spaceland. Obviously the measurements of a single angle would no longer be sufficient under such portentous circumstances; one's whole life would be taken up in feeling or surveying the perimeter of one's acquaintances. Already the difficulties of avoiding a collision in a crowd are enough to tax the sagacity of even a well-educated Square; but if no one could calculate the Regularity of a single figure in the company, all would be chaos and confusion, and the slightest panic would cause serious injuries, or – if there happened to be any Women or Soldiers present – perhaps considerable loss of life.

Expediency therefore concurs with Nature in stamping the seal of its approval upon Regularity of conformation: nor has the Law been backward in seconding their efforts. "Irregularity of Figure" means with us the same as, or more than, a combination of moral obliquity and criminality with you, and is treated accordingly. There are not wanting, it is true, some promulgators of paradoxes who maintain that there is no necessary connection between geometrical and moral Irregularity. "The Irregular," they say, "is from his birth scouted by his own parents, derided by his brothers and sisters, neglected by the domestics, scorned and suspected by society, and excluded from all posts of responsibility, trust, and useful activity. His every movement is jealously watched by the police till he comes of age and presents himself for inspection; then he is either destroyed, if he is found to exceed the fixed margin of deviation, at an uninteresting occupation for a miserable stipend; obliged to live and board at the office, and to take even his vacation under close supervision; what wonder that human nature, even in the best and purest, is embittered and perverted by such surroundings!"

All this very plausible reasoning does not convince me, as it has not convinced the wisest of our Statesmen, that our ancestors erred in laying it down as an axiom of policy that the toleration of Irregularity is incompatible with the safety of the State. Doubtless, the life of an Irregular is hard; but the interests of the Greater Number require that it shall be hard. If a man with a triangular front and a polygonal back were allowed to exist and to propagate a still more Irregular posterity, what would become of the arts of life? Are the houses and doors and churches in Flatland to be altered in order to accommodate such monsters? Are our ticket-collectors to be required to measure every man's perimeter before they allow him to enter a theatre, or to take his place in a lecture room? Is an Irregular to be exempted from the militia? And if not, how is he to be prevented from carrying desolation into the ranks of his comrades? Again, what irresistible temptations to fraudulent impostures must needs beset such a creature! How easy for him to enter a shop with his polygonal front foremost, and to order goods to any extent from a confiding tradesman! Let the advocates of a falsely called Philanthropy plead as they may for the abrogation of the Irregular Penal Laws, I for my part have never known an Irregular who was not also what Nature evidently intended him to be – a hypocrite, a misanthropist, and, up to the limits of his power, a perpetrator of all manner of mischief.

Not that I should be disposed to recommend (at present) the extreme measures adopted by some States, where an infant whose angle deviates by half a degree from the correct angularity is summarily destroyed at birth. Some of our highest and ablest men, men of real genius, have during their earliest days laboured under deviations as great as, or even greater than forty-five minutes: and the loss of their precious lives would have been an irreparable injury to the State. The art of healing also has achieved some of its most glorious triumphs in the compressions, extensions, trepannings, colligations, and other surgical or diaetetic operations by which Irregularity has been partly or wholly cured. Advocating therefore a via media, I would lay down no fixed or absolute line of demarcation; but at the period when the frame is just beginning to set, and when the Medical Board has reported that recovery is improbably, I would suggest that the Irregular offspring be painlessly and mercifully consumed.

Section 8: Of the Ancient Practice of Painting

IF MY READERS have followed me with any attention up to this point, they will not be surprised to hear that life is somewhat dull in Flatland. I do not, of course, mean that there are not battles, conspiracies, tumults, factions, and all those other phenomena which are supposed to make History interesting; nor would I deny that the strange mixture of the problems of life and the problems of Mathematics, continually inducing conjecture and giving an opportunity of immediate verification, imparts to our existence a zest which you in Spaceland can hardly comprehend. I speak now from the aesthetic and artistic point of view when I say that life with us is dull; aesthetically and artistically, very dull indeed.

How can it be otherwise, when all one's prospect, all one's landscapes, historical pieces, portraits, flowers, still life, are nothing but a single line, with no varieties except degrees of brightness and obscurity?

It was not always thus. Colour, if Tradition speaks the truth, once for the space of half a dozen centuries or more, threw a transient splendour over the lives of our ancestors in the remotest ages. Some private individual – a Pentagon whose name is variously reported – having casually discovered the constituents of the simpler colours and a rudimentary method of painting, is said to have begun by decorating first his house, then his slaves, then his Father, his Sons, and Grandsons, lastly himself. The convenience as well as the beauty of the results commended themselves to all. Wherever Chromatistes, – for by that name the most trustworthy authorities concur in calling him, – turned his variegated frame, there he at once excited attention, and attracted respect. No one now needed to "feel" him; no one mistook his front for his back; all his movements were readily ascertained by his neighbours without the slightest strain on their powers of calculation; no one jostled him, or failed to make way for him; his voice was saved the labour of that exhausting utterance by which we colourless Squares and Pentagons are often forced to proclaim our individuality when we move amid a crowd of ignorant Isosceles.

The fashion spread like wildfire. Before a week was over, every Square and Triangle in the district had copied the example of Chromatistes, and only a few of the more conservative Pentagons still held out. A month or two found even the Dodecagons infected with the innovation. A year had not elapsed before the habit had spread to all but the very highest of the Nobility. Needless to say, the custom soon made its way from the district of

Chromatistes to surrounding regions; and within two generations no one in all Flatland was colourless except the Women and the Priests.

Here Nature herself appeared to erect a barrier, and to plead against extending the innovations to these two classes. Many-sidedness was almost essential as a pretext for the Innovators. "Distinction of sides is intended by Nature to imply distinction of colours" – such was the sophism which in those days flew from mouth to mouth, converting whole towns at a time to a new culture. But manifestly to our Priests and Women this adage did not apply. The latter had only one side, and therefore – plurally and pedantically speaking – no sides. The former – if at least they would assert their claim to be readily and truly Circles, and not mere high-class Polygons, with an infinitely large number of infinitesimally small sides – were in the habit of boasting (what Women confessed and deplored) that they also had no sides, being blessed with a perimeter of only one line, or, in other words, a Circumference. Hence it came to pass that these two Classes could see no force in the so-called axiom about "Distinction of Sides implying Distinction of Colour;" and when all others had succumbed to the fascinations of corporal decoration, the Priests and the Women alone still remained pure from the pollution of paint.

Immoral, licentious, anarchical, unscientific – call them by what names you will – yet, from an aesthetic point of view, those ancient days of the Colour Revolt were the glorious childhood of Art in Flatland – a childhood, alas, that never ripened into manhood, nor even reached the blossom of youth. To live then in itself a delight, because living implied seeing. Even at a small party, the company was a pleasure to behold; the richly varied hues of the assembly in a church or theatre are said to have more than once proved too distracting from our greatest teachers and actors; but most ravishing of all is said to have been the unspeakable magnificence of a military review.

The sight of a line of battle of twenty thousand Isosceles suddenly facing about, and exchanging the sombre black of their bases for the orange of the two sides including their acute angle; the militia of the Equilateral Triangles tricoloured in red, white, and blue; the mauve, ultra-marine, gamboge, and burnt umber of the Square artillerymen rapidly rotating near their vermillion guns; the dashing and flashing of the five-coloured and six-coloured Pentagons and Hexagons careering across the field in their offices of surgeons, geometricians and aides-de-camp – all these may well have been sufficient to render credible the famous story how an illustrious Circle, overcome by the artistic beauty of the forces under his command, threw aside his marshal's baton and his royal crown, exclaiming that he henceforth exchanged them for the artist's pencil. How great and glorious the sensuous development of these days must have been is in part indicated by the very language and vocabulary of the period. The commonest utterances of the commonest citizens in the time of the Colour Revolt seem to have been suffused with a richer tinge of word or thought; and to that era we are even now indebted for our finest poetry and for whatever rhythm still remains in the more scientific utterance of those modern days.

Section 9: Of the Universal Colour Bill

BUT MEANWHILE the intellectual Arts were fast decaying.

The Art of Sight Recognition, being no longer needed, was no longer practised; and the studies of Geometry, Statics, Kinetics, and other kindred subjects, came soon to be considered superfluous, and fell into disrespect and neglect even at our University. The inferior Art of Feeling speedily experienced the same fate at our Elementary Schools. Then the Isosceles classes, asserting that the Specimens were no longer used nor needed, and refusing to pay the customary tribute from the Criminal classes to the service of Education, waxed daily more numerous and more insolent on the strength of their immunity from the old burden which had formerly exercised the twofold wholesome effect of at once taming their brutal nature and thinning their excessive numbers.

Year by year the Soldiers and Artisans began more vehemently to assert – and with increasing truth – that there was no great difference between them and the very highest class of Polygons, now that they were raised to an equality with the latter, and enabled to grapple with all the difficulties and solve all the problems of life, whether Statical or Kinetical, by the simple process of Colour Recognition. Not content with the natural neglect into which Sight Recognition was falling, they began boldly to demand the legal prohibition of all "monopolizing and aristocratic Arts" and the consequent abolition of all endowments for the studies of Sight Recognition, Mathematics, and Feeling. Soon, they began to insist that inasmuch as Colour, which was a second Nature, had destroyed the need of aristocratic distinctions, the Law should follow in the same path, and that henceforth all individuals and all classes should be recognized as absolutely equal and entitled to equal rights.

Finding the higher Orders wavering and undecided, the leaders of the Revolution advanced still further in their requirements, and at last demanded that all classes alike, the Priests and the Women not excepted, should do homage to Colour by submitting to be painted. When it was objected that Priests and Women had no sides, they retorted that Nature and Expediency concurred in dictating that the front half of every human being (that is to say, the half containing his eye and mouth) should be distinguishable from his hinder half. They therefore brought before a general and extraordinary Assembly of all the States of Flatland a Bill proposing that in every Woman the half containing the eye and mouth should be coloured red, and the other half green. The Priests were to be painted in the same way, red being applied to that semicircle in which the eye and mouth formed the middle point; while the other or hinder semicircle was to be coloured green.

There was no little cunning in this proposal, which indeed emanated not from any Isosceles – for no being so degraded would have angularity enough to appreciate, much less to devise, such a model of state-craft – but from an Irregular Circle who, instead of being destroyed in his childhood, was reserved by a foolish indulgence to bring desolation on his country and destruction on myriads of followers.

On the one hand the proposition was calculated to bring the Women in all classes over to the side of the Chromatic Innovation. For by assigning to the Women the same two colours as were assigned to the Priests, the Revolutionists thereby ensured that, in certain positions, every Woman would appear as a Priest, and be treated with corresponding respect and deference – a prospect that could not fail to attract the Female Sex in a mass.

But by some of my Readers the possibility of the identical appearance of Priests and Women, under a new Legislation, may not be recognized; if so, a word or two will make it obvious.

Imagine a woman duly decorated, according to the new Code; with the front half (i.e., the half containing the eye and mouth) red, and with the hinder half green. Look at her from one side. Obviously you will see a straight line, half red, half green.

Now imagine a Priest, whose mouth is at M, and whose front semicircle (AMB) is consequently coloured red, while his hinder semicircle is green; so that the diameter AB divides the green from the red. If you contemplate the Great Man so as to have your eye in the same straight line as his dividing diameter (AB), what you will see will be a straight line (CBD), of which one half (CB) will be red, and the other (BD) green. The whole line

(CD) will be rather shorter perhaps than that of a full-sized Woman, and will shade off more rapidly towards its extremities; but the identity of the colours would give you an immediate impression of identity in Class, making you neglectful of other details. Bear in mind the decay of Sight Recognition which threatened society at the time of the Colour revolt; add too the certainty that Woman would speedily learn to shade off their extremities so as to imitate the Circles; it must then be surely obvious to you, my dear Reader, that the Colour Bill placed us under a great danger of confounding a Priest with a young Woman.

How attractive this prospect must have been to the Frail Sex may readily be imagined. They anticipated with delight the confusion that would ensue. At home they might hear political and ecclesiastical secrets intended not for them but for their husbands and brothers, and might even issue some commands in the name of a priestly Circle; out of doors the striking combination of red and green without addition of any other colours, would be sure to lead the common people into endless mistakes, and the Woman would gain whatever the Circles lost, in the deference of the passers by. As for the scandal that would befall the Circular Class if the frivolous and unseemly conduct of the Women were imputed to them, and as to the consequent subversion of the Constitution, the Female Sex could not be expected to give a thought to these considerations. Even in the households of the Circles, the Women were all in favour of the Universal Colour Bill.

The second object aimed at by the Bill was the gradual demoralization of the Circles themselves. In the general intellectual decay they still preserved their pristine clearness and strength of understanding. From their earliest childhood, familiarized in their Circular households with the total absence of Colour, the Nobles alone preserved the Sacred Art of Sight Recognition, with all the advantages that result from that admirable training of the intellect. Hence, up to the date of the introduction of the Universal Colour Bill, the Circles had not only held their own, but even increased their lead of the other classes by abstinence from the popular fashion.

Now therefore the artful Irregular whom I described above as the real author of this diabolical Bill, determined at one blow to lower the status of the Hierarchy by forcing them to submit to the pollution of Colour, and at the same time to destroy their domestic opportunities of training in the Art of Sight Recognition, so as to enfeeble their intellects by depriving them of their pure and colourless homes. Once subjected to the chromatic taint, every parental and every childish Circle would demoralize each other. Only in discerning between the Father and the Mother would the Circular infant find problems for the exercise of his understanding – problems too often likely to be corrupted by maternal impostures with the result of shaking the child's faith in all logical conclusions. Thus by degrees the intellectual lustre of the Priestly Order would wane, and the road would then lie open for a total destruction of all Aristocratic Legislature and for the subversion of our Privileged Classes.

Section 10: Of the Suppression of the Chromatic Sedition

THE AGITATION for the Universal Colour Bill continued for three years; and up to the last moment of that period it seemed as though Anarchy were destined to triumph.

A whole army of Polygons, who turned out to fight as private soldiers, was utterly annihilated by a superior force of Isosceles Triangles – the Squares and Pentagons meanwhile remaining neutral.

Worse than all, some of the ablest Circles fell a prey to conjugal fury. Infuriated by political animosity, the wives in many a noble household wearied their lords with prayers to give up their opposition to the Colour Bill; and some, finding their entreaties fruitless, fell on and slaughtered their innocent children and husband, perishing themselves in the act of carnage. It is recorded that during that triennial agitation no less than twenty-three Circles perished in domestic discord.

Great indeed was the peril. It seemed as though the Priests had no choice between submission and extermination; when suddenly the course of events was completely changed by one of those picturesque incidents which Statesmen ought never to neglect, often to anticipate, and sometimes perhaps to originate, because of the absurdly disproportionate power with which they appeal to the sympathies of the populace.

It happened that an Isosceles of a low type, with a brain little if at all above four degrees – accidentally dabbling in the colours of some Tradesman whose shop he had plundered – painted himself, or caused himself to be painted (for the story varies) with the twelve colours of a Dodecagon. Going into the Market Place he accosted in a feigned voice a maiden, the orphan daughter of a noble Polygon, whose affection in former days he had sought in vain; and by a series of deceptions – aided, on the one side, by a string of lucky accidents too long to relate, and, on the other, by an almost inconceivable fatuity and neglect of ordinary precautions on the part of the relations of the bride – he succeeded in consummating the marriage. The unhappy girl committed suicide on discovering the fraud to which she had been subjected.

When the news of this catastrophe spread from State to State the minds of the Women were violently agitated. Sympathy with the miserable victim and anticipations of similar deceptions for themselves, their sisters, and their daughters, made them now regard the Colour Bill in an entirely new aspect. Not a few openly avowed themselves converted to antagonism; the rest needed only a slight stimulus to make a similar avowal. Seizing this favourable opportunity, the Circles hastily convened an extraordinary Assembly of the States; and besides the usual guard of Convicts, they secured the attendance of a large number of reactionary Women.

Amidst an unprecedented concourse, the Chief Circle of those days – by name Pantocyclus – arose to find himself hissed and hooted by a hundred and twenty thousand Isosceles. But he secured silence by declaring that henceforth the Circles would enter on a policy of Concession; yielding to the wishes of the majority, they would accept the Colour Bill. The uproar being at once converted to applause, he invited Chromatistes, the leader of the Sedition, into the centre of the hall, to receive in the name of his followers the submission of the Hierarchy. Then followed a speech, a masterpiece of rhetoric, which occupied nearly a day in the delivery, and to which no summary can do justice.

With a grave appearance of impartiality he declared that as they were now finally committing themselves to Reform or Innovation, it was desirable that they should take one last view of the perimeter of the whole subject, its defects as well as its advantages. Gradually introduction the mention of the dangers to the Tradesmen, the Professional Classes and the Gentlemen, he silenced the rising murmurs of the Isosceles by reminding them that, in spite of all these defects, he was willing to accept the Bill if it was approved by the majority. But it was manifest that all, except the Isosceles, were moved by his words and were either neutral or averse to the Bill.

Turning now to the Workmen he asserted that their interests must not be neglected, and that, if they intended to accept the Colour Bill, they ought at least to do so with full view of the consequences. Many of them, he said, were on the point of being admitted to the class of the Regular Triangles; others anticipated for their children a distinction they could not hope for themselves. That honourable ambition would not have to be sacrificed. With the universal adoption of Colour, all distinctions would cease; Regularity would be confused with Irregularity; development would give place to retrogression; the Workman would in a few generations be degraded to the level of the Military, or even the Convict Class; political power would be in the hands of the greatest number, that is to say the Criminal Classes, who were already more numerous than the Workmen, and would soon out-number all the other Classes put together when the usual Compensative Laws of Nature were violated.

A subdued murmur of assent ran through the ranks of the Artisans, and Chromatistes, in alarm, attempted to step forward and address them. But he found himself encompassed with guards and forced to remain silent while the Chief Circle in a few impassioned words made a final appeal to the Women, exclaiming that, if the Colour Bill passed, no marriage would henceforth be safe, no woman's honour secure; fraud, deception, hypocrisy would pervade every household; domestic bliss would share the fate of the Constitution and pass to speedy perdition. "Sooner than this," he cried, "come death."

At these words, which were the preconcerted signal for action, the Isosceles Convicts fell on and transfixed the wretched Chromatistes; the Regular Classes, opening their ranks, made way for a band of Women who, under direction of the Circles, moved back foremost, invisibly and unerringly upon the unconscious soldiers; the Artisans, imitating the example of their betters, also opened their ranks. Meantime bands of Convicts occupied every entrance with an impenetrable phalanx.

The battle, or rather carnage, was of short duration. Under the skillful generalship of the Circles almost every Woman's charge was fatal and very many extracted their sting uninjured, ready for a second slaughter. But no second blow was needed; the rabble of the Isosceles did the rest of the business for themselves. Surprised, leader-less, attacked in front by invisible foes, and finding egress cut off by the Convicts behind them, they at once – after their manner – lost all presence of mind, and raised the cry of "treachery." This sealed their fate. Every Isosceles now saw and felt a foe in every other. In half an hour not one of that vast multitude was living; and the fragments of seven score thousand of the Criminal Class slain by one another's angles attested the triumph of Order.

The Circles delayed not to push their victory to the uttermost. The Working Men they spared but decimated. The Militia of the Equilaterals was at once called out, and every Triangle suspected of Irregularity on reasonable grounds, was destroyed by Court Martial, without the formality of exact measurement by the Social Board. The homes of the Military and Artisan classes were inspected in a course of visitation extending through upwards of a year; and during that period every town, village, and hamlet was systematically purged of that excess of the lower orders which had been brought about by the neglect to pay the tribute of Criminals to the Schools and University, and by the violation of other natural Laws of the Constitution of Flatland. Thus the balance of classes was again restored.

Needless to say that henceforth the use of Colour was abolished, and its possession prohibited. Even the utterance of any word denoting Colour, except by the Circles or by qualified scientific teachers, was punished by a severe penalty. Only at our University in some of the very highest and most esoteric classes – which I myself have never been privileged to attend – it is understood that the sparing use of Colour is still sanctioned for the purpose of illustrating some of the deeper problems of mathematics. But of this I can only speak from hearsay.

Elsewhere in Flatland, Colour is now non-existent. The art of making it is known to only one living person, the Chief Circle for the time being; and by him it is handed down on his death-bed to none but his Successor. One manufactory alone produces it; and, lest the secret should be betrayed, the Workmen are annually consumed, and fresh ones introduced. So great is the terror with which even now our Aristocracy looks back to the far-distant days of the agitation for the Universal Colour Bill.

Section 11: Concerning our Priests

IT IS HIGH TIME that I should pass from these brief and discursive notes about things in Flatland to the central event of this book, my initiation into the mysteries of Space. That is my subject; all that has gone before is merely preface.

For this reason I must omit many matters of which the explanation would not, I flatter myself, be without interest for my Readers: as for example, our method of propelling and stopping ourselves, although destitute of feet; the means by which we give fixity to structures of wood, stone, or brick, although of course we have no hands, nor can we lay foundations as you can, nor avail ourselves of the lateral pressure of the earth; the manner in which the rain originates in the intervals between our various zones, so that the northern regions do not intercept the moisture falling on the southern; the nature of our hills and mines, our trees and vegetables, our seasons and harvests; our Alphabet and method of writing, adapted to our linear tablets; these and a hundred other details of our physical existence I must pass over, nor do I mention them now except to indicate to my readers that their omission proceeds not from forgetfulness on the part of the author, but from his regard for the time of the Reader.

Yet before I proceed to my legitimate subject some few final remarks will no doubt be expected by my Readers upon these pillars and mainstays of the Constitution of Flatland, the controllers of our conduct and shapers of our destiny, the objects of universal homage and almost of adoration: need I say that I mean our Circles or Priests?

When I call them Priests, let me not be understood as meaning no more than the term denotes with you. With us, our Priests are Administrators of all Business, Art, and Science; Directors of Trade, Commerce, Generalship, Architecture, Engineering, Education, Statesmanship, Legislature, Morality, Theology; doing nothing themselves, they are the Causes of everything worth doing, that is done by others.

Although popularly everyone called a Circle is deemed a Circle, yet among the better educated Classes it is known that no Circle is really a Circle, but only a Polygon with a very large number of very small sides. As the number of the sides increases, a Polygon approximates to a Circle; and, when the number is very great indeed, say for example three or four hundred, it is extremely difficult for the most delicate touch to feel any polygonal angles. Let me say rather it would be difficult: for, as I have shewn above, Recognition by Feeling is unknown among the highest society, and to feel a Circle would be considered a most audacious insult. This habit of abstention from Feeling in the best society enables a Circle the more easily to sustain the veil of mystery in which, from his earliest years, he is wont to enwrap the exact nature of his Perimeter or Circumference. Three feet being the average Perimeter it follows that, in a Polygon of three hundred sides each side will be no more than the hundredth part of a foot in length, or little more than the tenth part of an inch; and in a Polygon of six or seven hundred sides the sides are little larger than the diameter of a Spaceland pin-head. It is always assumed, by courtesy, that the Chief Circle for the time being has ten thousand sides.

The ascent of the posterity of the Circles in the social scale is not restricted, as it is among the lower Regular classes, by the Law of Nature which limits the increase of sides to one in each generation. If it were so, the number of sides in the Circle would be a mere question of pedigree and arithmetic, and the four hundred and ninety-seventh descendant of an Equilateral Triangle would necessarily be a polygon with five hundred sides. But this is not the case. Nature's Law prescribes two antagonistic decrees affecting Circular propagation; first, that as the race climbs higher in the scale of development, so development shall proceed at an accelerated pace; second, that in the same proportion, the race shall become less fertile. Consequently in the home of a Polygon of four or five hundred sides it is rare to find a son; more than one is never seen. On the other hand the son of a five-hundred-sided Polygon has been known to possess five hundred and fifty, or even six hundred sides.

Art also steps in to help the process of higher Evolution. Our physicians have discovered that the small and tender sides of an infant Polygon of the higher class can be fractured, and his whole frame re-set, with such exactness that a Polygon of two or three hundred sides sometimes – by no means always, for the process is attended with serious risk – but sometimes overleaps two or three hundred generations, and as it were double at a stroke, the number of his progenitors and the nobility of his descent.

Many a promising child is sacrificed in this way. Scarcely one out of ten survives. Yet so strong is the parental ambition among those Polygons who are, as it were, on the fringe of the Circular class, that it is very rare to find the Nobleman of that position in society, who has neglected to place his first-born in the Circular Neo-Therapeutic Gymnasium before he has attained the age of a month.

One year determines success or failure. At the end of that time the child has, in all probability, added one more to the tombstones that crowd the Neo-Therapeutic Cemetery; but on rare occasional a glad procession bears back the little one to his exultant parents, no longer a Polygon, but a Circle, at least by courtesy: and a single instance of so blessed a result induces multitudes of Polygonal parents to submit to similar domestic sacrifice, which have a dissimilar issue.

Section 12: Of the Doctrine of our Priests

AS TO THE DOCTRINE of the Circles it may briefly be summed up in a single maxim, "Attend to your Configuration." Whether political, ecclesiastical, or moral, all their teaching has for its object the improvement of individual and collective Configuration – with special reference of course to the Configuration of the Circles, to which all other objects are subordinated.

It is the merit of the Circles that they have effectually suppressed those ancient heresies which led men to waste energy and sympathy in the vain belief that conduct depends upon will, effort, training, encouragement, praise, or anything else but Configuration. It was Pantocyclus – the illustrious Circle mentioned above, as the queller of the Colour Revolt – who first convinced mankind that Configuration makes the man; that if, for example, you are born an Isosceles with two uneven sides, you will assuredly go wrong unless you have them made even – for which purpose you must go to the Isosceles Hospital; similarly, if you are a Triangle, or Square, or even a Polygon, born with any Irregularity, you must be taken to one of the Regular Hospitals to have your disease cured; otherwise you will end your days in the State Prison or by the angle of the State Executioner.

All faults or defects, from the slightest misconduct to the most flagitious crime, Pantocyclus attributed to some deviation from perfect Regularity in the bodily figure, caused perhaps (if not congenital) by some collision in a crowd; by neglect to take exercise, or by taking too much of it; or even by a sudden change of temperature, resulting in a shrinkage or expansion in some too susceptible part of the frame. Therefore, concluded that illustrious Philosopher, neither good conduct nor bad conduct is a fit subject, in any sober estimation, for either praise or blame. For why should you praise, for example, the integrity of a Square who faithfully defends the interests of his client, when you ought in reality rather to admire the exact precision of his right angles? Or again, why blame a lying, thievish Isosceles, when you ought rather to deplore the incurable inequality of his sides?

Theoretically, this doctrine is unquestionable; but it has practical drawbacks. In dealing with an Isosceles, if a rascal pleads that he cannot help stealing because of his unevenness, you reply that for that very reason, because he cannot help being a nuisance to his neighbours, you, the Magistrate, cannot help sentencing him to be consumed – and there's an end of the matter. But in little domestic difficulties, when the penalty of consumption, or death, is out of the question, this theory of Configuration sometimes comes in awkwardly; and I must confess that occasionally when one of my own Hexagonal Grandsons pleads as an excuse for his disobedience that a sudden change of temperature has been too much for his Perimeter, and that I ought to lay the blame not on him but on his Configuration, which can only be strengthened by abundance of the choicest sweetmeats, I neither see my way logically to reject, nor practically to accept, his conclusions.

For my own part, I find it best to assume that a good sound scolding or castigation has some latent and strengthening influence on my Grandson's Configuration; though I own that I have no grounds for thinking so. At all events I am not alone in my way of extricating myself from this dilemma; for I find that many of the highest Circles, sitting as Judges in law courts, use praise and blame towards Regular and Irregular Figures; and in their homes I know by experience that, when scolding their children, they speak about "right" and "wrong" as vehemently and passionately as if they believe that these names represented real existence, and that a human Figure is really capable of choosing between them.

Constantly carrying out their policy of making Configuration the leading idea in every mind, the Circles reverse the nature of that Commandment which in Spaceland regulates the relations between parents and children. With you, children are taught to honour their parents; with us – next to the Circles, who are the chief object of universal homage – a man is taught to honour his Grandson, if he has one; or, if not, his Son. By "honour," however, is by no means mean "indulgence," but a reverent regard for their highest interests: and the Circles teach that the duty of fathers is to subordinate their own interests to those of posterity, thereby advancing the welfare of the whole State as well as that of their own immediate descendants.

The weak point in the system of the Circles – if a humble Square may venture to speak of anything Circular as containing any element of weakness – appears to me to be found in their relations with Women.

As it is of the utmost importance for Society that Irregular births should be discouraged, it follows that no Woman who has any Irregularities in her ancestry is a fit partner for one who desires that his posterity should rise by regular degrees in the social scale.

Now the Irregularity of a Male is a matter of measurement; but as all Women are straight, and therefore visibly Regular so to speak, one has to devise some other means of ascertaining what I may call their invisible Irregularity, that is to say their potential Irregularities as regards possible offspring. This is effected by carefully-kept pedigrees, which are preserved and supervised by the State; and without a certified pedigree no Woman is allowed to marry.

Now it might have been supposed the a Circle – proud of his ancestry and regardful for a posterity which might possibly issue hereafter in a Chief Circle – would be more careful than any other to choose a wife who had no blot on her escutcheon. But it is not so. The care in choosing a Regular wife appears to diminish as one rises in the social scale. Nothing would induce an aspiring Isosceles, who has hopes of generating an Equilateral Son, to take a wife who reckoned a single Irregularity among her Ancestors; a Square or Pentagon, who is confident that his family is steadily on the rise, does not inquire above the five-hundredth generation; a Hexagon or Dodecagon is even more careless of the wife's pedigree; but a Circle has been known deliberately to take a wife who has had an Irregular Great-Grandfather, and all because of some slight superiority of lustre, or because of the charms of a low voice – which, with us, even more than with you, is thought "an excellent thing in a Woman."

Such ill-judged marriages are, as might be expected, barren, if they do not result in positive Irregularity or in diminution of sides; but none of these evils have hitherto provided sufficiently deterrent. The loss of a few sides in a highly-developed Polygon is not easily noticed, and is sometimes compensated by a successful operation in the Neo-Therapeutic Gymnasium, as I have described above; and the Circles are too much disposed to acquiesce in infecundity as a law of the superior development. Yet, if this evil be not arrested, the gradual diminution of the Circular class may soon become more rapid, and the time may not be far distant when, the race being no longer able to produce a Chief Circle, the Constitution of Flatland must fall.

One other word of warning suggest itself to me, though I cannot so easily mention a remedy; and this also refers to our relations with Women. About three hundred years ago, it was decreed by the Chief Circle that, since women are deficient in Reason but abundant in Emotion, they ought no longer to be treated as rational, nor receive any mental education. The consequence was that they were no longer taught to read, nor even to master Arithmetic enough to enable them to count the angles of their husband or children; and hence they sensibly declined during each generation in intellectual power. And this system of female non-education or quietism still prevails.

My fear is that, with the best intentions, this policy has been carried so far as to react injuriously on the Male Sex.

For the consequence is that, as things now are, we Males have to lead a kind of bi-lingual, and I may almost say bi-mental, existence. With Women, we speak of "love," "duty," "right," "wrong," "pity," "hope," and other irrational and emotional conceptions, which have no existence, and the fiction of which has no object except to control feminine exuberances; but among ourselves, and in our books, we have an entirely different vocabulary and I may also say, idiom. "Love" them becomes "the anticipation of benefits"; "duty" becomes "necessity" or "fitness"; and other words are correspondingly transmuted. Moreover, among Women, we use language implying the utmost deference for their Sex; and they fully believe that the Chief Circle Himself is not more devoutly adored by us than they are: but behind their backs they are both regarded and spoken of – by all but the very young – as being little better than "mindless organisms."

Our Theology also in the Women's chambers is entirely different from our Theology elsewhere.

Now my humble fear is that this double training, in language as well as in thought, imposes somewhat too heavy a burden upon the young, especially when, at the age of three years old, they are taken from the maternal care and taught to unlearn the old language

– except for the purpose of repeating it in the presence of the Mothers and Nurses – and to learn the vocabulary and idiom of science. Already methinks I discern a weakness in the grasp of mathematical truth at the present time as compared with the more robust intellect of our ancestors three hundred years ago. I say nothing of the possible danger if a Woman should ever surreptitiously learn to read and convey to her Sex the result of her perusal of a single popular volume; nor of the possibility that the indiscretion or disobedience of some infant Male might reveal to a Mother the secrets of the logical dialect. On the simple ground of the enfeebling of the male intellect, I rest this humble appeal to the highest Authorities to reconsider the regulations of Female education.

Part II: Other Worlds

Section 13: How I had a Vision of Lineland

IT WAS THE last day but one of the 1999th year of our era, and the first day of the Long Vacation. Having amused myself till a late hour with my favourite recreation of Geometry, I had retired to rest with an unsolved problem in my mind. In the night I had a dream.

I saw before me a vast multitude of small Straight Lines (which I naturally assumed to be Women) interspersed with other Beings still smaller and of the nature of lustrous points – all moving to and fro in one and the same Straight Line, and, as nearly as I could judge, with the same velocity.

A noise of confused, multitudinous chirping or twittering issued from them at intervals as long as they were moving; but sometimes they ceased from motion, and then all was silence.

Approaching one of the largest of what I thought to be Women, I accosted her, but received no answer. A second and third appeal on my part were equally ineffectual. Losing patience at what appeared to me intolerable rudeness, I brought my mouth to a position full in front of her mouth so as to intercept her motion, and loudly repeated my question, "Woman, what signifies this concourse, and this strange and confused chirping, and this monotonous motion to and fro in one and the same Straight Line?"

"I am no Woman," replied the small Line: "I am the Monarch of the world. But thou, whence intrudest thou into my realm of Lineland?" Receiving this abrupt reply, I begged pardon if I had in any way startled or molested his Royal Highness; and describing myself as a stranger I besought the King to give me some account of his dominions. But I had the greatest possible difficulty in obtaining any information on points that really interested me; for the Monarch could not refrain from constantly assuming that whatever was familiar to him must also be known to me and that I was simulating ignorance in jest. However, by preserving questions I elicited the following facts:

It seemed that this poor ignorant Monarch – as he called himself – was persuaded that the Straight Line which he called his Kingdom, and in which he passed his existence, constituted the whole of the world, and indeed the whole of Space. Not being able either to move or to see, save in his Straight Line, he had no conception of anything out of it. Though he had heard my voice when I first addressed him, the sounds had come to him in a manner so contrary to his experience that he had made no answer, "seeing no man," as he expressed it, "and hearing a voice as it were from my own intestines." Until the moment when I placed my mouth in his World, he had neither seen me, nor heard anything except confused sounds beating against, what I called his side, but what he called his inside or stomach; nor had he even now the least conception of the region from which I had come. Outside his World, or Line, all was a blank to him; nay, not even a blank, for a blank implies Space; say, rather, all was non-existent.

His subjects – of whom the small Lines were men and the Points Women – were all alike confined in motion and eyesight to that single Straight Line, which was their World. It need scarcely be added that the whole of their horizon was limited to a Point; nor could any one ever see anything but a Point. Man, woman, child, thing – each as a Point to the eye of a Linelander. Only by the sound of the voice could sex or age be distinguished. Moreover, as each individual occupied the whole of the narrow path, so to speak, which constituted his Universe, and no one could move to the right or left to make way for passers by, it followed that no Linelander could ever pass another. Once neighbours, always neighbours. Neighbourhood with them was like marriage with us. Neighbours remained neighbours till death did them part.

Such a life, with all vision limited to a Point, and all motion to a Straight Line, seemed to me inexpressibly dreary; and I was surprised to note that vivacity and cheerfulness of the King. Wondering whether it was possible, amid circumstances so unfavourable to domestic relations, to enjoy the pleasures of conjugal union, I hesitated for some time to question his Royal Highness on so delicate a subject; but at last I plunged into it by abruptly inquiring as to the health of his family. "My wives and children," he replied, "are well and happy."

Staggered at this answer – for in the immediate proximity of the Monarch (as I had noted in my dream before I entered Lineland) there were none but Men – I ventured to reply, "Pardon me, but I cannot imagine how your Royal Highness can at any time either see or approach their Majesties, when there at least half a dozen intervening individuals, whom you can neither see through, nor pass by? Is it possible that in Lineland proximity is not necessary for marriage and for the generation of children?"

"How can you ask so absurd a question?" replied the Monarch. "If it were indeed as you suggest, the Universe would soon be depopulated. No, no; neighbourhood is needless for the union of hearts; and the birth of children is too important a matter to have been allowed to depend upon such an accident as proximity. You cannot be ignorant of this. Yet since you are pleased to affect ignorance, I will instruct you as if you were the veriest baby in Lineland. Know, then, that marriages are consummated by means of the faculty of sound and the sense of hearing.

"You are of course aware that every Man has two mouths or voices – as well as two eyes – a bass at one and a tenor at the other of his extremities. I should not mention this, but that I have been unable to distinguish your tenor in the course of our conversation." I replied that I had but one voice, and that I had not been aware that his Royal Highness had two. "That confirms my impression," said the King, "that you are not a Man, but a feminine Monstrosity with a bass voice, and an utterly uneducated ear. But to continue.

"Nature having herself ordained that every Man should wed two wives – " "Why two?" asked I. "You carry your affected simplicity too far," he cried. "How can there be a completely harmonious union without the combination of the Four in One, viz. the Bass and Tenor of the Man and the Soprano and Contralto of the two Women?" "But supposing," said I, "that a man should prefer one wife or three?" "It is impossible," he said; "it is as inconceivable as that two and one should make five, or that the human eye should see a Straight Line." I would have interrupted him; but he proceeded as follows:

"Once in the middle of each week a Law of Nature compels us to move to and fro with a rhythmic motion of more than usual violence, which continues for the time you would take to count a hundred and one. In the midst of this choral dance, at the fifty-first pulsation, the inhabitants of the Universe pause in full career, and each individual sends forth his richest, fullest, sweetest strain. It is in this decisive moment that all our marriages are made. So exquisite is the adaptation of Bass and Treble, of Tenor to Contralto, that oftentimes the Loved Ones, though twenty thousand leagues away, recognize at once the responsive note of their destined Lover; and, penetrating the paltry obstacles of distance, Love unites the three. The marriage in that instance consummated results in a threefold Male and Female offspring which takes its place in Lineland."

"What! Always threefold?" said I. "Must one wife then always have twins?"

"Bass-voice Monstrosity! Yes," replied the King. "How else could the balance of the Sexes be maintained, if two girls were not born for every boy? Would you ignore the very Alphabet of Nature?" He ceased, speechless for fury; and some time elapsed before I could induce him to resume his narrative.

"You will not, of course, suppose that every bachelor among us finds his mates at the first wooing in this universal Marriage Chorus. On the contrary, the process is by most of us many times repeated. Few are the hearts whose happy lot is at once to recognize in each other's voice the partner intended for them by Providence, and to fly into a reciprocal and perfectly harmonious embrace. With most of us the courtship is of long duration. The Wooer's voices may perhaps accord with one of the future wives, but not with both; or not, at first, with either; or the Soprano and Contralto may not quite harmonize. In such cases Nature has provided that every weekly Chorus shall bring the three Lovers into closer harmony. Each trial of voice, each fresh discovery of discord, almost imperceptibly induces the less perfect to modify his or her vocal utterance so as to approximate to the more perfect. And after many trials and many approximations, the result is at last achieved. There comes a day at last when, while the wonted Marriage Chorus goes forth from universal Lineland, the three far-off Lovers suddenly find themselves in exact harmony, and, before they are aware, the wedded Triplet is rapt vocally into a duplicate embrace; and Nature rejoices over one more marriage and over three more births."

Section 14: How I Vainly Tried to Explain the Nature of Flatland

THINKING THAT it was time to bring down the Monarch from his raptures to the level of common sense, I determined to endeavour to open up to him some glimpses of the truth, that is to say of the nature of things in Flatland. So I began thus: "How does your Royal Highness distinguish the shapes and positions of his subjects? I for my part noticed by the sense of sight, before I entered your Kingdom, that some of your people are lines and others Points; and that some of the lines are larger – " "You speak of an impossibility," interrupted the King; "you must have seen a vision; for to detect the difference between a Line and a Point by the sense of sight is, as every one knows, in the nature of things, impossible; but it can be detected by the sense of hearing, and by the same means my shape can be exactly ascertained. Behold me – I am a Line, the longest in Lineland, over six inches of Space – " "Of Length," I ventured to suggest. "Fool," said he, "Space is Length. Interrupt me again, and I have done."

I apologized; but he continued scornfully, "Since you are impervious to argument, you shall hear with your ears how by means of my two voices I reveal my shape to my Wives, who are at this moment six thousand miles seventy yards two feet eight inches away, the one to the North, the other to the South. Listen, I call to them."

He chirruped, and then complacently continued: "My wives at this moment receiving the sound of one of my voice, closely followed by the other, and perceiving that the latter reaches them after an interval in which sound can traverse 6.457 inches, infer that one of my mouths is 6.457 inches further from them than the other, and accordingly know my shape to be 6.457 inches. But you will of course understand that my wives do not make this calculation every time they hear my two voices. They made it, once for all, before we were married. But they could make it at any time. And in the same way I can estimate the shape of any of my Male subjects by the sense of sound."

"But how," said I, "if a Man feigns a Woman's voice with one of his two voices, or so disguises his Southern voice that it cannot be recognized as the echo of the Northern? May not such deceptions cause great inconvenience? And have you no means of checking frauds of this kind by commanding your neighbouring subjects to feel one another?" This of course was a very stupid question, for feeling could not have answered the purpose; but I asked with the view of irritating the Monarch, and I succeeded perfectly.

"What!" cried he in horror, "explain your meaning." "Feel, touch, come into contact," I replied. "If you mean by feeling," said the King, "approaching so close as to leave no space between two individuals, know, Stranger, that this offence is punishable in my dominions by death. And the reason is obvious. The frail form of a Woman, being liable to be shattered by such an approximation, must be preserved by the State; but since Women cannot be distinguished by the sense of sight from Men, the Law ordains universally that neither Man nor Woman shall be approached so closely as to destroy the interval between the approximator and the approximated.

"And indeed what possible purpose would be served by this illegal and unnatural excess of approximation which you call touching, when all the ends of so brutal and course a process are attained at once more easily and more exactly by the sense of hearing? As to your suggested danger of deception, it is non-existent: for the Voice, being the essence of one's Being, cannot be thus changed at will. But come, suppose that I had the power of passing through solid things, so that I could penetrate my subjects, one after another, even to the number of a billion, verifying the size and distance of each by the sense of feeling: How much time and energy would be wasted in this clumsy and inaccurate method! Whereas now, in one moment of audition, I take as it were the census and statistics, local, corporeal, mental and spiritual, of every living being in Lineland. Hark, only hark!"

So saying he paused and listened, as if in an ecstasy, to a sound which seemed to me no better than a tiny chirping from an innumerable multitude of lilliputian grasshoppers.

"Truly," replied I, "your sense of hearing serves you in good stead, and fills up many of your deficiencies. But permit me to point out that your life in Lineland must be deplorably dull. To see nothing but a Point! Not even to be able to contemplate a Straight Line! Nay, not even to know what a Straight Line is! To see, yet to be cut off from those Linear prospects which are vouchsafed to us in Flatland! Better surely to have no sense of sight at all than to see so little! I grant you I have not your discriminative faculty of hearing; for the concert of all Lineland which gives you such intense pleasure, is to me no better than a multitudinous twittering or chirping. But at least I can discern, by sight, a Line from a Point. And let me prove it. Just before I came into your kingdom, I saw you dancing from left to right, and then from right to left, with Seven Men and a Woman in your immediate proximity on the left, and eight Men and two Women on your right. Is not this correct?"

"It is correct," said the King, "so far as the numbers and sexes are concerned, though I know not what you mean by 'right' and 'left.' But I deny that you saw these things. For how could you see the Line, that is to say the inside, of any Man? But you must have heard these things, and then dreamed that you saw them. And let me ask what you mean by those words 'left' and 'right.' I suppose it is your way of saying Northward and Southward."

"Not so," replied I; "besides your motion of Northward and Southward, there is another motion which I call from right to left."

King: Exhibit to me, if you please, this motion from left to right.

I: Nay, that I cannot do, unless you could step out of your Line altogether.

King: Out of my Line? Do you mean out of the world? Out of Space?

I: Well, yes. Out of your world. Out of your Space. For your Space is not the true Space. True Space is a Plane; but your Space is only a Line.

King: If you cannot indicate this motion from left to right by yourself moving in it, then I beg you to describe it to me in words.

I: If you cannot tell your right side from your left, I fear that no words of mine can make my meaning clearer to you. But surely you cannot be ignorant of so simple a distinction.

King: I do not in the least understand you.

I: Alas! How shall I make it clear? When you move straight on, does it not sometimes occur to you that you could move in some other way, turning your eye round so as to look in the direction towards which your side is now fronting? In other words, instead of always moving in the direction of one of your extremities, do you never feel a desire to move in the direction, so to speak, of your side?

King: Never. And what do you mean? How can a man's inside "front" in any direction? Or how can a man move in the direction of his inside?

I: Well then, since words cannot explain the matter, I will try deeds, and will move gradually out of Lineland in the direction which I desire to indicate to you.

At the word I began to move my body out of Lineland. As long as any part of me remained in his dominion and in his view, the King kept exclaiming, "I see you, I see you still; you are not moving." But when I had at last moved myself out of his Line, he cried in his shrillest voice, "She is vanished; she is dead." "I am not dead," replied I; "I am simply out of Lineland, that is to say, out of the Straight Line which you call Space, and in the true Space, where I can see things as they are. And at this moment I can see your Line, or side – or inside as you are pleased to call it; and I can see also the Men and Women on the North and South of you, whom I will now enumerate, describing their order, their size, and the interval between each."

When I had done this at great length, I cried triumphantly, "Does that at last convince you?" And, with that, I once more entered Lineland, taking up the same position as before.

But the Monarch replied, "If you were a Man of sense – though, as you appear to have only one voice I have little doubt you are not a Man but a Woman – but, if you had a particle of sense, you would listen to reason. You ask me to believe that there is another Line besides that which my senses indicate, and another motion besides that of which I am daily conscious. I, in return, ask you to describe in words or indicate by motion that other Line of which you speak. Instead of moving, you merely exercise some magic art of vanishing and returning to sight; and instead of any lucid description of your new World, you simply tell me the numbers and sizes of some forty of my retinue, facts known to any child in my capital. Can anything be more irrational or audacious? Acknowledge your folly or depart from my dominions."

Furious at his perversity, and especially indignant that he professed to be ignorant of my sex, I retorted in no measured terms, "Besotted Being! You think yourself the perfection of existence, while you are in reality the most imperfect and imbecile. You profess to see, whereas you see nothing but a Point! You plume yourself on inferring the existence of a Straight Line; but I can see Straight Lines, and infer the existence of Angles, Triangles, Squares, Pentagons, Hexagons, and even Circles. Why waste more words? Suffice it that I am the completion of your incomplete self. You are a Line, but I am a Line of Lines called in my country a Square: and even I, infinitely superior though I am to you, am of little account among the great nobles of Flatland, whence I have come to visit you, in the hope of enlightening your ignorance."

Hearing these words the King advanced towards me with a menacing cry as if to pierce me through the diagonal; and in that same movement there arose from myriads of his subjects a multitudinous war-cry, increasing in vehemence till at last methought it rivalled the roar of an army of a hundred thousand Isosceles, and the artillery of a thousand Pentagons. Spell-bound and motionless, I could neither speak nor move to avert the impending destruction; and still the noise grew louder, and the King came closer, when I awoke to find the breakfast-bell recalling me to the realities of Flatland.

Section 15: Concerning a Stranger from Spaceland

FROM DREAMS I proceed to facts.

It was the last day of our 1999th year of our era. The patterning of the rain had long ago announced nightfall; and I was sitting **(footnote 2)** in the company of my wife, musing on the events of the past and the prospects of the coming year, the coming century, the coming Millennium.

My four Sons and two orphan Grandchildren had retired to their several apartments; and my wife alone remained with me to see the old Millennium out and the new one in.

I was rapt in thought, pondering in my mind some words that had casually issued from the mouth of my youngest Grandson, a most promising young Hexagon of unusual brilliancy and perfect angularity. His uncles and I had been giving him his usual practical lesson in Sight Recognition, turning ourselves upon our centres, now rapidly, now more slowly, and questioning him as to our positions; and his answers had been so satisfactory that I had been induced to reward him by giving him a few hints on Arithmetic, as applied to Geometry.

Taking nine Squares, each an inch every way, I had put them together so as to make one large Square, with a side of three inches, and I had hence proved to my little Grandson that – though it was impossible for us to see the inside of the Square – yet we might ascertain the number of square inches in a Square by simply squaring the number of inches in the side: "and thus," said I, "we know that three-to-the-second, or nine, represents the number of square inches in a Square whose side is three inches long."

The little Hexagon meditated on this a while and then said to me; "But you have been teaching me to raise numbers to the third power: I suppose three-to-the-third must mean something in Geometry; what does it mean?" "Nothing at all," replied I, "not at least in Geometry; for Geometry has only Two Dimensions." And then I began to shew the boy how a Point by moving through a length of three inches makes a Line of three inches, which may be represented by three; and how a Line of three inches, moving parallel to itself through a length of three inches, makes a Square of three inches every way, which may be represented by three-to-the-second. Upon this, my Grandson, again returning to his former suggestion, took me up rather suddenly and exclaimed, "Well, then, if a Point by moving three inches, makes a Line of three inches represented by three; and if a straight Line of three inches, moving parallel to itself, makes a Square of three inches every way, represented by three-to-the-second; it must be that a Square of three inches every way, moving somehow parallel to itself (but I don't see how) must make Something else (but I don't see what) of three inches every way – and this must be represented by three-to-the-third."

"Go to bed," said I, a little ruffled by this interruption: "if you would talk less nonsense, you would remember more sense."

So my Grandson had disappeared in disgrace; and there I sat by my Wife's side, endeavouring to form a retrospect of the year 1999 and of the possibilities of the year 2000; but not quite able to shake of the thoughts suggested by the prattle of my bright little Hexagon. Only a few sands now remained in the half-hour glass. Rousing myself from my reverie I turned the glass Northward for the last time in the old Millennium; and in the act, I exclaimed aloud, "The boy is a fool."

Straightway I became conscious of a Presence in the room, and a chilling breath thrilled through my very being. "He is no such thing," cried my Wife, "and you are breaking the Commandments in thus dishonouring your own Grandson." But I took no notice of her. Looking around in every direction I could see nothing; yet still I felt a Presence, and shivered as the cold whisper came again. I started up. "What is the matter?" said my Wife, "there is no draught; what are you looking for? There is nothing." There was nothing; and I resumed my seat, again exclaiming, "The boy is a fool, I say; three-to-the-third can have no meaning in Geometry." At once there came a distinctly audible reply, "The boy is not a fool; and three-to-the-third has an obvious Geometrical meaning."

My Wife as well as myself heard the words, although she did not understand their meaning, and both of us sprang forward in the direction of the sound. What was our horror when we saw before us a Figure! At the first glance it appeared to be a Woman, seen sideways; but a moment's observation shewed me that the extremities passed into dimness too rapidly to represent one of the Female Sex; and I should have thought it a Circle, only that it seemed to change its size in a manner impossible for a Circle or for any regular Figure of which I had had experience.

But my Wife had not my experience, nor the coolness necessary to note these characteristics. With the usual hastiness and unreasoning jealousy of her Sex, she flew at once to the conclusion that a Woman had entered the house through some small aperture. "How comes this person here?" she exclaimed, "you promised me, my dear, that there should be no ventilators in our new house." "Nor are they any," said I; "but what makes you think that the stranger is a Woman? I see by my power of Sight Recognition – "

"Oh, I have no patience with your Sight Recognition," replied she, "'Feeling is believing' and 'A Straight Line to the touch is worth a Circle to the sight'" – two Proverbs, very common with the Frailer Sex in Flatland.

"Well," said I, for I was afraid of irritating her, "if it must be so, demand an introduction." Assuming her most gracious manner, my Wife advanced towards the Stranger, "Permit me, Madam to feel and be felt by – " then, suddenly recoiling, "Oh! it is not a Woman, and there are no angles either, not a trace of one. Can it be that I have so misbehaved to a perfect Circle?"

"I am indeed, in a certain sense a Circle," replied the Voice, "and a more perfect Circle than any in Flatland; but to speak more accurately, I am many Circles in one." Then he added more mildly, "I have a message, dear Madam, to your husband, which I must not deliver in your presence; and, if you would suffer us to retire for a few minutes – " But my wife would not listen to the proposal that our august Visitor should so incommode himself, and assuring the Circle that the hour of her own retirement had long passed, with many reiterated apologies for her recent indiscretion, she at last retreated to her apartment.

I glanced at the half-hour glass. The last sands had fallen. The third Millennium had begun.

Footnote 2. When I say "sitting," of course I do not mean any change of attitude such as you in Spaceland signify by that word; for as we have no feet, we can no more "sit" nor "stand" (in your sense of the word) than one of your soles or flounders.

Nevertheless, we perfectly well recognize the different mental states of volition implied by "lying," "sitting," and "standing," which are to some extent indicated to a beholder by a slight increase of lustre corresponding to the increase of volition.

But on this, and a thousand other kindred subjects, time forbids me to dwell.

Section 16: How the Stranger Vainly Endeavoured to Reveal to me in Words the Mysteries of Spaceland

AS SOON as the sound of the Peace-cry of my departing Wife had died away, I began to approach the Stranger with the intention of taking a nearer view and of bidding him be seated: but his appearance struck me dumb and motionless with astonishment. Without the slightest symptoms of angularity he nevertheless varied every instant with graduations of size and brightness scarcely possible for any Figure within the scope of my experience. The thought flashed across me that I might have before me a burglar or cut-throat, some monstrous Irregular Isosceles, who, by feigning the voice of a Circle, had obtained admission somehow into the house, and was now preparing to stab me with his acute angle.

In a sitting-room, the absence of Fog (and the season happened to be remarkably dry), made it difficult for me to trust to Sight Recognition, especially at the short distance at which I was standing. Desperate with fear, I rushed forward with an unceremonious, "You must permit me, Sir – " and felt him. My Wife was right. There was not the trace of an angle, not the slightest roughness or inequality: never in my life had I met with a more perfect Circle. He remained motionless while I walked around him, beginning from his eye and returning to it again. Circular he was throughout, a perfectly satisfactory Circle; there could not be a doubt of it. Then followed a dialogue, which I will endeavour to set down as near as I can recollect it, omitting only some of my profuse apologies – for I was covered with shame and humiliation that I, a Square, should have been guilty of the impertinence of feeling a Circle. It was commenced by the Stranger with some impatience at the lengthiness of my introductory process.

Stranger: Have you felt me enough by this time? Are you not introduced to me yet?

I: Most illustrious Sir, excuse my awkwardness, which arises not from ignorance of the usages of polite society, but from a little surprise and nervousness, consequent on this somewhat unexpected visit. And I beseech you to reveal my indiscretion to no one, and especially not to my Wife. But before your Lordship enters into further communications, would he deign to satisfy the curiosity of one who would gladly know whence his visitor came?

Stranger: From Space, from Space, Sir: whence else?

I: Pardon me, my Lord, but is not your Lordship already in Space, your Lordship and his humble servant, even at this moment?

Stranger: Pooh! what do you know of Space? Define Space.

I: Space, my Lord, is height and breadth indefinitely prolonged.

Stranger: Exactly: you see you do not even know what Space is. You think it is of Two Dimensions only; but I have come to announce to you a Third – height, breadth, and length.

I: Your Lordship is pleased to be merry. We also speak of length and height, or breadth and thickness, thus denoting Two Dimensions by four names.

Stranger: But I mean not only three names, but Three Dimensions.

I: Would your Lordship indicate or explain to me in what direction is the Third Dimension, unknown to me?

Stranger: I came from it. It is up above and down below.

I: My Lord means seemingly that it is Northward and Southward.

Stranger: I mean nothing of the kind. I mean a direction in which you cannot look, because you have no eye in your side.

I: Pardon me, my Lord, a moment's inspection will convince your Lordship that I have a perfectly luminary at the juncture of my two sides.

Stranger: Yes: but in order to see into Space you ought to have an eye, not on your Perimeter, but on your side, that is, on what you would probably call your inside; but we in Spaceland should call it your side.

I: An eye in my inside! An eye in my stomach! Your Lordship jests.

Stranger: I am in no jesting humour. I tell you that I come from Space, or, since you will not understand what Space means, from the Land of Three Dimensions whence I but lately looked down upon your Plane which you call Space forsooth. From that position of advantage I discerned all that you speak of as SOLID (by which you mean "enclosed on four sides"), your houses, your churches, your very chests and safes, yes even your insides and stomachs, all lying open and exposed to my view.

I: Such assertions are easily made, my Lord.

Stranger: But not easily proved, you mean. But I mean to prove mine.

When I descended here, I saw your four Sons, the Pentagons, each in his apartment, and your two Grandsons the Hexagons; I saw your youngest Hexagon remain a while with you and then retire to his room, leaving you and your Wife alone. I saw your Isosceles servants, three in number, in the kitchen at supper, and the little Page in the scullery. Then I came here, and how do you think I came?

I: Through the roof, I suppose.

Stranger: Not so. Your roof, as you know very well, has been recently repaired, and has no aperture by which even a Woman could penetrate. I tell you I come from Space. Are you not convinced by what I have told you of your children and household?

I: Your Lordship must be aware that such facts touching the belongings of his humble servant might be easily ascertained by any one of the neighbourhood possessing your Lordship's ample means of information.

Stranger: (To himself). What must I do? Stay; one more argument suggests itself to me. When you see a Straight Line – your wife, for example – how many Dimensions do you attribute to her?

I: Your Lordship would treat me as if I were one of the vulgar who, being ignorant of Mathematics, suppose that a Woman is really a Straight Line, and only of One Dimension. No, no, my Lord; we Squares are better advised, and are as well aware of your Lordship that a Woman, though popularly called a Straight Line, is, really and scientifically, a very thin Parallelogram, possessing Two Dimensions, like the rest of us, viz., length and breadth (or thickness).

Stranger: But the very fact that a Line is visible implies that it possesses yet another Dimension.

I: My Lord, I have just acknowledged that a Woman is broad as well as long. We see her length, we infer her breadth; which, though very slight, is capable of measurement.

Stranger: You do not understand me. I mean that when you see a Woman, you ought – besides inferring her breadth – to see her length, and to see what we call her height; although the last Dimension is infinitesimal in your country. If a Line were mere length without "height," it would cease to occupy Space and would become invisible. Surely you must recognize this?

I: I must indeed confess that I do not in the least understand your Lordship. When we in Flatland see a Line, we see length and BRIGHTNESS. If the brightness disappears, the Line is extinguished, and, as you say, ceases to occupy Space. But am I to suppose that your Lordship gives the brightness the title of a Dimension, and that what we call "bright" you call "high"?

Stranger: No, indeed. By "height" I mean a Dimension like your length: only, with you, "height" is not so easily perceptible, being extremely small.

I: My Lord, your assertion is easily put to the test. You say I have a Third Dimension, which you call "height." Now, Dimension implies direction and measurement. Do but measure my "height," or merely indicate to me the direction in which my "height" extends, and I will become your convert. Otherwise, your Lordship's own understand must hold me excused.

Stranger: (To himself). I can do neither. How shall I convince him? Surely a plain statement of facts followed by ocular demonstration ought to suffice – Now, Sir; listen to me.

You are living on a Plane. What you style Flatland is the vast level surface of what I may call a fluid, or in, the top of which you and your countrymen move about, without rising above or falling below it.

I am not a plane Figure, but a Solid. You call me a Circle; but in reality I am not a Circle, but an infinite number of Circles, of size varying from a Point to a Circle of thirteen inches in diameter, one placed on the top of the other. When I cut through your plane as I am now doing, I make in your plane a section which you, very rightly, call a Circle. For even a Sphere – which is my proper name in my own country – if he manifest himself at all to an inhabitant of Flatland – must needs manifest himself as a Circle.

Do you not remember – for I, who see all things, discerned last night the phantasmal vision of Lineland written upon your brain – do you not remember, I say, how when you entered the realm of Lineland, you were compelled to manifest yourself to the King, not as a Square, but as a Line, because that Linear Realm had not Dimensions enough to represent the whole of you, but only a slice or section of you? In precisely the same way, your country of Two Dimensions is not spacious enough to represent me, a being of Three, but can only exhibit a slice or section of me, which is what you call a Circle.

The diminished brightness of your eye indicates incredulity. But now prepare to receive proof positive of the truth of my assertions. You cannot indeed see more than one of my sections, or Circles, at a time; for you have no power to raise your eye out of the plane of Flatland; but you can at least see that, as I rise in Space, so my sections become smaller. See now, I will rise; and the effect upon your eye will be that my Circle will become smaller and smaller till it dwindles to a point and finally vanishes.

There was no "rising" that I could see; but he diminished and finally vanished. I winked once or twice to make sure that I was not dreaming. But it was no dream. For from the depths of nowhere came forth a hollow voice – close to my heart it seemed – "Am I quite gone? Are you convinced now? Well, now I will gradually return to Flatland and you shall see my section become larger and larger."

Every reader in Spaceland will easily understand that my mysterious Guest was speaking the language of truth and even of simplicity. But to me, proficient though I was in Flatland Mathematics, it was by no means a simple matter. The rough diagram given above will make it clear to any Spaceland child that the Sphere, ascending in the three positions indicated there, must needs have manifested himself to me, or to any Flatlander, as a Circle, at first of full size, then small, and at last very small indeed, approaching to a Point. But to me, although I saw the facts before me, the causes were as dark as ever. All that I could comprehend was, that the Circle had made himself smaller and vanished, and that he had now re-appeared and was rapidly making himself larger.

When he regained his original size, he heaved a deep sigh; for he perceived by my silence that I had altogether failed to comprehend him. And indeed I was now inclining to the belief that he must be no Circle at all, but some extremely clever juggler; or else that the old wives' tales were true, and that after all there were such people as Enchanters and Magicians.

After a long pause he muttered to himself, "One resource alone remains, if I am not to resort to action. I must try the method of Analogy." Then followed a still longer silence, after which he continued our dialogue.

Sphere. Tell me, Mr Mathematician; if a Point moves Northward, and leaves a luminous wake, what name would you give to the wake?

I: A straight Line.

Sphere: And a straight Line has how many extremities?

I: Two.

Sphere: Now conceive the Northward straight Line moving parallel to itself, East and West, so that every point in it leaves behind it the wake of a straight Line. What name will you give to the Figure thereby formed? We will suppose that it moves through a distance equal to the original straight line. – What name, I say?

I: A square.

Sphere: And how many sides has a Square? How many angles?

I: Four sides and four angles.

Sphere: Now stretch your imagination a little, and conceive a Square in Flatland, moving parallel to itself upward.

I: What? Northward?

Sphere: No, not Northward; upward; out of Flatland altogether.

If it moved Northward, the Southern points in the Square would have to move through the positions previously occupied by the Northern points. But that is not my meaning.

I mean that every Point in you – for you are a Square and will serve the purpose of my illustration – every Point in you, that is to say in what you call your inside, is to pass upwards through Space in such a way that no Point shall pass through the position previously occupied by any other Point; but each Point shall describe a straight Line of its own. This is all in accordance with Analogy; surely it must be clear to you.

Restraining my impatience – for I was now under a strong temptation to rush blindly at my Visitor and to precipitate him into Space, or out of Flatland, anywhere, so that I could get rid of him – I replied:

"And what may be the nature of the Figure which I am to shape out by this motion which you are pleased to denote by the word 'upward'? I presume it is describable in the language of Flatland."

Sphere: Oh, certainly. It is all plain and simple, and in strict accordance with Analogy – only, by the way, you must not speak of the result as being a Figure, but as a Solid. But I will describe it to you. Or rather not I, but Analogy.

We began with a single Point, which of course – being itself a Point – has only one terminal Point.

One Point produces a Line with two terminal Points.

One Line produces a Square with four terminal Points.

Now you can give yourself the answer to your own question: 1, 2, 4, are evidently in Geometrical Progression. What is the next number?

I: Eight.

Sphere: Exactly. The one Square produces a something-which-you-do-not-as-yet-know-a-name-for-but-which-we-call-a-cube with eight terminal Points. Now are you convinced?

I: And has this Creature sides, as well as Angles or what you call "terminal Points"?

Sphere: Of course; and all according to Analogy. But, by the way, not what you call sides, but what we call sides. You would call them solids.

I: And how many solids or sides will appertain to this Being whom I am to generate by the motion of my inside in an "upward" direction, and whom you call a Cube?

Sphere: How can you ask? And you a mathematician! The side of anything is always, if I may so say, one Dimension behind the thing. Consequently, as there is no Dimension behind a Point, a Point has 0 sides; a Line, if I may so say, has 2 sides (for the points of a Line may be called by courtesy, its sides); a Square has 4 sides; 0, 2, 4; what Progression do you call that?

I: Arithmetical.

Sphere: And what is the next number?

I: Six.

Sphere: Exactly. Then you see you have answered your own question. The Cube which you will generate will be bounded by six sides, that is to say, six of your insides. You see it all now, eh?

"Monster," I shrieked, "be thou juggler, enchanter, dream, or devil, no more will I endure thy mockeries. Either thou or I must perish." And saying these words I precipitated myself upon him.

Section 17: How the Sphere, Having in Vain Tried Words, Resorted to Deeds

IT WAS IN VAIN. I brought my hardest right angle into violent collision with the Stranger, pressing on him with a force sufficient to have destroyed any ordinary Circle: but I could feel him slowly and unarrestably slipping from my contact; not edging to the right nor to the left, but moving somehow out of the world, and vanishing into nothing. Soon there was a blank. But still I heard the Intruder's voice.

Sphere: Why will you refuse to listen to reason? I had hoped to find in you – as being a man of sense and an accomplished mathematician – a fit apostle for the Gospel of the Three Dimensions, which I am allowed to preach once only in a thousand years: but now I know not how to convince you. Stay, I have it. Deeds, and not words, shall proclaim the truth. Listen, my friend.

I have told you I can see from my position in Space the inside of all things that you consider closed. For example, I see in yonder cupboard near which you are standing, several of what you call boxes (but like everything else in Flatland, they have no tops or bottom) full of money; I see also two tablets of accounts. I am about to descend into that cupboard and to bring you one of those tablets. I saw you lock the cupboard half an hour ago, and I know you have the key in your possession. But I descend from Space; the doors, you see, remain unmoved. Now I am in the cupboard and am taking the tablet. Now I have it. Now I ascend with it.

I rushed to the closet and dashed the door open. One of the tablets was gone. With a mocking laugh, the Stranger appeared in the other corner of the room, and at the same time the tablet appeared upon the floor. I took it up. There could be no doubt – it was the missing tablet.

I groaned with horror, doubting whether I was not out of my sense; but the Stranger continued: "Surely you must now see that my explanation, and no other, suits the phenomena. What you call Solid things are really superficial; what you call Space is really nothing but a great Plane. I am in Space, and look down upon the insides of the things of which you only see the outsides. You could leave the Plane yourself, if you could but summon up the necessary volition. A slight upward or downward motion would enable you to see all that I can see.

"The higher I mount, and the further I go from your Plane, the more I can see, though of course I see it on a smaller scale. For example, I am ascending; now I can see your neighbour the Hexagon and his family in their several apartments; now I see the inside of the Theatre, ten doors off, from which the audience is only just departing; and on the other side a Circle in his study, sitting at his books. Now I shall come back to you. And, as a crowning proof, what do you say to my giving you a touch, just the least touch, in your stomach? It will not seriously injure you, and the slight pain you may suffer cannot be compared with the mental benefit you will receive."

Before I could utter a word of remonstrance, I felt a shooting pain in my inside, and a demoniacal laugh seemed to issue from within me. A moment afterwards the sharp agony had ceased, leaving nothing but a dull ache behind, and the Stranger began to reappear, saying, as he gradually increased in size, "There, I have not hurt you much, have I? If you are not convinced now, I don't know what will convince you. What say you?"

My resolution was taken. It seemed intolerable that I should endure existence subject to the arbitrary visitations of a Magician who could thus play tricks with one's very stomach. If only I could in any way manage to pin him against the wall till help came!

Once more I dashed my hardest angle against him, at the same time alarming the whole household by my cries for aid. I believe, at the moment of my onset, the Stranger had sunk below our Plane, and really found difficulty in rising. In any case he remained motionless, while I, hearing, as I thought, the sound of some help approaching, pressed against him with redoubled vigor, and continued to shout for assistance.

A convulsive shudder ran through the Sphere. "This must not be," I thought I heard him say: "either he must listen to reason, or I must have recourse to the last resource of civilization." Then, addressing me in a louder tone, he hurriedly exclaimed, "Listen: no stranger must witness what you have witnessed. Send your Wife back at once, before she enters the apartment. The Gospel of Three Dimensions must not be thus frustrated. Not thus must the fruits of one thousand years of waiting be thrown away. I hear her coming. Back! back! Away from me, or you must go with me – wither you know not – into the Land of Three Dimensions!"

"Fool! Madman! Irregular!" I exclaimed; "never will I release thee; thou shalt pay the penalty of thine impostures."

"Ha! Is it come to this?" thundered the Stranger: "then meet your fate: out of your Plane you go. Once, twice, thrice! 'Tis done!"

48

Section 18: How I came to Spaceland, and What I Saw There

AN UNSPEAKABLE HORROR seized me. There was a darkness; then a dizzy, sickening sensation of sight that was not like seeing; I saw a Line that was no Line; Space that was not Space: I was myself, and not myself. When I could find voice, I shrieked loud in agony, "Either this is madness or it is Hell." "It is neither," calmly replied the voice of the Sphere, "it is Knowledge; it is Three Dimensions: open your eye once again and try to look steadily."

I looked, and, behold, a new world! There stood before me, visibly incorporate, all that I had before inferred, conjectured, dreamed, of perfect Circular beauty. What seemed the centre of the Stranger's form lay open to my view: yet I could see no heart, lungs, nor arteries, only a beautiful harmonious Something – for which I had no words; but you, my Readers in Spaceland, would call it the surface of the Sphere.

Prostrating myself mentally before my Guide, I cried, "How is it, O divine ideal of consummate loveliness and wisdom that I see thy inside, and yet cannot discern thy heart, thy lungs, thy arteries, thy liver?" "What you think you see, you see not," he replied; "it is not giving to you, nor to any other Being, to behold my internal parts. I am of a different order of Beings from those in Flatland. Were I a Circle, you could discern my intestines, but I am a Being, composed as I told you before, of many Circles, the Many in the One, called in this country a Sphere. And, just as the outside of a Cube is a Square, so the outside of a Sphere represents the appearance of a Circle."

Bewildered though I was by my Teacher's enigmatic utterance, I no longer chafed against it, but worshipped him in silent adoration. He continued, with more mildness in his voice. "Distress not yourself if you cannot at first understand the deeper mysteries of Spaceland. By degrees they will dawn upon you. Let us begin by casting back a glance at the region whence you came. Return with me a while to the plains of Flatland and I will shew you that which you have often reasoned and thought about, but never seen with the sense of sight – a visible angle." "Impossible!" I cried; but, the Sphere leading the way, I followed as if in a dream, till once more his voice arrested me: "Look yonder, and behold your own Pentagonal house, and all its inmates."

I looked below, and saw with my physical eye all that domestic individuality which I had hitherto merely inferred with the understanding. And how poor and shadowy was the inferred conjecture in comparison with the reality which I now behold! My four Sons calmly asleep in the North-Western rooms, my two orphan Grandsons to the South; the Servants, the Butler, my Daughter, all in their several apartments. Only my affectionate Wife, alarmed by my continued absence, had quitted her room and was roving up and down in the Hall, anxiously awaiting my return. Also the Page, aroused by my cries, had left his room, and under pretext of ascertaining whether I had fallen somewhere in a faint, was prying into the cabinet in my study. All this I could now see, not merely infer; and as we came nearer and nearer, I could discern even the contents of my cabinet, and the two chests of gold, and the tablets of which the Sphere had made mention.

Touched by my Wife's distress, I would have sprung downward to reassure her, but I found myself incapable of motion. "Trouble not yourself about your Wife," said my Guide: "she will not be long left in anxiety; meantime, let us take a survey of Flatland."

Once more I felt myself rising through space. It was even as the Sphere had said. The further we receded from the object we beheld, the larger became the field of vision. My native city, with the interior of every house and every creature therein, lay open to my view in miniature. We mounted higher, and lo, the secrets of the earth, the depths of the mines and inmost caverns of the hills, were bared before me.

Awestruck at the sight of the mysteries of the earth, thus unveiled before my unworthy eye, I said to my Companion, "Behold, I am become as a God. For the wise men in our country say that to see all things, or as they express it, omnividence, is the attribute of God alone." There was something of scorn in the voice of my Teacher as he made answer: "it is so indeed? Then the very pick-pockets and cut-throats of my country are to be worshipped by your wise men as being Gods: for there is not one of them that does not see as much as you see now. But trust me, your wise men are wrong."

I: Then is omnividence the attribute of others besides Gods?

Sphere: I do not know. But, if a pick-pocket or a cut-throat of our country can see everything that is in your country, surely that is no reason why the pick-pocket or cut-throat should be accepted by you as a God. This omnividence, as you call it – it is not a common word in Spaceland – does it make you more just, more merciful, less selfish, more loving? Not in the least. Then how does it make you more divine?

I: "More merciful, more loving!" But these are the qualities of women! And we know that a Circle is a higher Being than a Straight Line, in so far as knowledge and wisdom are more to be esteemed than mere affection.

Sphere: It is not for me to classify human faculties according to merit. Yet many of the best and wisest in Spaceland think more of the affections than of the understand, more of your despised Straight Lines than of your belauded Circles. But enough of this. Look yonder. Do you know that building?

I looked, and afar off I saw an immense Polygonal structure, in which I recognized the General Assembly Hall of the States of Flatland, surrounded by dense lines of Pentagonal buildings at right angles to each other, which I knew to be streets; and I perceived that I was approaching the great Metropolis.

"Here we descend," said my Guide. It was now morning, the first hour of the first day of the two thousandth year of our era. Acting, as was their wont, in strict accordance with precedent, the highest Circles of the realm were meeting in solemn conclave, as they had met on the first hour of the first day of the year 1000, and also on the first hour of the first day of the year 0.

The minutes of the previous meetings were now read by one whom I at once recognized as my brother, a perfectly Symmetrical Square, and the Chief Clerk of the High Council. It was found recorded on each occasion that: "Whereas the States had been troubled by divers ill-intentioned persons pretending to have received revelations from another World, and professing to produce demonstrations whereby they had instigated to frenzy both themselves and others, it had been for this cause unanimously resolved by the Grand Council that on the first day of each millenary, special injunctions be sent to the Prefects in the several districts of Flatland, to make strict search for such misguided persons, and without formality of mathematical examination, to destroy all such as were Isosceles of any degree, to scourge and imprison any regular Triangle, to cause any Square or Pentagon to be sent to the district Asylum, and to arrest any one of higher rank, sending him straightway to the Capital to be examined and judged by the Council."

"You hear your fate," said the Sphere to me, while the Council was passing for the third time the formal resolution. "Death or imprisonment awaits the Apostle of the Gospel of Three Dimensions." "Not so," replied I, "the matter is now so clear to me, the nature of real space so palpable, that methinks I could make a child understand it. Permit me but to descend at this moment and enlighten them." "Not yet," said my Guide, "the time will come for that. Meantime I must perform my mission. Stay thou there in thy place." Saying these words, he leaped with great dexterity into the sea (if I may so call it) of Flatland, right in the midst of the ring of Counsellors. "I come," said he, "to proclaim that there is a land of Three Dimensions."

I could see many of the younger Counsellors start back in manifest horror, as the Sphere's circular section widened before them. But on a sign from the presiding Circle – who shewed not the slightest alarm or surprise – six Isosceles of a low type from six different quarters rushed upon the Sphere. "We have him," they cried; "No; yes; we have him still! he's going! he's gone!"

"My Lords," said the President to the Junior Circles of the Council, "there is not the slightest need for surprise; the secret archives, to which I alone have access, tell me that a similar occurrence happened on the last two millennial commencements. You will, of course, say nothing of these trifles outside the Cabinet."

Raising his voice, he now summoned the guards. "Arrest the policemen; gag them. You know your duty." After he had consigned to their fate the wretched policemen – ill-fated and unwilling witnesses of a State-secret which they were not to be permitted to reveal – he again addressed the Counsellors. "My Lords, the business of the Council being concluded, I have only to wish you a happy New Year." Before departing, he expressed, at some length, to the Clerk, my excellent but most unfortunate brother, his sincere regret that, in accordance with precedent and for the sake of secrecy, he must condemn him to perpetual imprisonment, but added his satisfaction that, unless some mention were made by him of that day's incident, his life would be spared.

Section 19: How, Though the Sphere Shewed Me Other Mysteries of Spaceland, I Still Desire More; and What Came of It

WHEN I SAW my poor brother led away to imprisonment, I attempted to leap down into the Council Chamber, desiring to intercede on his behalf, or at least bid him farewell. But I found that I had no motion of my own. I absolutely depended on the volition of my Guide, who said in gloomy tones, "Heed not thy brother; haply thou shalt have ample time hereafter to condole with him. Follow me."

Once more we ascended into space. "Hitherto," said the Sphere, "I have shewn you naught save Plane Figures and their interiors. Now I must introduce you to Solids, and reveal to you the plan upon which they are constructed. Behold this multitude of moveable square cards. See, I put one on another, not, as you supposed, Northward of the other, but on the other. Now a second, now a third. See, I am building up a Solid by a multitude of Squares parallel to one another. Now the Solid is complete, being as high as it is long and broad, and we call it a Cube."

"Pardon me, my Lord," replied I; "but to my eye the appearance is as of an Irregular Figure whose inside is laid open to view; in other words, methinks I see no Solid, but a Plane such as we infer in Flatland; only of an Irregularity which betokens some monstrous criminal, so that the very sight of it is painful to my eyes."

"True," said the Sphere; "it appears to you a Plane, because you are not accustomed to light and shade and perspective; just as in Flatland a Hexagon would appear a Straight Line to one who has not the Art of Sight Recognition. But in reality it is a Solid, as you shall learn by the sense of Feeling."

He then introduced me to the Cube, and I found that this marvellous Being was indeed no Plane, but a Solid; and that he was endowed with six plane sides and eight terminal points called solid angles; and I remembered the saying of the Sphere that just such a Creature as this would be formed by the Square moving, in Space, parallel to himself: and I rejoiced to think that so insignificant a Creature as I could in some sense be called the Progenitor of so illustrious an offspring.

But still I could not fully understand the meaning of what my Teacher had told me concerning "light" and "shade" and "perspective"; and I did not hesitate to put my difficulties before him.

Were I to give the Sphere's explanation of these matters, succinct and clear though it was, it would be tedious to an inhabitant of Space, who knows these things already. Suffice it, that by his lucid statements, and by changing the position of objects and lights, and by allowing me to feel the several objects and even his own sacred Person, he at last made all things clear to me, so that I could now readily distinguish between a Circle and a Sphere, a Plane Figure and a Solid.

This was the Climax, the Paradise, of my strange eventful History. Henceforth I have to relate the story of my miserable Fall: most miserable, yet surely most undeserved! For why should the thirst for knowledge be aroused, only to be disappointed and punished? My volition shrinks from the painful task of recalling my humiliation; yet, like a second Prometheus, I will endure this and worse, if by any means I may arouse in the interiors of Plane and Solid Humanity a spirit of rebellion against the Conceit which would limit our Dimensions to Two or Three or any number short of Infinity. Away then with all personal considerations! Let me continue to the end, as I began, without further digressions or anticipations, pursuing the plain path of dispassionate History. The exact facts, the exact words – and they are burnt in upon my brain – shall be set down without alteration of an iota; and let my Readers judge between me and Destiny.

The Sphere would willingly have continued his lessons by indoctrinating me in the conformation of all regular Solids, Cylinders, Cones, Pyramids, Pentahedrons, Hexahedrons, Dodecahedrons, and Spheres: but I ventured to interrupt him. Not that I was wearied of knowledge. On the contrary, I thirsted for yet deeper and fuller draughts than he was offering to me.

"Pardon me," said I, "O Thou Whom I must no longer address as the Perfection of all Beauty; but let me beg thee to vouchsafe thy servant a sight of thine interior."

Sphere: My what?

I: Thine interior: thy stomach, thy intestines.

Sphere: Whence this ill-timed impertinent request? And what mean you by saying that I am no longer the Perfection of all Beauty?

I: My Lord, your own wisdom has taught me to aspire to One even more great, more beautiful, and more closely approximate to Perfection than yourself. As you yourself, superior to all Flatland forms, combine many Circles in One, so doubtless there is One above you who combines many Spheres in One Supreme Existence, surpassing even the Solids of Spaceland. And even as we, who are now in Space, look down on Flatland and see the insides of all things, so of a certainty there is yet above us some higher, purer region, whither thou dost surely purpose to lead me – O Thou Whom I shall always call, everywhere and in all Dimensions, my Priest, Philosopher, and Friend – some yet more spacious Space, some more dimensionable Dimensionality, from the vantage-ground of which we shall look down together upon the revealed insides of Solid things, and where thine own intestines, and those of thy kindred Spheres, will lie exposed to the view of the poor wandering exile from Flatland, to whom so much has already been vouchsafed.

Sphere: Pooh! Stuff! Enough of this trifling! The time is short, and much remains to be done before you are fit to proclaim the Gospel of Three Dimensions to your blind benighted countrymen in Flatland.

I: Nay, gracious Teacher, deny me not what I know it is in thy power to reform. Grant me but one glimpse of thine interior, and I am satisfied for ever, remaining henceforth thy docile pupil, thy unemancipable slave, ready to receive all thy teachings and to feed upon the words that fall from thy lips.

Sphere: Well, then, to content and silence you, let me say at once, I would shew you what you wish if I could; but I cannot. Would you have me turn my stomach inside out to oblige you?

I: But my Lord has shewn me the intestines of all my countrymen in the Land of Two Dimensions by taking me with him into the Land of Three. What therefore more easy than now to take his servant on a second journey into the blessed region of the Fourth Dimension, where I shall look down with him once more upon this land of Three Dimensions, and see the inside of every three-dimensioned house, the secrets of the solid earth, the treasures of the mines of Spaceland, and the intestines of every solid living creature, even the noble and adorable Spheres.

Sphere: But where is this land of Four Dimensions?

I: I know not: but doubtless my Teacher knows.

Sphere: Not I. There is no such land. The very idea of it is utterly inconceivable.

I: Not inconceivable, my Lord, to me, and therefore still less inconceivable to my Master. Nay, I despair not that, even here, in this region of Three Dimensions, your Lordship's art may make the Fourth Dimension visible to me; just as in the Land of Two Dimensions my Teacher's skill would fain have opened the eyes of his blind servant to the invisible presence of a Third Dimension, though I saw it not.

Let me recall the past. Was I not taught below that when I saw a Line and inferred a Plane, I in reality saw a Third unrecognized Dimension, not the same as brightness, called "height"? And does it not now follow that, in this region, when I see a Plane and infer a Solid, I really see a Fourth unrecognized Dimension, not the same as colour, but existent, though infinitesimal and incapable of measurement?

And besides this, there is the Argument from Analogy of Figures.

Sphere: Analogy! Nonsense: what analogy?

I: Your Lordship tempts his servant to see whether he remembers the revelations imparted to him. Trifle not with me, my Lord; I crave, I thirst, for more knowledge. Doubtless we cannot see that other higher Spaceland now, because we have no eye in our stomachs. But, just as there was the realm of Flatland, though that poor puny Lineland Monarch could neither turn to left nor right to discern it, and just as there WAS close at hand, and touching my frame, the land of Three Dimensions, though I, blind senseless wretch, had no power to touch it, no eye in my interior to discern it, so of a surety there is a Fourth Dimension, which my Lord perceives with the inner eye of thought. And that it must exist my Lord himself has taught me. Or can he have forgotten what he himself imparted to his servant?

In One Dimension, did not a moving Point produce a Line with two terminal points?

In Two Dimensions, did not a moving Line produce a Square with four terminal points?

In Three Dimensions, did not a moving Square produce – did not this eye of mine behold it – that blessed Being, a Cube, with eight terminal points?

And in Four Dimensions shall not a moving Cube – alas, for Analogy, and alas for the Progress of Truth, if it be not so – shall not, I say, the motion of a divine Cube result in a still more divine Organization with sixteen terminal points?

Behold the infallible confirmation of the Series, 2, 4, 8, 16: is not this a Geometrical Progression? Is not this – if I might quote my Lord's own words – "strictly according to Analogy"?

Again, was I not taught by my Lord that as in a Line there are two bounding Points, and in a Square there are four bounding Lines, so in a Cube there must be six bounding Squares? Behold once more the confirming Series, 2, 4, 6: is not this an Arithmetical Progression? And consequently does it not of necessity follow that the more divine offspring of the divine Cube in the Land of Four Dimensions, must have 8 bounding Cubes: and is not this also, as my Lord has taught me to believe, "strictly according to Analogy"? O, my Lord, my Lord, behold, I cast myself in faith upon conjecture, not knowing the facts; and I appeal to your Lordship to confirm or deny my logical anticipations. If I am wrong, I yield, and will no longer demand a Fourth Dimension; but, if I am right, my Lord will listen to reason.

I ask therefore, is it, or is it not, the fact, that ere now your countrymen also have witnessed the descent of Beings of a higher order than their own, entering closed rooms, even as your Lordship entered mine, without the opening of doors or windows, and appearing and vanishing at will? On the reply to this question I am ready to stake everything. Deny it, and I am henceforth silent. Only vouchsafe an answer.

Sphere: (After a pause). It is reported so. But men are divided in opinion as to the facts. And even granting the facts, they explain them in different ways. And in any case, however great may be the number of different explanations, no one has adopted or suggested the theory of a Fourth Dimension. Therefore, pray have done with this trifling, and let us return to business.

I: I was certain of it. I was certain that my anticipations would be fulfilled. And now have patience with me and answer me yet one more question, best of Teachers! Those who have thus appeared – no one knows whence – and have returned – no one knows whither – have they also contracted their sections and vanished somehow into that more Spacious Space, whither I now entreat you to conduct me?

Sphere: (Moodily). They have vanished, certainly – if they ever appeared. But most people say that these visions arose from the thought – you will not understand me – from the brain; from the perturbed angularity of the Seer.

I: Say they so? Oh, believe them not. Or if it indeed be so, that this other Space is really Thoughtland, then take me to that blessed Region where I in Thought shall see the insides of all solid things. There, before my ravished eye, a Cube moving in some altogether new direction, but strictly according to Analogy, so as to make every particle of his interior pass through a new kind of Space, with a wake of its own – shall create a still more perfect perfection than himself, with sixteen terminal Extra-solid angles, and Eight solid Cubes for his Perimeter. And once there, shall we stay our upward course? In that blessed region of Four Dimensions, shall we linger at the threshold of the Fifth, and not enter therein? Ah, no! Let us rather resolve that our ambition shall soar with our corporal ascent. Then, yielding to our intellectual onset, the gates of the Six Dimension shall fly open; after that a Seventh, and then an Eighth –

How long I should have continued I know not. In vain did the Sphere, in his voice of thunder, reiterate his command of silence, and threaten me with the direst penalties if I persisted. Nothing could stem the flood of my ecstatic aspirations. Perhaps I was to blame; but indeed I was intoxicated with the recent draughts of Truth to which he himself had introduced me. However, the end was not long in coming. My words were cut short by a crash outside, and a simultaneous crash inside me, which impelled me through space with a velocity that precluded speech. Down! down! down! I was rapidly descending; and I knew that return to Flatland was my doom. One glimpse, one last and never-to-be-forgotten glimpse I had of that dull level wilderness – which was now to become my Universe again – spread out before my eye. Then a darkness. Then a final, all-consummating thunder-peal; and, when I came to myself, I was once more a common creeping Square, in my Study at home, listening to the Peace-Cry of my approaching Wife.

Section 20: How the Sphere Encouraged Me in a Vision

ALTHOUGH I HAD less than a minute for reflection, I felt, by a kind of instinct, that I must conceal my experiences from my Wife. Not that I apprehended, at the moment, any danger from her divulging my secret, but I knew that to any Woman in Flatland the narrative of my adventures must needs be unintelligible. So I endeavoured to reassure her by some story, invented for the occasion, that I had accidentally fallen through the trap-door of the cellar, and had there lain stunned.

The Southward attraction in our country is so slight that even to a Woman my tale necessarily appeared extraordinary and well-nigh incredible; but my Wife, whose good sense far exceeds that of the average of her Sex, and who perceived that I was unusually excited, did not argue with me on the subject, but insisted that I was ill and required repose. I was glad of an excuse for retiring to my chamber to think quietly over what had happened. When I was at last by myself, a drowsy sensation fell on me; but before my eyes closed I endeavoured to reproduce the Third Dimension, and especially the process by which a Cube is constructed through the motion of a Square. It was not so clear as I could have wished; but I remembered that it must be "Upward, and yet not Northward," and I determined steadfastly to retain these words as the clue which, if firmly grasped, could not fail to guide me to the solution. So mechanically repeating, like a charm, the words, "Upward, yet not Northward," I fell into a sound refreshing sleep.

During my slumber I had a dream. I thought I was once more by the side of the Sphere, whose lustrous hue betokened that he had exchanged his wrath against me for perfectly placability. We were moving together towards a bright but infinitesimally small Point, to which my Master directed my attention. As we approached, methought there issued from it a slight humming noise as from one of your Spaceland bluebottles, only less resonant by far, so slight indeed that even in the perfect stillness of the Vacuum through which we soared, the sound reached not our ears till we checked our flight at a distance from it of something under twenty human diagonals.

"Look yonder," said my Guide, "in Flatland thou hast lived; of Lineland thou hast received a vision; thou hast soared with me to the heights of Spaceland; now, in order to complete the range of thy experience, I conduct thee downward to the lowest depth of existence, even to the realm of Pointland, the Abyss of No dimensions.

"Behold yon miserable creature. That Point is a Being like ourselves, but confined to the non-dimensional Gulf. He is himself his own World, his own Universe; of any other than himself he can form no conception; he knows not Length, nor Breadth, nor Height, for he has had no experience of them; he has no cognizance even of the number Two; nor has he a thought of Plurality; for he is himself his One and All, being really Nothing. Yet mark his perfect self-contentment, and hence learn his lesson, that to be self-contented is to be vile and ignorant, and that to aspire is better than to be blindly and impotently happy. Now listen."

He ceased; and there arose from the little buzzing creature a tiny, low, monotonous, but distinct tinkling, as from one of your Spaceland phonographs, from which I caught these words, "Infinite beatitude of existence! It is; and there is nothing else beside It."

"What," said I, "does the puny creature mean by 'it'?" "He means himself," said the Sphere: "have you not noticed before now, that babies and babyish people who cannot distinguish themselves from the world, speak of themselves in the Third Person? But hush!"

"It fills all Space," continued the little soliloquizing Creature, "and what It fills, It is. What It thinks, that It utters; and what It utters, that It hears; and It itself is Thinker, Utterer, Hearer, Thought, Word, Audition; it is the One, and yet the All in All. Ah, the happiness, ah, the happiness of Being!"

"Can you not startle the little thing out of its complacency?" said I. "Tell it what it really is, as you told me; reveal to it the narrow limitations of Pointland, and lead it up to something higher." "That is no easy task," said my Master; "try you."

Hereon, raising by voice to the uttermost, I addressed the Point as follows:

"Silence, silence, contemptible Creature. You call yourself the All in All, but you are the Nothing: your so-called Universe is a mere speck in a Line, and a Line is a mere shadow as compared with – " "Hush, hush, you have said enough," interrupted the Sphere, "now listen, and mark the effect of your harangue on the King of Pointland."

The lustre of the Monarch, who beamed more brightly than ever upon hearing my words, shewed clearly that he retained his complacency; and I had hardly ceased when he took up his strain again. "Ah, the joy, ah, the joy of Thought! What can It not achieve by thinking! Its own Thought coming to Itself, suggestive of its disparagement, thereby to enhance Its happiness! Sweet rebellion stirred up to result in triumph! Ah, the divine creative power of the All in One! Ah, the joy, the joy of Being!"

"You see," said my Teacher, "how little your words have done. So far as the Monarch understand them at all, he accepts them as his own – for he cannot conceive of any other except himself – and plumes himself upon the variety of 'Its Thought' as an instance of creative Power. Let us leave this God of Pointland to the ignorant fruition of his omnipresence and omniscience: nothing that you or I can do can rescue him from his self-satisfaction."

After this, as we floated gently back to Flatland, I could hear the mild voice of my Companion pointing the moral of my vision, and stimulating me to aspire, and to teach others to aspire. He had been angered at first – he confessed – by my ambition to soar to Dimensions above the Third; but, since then, he had received fresh insight, and he was not too proud to acknowledge his error to a Pupil. Then he proceeded to initiate me into mysteries yet higher than those I had witnessed, shewing me how to construct Extra-Solids by the motion of Solids, and Double Extra-Solids by the motion of Extra-Solids, and all "strictly according to Analogy," all by methods so simple, so easy, as to be patent even to the Female Sex.

Section 21: How I Tried to Teach the Theory of Three Dimensions to My Grandson, and With What Success

I AWOKE REJOICING, and began to reflect on the glorious career before me. I would go forth, methought, at once, and evangelize the whole of Flatland. Even to Women and Soldiers should the Gospel of Three Dimensions be proclaimed. I would begin with my Wife.

Just as I had decided on the plan of my operations, I heard the sound of many voices in the street commanding silence. Then followed a louder voice. It was a herald's proclamation.

Listening attentively, I recognized the words of the Resolution of the Council, enjoining the arrest, imprisonment, or execution of any one who should pervert the minds of people by delusions, and by professing to have received revelations from another World.

I reflected. This danger was not to be trifled with. It would be better to avoid it by omitting all mention of my Revelation, and by proceeding on the path of Demonstration – which after all, seemed so simple and so conclusive that nothing would be lost by discarding the former means. "Upward, not Northward" – was the clue to the whole proof. It had seemed to me fairly clear before I fell asleep; and when I first awoke, fresh from my dream, it had appeared as patent as Arithmetic; but somehow it did not seem to me quite so obvious now. Though my Wife entered the room opportunely at just that moment, I decided, after we had exchanged a few words of commonplace conversation, not to begin with her.

My Pentagonal Sons were men of character and standing, and physicians of no mean reputation, but not great in mathematics, and, in that respect, unfit for my purpose. But it occurred to me that a young and docile Hexagon, with a mathematical turn, would be a most suitable pupil. Why therefore not make my first experiment with my little precocious Grandson, whose casual remarks on the meaning of three-to-the-third had met with the approval of the Sphere? Discussing the matter with him, a mere boy, I should be in perfect safety; for he would know nothing of the Proclamation of the Council; whereas I could not feel sure that my Sons – so greatly did their patriotism and reverence for the Circles predominate over mere blind affection – might not feel compelled to hand me over to the Prefect, if they found me seriously maintaining the seditious heresy of the Third Dimension.

But the first thing to be done was to satisfy in some way the curiosity of my Wife, who naturally wished to know something of the reasons for which the Circle had desired that mysterious interview, and of the means by which he had entered the house. Without entering into the details of the elaborate account I gave her – an account, I fear, not quite so consistent with truth as my Readers in Spaceland might desire – I must be content with saying that I succeeded at last in persuading her to return quietly to her household duties without eliciting from me any reference to the World of Three Dimensions. This done, I immediately sent for my Grandson; for, to confess the truth, I felt that all that I had seen and heard was in some strange way slipping away from me, like the image of a half-grasped, tantalizing dream, and I longed to essay my skill in making a first disciple.

When my Grandson entered the room I carefully secured the door. Then, sitting down by his side and taking our mathematical tablets, – or, as you would call them, Lines – I told him we would resume the lesson of yesterday. I taught him once more how a Point by motion in One Dimension produces a Line, and how a straight Line in Two Dimensions produces a Square. After this, forcing a laugh, I said, "And now, you scamp, you wanted to make believe that a Square may in the same way by motion 'Upward, not Northward' produce another figure, a sort of extra square in Three Dimensions. Say that again, you young rascal."

At this moment we heard once more the herald's "O yes! O yes!" outside in the street proclaiming the Resolution of the Council. Young though he was, my Grandson – who was unusually intelligent for his age, and bred up in perfect reverence for the authority of the Circles – took in the situation with an acuteness for which I was quite unprepared. He remained silent till the last words of the Proclamation had died away, and then, bursting into tears, "Dear Grandpapa," he said, "that was only my fun, and of course I meant nothing at all by it; and we did not know anything then about the new Law; and I don't think I said anything about the Third Dimension; and I am sure I did not say one word about 'Upward, not Northward,' for that would be such nonsense, you know. How could a thing move

Upward, and not Northward? Upward and not Northward! Even if I were a baby, I could not be so absurd as that. How silly it is! Ha! Ha! Ha!"

"Not at all silly," said I, losing my temper; "here for example, I take this Square," and, at the word, I grasped a moveable Square, which was lying at hand – "and I move it, you see, not Northward but – yes, I move it Upward – that is to say, Northward but I move it somewhere – not exactly like this, but somehow – " Here I brought my sentence to an inane conclusion, shaking the Square about in a purposeless manner, much to the amusement of my Grandson, who burst out laughing louder than ever, and declared that I was not teaching him, but joking with him; and so saying he unlocked the door and ran out of the room. Thus ended my first attempt to convert a pupil to the Gospel of Three Dimensions.

Section 22: How I Then Tried to Diffuse the Theory of Three Dimensions by Other Means, and of the Result

MY FAILURE with my Grandson did not encourage me to communicate my secret to others of my household; yet neither was I led by it to despair of success. Only I saw that I must not wholly rely on the catch-phrase, "Upward, not Northward," but must rather endeavour to seek a demonstration by setting before the public a clear view of the whole subject; and for this purpose it seemed necessary to resort to writing.

So I devoted several months in privacy to the composition of a treatise on the mysteries of Three Dimensions. Only, with the view of evading the Law, if possible, I spoke not of a physical Dimension, but of a Thoughtland whence, in theory, a Figure could look down upon Flatland and see simultaneously the insides of all things, and where it was possible that there might be supposed to exist a Figure environed, as it were, with six Squares, and containing eight terminal Points. But in writing this book I found myself sadly hampered by the impossibility of drawing such diagrams as were necessary for my purpose: for of course, in our country of Flatland, there are no tablets but Lines, and no diagrams but Lines, all in one straight Line and only distinguishable by difference of size and brightness; so that, when I had finished my treatise (which I entitled, "Through Flatland to Thoughtland") I could not feel certain that many would understand my meaning.

Meanwhile my wife was under a cloud. All pleasures palled upon me; all sights tantalized and tempted me to outspoken treason, because I could not compare what I saw in Two Dimensions with what it really was if seen in Three, and could hardly refrain from making my comparisons aloud. I neglected my clients and my own business to give myself to the contemplation of the mysteries which I had once beheld, yet which I could impart to no one, and found daily more difficult to reproduce even before my own mental vision. One day, about eleven months after my return from Spaceland, I tried to see a Cube with my eye closed, but failed; and though I succeeded afterwards, I was not then quite certain (nor have I been ever afterwards) that I had exactly realized the original. This made me more melancholy than before, and determined me to take some step; yet what, I knew not. I felt that I would have been willing to sacrifice my life for the Cause, if thereby I could have produced conviction. But if I could not convince my Grandson, how could I convince the highest and most developed Circles in the land?

And yet at times my spirit was too strong for me, and I gave vent to dangerous utterances. Already I was considered heterodox if not treasonable, and I was keenly alive to the danger of my position; nevertheless I could not at times refrain from bursting out into suspicious or half-seditious utterances, even among the highest Polygonal or Circular society. When, for example, the question arose about the treatment of those lunatics who said that they had received the power of seeing the insides of things, I would quote the saying of an ancient Circle, who declared that prophets and inspired people are always considered by the majority to be mad; and I could not help occasionally dropping such expressions as "the eye that discerns the interiors of things," and "the all-seeing land"; once or twice I even let fall the forbidden terms "the Third and Fourth Dimensions." At last, to complete a series of minor indiscretions, at a meeting of our Local Speculative Society held at the palace of the Prefect himself – some extremely silly person having read an elaborate paper exhibiting the precise reasons why Providence has limited the number of Dimensions to Two, and why the attribute of omnividence is assigned to the Supreme alone – I so far forgot myself as to give an exact account of the whole of my voyage with the Sphere into Space, and to the Assembly Hall in our Metropolis, and then to Space again, and of my return home, and of everything that I had seen and heard in fact or vision. At first, indeed, I pretended that I was describing the imaginary experiences of a fictitious person; but my enthusiasm soon forced me to throw off all disguise, and finally, in a fervent peroration, I exhorted all my hearers to divest themselves of prejudice and to become believers in the Third Dimension.

Need I say that I was at once arrested and taken before the Council?

Next morning, standing in the very place where but a very few months ago the Sphere had stood in my company, I was allowed to begin and to continue my narration unquestioned and uninterrupted. But from the first I foresaw my fate; for the President, noting that a guard of the better sort of Policemen was in attendance, of angularity little, if at all, under 55 degrees, ordered them to be relieved before I began my defence, by an inferior class of 2 or 3 degrees. I knew only too well what that meant. I was to be executed or imprisoned, and my story was to be kept secret from the world by the simultaneous destruction of the officials who had heard it; and, this being the case, the President desired to substitute the cheaper for the more expensive victims.

After I had concluded my defence, the President, perhaps perceiving that some of the junior Circles had been moved by evident earnestness, asked me two questions:

1. Whether I could indicate the direction which I meant when I used the words "Upward, not Northward"?
2. Whether I could by any diagrams or descriptions (other than the enumeration of imaginary sides and angles) indicate the Figure I was pleased to call a Cube?

I declared that I could say nothing more, and that I must commit myself to the Truth, whose cause would surely prevail in the end.

The President replied that he quite concurred in my sentiment, and that I could not do better. I must be sentenced to perpetual imprisonment; but if the Truth intended that I should emerge from prison and evangelize the world, the Truth might be trusted to bring that result to pass. Meanwhile I should be subjected to no discomfort that was not necessary to preclude escape, and, unless I forfeited the privilege by misconduct, I should be occasionally permitted to see my brother who had preceded me to my prison.

Seven years have elapsed and I am still a prisoner, and – if I except the occasional visits of my brother – debarred from all companionship save that of my jailers. My brother is one of the best of Squares, just sensible, cheerful, and not without fraternal affection; yet I confess that my weekly interviews, at least in one respect, cause me the bitterest pain. He was present when the Sphere manifested himself in the Council Chamber; he saw the Sphere's changing sections; he heard the explanation of the phenomena then give to the Circles. Since that time, scarcely a week has passed during seven whole years, without his hearing from me a repetition of the part I played in that manifestation, together with ample descriptions of all the phenomena in Spaceland, and the arguments for the existence of Solid things derivable from Analogy. Yet – I take shame to be forced to confess it – my brother has not yet grasped the nature of Three Dimensions, and frankly avows his disbelief in the existence of a Sphere.

Hence I am absolutely destitute of converts, and, for aught that I can see, the millennial Revelation has been made to me for nothing. Prometheus up in Spaceland was bound for bringing down fire for mortals, but I – poor Flatland Prometheus – lie here in prison for bringing down nothing to my countrymen. Yet I existing the hope that these memoirs, in some manner, I know not how, may find their way to the minds of humanity in Some Dimension, and may stir up a race of rebels who shall refuse to be confined to limited Dimensionality.

That is the hope of my brighter moments. Alas, it is not always so. Heavily weights on me at times the burdensome reflection that I cannot honestly say I am confident as to the exact shape of the once-seen, oft-regretted Cube; and in my nightly visions the mysterious precept, "Upward, not Northward," haunts me like a soul-devouring Sphinx. It is part of the martyrdom which I endure for the cause of Truth that there are seasons of mental weakness, when Cubes and Spheres flit away into the background of scarce-possible existences; when the Land of Three Dimensions seems almost as visionary as the Land of One or None; nay, when even this hard wall that bars me from my freedom, these very tablets on which I am writing, and all the substantial realities of Flatland itself, appear no better than the offspring of a diseased imagination, or the baseless fabric of a dream.

The Body Surfer

Edward Ahern

DANTON ROUSED to the sense turmoil of his new host - gasoline smoke, dung flavored dust, lice bites, the taste of spiced mutton, the ache of hernia, tiny horns, and blurred vision of a tent stocked with cloth.

The last host had been driving to this village when it was broadsided by a Mercedes truck. It had bled out, forcing Danton to blindly flee into a new body.

Burrow now, burrow. Slide past the thinking and the seeing and the hearing. Deeper, hiding depth at the bottom of the mind.

Danton waits, measuring time by his host's body rhythms. He hibernates, sipping from its energy and cradling in its rhythms.

Motions ebb. Breathing slows. Pulse lowers. Now, Danton thinks, let's see what I'm riding. Gently creep up from the lair. Seep upward, deadening and oozing, an invasive well spring. Pluck from the sleeping sensations. Fat circulating from the evening meal. New sweat coating old. Rasping tobacco breath. Eyelid flutter. Dream of saffron rice.

Fleas, they called themselves, hopping on and off hosts until they found the quarry. His last host had known that the quarry lived in this village. Luckily, it had died close.

Slither into the sleeping library. It is Khalil. Sells fabrics. Poor. Seven children, three dead. Ignored wife. Timid thief. Ah, knows the prey's relatives but not the prey. Bad, only the women in the target family come to the shop. Can't be helped.

Danton swirls, gelling brain fluid into a cocoon for himself. Khalil will never know he's being ridden. Danton waits. He cannot sleep, but shrivels his thoughts, aware only of the host's physical sensations. Body temperature rises slightly. The gray light of false dawn creeps into the room.

Stirrings. Stiff muscles flex. Flatulence. Its eyes open. It needs glasses. It washes body parts, dresses and eats. Khalil walks to its stall in the souk. It hates many people here. Danton waits. A bird dog, he thinks, just a bird dog. But instead of scents he prowls for thoughts. The closer to the quarry, the stronger the thought scent. No, not quite a bird dog. Danton retrieved thoughts but killed his quarry. And he relished the kill.

One day. Two. Three. It prays, sells cloth. Eats. Defecates. Sleeps. Once, it beats its wife.

Danton holds to his perch, insulated from the host. In it but not of it. A deer tick that wants no host diseases.

On the fourth day two wrapped women enter the souk. Khalil recognizes them, they are kin of the quarry. Danton has more difficulty infiltrating into women. The younger, ride the younger, there will be fewer hard thought patterns. With both hosts awake Danton must take great care.

Danton stretches out gently from Khalil and touches the girl's head like a blessing. Ooze inward from the skin. Confirm. Quarry's daughter. Lives with prey. Curl back to cup the neck nape. Glide through hairs, black and clean. Poise at the skin, then flow in through a hole smaller than a pore. Once at the mind bottom, hollow out a sac. Bulge his stream to accommodate a morsel of himself and leave it behind. It shivers as Danton's bit of consciousness nestles in.

Draw back like ebbing water. Resettle on his perch in Khalil.

The two women buy nothing. Khalil is annoyed.

The day passes. Khalil is ignored. A cab ride, Danton is taught, just a cab ride. He subsides, becoming only what Khalil senses.

Light fades. It prays, eats and argues with the woman. It falls asleep. The night gradually chills. At its coldest, Danton winds himself and glides out without damaging Khalil, who is left behind unknowing and alive.

He glides from the hut and moves into the light spattered dark and holds, swaying at rooftop level. The mind morsel that he infested the girl with pulses and he moves forward and side to side, keeping in the spoor of himself. His reach is about as long as he can hold his breath. Mistakes cause delays which will kill him. The roads below are traps, almost never going in the direction he needs. Slide around a taller building, around another. The walled compound ahead. Left, near the back wall. First, no, second floor, open window, not that it mattered.

The girl's bed is in a darkened corner, but he did not need light to see it and the pulsing germ of himself. He swirls so close that were he breathing his breath would flutter its hair. Touch with the lightness of dust fall.

Sleeping.

He flows in. The smell of sandalwood soap and the pungent smell of a child. Fan whirr. Tongue taste of sugared cake. Barked knuckle ache. Swells of growth and wellness. Burrow, burrow down until only heat and pulse and motion are sensible. Hollow out the lair.

Sleeping still. Swim upward. Deaden and seep, deaden and seep. Explore the library. Amira. Five. Father equals quarry. Father is away, back perhaps tomorrow. Dream of moving through a wheat field. Certainty that Amira is exactly where she should be. The perch in her consciousness is spun. Danton slides back down. He waits.

Target does not return the next day. Danton is cocooned but cannot settle into dormancy. He is taught not to commingle with hosts, but is restless. After half a day, he seeps into her mind and explores. Beliefs. Warm beliefs wash over him. Father, mother, something called Allah, hazy but protective. The day's purpose is itself. Mutton, rice, bread tastes, all new and sharp. Running without restraint. So little difference between waking and sleeping. He is uncomfortable and slides back down.

The quarry is another day late. He moves back into her consciousness. Delicacies of soft touch. Annoyance at an older sister. Attending with vigor to a small cat. Water has taste. Small pains are newly discovered. He holds at sense level, unwilling to return to the lair. Finally she sleeps and Danton drops back down. He does not wish to share her dreams.

Amira is in a state of high excitement. Her father has returned. Quarry spends time with assistants and wife, then takes Amira on to his lap. Questions back and forth. He reads Amira's senses of the quarry's warmth and odors and muscles. Target is uneasy, it asks Amira several times if she is unwell, or has troubles.

Target wraps its arms around Amira more tightly and opens up to absorb everything it can about her. Amira is completely open to his gentle probing. Danton is trained to the stillness of a hunting cat, but senses his own fear despite his sealed cocoon. He drops from his perch, down the deadened channel into the lair, landing hard. Too hard. Bleeding starts, couldn't be helped. He knows by training that the target cannot have sensed him, but fear lingers.

Danton waits in the lightlessness. Breathing slows, pulse slows. Motion almost stops. Wait. Wait. Wait. Judge time by the falling night temperature.

If the target did sense him its defenses will be up. The target travels constantly, and could be off again the next day. There may be only this night, Danton takes energy from her. The kill, so close to the kill. There is only one suitable technique, nice in the sense of elegance. Danton poises, flexing for departure.

He wraps himself around himself and glides out. Amira is left in her bed unaware and dreaming. She is still bleeding internally and will die.

Floor slide without resistance into the targets room. Observe. Wait. Target sleeps. Unfold and reach out. Gently, gently touch, not the head, but lower down, the nape of the neck. Gray frizzled hair. Acne-pored skin. Breathing slow, and even. Pulse slow, soft. Deaden and slide in. Deaden and slide deeper. Deaden and slide deeper. This leaves blood spotting, but no matter. He pushes himself into the brain stem.

He is cord bound. No references but up and down, stem tissue and not stem tissue. Swirling blood in veins. And touch, his own touch to use. Touch, touch again and again, and again. Ah. Numb this spot. Carve. Cut close by. Cut again. Fuzzy, aching. The killing cuts always demand such energy. It is done. Danton rests in the blood of his kill.

He cannot leave from this depth and must move upward. Target's body is inactive, its pulse rate slow. The target sleeps as it dies. Deaden and slither upward.

Clear out a lair and climb past, up, and up. Cradle quickly at the level of thought. Enter the library.

Shaikh Rhaman. Confirmed. A flip flop procedure, first the kill then extract information before thought is lost. Query, answer. Query, answer. Query, answer. Dawn swells into the room. A good performer, Danton thinks, knows when to exit. Two associates in the house, Khalil and Faisal. Faisal is trusted to travel. Faisal it is. Store intelligence. Slide down into the lair. Rest. Draw energy from the sleeping, dying Shaikh.

Wait.

Wait.

Quickening pulse. Motion. Movement. Disturbed motion. Thready pulse. Danton is curled tightly in the lair. Wait.

From motions Danton infers that the Shaikh performs his ablutions. The killing cuts are bleeding nicely. The Shaikh begins having trouble breathing and thinking. Wait. The Shaikh's body falls sideways and begins to tremble and lose function. Danton swells quickly upward into his perch.

But then, without thinking, like a relapsing alcoholic taking a drink, Danton reaches outside the cocoon to the dying Shaikh. His action violates his training and Danton is shocked at himself.

Bloated fear of dying, swelling, blobby. The Shaikh has no reference for Danton's invasion. Just weak hatred.

Its thoughts are swirling wildly. It does not realize that its thinking flows into Danton like river water. Floating in the water are memories, sensations. More than Danton wants to know. Confusing. Pain, he begins to sense the Shaikh's pain.

The Shaikh has weak dying thoughts, and Danton easily out shouts him.

"Shaikh Rahman. You have no bodily control and very little time. Listen to me. I will help you scream for help. I will let you ask one thing – that you be taken to Amira. You need to say goodbye to her. If you fight me I will leave you on the floor to die in your feces."

The Shaikh sputters out hatred, and horror at his weakness, and disbelief, and then grudging agreement in the hope that he can somehow trick or overpower this hallucination. Its thoughts begin to flicker.

Danton has stolen energy from the Shaikh and must now give some of it back. The Shaikh screams. His wife hears and finds the Shaikh on the floor.

Screams, motion, bodies filling the small bathroom. The Shaikh tries to shout a warning but Danton chokes its vocal cords, and then plays them. "Take me to Amira now!"

Shouting, calls for a doctor, an ambulance. The wife, who has been screaming the loudest, is obedient. She speaks.

"While the ambulance is coming, carry him to Amira's room. It is closer to the entry way."

The Shaikh is picked up by his arms and legs and carried to the girl's room. The wife screams again, for Amira cannot be awakened. Faisal stays in the room. Danton swells outward for eight feet and cradles the nape of Faisal's neck. He inserts his morsel seed and moves back. Faisal is bleeding from his neck but no one will notice.

The Shaikh is beyond making sounds.

"Listen to me Shaikh. You are dying. Amira is dying. Can't be helped. You should say your goodbye. I will help you. Do you understand?"

Confused thoughts, fear for Amira but no longer for himself. Vaguely, what, not grateful, accepting.

Danton has little energy left, but plays the vocal cords again.

"Goodbye Amira."

Wasted, Danton thinks, with drinker's remorse. Foolishly wasted energy.

He has left the dead only once, and hated it. His host is his world, and once death begins its cloying process he must fight hard to escape. He claws in as much as he can of the Shaikh's energy and swirls about himself.

The Shaikh fails. Fading screams. Gray, clotting gray, must kick loose from the spreading nothing, must flee. Out, swirling and disheveled, only partially wrapped about himself. He seeps quickly into Faisal. Down, quickly, burrow down into the black comfort at the bottom of mind. Wait.

Faisal does not travel for two weeks after the funerals, but finally flies out of country. It carries instructions which Danton records. Danton knows he should try to leave Faisal alive, so the known instructions can be passed along. Faisal should voyage onward as an unwitting Judas goat.

The commute by body begins. Hardest to find that first air traveler. Then traveler to traveler, airport to airport to airport. Child, stewardess, salesman, child. They are disposable, more roughly handled than their baggage. He does not explore them beyond confirming a destination.

Danton relishes his kills and normally relives them several times. But he drifts instead to the flowing, almost directionless thoughts of Amira, and they sour the lingering lust from his killing. Her sensations, so open and strong, bathe him and wash off his pleasure from the kill.

Danton's last host deplanes at the airport where he is housed. He wraps himself about himself, seeps out of his host, and dives easily back into his body. Monitors record his re-entry.

He has been absent for two months and his body has vegetated. His withered muscles twitch as he prods them awake. The reopened senses seem stale, like bad air conditioning. Not like Amira's senses, he thinks.

His minders are careful but uncaring. Before any other muscles, Danton's vocal cords are made pliable enough that he can recite the stored information. Danton expects nothing different.

Then therapy. Body and mind. From the careful ministrations of many people Danton senses that he is one of very few, that the bird dog is so caringly tended to because his masters have so few dogs with which to hunt.

Four months are spent reconditioning his body and oh so gently assessing his mind. Occasional women are provided to him for one night each so that they learn nothing and no attachments are formed. He is allowed two drunken evenings of his choice.

And he is judged to be field ready again.

As Danton receives instructions, he hesitates. What happens, he wonders, to fleas too weak to hop, to crippled hunting dogs. Amira, with no duplicity of her own, has made him wary. But as the briefing continues the sickly-sweet killing expectation rises. He wants again to jaguar-prowl in darkness, to ride the many hosts to prey. And most of all, perhaps he wants to leave himself behind.

Behind the First Years

Stewart C. Baker

FIVE SHORT HOURS to planet-fall, Pete sat watching Magda die. Her hands were thin and wrinkle-fine, the leathern colour of paper five hundred years old. She had been Archivist sixty years before him there in the great, silent bulk of the ship.

"But what am I to do when we land?" he asked. "I have only been Transcriber, Magda. I never–"

"You must look behind the shelf of the first years."

"The shelf of the first years is empty."

"Did I say *on*, foolish man?" Magda asked. "How can you record history if you do not listen?" Her eyes were as sharp as her voice, clear and precise, honed from the long years of watching that her duties entailed.

Pete flushed and bowed his head. "Behind the shelf, Magda. I understand."

How can she possibly die? he thought. Yet the grey-white walls of her quarters were hung with freshly picked jasmine to hide the stink of it.

"You understand nothing, foolish man. Look at me." And again, kinder, when he did not. "Look at me."

"Yes, Magda."

"What lies behind the shelf of the first years is important, but does not change your duty. You must record all things, as I have. Record and preserve, Peter. In all these lifetimes under space, that has been our calling."

"Record and preserve. Yes, Magda."

He had first spoken the words fifteen years prior, when he became Transcriber. His parents cried during the ceremony, then left him to go back to Bottom. Magda had been old even then, and Pete used to go to bed terrified of finding her dead when he woke, and him still an untrained youth. Now she was going at last.

She coughed once, twice, making no move to clean the deep red flecks from her lips. Her eyes had gone dim.

"Peter," she said, "Peter."

She reached out with one frail hand and he took it: "Yes, Magda."

"You will be building the history of a world. Remember... the first years."

Pete did not respond: she was gone. He placed her hand back on her stomach and wiped her lips one last time with the damp cloth the ship's doctor had left him. The man waited outside the door, polite and sympathetic.

"I know it's hard, but it may be for the best. The dispersal would have been hard on her."

Pete nodded, not trusting himself to speak, and left the doctor to his work. It was eighteen floors down to the archives, but instead of the express lift he took the stairs. Something Magda had said didn't sit right, but he could not put his finger on it. Walking helped him think.

'Remember the first years' was a strange directive. The people of that time had been content to track their history in transient digital form, with the result that little was left. Pete thought with regret of the few scraps of paper that had come down to them.

Scrawled inventories, engineer-neat lists of meaningless names. In his darker moments, Pete felt the first people were mocking him, conspiring to erase all knowledge of why they had been sent away, what calamity had befallen Earth.

But what did it matter? Earth was a planet he would never see, and in just over four hours he would be walking the surface of a world untouched by human hands. A place to start anew. Even Magda's death could not entirely remove the thrill of it. She had died well, clear and alert until the last. And it was true the dispersal would have been hard on her.

Dispersal! Soon they would spread across the surface of the unsullied planet, down amidst the mottled green and black they had so far seen only on the vid-screens, where it hung in the middle distance between the ship and the system's star.

He came out on the archives level and picked up his pace. He had set up an interview with Captain McAllister-Xo the night before, the first part of his duty. He would not have long to examine the shelf of the first years. He was reaching for the panel to open the ever-dimmed rooms of the archives when he realized.

Under. Magda had said under space.

* * *

Captaincy was in McAllister-Xo's bones. His family had guided the ship since the time of the first people – or so it was said. He greeted Pete and spoke to him of approach vectors and automated systems, stopping occasionally to check in with an officer or to type arcane sequences of keys into the mem-pad before him.

In one of these pauses, Pete told him of Magda's death.

"That old witch," the captain said. "I always thought she'd live for ever." He paused, coughed, scratched his temple with his middle finger. "Sorry. I know you were close."

"It was her time. But there was something she said before she passed that I thought you might be able to explain."

"Shoot."

"She was talking of the Archivists' Code: record and preserve."

"I've heard it."

"Um, yes. But it was how she described it: 'In all these lifetimes under space, that has been our calling.' She said 'under,' not 'in.' What do you make of that?"

The captain shrugged. "She was old. She was dying. A slip of the tongue, some missed connection between her brain and her lips. What's to make of it?"

The explanation made as much sense as any Pete could think of, but McAllister-Xo had not been there. Magda had been too alert, her voice too clear and strong for the word to be delirium or sickness. He remembered the way she had taken him to task for not listening clearly. There was something to what she had said, he was sure of it.

He thanked the captain and made his way to Bottom. Perhaps popular memory could tell him what high command could not.

* * *

Bottom, so called for its location at the lowest part of the ship, was a vast expanse of inspired agro-engineering which doubled as the ship's food supply and as a living space for most of its population. It was as large as the rest of the ship.

The express lift plunged from the light-specked ceiling and sank past moisture sprays and clouds. The rolling green landscape that sped to meet him was the same as he remembered from before he had been taken above to the archives. He could just make out the pale, blue-tinged metal of the inner bulkhead a kilometre or so away. Then the trees rushed up and overhead, and the lift doors hissed open.

The smell of Bottom was earthy and moist, as different from the paper-dry odours of the archives as possible. He strode past farms and villages he knew from his childhood, passing within metres of the homes where his family and friends still lived. But he did not have time for a visit today.

At last, he reached his destination. Old Jadwiga had been ancient when he was still a child and, unlike Magda, had lived the hard life of a Bottom woman. She walked with a cane, bent over and shuffling, and her hands trembled as she invited him to sit. Her eyes were rheumy, and he had to repeat Magda's dying words several times before she understood him.

"Under space, hmmm?"

She sat quiet for a few minutes after that, but Pete waited patiently. As slow as it was, even Old Jadwiga's memory would be faster than trying to find just the right Bottom lore in the archives' massive collection, which filled kilometres of shelving.

Just as Pete began to doubt his assessment, the old woman spoke again: "I remember ... under the time of Captain Xo, there was a great anger among the people."

"Captain *Xo*?" But that was ridiculous – the last captain of that name had served almost one hundred years ago. Jadwiga couldn't possibly be that old, could she?

"Yes. Yes. People were angry, for the upper deck families took the best crops and we in Bottom had always to make do with their leavings. One year when I was a young girl ..."

Jadwiga continued to speak, drawing out story after story of the actions of those long-dead. Pete let her voice fade into the background, half-listening for anything about the ship being "under" space instead of in it. After an hour, he excused himself and left the old woman to her memories. They were fascinating enough, but of all she had said there were only two things relevant to Magda's words.

First, something he'd forgotten from his childhood: people here took the designation of "Bottom" with pride. They were liable to refer to any other part of the ship as "above." But Magda had come from an upper deck family, and in any case she had placed the entire ship under space, not just Bottom.

The second was a children's rhyme, cryptic to the point of uselessness:

> *Under space and over all,*
> *Ship-bound people standing tall;*
> *When they reach their destination,*
> *They will build a new old nation.*

He shook his head as he re-entered the lift. Even the stacks, with their information overload, would likely have given him more than that.

There were only two hours left to landing, and Captain McAllister-Xo expected Pete to make a record of the dispersal. He hoped there would still be time to make it to the shelf of the first years and retrieve whatever Magda had hidden there.

* * *

The stacks were dark, but Pete did not bother with a light. The shelf of the first years was easy enough to find without looking: it was the only one empty.

He ran his hands over the smooth metal surface, then crouched down, feeling around behind the shelf with one awkward, outstretched arm. There was only open space. He wondered if he had, after all, put too much stock in the words of an old, dying woman.

Then, just as he was standing, giving up, something brushed the tips of his fingers. Something hard, with the texture of rough-spun cloth. He leaned his shoulder into the shelf, extending his arm until the muscles burned, and closed his hand around the item. A book.

Back in the lift, on the way to the McAllister-Xo and the ceremony, he brushed dust off the cover and read the title, embossed in the spine: *The Book of the Ship*.

He had expected something grander from the way the book was hidden, and Magda's cryptic promises. He flipped to a random page, hoping it would make the book's purpose clear. It was in one of the old languages: "... extended isolation studies, which have shown the feasibility of interplanetary travel, were first carried out... " Other pages were filled with similar stuff. Exciting as it was from an archival point of view – it was clearly very old – how could any of it be important to him in the days to come?

Perhaps he was misunderstanding the text, he thought. He had never mastered the old languages as Magda had. But he remembered her words as she lay dying. *How can you record if you do not listen?*

The same must be true of reading, of observation in general. He would have to take the time to decipher it, but time was something he did not have – he would have to wait until the dispersal had begun.

* * *

McCallister-Xo and half a dozen officers were crammed into the control room with Pete, the captain going through the schedule one last time before the live broadcast began.

"First Officer Seong, you will say the words to set us on our way. I will then inform the ship about the dispersal order, and the dangers that may await them on the planet."

He had rehearsed these briefly already, his voice terse as he rattled off the items of a list apparently long memorized. The possibility of indigenous flora and fauna, dangerous or benign. Likely meteorological phenomena, dangerous or benign. How to handle riots from the people of Bottom, who were unused to change.

"We touched down three hours ago, ahead of schedule," the captain concluded. "All systems show a planet which matches the specifications from the few remaining scientific records of the first people. Oxygen content and purity is similar to Earth's and the ship's, and our exterior sensors show pressure well within comfort range."

Not for the first time, Pete marvelled at the shipbuilding genius of the first people. He had felt nothing whatsoever during the landing: the ship was as silent and still as before. His regret for their missing records intensified, but at least he had the book.

The ceremony made up little more than a scant few words directed at the present, not the future. Vague and visionary things Pete did not bother to remember – the first moments of the dispersal would be infinitely more important, and anyway an officer with a vid-crew was transmitting it all live to the entire ship.

They filed into the airlock, thick with the dry smell of centuries of stale emptiness. Pete, at the front of the crowd with the captain, watched the dull steel of the outer door. He wished the first people had put in windows – the scenes from the vid-display had done little to whet his appetite for the new world. Yet as the door hissed open, he could not help closing his eyes tight, preparing poetic turns of phrase to use later when he wrote the events of this day, their first on the planet, the fruition of all their long labours.

But there was a black void beyond the ship when he did look, the only light a dim yellow that spilled from the airlock and illuminated little save a narrow, steel ledge jutting up against the ship. The vid-screen had shown hills, rock-strewn but wide and gentle. There was a sudden surge as the officers at the back tried to push forward out into the planet. Pete stumbled back, jostling against the press of bodies. He felt more than saw the newly empty space beside him – McCallister-Xo had fallen over the side of the ledge. His hoarse yells echoed down and away, punctuated in jerking thuds until at last all was silent.

One of the officers took out a maintenance flashlight. The stark white beam pulled fragments of horror out of the dark: bloody streaks left by the captain's fall on the side of the ship; the hull stretching endlessly down, juxtaposed not against some outcropping of rock or grass but hard, slick steel. Dust and mildewed greens.

Across the ledge was a vast platform, similar in design to the ship itself. The far wall was rough stone and stretched up into darkness beyond the range of their vision; set into it were two massive steel doors, the words *May God forgive us what we have done* scrawled rust-coloured and huge above them in one of the ancient Earth languages. Pete translated for the others, his mind numb.

Captainless and bewildered – were they still on Earth? How? And why? – they wandered around the platform in disarray, all thoughts of their grand journey's fated destination fallen away into the dark. Three of the officers joined McCallister-Xo, walking slow, deliberate steps off the ledge, their descent all the more harrowing for its silence. Pete and the others heard only soft thuds and scratches as they tumbled off the hull of the ship they had served.

At last Pete remembered the book, Magda's dying words. She had known – all the archivists had. His head felt loose on his shoulders as he staggered back to the airlock to read by its light.

* * *

It took a team of six rugged Bottom labourers several hours to shift the doors at the cavern's edge. While they worked, other teams walked its interior, measuring and probing, trying to find some sort of explanation.

Pete read.

The book turned out to hold two separate texts, joined who knew when. The first older text was the shorter of the two and so, despite the difficulty of its language, Pete tackled it first. It was set on official looking paper and dated in the old style, which had not been used as far as Pete was aware since the second or third generation.

This was the portion of the book he had turned to when he first found it. The terminology seemed wilfully obscure at points, and even when the words were clear the grammar was strange to him, but eventually Pete determined that it was a study on simulated space travel, commissioned by some long-ago Earth government.

He had struggled through half of it before the team breached the door, revealing empty, winding caves that branched and joined in maze-like arrays. The ship crew abandoned their search of the cavern where the ship sat and spread outward. It was dispersal of a sort, but tethered and impermanent, a ranging into the caves which always returned to the bulk of the ship.

They found none of the promised meadows, no life of any sort save mildew and fungi. There were streams, little trickling spots of damp, which were clear and cool as promises on their tongue, filtered by the endless rock. The water tasted bitter in the dankness of their underground prison.

The teams were always careful to mark the way back to the ship, placing fluorescent strips from long-term storage on the walls or floors of the caves. But even so, some did not return. Other teams would come across markings which simply stopped, with no sign of life nearby and nobody to answer their calls.

When he was not ranging, Pete read the book. By now it was clear the ship had never left Earth, although the reason for this eluded them all. Pete skipped the rest of the first text and moved to the second, which was actually harder to read despite its language being more recognisably his own. It was technical in nature, describing systems the ship used to simulate space travel. Even though he didn't understand most of what it said, Pete continued to read.

Then one day Pete's team found the wall. It was at the end of a long passage which wound inexorably upwards, and it was made of brick. Pete watched, glad he had been there when it happened, as two Bottom men scrabbled at the caulking, hammered at the bricks with stalagmites they ripped from the cave floor, breaking down the dirt and rocks and scree beyond with equal fervour. He made no move to participate, caught up in fantasies of what they would find on the other side and readying what he would say when they returned to the ship.

All they found was ruin and stagnation, silence and death – an ash-choked swathe of land which stretched away beyond their newly made exit in the brick. Clouds of the dust blew past what must have once been a town, billowing out grey plumes from shattered buildings and tugging formless bundles of stuff.

The two men who had torn down the wall walked off into the dust, searching for life, supplies, or signs of what had happened. After an hour or two, with weak sunlight ribboning down, the other members of the party went too. Pete stayed: he would report back to the ship, he told them.

And so he watched and waited until the sun died a fiery red and the cold of evening set in. In the dim emptiness, he seemed to hear sounds in the distance, low sinuous hissings from the depths of history. The clouds of ash seemed to hide shadowy figures, but when they swirled away revealed only a shattered building, a rusting, useless metal hulk, or nothing at all. He shuddered and returned to the ship's resting place, alone.

When he arrived, they questioned him. Why had he returned alone? Where was his team? What of the time they had spent out in the caves? *He only shook his head, filled with grief, and passed them by.*

* * *

"The secrets of the ship?"

"Yes, Captain Seong. Nothing of why we're here, who the first people were or what purpose they hoped to achieve. But all the secrets of the ship's systems, everything we need to prolong the illusion."

"And we should do this even though you *found a way out*?"

"Just come with me, Captain. Come with me and you will understand. Hope, purpose, meaning, happiness of a sort – what we had in the years before was infinitely, unthinkably better than what awaits us without."

* * *

Captain Seong took little convincing once he had seen the desolation that lay beyond the caves. He and Pete took a few steps out down the hillside until the ash began to choke them, cold acrid fingers down their throats. They heard the sounds, saw things that were not there. Captain Seong swore he felt something brush his shoulder, though Pete was only a few feet away and saw nothing but ash. They turned back lest they lose sight of the entrance: Earth held nothing for them and if it did they were terrified of it.

Inside the cave mouth, the other officers waited. At a shake of the head from Captain Seong, they began to rebuild the wall, working in silence. On the walk back to the ship, they tore up the guide-strips. Over the next few days, as Bottom teams tore up the other strips, removing all signs which pointed to their ship, Pete and the officers between them got the ship's systems rebooted.

When all was complete, they sealed the cavern doors and closed off the ship once more. The ship's journey was a lie, but it was one with promise that they would pass on to later generations.

* * *

Pete finished transcribing the last of the records from the dispersal and sat back, cracking his knuckles. It was only right, he thought, that he complete his duty as Archivist before betraying it. His generation would keep few records, and preserve none of them.

He lifted the paper from the desk and set it in the book he held, behind the two older sets of papers, then walked with it from the stacks, nodding to the two officers who stood at the ready with vid-cams and torches.

At the door, he stopped to watch. One last time, one last event: the fire-swept cleansing of all they had recorded, all their history and lore. He felt no regret at the destruction of their legends and dreams, their pasts and their futures.

After a while, he set the book firmly under his arm, turned on his heel, and walked to the express lift and the rich, verdant hills of Bottom. Behind him, the tongues of flame licked over everything but the shelf of the first years, already long since empty.

Genetic Changelings

Keyan Bowes

"RANDALL, NO! Get your tail off Imran's neck right now!" I call to the little boys. Though it's an unseasonably wet spring day, two dozen squealing preschoolers scamper around the rubber-matted playground, making infant mischief. They're all Dezzies, designer kids, and they're a handful.

Going over to the two boys, I crouch down to their level. "I've told you not to wrap your tail round anyone's neck. I don't care if Imran raised his crest at you. Look guys, you're both too smart to keep getting in trouble."

Randall's impish face, curly red hair and freckles somehow match his prehensile monkey tail. Imran is darkly handsome, with a crest that lies flat along his head, neck and back. It's mostly hidden under his weatherproof jacket, but he raises the red bit on top of his head to show me.

It's bittersweet for me, being around small children – even these cute lovable not-quite-humans.

But here I am. Tessa's assistant is out sick; if she doesn't maintain her adult-kid ratio, her school could lose its license. I'm her oldest friend, and if she can't count on me, then who? As a science writer, my schedule is flexible – at least until my publisher says it isn't. But they're still digesting my latest book, *Genetic Changelings: The Slippery Slope From Normalcy.*

Tessa's bending over two kids next to the play structure. "Hold still while I get you free of Kwok Kin's jacket," she tells the girl. "There. You have to keep those claws retracted, Priya. It could easily be someone's skin next time."

"I'm sorry, I got excited," Priya says to Kwok Kin.

"S'okay," he replies, and runs off to play. His face has faint tiger stripes. Priya, Randall and Imran give chase, racing around the playground in a frenetic game of tag.

These kids. So smart, so adorable, so wrong. It's the parents I blame for creating these genetic changelings. The kids didn't have a choice.

* * *

My phone pings. It's Vimla, my sister. "Deepali, I need to see you," she says, "I'm coming over."

"I'm not home. I'm helping out at Tessa's pre-school, I'll be done in an hour."

"Meet you there," she says.

"Is Edward coming?" I ask her. If he is, I'll pick up a bottle of my brother-in-law's favorite wine.

"No... he's in Sweden. He's traveling a lot in this new consulting job."

Vimla arrives early. She makes her way over to me, gingerly picking her way through the careening kids. Tessa waves and joins us.

"Sorry Vim," Tessa says. "This place is a zoo around closing time."

"Sure," Vim says, looking a bit stunned at the playground chaos. "Anything I can do?"

"Want to help with the wingers? It takes for ever to get their coats on." Tessa hands off the playground to her two teenage interns, who start a game of "*Horns, Feathers, Knees and Toes*" to calm the kids.

In the warm and cocoa-fragrant hallway, four children are waiting for their coats. Four little voices chorus a hello when Tessa introduces us: "Anh, Samira, Alain, Maia... you know Miss Dee, and this is her sister Miss Vimla."

Little Anh's wings are scaly and golden, like a small dragon's. His matching, pointed, gold ears stick up through his straight black hair. Samira's perfect round brown face is framed by a cloud of dark curls; her wing feathers are raven-black. Alain standing beside her has the pale features of an icon, and creamy wings that rise above his head. Cherubic rosy-feathered Maia looks like she escaped from a gold-dusted Victorian greeting card.

Vimla's entranced.

"What's a sister?" Anh asks.

"It's when there are two of you, but one's a girl," Maia explains confidently. "Imran's got a sister. You know the soft furry baby his mom brings sometimes? That's her."

Tessa demonstrates the coat process on Alain. His dark red coat fits between the shoulders and zips below the wing-slits. She's careful to avoid damaging the feathers on his wings.

"Fold your wings, sweetie." When Alain flattens his wings, Tessa fastens the cape over them. "They chill easily if their wings get wet," she explains. "Off you go. You still have playtime before your dad comes."

Samira marches up to Vim, lifting her wings. "Are you coming to work here?" she demands as she manoeuvres into her coat.

"I work at a museum," Vimla says. The child nods; she knows about museums. Dezzies' parents typically start culture early. I finish with Anh and Maia, and we follow the wingers outside.

"Are all your kids Enhanced?" Vimla asks Tessa. "I've never seen so many Dezzies in my life!"

"We're a premium private preschool... it sort of goes with the turf," Tessa responds, her attention on the children and the arriving adults. In the background, the game continues with its familiar tune, Eyes and tails and mouth and nose / Horns and feathers, knees and toes, knees and toes.

"The wingers are adorable," Vimla says. "What's it like teaching here? Compared with a regular daycare? Have you taught Normies?"

Tessa nods. "Different. These kids are brighter, easier to talk to." She starts tidying, getting ready to lock up. "But they get into their own kinds of mischief. And the Enhancements, the external ones, anyway – they're a trip. When I have kids, they'll be Normies."

Yeah. Me too. Me three, in fact, if any of my babies had actually lived. I'd held the tiny, premature bodies of my sons and daughter. They hadn't breathed even once.

* * *

My publisher calls as we leave. I grimace an apology at Vimla and take the call. It's fantastic news. My book has really taken off. It's generating a lot of discussion about Enhancements and Modifications, and it's up for three different awards. I'm floating out the door.

But Vim isn't. There's tension under the calm front she put on for Tessa. "So, what's up?" I ask as we get to my cottage.

She steps inside and inhales the lingering scent of the incense I lit last night. "That incense always reminds me of Mom," she says.

"Yeah, me too." It's what Mom used to light on the prayer shelf. I don't have a prayer shelf, but the fragrance feels like home.

Vimla curls up on my couch and fiddles nervously with my little marble Ganesh, Remover of Obstacles. I pour Chardonnay. She puts down the figurine and raises her glass in a silent toast. Then she looks up at me and blurts, "Deepali ... well, did you know I'm Enhanced?"

What the hell is she talking about?

She smiles weakly. "Dad said you didn't know."

"No shit I didn't! Because it's not true. I'm your big sister. I was there when you were born." Was she delusional?

"You don't even look Enhanced. I see designer kids all the time. And Dezzie parents, too."

"It's not obvious. No externals, except for two extra inches of height. But they put in extra IQ, and good disease resistance." She sips the wine and looks away. Her gaze rests on my cat Goofy, sitting on the window sill. The sun has finally come out, and he's washing his magenta face with a dark purple paw. "Mom and Dad didn't tell you. Nor me, either, until the end. I thought Dad had started to imagine things. But last week I found the certificates."

"So that explains it." I plonk down on the couch. "You were always the one with the terrific grades. And I was the one with the flu and the head colds." I have a sudden thought. "Unless... am I designer too?"

How do I explain this to my publisher and my readers?

Vim shakes her head. I'm flooded with relief - and, to my surprise, resentment. "Dad said they couldn't afford it when you were born. They'd just moved here from India with no money. They had me after Mom's stock options paid off. That's why they never said anything. They didn't want you to feel bad, or me to feel different. Anyway, back then people didn't talk about it."

I close my eyes. My own sister, the closest family I have left in the world, feels like a stranger.

"I know it's weird, Dee," she says. "How d'you think I felt? That the real me would have been two inches shorter and 20% stupider? That all those honors and things weren't me – they were the Enhancements."

"Don't be dumb, Vimsy," I say, giving her a hug. "You're the real you."

"There's more," she says.

I look at her.

"We're having a baby," she says.

"What? Oh, wow, Vim, that's awesome!" It's thrilling news, even more thrilling than my book sales. I'm going to be an aunty! I ruthlessly suppress a tiny twinge of jealousy. After that third miscarriage, I gave up. This baby will be the nearest thing to mine, my flesh and blood at one remove.

She sort of smiles and takes a swig of Chardonnay, not looking at me. "I should tell you... I sort of feel differently about Enhancement now. It wouldn't be fair to give my child any less than what I got. It's maybe the new Normal."

What? We'd *had* this discussion. All the babies in our family were going to be Normal. *You're nuts, Vim,* I want to say. *You're not modifying your baby. Apart from everything else, what about long-term effects? The first wave Dezzies aren't even fifty years old now. What if some Enhancements are dangerous? We're hearing stuff. Like cancers and metabolic disorders.* Only, how can I say anything without implying there's something wrong with her, too?

And – "any less?" Like me? I'm the old Normal now? But I can't call her on it. Instead, I ask, "So what about all the things we talked about? About designer babies breeding conditional love in the parents? About not creating a wealthy uber-class of Dezzies?"

"That's all theoretical, Dee. I'm not making social policy on the back of my baby."

Goofy climbs into Vim's lap and purrs, brilliant green eyes half-closed. Vim strokes him, apparently engrossed in examining the magenta coat that darkens to purple on the face, legs, and tail. The cat's coloring clashes magnificently with her brick-red top. "Just like you're not making it on the back of your cat," she adds.

"Goofy's a rescue! The idiots who sold the house next door abandoned him. Probably didn't match their new décor. Or maybe they upgraded to a non-shedding model." Was that what my folks did, upgrade to Vimla? There's no one left to ask.

The stale incense overlaid with the smell of the wine is suddenly cloying. The cottage feels claustrophobic. We adjourn to the Arbor Mall for an early dinner. Vimla looks visibly brighter, probably relieved that the difficult talk is over.

Now it's my turn to be silent, focusing on anything but the issue at hand. The evening sun shines through the glass roof into the atrium garden of sixty-foot trees towering over tree-ferns and clivia, and sparkles off a stream feeding into a waterfall. There's a scent of damp earth. Flights of Designer sparrows dart around the miniature forest like reef fish in distracting bursts of color: peacock blue, cardinal red, oriole yellow, parrot green. We run into Tessa at a book store, and invite her to join us. She's got a print copy of *Genetic Changelings*, and I sign it for her.

We pick at an outside table near the garden. A short girl with three breasts and an extra eyebrow takes our orders. They aren't actual Enhancements, but falsies made to emulate them. A dissatisfied Normie. Tri-boobs and tri-brows are in for spring.

"How does it work, this designer stuff?" Vim asks, brushing bread crumbs off the table. "Wouldn't the baby inherit my Enhancements anyway?"

"Nah," I say, watching the gaudy Modified birds descend on the crumbs. "The Enhancements to the embryo are designed to turn off in the reproductive cells so they don't go into the germ line."

"Why would they do that? It's not fair!"

"Too many complications. They're afraid of what would happen if two Dezzies got together. Imagine a kid with Priya's claws and Randall's tail and maybe feathers and fur."

I didn't mention the homozygous IQ Enhancements that sometimes produced schizophrenia, or the amped up immune systems that could trigger autoimmune diseases. The scientists said they'd ironed out all the bugs by making human Enhancements non-heritable and Enhanced animals sterile. It suited the industry too, not to have amateur breeding attempts competing with their products.

"Since we're doing Enhancements, I'm thinking we might as well go all the way, and have external mods," Vimla says, looking at me cautiously. She turns to Tessa. "Those winged kids looked so darling!"

"They do," Tessa agrees, "But those wings have been covered all winter. Wait for summer. The feathers get muddy and broken, kids unfurl them like umbrellas and they go in someone's eye, and Maia got bird lice from the pigeons last year. We had to quarantine all the feathered wingers. I tell you, my kids will be Normies."

"Winged kids are often small for their age, too," I remark, determinedly staying calm. "Metabolically expensive. They have to grow wings as well as everything else."

Tessa nods. "We're always on guard so they don't get hurt romping on the playground. Not much good for sports, either." A bright green bird lands by her plate and she shoos it off.

Vimla says nothing, but I know the look.

I'm appalled she's even considering it. "Look, Vim, I kind of understand extra IQ for the baby," I say. "But wings? Claws? Crests? That's ridiculous!"

"That's unfair," Vimla retorts. "I'm not saying claws or crests. But without externals, who'll even know it's a Designer child? It's not something to hide any more, like you're ashamed."

"Are you?" I ask, curiously.

"I am not ashamed! I just don't flaunt it!"

No shit you don't. Even your big sister didn't know. But I keep quiet.

I turn to Tessa for support. "So Tessa, how would you feel if you had tiger stripes?"

"Truthfully?" She gazes down at her coffee cup and takes a deep breath. "Younger," she admits.

Vim and I both look question marks at her.

"Remember Jules? The ex? I saw him at the movie theater yesterday with this twenty-something woman. With bat ears." She waggles her hands behind her ears. "The younger Dezzies do flaunt it."

There's silence. A crimson sparrow with a shiny blue-green tail hops on to the table, grabs a crumb and flies off to perch on a nearby "Do Not Feed The Birds" sign. I can't help feeling second best, an ugly duckling that will never be a swan. But wait, I'm the Normal one. Right?

* * *

Genetic Changelings is doing brilliantly. My previous books sold moderately well, but this one has clearly touched a nerve with a lot of people. My publisher calls me every morning with sales figures. They want to start some tours, initially virtual ones on the web.

Vim and Edward, meanwhile, are deep into baby plans. Edward's apparently bought into Vim's ideas, and I wonder if he's secretly Enhanced, too. I'm hesitant to ask.

"Dee, are you free tomorrow?" Vim calls up to ask. "We have an appointment at BabyMakers Inc. but Edward had to go to Hong Kong. Come with me?" Against my better judgment I agree to come anonymously. My name's beginning to get recognized as the Normalist author. I don't want to make waves. But I'm also feeling increasingly guilty about my diplomatic silence.

With no parents or aunts or uncles to fill that role, I feel the family responsibility. As the didi, big sister, what am I doing to protect this helpless baby who will continue our family into the next generation?

When I arrive at their office on the 23rd floor of a smart downtown building, Vim is already waiting for me. Dr Estevan's assistant appears. He's cute and dark-skinned, with snaky hair and flame-colored eyes meant to suggest Enhancement. He escorts us to a glass-walled meeting room with a view over the bay and gets us coffee. Then he flips on the screen.

"Kids just love tails," he says and selects an icon. A series of pictures tile the screen, showing bare baby bottoms with animal tails of one kind or another – zebra or leopard, horse or lion, golden retriever or rabbit. It's adorable but grotesque, seeing a furry animal tail emerge from the base of a human spine. I've only ever seen Tessa's little Dezzie students fully dressed.

To my relief, Vimla shakes her head no. "I guess we should keep it mostly internal," she says to me. "I was talking with Edward. But Dee – those adorable baby angels at Tessa's preschool!"

My mind goes to my own baby angels at the Angel Garden Cemetery for the unborn. I turn away, look out over the water.

Dr Estevan enters and we all shake hands. The flame-eyed assistant pulls our spreadsheet down on the screen.

"So now let's go over your choices for Kris," says Dr Estevan, viewing the spreadsheet. "Ah, yes. The full disease-resistant package. IQ, yes, very nice, high but not enough to cause social problems. Oh, lovely temperament, with a little extra competitive edge. I see you've chosen a monogamous personality-type? Is that based on your religious beliefs?"

He continues through the choices they've already selected. There are a lot. This kid is being engineered from head to toe. I'm increasingly uncomfortable with the whole situation.

"Wait, I seem to have missed something. Gender?"

"We haven't decided..." Vim sounds embarrassed.

"Oh?" He looks disconcerted. Then he smiles. "We"ll come back to that. Or not, of course. Some parents are selecting none of the above."

It's one thing to know about the procedure in theory, but when it's your own family... This is making me crazy, special-ordering a baby like options on an automobile.

Dr Estevan is talking again. "In just a minute, we'll give you a simulation of what your baby will look like, and the performance parameters. Then we'll age-progress it... Now, when were you planning to incubate?"

"I want to carry the baby," says Vimla.

"Ah, yes." Dr Estevan pushes over a pamphlet. "BabyMakers is the only major company still offering the natural birth option. We'll need to optimize your hormone cycle, then implant the embryo. Few doctors are certified for these special deliveries, but we have several."

Why on earth does Vim want a "natural" birth, having decided on a Designer kid? I glance through the leaflet and whistle at the cost. "Prenatal check-ups. Special diet. Hospital stay...?" It's ridiculously extravagant.

"Incubation is much less expensive," Dr Estevan says hastily. "We pop the embryo into the Optimized Womb, and when the baby's ready, we lift it out."

Like a pizza with customized toppings.

I can feel my fury building. "Doctor?" I say.

He looks at me.

"What would the baby look like with a tail? And bat ears? And wings? And claws? And fur? And tiger stripes?" My rising voice sounds loud and squeaky in my ears.

Vim looks stunned. The doctor keeps his cool. "I can show you all that on a generic model. Not a combination I'd recommend, of course..." His assistant flips the setting on the screen. A 3D hologram of a baby appears above the table, and he adds a tiger's tail, bat ears, and wings, claws, and striped fur to the image. The tiger-bat-cub rotates slowly in the air.

I stand up, turn to Vim. "There! Is that what you want for our baby? A fucking freak!"

Vim's on her feet too. "It's not our baby to you, Deepali. And your Normie babies didn't make it!"

I'm completely losing it. I stomp out before I beat someone up or burst into tears. As I leave, I hear Dr Estevan say something about Genetic Changelings. So he did recognize me. I make it to my car and drive with exaggerated care, concentrating hard on the road and the vista of silvery clouds piled behind dark green hills. My mind churns with fury at Vim and Dr Estevan and myself and my parents.

At my cottage, I take several deep breaths, let myself in and disentangle Goofy from around my ankles where he's leaving a layer of magenta hair. Then I pour myself a glass of Merlot. A few glasses of wine later, I'm slumped in my armchair with Goofy in my lap and stupid tears all over my face, clutching my little Ganesh statue as though it really can remove obstacles. I empty the bottle, stagger off to bed. Vimla's right. My dead babies had different gene-dads, so it wasn't them, it was me. Did I kill my children?

* * *

My book keeps me busy. I'm invited to speak, to join debates, to participate in forums on the web and in person. In just a few weeks, I've somehow become the voice of the Normalist movement, and it's gaining traction. Tessa can't ask me back to her preschool now, the parents would object. It's that controversial.

Vimla posts pregnancy bulletins on her social networks, with pictures of her growing belly. I'm not sure how I feel about this. We haven't talked since that day. But I keep reading.

Back in India, my mom said, a woman returned to her parents' home to have her babies so she could be pampered and cared for and have help with the little ones. Not that mom had that luxury; Vimla and I were born in American hospitals. Nor did I. By the time I was pregnant, Mom was gone. But irrationally, reading Vim's posts, I feel I should be caring for her.

It happens one evening, when I'm exhausted. Three meetings, each in different time zones. The last one was a debate against someone who was very reasonable, but adamant that Modifications were fine. The human race had always modified their bodies within the limits of the available technology. Pierced ears. Tattoos. Circumcision. New teeth. Cosmetic surgery.

"Are you saying that these Mods are the new foot binding?" I asked, and the audience erupted. "Would you do that to your kids?"

Afterward, my own words echo in my head. "Would you do that to your kids?"

A design firm could modify my embryo to be viable, change it just enough to live. A near-Normie, born of a laboratory and a bank loan against my currently debt free cottage.

Otherwise… no. Not another little marker in the Angel Garden. I pull up the pictures from my last visit to the hillside garden, three markers among maybe a hundred. When I realize that all the other markers predate mine, I start crying again.

That's when the phone rings. It's Edward. "Deepali, can you come? Vim wants you. Please?" I don't even know if I'm having a nephew or a niece or "none of the above."

* * *

Vimla's in labor by the time I arrive. She cries when she sees me. "Deepali! I wasn't sure you'd come. I'm so, so sorry! Of course this is your baby too, Didi."

"Shush, don't worry about that," I tell her. "You were right anyway..." And then I'm holding her hand and telling her to breathe.

Vim's labor goes on and on, bringing back bad memories. Why the hell didn't she go with the safe and easy artificial womb? At last, I can't stand it any more and step out. She's too focused to care now.

Through the door, I hear someone say "One more time!" and "Aha, here we go..." and a newborn cry. After a bit, Edward comes out dressed in scrubs proudly holding the child. "Deepali?"

My face is wet with tears as I turn around.

"Meet your niece," he says softly, handing me the baby. "Here's Kris."

Two huge dark eyes look up at me. Vimla's eyes, just like our mom's. Krissie has tiny bumps on her back. Wing-buds. "She's beautiful, Edward. She's absolutely beautiful."

Holding her, I imagine Krissie in preschool, looking like Vimla did at four, but with soft brown wings arcing above her shoulders. She's playing Knees and Toes with her little Normie cousin, who looks a lot like me. As the song goes into the second verse, Tail and eyes and ears and nose, my imagination unbidden adds a cute little tail to my baby. I ruthlessly delete it. And the tiny elf-ears, the luminous third eye, the darling puppy nose.

Near-Normie, I tell myself, Near-Normie.

What do I tell my readers?

※

Overlap

Beth Cato

TODAY WAS THE DAY Reyna Aguilar's Goodwill and junkyard jury-rigged teleporter was going to win her the New Avalon Scientific Innovators Prize. No more setbacks, no more failures. This was it. The deadline was tomorrow.

The heavy industrial door clanged behind her as she hopped down two flights of concrete steps to her basement bungalow. Her lab/bedroom/home sweet home was complete with a borrowed portable toilet stuck in a far corner. Reyna liked to think that the smell granted the place some ambience.

The plastic grocery bag rattled against her thigh. In honor of the day, she had gone all out: a Marie Callender's Chocolate Satin Pie. That sucker wasn't even on sale, costing as much as ten of her usual ramen cups. Reyna stashed the pie in the freezer; the lower part of the fridge didn't work anymore. That's what happened when you mined electronics for spare parts that turned out to not be spare.

"Okay." She clapped her hands and looked around the basement.

Most of the space was devoted to her laboratory. Monitors cluttered several attached desks, while two teleporter pads sat about ten feet apart. They looked like showers because that's what they had been in their previous incarnation. She had ripped out the bases and replaced them with smooth steel and data receivers. Crammed in one corner, not far from her destination unit, was her mattress with its crumpled blankets.

Adrenaline thrumming, Reyna began her systems checklist and reviewed the contents on her screens. The list had been printed out for weeks, read to the point of memorization, but her gaze still traced every syllable. Long lines of numerals expanded on the monitors as she scrolled down.

She could not afford to screw this up, not if she wanted the NASIP and its million dollar prize, not if she wanted to attract the attention of hiring managers at CERN, not if she wanted to prove she wasn't a freaking failure.

Reyna had dropped out of college, five units shy of graduation, because of some stupid financial aid deadline. Then three weeks back, Taco Bell had fired her. Goddamned Taco Bell.

Three years working there, shift manager and all, and they fired her because some punk wrote a letter to the district manager. Because Reyna told the jerk not to grab hot sauce packets by the fistful as he walked out the door.

Her teleporter was going to work. It had to.

Her checklist and data looked good to go. Next she had to satisfy the requisites for the prize. She climbed a rickety ladder to where a mesh sling cradled her smartphone. That vantage point provided a perfect view of both teleporters. To reduce digital manipulation, contestants had to upload the raw feed of their experiments as they happened. It would go directly to New Avalon's databanks. Reyna could still edit the feed – and she would, for presentation's sake – but that raw version was required. She set the phone to start recording and placed it in its niche.

"My name is Reyna Aguilar," she said, voice raspy. She knew her face filled the lens. "And I'm about to make history."

This was a moment she'd been working towards since age five when she spied the cover of *A Brief History of Time*, wondered about the guy in the wheelchair, and started reading. Other kids in Fresno's south side read graffiti and emulated gang signs for fun; instead, in first grade she declared she was going to be a particle physicist when she grew up.

"I'm going to win, I'm going to win," she whispered beneath her breath.

She checked the teleporter pads. She had mapped their surface area and calibrated down to the micrometer so she could land within a precise zone. Reyna's basic data was greatly modified from laboratory work from the UK, where scientists had successfully beamed objects like pencils from room to room. What they had spent ten years researching, she had replicated in six months. She had tested a dozen inanimate objects, but she wasn't going to win the NASIP by zapping a talking Furby from point A to point B. To win, she had to go big. Animal testing should be the next step, but Reyna wasn't going to risk any living creature on something she wasn't willing to try herself.

So that's exactly what she planned to do.

It was dangerous. It was hella scary. One of the big theories was that teleporters didn't transfer exact material. Reyna could very well be killing herself, and then emerge on the other side as a copy. Or, by more crazy science fiction theories, she could rip holes in space time or invite in an alien race or something.

Well, that might win the NASIP, too. Or a Nobel.

Her computers hummed. The sound was comforting white noise, as she removed her socks and shoes and tossed them beside her bed. She wanted to describe every sensation of transit, how it felt from the callused skin of her heels to the very taste of the air against her tongue.

Reyna took a deep breath. Glanced at the clock. 10:31. Years of work for something that would take less than ten seconds. She'd need to spend the rest of the day editing footage, perfecting her presentation. Eating that pie.

All systems were ready. She stared, absorbing that fact, then nodded. Okay then. She crossed herself as a precaution. Fingers shaking, Reyna clicked the mouse and began the countdown sequence. One minute.

God, oh God. The ten feet to the teleporter felt like a mile, or two steps. So far yet so close. She entered and closed the door behind her. Her thudding heart threatened to clog her throat, the world all a hum of electricity. She centered herself on the X and pressed her arms tightly against her sides, her chin up. Steel was cold and smooth beneath her bare feet. In the shadows, the green light of her phone's camera stared down. She raised an arm in a brief wave. A hello, not a goodbye.

The seconds ticked by as eternities. She stared up at the light, willing herself not to panic. It was going to happen, it was going to happen.

It happened.

The light was brilliant blue, dazzling like a Caribbean sea. Reyna felt her lips part in a gasp, but no sound registered in her ears. Sound ceased existing at all.

Then the light was gone. All light was gone. Then came the pain. Excruciating agony extended from both feet, its suddenness ripping a scream from her throat. Pain? Why was there pain? Where was she? The smell – the sharpness of ozone. The hum was gone – the computers were off? But the green light above, it was still there. She tried to move. Her right foot scuttled forward, slick with agony, but her left was anchored in place. She fell. Screaming, she dropped face first into something soft. Her body bounced. White lightning bolts of agony zinged up both legs, and then blackness claimed her.

* * *

Searing agony woke her, and wetness, and cold.

Reyna's lips pressed against softness beneath her. Where was she? What happened? That pain – she gasped, reeling, fighting to stay conscious. Even in the darkness, white spots of agony dappled her sight. She forced herself on to her knees; one knee was higher, and the cushioning beneath adjusted to the movement, like a bed. A bed?

Her fingers explored, finding cloth. Sheets, blankets. Hers? She reached back along the length of her body, where wetness lingered, and grasped at her left foot, the one that didn't move.

It was inside the mattress.

Inside, literally. She felt strained cloth just above where her ankle should be, where it fused with her flesh. She hadn't landed on telepad B. She had landed in the mattress. Fused with it on an atomic level. Above the overlap, her calf swelled like a sausage casing. Shock and nausea rose in her throat, and she retched. Heaving only worsened the pain, driving her flat on her belly again in a pool of her own vomit and blood.

Something had gone very, very wrong.

Her mind raced over the algorithms. Something – something was off, some calculation. Damn it. She wanted to see her screens, figure out what happened. Even bleeding out, dying, this was a puzzle that needed solving. Dying. She could die.

That rational thought forced back the nausea and terror. Grinding her teeth, she reared on to her knees and probed with her hands again, this time reaching for her right foot. The leg wasn't locked in place, but something was still wrong. She grappled at her heel, pain causing her to dry heave for a moment. A flag of cloth covered most of her sole and was merged with her flesh. It was sopping with hot blood but the weave of the cloth was familiar. Her sock – she had landed partially on her discarded sock. Dizziness overtook her again and her face met the foul mattress.

It could have been worse. She could have landed in the wall, inside the floor. Died instantly. Melded with that port-a-potty across the room. Reyna tried to laugh and it emerged somewhere between a screech and a sob.

She refused to die here, alone. She pushed up on to her elbows. Okay. The power was out for some reason. The calculations – she should have landed on the second pad, just as the other test objects had. What had gone wrong? Reyna shivered. Cold – that was a sign of shock, right? Loss of body temperature because of the blood. She had to get out of the mattress, out of the basement. No time to analyze, not now.

Her fingers tested the fabric where her leg met the cloth. The strands were pulled tight, frazzled, soaked by blood. Thank God it was a ratty old Craigslist mattress, already weakened by wear. Gritting her teeth, she shredded the threads with her nails and dug deeper, digging her foot out from a mash of sponge and fluff. She couldn't feel many sensations from her foot now, but her calf was hot, bulging. No blood was circulating downward. Taking a deep breath, she yanked her foot upward. It jerked free and met the coolness of the concrete, something metallic clattering at one side of her foot. A spring. Nausea threatened her again, and she forced down bile.

If she didn't get out of here, she would go mad in the darkness with freaking feet joined with polyester and cotton and a goddamned spring. Everyone used to say she was crazy, anyway, making her own teleporter. Saying she was going to win.

The light of her phone remained steady as it recorded. Oh, God – the NASIP. No, she couldn't think of that now, that failure. She just had to get out of here.

Grinding her teeth to block out the pain, she eased her entire body on to the floor. She was cold. So cold. Thirsty. The fridge – it was so damn close, but the bottom compartment was empty. Her phone – seven feet up an already rickety ladder. She had to make the stairs, both flights. The door on the top – God, that thing was heavy on an average day.

The concrete floor was icy cold beneath her palms, causing her to shiver more. Move. Don't dawdle. Reyna dragged herself forward. The spring rattled and jostled from one foot, and the merged sock was heavy and dragging from the other. She found the plastic mats that covered the spiderwebbing of wires across the floor. Her legs, her body, felt compressed by gravity. Sweat beaded on her skin, dripped from her nose. The room should be thirty feet across. She knew the direction, roughly. It would be mostly open space.

The lights flicked on.

Blinded, surprised, Reyna cried out, dropping her head towards the floor. She panted, quivering. Lights. The teleporter must have knocked out the power within a radius. She raised her head again. The stairs, ten feet away, stretched into the ceiling in stern grey.

She couldn't help it. She glanced back.

A snail's trail of blood lead back to the mattress. The computer monitors were all on start-up screens. Well, her server should have backed up everything to the moment of the outage. The camera would see her clearly now, too, if it was still streaming. Too bad it was all going straight to some NASIP storage server along with 1,300 other attempts at the prize. No one would see this as a live feed and call for help.

She turned back around, curling her body like a pill bug. God. What happened? How did she screw up this badly? The NASIP. This place, no job, no money – she would be homeless. The medical bills. End up back at her parents, cocooned by their pity, their murmured "there-there, you'll get all better, chica" condolences as they knowingly nodded amongst themselves. Because they knew she'd screw this up, just like everything else, and end up back home. No degree, not even a job at freaking Taco Bell.

Reyna screamed, but this time it wasn't from pain. It was from honest to God rage.

"I am not a failure!" she yelled, her voice bouncing back against the high ceiling. "I am not going to die, I am not going to fail!"

And she moved forward. Tears flowing, breaths heaving. Using her hands, she pushed herself up to the first step, and paused. Reality wobbled around her. Sitting upright – not a good idea – she lowered her torso against the concrete steps, then she began to climb.

She didn't count stairs, or flights. It was all about moving up, one at a time. Having committed some terrible mathematical error in her algorithms, this was all about basic math. One plus one plus one. To infinity, it seemed. Then she was staring at the dark gray of the door.

Placing her weight against her sock-merged foot sent white sparkles of agony dancing across her vision, but she propped herself against the door. Leaned on the push bar. Leaned harder. The door opened.

Reyna had rented the basement in an old commercial complex. Most of the places were vacant. The heavy door echoed as it shut behind her, the automatic lock clattering. Down the hallway she dragged herself. Almost out. There was daylight now, slits of summer sun through the high windows. Her elbows ached and bled, bone and blisters grinding on concrete. The next door was lighter, easier.

Reyna was on the sidewalk. It was hot, gritty, and stank of oil, asphalt and exhaust. There weren't any pedestrians, not here. There was only one way to get attention.

She dragged herself into the road.

The asphalt ripped at whatever flesh remained at her elbows. She was past sobbing, past pain. The world was brightness and heat and cold. The yellow lines on the road – those were her goal. She felt the truck coming, the mighty rumbles of a behemoth. She lacked the strength to move her head. The roaring grew louder, the stink of fumes increasing, then it stopped. Footsteps. Feet, in her vision.

"Hey, what happened? You all right?"

"No," she said, and rested her cheek on the pavement.

* * *

The best part of being knocked out at the hospital wasn't the blissful absence of pain, though that was a major perk. No, it was that she slept through the deadline for the New Avalon Scientifics Innovators Prize.

Upon awakening, however, her consciousness didn't go straight to the beeping monitors, the draping intravenous lines, or the long creases of worry in her mother's face as she waited there at Reyna's bedside. It went straight to one thought: I failed.

If she hadn't just fought so damn hard to stay alive, she might have been suicidal. Instead, she lay there, accepting Mama's fervent prayers, tears, and exclamations of joy; Papa's stoic hand-clasp; even her brother's tearful hug.

The doctors came next, then the police. She answered their questions as best she could and asked plenty of her own, making sure no one had messed with her laboratory.

Then the flowers started arriving.

"What the hell?" Reyna asked, as an attendant wheeled in an entire cart of vases and balloons.

"It's 'cause of that contest and your weird-ass injuries," said her brother, shrugging. "You been all over the news."

"Oh." Pity flowers. How nice. She looked to the attendant. "Can you take these to the pediatric or cancer wing or something?"

The flowers kept coming, then relayed requests from the media. A police officer was stationed at her door to keep out the nosey. Reyna slipped in and out of sleep. When she was awake, she lay there. She could see the algorithms in her mind. She traced over them, searching for the flaw, whispering beneath her breath.

Her ruminations were interrupted by a knock at the door. At her bedside, Papa jerked awake, eyes wide.

"Pardon me, ma'am." It was the police officer on duty. "There's a lawyer here, says she's from New Avalon."

Reyna's mental number stream froze in place. "New Avalon? Let her in." The officer nodded and motioned behind him.

"A lawyer?" repeated Papa, frowning.

The woman who entered was petite and precise in a white pantsuit. Tousled blonde hair framed her face and contrasted with thick black glasses. "I'm Lilah Caputo. You're Reyna Aguilar?"

"Yeah. Why are you here?"

"How are you recovering?" The woman's tone was even, as though Reyna hadn't asked a thing. She set a briefcase on a side table.

"I'm shorter. They had to cut off both feet, but they're already talking about prosthetics." Like Reyna could afford them. "But why's a lawyer from New Avalon here? I didn't complete my submission, but I signed off on the legal stuff. I'm not going to sue you." Not when this was her own stupid fault somehow.

"I'm not here regarding any lawsuit. I'm here because of your video."

Reyna sat up, wincing at pain from the motion. "The upload? New Avalon owns that video, I remember that much from the fine print. I'm not going to turn around and upload it to YouTube or anything. But my invention is still mine, as it is." Bitterness crept into her voice.

"As it is. You are the first teleported human being."

"Yeah. Minus my feet because I screwed up and missed my target."

"You teleported. You lived. You recorded everything. The dark portions were easily lightened for visibility. It's not simply what you've created, and what you have the potential to create. It's who you are. New Avalon needs people with that kind of tenacity, that resilience." Her voice softened, and she unlatched the suitcase. "I have paperwork, offering you a job with our company. The details are here. Actually, there are several jobs, depending on your interests."

Reyna only stared. "...Jobs?"

"Of course, there may be other forthcoming offers as well," Lilah continued. "Would you like to look at our paperwork?"

"Yeah. Sure." Reyna accepted the packet, blinking in disbelief. Her eyes scanned the sheets. Numbers stood out the most; numbers always did. For the first time in days, she had keen awareness of her heartbeat. "Oh."

"Ray-ray, you okay?" Papa leaned closer.

"Yeah. I'm... okay." She stared at the numbers again, comprehending. Job offers. CERN might even come knocking, but even if not, New Avalon... was New Avalon. That equipment, those extra resources, might be what she needed to get her teleporter working again – hers. She needed to make sure it still belonged to her, no matter who she worked for.

"I also had a favor to ask you. Don't feel any obligation, of course." Lilah's smile turned surprisingly shy. "I was wondering if someone in your family could show me to the basement where everything happened. I wouldn't touch anything, but I – and my peers – would love to have pictures of it all."

Reyna bet they would. She met Lilah's gaze. The lawyer might be poaching, but there was genuine joy and curiosity behind it.

"Papa?" she asked. He leaned closer, clasping her wrist. "I need a lawyer. The best damn lawyer you can get. I don't think money will be an object, not anymore. Call up some people and have them come here so I can interview them, okay?" She looked at Lilah, challenging her.

Lilah arched an eyebrow, but if anything her smile grew. "You have to look out for yourself. I can wait."

Papa stood and shuffled to the door, already pulling out his cell phone.

"No one in my family has wanted to go in... there," Reyna said. "But once I have this lawyer, I'll talk to them, see if they can walk you in. But we'll talk details later."

"Of course. No pressure."

Reyna may have screwed up, but this was her chance at redemption. She could make this right, make her teleporter right. New Avalon wanted to use her and her machine – all right. She could use them, too.

She looked at the papers resting against her chest. "There's one big favor you can do for me at my place, though."

Lilah tilted forward. "Oh?"

"There's a pie in my freezer that needs to be brought here to the hospital." Reyna grinned as algorithms danced in her head. "I think it'd taste really good about now."

Phantoms of Reality

Ray Cummings

Chapter I: Wall Street – or the Open Road?

WHEN I WAS some fifteen years old, I once made the remark, "Why, that's impossible."

The man to whom I spoke was a scientist. He replied gently, "My boy, when you are grown older and wiser you will realize that nothing is impossible."

Somehow, that statement stayed with me. In our swift-moving wonderful world I have seen it proven many times. They once thought it impossible to tell what lay across the broad, unknown Atlantic Ocean. They thought the vault of the heavens revolved around the earth. It was impossible for it to do anything else, because they could see it revolve. It was impossible, too, for anything to be alive and yet be so small that one might not see it. But the microscope proved the contrary. Or again, to talk beyond the normal range of the human voice was impossible, until the telephone came to show how simply and easily it might be done.

I never forgot that physician's remark. And it was repeated to me some ten years later by my friend, Captain Derek Mason, on that memorable June night of 1929.

My name is Charles Wilson. I was twenty-five that June of 1929. Although I had lived all of my adult life in New York City, I had no relatives there and few friends.

I had known Captain Mason for several years. Like myself, he seemed one who walked alone in life. He was an English gentleman, perhaps thirty years old. He had been stationed in the Bermudas, I understood, though he seldom spoke of it.

I always felt that I had never seen so attractive a figure of a man as this Derek Mason. An English aristocrat, he was straight and tall and dark, and rather rakish, with a military swagger. He affected a small, black mustache. A handsome, debonair fellow, with an easy grace of manner: a modern d'Artagnan. In an earlier, less civilized age, he would have been expert with sword and stick, I could not doubt. A man who could capture the hearts of women with a look. He had always been to me a romantic figure, and a mystery that seemed to shroud him made him no less so.

A friendship had sprung up between Derek Mason and me, perhaps because we were such opposite types! I am an American, of medium height, and medium build. Ruddy, with sandy hair. Derek Mason was as meticulous of his clothes, his swagger uniforms, as the most perfect Beau Brummel. Not so myself. I am careless of dress and speech.

I had not seen Derek Mason for at least a month when, one June afternoon, a note came from him. I went to his apartment at eight o'clock the same evening. Even about his home there seemed a mystery. He lived alone with one man servant. He had taken quarters in a high-class bachelor apartment building near lower Fifth Avenue, at the edge of Greenwich Village.

All of which no doubt was rational enough, but in this building he had chosen the lower apartment at the ground-floor level. It adjoined the cellar. It was built for the janitor, but Derek had taken it and fixed it up in luxurious fashion. Near it, in a corner of the cellar, he had boarded off a square space into a room. I understood vaguely that it was a chemical laboratory. He had never discussed it, nor had I ever been shown inside it. Unusual, mysterious enough, and that a captain of the British military should be an experimental scientist was even more unusual. Yet I had always believed that for a year or two Derek had been engaged in some sort of chemical or physical experiment. With all his military swagger he had the precise, careful mode of thought characteristic of the man of scientific mind.

I recall that when I got his note with its few sentences bidding me come to see him, I had a premonition that it marked the beginning of something strange. As though the portals of a mystery were opening to me!

Nothing is impossible! Nevertheless I record these events into which I was plunged that June evening with a very natural reluctance. I expect no credibility. If this were the year 2000, my narrative doubtless would be tame enough. Yet in 1929 it can only be called a fantasy. Let it go at that. The fantasy of today is the sober truth of tomorrow. And by the day after, it is a mere platitude. Our world moves swiftly.

Derek received me in his living-room. He admitted me himself. He told me that his man servant was out. It was a small room, with leather-covered easy chairs, rugs on its hardwood floor, and sober brown portieres at its door and windows. A brown parchment shade shrouded the electrolier on the table. It was the only light in the room. It cast its mellow sheen upon Derek's lean graceful figure as he flung himself down and produced cigarettes.

He said, "Charlie, I want a little talk with you. I've something to tell you – something to offer you."

He held his lighter out to me, with its tiny blue alcohol flame under my cigarette. And I saw that his hand was trembling.

"But I don't understand what you mean," I protested.

He retorted, "I'm suggesting that you might be tired of being a clerk in a brokerage office. Tired of this humdrum world that we call civilization. Tired of Wall Street."

"I am, Derek. Heavens, that's true enough."

His eyes held me. He was smiling half whimsically: his voice was only half serious. Yet I could see, in the smoldering depths of those luminous dark eyes, a deadly seriousness that belied his smiling lips and his gay tone.

He interrupted me with, "And I offer you a chance for deeds of high adventuring. The romance of danger, of pitting your wits against villainy to make right triumph over wrong, and to win for yourself power and riches – and perhaps a fair lady..."

"Derek, you talk like a swashbuckler of the middle ages."

I thought he would grin, but he turned suddenly solemn.

"I'm offering to make you henchman to a king, Charlie."

"King of what? Where?"

He spread his lean brown hands with a gesture. He shrugged. "What matter? If you seek adventure, you can find it – somewhere. If you feel the lure of romance – it will come to you."

I said, "Henchman to a king?"

But still he would not smile. "Yes. If I were king. I'm serious. Absolutely. In all this world there is no one who cares a damn about me. Not in this world, but..."

He checked himself. He went on, "You are the same. You have no relatives?"

"No. None that ever think of me."

"Nor a sweetheart. Or have you?"

"No," I smiled. "Not yet. Maybe never."

"But you are too interested in Wall Street to leave it for the open road?" He was sarcastic now. "Or do you fear deeds of daring? Do you want to right a great wrong? Rescue an oppressed people, overturn the tyranny of an evil monarch, and put your friend and the girl he loves upon the throne? Or do you want to go down to work as usual in the subway tomorrow morning? Are you afraid that in this process of becoming henchman to a king you may perchance get killed?"

I matched his caustic tone. "Let's hear it, Derek."

Chapter II: The Challenge of the Unknown

INCREDIBLE! Impossible! I did not say it, though my thoughts were written on my face, no doubt.

Derek said quietly, "Difficult to believe, Charlie? Yes! But it happens to be true. The girl I love is not of this world, but she lives nevertheless. I have seen her, talked with her. A slim little thing – beautiful..."

He sat staring. "This is nothing supernatural, Charlie. Only the ignorant savages of our past called the unknown – the unusual – supernatural. We know better now."

I said, "This girl –"

He gestured. "As I told you, I have for years been working on the theory that there is another world, existing here in this same space with us. The Fourth Dimension! Call it that it you like. I have found it, proved its existence! And this girl – her name is Hope – lives in it. Let me tell you about her and her people. Shall I?"

My heart was pounding so that it almost smothered me. "Yes, Derek."

"She lives here, in this Space we call New York City. She and her people use this same Space at the same time that we use it. A different world from ours, existing here now with us! Unseen by us. And we are unseen by them!"

"A different form of matter, Charlie. As tangible to the people of the other realm as we are to our own world. Humans like ourselves."

He paused, but I could find no words to fill the gap. And presently he went on:

"Hope's world, co-existing here with us, is dependent upon us. They speak what we call English. They shadow us."

I murmured, "Phantoms of reality."

"Yes. A world very like ours. But primitive, where ours is civilized."

He paused again. His eyes were staring past me as though he could see through the walls of the cellar room into great reaches of the unknown. What a strange mixture was this Derek Mason! What a strange compound of the cold reality of the scientist and the fancy of the romantic dreamer! Yet I wonder if that is not what science is. There is no romantic lover gawping at the moon who could have more romance in his soul, or see in the moonlit eyes of his loved one more romance than the scientist finds in the wonders of his laboratory.

Derek went on slowly:

"A primitive world, primitive nation, primitive passions! As I see it now, Charlie – as I know it to be – it seems as though perhaps Hope's world is merely a replica of ours, stripped to the primitive. As though it might be the naked soul of our modern New York, ourselves as we really are, not as we pretend to be."

He roused himself from his reverie.

"Hope's nation is ruled by a king. An emperor, if you like. A monarch, beset with the evils of luxury and ease, and wine and women. He is surrounded by his nobles, the idle aristocracy, by virtue of their birth proclaiming themselves of too fine a clay to work. The crimson nobles, they are called. Because they affect crimson cloaks, and their beautiful women, voluptuous, sex-mad, are wont to bedeck themselves in veils and robes of crimson.

"And there are workers, toilers they call them. Oppressed, down-trodden toilers, with hate for the nobles and the king smoldering within them. In France there was such a condition, and the bloody revolution came of it. It exists here now. Hope was born in the ranks of these toilers, but has risen by her grace and beauty to a position in the court of this graceless monarch."

He leaped from his chair and began pacing the room. I sat silent, staring at him. So strange a thing! Impossible? I could not say that. I could only say, incredible to me. And as I framed the thought I knew its incredibility was the very measure of my limited intelligence, my lack of knowledge. The vast unknown of nature, so vast that everything which was real to me, understandable to me, was a mere drop in the ocean of the existing unknown.

"Don't you understand me now?" Derek added vehemently. "I'm not talking fantasy. Cold reality! I've found a way to transport myself – and you – into this different state of matter, into this other world! I've already made a test. I went there and stayed just for a few moments, a night or so ago."

It made my heart leap wildly. He went on: "There is chaos there. Smoldering revolution which at any time – tonight perhaps – may burst into conflagration and destroy this wanton ruling class." He laughed harshly. "In Hope's world the workers are a primitive, ignorant people. Superstitious. Like the peons of Mexico, they're all primed and ready to shout for any leader who sets himself up. My chance – our chance –"

He suddenly stopped his pacing and stood before me. "Don't you feel the lure of it? The open road? 'The road is straight before me and the Red Gods call for me!' I'm going, Charlie. Going tonight – and I want you to go with me! Will you?"

Would I go? The thing leaped like a menacing shadow risen solidly to confront me. Would I go?

Suddenly there was before me the face of a girl. White. Apprehensive. It seemed almost pleading. A face beautiful, with a mouth of parted red lips. A face framed in long, pale-golden hair with big staring blue eyes. Wistful eyes, wan with starlight – eyes that seemed to plead.

I thought, "Why, this is madness!" I was not seeing this face with my eyes. There was nothing, no one here in the room with me but Derek. I knew it. The shadows about us were empty. I was conjuring the face only from Derek's words, making real that which existed only in my imagination.

Yet I knew that in another realm, with my thoughts now bridging the gap, the girl was real. Would I go into the unknown?

The quest of the unknown. The gauntlet of the unknown flung down now before me, as it was flung down before the ancient explorers who picked up its challenge and mounted the swaying decks of their little galleons and said, "We'll go and see what lies off there in the unknown."

That same lure was on me now. I heard my voice saying, "Why yes, I guess I'll go, Derek."

Chapter III: Into the Unknown

WE STOOD in the boarded room which was Derek's laboratory. Our preparations had been simple: Derek had made them all in advance. There was little left to do. The laboratory was a small room of board walls, board ceiling and floor. Windowless, with a single door opening into the cellar of the apartment house.

Derek had locked the door after us as we entered. He said, "I have sent my man servant away for a week. The people in the house here think I have gone away on a vacation. No one will miss us, Charlie – not for a time, anyway."

No one would miss me, save my employers, and to them I would no doubt be a small loss.

We had put out the light in Derek's apartment and locked it carefully after us. This journey! I own that I was trembling, and frightened. Yet a strange eagerness was on me.

The cellar room was comfortably furnished. Rugs were on its floor. Whatever apparatus of a research laboratory had been here was removed now. But the evidence of it remained – Derek's long search for this secret which now he was about to use. A row of board shelves at one side of the room showed where bottles and chemical apparatus had stood. A box of electrical tools and odds and ends of wire still lay discarded in a corner of the room. There was a tank of running water, and gas connections, where no doubt Bunsen burners had been.

Derek produced his apparatus. I sat on a small low couch against the wall and watched him as he stripped himself of his clothes. Around his waist he adjusted a wide, flat, wire-woven belt. A small box was fastened to it in the middle of the back – a wide, flat thing of metal, a quarter of an inch thick, and curved to fit his body.

It was a storage battery of the vibratory current he was using. From the battery, tiny threads of wire ran up his back to a wire necklace flat against his throat. Other wires extended down his arms to the wrists. Still others down his legs to the ankles. A flat electrode was connected to the top of his head like a helmet. I was reminded as he stood there, of medical charts of the human body with the arterial system outlined. But when he dressed again and put on his jaunty captain's uniform, only the electrode clamped to his head and the thin wires dangling from it in the back were visible to disclose that there was anything unusual about him.

He said smilingly, "Don't stare at me like that."

I took a grip on myself. This thing was frightening, now that I actually was embarked on it. Derek had explained to me briefly the workings of his apparatus. A vibratory electronic current, for which as yet he had no name, was stored in the small battery. He had said:

"There's nothing incomprehensible about this, Charlie. It's merely a changing of the vibration rate of the basic substance out of which our bodies are made. Vibration is the governing factor of all states of matter. In its essence what we call substance is wholly intangible. That is already proven. A vortex! A whirlpool of nothingness! It creates a pseudo-substance which is the only material in the universe. And from this, by vibration, is built the complicated structure of things as we see and feel them to be, all dependent upon vibration. Everything is altered, directly as the vibratory rate is changed. From the most tenuous gas, to fluids to solids – throughout all the different states of matter the only fundamental difference is the rate of vibration."

I understood the basic principle of this that he was explaining – that now when this electronic current which he had captured and controlled was applied to our physical body, the vibration rate of every smallest and most minute particle of our physical being was altered. There is so little in the vast scale of natural phenomena of which our human senses are cognizant! Our eyes see the colors of the spectrum, from red to violet. But a vast invisible world of color lies below the red of the rainbow! Physicists call it the infra-red. And beyond the violet, another realm – the ultra-violet. With sound it is the same. Our audible range of sound is very small. There are sounds with too slow a vibratory rate for us to hear, and others too rapid. The differing vibratory rate from most tenuous gas to most substantial solid is all that we can perceive in this physical world of ours. Yet of the whole, it is so very little! This other realm to which we were now going lay in the higher, more rapid vibratory scale. To us, by comparison, a more tenuous world, a shadow realm.

I listened to Derek's words, but my mind was on the practicality of what lay ahead. An explorer, standing upon his ship, may watch his men bending the sails, raising the anchor, but his mind flings out to the journey's end...

We were soon ready. Derek wore his jaunty uniform, I wore my ordinary business suit. A magnetic field would be about us, so that in the transition anything in fairly close contact with our bodies was affected by the current.

Derek said, "I will go first, Charlie."

"But, Derek –" A fear, greater than the trembling I had felt before, leaped at me. Left here alone, with no one on whom to depend!

He spoke with careful casualness, but his eyes were burning me. "Just sit there, and watch. When I am gone, turn on the current as I showed you and come after me. I'll wait for you."

"Where?" I stammered.

He smiled faintly. "Here. Right here. I'm not going away! Not going to move. I'll be here on the couch waiting for you."

Terrifying words! He had lowered the couch, bending out its short legs until the frame of it rested on the board floor. He drew a chair up before it and seated me. He sat down on the couch.

He said, "Oh, one other thing. Just before you start, put out the light. We can't tell how long it will be before we return."

Terrifying words!

His right hand was on his left wrist where the tiny switch was placed. He smiled again. "Good luck to us, Charlie!"

Good luck to us! The open road, the unknown!

I sat there staring. He was partly in shadow. The room was very silent. Derek lay propped up on one elbow. His hand threw the tiny switch.

There was a breathless moment. Derek's face was set and white, but no whiter than my own, I was sure. His eyes were fixed on me. I saw him suddenly quiver and twitch a little.

I murmured, "Derek –"

At once he spoke, to reassure me. "I'm all right, Charlie. That was just the first feel of it."

There was a faint quivering throb in the room, like a tiny distant dynamo throbbing. The current was surging over Derek; his legs twitched.

A moment. The faint throbbing intensified. No louder, but rapid, infinitely more rapid. A tiny throb, an aerial whine, faint as the whirring wings of a humming bird. It went up the scale, ascending in pitch, until presently it was screaming with an aerial microscopic voice.

But there seemed no change in Derek. His uniform was glowing a trifle, that was all. His face was composed now; he smiled, but did not speak. His eyes roved away from me, as though now he were seeing things that I could not see.

Another moment. No change.

Why, what was this? I blinked, gasped. There was a change! My gaze was fastened upon Derek's white face. White? It was more than white now! A silver sheen seemed to be coming to his skin!

I think no more than a minute had passed. His face was glowing, shimmering. A transparent look was coming to it, a thinness, a sudden unsubstantiality! He dropped his elbow and lay on the couch, stretched at full length at my feet. His eyes were staring.

And suddenly I realized that the face that held those staring eyes was erased! A shimmering apparition of Derek was stretched here before me. I could see through it now! Beneath the shimmering, blurred outlines of his body I could see the solid folds of the couch cover. A ghost of Derek here. An apparition – fading – dissipating!

A gossamer outline of him, imponderable, intangible.

I leaped to my feet, staring down over him.

"Derek!"

The shape of him did not move. Every instant it was more vaporous, more unreal.

I thought, "He's gone!"

No! He was still there. A white mist of his form on the couch. Melting, dissipating in the light like a fog before sunshine. A wisp of it left, like a breath, and then there was nothing.

I sat on the couch. I had put out the light. Around me the room was black. My fingers found the small switch at my wrist. I pressed it across its tiny arc.

The first shock was slight, but infinitely strange. A shuddering, twitching sensation ran all over me. It made my head reel, swept a wave of nausea over me, a giddiness, a feeling that I was falling through darkness.

I lay on the couch, bracing myself. The current was whining up its tiny scale. I could feel it now. A tiny throbbing, communicating itself to my physical being.

And then in a moment I realized that my body was throbbing. The vibration of the current was communicating itself to the most minute cells of my body. An indescribable tiny quivering within me. Strange, frightening, sickening at first. But the sickness passed, and in a moment I found it almost pleasant.

I could see nothing. The room was wholly dark. I lay on my side on the couch, my eyes staring into the blackness around me. I could hear the humming of the current, and then it seemed to fade. Abruptly I felt a sense of lightness. My body, lying on the couch, pressed less heavily.

I gripped my arm. I was solid, substantial as before. I touched the couch. It was the couch which was changing, not I! The couch cover queerly seemed to melt under my hand!

The sense of my own lightness grew upon me. A lightness, a freedom, pressed me, as though chains and shackles which all my life had encompassed me were falling away. A wild, queer freedom.

I wondered where Derek was. Had I arrived in the other realm? Was he here? I had no idea how much time had passed: a minute or two, perhaps.

Or was I still in Derek's laboratory? The darkness was as solid, impenetrable as ever. No, not quite dark! I saw something now. A glowing, misty outline around me. Then I saw that it was not the new, unknown realm, but still Derek's room. A shadowy, spectral room, and the light, which dimly illumined it, was from outside.

I lay puzzling, my own situation forgotten for the moment. The light came from overhead, in another room of the apartment house. I stared. Around me now was a dim vista of distance, and vague, blurred, misty outlines of the apartment building above me. The shadowy world I had left now lay bare. There was a moment when I thought I could see far away across a spectral city street. The shadows of the great city were around me. They glowed, and then were gone.

A hand gripped my arm in a solid grip. Derek's voice sounded.

"Are you all right?"

"Yes," I murmured. The couch had faded. I was conscious that I had floated or drifted down a few inches, to a new level. The level of the cellar floor beneath the couch. Cellar floor! It was not that now. Yet there was something solid here, a solid ground, and I was lying upon it, with Derek sitting beside me.

I murmured again, "Yes, I'm all right."

My groping hand felt the ground. It was soil, with a growth of vegetation like a grass sward on it. Were we outdoors? It suddenly seemed so. I could feel soft, warm air on my face and had a sense of open distance around me. A light was growing, a vague, diffused light, as though day were swiftly coming upon us.

I felt Derek fumbling at my wrist. "That's all, Charlie."

There was a slight shock. Derek was pulling me up beside him. I found myself on my feet, with light around me. I stood wavering, gripping Derek. It was as though I had closed my eyes, and now they were suddenly open. I was aware of daylight, color, and movement. A world of normality here, normal to me now because I was part of it. The realm of the unknown!

Chapter IV: "Hope, I Came..."

I THINK I was first conscious of a queer calmness which had settled upon me, as though now I had withdrawn contact with the turmoil of our world! Something was gone, and in its place came a calmness. But that was a mere transition. It had passed in a moment. I stood trembling with eagerness, as I know Derek was trembling.

A radiant effulgence of light was around us, clarifying, growing. There was ground beneath our feet, and sky overhead. A rational landscape, strangely familiar. A physical world like my own, but, it seemed, with a new glory upon it. Nature, calmly serene.

I had thought we were standing in daylight. I saw now it was bright starlight. An evening, such as the evening we had just left in our own world. The starlight showed everything clearly. I could see a fair distance.

We stood at the top of a slight rise. I saw gentle, slightly undulating country. A brook nearby wound through a grove of trees and lost itself. Suddenly, with a shock, I realized how familiar this was! We stood facing what in New York City we call West. The contour of this land was familiar enough for me to identify it. A mile or so ahead lay a river; it shimmered in its valley, with cliffs on its further side. Near at hand the open country was dotted with trees and checkered with round patches of cultivated fields. And there were occasional habitations, low, oval houses of green thatch.

The faint flush of a recent sunset lay upon the landscape, mingled with the starlight. A road – a white ribbon in the starlight – wound over the countryside toward the river. Animals, strange of aspect, were slowly dragging carts. There were distant figures working in the fields.

A city lay ahead of us, set along this nearer bank of the river. A city! It seemed a primitive village. All was primitive, as though here might be some lost Indian tribe of our early ages. The people were picturesque, the field workers garbed in vivid colors. The flat little carts, slow moving, with broad-horned oxen.

This quiet village, drowsing beside the calm-flowing river, seemed all very normal. I could fancy that it was just after sundown of a quiet workday. There was a faint flush of pink upon everything: the glory of the sun just set. And as though to further my fancy, in the village by the river, like an angelus, a faint-toned bell was chiming.

We stood for a moment gazing silently. I felt wholly normal. A warm, pleasant wind fanned my hot face. The sense of lightness was gone. This was normality to me.

Derek murmured, "Hope was to meet me here."

And then we both saw her. She was coming toward us along the road. A slight, girlish figure, clothed in queerly vivid garments: a short jacket of blue cloth with wide-flowing sleeves, knee-length pantaloons of red, with tassels dangling from them, and a wide red sash about her waist. Pale golden hair was piled in a coil upon her head...

She was coming toward us along the edge of the road, from the direction of the city. She was only a few hundred feet from us when we first saw her, coming swiftly, furtively it seemed. A low pike fence bordered the road. She seemed to be shielding herself in the shadows beside it.

We stood waiting in the starlight. The nearest figures in the field and on the road were too far away to notice us. The girl advanced. Her white arm went up in a gesture, and Derek answered. She left the road, crossing the field toward us. As she came closer, I saw how very beautiful she was. A girl of eighteen, perhaps, a fantastic little figure with her vivid garments. The starlight illumined her white face, anxious, apprehensive, but eager.

"Derek!"

He said, "Hope, I came..."

I stood silently watching. Derek's arms went out, and the girl, with a little cry, came running forward and threw herself into them.

Chapter V: Intrigue

"AM I in time, Hope?"

"Yes, but the festival is tonight. In an hour or two now. Oh Derek, if the king holds this festival, the toilers will revolt. They won't stand it –"

"Tonight! It mustn't be held tonight! It doesn't give me time, time to plan."

I stood listening to their vehement, half-whispered words. For a moment or two, absorbed, they ignored me.

"The king will make his choice tonight, Derek. He has announced it. Blanca or Sensua for his queen. And if he chooses the Crimson Sensua –"–" She stammered, then she went on:

"If he does – there will be bloodshed. The toilers are waiting, just to learn his choice."

Derek exclaimed, "But tonight is too soon! I've got to plan. Hope, where does Rohbar stand in this?"

Strange intrigue! I pieced it together now, from their words, and from what presently they briefly told me. A festival was about to be held, an orgy of feasting and merrymaking, of music and dancing. And during it, this young King Leonto was to choose his queen. There were two possibilities. The Crimson Sensua, a profligate, debauched woman who, as queen, would further oppress the workers. And Blanca, a white beauty, risen from the toilers to be a favorite at the Court. Hope was her handmaiden.

If Blanca were chosen, the toilers would be appeased. She was one of them. She would lead this king from his profligate ways, would win from him justice for the workers.

But Derek and Hope both knew that the pure and gentle Blanca would never be the king's choice. And tonight the toilers would definitely know it, and the smoldering revolt would burst into flame.

And there was this Rohbar. Derek said, "He is the king's henchman, Charlie."

I stood here in the starlight, listening to them. This strange primitive realm. There were no modern weapons here. We had brought none. The current used in our transition would have exploded the cartridges of a revolver. I had a dirk which Hope now gave me, and that was all.

Primitive intrigue. I envisaged this chaotic nation, with its toilers ignorant as the oppressed Mexican peons at their worst. Striving to better themselves, yet, not knowing how. Ready to shout for any leader who might with vainglorious words set himself up as a patriot.

This Rohbar, perhaps, was planning to do just that.

And so was Derek! He said, "Hope, if you could persuade the king to postpone the festival – if Blanca would help persuade him – just until tomorrow night..."

"I can try, Derek. But the festival is planned for an hour or two from now."

"Where is the king?"

"In his palace, near the festival gardens."

She gestured to the south. My mind went back to New York City. This hillock, where we were standing in the starlight beside a tree, was in my world about Fifth Avenue and Sixteenth Street. The king's palace – the festival gardens – stood down at the Battery, where the rivers met in the broad water of the harbor.

Derek was saying, "We haven't much time: can you get us to the palace?"

"Yes. I have a cart down there on the road."

"And the cloaks for Charlie and me?"

"Yes."

"Good!" said Derek. "We'll go with you. It's a long chance; he probably won't postpone it. If he does not, we'll be among the audience. And when he chooses the Red Sensua –"

She shuddered, "Oh, Derek –" And I thought I heard her whisper, "Oh, Alexandre –" and I saw his finger go to his lips.

His arm went around her. She huddled, small as a child against his tall, muscular body. He said gently, "Don't be afraid, little Hope."

His face was grim, his eyes were gleaming. I saw him suddenly as an instinctive military adventurer. An anachronism in our modern New York City. Born in a wrong age. But here in this primitive realm he was at home.

I plucked at him. "How can you – how can we dare plunge into this thing? Hidden with cloaks, yes. But you talk of leading these toilers."

He cast Hope away and confronted me. "I can do it! You'll see, Charlie." He was very strangely smiling. "You'll see. But I don't want to come into the open right away. Not tonight. But if we can only postpone this accursed festival."

We had been talking perhaps five minutes. We were ready now to start away. Derek said: "Whatever comes, Charlie, I want you to take care of Hope. Guard her for me, will you?"

I said, "Yes, I will try to."

Hope smiled as she held out her hand to me. "I will not be afraid, with Derek's friend."

Her English was of different intonation from our own, but it was her native language, I could not doubt.

I took her cold, slightly trembling hand. "Thank you, Hope."

Her eyes were misty with starlight. Tender eyes, but the tenderness was not for me.

"Yes," I repeated. "You can depend upon me, Derek."

We left the hillock. A food-laden cart came along the road. The driver, a boy vivid in jacket and wide trousers of red and blue, bravely worn but tattered, ran alongside guiding the oxen. When they had passed we followed, and presently we came to the cloaks Hope had hidden. Derek and I donned them. They were long crimson cloaks with hoods.

Hope said, "Many are gathering for the festival shrouded like that. You will not be noticed now."

Further along the road we reached a little eminence. I saw the river ahead of us, and a river behind us. And a few miles to the south, an open spread of water where the rivers joined. Familiar contours! The Hudson River! The East River. And down at the end of the island, New York Harbor.

Hope gestured that way. "The king's palace is there."

We were soon passing occasional houses, primitive thatched dwellings. I saw inside one. Workers were seated over their frugal evening meal. Always the same vivid garments, jaunty but tattered. We passed one old fellow in a field, working late in the starlight. A man bent with age, but still a tiller of the soil. Hope waved to him and he responded, but the look he gave us as we hurried by shrouded in our crimson cloaks was sullenly hostile.

We came to an open cart. It stood by the roadside. An ox with shaggy coat and spreading horns was fastened to the fence. It was a small cart with small rollers like wheels. Seats were in it and a vivid canopy over it. We climbed in and rumbled away.

And this starlit road in our own world was Broadway! We were presently passing close to the river's edge. This quiet, peaceful, starlit river! Why, in our world it was massed with docks! Great ocean liners, huge funneled, with storied decks lay here! Under this river, tunnels with endless passing vehicles! Tubes, with speeding trains crowded with people!

The reality here was so different! Behind us what seemed an upper city was strung along the river. Ahead of us also there were streets and houses, the city of the workers. A bell was tolling. Along all the roads now we could see the moving yellow spots of lights on the holiday carts headed for the festival. And there were spots of yellow torchlight from boats on the river.

We soon were entering the city streets. Narrow dirt streets they were, with primitive shacks to the sides. Women came to the doorways to stare at our little cart rumbling hastily past. I was conscious of my crimson cloak, and conscious of the sullen glances of hate which were flung at it from every side, here in this squalid, forlorn section where the workers lived.

Along every street now the carts were passing, converging to the south. They were filled, most of them, with young men and girls, all in gaudy costumes. Some of them, like ourselves, were shrouded in crimson cloaks. The carts occasionally were piled with flowers. As one larger than us, and moving faster rumbled by, a girl in it stood up and pelted me with blossoms. She wore a crimson robe, but it had fallen from her shoulders. I caught a glimpse of her face, framed in flowing dark hair, and of eyes with laughter in them, mocking me, alluring.

We came at last to the end of the island. There seemed to be a thousand or more people arriving, or here already. The tip of the island had an esplanade with a broad canopy behind it. Burning torches of wood gave flames of yellow, red and blue fire. A throng of gay young people promenaded the walk, watching the arriving boats.

And here, behind the walk at the water's edge, was a garden of trees and lawn, shrubs and beds of tall vivid flowers. Nooks were here to shelter lovers, pools of water glinted red and green with the reflected torchlight. In one of the pools I saw a group of girls bathing, sportive as dolphins.

To one side at a little distance up the river, banked against the water, was a broad, low building: the palace of the king. About it were broad gardens, with shrubs and flowers. The whole was surrounded by a high metal fence, spiked on top.

The main gate was near at hand; we left our cart. Close to the gate was a guard standing alert, a jaunty fellow in leather pantaloons and leather jacket, with a spiked helmet, and in his hand a huge, sharp-pointed lance. The gardens of the palace, what we could see of them, seemed empty – none but the favored few might enter here. But as I climbed from the cart, I got the impression that just inside the fence a figure was lurking. It started away as we approached the gate. The guard had not seen it – the drab figure of a man in what seemed to be dripping garments, as though perhaps he had swum in from the water.

And Derek saw him. He muttered, "They are everywhere."

Hope led us to the gate. The guard recognized her. At her imperious gesture he stood aside. We passed within. I saw the palace now as a long winged structure of timber and stone, with a high tower at the end of one wing. The building fronted the river, but here on the garden side there was a broad doorway up an incline, twenty feet up and over a small bridge, spanning what seemed a dry moat. Beyond it, a small platform, then an oval archway, the main entrance to the building.

Derek and I, shrouded in our crimson cloaks with hoods covering us to the eyes, followed Hope into the palace.

Chapter VI: The King's Henchman

THE LONG ROOM was bathed in colored lights. There was an ornate tiled floor. Barbaric draperies of heavy fabric shrouded the archways and windows. It was a totally barbaric apartment. It might have been the audience chamber of some fabled Eastern Prince of our early ages. Yet not quite that either. There was a primitive modernity here. I could not define it, could not tell why I felt this strangeness. Perhaps it was the aspect of the people.

The room was crowded with men and gay laughing girls in fancy dress costumes. Half of them at least were shrouded in crimson cloaks, but most of the hoods were back. They moved about, laughing and talking, evidently waiting for the time to come for them to go to the festival. We pushed our way through them.

Derek murmured, "Keep your hood up, Charlie."

A girl plucked at me. "Handsome man, let me see." She thrust her painted lips up to mine as though daring me to kiss them. Hope shoved her away. Her parted cloak showed her white, beautiful body with the dark tresses of her hair shrouding it. Exotically lovely she was, with primitive, unrestrained passions – typical of the land in which she lived.

"This way," whispered Hope. "Keep close together. Do not speak!"

We moved forward and stood quietly against the wall of the room, where great curtains hid us partly from view. Under a canopy, at a table on a raised platform near one end of the apartment, sat the youthful monarch. I saw him as a man of perhaps thirty. He was in holiday garb, robed in silken hose of red and white, a strangely fashioned doublet, and a close-fitting shirt. Bare-headed, with thick black hair, long to the base of his neck.

He sat at the table with a calm dignity. But he relaxed here in the presence of his favored courtiers. He was evidently in a high good humor this night, giving directions for the staging of the spectacle, despatching messengers. I stood gazing at him. A very kingly fellow this. There was about him that strange mingled look of barbarism and modernity.

Hope approached him and knelt. Derek and I could hear their voices, although the babble of the crowd went on.

"My little Hope, what is it? Stand up, child."

She said, "Your Highness, a message from Blanca."

He laughed. "Say no more! I know it already! She does not want this festival. The workers," – what a world of sardonic contempt he put into that one word! – "the workers will be offended because we take pleasure tonight. Bah!" But he was still laughing. "Say no more, little Hope. Tell Blanca to dance and sing her best this night. I am making my choice. Did you know that?"

Hope was silent. He repeated, "Did you know that?"

"Yes, Your Highness," she murmured.

"I choose our queen tonight, child. Blanca or Sensua." He sighed. "Both are very beautiful. Do you know which one I am going to choose?"

"No," she said.

"Nor do I, little Hope. Nor do I."

He dismissed her. "Go now. Don't bother me."

She parted her lips as though to make another protest, but his eyes suddenly flashed.

"I would not have you annoy me again. Do you understand?"

She turned away, back toward where Derek and I were lurking. The chattering crowd in the room had paid no attention to Hope, but before she could reach us a man detached himself from a nearby group and accosted her. A commanding figure, he was, I think, quite the largest man in the room. An inch or two taller than Derek, at the least. He wore his red cloak with the hood thrown back upon his wide heavy shoulders. A bullet-head with close-clipped black hair. A man of about the king's age, he had a face of heavy features, and flashing dark eyes. A scoundrel adventurer, this king's henchman.

Hope said, "What is it, Rohbar?"

"You will join our party, little Hope?" He laid a heavy hand on her white arm. His face was turned toward me. I could not miss the gleaming look in his eyes as he regarded her.

"No," she said.

It seemed that he twitched at her, but she broke away from him.

Anger crossed his face, but the desirous look in his eyes remained.

"You are very bold, Hope, to spurn me like this." He had lowered his voice as though fearful that the king might hear him.

"Let me alone!" she said.

She darted away from him, but before she joined us she stood waiting until he turned away.

"No use," Hope whispered. "There is nothing we can do here. You heard what the king said – and the festival is already begun."

Derek stood a moment, lost in thought. He was gazing across the room to where Rohbar was standing with a group of girls. He said at last:

"Come on, Charlie. We'll watch this festival. This damn fool king will choose the Red Sensua." He shrugged. "There will be chaos…"

We shoved our way from the room, went out of the main doorway and hurried through the gardens of the palace. The red-cloaked figures were leaving the building now for the festival grounds. We waited for a group of them to pass so that we might walk alone. As we neared the gate, passing through the shadows of high flowered shrubs, a vague feeling that we were being followed shot through me. In a moment there was so much to see that I forgot it, but I held my hand on my dirk and moved closer to Hope.

We reached the entrance to the canopy. A group of girls, red-cloaked, were just coming out. They rushed past us. They ran, discarding their cloaks. Their white bodies gleamed under the colored lights as they rushed to the pool and dove.

We were just in time. Hope whispered, "The king will be here any moment."

Beneath the canopy was a broad arena of seats. A platform, like a stage, was at one end. It was brilliantly illuminated with colored torches held aloft by girls in flowing robes, each standing like a statue with her light held high. The place was crowded. In the gloom of the darkened auditorium we found seats off to one side, near the open edge of the canopy. We sat, with Hope between us.

Derek whispered, "Shakespeare might have staged a play in a fashion like this."

A primitive theatrical performance. There was no curtain for interlude between what might have been the acts of a vaudeville. The torch girls, like pages, ranged themselves in a line across the front of the stage. They were standing there as we took our seats. The vivid glare of their torches concealed the stage behind them.

There was a few moments wait, then, amid hushed silence, the king with his retinue came in. He sat in a canopied box off to one side. When he was seated, he raised his arm and the buzz of conversation in the audience began again.

Presently the page girls moved aside from the stage. The buzz of the audience was stilted. The performance, destined to end so soon in tragedy, now began.

Chapter VII: The Crimson Murderess

HOPE MURMURED. "The three-part music comes first. There will first be the spiritual."

An orchestra was seated on the stage in a semi-circle. It was composed of men and women musicians, and there seemed to be over a hundred of them. They sat in three groups; the center group was about to play. In a solemn hush the leaderless choirs, with all its players garbed in white, began its first faint note. I craned to get a clear view of the stage. This white choir seemed almost all wood-wind. There were tiny pipes in little series such as Pan might have used. Flutes, and flageolets; and round-bellied little instruments of clay, like ocarinas. And pitch-pipes, long and slender as a marsh reed.

In a moment I was lost in the music. It began softly, with single muted notes from a single instrument, echoed by the others, running about the choir like a will-o'-the-wisp. It was faint, as though very far away, made more sweet by distance. And then it swelled, came nearer.

I had never heard such music as this. Primitive! It was not that. Nor barbaric! Nothing like the music of our ancient world. Nor was it what I might conceive to be the music of our future. A thing apart, unworldly, ethereal. It swept me, carried me off; it was an exaltation of the spirit lifting me. It was triumphant now. It surged, but there was in its rhythm, the beat of its every instrument, nothing but the soul of purity. And then it shimmered into distance again, faint and exquisite music of a dream. Crooning, pleading, the speech of whispering angels.

It ceased. There was a storm of applause.

I breathed again. Why, this was what music might be in our world but was not. I thought of our blaring jazz.

Hope said, "Now they play the physical music. Then Sensua will dance with Blanca. We will see then which one the king chooses."

On the stage all the torches were extinguished save those which were red. The arena was darker than before. The stage was bathed with a deep crimson. Music of the physical senses! It was, indeed, no more like the other choir than is the body to the spirit.

There were stringed instruments playing now; deep-toned, singing zithers, and instruments of rounded, swelling bodies, like great viols with sensuous, throbbing voices. Music with a swift rhythm, marked by the thump of hollow gourds. It rose with its voluptuous swell into a paean of abandonment, and upon the tide of it, the crimson Sensua flung herself upon the stage. She stood motionless for a moment that all might regard her. The crimson torchlight bathed her, stained crimson the white flush of her limbs, her heavy shoulders, her full, rounded throat.

A woman in her late twenties. Voluptuous of figure, with crimson veils half-hiding, half-revealing it. A face of coarse, sensuous beauty. A face wholly evil, and it seemed to me wholly debauched. Dark eyes with beaded lashes. Heavy lips painted scarlet. A pagan woman of the streets. One might have encountered such a woman swaggering in some ancient street of some ancient city, flaunting the finery given her by a rich and profligate eastern prince.

She stood a moment with smoldering, passion-filled eyes, gazing from beneath her lowered lids. Her glance went to the king's canopy, and flashed a look of confidence, of triumph. The king answered it with a smile. He leaned forward over his railing, watching her intently.

With the surge of the music she moved into her dance. Slowly she began, quite slowly. A posturing and swaying of hips like a nautch girl. She made the rounds of the musicians, leering at them. She stood in the whirl of the music, almost ignoring it, stood at the front of the stage with a gaze of slumberous, insolent passion flung at the king. A knife was in her hand now. She held it aloft. The red torchlight caught its naked blade. With shuddering fancy I seemed to see it dripping crimson. She frowned, and struck it at a phantom lover. She backed away. She stooped and knelt. She knelt and seemed with her empty arms to be caressing a murdered lover's head. She kissed him, rained upon his dead lips her macabre kisses.

And then she was up on her bare feet, again circling the stage. Her anklets clanked as she moved with the tread of a tigress. The musicians shrank from her waving blade.

A girl in white veils was suddenly disclosed standing at the back of the stage.

Derek whispered, "Is that Blanca?"

"Yes," whispered Hope.

Blanca stood watching her rival. The crimson Sensua passed her, took her suddenly by the wrist, drew her forward. For an instant I thought it might have been rehearsed. I saw Blanca as a slim, gentle girl in white, with a white head-dress. A dancer who could symbolize purity, now in the grip of red passion.

An instant, and then horror struck us. And I could feel it surge over the audience. A gasp of horror. The frightened girl in white tried to escape. The musicians wavered and broke. I stared, stricken, with freezing blood. Upon the stage the knife went swiftly up; it came down; then up again. The red Sensua stood gloating. The knife she waved aloft was truly dripping crimson now.

With a choked, gasping scream the white girl of the toilers crumpled and fell... She lay motionless, at the feet of the crimson murderess.

Chapter VIII: "Why, This Is Treason!"

THERE WAS A GASP. The audience sat frozen. On the stage, with no one lifting a hand to stop her, the crimson murderess made a leap and vanished. A moment, and then the spell broke. A girl in the audience screamed. Some one moved to stand up and overturned a seat with a crash.

The amphitheater under the canopy broke into a pandemonium. Screams and shouts, crashing of seats, screaming, frightened people struggling to get out of the darkness. The torches on the stage were dropped and extinguished. The darkness leaped upon us.

Derek and I were gripping Hope. We were struck by a bench flung backward from in front. People were rushing at us. We were swept along in the panic of the crowd.

I heard Derek shout, "We must keep together!"

We fought, but we were swept backward. We found ourselves outside the canopy. Torchlight was here. It glimmered on the pool of water. People were everywhere rushing past us, some one way, some another. Aimless, with the shock of terror upon them. Under the canopy they were still screaming.

I was momentarily separated from Derek and Hope. I very nearly stumbled into the pool. A girl was here, crouched on the stone bank. Her wet crimson veils clung to her white body. Her long, wet hair lay on her. I stumbled against her. She raised her face. Eyes, wide with terror. Mute, painted red lips...

I heard Derek calling again, "Charlie!" I shoved my way back to him. The crowd was thinning out around us. Girls were climbing from the pool, rushing off in terror, to mingle with the milling throng. Among the crowd now, down by the edge of the bay, I saw the sinister figures of men come running. The toilers, miraculously appearing everywhere! I saw, across the pool, a terrified girl crouching. A huge man in a black cloak came leaping. The colored lights in the trees glittered on his upraised knife blade as it descended. The girl fell with a shuddering scream. The murderer turned and whirled away into the crowd.

"Charlie!"

I was back with Derek and Hope. Hope stood trembling, with her hand pressed against her mouth. Derek gripped me.

"That cloak, get it off!" He ripped his crimson cloak from him and tossed it away. He jerked mine off. "Too dangerous! That's the crimson badge of death tonight."

We stood revealed in the clothes of our own world. My business suit, in which that day I had worked in Wall Street. Derek in his swagger uniform. He stood drawn to his full height, a powerful figure. The wires of our mechanism showed at his wrists. They dangled at the back of his neck, mounting to that strangely fashioned electrode clamped to his head. Strange, awe-inspiring figure of a man!

We were momentarily alone under the colored lights of the trees. Hope murmured, "But they will see us – see you..."

Derek's face was grim, but at her words he laughed harshly. "See us! What matter?" He swung on me. "It forces our hand; we've got to come out in the open now! This murder – this king! My God, what a fool to let himself get into such a condition as this! His people – this chaos – what a fool!"

He had drawn his dirk. I realized that I was holding mine. Near us the body of a crimson noble was lying under a tree. A sword was there on the ground. Derek sprang for it, waved it aloft.

I think that no more than a minute or two had passed since the murder. Down by the water the boats were hastily loading and leaving the dock. One of them overturned. There were screams everywhere. Red forms lay inert upon the ground where they had been trampled, or stabbed. But the prowling figures of the toilers now seemed to have vanished.

Derek gestured. "Look at the palace! The garden!"

Beyond the canopy I could see the dim gardens surrounding the palace. I glimpsed the high fence, and the gateway in front. A mob of toilers was there. The guard at the gate had fled. The mob was surging through. Men and women in the vivid garments of the fields, armed with sticks and clubs and stones and the implements of agriculture. They milled at the gate; rushed through; scattered over the garden. Their shouts floated back to us in a blended murmur.

We were standing only a dozen feet from the edge of the pavilion. No one seemed yet to have noticed us. A few straggling lights had come on under the canopy. I could see the dead lying there in the wreckage of overturned seats.

Derek said, "We can't help it – it's done. Look at them! They're attacking the palace!"

This mob springing miraculously into existence! I realized that the toilers had planned that if Sensua were chosen they would attack the festival. The murder of Blanca had come as big a surprise to them as to us...

"Come on! Can you get into the palace, Hope? The king must have gotten back there. Get your wits, girl!" Derek stood gripping her, shaking her.

"Yea, there's an underground passage. He probably went that way."

From the palace gardens the shouts of the mob sounded louder now. And from within the building there was an alarm bell tumultuously clanging.

Hope gasped, "This way."

She led us back into the pavilion. We clambered over its broken seats, past its gruesome huddled figures. Some were still moving... We went to a small door under the platform. A dim room was here, deserted now. Against the wall was a large wardrobe closet; stage costumes were hanging in it. The closet was fully twenty feet deep. We pushed our way through the hanging garments. Hope fumbled at the blank board wall in the rear. Her groping fingers found a secret panel. A door swung aside and a rush of dank cool air came at us. The dark outlines of a tunnel stretched ahead.

"In, Charlie!"

I crouched and stepped through the door. Hope closed it behind us. The tunnel passage was black, but soon we began to see its vague outlines. Derek, sword in hand, led us. I clutched my dirk. We went perhaps five hundred feet. Down at first, then up again. I figured we were under the palace gardens now, as the tunnel was winding to the left. There were occasional small lights.

Derek whispered to Hope, "The toilers don't know of this?"

"No."

"Where does it bring us out?" I whispered.

"Into the lower floor of the castle. The king must have gone this way. There might be a guard, Derek. What will you do?"

He laughed. "I can handle this mob. Disperse it! You'll see! And handle the king." He laughed again grimly. "There is no Blanca to choose now."

The tunnel went round a sharp angle and began steeply ascending. Derek stopped.

"How much further, Hope?"

"Not far," she whispered.

We crept forward. The tunnel was more like a small corridor now. Beyond Derek's crouching figure, in the dimness I could see a doorway. Derek turned and gestured to us to keep back. A palace guard was standing there. His pike went up.

"Who are you?"

"A friend."

But the man lunged with his pike. Derek leaped aside. His sword flashed; the flat of it struck the fellow in the face. Derek, with incredible swiftness, was upon him. They went down together and before the man could shout, Derek had struck him on the head with the sword hilt. The guard lay motionless. Derek climbed up as we ran forward to join him.

I noticed now, for the first time, that in his left hand Derek held a small metal cylinder. A weapon, strange to me, which he had brought with him. He had not mentioned it. He had produced it, when menaced by this guard. Then he evidently decided not to use it.

He shoved it back in his pocket. He whirled on us, panting. "Hurry! Close that door!"

We closed the door of the tunnel.

"Charlie, help me move him!"

We dragged the prostrate figure of the unconscious guard aside into a shadow of the wall. We were in a lower room of the palace. It seemed momentarily unoccupied. Overhead we could hear the footsteps of running people. A confusion in the palace, and outside in the garden the shouts of the menacing throng of toilers. And above it all, the wild clanging of the alarm bell from the palace tower.

Derek said swiftly, "Get us to the king!"

Hope led us through the castle corridors, and up a flight of steps to the main floor. The rooms here were thronged with terrified people – crimson nobles in their bedraggled finery of the festival. In all the chaos no one seemed to notice us.

We mounted another staircase. We found a vacant room; through its windows we looked a moment, gazing into the garden. It was jammed with a menacing mob, which milled about, leaderless, waving crude weapons, shouting imprecations at the palace. At the foot of the main steps the throng stood packed, but none dared to mount. A group of the palace guards stood on the platform over the moat.

Derek turned away impatiently. "Let's get to the king."

We mounted to the upper story. The castle occupants stared at Derek and me as we passed them. A group of girls at the head of the staircase fled before us.

"The king," Derek demanded, "Which is his apartment? Hurry, Hope, we've no time now!"

We found the frightened king seated on a couch with his counselors around him. It was a small room in this top story of the castle, with long windows to the floor. I saw that they gave onto a balcony which overlooked the gardens. There were perhaps twenty or thirty people huddled in the room. A confusion existed here as everywhere else – no one knowing what to do in this crisis. And that cursed alarm bell wildly adding to the turmoil. We paused at the doorway.

"Now," whispered Derek. He drew himself to his full height. His eyes were flashing. It was a Derek I had not seen before; he wore an air of mastery. As though he, and not the frightened, trembling monarch on the couch, were master here. And as I stared at him that instant in this primitive chaotic environment, the power of him swept me. A conqueror. The strange electrode clamped to his head gave him an aspect miraculous, awe inspiring.

He strode forward across the apartment. The king was just giving some futile, vague command to be transmitted to his guards down below. A hush fell over the room at our appearance. The king half stood up, then sank back.

"Why – why – who –"

I saw Rohbar here. His long crimson cloak hung from his shoulders, with its hood thrown back. Beneath it, as it parted in front, his leather uniform was visible. A sword was strapped to his waist. He was striding back and forth with folded arms, frowning, but his gaze was very keen. Rohbar was not frightened. He seemed rather to be gauging the situation, pondering how he might turn it to his own ends. He stopped short and swung about to face us. His jaw dropped with surprise, amazement, at our strangeness.

Derek confronted him. His bulk, and huge weight towered even over Derek. The king gasped and sat helplessly staring.

Rohbar spoke first. "Who are you?"

"This mob must be dispersed. Don't stand looking at me like that, man!"

Derek spoke in friendly fashion, but vehemently. "This is no time for explanations."

They were menacing each other. Rohbar's heavy hand fell to his sword, but Derek boldly pushed him away. He faced the king.

"Your Majesty..."

The king stared blankly at him. The title was no doubt strange to this realm, but no stranger than Derek's aspect.

"Your Majesty..."

But the noise from the garden, the confusion which now broke out in the room, and that damnable clattering bell, drowned his words.

The king found his voice. "Be quiet, all of you!" He was on his feet. He demanded of Derek again, "Who are you?"

Derek said swiftly, "I'll show you. I can disperse this mob! Charlie, come."

It seemed as though the gaze of everyone in the room went to me. I drew myself up and flashed defiance back at them. And I followed Derek to one of the balcony windows. He went through it, with me after him. I stood at the threshold, watchful of the room behind us. Rohbar was standing aside, and I saw now the woman Sensua with him. They were whispering, staring at me and Derek.

I had been wondering why, when Sensua must have known that the king would choose her – why she had dared to murder her rival. I thought now – as I saw her with Rohbar – that I could guess the reason. She loved Rohbar, not the king. Rohbar was plotting to put himself on the throne, using Sensua as a lover to that end. He had doubtless persuaded her to this murder, knowing it would arouse the toilers, precipitate this chaos which was what he wanted. Scheming scoundrel! I could not forget the look of desire on his face as he had accosted Hope...

And now Derek appeared, to add an unknown element to Rohbar's plans. There was no way he could guess who or what we were. I saw that he was puzzled, was whispering to Sensua about us, doubtless wondering how to handle us.

I saw too, that there were half a dozen crimson cloaked men here who were not frightened. They had gathered in a group. They stood with hands upon their swords, eyeing me, and watching Rohbar – as though at a sign from him they would rush me.

On the balcony Derek stood with the light from the room upon him. The crowd saw him. The main gateway of the palace was just under his balcony. The crowd had now started up the steps to where the guards were standing at the top. At the sight of Derek the mob let out a roar, and those on the steps retreated down again.

Derek stood at the balcony rail, silent, with upraised arms, gazing down upon the menacing throng. There was a moment of startled silence as he appeared. Then the shout broke out louder than before. The crowd was milling and pushing, but still leaderless. An aimless activity. Someone threw a stone. It came hurtling up. It missed Derek and struck the castle wall, falling almost at my feet.

Derek did not move. He stood calmly gazing down; stood like an orator waiting for the confusion to die before he would speak.

From the platform, just beneath Derek, the guards were staring wonderingly up, awed, startled. To the right a wing of the building turned an angle. The castle tower was there:

it rose perhaps a hundred feet higher than our balcony. On the railed platform-balcony girding its top I saw the figures of other guards standing, gazing down at Derek. The clanging bell up there was suddenly stilled.

I became aware of the king close behind me. His voice rang out: "What are you doing? How dare you?"

Derek whirled, "You fool! To what a pass you have come! Your people in arms against you..."

His violent words brought the king's anger. "How dare you! This is treason!"

I stood alert, with my hand upon my dirk.

There would be conflict here, I felt that we could not hold it off more than a moment longer. My mind leaped to that metal cylinder Derek had concealed. A weapon? Then why did he not have it out now? His eyes were flashing. The aspect of power, of confidence, upon him was unmistakable. It heartened me. I took a step toward him.

He smiled faintly. "Wait, Charlie."

The king gasped again. "How dare you? Why, this is treason! Rohbar, seize him!"

Hope was beside me, her eyes watching the room. Rohbar came striding forward. Derek rasped, "You perhaps have some sense! Lead His Majesty away. Take care of him until this is over."

They stood with crossing glances. And upon Rohbar's face a look, queerly sinister, had come. A smile, sardonic.

He said abruptly to the king, "I think we should let him have his way. What harm?"

He gestured and Sensua came forward. The crimson murderess! Her voluptuous figure was shrouded in a crimson cloak. Her heavy painted lips smiled at the king. Her rounded white arms went over his shoulders.

"Leonto, do as Rohbar says. Let this stranger try. It can do no harm."

The king yielded to her; I watched as she and Rohbar urged him through an archway that gave into the adjoining apartment.

No wonder Rohbar was sardonically smiling! Derek had played into his hand. We did not know it then, but we were soon to find it out.

Chapter IX: "Alexandre – "

DEREK TURNED back to the balcony. It had been a brief interlude. The mob in the garden, the soldiers at the top of the stairway, and the other guards high on the bridge of the tower were all standing gazing. Shouts again arose as Derek appeared. Again he raised his arms. This time his voice rang out.

"Silence all of you! I am a friend! Silence!"

At first they did not heed him; then someone shouted:

"Quiet! Listen to him! Let him talk!"

The crowd was bellowing, and then they ceased. The bell was still. In the hush came Derek's voice:

"I am a friend. I come from foreign lands, from distant lands of strange people and strange magic."

For answer the crowd shouted and milled in confusion. A stone came up and then another. Derek stood immovable, like a statue gazing down at them.

"I command you to disperse. You will not? Then look at me! Look at me, all of you. My will is law beyond this king – beyond these palace soldiers – beyond any power you have ever known."

Then I knew a part of Derek's purpose! He had pressed the mechanism at his wrist. He stood imperious with upraised arms. The garden was in a tumult, but in a moment it died. A wave of horror swept the crowd. A freezing, incredulous horror. They stood staring, incredulous, silent, swept with a widening wave of horror.

The figure of Derek on the balcony was fading, turning luminous. A wraith, a ghost of his menacing shape standing there. It faded until it was almost gone, and then, as he reversed the mechanism, it materialized again. A moment passed, then he stood again solid before them.

His voice rang out, "Will you obey me now? I am a friend of the toilers!"

They were prostrate before him. There is no fear more terrible than the fear of the supernatural. In all of history there has been in our world no worship more abject than the worship and fear of a primitive people for its supernatural God. On the platform beneath the balcony, the palace soldiers stared up, horrified. Then they too were prostrate before Derek's threatening gestures and commanding voice.

I stood watching, listening. And suddenly, from the prostrate crowd, a man leaped up. In the silence his amazed voice carried over the garden.

"Alexandre! It is our Prince Alexandre! Our lost prince!"

He stood staring at Derek, his arms gesturing to his comrade around him. He shouted it again:

"Our rightful king, come back to us! Don't you recognize him? I saw him go! He went like that – fading into a ghost. Ten years ago, when Leonto killed his father and would have killed him had he not escaped!"

The crowd was standing up now. They recognized Derek! There was no doubt of it. The garden was ringing with the tumultuous shouts,

"Alexandre! Our lost prince has come back to us!"

My head was whirling with it. Derek, prince of this realm? I could see that it was true. Escaped from here as a young lad, when his throne was usurped. Returning now, a man, to claim his own.

And suddenly he turned and flashed me his smile.

The din from the garden drowned his words. The crowd was shouting: "Alexandre! Our lost prince!"

The king's guards on the lower platform stood sullen, confused. I heard footsteps behind me. I whirled around.

From the room, the group of Rohbar's crimson nobles were rushing toward me! Their swords were out. One of them shouted, "Kill them now! We must kill them and have done!"

There were five or six men in the group. They were no more than ten feet away from me. They came leaping.

I stood in the window opening, with only my dirk to oppose them. I shouted, "Derek! Derek!"

I think I took a step backward. I was out on the balcony. It flashed over me – Derek and I were caught out here!

The first of the red-cloaked figures came hurtling through the doorway. I leaped to avoid his sword. I saw the others crowding behind him.

Then I felt Derek shove me violently aside. I half fell, but recovered myself at the balcony rail. Five of the crimson nobles were on the balcony. Derek confronted them. His aspect made them pause. They stood, with outstretched swords. The garden was silent; the crowd stared up. And in the silence Derek roared:

"Get back! All of you, go back inside! Back, or I'll kill you!"

In Derek's right hand he held the cylinder outstretched, leveled at the menacing nobles. "Back, I say!"

But instead they rushed him. There was a flash. From the cylinder it seemed that a ray spat out, a flash of silver light. It caught the three men who were in advance of the others. Their swords dropped with a clatter to the balcony floor. They stood, transfixed.

An instant. Derek's silver ray played upon them. Their red cloaks were painted with its silver sheen.

They were shimmering! I gasped, staring. The other nobles, beyond the ray, had fallen back. And they too stood staring in horror.

Another instant the three figures wavered. I saw the face of one of them, with the shock of incredulous horror still upon it. A face turning luminous! A face, erased, with only the staring eyes to mark where it had been!

There was a moment when the three stricken men stood like shimmering ghosts, with Derek's deadly ray upon them. Then they were gone! It seemed, just as they vanished, that they were falling through the balcony floor...

Derek snapped off his ray. He rasped, "Back into that room, I tell you!"

The remaining nobles fled before him. He turned again to the balcony rail.

"My people – yes, I am Alexandre – I had not thought you would recognize me so soon. But you are right – the time has come for me to claim my inheritance. And I will rule you justly."

His cylinder was still in his hand; he swept a watchful glance behind him. I thought of Rohbar. He was in the next room, with the king. Had they seen this attack upon Derek? They must have heard the crowd shouting, "Alexandre!" It seemed strange they did not appear.

I recall now, as I look back to this moment on the balcony, that I suddenly thought of Hope. She had been beside me just before the nobles attacked. I did not see her now. I was startled, but thought of her was driven from my mind. From within the palace a scream sounded. A girl screaming.

But it was not Hope's voice. A girl, screaming, and then shouting:

"The king is dead!"

Derek came rushing at me. "Charlie, that –".

We heard it again. "The king is dead!"

We hurried into the adjoining room. There was no one to stop us – no one up here now who dared oppose Derek. The terrified nobles in the room fell cringing before him.

"Alexandre – spare us! We are loyal to you!"

He strode past them. In the adjacent apartment we found the king lying upon the floor. A wound in his throat welled crimson. He had evidently been lying here alone, and had just now been found by a girl who had entered. He was not quite dead. Derek bent over him. He opened his eyes.

He gasped faintly: "Rohbar – killed me. Rohbar and that – accursed crimson Sensua..."

His voice trailed away. The light went out of his staring eyes. Derek laid him gently back on the floor.

And as though already the news of his death had miraculously spread, the bell in the castle tower began tolling. Not clanging now. Tolling, with slow, solemn accent. The crowd evidently recognized it. We could hear the shouts: "Death! Death has come!"

Derek's eyes ware blazing as he stood up. "The end, Charlie! I would not have planned this, and yet..."

He did not finish. He whirled, rushed back to the other room and to the balcony. The scene was again in confusion the crowd milling, voices shouting:

"The king is dead!"

At the edge of the garden a woman's shrill, hysterical laughter rose over the din.

Derek called, "Yes, the king is dead!" He paused. Then he added, "If you want me – if I have your loyalty – I will claim my throne."

A tumult interrupted him. "Alexandre! King Alexandre!"

He spread his arms, but he could not silence them.

"The king is dead. Long live King Alexandre!"

A wave of it swept over the garden, engulfing the castle. At the main entrance Leonto's soldiers stood sullen, listening to it.

Derek stood triumphant. His hands were outstretched, palms down. But up on the circular bridge at the top of the tower there was a sudden commotion. The soldiers up there had vanished, moved back within the tower to make room for other figures. I stared amazed, transfixed. A huge man in leather garments was there, with a sword stuck in his wide belt. A man with a bullet head, a heavy face, gazing down...

Rohbar!

And held in front of him the slender figure of a girl. Hope! He clutched her, his thick arm encircling her breast. With sinking heart I realized what had happened. Hope had moved away from me. Every one in the room had been intent upon Derek. Rohbar had come quietly in, after murdering the king, had seized Hope, stifled her outcry, and had taken her up into the tower.

And I had promised Derek that I would shield this girl from harm! The horror of it – the self-condemnation of it – swept me, froze me to numbness. I could not think; I could only stand and stare. Rohbar held Hope like a shield before him. The low railing hardly reached her knees. A sheer drop to the garden beneath. He held her tightly, and in his free hand I saw his dirk come up menacingly against her white throat. His voice called:

"Silent, down there! Alexandre, you traitor! Silence!"

Derek stared up. The triumph faded from him. He stared, stricken. The crowd stared. The soldiers on the lower platform ceased their shouting and gazed up at these new actors, come so unexpectedly upon the stage. Again Rohbar called, to the guards this time:

"I represent your King Leonto. This Alexandre is a traitor to us all. And he cannot harm me! I defy him. Look at him! I defy him to use his evil weapon upon me!"

Derek was silent. A single adverse move and Rohbar's knife would stab into Hope's throat. Derek's ray was powerless. A flash from it would have killed Hope, not Rohbar.

The king's soldiers saw Derek's indecision. One of them shouted, "He cannot harm us! Look, he is frightened!"

The crowd recognized Hope. They began calling her name. And calling, "Master Rohbar, do not harm our Hope!"

"I will not harm her! Not if you do what I tell you! Leave the garden – go quietly! I will deal with this traitor!"

He added to the guards, "Go up and seize him! He cannot hurt you! Traitor! Seize him! If he does not yield – if any of this crowd attacks you – then I will kill Hope."

Derek stood clinging to the balcony rail. With Rohbar's watchful gaze upon him he did not dare turn or move. I was standing back from the balcony, behind Derek and partly in the room. No one thought of me. No one from outside could see me. And I, who had played no part in this, save that one I had neglected, suddenly saw my role. My cue was sounding. My role to play, here upon this tumultuous stage.

I turned back into the dim room. A few frightened men and girls were here. They were all crowding forward, gazing through the windows at the scene outside. No one noticed me, but I saw, with sudden realization, my role to play.

I darted across the room, out into the dim, deserted corridor of the castle.

Chapter X: My Role to Play

I SLIPPED like a shadow through the almost empty corridors. Down on the lower floor I found that many of the soldiers were on the inside, standing about the corridors in groups, waiting for word from their comrades on the platform to indicate what action they should take. My time was short; I knew that within a few minutes they would be rushing up to overpower Derek.

I stood unseen against the wall near the main entrance. I could not get outside. There were too many soldiers there.

I tried to keep my sense of direction. The wing upon which the tower stood was about two hundred feet from me here. If I could not get outside I would have to try the inside, along this corridor. I prayed that I might not make an error. I tried to gauge exactly where the tower would be.

The hallway was almost dark and in this wing there chanced to be no one at the moment. I came to the angle and turned it to the left. I was unarmed save my dirk. I drew it. But I encountered no one. I passed the doors of many empty rooms. The windows were all barred on this lower floor. I could hear the shouts of the crowd outside.

I came at last to the end of the wing. A staircase here led upward. I guessed that I was directly under the tower now, and that this staircase undoubtedly led upward into it. I mounted a few steps to verify what I was sure would be the condition. It was as I thought. Rohbar had won over the soldiers who were here. He had sent them down from the tower bridge. They were guarding this staircase.

I crept up another few steps, very cautiously. I could hear their voices on the stairs. A light was up there. I could see the legs of some of them as they crowded the stairs. I softly retreated.

There was no way of getting up into the tower here. Alone and armed only with my dirk, I could not mount these stairs and assail a dozen armed men standing above me; especially when, if I raised an alarm, Rohbar overhead might be startled into killing Hope.

I stood another moment, thinking, planning my actions. I was trembling. Everything depended upon me now. I must get up into the tower. And, above everything, haste was necessary.

I retreated back to the lower floor. I was still some twenty feet above the ground, I judged. That was too far. A dozen paces along the hall I saw a stairway leading downward into the ground level cellar of the castle. I marked in my mind exactly in which direction I turned, and how far. I went down the stairs.

There was an empty lower room. It was pitch black. I lay down on its earthen floor. Above me, a few paces off to one side I could visualize the tower. A hundred and fifty feet above me, at least, up to that bridge balcony, where Rohbar stood with Hope. I kept my mind on it and prayed that I might not be making an error, a miscalculation.

I prayed, too, that luck would be with me. A desperate chance, yet I thought I knew what was here, or about here, in New York City. I lay on my side, alone in the blackness, and pressed the switch at my wrist...

The familiar sensation of the transition began. The darkness grew luminous. Around me shadows were taking form. My body was humming, thrilling with the vibrations within it. I could feel the ground under me seeming to melt. My head was reeling. Nausea swept me, but with it all I tried to keep my wits. I must watch this new Space into which I was going. Space? I prayed that here on this spot in New York City there would be empty space! If not, at the first warning, I was prepared to stop my mechanism.

The shadows grew around me. There was a moment or two when I felt as though I were floating. Weightless. The sense of my body hovering in a void, intangible, imponderable, with only my struggling mentality holding it together...

And then I felt myself materializing. Around me walls were taking form. I floated down a foot or two and came to rest upon a new floor. My hand brushed it. My physical senses were returning. I could feel a floor of concrete. A vague, shimmering light was near me. It seemed to outline the rectangle of a window. All around was darkness. Empty darkness. Soundless, with only the throbbing hum of the mechanism...

I was indoors, in a room. I felt suddenly almost normal, except for the whirring vibration. I flung the switch again. There was a shock. A whirling of my senses. Then I sat up; my head steadied. The nausea passed.

I was back in my own world, in New York City. This was night: I tried to calculate the time. Derek and I had departed about midnight. This would be, then some time before dawn. I was in a cellar room, lying on its cement floor. There was a window, with a faint light outside it. A window up near the ceiling. A straggling illumination showed me a bin, a few barrels, a door leading into another room which looked as though it might be a machine shop.

I sat up, calculating. I was a thousand feet perhaps from the Battery wall, two hundred feet from the Hudson River. This was an office building, and I was in one of its cellar rooms, at the ground level.

Near dawn? I tried to calculate what might be overhead. A deserted office building. Too early yet for the scrub-women. The elevator would not be running. I laughed to myself. Of what use to me an elevator, if it had been running? How could I, a midnight prowler, appear from the cellar of this building, and demand to be taken upstairs! There would be no elevator, but there would be watchmen. I would avoid them.

I found a door. My heart leaped with a sudden fear that it would be locked, but it was not. I went through it into a passage and found the staircase. I made two turns. I tried again to keep my mind on this Space here. I stood, carefully thinking. I had it clear. I had made no move without careful thought. The tower with Rohbar was still to my left, and about directly above me.

I went up the short stone staircase, opened another door carefully. I was in the dim lower hall of the office building. I found myself beside the deserted elevator shaft. A light was burning on the night attendant's table in an alcove, on the other side of the shaft. He sat there with his back to me. I closed the door soundlessly.

The stairway upward beside the elevator was here. I watched my chance. I darted around the angle and went up. I met no one. The concrete staircase had a light at each floor. Four floors up. No, not enough! I opened the fourth floor door. The marble hall of the office building was empty and silent. Rows of locked office doors with their gold-leaf names and numbers. A single dim light to illumine the silent emptiness...

I retreated into the staircase shaft and mounted higher. My dirk was in my hand. Charlie Wilson, the Wall Street brokerage clerk, prowling here! And upon what a strange adventure!

I came to what I thought was the proper floor. In the hall I selected a room. The door was securely locked. I had no way of breaking the lock, but the panel was of opaque glass. I would have to chance the noise. I rushed the length of the hall, to where a red fire-ax hung in a bracket. I came back with it. I smashed the glass panel of the door.

Would a watchman hear me? I did not wait to find out. With the ax I scraped away the splinters of glass. I climbed through the opening. My hand was cut, but I did not heed it.

I was in a dim, silent office, with rugs on the floor, desks standing about, filing cases, a water-cooler, and a safe in the corner. I rushed to one of the windows. It looked over Battery Park and the upper bay. The stars were shining, but to the east over Brooklyn I could see them paling with the coming dawn. I gazed down to try and calculate my height. Yes, this would be about right. And my position. I could see the outline of the shore, the trees of Battery Park, the busy harbor, even at this hour before dawn, thronged with the moving lights of its boats.

I saw all this with my eyes, but with my mind I saw the wrecked, deserted pavilion, and the gardens of Leonto's castle. The threatening mob would be below me. The palace entrance would be here to my left, down in the street where those taxis were parked. There was a commotion down there by the office building entrance. I know now what caused it, but at the time I did not notice. The wing of the castle was under me. This would be the tower. Its upper room, or the balcony, just about where I was standing. I prayed that it might be so. I seemed with my mind to see it all.

I lay down on the floor by the window. Out in the office building hallway I heard heavy footsteps come running. One of the night watchmen had evidently heard the glass crashed.

I laughed. I pressed the switch at my wrist...

Chapter XI: The Fight on the Tower Balcony

THE SENSATIONS swept me again. The room faded. Whether the watchmen came in to see a ghost of me lying there on the floor I did not know, nor did I care. I whirled into the shadows. And came in a moment out of the black silence. The office room was gone. I seemed to have fallen or floated down – how far I do not know. A triumph swept me. I was lying on another floor. I could see a doorway materializing. I was not upon the balcony as I had calculated, but within the tower room. New walls sprang around me.

I did not heed it, this time, the sensation, of the transition. I was too alert to what new situation might come upon me. The tower room. I could see it. I could see its oval windows close at hand. The doorway to its balcony. Sounds flooded me, mingled with the humming within me. Familiar sounds. The crowd shouting. And a single voice – the voice of Rohbar. Vague and blurred, but as I materialized it became clearer.

I was suddenly aware that there was a man beside me. One of the palace soldiers. He saw me materialize. He leaped backward in horror. I flung my switch. I was on my feet, swaying, and then I leaped upon him. My dirk plunged downward into his chest.

The thing made me shudder. I reeled with the sickness of it, but as he fell I clung to the dirk and ripped it out of him. It was dripping with his blood.

I stood trembling. The small tower room had no other occupants. I turned toward the door. I could see a patch of stars, paling with the coming dawn. I crouched in the small doorway which gave onto the balcony, staring, swiftly calculating. The scene had scarcely changed. But, some of the soldiers had left the entrance platform, gone, no doubt, into the castle on their way upstairs to seize Derek.

On this upper balcony, no more than ten feet before me, Rohbar still stood gripping Hope. She was in front of him. His back was to me. A sudden jump, and I could plunge my dagger into his back.

Rohbar was shouting, "King Leonto is dead. If you should want me to succeed him, I will take this girl Hope for my queen. You all love her..."

I was tense to spring. Then out in the balcony, to one side, I saw Sensua crouching. Her crimson robe fell away to bare her white limbs. Her hand fumbled in her robe. She had been Rohbar's dupe, and now she knew it. Her knife was in her hand. Frenzied with jealousy and rage she sprang upon Rohbar's back, trying to stab at Hope.

Perhaps he sensed her coming, heard her; or perhaps she was unskilful. Her knife only grazed Hope's shoulder. He released Hope. He roared. He turned and gripped his murderous assailant. A second or two while I stood watching. He caught Sensua's wrist, twisted the knife from it and plunged the knife into her breast. She sank with a scream at his feet, and as he straightened he saw me.

But I had leaped. I was upon him. His own knife had remained in Sensua's breast. As I raised mine in my leap, he caught at my wrist; twisted it, but I flung the knife away before he could get it. The knife fell over the balcony rail. The weight of my hurtling body flung him backward, but the rail caught him. His arms went around me. Powerful arms, crushing me. I gripped at his throat.

There was an instant when I thought that we would both topple over the railing. I felt Hope beside us. I heard her scream. We did not go over the rail, for Rohbar lurched and flung us back. We dropped to the balcony floor, rolling, locked together. He was far stronger and heavier than I. He came uppermost. He lunged and broke my hold upon his throat, but I was agile: I squirmed from under him. I almost regained my feet. He got up on one knee. He was trying to draw his sword. Then again I bore into him, kicking and tearing. He roared like a bull. And ignoring my plucking fingers, my flailing fists, he lunged to his feet with me gripping again at his throat.

His huge height swung me off the ground. I was aware that he had drawn his sword, but I was too close for him to use it. He swayed drunkenly with my weight; he was confused. I felt the rail behind us. We lunged again into it. Again I heard Hope scream in terror, and saw her leap at us. Rohbar stooped, trying to clutch the low rail. His bending down brought my feet to the balcony floor. With a last despairing effort I shoved him backward. And as he toppled at the rail, I fought to break his hold upon me. I felt us going and then I felt Hope reach me. Her arms flung about my waist. Her hold tore me loose. Rohbar's huge body fell away...

For an instant Rohbar seemed balanced upon the rail; then he went over. He gave a last long, agonized scream as he fell. I did not look down. I crouched by the rail. The crowd in the garden; Derek standing on the other balcony; the soldiers who now had appeared behind him – all were silent, and in the silence I heard the horrible thud of Rohbar's body as it struck...

I clung to Hope for an instant, and she shuddered against me. The scene broke again into chaos. I cast Hope away and leaped up. I stood at the balcony rail. My arms went up and gestured to Derek. Amazement was on his face, but he answered my gesture. Behind him the soldiers who had come to seize him were standing in a group, stricken at this new tragedy.

Derek swung on them. He was not powerless now! "Away with you!"

His cylinder menaced them, and they fell back in terror before him.

He darted past them and disappeared into the castle.

I felt Hope plucking at me. "I want to talk to the people."

She stood beside me, leaning over the rail. Gentle little figure. Familiar figure to them all. Their beloved Hope. Her voice rang out clearly through the hush.

"My people, we all want our beloved Alexandre – he has come back to us. He is our rightful king."

"King Alexandre! Long live King Alexandre!"

Derek in a moment appeared behind us. "My God, Charlie, I can't understand –"

I told him how I had done it. He gripped me. "I'll never be able to repay you for this!"

I pushed him forward and he joined Hope at the rail. Held her, and her arms went around his neck as she returned his kisses. The crowd gaped, then cheered.

I shouted, "Hope will be your queen – The reign of the crimson nobles is at an end!"

The wild cheering of the people, in which now the castle guards were joining, surged up to mingle with my words.

Chapter XII: One Tumultuous Night

I COME NOW with very little more to record.

I returned to my own world. And Derek stayed in his. Each to his own; one may rail at this allotted portion – but he does not lightly give it up.

The scientists who have examined the mechanism with which I returned very naturally are skeptical of me. Derek feared a further communication between his world, and mine. He smiled his quiet smile.

"Your modern world is very aggressive, Charlie. I would not want to chance having my mechanism duplicated – a conquering army coming in here."

And so he adjusted the apparatus to carry me back and then go dead. I have wires and electrodes to show in support of my narrative. But since they will not operate I cannot blame my hearers for smiling in derision.

Yet there is some contributing evidence. Derek Mason has vanished. A watchman in an office building near Battery Park reports that at dawn of that June morning he heard splintering glass. He found the office door with its broken panel, and the ax lying on the hall floor. He even thinks he saw a ghost stretched out by the window. But he is laughed at for saying it.

And there is still another circumstance. If you will trouble to examine the newspaper files of that time, you will find an occurrence headed "Inexplicable Tragedy at Battery Park." You will read that near dawn that morning, the bodies of three men in crimson cloaks came hurtling down through the air and fell in the street near where several taxis were parked. Strange, unidentified men. Of extraordinary aspect. The flesh burned, perhaps. All three were dead; the bodies were mangled by falling some considerable height.

An inexplicable tragedy. Why should anyone believe that they were the three crimson nobles whom Derek attacked with his strange ray?

I am only Charles Wilson, clerk in a Wall Street brokerage office. If you met me, you would find me a very average, prosaic sort of fellow. You would never think that deeds of daring were in my line at all. Yet I have lived this one strange tumultuous night, and I shall always cherish the memory.

The Disintegration Machine

Arthur Conan Doyle

PROFESSOR CHALLENGER was in the worst possible humour. As I stood at the door of his study, my hand upon the handle and my foot upon the mat, I heard a monologue which ran like this, the words booming and reverberating through the house: "Yes, I say it is the second wrong call. The second in one morning. Do you imagine that a man of science is to be distracted from essential work by the constant interference of some idiot at the end of a wire? I will not have it. Send this instant for the manager. Oh! you are the manager. Well, why don't you manage? Yes, you certainly manage to distract me from work the importance of which your mind is incapable of understanding. I want the superintendent. He is away? So I should imagine. I will carry you to the law courts if this occurs again. Crowing cocks have been adjudicated upon. I myself have obtained a judgement. If crowing cocks, why not jangling bells? The case is clear. A written apology. Very good. I will consider it. Good morning."

It was at this point that I ventured to make my entrance. It was certainly an unfortunate moment. I confronted him as he turned from the telephone – a lion in its wrath. His huge black beard was bristling, his great chest was heaving with indignation, and his arrogant grey eyes swept me up and down as the backwash of his anger fell upon me.

"Infernal, idle, overpaid rascals!" he boomed. "I could hear them laughing while I was making my just complaint. There is a conspiracy to annoy me. And now, young Malone, you arrive to complete a disastrous morning. Are you here, may I ask, on your own account, or has your rag commissioned you to obtain an interview? As a friend you are privileged – as a journalist you are outside the pale."

I was hunting in my pocket for McArdle's letter when suddenly some new grievance came to his memory. His great hairy hands fumbled about among the papers upon his desk and finally extracted a press cutting.

"You have been good enough to allude to me in one of your recent lucubrations," he said, shaking the paper at me. "It was in the course of your somewhat fatuous remarks concerning the recent Saurian remains discovered in the Solenhofen Slates. You began a paragraph with the words: 'Professor G.E. Challenger, who is among our greatest living scientists–'"

"Well, sir?" I asked.

"Why these invidious qualifications and limitations? Perhaps you can mention who these other predominant scientific men may be to whom you impute equality, or possibly superiority to myself?"

"It was badly worded. I should certainly have said: 'Our greatest living scientist,'" I admitted. It was after all my own honest belief. My words turned winter into summer.

"My dear young friend, do not imagine that I am exacting, but surrounded as I am by pugnacious and unreasonable colleagues, one is forced to take one's own part. Self-assertion is foreign to my nature, but I have to hold my ground against opposition. Come now! Sit here! What is the reason of your visit?"

I had to tread warily, for I knew how easy it was to set the lion roaring once again. I opened McArdle's letter. "May I read you this, sir? It is from McArdle, my editor."

"I remember the man – not an unfavourable specimen of his class."

"He has, at least, a very high admiration for you. He has turned to you again and again when he needed the highest qualities in some investigation. That is the case now."

"What does he desire?" Challenger plumed himself like some unwieldy bird under the influence of flattery. He sat down with his elbows upon the desk, his gorilla hands clasped together, his beard bristling forward, and his big grey eyes, half-covered by his drooping lids, fixed benignly upon me. He was huge in all that he did, and his benevolence was even more overpowering than his truculence.

"I'll read you his note to me. He says:

> Please call upon our esteemed friend, Professor Challenger, and ask for his co-operation in the following circumstances. There is a Latvian gentleman named Theodore Nemor living at White Friars Mansions, Hampstead, who claims to have invented a machine of a most extraordinary character which is capable of disintegrating any object placed within its sphere of influence. Matter dissolves and returns to its molecular or atomic condition. By reversing the process it can be reassembled. The claim seems to be an extravagant one, and yet there is solid evidence that there is some basis for it and that the man has stumbled upon some remarkable discovery.
>
> I need not enlarge upon the revolutionary character of such an invention, nor of its extreme importance as a potential weapon of war. A force which could disintegrate a battleship, or turn a battalion, if it were only for a time, into a collection of atoms, would dominate the world. For social and for political reasons not an instant is to be lost in getting to the bottom of the affair. The man courts publicity as he is anxious to sell his invention, so that there is no difficulty in approaching him. The enclosed card will open his doors. What I desire is that you and Professor Challenger shall call upon him, inspect his invention, and write for the Gazette a considered report upon the value of the discovery. I expect to hear from you tonight.
>
> R. MCARDLE."

"There are my instructions, Professor," I added, as I refolded the letter. "I sincerely hope that you will come with me, for how can I, with my limited capacities, act alone in such a matter?"

"True, Malone! True!" purred the great man. "Though you are by no means destitute of natural intelligence, I agree with you that you would be somewhat overweighted in such a matter as you lay before me. These unutterable people upon the telephone have already ruined my morning's work, so that a little more can hardly matter. I am engaged in answering that Italian buffoon, Mazotti, whose views upon the larval development of the tropical termites have excited my derision and contempt, but I can leave the complete exposure of the impostor until evening. Meanwhile, I am at your service."

And thus it came about that on that October morning I found myself in the deep level tube with the Professor speeding to the North of London in what proved to be one of the most singular experiences of my remarkable life.

I had, before leaving Enmore Gardens, ascertained by the much-abused telephone that our man was at home, and had warned him of our coming. He lived in a comfortable flat in Hampstead, and he kept us waiting for quite half an hour in his ante-room whilst he carried on an animated conversation with a group of visitors, whose voices, as they finally bade farewell in the hall, showed that they were Russians. I caught a glimpse of them through the half-opened door, and had a passing impression of prosperous and intelligent men, with astrakhan collars to their coats, glistening top-hats, and every appearance of that bourgeois well-being which the successful Communist so readily assumes. The hall door closed behind them, and the next instant Theodore Nemor entered our apartment. I can see him now as he stood with the sunlight full upon him, rubbing his long, thin hands together and surveying us with his broad smile and his cunning yellow eyes.

He was a short, thick man, with some suggestion of deformity in his body, though it was difficult to say where that suggestion lay. One might say that he was a hunchback without the hump. His large, soft face was like an underdone dumpling, of the same colour and moist consistency, while the pimples and blotches which adorned it stood out the more aggressively against the pallid background. His eyes were those of a cat, and catlike was the thin, long, bristling moustache above his loose, wet, slobbering mouth. It was all low and repulsive until one came to the sandy eyebrows. From these upwards there was a splendid cranial arch such as I have seldom seen. Even Challenger's hat might have fitted that magnificent head. One might read Theodore Nemor as a vile, crawling conspirator below, but above he might take rank with the great thinkers and philosophers of the world.

"Well, gentlemen," said he, in a velvety voice with only the least trace of a foreign accent, "you have come, as I understand from our short chat over the wires, in order to learn more of the Nemor Disintegrator. Is it so?"

"Exactly."

"May I ask whether you represent the British Government?"

"Not at all. I am a correspondent of the Gazette, and this is Professor Challenger."

"An honoured name – a European name." His yellow fangs gleamed in obsequious amiability. "I was about to say that the British Government has lost its chance. What else it has lost it may find out later. Possibly its Empire as well. I was prepared to sell to the first Government which gave me its price, and if it has now fallen into hands of which you may disapprove, you have only yourselves to blame."

"Then you have sold your secret?"

"At my own price."

"You think the purchaser will have a monopoly?"

"Undoubtedly he will."

"But others know the secret as well as you."

"No, sir." He touched his great forehead.

"This is the safe in which the secret is securely locked – a better safe than any of steel, and secured by something better than a Yale key. Some may know one side of the matter: others may know another. No one in the world knows the whole matter save only I."

"And these gentlemen to whom you have sold it."

"No, sir; I am not so foolish as to hand over the knowledge until the price is paid. After that it is I whom they buy, and they move this safe' he again tapped his brow 'with all its contents to whatever point they desire. My part of the bargain will then be done – faithfully, ruthlessly done. After that, history will be made." He rubbed his hands together and the fixed smile upon his face twisted itself into something like a snarl.

"You will excuse me, sir," boomed Challenger, who had sat in silence up to now, but whose expressive face registered most complete disapproval of Theodore Nemor, "we should wish before we discuss the matter to convince ourselves that there is something to discuss. We have not forgotten a recent case where an Italian, who proposed to explode mines from a distance, proved upon investigation to be an arrant impostor. History may well repeat itself. You will understand, sir, that I have a reputation to sustain as a man of science – a reputation which you have been good enough to describe as European, though I have every reason to believe that it is not less conspicuous in America. Caution is a scientific attribute, and you must show us your proofs before we can seriously consider your claims."

Nemor cast a particularly malignant glance from the yellow eyes at my companion, but the smile of affected geniality broadened his face.

"You live up to your reputation, Professor. I had always heard that you were the last man in the world who could be deceived. I am prepared to give you an actual demonstration which cannot fail to convince you, but before we proceed to that I must say a few words upon the general principle."

"You will realize that the experimental plant which I have erected here in my laboratory is a mere model, though within its limits it acts most admirably. There would be no possible difficulty, for example, in disintegrating you and reassembling you, but it is not for such a purpose as that that a great Government is prepared to pay a price which runs into millions. My model is a mere scientific toy. It is only when the same force is invoked upon a large scale that enormous practical effects could be achieved."

"May we see this model?"

"You will not only see it, Professor Challenger, but you will have the most conclusive demonstration possible upon your own person, if you have the courage to submit to it."

"If!" the lion began to roar. "Your 'if,' sir, is in the highest degree offensive."

"Well, well. I had no intention to dispute your courage. I will only say that I will give you an opportunity to demonstrate It. But I would first say a few words upon the underlying laws which govern the matter."

"When certain crystals, salt, for example, or sugar, are placed in water they dissolve and disappear. You would not know that they have ever been there. Then by evaporation or otherwise you lessen the amount of water, and lo! there are your crystals again, visible once more and the same as before. Can you conceive a process by which you, an organic being, are in the same way dissolved into the cosmos, and then by a subtle reversal of the conditions reassembled once more?"

"The analogy is a false one," cried Challenger. "Even if I make so monstrous an admission as that our molecules could be dispersed by some disrupting power, why should they reassemble in exactly the same order as before?"

"The objection is an obvious one, and I can only answer that they do so reassemble down to the last atom of the structure. There is an invisible framework and every brick flies into its true place. You may smile, Professor, but your incredulity and your smile may soon be replaced by quite another emotion."

Challenger shrugged his shoulders. "I am quite ready to submit it to the test."

"There is another case which I would impress upon you, gentlemen, and which may help you to grasp the idea. You have heard both in Oriental magic and in Western occultism of the phenomenon of the apport when some object is suddenly brought from a distance and appears in a new place. How can such a thing be done save by the loosening of the molecules, their conveyance upon an etheric wave, and their reassembling, each exactly in its own place, drawn together by some irresistible law? That seems a fair analogy to that which is done by my machine."

"You cannot explain one incredible thing by quoting another incredible thing," said Challenger. "I do not believe in your apports, Mr Nemor, and I do not believe in your machine. My time is valuable, and if we are to have any sort of demonstration I would beg you to proceed with it without further ceremony."

"Then you will be pleased to follow me," said the inventor. He led us down the stair of the flat and across a small garden which lay behind. There was a considerable outhouse, which he unlocked and we entered.

Inside was a large whitewashed room with innumerable copper wires hanging in festoons from the ceiling, and a huge magnet balanced upon a pedestal. In front of this was what looked like a prism of glass, three feet in length and about a foot in diameter. To the right of it was a chair which rested upon a platform of zinc, and which had a burnished copper cap suspended above it. Both the cap and the chair had heavy wires attached to them, and at the side was a sort of ratchet with numbered slots and a handle covered with india rubber which lay at present in the slot marked zero.

"Nemor's Disintegrator," said this strange man, waving his hand towards the machine.

"This is the model which is destined to be famous, as altering the balance of power among the nations. Who holds this rules the world. Now, Professor Challenger, you have, if I may say so, treated me with some lack of courtesy and consideration in this matter. Will you dare to sit upon that chair and to allow me to demonstrate upon your own body the capabilities of the new force?"

Challenger had the courage of a lion, and anything in the nature of a defiance roused him in an instant to a frenzy He rushed at the machine, but I seized his arm and held him back.

"You shall not go," I said. "Your life is too valuable. It is monstrous. What possible guarantee of safety have you? The nearest approach to that apparatus which I have ever seen was the electrocution chair at Sing Sing."

"My guarantee of safety," said Challenger, "is that you are a witness and that this person would certainly be held for manslaughter at the least should anything befall me."

"That would be a poor consolation to the world of science, when you would leave work unfinished which none but you can do. Let me, at least, go first, and then, when the experience proves to be harmless, you can follow."

Personal danger would never have moved Challenger, but the idea that his scientific work might remain unfinished hit him hard. He hesitated, and before he could make up his mind I had dashed forward and jumped into the chair. I saw the inventor put his hand to the handle. I was aware of a click. Then for a moment there was a sensation of confusion and a mist before my eyes. When they cleared, the inventor with his odious smile was standing before me, and Challenger, with his apple-red cheeks drained of blood and colour, was staring over his shoulder.

"Well, get on with it!" said I.

"It is all over. You responded admirably," Nemor replied. "Step out, and Professor Challenger will now, no doubt, be ready to take his turn."

I have never seen my old friend so utterly upset. His iron nerve had for a moment completely failed him. He grasped my arm with a shaking hand.

"My God, Malone, it is true," said he. "You vanished. There is not a doubt of it. There was a mist for an instant and then vacancy."

"How long was I away?"

"Two or three minutes. I was, I confess, horrified. I could not imagine that you would return. Then he clicked this lever, if it is a lever, into a new slot and there you were upon the chair, looking a little bewildered but otherwise the same as ever. I thanked God at the sight of you!" He mopped his moist brow with his big red handkerchief.

"Now, sir," said the inventor. "Or perhaps your nerve has failed you?"

Challenger visibly braced himself. Then, pushing my protesting hand to one side, he seated himself upon the chair. The handle clicked into number three. He was gone.

I should have been horrified but for the perfect coolness of the operator. "It is an interesting process, is it not?" he remarked. "When one considers the tremendous individuality of the Professor it is strange to think that he is at present a molecular cloud suspended in some portion of this building. He is now, of course, entirely at my mercy. If I choose to leave him in suspension there is nothing on earth to prevent me."

"I would very soon find means to prevent you."

The smile once again became a snarl. "You cannot imagine that such a thought ever entered my mind. Good heavens! Think of the permanent dissolution of the great Professor Challenger vanished into cosmic space and left no trace! Terrible! Terrible! At the same time he has not been as courteous as he might. Don't you think some small lesson —?"

"No, I do not."

"Well, we will call it a curious demonstration. Something that would make an interesting paragraph in your paper. For example, I have discovered that the hair of the body being on an entirely different vibration to the living organic tissues can be included or excluded at will. It would interest me to see the bear without his bristles. Behold him!"

There was the click of the lever. An instant later Challenger was seated upon the chair once more. But what a Challenger! What a shorn lion! Furious as I was at the trick that had been played upon him I could hardly keep from roaring with laughter.

His huge head was as bald as a baby's and his chin was as smooth as a girl's. Bereft of his glorious mane the lower part of his face was heavily jowled and ham-shaped, while his whole appearance was that of an old fighting gladiator, battered and bulging, with the jaws of a bulldog over a massive chin.

It may have been some look upon our faces – I have no doubt that the evil grin of my companion had widened at the sight – but, however that may be, Challenger's hand flew up to his head and he became conscious of his condition. The next instant he had sprung out of his chair, seized the inventor by the throat, and had hurled him to the ground. Knowing Challenger's immense strength I was convinced that the man would be killed.

"For God's sake be careful. If you kill him we can never get matters right again!" I cried.

That argument prevailed. Even in his maddest moments Challenger was always open to reason. He sprang up from the floor, dragging the trembling inventor with him. "I give you five minutes," he panted in his fury. "If in five minutes I am not as I was, I will choke the life out of your wretched little body."

Challenger in a fury was not a safe person to argue with. The bravest man might shrink from him, and there were no signs that Mr Nemor was a particularly brave man. On the contrary, those blotches and warts upon his face had suddenly become much more conspicuous as the face behind them changed from the colour of putty, which was normal, to that of a fish's belly. His limbs were shaking and he could hardly articulate.

"Really, Professor!" he babbled, with his hand to his throat, "this violence is quite unnecessary. Surely a harmless joke may pass among friends. It was my wish to demonstrate the powers of the machine. I had imagined that you wanted a full demonstration. No offence, I assure you. Professor, none in the world!"

For answer Challenger climbed back into the chair.

"You will keep your eye upon him, Malone. Do not permit any liberties."

"I'll see to it, sir."

"Now then, set that matter right or take the consequences."

The terrified inventor approached his machine. The reuniting power was turned on to the full, and in an instant, there was the old lion with his tangled mane once more. He stroked his beard affectionately with his hands and passed them over his cranium to be sure that the restoration was complete. Then he descended solemnly from his perch.

"You have taken a liberty, sir, which might have had very serious consequences to yourself. However, I am content to accept your explanation that you only did it for purposes of demonstration. Now, may I ask you a few direct questions upon this remarkable power which you claim to have discovered?"

"I am ready to answer anything save what the source of the power is. That is my secret."

"And do you seriously inform us that no one in the world knows this except yourself?"

"No one has the least inkling."

"No assistants?"

"No, sir. I work alone."

"Dear me! That is most interesting. You have satisfied me as to the reality of the power, but I do not yet perceive its practical bearings."

"I have explained, sir, that this is a model. But it would be quite easy to erect a plant upon a large scale. You understand that this acts vertically. Certain currents above you, and certain others below you, set up vibrations which either disintegrate or reunite. But the process could be lateral. If it were so conducted it would have the same effect, and cover a space in proportion to the strength of the current."

"Give an example."

"We will suppose that one pole was in one small vessel and one in another; a battleship between them would simply vanish into molecules. So also with a column of troops."

"And you have sold this secret as a monopoly to a single European Power?"

"Yes, sir, I have. When the money is paid over they shall have such power as no nation ever had yet. You don't even now see the full possibilities if placed in capable hands which did not fear to wield the weapon which they held. They are immeasurable.' A gloating smile passed over the man's evil face. 'Conceive a quarter of London in which such machines have been erected. Imagine the effect of such a current upon the scale which could easily be adopted. Why," he burst into laughter, "I could imagine the whole Thames valley being swept clean, and not one man, woman, or child left of all these teeming millions!"

The words filled me with horror – and even more the air of exultation with which they were pronounced. They seemed, however, to produce quite a different effect upon my companion. To my surprise he broke into a genial smile and held out his hand to the inventor.

"Well, Mr Nemor, we have to congratulate you," said he. "There is no doubt that you have come upon a remarkable property of nature which you have succeeded in harnessing for the use of man. That this use should be destructive is no doubt very deplorable, but Science knows no distinctions of the sort, but follows knowledge wherever it may lead. Apart from the principle involved you have, I suppose, no objection to my examining the construction of the machine?"

"None in the least. The machine is merely the body. It is the soul of it, the animating principle, which you can never hope to capture."

"Exactly. But the mere mechanism seems to be a model of ingenuity." For some time he walked round it and fingered its several parts. Then he hoisted his unwieldy bulk into the insulated chair.

"Would you like another excursion into the cosmos?" asked the inventor.

"Later, perhaps – later! But meanwhile there is, as no doubt you know, some leakage of electricity. I can distinctly feel a weak current passing through me."

"Impossible. It is quite insulated."

"But I assure you that I feel it." He levered himself down from his perch.

The inventor hastened to take his place.

"I can feel nothing."

"Is there not a tingling down your spine?"

"No, sir, I do not observe it."

There was a sharp click and the man had disappeared. I looked with amazement at Challenger. "Good heavens! Did you touch the machine, Professor?"

He smiled at me benignly with an air of mild surprise.

"Dear me! I may have inadvertently touched the handle," said he. "One is very liable to have awkward incidents with a rough model of this kind. This lever should certainly be guarded."

"It is in number three. That is the slot which causes disintegration."

"So I observed when you were operated upon."

"But I was so excited when he brought you back that I did not see which was the proper slot for the return. Did you notice it?"

"I may have noticed it, young Malone, but I do not burden my mind with small details. There are many slots and we do not know their purpose. We may make the matter worse if we experiment with the unknown. Perhaps it is better to leave matters as they are."

"And you would –"

"Exactly. It is better so. The interesting personality of Mr Theodore Nemor has distributed itself throughout the cosmos, his machine is worthless, and a certain foreign Government has been deprived of knowledge by which much harm might have been wrought. Not a bad morning's work, young Malone. Your rag will no doubt have an interesting column upon the inexplicable disappearance of a Latvian inventor shortly after the visit of its own special correspondent. I have enjoyed the experience. These are the lighter moments which come to brighten the dull routine of study. But life has its duties as well as its pleasures, and I now return to the Italian Mazotti and his preposterous views upon the larval development of the tropical termites."

Looking back, it seemed to me that a slight oleaginous mist was still hovering round the chair. "But surely –" I urged.

"The first duty of the law-abiding citizen is to prevent murder," said Professor Challenger. "I have done so. Enough, Malone, enough! The theme will not bear discussion. It has already disengaged my thoughts too long from matters of more importance."

The Machine Stops

E.M. Forster

Chapter I: The Air-Ship

IMAGINE, if you can, a small room, hexagonal in shape, like the cell of a bee. It is lighted neither by window nor by lamp, yet it is filled with a soft radiance. There are no apertures for ventilation, yet the air is fresh. There are no musical instruments, and yet, at the moment that my meditation opens, this room is throbbing with melodious sounds. An armchair is in the centre, by its side a reading-desk – that is all the furniture. And in the armchair there sits a swaddled lump of flesh – a woman, about five feet high, with a face as white as a fungus. It is to her that the little room belongs.

An electric bell rang.

The woman touched a switch and the music was silent.

"I suppose I must see who it is," she thought, and set her chair in motion. The chair, like the music, was worked by machinery and it rolled her to the other side of the room where the bell still rang importunately.

"Who is it?" she called. Her voice was irritable, for she had been interrupted often since the music began. She knew several thousand people, in certain directions human intercourse had advanced enormously.

But when she listened into the receiver, her white face wrinkled into smiles, and she said: "Very well. Let us talk, I will isolate myself. I do not expect anything important will happen for the next five minutes -for I can give you fully five minutes, Kuno. Then I must deliver my lecture on 'Music during the Australian Period'."

She touched the isolation knob, so that no one else could speak to her. Then she touched the lighting apparatus, and the little room was plunged into darkness.

"Be quick!" she called, her irritation returning. "Be quick, Kuno; here I am in the dark wasting my time."

But it was fully fifteen seconds before the round plate that she held in her hands began to glow. A faint blue light shot across it, darkening to purple, and presently she could see the image of her son, who lived on the other side of the earth, and he could see her.

"Kuno, how slow you are."

He smiled gravely.

"I really believe you enjoy dawdling."

"I have called you before, mother, but you were always busy or isolated. I have something particular to say."

"What is it, dearest boy? Be quick. Why could you not send it by pneumatic post?"

"Because I prefer saying such a thing. I want –"

"Well?"

"I want you to come and see me."

Vashti watched his face in the blue plate.

"But I can see you!" she exclaimed. "What more do you want?"

"I want to see you not through the Machine," said Kuno. "I want to speak to you not through the wearisome Machine."

"Oh, hush!" said his mother, vaguely shocked. "You mustn't say anything against the Machine."

"Why not?"

"One mustn't."

"You talk as if a god had made the Machine," cried the other.

"I believe that you pray to it when you are unhappy. Men made it, do not forget that. Great men, but men. The Machine is much, but it is not everything. I see something like you in this plate, but I do not see you. I hear something like you through this telephone, but I do not hear you. That is why I want you to come. Pay me a visit, so that we can meet face to face, and talk about the hopes that are in my mind."

She replied that she could scarcely spare the time for a visit.

"The air-ship barely takes two days to fly between me and you."

"I dislike air-ships."

"Why?"

"I dislike seeing the horrible brown earth, and the sea, and the stars when it is dark. I get no ideas in an air- ship."

"I do not get them anywhere else."

"What kind of ideas can the air give you?" He paused for an instant.

"Do you not know four big stars that form an oblong, and three stars close together in the middle of the oblong, and hanging from these stars, three other stars?"

"No, I do not. I dislike the stars. But did they give you an idea? How interesting; tell me."

"I had an idea that they were like a man."

"I do not understand."

"The four big stars are the man's shoulders and his knees. The three stars in the middle are like the belts that men wore once, and the three stars hanging are like a sword."

"A sword?"

"Men carried swords about with them, to kill animals and other men."

"It does not strike me as a very good idea, but it is certainly original. When did it come to you first?"

"In the air-ship–" He broke off, and she fancied that he looked sad. She could not be sure, for the Machine did not transmit nuances of expression. It only gave a general idea of people – an idea that was good enough for all practical purposes, Vashti thought. The imponderable bloom, declared by a discredited philosophy to be the actual essence of intercourse, was rightly ignored by the Machine, just as the imponderable bloom of the grape was ignored by the manufacturers of artificial fruit. Something "good enough" had long since been accepted by our race.

"The truth is," he continued, "that I want to see these stars again. They are curious stars. I want to see them not from the air-ship, but from the surface of the earth, as our ancestors did, thousands of years ago. I want to visit the surface of the earth."

She was shocked again.

"Mother, you must come, if only to explain to me what is the harm of visiting the surface of the earth."

"No harm," she replied, controlling herself. "But no advantage. The surface of the earth is only dust and mud, no advantage. The surface of the earth is only dust and mud, no life remains on it, and you would need a respirator, or the cold of the outer air would kill you. One dies immediately in the outer air."

"I know; of course I shall take all precautions."

"And besides –"

"Well?"

She considered, and chose her words with care. Her son had a queer temper, and she wished to dissuade him from the expedition.

"It is contrary to the spirit of the age," she asserted.

"Do you mean by that, contrary to the Machine?"

"In a sense, but –"

His image is the blue plate faded.

"Kuno!"

He had isolated himself.

For a moment Vashti felt lonely.

Then she generated the light, and the sight of her room, flooded with radiance and studded with electric buttons, revived her. There were buttons and switches everywhere – buttons to call for food for music, for clothing. There was the hot-bath button, by pressure of which a basin of (imitation) marble rose out of the floor, filled to the brim with a warm deodorized liquid. There was the cold-bath button. There was the button that produced literature. And there were of course the buttons by which she communicated with her friends. The room, though it contained nothing, was in touch with all that she cared for in the world.

Vashti's next move was to turn off the isolation switch, and all the accumulations of the last three minutes burst upon her. The room was filled with the noise of bells, and speaking-tubes. What was the new food like? Could she recommend it? Has she had any ideas lately? Might one tell her one's own ideas? Would she make an engagement to visit the public nurseries at an early date? Say this day month.

To most of these questions she replied with irritation – a growing quality in that accelerated age. She said that the new food was horrible. That she could not visit the public nurseries through press of engagements. That she had no ideas of her own but had just been told one – that four stars and three in the middle were like a man: she doubted there was much in it.

Then she switched off her correspondents, for it was time to deliver her lecture on Australian music.

The clumsy system of public gatherings had been long since abandoned; neither Vashti nor her audience stirred from their rooms. Seated in her armchair she spoke, while they in their armchairs heard her, fairly well, and saw her, fairly well. She opened with a humorous account of music in the pre-Mongolian epoch, and went on to describe the great outburst of song that followed the Chinese conquest. Remote and primæval as were the methods of I-San-So and the Brisbane school, she yet felt (she said) that study of them might repay the musicians of today: they had freshness; they had, above all, ideas. Her lecture, which lasted ten minutes, was well received, and at its conclusion she and many of her audience listened to a lecture on the sea; there were ideas to be got from the sea; the speaker had donned a respirator and visited it lately. Then she fed, talked to many friends, had a bath, talked again, and summoned her bed.

The bed was not to her liking. It was too large, and she had a feeling for a small bed. Complaint was useless, for beds were of the same dimension all over the world, and to have had an alternative size would have involved vast alterations in the Machine. Vashti isolated herself – it was necessary, for neither day nor night existed under the ground – and reviewed all that had happened since she had summoned the bed last. Ideas? Scarcely any. Events – was Kuno's invitation an event?

By her side, on the little reading-desk, was a survival from the ages of litter – one book. This was the Book of the Machine. In it were instructions against every possible contingency. If she was hot or cold or dyspeptic or at a loss for a word, she went to the book, and it told her which button to press. The Central Committee published it. In accordance with a growing habit, it was richly bound.

Sitting up in the bed, she took it reverently in her hands. She glanced round the glowing room as if some one might be watching her. Then, half ashamed, half joyful, she murmured "O Machine! O Machine!" and raised the volume to her lips. Thrice she kissed it, thrice inclined her head, thrice she felt the delirium of acquiescence. Her ritual performed, she turned to page 1367, which gave the times of the departure of the air ships from the island in the southern hemisphere, under whose soil she lived, to the island in the northern hemisphere, whereunder lived her son.

She thought, "I have not the time."

She made the room dark and slept; she awoke and made the room light; she ate and exchanged ideas with her friends, and listened to music and attended lectures; she make the room dark and slept. Above her, beneath her, and around her, the Machine hummed eternally; she did not notice the noise, for she had been born with it in her ears. The earth, carrying her, hummed as it sped through silence, turning her now to the invisible sun, now to the invisible stars. She awoke and made the room light.

"Kuno!"

"I will not talk to you." He answered, "until you come."

"Have you been on the surface of the earth since we spoke last?"

His image faded.

Again she consulted the book. She became very nervous and lay back in her chair palpitating. Think of her as without teeth or hair. Presently she directed the chair to the wall, and pressed an unfamiliar button. The wall swung apart slowly. Through the opening she saw a tunnel that curved slightly, so that its goal was not visible. Should she go to see her son, here was the beginning of the journey.

Of course she knew all about the communication-system. There was nothing mysterious in it. She would summon a car and it would fly with her down the tunnel until it reached the lift that communicated with the air-ship station: the system had been in use for many, many years, long before the universal establishment of the Machine. And of course she had studied the civilization that had immediately preceded her own – the civilization that had mistaken the functions of the system, and had used it for bringing people to things, instead of for bringing things to people. Those funny old days, when men went for change of air instead of changing the air in their rooms! And yet – she was frightened of the tunnel: she had not seen it since her last child was born. It curved – but not quite as she remembered; it was brilliant – but not quite as brilliant as a lecturer had suggested. Vashti was seized with the terrors of direct experience. She shrank back into the room, and the wall closed up again.

"Kuno," she said, "I cannot come to see you. I am not well."

Immediately an enormous apparatus fell on to her out of the ceiling, a thermometer was automatically laid upon her heart.

She lay powerless. Cool pads soothed her forehead. Kuno had telegraphed to her doctor.

So the human passions still blundered up and down in the Machine. Vashti drank the medicine that the doctor projected into her mouth, and the machinery retired into the ceiling. The voice of Kuno was heard asking how she felt.

"Better." Then with irritation: "But why do you not come to me instead?"

"Because I cannot leave this place."

"Why?"

"Because, any moment, something tremendous many happen."

"Have you been on the surface of the earth yet?"

"Not yet."

"Then what is it?"

"I will not tell you through the Machine."

She resumed her life.

But she thought of Kuno as a baby, his birth, his removal to the public nurseries, her own visit to him there, his visits to her-visits which stopped when the Machine had assigned him a room on the other side of the earth. "Parents, duties of," said the book of the Machine, "cease at the moment of birth. P.422327483." True, but there was something special about Kuno – indeed there had been something special about all her children -and, after all, she must brave the journey if he desired it. And "something tremendous might happen." What did that mean? The nonsense of a youthful man, no doubt, but she must go. Again she pressed the unfamiliar button, again the wall swung back, and she saw the tunnel that curves out of sight. Clasping the Book, she rose, tottered on to the platform, and summoned the car. Her room closed behind her: the journey to the northern hemisphere had begun.

Of course it was perfectly easy. The car approached and in it she found armchairs exactly like her own. When she signalled, it stopped, and she tottered into the lift. One other passenger was in the lift, the first fellow creature she had seen face to face for months. Few travelled in these days, for, thanks to the advance of science, the earth was exactly alike all over. Rapid intercourse, from which the previous civilization had hoped so much, had ended by defeating itself. What was the good of going to Peking when it was just like Shrewsbury? Why return to Shrewsbury when it would all be like Peking? Men seldom moved their bodies; all unrest was concentrated in the soul.

The air-ship service was a relic from the former age. It was kept up, because it was easier to keep it up than to stop it or to diminish it, but it now far exceeded the wants of the population. Vessel after vessel would rise from the vomitories of Rye or of Christchurch (I use the antique names), would sail into the crowded sky, and would draw up at the wharves of the south – empty. So nicely adjusted was the system, so independent of meteorology, that the sky, whether calm or cloudy, resembled a vast kaleidoscope whereon the same patterns periodically recurred. The ship on which Vashti sailed started now at sunset, now at dawn. But always, as it passed above Rheas, it would neighbour the ship that served between Helsingfors and the Brazils, and, every third time it surmounted the Alps, the fleet of Palermo would cross its track behind. Night and day, wind and storm, tide and earthquake, impeded man no longer. He had harnessed Leviathan. All the old literature, with its praise of Nature, and its fear of Nature, rang false as the prattle of a child.

Yet as Vashti saw the vast flank of the ship, stained with exposure to the outer air, her horror of direct experience returned. It was not quite like the air-ship in the cinematophote. For one thing it smelt – not strongly or unpleasantly, but it did smell, and with her eyes shut she should have known that a new thing was close to her. Then she had to walk to it from the lift, had to submit to glances from the other passengers. The man in front dropped his Book – no great matter, but it disquieted them all. In the rooms, if the Book was dropped, the floor raised it mechanically, but the gangway to the air-ship was not so prepared, and the sacred volume lay motionless. They stopped – the thing was unforeseen – and the man, instead of picking up his property, felt the muscles of his arm to see how they had failed him. Then some one actually said with direct utterance: 'We shall be late' -and they trooped on board, Vashti treading on the pages as she did so.

Inside, her anxiety increased. The arrangements were old-fashioned and rough. There was even a female attendant, to whom she would have to announce her wants during the voyage. Of course a revolving platform ran the length of the boat, but she was expected to walk from it to her cabin. Some cabins were better than others, and she did not get the best. She thought the attendant had been unfair, and spasms of rage shook her. The glass valves had closed, she could not go back. She saw, at the end of the vestibule, the lift in which she had ascended going quietly up and down, empty. Beneath those corridors of shining tiles were rooms, tier below tier, reaching far into the earth, and in each room there sat a human being, eating, or sleeping, or producing ideas. And buried deep in the hive was her own room. Vashti was afraid.

"O Machine!" she murmured, and caressed her Book, and was comforted.

Then the sides of the vestibule seemed to melt together, as do the passages that we see in dreams, the lift vanished, the Book that had been dropped slid to the left and vanished, polished tiles rushed by like a stream of water, there was a slight jar, and the air-ship, issuing from its tunnel, soared above the waters of a tropical ocean.

It was night. For a moment she saw the coast of Sumatra edged by the phosphorescence of waves, and crowned by lighthouses, still sending forth their disregarded beams. These also vanished, and only the stars distracted her. They were not motionless, but swayed to and fro above her head, thronging out of one sky-light into another, as if the universe and not the airship was careening. And, as often happens on clear nights, they seemed now to be in perspective, now on a plane; now piled tier beyond tier into the infinite heavens, now concealing infinity, a roof limiting for ever the visions of men. In either case they seemed intolerable. "Are we to travel in the dark?" called the passengers angrily, and the attendant, who had been careless, generated the light, and pulled down the blinds of pliable metal. When the air-ships had been built, the desire to look direct at things still lingered in the world. Hence the extraordinary number of skylights and windows, and the proportionate discomfort to those who were civilized and refined. Even in Vashti's cabin one star peeped through a flaw in the blind, and after a few hours uneasy slumber, she was disturbed by an unfamiliar glow, which was the dawn.

Quick as the ship had sped westwards, the earth had rolled eastwards quicker still, and had dragged back Vashti and her companions towards the sun. Science could prolong the night, but only for a little, and those high hopes of neutralizing the earth's diurnal revolution had passed, together with hopes that were possibly higher. To "keep pace with the sun," or even to outstrip it, had been the aim of the civilization preceding this. Racing aeroplanes had been built for the purpose, capable of enormous speed, and steered by the greatest intellects of the epoch. Round the globe they went, round and round, westward, westward, round and round, amidst humanity's applause. In vain. The globe went eastward quicker still, horrible accidents occurred, and the Committee of the Machine, at the time rising into prominence, declared the pursuit illegal, unmechanical, and punishable by Homelessness.

Of Homelessness more will be said later.

Doubtless the Committee was right. Yet the attempt to "defeat the sun" aroused the last common interest that our race experienced about the heavenly bodies, or indeed about anything. It was the last time that men were compacted by thinking of a power outside the world. The sun had conquered, yet it was the end of his spiritual dominion. Dawn, midday, twilight, the zodiacal path, touched neither men's lives nor their hearts, and science retreated into the ground, to concentrate herself upon problems that she was certain of solving.

So when Vashti found her cabin invaded by a rosy finger of light, she was annoyed, and tried to adjust the blind. But the blind flew up altogether, and she saw through the skylight small pink clouds, swaying against a background of blue, and as the sun crept higher, its radiance entered direct, brimming down the wall, like a golden sea. It rose and fell with the airship's motion, just as waves rise and fall, but it advanced steadily, as a tide advances. Unless she was careful, it would strike her face. A spasm of horror shook her and she rang for the attendant. The attendant too was horrified, but she could do nothing; it was not her place to mend the blind. She could only suggest that the lady should change her cabin, which she accordingly prepared to do.

People were almost exactly alike all over the world, but the attendant of the air-ship, perhaps owing to her exceptional duties, had grown a little out of the common. She had often to address passengers with direct speech, and this had given her a certain roughness and originality of manner. When Vashti swerved away from the sunbeams with a cry, she behaved barbarically – she put out her hand to steady her.

"How dare you!" exclaimed the passenger. "You forget yourself!"

The woman was confused, and apologized for not having let her fall. People never touched one another. The custom had become obsolete, owing to the Machine.

"Where are we now?" asked Vashti haughtily.

"We are over Asia," said the attendant, anxious to be polite.

"Asia?"

"You must excuse my common way of speaking. I have got into the habit of calling places over which I pass by their unmechanical names."

"Oh, I remember Asia. The Mongols came from it."

Beneath us, in the open air, stood a city that was once called Simla. "Have you ever heard of the Mongols and of the Brisbane school?"

"No."

"Brisbane also stood in the open air."

"Those mountains to the right – let me show you them." She pushed back a metal blind. The main chain of the Himalayas was revealed. "They were once called the Roof of the World, those mountains."

"You must remember that, before the dawn of civilization, they seemed to be an impenetrable wall that touched the stars. It was supposed that no one but the gods could exist above their summits. How we have advanced, thanks to the Machine!"

"How we have advanced, thanks to the Machine!" said Vashti.

"How we have advanced, thanks to the Machine!" echoed the passenger who had dropped his Book the night before, and who was standing in the passage.

"And that white stuff in the cracks? What is it?"

"I have forgotten its name."

"Cover the window, please. These mountains give me no ideas."

The northern aspect of the Himalayas was in deep shadow: on the Indian slope the sun had just prevailed. The forests had been destroyed during the literature epoch for the purpose of making newspaper-pulp, but the snows were awakening to their morning glory, and clouds still hung on the breasts of Kinchinjunga. In the plain were seen the ruins of cities, with diminished rivers creeping by their walls, and by the sides of these were sometimes the signs of vomitories, marking the cities of to day. Over the whole prospect air-ships rushed, crossing the inter-crossing with incredible aplomb, and rising nonchalantly when they desired to escape the perturbations of the lower atmosphere and to traverse the Roof of the World.

"We have indeed advanced, thanks to the Machine," repeated the attendant, and hid the Himalayas behind a metal blind.

The day dragged wearily forward. The passengers sat each in his cabin, avoiding one another with an almost physical repulsion and longing to be once more under the surface of the earth. There were eight or ten of them, mostly young males, sent out from the public nurseries to inhabit the rooms of those who had died in various parts of the earth. The man who had dropped his Book was on the homeward journey. He had been sent to Sumatra for the purpose of propagating the race. Vashti alone was travelling by her private will.

At midday she took a second glance at the earth. The air-ship was crossing another range of mountains, but she could see little, owing to clouds. Masses of black rock hovered below her, and merged indistinctly into grey. Their shapes were fantastic; one of them resembled a prostrate man.

"No ideas here," murmured Vashti, and hid the Caucasus behind a metal blind.

In the evening she looked again. They were crossing a golden sea, in which lay many small islands and one peninsula. She repeated, "No ideas here," and hid Greece behind a metal blind.

Chapter II: The Mending Apparatus

BY A VESTIBULE, by a lift, by a tubular railway, by a platform, by a sliding door – by reversing all the steps of her departure did Vashti arrive at her son's room, which exactly resembled her own. She might well declare that the visit was superfluous. The buttons, the knobs, the reading-desk with the Book, the temperature, the atmosphere, the illumination – all were exactly the same. And if Kuno himself, flesh of her flesh, stood close beside her at last, what profit was there in that? She was too well-bred to shake him by the hand.

Averting her eyes, she spoke as follows: "Here I am. I have had the most terrible journey and greatly retarded the development of my soul. It is not worth it, Kuno, it is not worth it. My time is too precious. The sunlight almost touched me, and I have met with the rudest people. I can only stop a few minutes. Say what you want to say, and then I must return."

"I have been threatened with Homelessness," said Kuno.

She looked at him now.

"I have been threatened with Homelessness, and I could not tell you such a thing through the Machine."

Homelessness means death. The victim is exposed to the air, which kills him.

"I have been outside since I spoke to you last. The tremendous thing has happened, and they have discovered me."

"But why shouldn't you go outside?" she exclaimed, "It is perfectly legal, perfectly mechanical, to visit the surface of the earth. I have lately been to a lecture on the sea; there is no objection to that; one simply summons a respirator and gets an Egression-permit. It is not the kind of thing that spiritually minded people do, and I begged you not to do it, but there is no legal objection to it."

"I did not get an Egression-permit."

"Then how did you get out?"

"I found out a way of my own."

The phrase conveyed no meaning to her, and he had to repeat it.

"A way of your own?" she whispered. "But that would be wrong."

"Why?"

The question shocked her beyond measure.

"You are beginning to worship the Machine," he said coldly.

"You think it irreligious of me to have found out a way of my own. It was just what the Committee thought, when they threatened me with Homelessness."

At this she grew angry. "I worship nothing!" she cried. "I am most advanced. I don't think you irreligious, for there is no such thing as religion left. All the fear and the superstition that existed once have been destroyed by the Machine. I only meant that to find out a way of your own was – besides, there is no new way out."

"So it is always supposed."

"Except through the vomitories, for which one must have an Egression-permit, it is impossible to get out. The Book says so."

"Well, the Book's wrong, for I have been out on my feet."

For Kuno was possessed of a certain physical strength.

By these days it was a demerit to be muscular. Each infant was examined at birth, and all who promised undue strength were destroyed. Humanitarians may protest, but it would have been no true kindness to let an athlete live; he would never have been happy in that state of life to which the Machine had called him; he would have yearned for trees to climb, rivers to bathe in, meadows and hills against which he might measure his body. Man must be adapted to his surroundings, must he not? In the dawn of the world our weakly must be exposed on Mount Taygetus, in its twilight our strong will suffer euthanasia, that the Machine may progress, that the Machine may progress, that the Machine may progress eternally.

"You know that we have lost the sense of space. We say 'space is annihilated,' but we have annihilated not space, but the sense thereof. We have lost a part of ourselves. I determined to recover it, and I began by walking up and down the platform of the railway outside my room. Up and down, until I was tired, and so did recapture the meaning of 'Near' and 'Far.' 'Near' is a place to which I can get quickly on my feet, not a place to which the train or the air-ship will take me quickly. 'Far' is a place to which I cannot get quickly on my feet; the vomitory is 'far,' though I could be there in thirty-eight seconds by summoning the train. Man is the measure. That was my first lesson. Man's feet are the measure for distance, his hands are the measure for ownership, his body is the measure for all that is lovable and desirable and strong. Then I went further: it was then that I called to you for the first time, and you would not come.

"This city, as you know, is built deep beneath the surface of the earth, with only the vomitories protruding. Having paced the platform outside my own room, I took the lift to the next platform and paced that also, and so with each in turn, until I came to the topmost, above which begins the earth. All the platforms were exactly alike, and all that I gained by visiting them was to develop my sense of space and my muscles. I think I should have been content with this – it is not a little thing, but as I walked and brooded, it occurred to me that our cities had been built in the days when men still breathed the outer air, and that there had been ventilation shafts for the workmen. I could think of nothing but these ventilation shafts. Had they been destroyed by all the food-tubes and medicine-tubes and music-tubes that the Machine has evolved lately? Or did traces of them remain? One thing was certain. If I came upon them anywhere, it would be in the railway-tunnels of the topmost storey. Everywhere else, all space was accounted for.

"I am telling my story quickly, but don't think that I was not a coward or that your answers never depressed me. It is not the proper thing, it is not mechanical, it is not decent to walk along a railway-tunnel. I did not fear that I might tread upon a live rail and be killed. I feared something far more intangible – doing what was not contemplated by the Machine. Then I said to myself, 'Man is the measure,' and I went, and after many visits I found an opening.

"The tunnels, of course, were lighted. Everything is light, artificial light; darkness is the exception. So when I saw a black gap in the tiles, I knew that it was an exception, and rejoiced. I put in my arm – I could put in no more at first – and waved it round and round in ecstasy. I loosened another tile, and put in my head, and shouted into the darkness: 'I am coming, I shall do it yet,' and my voice reverberated down endless passages. I seemed to hear the spirits of those dead workmen who had returned each evening to the starlight and to their wives, and all the generations who had lived in the open air called back to me, 'You will do it yet, you are coming.'"

He paused, and, absurd as he was, his last words moved her.

For Kuno had lately asked to be a father, and his request had been refused by the Committee. His was not a type that the Machine desired to hand on.

"Then a train passed. It brushed by me, but I thrust my head and arms into the hole. I had done enough for one day, so I crawled back to the platform, went down in the lift, and summoned my bed. Ah what dreams! And again I called you, and again you refused."

She shook her head and said: "Don't. Don't talk of these terrible things. You make me miserable. You are throwing civilization away."

"But I had got back the sense of space and a man cannot rest then. I determined to get in at the hole and climb the shaft. And so I exercised my arms. Day after day I went through ridiculous movements, until my flesh ached, and I could hang by my hands and hold the pillow of my bed outstretched for many minutes. Then I summoned a respirator, and started.

"It was easy at first. The mortar had somehow rotted, and I soon pushed some more tiles in, and clambered after them into the darkness, and the spirits of the dead comforted me. I don't know what I mean by that. I just say what I felt. I felt, for the first time, that a protest had been lodged against corruption, and that even as the dead were comforting me, so I was comforting the unborn. I felt that humanity existed, and that it existed without clothes. How can I possibly explain this? It was naked, humanity seemed naked, and all these tubes and buttons and machineries neither came into the world with us, nor will they follow us out, nor do they matter supremely while we are here. Had I been strong, I would have torn off every garment I had, and gone out into the outer air unswaddled. But this is not for me, nor perhaps for my generation. I climbed with my respirator and my hygienic clothes and my dietetic tabloids! Better thus than not at all.

"There was a ladder, made of some primæval metal. The light from the railway fell upon its lowest rungs, and I saw that it led straight upwards out of the rubble at the bottom of the shaft. Perhaps our ancestors ran up and down it a dozen times daily, in their building. As I climbed, the rough edges cut through my gloves so that my hands bled. The light helped me for a little, and then came darkness and, worse still, silence which pierced my ears like a sword. The Machine hums! Did you know that? Its hum penetrates our blood, and may even guide our thoughts. Who knows! I was getting beyond its power. Then I thought: 'This silence means that I am doing wrong.' But I heard voices in the silence, and again they strengthened me." He laughed. "I had need of them. The next moment I cracked my head against something."

She sighed.

"I had reached one of those pneumatic stoppers that defend us from the outer air. You may have noticed them no the airship. Pitch dark, my feet on the rungs of an invisible ladder, my hands cut; I cannot explain how I lived through this part, but the voices still comforted me, and I felt for fastenings. The stopper, I suppose, was about eight feet across. I passed my hand over it as far as I could reach. It was perfectly smooth. I felt it almost to the centre. Not quite to the centre, for my arm was too short. Then the voice said: 'Jump. It is worth it. There may be a handle in the centre, and you may catch hold of it and so come to us your own way. And if there is no handle, so that you may fall and are dashed to pieces – it is till worth it: you will still come to us your own way.' So I jumped. There was a handle, and –"

He paused. Tears gathered in his mother's eyes. She knew that he was fated. If he did not die today he would die tomorrow. There was not room for such a person in the world. And with her pity disgust mingled. She was ashamed at having borne such a son, she who had always been so respectable and so full of ideas. Was he really the little boy to whom she had taught the use of his stops and buttons, and to whom she had given his first lessons in the Book? The very hair that disfigured his lip showed that he was reverting to some savage type. On atavism the Machine can have no mercy.

"There was a handle, and I did catch it. I hung tranced over the darkness and heard the hum of these workings as the last whisper in a dying dream. All the things I had cared about and all the people I had spoken to through tubes appeared infinitely little. Meanwhile the handle revolved. My weight had set something in motion and I span slowly, and then –"

"I cannot describe it. I was lying with my face to the sunshine. Blood poured from my nose and ears and I heard a tremendous roaring. The stopper, with me clinging to it, had simply been blown out of the earth, and the air that we make down here was escaping through the vent into the air above. It burst up like a fountain. I crawled back to it – for the upper air hurts – and, as it were, I took great sips from the edge. My respirator had flown goodness knows here, my clothes were torn. I just lay with my lips close to the hole, and I sipped until the bleeding stopped. You can imagine nothing so curious. This hollow in the grass – I will speak of it in a minute – the sun shining into it, not brilliantly but through marbled clouds, the peace, the nonchalance, the sense of space, and, brushing my cheek, the roaring fountain of our artificial air!

Soon I spied my respirator, bobbing up and down in the current high above my head, and higher still were many air-ships. But no one ever looks out of air-ships, and in any case they could not have picked me up. There I was, stranded. The sun shone a little way down the shaft, and revealed the topmost rung of the ladder, but it was hopeless trying to reach it. I should either have been tossed up again by the escape, or else have fallen in, and died. I could only lie on the grass, sipping and sipping, and from time to time glancing around me.

"I knew that I was in Wessex, for I had taken care to go to a lecture on the subject before starting. Wessex lies above the room in which we are talking now. It was once an important state. Its kings held all the southern coast from the Andredswald to Cornwall, while the Wansdyke protected them on the north, running over the high ground. The lecturer was only concerned with the rise of Wessex, so I do not know how long it remained an international power, nor would the knowledge have assisted me. To tell the truth I could do nothing but laugh, during this part. There was I, with a pneumatic stopper by my side and a respirator bobbing over my head, imprisoned, all three of us, in a grass-grown hollow that was edged with fern.'

Then he grew grave again.

'Lucky for me that it was a hollow. For the air began to fall back into it and to fill it as water fills a bowl. I could crawl about. Presently I stood. I breathed a mixture, in which the air that hurts predominated whenever I tried to climb the sides. This was not so bad. I had not lost my tabloids and remained ridiculously cheerful, and as for the Machine, I forgot about it altogether. My one aim now was to get to the top, where the ferns were, and to view whatever objects lay beyond.

"I rushed the slope. The new air was still too bitter for me and I came rolling back, after a momentary vision of something grey. The sun grew very feeble, and I remembered that he was in Scorpio – I had been to a lecture on that too. If the sun is in Scorpio, and you are in Wessex, it means that you must be as quick as you can, or it will get too dark. (This is the first bit of useful information I have ever got from a lecture, and I expect it will be the last). It made me try frantically to breathe the new air, and to advance as far as I dared out of my pond. The hollow filled so slowly. At times I thought that the fountain played with less vigour. My respirator seemed to dance nearer the earth; the roar was decreasing."

He broke off.

"I don't think this is interesting you. The rest will interest you even less. There are no ideas in it, and I wish that I had not troubled you to come. We are too different, mother."

She told him to continue.

"It was evening before I climbed the bank. The sun had very nearly slipped out of the sky by this time, and I could not get a good view. You, who have just crossed the Roof of the World, will not want to hear an account of the little hills that I saw low colourless hills. But to me they were living and the turf that covered them was a skin, under which their muscles rippled, and I felt that those hills had called with incalculable force to men in the past, and that men had loved them. Now they sleep – perhaps for ever. They commune with humanity in dreams. Happy the man, happy the woman, who awakes the hills of Wessex. For though they sleep, they will never die."

His voice rose passionately.

"Cannot you see, cannot all you lecturers see, that it is we that are dying, and that down here the only thing that really lives is the Machine? We created the Machine, to do our will, but we cannot make it do our will now. It has robbed us of the sense of space and of the sense of touch, it has blurred every human relation and narrowed down love to a carnal act, it has paralysed our bodies and our wills, and now it compels us to worship it. The Machine develops – but not on our lies. The Machine proceeds – but not to our goal. We only exist as the blood corpuscles that course through its arteries, and if it could work without us, it would let us die. Oh, I have no remedy – or, at least, only one – to tell men again and again that I have seen the hills of Wessex as Aelfrid saw them when he overthrew the Danes. So the sun set. I forgot to mention that a belt of mist lay between my hill and other hills, and that it was the colour of pearl."

He broke off for the second time.

"Go on," said his mother wearily.

He shook his head.

"Go on. Nothing that you say can distress me now. I am hardened."

"I had meant to tell you the rest, but I cannot: I know that I cannot: goodbye."

Vashti stood irresolute. All her nerves were tingling with his blasphemies. But she was also inquisitive.

"This is unfair," she complained. "You have called me across the world to hear your story, and hear it I will. Tell me – as briefly as possible, for this is a disastrous waste of time – tell me how you returned to civilization."

"Oh – that!" he said, starting. "You would like to hear about civilization. Certainly. Had I got to where my respirator fell down?"

"No – but I understand everything now. You put on your respirator, and managed to walk along the surface of the earth to a vomitory, and there your conduct was reported to the Central Committee."

"By no means."

He passed his hand over his forehead, as if dispelling some strong impression. Then, resuming his narrative, he warmed to it again.

"My respirator fell about sunset. I had mentioned that the fountain seemed feebler, had I not?"

"Yes."

"About sunset, it let the respirator fall. As I said, I had entirely forgotten about the Machine, and I paid no great attention at the time, being occupied with other things. I had my pool of air, into which I could dip when the outer keenness became intolerable, and which would possibly remain for days, provided that no wind sprang up to disperse it. Not until it was too late did I realize what the stoppage of the escape implied. You see – the gap in the tunnel had been mended; the Mending Apparatus; the Mending Apparatus, was after me.

"One other warning I had, but I neglected it. The sky at night was clearer than it had been in the day, and the moon, which was about half the sky behind the sun, shone into the dell at moments quite brightly. I was in my usual place – on the boundary between the two atmospheres – when I thought I saw something dark move across the bottom of the dell, and vanish into the shaft. In my folly, I ran down. I bent over and listened, and I thought I heard a faint scraping noise in the depths.

"At this – but it was too late – I took alarm. I determined to put on my respirator and to walk right out of the dell. But my respirator had gone. I knew exactly where it had fallen between the stopper and the aperture – and I could even feel the mark that it had made in the turf. It had gone, and I realized that something evil was at work, and I had better escape to the other air, and, if I must die, die running towards the cloud that had been the colour of a pearl. I never started. Out of the shaft – it is too horrible. A worm, a long white worm, had crawled out of the shaft and was gliding over the moonlit grass.

"I screamed. I did everything that I should not have done, I stamped upon the creature instead of flying from it, and it at once curled round the ankle. Then we fought. The worm let me run all over the dell, but edged up my leg as I ran. 'Help!' I cried. (That part is too awful. It belongs to the part that you will never know). 'Help!' I cried. (Why cannot we suffer in silence?) 'Help!' I cried. When my feet were wound together, I fell, I was dragged away from the dear ferns and the living hills, and past the great metal stopper (I can tell you this part), and I thought it might save me again if I caught hold of the handle. It also was enwrapped, it also. Oh, the whole dell was full of the things. They were searching it in all directions, they were denuding it, and the white snouts of others peeped out of the hole, ready if needed. Everything that could be moved they brought – brushwood, bundles of fern, everything, and down we all went intertwined into hell. The last things that I saw, ere the stopper closed after us, were certain stars, and I felt that a man of my sort lived in the sky. For I did fight, I fought till the very end, and it was only my head hitting against the ladder that quieted me. I woke up in this room. The worms had vanished. I was surrounded by artificial air, artificial light, artificial peace, and my friends were calling to me down speaking-tubes to know whether I had come across any new ideas lately."

Here his story ended. Discussion of it was impossible, and Vashti turned to go.

"It will end in Homelessness," she said quietly.

"I wish it would," retorted Kuno.

"The Machine has been most merciful."

"I prefer the mercy of God.'

'By that superstitious phrase, do you mean that you could live in the outer air?"

"Yes."

"Have you ever seen, round the vomitories, the bones of those who were extruded after the Great Rebellion?"

"Yes."

"They were left where they perished for our edification. A few crawled away, but they perished, too – who can doubt it? And so with the Homeless of our own day. The surface of the earth supports life no longer."

"Indeed."

"Ferns and a little grass may survive, but all higher forms have perished. Has any air-ship detected them?"

"No."

"Has any lecturer dealt with them?"

"No."

"Then why this obstinacy?"

"Because I have seen them," he exploded.

"Seen what?"

"Because I have seen her in the twilight –because she came to my help when I called – because she, too, was entangled by the worms, and, luckier than I, was killed by one of them piercing her throat."

He was mad. Vashti departed, nor, in the troubles that followed, did she ever see his face again.

Chapter III: The Homeless

DURING THE YEARS that followed Kuno's escapade, two important developments took place in the Machine. On the surface they were revolutionary, but in either case men's minds had been prepared beforehand, and they did but express tendencies that were latent already.

The first of these was the abolition of respirators.

Advanced thinkers, like Vashti, had always held it foolish to visit the surface of the earth. Air-ships might be necessary, but what was the good of going out for mere curiosity and crawling along for a mile or two in a terrestrial motor? The habit was vulgar and perhaps faintly improper: it was unproductive of ideas, and had no connection with the habits that really mattered. So respirators were abolished, and with them, of course, the terrestrial motors, and except for a few lecturers, who complained that they were debarred access to their subject-matter, the development was accepted quietly. Those who still wanted to know what the earth was like had after all only to listen to some gramophone, or to look into some cinematophote. And even the lecturers acquiesced when they found that a lecture on the sea was none the less stimulating when compiled out of other lectures that had already been delivered on the same subject. "Beware of first-hand ideas!" exclaimed one of the most advanced of them. "First-hand ideas do not really exist. They are but the physical impressions produced by live and fear, and on this gross foundation who could erect a philosophy? Let your ideas be second-hand, and if possible tenth-hand, for then they will be far removed from that disturbing element – direct observation. Do not learn anything about this subject of mine – the French Revolution. Learn instead what I think that Enicharmon thought Urizen thought Gutch thought Ho-Yung thought Chi-Bo-Sing thought Lafcadio Hearn thought Carlyle thought Mirabeau said about the French Revolution. Through the medium of these ten great minds, the blood that was shed at Paris and the windows that were broken at Versailles will be clarified to an idea which you may employ most profitably in your daily lives. But be sure that the intermediates are many and varied, for in history one authority exists to counteract another. Urizen must counteract the scepticism of Ho-Yung and Enicharmon, I must myself counteract the impetuosity of Gutch. You who listen to me are in a better position to judge about the French Revolution than I am. Your descendants will be even in a better position than you, for they will learn what you think I think, and yet another intermediate will be added to the chain. And in time" – his voice rose – "there will come a generation that had got beyond facts, beyond impressions, a generation absolutely colourless, a generation seraphically free from taint of personality, which will see the French Revolution not as it happened, nor as they would like it to have happened, but as it would have happened, had it taken place in the days of the Machine."

Tremendous applause greeted this lecture, which did but voice a feeling already latent in the minds of men – a feeling that terrestrial facts must be ignored, and that the abolition of respirators was a positive gain. It was even suggested that airships should be abolished too. This was not done, because airships had somehow worked themselves into the Machine's system. But year by year they were used less, and mentioned less by thoughtful men.

The second great development was the re-establishment of religion.

This, too, had been voiced in the celebrated lecture. No one could mistake the reverent tone in which the peroration had concluded, and it awakened a responsive echo in the heart of each. Those who had long worshipped silently, now began to talk. They described the strange feeling of peace that came over them when they handled the Book of the Machine, the pleasure that it was to repeat certain numerals out of it, however little meaning those numerals conveyed to the outward ear, the ecstasy of touching a button, however unimportant, or of ringing an electric bell, however superfluously.

"The Machine," they exclaimed, "feeds us and clothes us and houses us; through it we speak to one another, through it we see one another, in it we have our being. The Machine is the friend of ideas and the enemy of superstition: the Machine is omnipotent, eternal; blessed is the Machine." And before long this allocution was printed on the first page of the Book, and in subsequent editions the ritual swelled into a complicated system of praise and prayer. The word "religion" was sedulously avoided, and in theory the Machine was still the creation and the implement of man. But in practice all, save a few retrogrades, worshipped it as divine. Nor was it worshipped in unity. One believer would be chiefly impressed by the blue optic plates, through which he saw other believers; another by the mending apparatus, which sinful Kuno had compared to worms; another by the lifts, another by the Book. And each would pray to this or to that, and ask it to intercede for him with the Machine as a whole. Persecution – that also was present. It did not break out, for reasons that will be set forward shortly. But it was latent, and all who did not accept the minimum known as "undenominational Mechanism" lived in danger of Homelessness, which means death, as we know.

To attribute these two great developments to the Central Committee, is to take a very narrow view of civilization. The Central Committee announced the developments, it is true, but they were no more the cause of them than were the kings of the imperialistic period the cause of war. Rather did they yield to some invincible pressure, which came no one knew whither, and which, when gratified, was succeeded by some new pressure equally invincible. To such a state of affairs it is convenient to give the name of progress. No one confessed the Machine was out of hand. Year by year it was served with increased efficiency and decreased intelligence. The better a man knew his own duties upon it, the less he understood the duties of his neighbour, and in all the world there was not one who understood the monster as a whole. Those master brains had perished. They had left full directions, it is true, and their successors had each of them mastered a portion of those directions. But Humanity, in its desire for comfort, had over-reached itself. It had exploited the riches of nature too far. Quietly and complacently, it was sinking into decadence, and progress had come to mean the progress of the Machine.

As for Vashti, her life went peacefully forward until the final disaster. She made her room dark and slept; she awoke and made the room light. She lectured and attended lectures. She exchanged ideas with her innumerable friends and believed she was growing more spiritual. At times a friend was granted Euthanasia, and left his or her room for the homelessness that is beyond all human conception. Vashti did not much mind. After an unsuccessful lecture, she would sometimes ask for Euthanasia herself. But the death-rate was not permitted to exceed the birth-rate, and the Machine had hitherto refused it to her.

The troubles began quietly, long before she was conscious of them.

One day she was astonished at receiving a message from her son. They never communicated, having nothing in common, and she had only heard indirectly that he was still alive, and had been transferred from the northern hemisphere, where he had behaved so mischievously, to the southern – indeed, to a room not far from her own.

"Does he want me to visit him?" she thought. "Never again, never. And I have not the time."

No, it was madness of another kind.

He refused to visualize his face upon the blue plate, and speaking out of the darkness with solemnity said: "The Machine stops."

"What do you say?"

"The Machine is stopping, I know it, I know the signs."

She burst into a peal of laughter. He heard her and was angry, and they spoke no more.

"Can you imagine anything more absurd?" she cried to a friend. "A man who was my son believes that the Machine is stopping. It would be impious if it was not mad."

"The Machine is stopping?" her friend replied. "What does that mean? The phrase conveys nothing to me."

"Nor to me."

"He does not refer, I suppose, to the trouble there has been lately with the music?"

"Oh no, of course not. Let us talk about music."

"Have you complained to the authorities?"

"Yes, and they say it wants mending, and referred me to the Committee of the Mending Apparatus. I complained of those curious gasping sighs that disfigure the symphonies of the Brisbane school. They sound like some one in pain. The Committee of the Mending Apparatus say that it shall be remedied shortly."

Obscurely worried, she resumed her life. For one thing, the defect in the music irritated her. For another thing, she could not forget Kuno's speech. If he had known that the music was out of repair – he could not know it, for he detested music –if he had known that it was wrong, "the Machine stops" was exactly the venomous sort of remark he would have made. Of course he had made it at a venture, but the coincidence annoyed her, and she spoke with some petulance to the Committee of the Mending Apparatus.

They replied, as before, that the defect would be set right shortly.

"Shortly! At once!" she retorted. "Why should I be worried by imperfect music? Things are always put right at once. If you do not mend it at once, I shall complain to the Central Committee."

"No personal complaints are received by the Central Committee," the Committee of the Mending Apparatus replied.

"Through whom am I to make my complaint, then?"

"Through us."

"I complain then."

"Your complaint shall be forwarded in its turn."

"Have others complained?"

This question was unmechanical, and the Committee of the Mending Apparatus refused to answer it.

"It is too bad!" she exclaimed to another of her friends.

"There never was such an unfortunate woman as myself. I can never be sure of my music now. It gets worse and worse each time I summon it."

"What is it?"

"I do not know whether it is inside my head, or inside the wall."

"Complain, in either case."

"I have complained, and my complaint will be forwarded in its turn to the Central Committee."

Time passed, and they resented the defects no longer. The defects had not been remedied, but the human tissues in that latter day had become so subservient, that they readily adapted themselves to every caprice of the Machine. The sigh at the crises of the Brisbane symphony no longer irritated Vashti; she accepted it as part of the melody. The jarring noise, whether in the head or in the wall, was no longer resented by her friend. And so with the mouldy artificial fruit, so with the bath water that began to stink, so with the defective rhymes that the poetry machine had taken to emit. All were bitterly complained of at first, and then acquiesced in and forgotten. Things went from bad to worse unchallenged.

It was otherwise with the failure of the sleeping apparatus. That was a more serious stoppage. There came a day when over the whole world – in Sumatra, in Wessex, in the innumerable cities of Courland and Brazil – the beds, when summoned by their tired owners, failed to appear. It may seem a ludicrous matter, but from it we may date the collapse of humanity. The Committee responsible for the failure was assailed by complainants, whom it referred, as usual, to the Committee of the Mending Apparatus, who in its turn assured them that their complaints would be forwarded to the Central Committee. But the discontent grew, for mankind was not yet sufficiently adaptable to do without sleeping.

"Some one is meddling with the Machine –" they began.

"Some one is trying to make himself king, to reintroduce the personal element."

"Punish that man with Homelessness."

"To the rescue! Avenge the Machine! Avenge the Machine!"

"War! Kill the man!"

But the Committee of the Mending Apparatus now came forward, and allayed the panic with well-chosen words. It confessed that the Mending Apparatus was itself in need of repair.

The effect of this frank confession was admirable.

"Of course," said a famous lecturer – he of the French Revolution, who gilded each new decay with splendour – "of course we shall not press our complaints now. The Mending Apparatus has treated us so well in the past that we all sympathize with it, and will wait patiently for its recovery. In its own good time it will resume its duties. Meanwhile let us do without our beds, our tabloids, our other little wants. Such, I feel sure, would be the wish of the Machine."

Thousands of miles away his audience applauded. The Machine still linked them. Under the seas, beneath the roots of the mountains, ran the wires through which they saw and heard, the enormous eyes and ears that were their heritage, and the hum of many workings clothed their thoughts in one garment of subserviency. Only the old and the sick remained ungrateful, for it was rumoured that Euthanasia, too, was out of order, and that pain had reappeared among men.

It became difficult to read. A blight entered the atmosphere and dulled its luminosity. At times Vashti could scarcely see across her room. The air, too, was foul. Loud were the complaints, impotent the remedies, heroic the tone of the lecturer as he cried: "Courage! Courage! What matter so long as the Machine goes on? To it the darkness and the light are one." And though things improved again after a time, the old brilliancy was never recaptured, and humanity never recovered from its entrance into twilight. There was an hysterical talk of "measures," of "provisional dictatorship," and the inhabitants of Sumatra were asked to familiarize themselves with the workings of the central power station, the said power station being situated in France. But for the most part panic reigned, and men spent their strength praying to their Books, tangible proofs of the Machine's omnipotence. There were gradations of terror – at times came rumours of hope-the Mending Apparatus was almost mended – the enemies of the Machine had been got under – new "nerve-centres" were evolving which would do the work even more magnificently than before. But there came a day when, without the slightest warning, without any previous hint of feebleness, the entire communication-system broke down, all over the world, and the world, as they understood it, ended.

Vashti was lecturing at the time and her earlier remarks had been punctuated with applause. As she proceeded the audience became silent, and at the conclusion there was no sound. Somewhat displeased, she called to a friend who was a specialist in sympathy. No sound: doubtless the friend was sleeping.

And so with the next friend whom she tried to summon, and so with the next, until she remembered Kuno's cryptic remark, "The Machine stops."

The phrase still conveyed nothing. If Eternity was stopping it would of course be set going shortly.

For example, there was still a little light and air – the atmosphere had improved a few hours previously. There was still the Book, and while there was the Book there was security.

Then she broke down, for with the cessation of activity came an unexpected terror – silence.

She had never known silence, and the coming of it nearly killed her – it did kill many thousands of people outright. Ever since her birth she had been surrounded by the steady hum. It was to the ear what artificial air was to the lungs, and agonizing pains shot across her head. And scarcely knowing what she did, she stumbled forward and pressed the unfamiliar button, the one that opened the door of her cell.

Now the door of the cell worked on a simple hinge of its own. It was not connected with the central power station, dying far away in France. It opened, rousing immoderate hopes in Vashti, for she thought that the Machine had been mended. It opened, and she saw the dim tunnel that curved far away towards freedom. One look, and then she shrank back. For the tunnel was full of people -she was almost the last in that city to have taken alarm.

People at any time repelled her, and these were nightmares from her worst dreams. People were crawling about, people were screaming, whimpering, gasping for breath, touching each other, vanishing in the dark, and ever and anon being pushed off the platform on to the live rail. Some were fighting round the electric bells, trying to summon trains which could not be summoned. Others were yelling for Euthanasia or for respirators, or blaspheming the Machine. Others stood at the doors of their cells fearing, like herself, either to stop in them or to leave them. And behind all the uproar was silence – the silence which is the voice of the earth and of the generations who have gone.

No, it was worse than solitude. She closed the door again and sat down to wait for the end. The disintegration went on, accompanied by horrible cracks and rumbling. The valves that restrained the Medical Apparatus must have weakened, for it ruptured and hung hideously from the ceiling. The floor heaved and fell and flung her from the chair. A tube oozed towards her serpent fashion. And at last the final horror approached – light began to ebb, and she knew that civilization's long day was closing.

She whirled around, praying to be saved from this, at any rate, kissing the Book, pressing button after button. The uproar outside was increasing, and even penetrated the wall. Slowly the brilliancy of her cell was dimmed, the reflections faded from the metal switches. Now she could not see the reading-stand, now not the Book, though she held it in her hand. Light followed the flight of sound, air was following light, and the original void returned to the cavern from which it has so long been excluded. Vashti continued to whirl, like the devotees of an earlier religion, screaming, praying, striking at the buttons with bleeding hands. It was thus that she opened her prison and escaped – escaped in the spirit: at least so it seems to me, ere my meditation closes. That she escapes in the body I cannot perceive that. She struck, by chance, the switch that released the door, and the rush of foul air on her skin, the loud throbbing whispers in her ears, told her that she was facing the tunnel again, and that tremendous platform on which she had seen men fighting. They were not fighting now. Only the whispers remained, and the little whimpering groans. They were dying by hundreds out in the dark.

She burst into tears.

Tears answered her.

They wept for humanity, those two, not for themselves. They could not bear that this should be the end. Ere silence was completed their hearts were opened, and they knew what had been important on the earth. Man, the flower of all flesh, the noblest of all creatures visible, man who had once made god in his image, and had mirrored his strength on the constellations, beautiful naked man was dying, strangled in the garments that he had woven. Century after century had he toiled, and here was his reward. Truly the garment had seemed heavenly at first, shot with colours of culture, sewn with the threads of self-denial. And heavenly it had been so long as man could shed it at will and live by the essence that is his soul, and the essence, equally divine, that is his body. The sin against the body – it was for that they wept in chief; the centuries of wrong against the muscles and the nerves, and those five portals by which we can alone apprehend – glozing it over with talk of evolution, until the body was white pap, the home of ideas as colourless, last sloshy stirrings of a spirit that had grasped the stars.

"Where are you?" she sobbed.

His voice in the darkness said, "Here."

"Is there any hope, Kuno?"

"None for us."

"Where are you?"

She crawled over the bodies of the dead. His blood spurted over her hands.

"Quicker," he gasped, "I am dying – but we touch, we talk, not through the Machine."

He kissed her.

"We have come back to our own. We die, but we have recaptured life, as it was in Wessex, when Aelfrid overthrew the Danes. We know what they know outside, they who dwelt in the cloud that is the colour of a pearl."

"But Kuno, is it true? Are there still men on the surface of the earth? Is this – tunnel, this poisoned darkness – really not the end?"

He replied: "I have seen them, spoken to them, loved them. They are hiding in the midst and the ferns until our civilization stops. Today they are the Homeless - tomorrow – "

"Oh, tomorrow – some fool will start the Machine again, tomorrow."

"Never," said Kuno, "never. Humanity has learnt its lesson."

As he spoke, the whole city was broken like a honeycomb. An air-ship had sailed in through the vomitory into a ruined wharf. It crashed downwards, exploding as it went, rending gallery after gallery with its wings of steel. For a moment they saw the nations of the dead, and, before they joined them, scraps of the untainted sky.

Smith and the Pharaohs

H. Rider Haggard

Chapter I

SCIENTISTS, or some scientists – for occasionally one learned person differs from other learned persons – tell us they know all that is worth knowing about man, which statement, of course, includes woman. They trace him from his remotest origin; they show us how his bones changed and his shape modified, also how, under the influence of his needs and passions, his intelligence developed from something very humble. They demonstrate conclusively that there is nothing in man which the dissecting table will not explain; that his aspirations towards another life have their root in the fear of death, or, say others of them, in that of earthquake or thunder; that his affinities with the past are merely inherited from remote ancestors who lived in that past, perhaps a million years ago; and that everything noble about him is but the fruit of expediency or of a veneer of civilisation, while everything base must be attributed to the instincts of his dominant and primeval nature. Man, in short, is an animal who, like every other animal, is finally subdued by his environment and takes his colour from his surroundings, as cattle do from the red soil of Devon. Such are the facts, they (or some of them) declare; all the rest is rubbish.

At times we are inclined to agree with these sages, especially after it has been our privilege to attend a course of lectures by one of them. Then perhaps something comes within the range of our experience which gives us pause and causes doubts, the old divine doubts, to arise again deep in our hearts, and with them a yet diviner hope.

Perchance when all is said, so we think to ourselves, man is something more than an animal. Perchance he has known the past, the far past, and will know the future, the far, far future. Perchance the dream is true, and he does indeed possess what for convenience is called an immortal soul, that may manifest itself in one shape or another; that may sleep for ages, but, waking or sleeping, still remains itself, indestructible as the matter of the Universe.

An incident in the career of Mr James Ebenezer Smith might well occasion such reflections, were any acquainted with its details, which until this, its setting forth, was not the case. Mr Smith is a person who knows when to be silent. Still, undoubtedly it gave cause for thought to one individual – namely, to him to whom it happened. Indeed, James Ebenezer Smith is still thinking over it, thinking very hard indeed.

J E Smith was well born and well educated. When he was a good-looking and able young man at college, but before he had taken his degree, trouble came to him, the particulars of which do not matter, and he was thrown penniless, also friendless, upon the rocky bosom of the world. No, not quite friendless, for he had a godfather, a gentleman connected with business whose Christian name was Ebenezer. To him, as a last resource, Smith went, feeling that Ebenezer owed him something in return for the awful appellation wherewith he had been endowed in baptism.

To a certain extent Ebenezer recognised the obligation. He did nothing heroic, but he found his godson a clerkship in a bank of which he was one of the directors – a modest clerkship, no more. Also, when he died a year later, he left him a hundred pounds to be spent upon some souvenir.

Smith, being of a practical turn of mind, instead of adorning himself with memorial jewellery for which he had no use, invested the hundred pounds in an exceedingly promising speculation. As it happened, he was not misinformed, and his talent returned to him multiplied by ten. He repeated the experiment, and, being in a position to know what he was doing, with considerable success. By the time that he was thirty he found himself possessed of a fortune of something over twenty-five thousand pounds. Then (and this shows the wise and practical nature of the man) he stopped speculating and put out his money in such a fashion that it brought him a safe and clear four per cent.

By this time Smith, being an excellent man of business, was well up in the service of his bank – as yet only a clerk, it is true, but one who drew his four hundred pounds a year, with prospects. In short, he was in a position to marry had he wished to do so. As it happened, he did not wish – perhaps because, being very friendless, no lady who attracted him crossed his path; perhaps for other reasons.

Shy and reserved in temperament, he confided only in himself. None, not even his superiors at the bank or the Board of Management, knew how well off he had become. No one visited him at the flat which he was understood to occupy somewhere in the neighbourhood of Putney; he belonged to no club, and possessed not a single intimate. The blow which the world had dealt him in his early days, the harsh repulses and the rough treatment he had then experienced, sank so deep into his sensitive soul that never again did he seek close converse with his kind. In fact, while still young, he fell into a condition of old-bachelorhood of a refined type.

Soon, however, Smith discovered – it was after he had given up speculating – that a man must have something to occupy his mind. He tried philanthropy, but found himself too sensitive for a business which so often resolves itself into rude inquiry as to the affairs of other people. After a struggle, therefore, he compromised with his conscience by setting aside a liberal portion of his income for anonymous distribution among deserving persons and objects.

While still in this vacant frame of mind Smith chanced one day, when the bank was closed, to drift into the British Museum, more to escape the vile weather that prevailed without than for any other reason. Wandering hither and thither at hazard, he found himself in the great gallery devoted to Egyptian stone objects and sculpture. The place bewildered him somewhat, for he knew nothing of Egyptology; indeed, there remained upon his mind only a sense of wonderment not unmixed with awe. It must have been a great people, he thought to himself, that executed these works, and with the thought came a desire to know more about them. Yet he was going away when suddenly his eye fell on the sculptured head of a woman which hung upon the wall.

Smith looked at it once, twice, thrice, and at the third look he fell in love. Needless to say, he was not aware that such was his condition. He knew only that a change had come over him, and never, never could he forget the face which that carven mask portrayed. Perhaps it was not really beautiful save for its wondrous and mystic smile; perhaps the lips were too thick and the nostrils too broad. Yet to him that face was Beauty itself, beauty which drew him as with a cart-rope, and awoke within him all kinds of wonderful imaginings, some of them so strange and tender that almost they partook of the nature of memories. He stared at the image, and the image smiled back sweetly at him, as doubtless it, or rather its original – for this was but a plaster cast – had smiled at nothingness in some tomb or hiding-hole for over thirty centuries, and as the woman whose likeness it was had once smiled upon the world.

A short, stout gentleman bustled up and, in tones of authority, addressed some workmen who were arranging a base for a neighbouring statue. It occurred to Smith that he must be someone who knew about these objects. Overcoming his natural diffidence with an effort, he raised his hat and asked the gentleman if he could tell him who was the original of the mask.

The official – who, in fact, was a very great man in the Museum – glanced at Smith shrewdly, and, seeing that his interest was genuine, answered –

"I don't know. Nobody knows. She has been given several names, but none of them have authority. Perhaps one day the rest of the statue may be found, and then we shall learn – that is, if it is inscribed. Most likely, however, it has been burnt for lime long ago."

"Then you can't tell me anything about her?" said Smith.

"Well, only a little. To begin with, that's a cast. The original is in the Cairo Museum. Mariette found it, I believe at Karnac, and gave it a name after his fashion. Probably she was a queen – of the eighteenth dynasty, by the work. But you can see her rank for yourself from the broken uraeus." (Smith did not stop him to explain that he had not the faintest idea what a uraeus might be, seeing that he was utterly unfamiliar with the snake-headed crest of Egyptian royalty.) "You should go to Egypt and study the head for yourself. It is one of the most beautiful things that ever was found. Well, I must be off. Good day."

And he bustled down the long gallery.

Smith found his way upstairs and looked at mummies and other things. Somehow it hurt him to reflect that the owner of yonder sweet, alluring face must have become a mummy long, long before the Christian era. Mummies did not strike him as attractive.

He returned to the statuary and stared at his plaster cast till one of the workmen remarked to his fellow that if he were the gent he'd go and look at "a live'un" for a change.

Then Smith retired abashed.

On his way home he called at his bookseller's and ordered "all the best works on Egyptology". When, a day or two later, they arrived in a packing-case, together with a bill for thirty-eight pounds, he was somewhat dismayed. Still, he tackled those books like a man, and, being clever and industrious, within three months had a fair working knowledge of the subject, and had even picked up a smattering of hieroglyphics.

In January – that was, at the end of those three months – Smith astonished his Board of Directors by applying for ten weeks' leave, he who had hitherto been content with a fortnight in the year. When questioned he explained that he had been suffering from bronchitis, and was advised to take a change in Egypt.

"A very good idea," said the manager; "but I'm afraid you'll find it expensive. They fleece one in Egypt."

"I know," answered Smith; "but I've saved a little and have only myself to spend it upon."

So Smith went to Egypt and saw the original of the beauteous head and a thousand other fascinating things. Indeed, he did more. Attaching himself to some excavators who were glad of his intelligent assistance, he actually dug for a month in the neighbourhood of ancient Thebes, but without finding anything in particular.

It was not till two years later that he made his great discovery, that which is known as Smith's Tomb. Here it may be explained that the state of his health had become such as to necessitate an annual visit to Egypt, or so his superiors understood.

However, as he asked for no summer holiday, and was always ready to do another man's work or to stop overtime, he found it easy to arrange for these winter excursions.

On this, his third visit to Egypt, Smith obtained from the Director-General of Antiquities at Cairo a licence to dig upon his own account. Being already well known in the country as a skilled Egyptologist, this was granted upon the usual terms – namely, that the Department of Antiquities should have a right to take any of the objects which might be found, or all of them, if it so desired.

Such preliminary matters having been arranged by correspondence, Smith, after a few days spent in the Museum at Cairo, took the night train to Luxor, where he found his head-man, an ex-dragoman named Mahomet, waiting for him and his fellaheen labourers already hired. There were but forty of them, for his was a comparatively small venture. Three hundred pounds was the amount that he had made up his mind to expend, and such a sum does not go far in excavations.

During his visit of the previous year Smith had marked the place where he meant to dig. It was in the cemetery of old Thebes, at the wild spot not far from the temple of Medinet Habu, that is known as the Valley of the Queens. Here, separated from the resting-places of their royal lords by the bold mass of the intervening hill, some of the greatest ladies of Egypt have been laid to rest, and it was their tombs that Smith desired to investigate. As he knew well, some of these must yet remain to be discovered. Who could say? Fortune favours the bold. It might be that he would find the holy grave of that beauteous, unknown Royalty whose face had haunted him for three long years!

For a whole month he dug without the slightest success. The spot that he selected had proved, indeed, to be the mouth of a tomb. After twenty-five days of laborious exploration it was at length cleared out, and he stood in a rude, unfinished cave. The queen for whom it had been designed must have died quite young and been buried elsewhere; or she had chosen herself another sepulchre, or mayhap the rock had proved unsuitable for sculpture.

Smith shrugged his shoulders and moved on, sinking trial pits and trenches here and there, but still finding nothing. Two-thirds of his time and money had been spent when at last the luck turned. One day, towards evening, with some half-dozen of his best men he was returning after a fruitless morning of labour, when something seemed to attract him towards a little wadi, or bay, in the hillside that was filled with tumbled rocks and sand. There were scores of such places, and this one looked no more promising than any of the others had proved to be. Yet it attracted him. Thoroughly dispirited, he walked past it twenty paces or more, then turned.

"Where go you, sah?" asked his head-man, Mahomet.

He pointed to the recess in the cliff.

"No good, sah," said Mahomet. "No tomb there. Bed-rock too near top. Too much water run in there; dead queen like keep dry!"

But Smith went on, and the others followed obediently.

He walked down the little slope of sand and boulders and examined the cliff. It was virgin rock; never a tool mark was to be seen. Already the men were going, when the same strange instinct which had drawn him to the spot caused him to take a spade from one of them and begin to shovel away the sand from the face of the cliff – for here, for some unexplained reason, were no boulders or debris. Seeing their master, to whom they were attached, at work, they began to work too, and for twenty minutes or more dug on cheerfully enough, just to humour him, since all were sure that here there was no tomb. At length Smith ordered them to desist, for, although now they were six feet down, the rock remained of the same virgin character.

With an exclamation of disgust he threw out a last shovelful of sand. The edge of his spade struck on something that projected. He cleared away a little more sand, and there appeared a rounded ledge which seemed to be a cornice. Calling back the men, he pointed to it, and without a word all of them began to dig again. Five minutes more of work made it clear that it was a cornice, and half an hour later there appeared the top of the doorway of a tomb.

"Old people wall him up," said Mahomet, pointing to the flat stones set in mud for mortar with which the doorway had been closed, and to the undecipherable impress upon the mud of the scarab seals of the officials whose duty it had been to close the last resting-place of the royal dead for ever.

"Perhaps queen all right inside," he went on, receiving no answer to his remark.

"Perhaps," replied Smith, briefly. "Dig, man, dig! Don't waste time in talking."

So they dug on furiously till at length Smith saw something which caused him to groan aloud. There was a hole in the masonry – the tomb had been broken into. Mahomet saw it too, and examined the top of the aperture with his skilled eye.

"Very old thief," he said. "Look, he try build up wall again, but run away before he have time finish." And he pointed to certain flat stones which had been roughly and hurriedly replaced.

"Dig – dig!" said Smith.

Ten minutes more and the aperture was cleared. It was only just big enough to admit the body of a man.

By now the sun was setting. Swiftly, swiftly it seemed to tumble down the sky. One minute it was above the rough crests of the western hills behind them; the next, a great ball of glowing fire, it rested on their topmost ridge. Then it was gone. For an instant a kind of green spark shone where it had been. This too went out, and the sudden Egyptian night was upon them.

The fellaheen muttered among themselves, and one or two of them wandered off on some pretext. The rest threw down their tools and looked at Smith. "Men say they no like stop here. They afraid of ghost! Too many afreet live in these tomb. That what they say. Come back finish tomorrow morning when it light. Very foolish people, these common fellaheen," remarked Mahomet, in a superior tone.

"Quite so," replied Smith, who knew well that nothing that he could offer would tempt his men to go on with the opening of a tomb after sunset. "Let them go away. You and I will stop and watch the place till morning."

"Sorry, sah," said Mahomet, "but I not feel quite well inside; think I got fever. I go to camp and lie down and pray under plenty blanket."

"All right, go," said Smith; "but if there is anyone who is not a coward, let him bring me my big coat, something to eat and drink, and the lantern that hangs in my tent. I will meet him there in the valley."

Mahomet, though rather doubtfully, promised that this should be done, and, after begging Smith to accompany them, lest the spirit of whoever slept in the tomb should work him a mischief during the night, they departed quickly enough.

Smith lit his pipe, sat down on the sand, and waited. Half an hour later he heard a sound of singing, and through the darkness, which was dense, saw lights coming up the valley.

"My brave men," he thought to himself, and scrambled up the slope to meet them.

He was right. These were his men, no less than twenty of them, for with a fewer number they did not dare to face the ghosts which they believed haunted the valley after nightfall. Presently the light from the lantern which one of them carried (not Mahomet, whose sickness had increased too suddenly to enable him to come) fell upon the tall form of Smith, who, dressed in his white working clothes, was leaning against a rock. Down went the lantern, and with a howl of terror the brave company turned and fled.

"Sons of cowards!" roared Smith after them, in his most vigorous Arabic. "It is I, your master, not an afreet."

They heard, and by degrees crept back again. Then he perceived that in order to account for their number each of them carried some article. Thus one had the bread, another the lantern, another a tin of sardines, another the sardine-opener, another a box of matches, another a bottle of beer, and so on. As even thus there were not enough things to go round, two of them bore his big coat between them, the first holding it by the sleeves and the second by the tail as though it were a stretcher.

"Put them down," said Smith, and they obeyed. "Now," he added, "run for your lives; I thought I heard two afreets talking up there just now of what they would do to any followers of the Prophet who mocked their gods, if perchance they should meet them in their holy place at night."

This kindly counsel was accepted with much eagerness. In another minute Smith was alone with the stars and the dying desert wind.

Collecting his goods, or as many of them as he wanted, he thrust them into the pockets of the great-coat and returned to the mouth of the tomb. Here he made his simple meal by the light of the lantern, and afterwards tried to go to sleep. But sleep he could not. Something always woke him. First it was a jackal howling amongst the rocks; next a sand-fly bit him in the ankle so sharply that he thought he must have been stung by a scorpion. Then, notwithstanding his warm coat, the cold got hold of him, for the clothes beneath were wet through with perspiration, and it occurred to him that unless he did something he would probably contract an internal chill or perhaps fever. He rose and walked about.

By now the moon was up, revealing all the sad, wild scene in its every detail. The mystery of Egypt entered his soul and oppressed him. How much dead majesty lay in the hill upon which he stood? Were they all really dead, he wondered, or were those fellaheen right? Did their spirits still come forth at night and wander through the land where once they ruled? Of course that was the Egyptian faith according to which the Ka, or Double, eternally haunted the place where its earthly counterpart had been laid to rest. When one came to think of it, beneath a mass of unintelligible symbolism there was much in the Egyptian faith which it was hard for a Christian to disbelieve. Salvation through a Redeemer, for instance, and the resurrection of the body. Had he, Smith, not already written a treatise upon these points of similarity which he proposed to publish one day, not under his own name? Well, he would not think of them now; the occasion seemed scarcely fitting – they came home too pointedly to one who was engaged in violating a tomb.

His mind, or rather his imagination – of which he had plenty – went off at a tangent. What sights had this place seen thousands of years ago! Once, thousands of years ago, a procession had wound up along the roadway which was doubtless buried beneath the sand whereon he stood towards the dark door of this sepulchre. He could see it as it passed in and out between the rocks. The priests, shaven-headed and robed in leopards' skins, or some of them in pure white, bearing the mystic symbols of their office. The funeral sledge drawn by oxen, and on it the great rectangular case that contained the outer and the inner coffins, and within them the mummy of some departed Majesty; in the Egyptian formula, "the hawk that had spread its wings and flown into the bosom of Osiris," God of Death. Behind, the mourners, rending the air with their lamentations. Then those who bore the funeral furniture and offerings. Then the high officers of State and the first priests of Amen and of the other gods. Then the sister queens, leading by the hand a wondering child or two. Then the sons of Pharaoh, young men carrying the emblems of their rank.

Lastly, walking alone, Pharaoh himself in his ceremonial robes, his apron, his double crown of linen surmounted by the golden snake, his inlaid bracelets and his heavy, tinkling earrings. Pharaoh, his head bowed, his feet travelling wearily, and in his heart – what thoughts? Sorrow, perhaps, for her who had departed. Yet he had other queens and fair women without count. Doubtless she was sweet and beautiful, but sweetness and beauty were not given to her alone. Moreover, was she not wont to cross his will and to question his divinity? No, surely it is not only of her that he thinks, her for whom he had prepared this splendid tomb with all things needful to unite her with the gods. Surely he thinks also of himself and that other tomb on the farther side of the hill whereat the artists labour day by day – yes, and have laboured these many years; that tomb to which before so very long he too must travel in just this fashion, to seek his place beyond the doors of Death, who lays his equal hand on king and queen and slave.

The vision passed. It was so real that Smith thought he must have been dreaming. Well, he was awake now, and colder than ever. Moreover, the jackals had multiplied. There were a whole pack of them, and not far away. Look! One crossed in the ring of the lamplight, a slinking, yellow beast that smelt the remains of dinner. Or perhaps it smelt himself. Moreover, there were bad characters who haunted these mountains, and he was alone and quite unarmed. Perhaps he ought to put out the light which advertised his whereabouts. It would be wise, and yet in this particular he rejected wisdom. After all, the light was some company.

Since sleep seemed to be out of the question, he fell back upon poor humanity's other anodyne, work, which has the incidental advantage of generating warmth. Seizing a shovel, he began to dig at the doorway of the tomb, whilst the jackals howled louder than ever in astonishment. They were not used to such a sight. For thousands of years, as the old moon above could have told, no man, or at least no solitary man, had dared to rob tombs at such an unnatural hour.

When Smith had been digging for about twenty minutes something tinkled on his shovel with a noise which sounded loud in that silence.

"A stone which may come in handy for the jackals," he thought to himself, shaking the sand slowly off the spade until it appeared. There it was, and not large enough to be of much service. Still, he picked it up, and rubbed it in his hands to clear off the encrusting dirt. When he opened them he saw that it was no stone, but a bronze.

"Osiris," reflected Smith, "buried in front of the tomb to hallow the ground. No, an Isis. No, the head of a statuette, and a jolly good one, too – at any rate, in moonlight. Seems to have been gilded." And, reaching out for the lamp, he held it over the object.

Another minute, and he found himself sitting at the bottom of the hole, lamp in one hand and statuette, or rather head, in the other.

"The Queen of the Mask!" he gasped. "The same – the same! By heavens, the very same!"

Oh, he could not be mistaken. There were the identical lips, a little thick and pouted; the identical nostrils, curved and quivering, but a little wide; the identical arched eyebrows and dreamy eyes set somewhat far apart. Above all, there was the identical alluring and mysterious smile. Only on this masterpiece of ancient art was set a whole crown of uraei surrounding the entire head. Beneath the crown and pressed back behind the ears was a full-bottomed wig or royal head-dress, of which the ends descended to the breasts. The statuette, that, having been gilt, remained quite perfect and uncorroded, was broken just above the middle, apparently by a single violent blow, for the fracture was very clean.

At once it occurred to Smith that it had been stolen from the tomb by a thief who thought it to be gold; that outside of the tomb doubt had overtaken him and caused him to break it upon a stone or otherwise. The rest was clear. Finding that it was but gold-washed bronze he had thrown away the fragments, rather than be at the pains of carrying them. This was his theory, probably not a correct one, as the sequel seems to show.

Smith's first idea was to recover the other portion. He searched quite a long while, but without success. Neither then nor afterwards could it be found. He reflected that perhaps this lower half had remained in the thief's hand, who, in his vexation, had thrown it far away, leaving the head to lie where it fell. Again Smith examined this head, and more closely. Now he saw that just beneath the breasts was a delicately cut cartouche.

Being by this time a master of hieroglyphics, he read it without trouble. It ran: "Ma-Mee, Great Royal Lady. Beloved of – " Here the cartouche was broken away.

"Ma-Me, or it might be Ma-Mi," he reflected. "I never heard of a queen called Ma-Me, or Ma-Mi, or Ma-Mu. She must be quite new to history. I wonder of whom she was beloved? Amen, or Horus, or Isis, probably. Of some god, I have no doubt, at least I hope so!"

He stared at the beautiful portrait in his hand, as once he had stared at the cast on the Museum wall, and the beautiful portrait, emerging from the dust of ages, smiled back at him there in the solemn moonlight as once the cast had smiled from the museum wall. Only that had been but a cast, whereas this was real. This had slept with the dead from whose features it had been fashioned, the dead who lay, or who had lain, within.

A sudden resolution took hold of Smith. He would explore that tomb, at once and alone. No one should accompany him on this his first visit; it would be a sacrilege that anyone save himself should set foot there until he had looked on what it might contain.

Why should he not enter? His lamp, of what is called the "hurricane" brand, was very good and bright, and would burn for many hours. Moreover, there had been time for the foul air to escape through the hole that they had cleared. Lastly, something seemed to call on him to come and see. He placed the bronze head in his breast-pocket over his heart, and, thrusting the lamp through the hole, looked down. Here there was no difficulty, since sand had drifted in to the level of the bottom of the aperture. Through it he struggled, to find himself upon a bed of sand that only just left him room to push himself along between it and the roof. A little farther on the passage was almost filled with mud.

Mahomet had been right when, from his knowledge of the bed-rock, he said that any tomb made in this place must be flooded. It had been flooded by some ancient rain-storm, and Smith began to fear that he would find it quite filled with soil caked as hard as iron. So, indeed, it was to a certain depth, a result that apparently had been anticipated by those who hollowed it, for this entrance shaft was left quite undecorated. Indeed, as Smith found afterwards, a hole had been dug beneath the doorway to allow the mud to enter after the burial was completed. Only a miscalculation had been made. The natural level of the mud did not quite reach the roof of the tomb, and therefore still left it open.

After crawling for forty feet or so over this caked mud, Smith suddenly found himself on a rising stair. Then he understood the plan; the tomb itself was on a higher level.

Here began the paintings. Here the Queen Ma-Mee, wearing her crowns and dressed in diaphanous garments, was presented to god after god. Between her figure and those of the divinities the wall was covered with hieroglyphs as fresh today as on that when the artist had limned them. A glance told him that they were extracts from the Book of the Dead. When the thief of bygone ages had broken into the tomb, probably not very long after the interment, the mud over which Smith had just crawled was still wet. This he could tell, since the clay from the rascal's feet remained upon the stairs, and that upon his fingers had stained the paintings on the wall against which he had supported himself; indeed, in one place was an exact impression of his hand, showing its shape and even the lines of the skin.

At the top of the flight of steps ran another passage at a higher level, which the water had never reached, and to right and left were the beginnings of unfinished chambers. It was clear to him that this queen had died young. Her tomb, as she or the king had designed it, was never finished. A few more paces, and the passage enlarged itself into a hall about thirty feet square. The ceiling was decorated with vultures, their wings outspread, the looped Cross of Life hanging from their talons. On one wall her Majesty Ma-Mee stood expectant while Anubis weighed her heart against the feather of truth, and Thoth, the Recorder, wrote down the verdict upon his tablets. All her titles were given to her here, such as – "Great Royal Heiress, Royal Sister, Royal Wife, Royal Mother, Lady of the Two Lands, Palm-branch of Love, Beautiful-exceedingly."

Smith read them hurriedly and noted that nowhere could he see the name of the king who had been her husband. It would almost seem as though this had been purposely omitted. On the other walls Ma-Mee, accompanied by her Ka, or Double, made offerings to the various gods, or uttered propitiatory speeches to the hideous demons of the underworld, declaring their names to them and forcing them to say: "Pass on. Thou art pure!"

Lastly, on the end wall, triumphant, all her trials done, she, the justified Osiris, or Spirit, was received by the god Osiris, Saviour of Spirits.

All these things Smith noted hurriedly as he swung the lamp to and fro in that hallowed place. Then he saw something else which filled him with dismay. On the floor of the chamber where the coffins had been – for this was the burial chamber – lay a heap of black fragments charred with fire. Instantly he understood. After the thief had done his work he had burned the mummy-cases, and with them the body of the queen. There could be no doubt that this was so, for look! Among the ashes lay some calcined human bones, while the roof above was blackened with the smoke and cracked by the heat of the conflagration. There was nothing left for him to find!

Oppressed with the closeness of the atmosphere, he sat down upon a little bench or table cut in the rock that evidently had been meant to receive offerings to the dead. Indeed, on it still lay the scorched remains of some votive flowers. Here, his lamp between his feet, he rested a while, staring at those calcined bones. See, yonder was the lower jaw, and in it some teeth, small, white, regular and but little worn. Yes, she had died young. Then he turned to go, for disappointment and the holiness of the place overcame him; he could endure no more of it that night.

Leaving the burial hall, he walked along the painted passage, the lamp swinging and his eyes fixed upon the floor. He was disheartened, and the paintings could wait till the morrow. He descended the steps and came to the foot of the mud slope. Here suddenly he perceived, projecting from some sand that had drifted down over the mud, what seemed to be the corner of a reed box or basket. To clear away the sand was easy, and – yes, it was a basket, a foot or so in length, such a basket as the old Egyptians used to contain the funeral figures which are called ushaptis, or other objects connected with the dead. It looked as though it had been dropped, for it lay upon its side. Smith opened it – not very hopefully, for surely nothing of value would have been abandoned thus.

The first thing that met his eyes was a mummied hand, broken off at the wrist, a woman's little hand, most delicately shaped. It was withered and paper-white, but the contours still remained; the long fingers were perfect, and the almond-shaped nails had been stained with henna, as was the embalmers' fashion. On the hand were two gold rings, and for those rings it had been stolen. Smith looked at it for a long while, and his heart swelled within him, for here was the hand of that royal lady of his dreams.

Indeed, he did more than look; he kissed it, and as his lips touched the holy relic it seemed to him as though a wind, cold but scented, blew upon his brow. Then, growing fearful of the thoughts that arose within him, he hurried his mind back to the world, or rather to the examination of the basket.

Here he found other objects roughly wrapped in fragments of mummy-cloth that had been torn from the body of the queen. These it is needless to describe, for are they not to be seen in the gold room of the Museum, labelled "Bijouterie de la Reine Ma-Me, XVIIIeme Dynastie. Thebes (Smith's Tomb)"? It may be mentioned, however, that the set was incomplete. For instance, there was but one of the great gold ceremonial ear-rings fashioned like a group of pomegranate blooms, and the most beautiful of the necklaces had been torn in two – half of it was missing.

It was clear to Smith that only a portion of the precious objects which were buried with the mummy had been placed in this basket. Why had these been left where he found them? A little reflection made that clear also. Something had prompted the thief to destroy the desecrated body and its coffin with fire, probably in the hope of hiding his evil handiwork. Then he fled with his spoil. But he had forgotten how fiercely mummies and their trappings can burn. Or perhaps the thing was an accident. He must have had a lamp, and if its flame chanced to touch this bituminous tinder!

At any rate, the smoke overtook the man in that narrow place as he began to climb the slippery slope of clay. In his haste he dropped the basket, and dared not return to search for it. It could wait till the morrow, when the fire would be out and the air pure. Only for this desecrator of the royal dead that morrow never came, as was discovered afterwards.

When at length Smith struggled into the open air the stars were paling before the dawn. An hour later, after the sky was well up, Mahomet (recovered from his sickness) and his myrmidons arrived.

"I have been busy while you slept," said Smith, showing them the mummied hand (but not the rings which he had removed from the shrunk fingers), and the broken bronze, but not the priceless jewellery which was hidden in his pockets.

For the next ten days they dug till the tomb and its approach were quite clear. In the sand, at the head of a flight of steps which led down to the doorway, they found the skeleton of a man, who evidently had been buried there in a hurried fashion. His skull was shattered by the blow of an axe, and the shaven scalp that still clung to it suggested that he might have been a priest.

Mahomet thought, and Smith agreed with him, that this was the person who had violated the tomb. As he was escaping from it the guards of the holy place surprised him after he had covered up the hole by which he had entered and purposed to return. There they executed him without trial and divided up the plunder, thinking that no more was to be found. Or perhaps his confederates killed him.

Such at least were the theories advanced by Mahomet. Whether they were right or wrong none will ever know. For instance, the skeleton may not have been that of the thief, though probability appears to point the other way.

Nothing more was found in the tomb, not even a scarab or a mummy-bead. Smith spent the remainder of his time in photographing the pictures and copying the inscriptions, which for various reasons proved to be of extraordinary interest. Then, having reverently buried the charred bones of the queen in a secret place of the sepulchre, he handed it over to the care of the local Guardian of Antiquities, paid off Mahomet and the fellaheen, and departed for Cairo. With him went the wonderful jewels of which he had breathed no word, and another relic to him yet more precious – the hand of her Majesty Ma-Mee, Palm-branch of Love.

And now follows the strange sequel of this story of Smith and the queen Ma-Mee.

Chapter II

SMITH WAS SEATED in the sanctum of the distinguished Director-General of Antiquities at the new Cairo Museum. It was a very interesting room. Books piled upon the floor; objects from tombs awaiting examination, lying here and there; a hoard of Ptolemaic silver coins, just dug up at Alexandria, standing on a table in the pot that had hidden them for two thousand years; in the corner the mummy of a royal child, aged six or seven, not long ago discovered, with some inscription scrawled upon the wrappings (brought here to be deciphered by the Master), and the withered lotus-bloom, love's last offering, thrust beneath one of the pink retaining bands.

"A touching object," thought Smith to himself. "Really, they might have left the dear little girl in peace."

Smith had a tender heart, but even as he reflected he became aware that some of the jewellery hidden in an inner pocket of his waistcoat (designed for bank-notes) was fretting his skin. He had a tender conscience also.

Just then the Director, a French savant, bustled in, alert, vigorous, full of interest.

"Ah, my dear Mr Smith!" he said, in his excellent English. "I am indeed glad to see you back again, especially as I understand that you are come rejoicing and bringing your sheaves with you. They tell me you have been extraordinarily successful. What do you say is the name of this queen whose tomb you have found – Ma-Mee? A very unusual name. How do you get the extra vowel? Is it for euphony, eh? Did I not know how good a scholar you are, I should be tempted to believe that you had misread it. Me-Mee, Ma-Mee! That would be pretty in French, would it not? Ma mie – my darling! Well, I dare say she was somebody's mie in her time. But tell me the story."

Smith told him shortly and clearly; also he produced his photographs and copies of inscriptions.

"This is interesting – interesting truly," said the Director, when he had glanced through them. "You must leave them with me to study. Also you will publish them, is it not so? Perhaps one of the Societies would help you with the cost, for it should be done in facsimile. Look at this vignette! Most unusual. Oh, what a pity that scoundrelly priest got off with the jewellery and burnt her Majesty's body!"

"He didn't get off with all of it."

"What, Mr Smith? Our inspector reported to me that you found nothing."

"I dare say, sir; but your inspector did not know what I found."

"Ah, you are a discreet man! Well, let us see."

Slowly Smith unbuttoned his waistcoat. From its inner pocket and elsewhere about his person he extracted the jewels wrapped in mummy-cloth as he had found them. First he produced a sceptre-head of gold, in the shape of a pomegranate fruit and engraved with the throne name and titles of Ma-Mee.

"What a beautiful object!" said the Director. "Look! the handle was of ivory, and that sacre thief of a priest smashed it out at the socket. It was fresh ivory then; the robbery must have taken place not long after the burial. See, this magnifying-glass shows it. Is that all?"

Smith handed him the surviving half of the marvellous necklace that had been torn in two.

"I have re-threaded it," he muttered, "but every bead is in its place."

"Oh, heavens! How lovely! Note the cutting of those cornelian heads of Hathor and the gold lotus-blooms between – yes, and the enamelled flies beneath. We have nothing like it in the Museum."

So it went on.

"Is that all?" gasped the Director at last, when every object from the basket glittered before them on the table.

"Yes," said Smith. "That is – no. I found a broken statuette hidden in the sand outside the tomb. It is of the queen, but I thought perhaps you would allow me to keep this."

"But certainly, Mr Smith; it is yours indeed. We are not niggards here. Still, if I might see it –"

From yet another pocket Smith produced the head. The Director gazed at it, then he spoke with feeling.

"I said just now that you were discreet, Mr Smith, and I have been reflecting that you are honest. But now I must add that you are very clever. If you had not made me promise that this bronze should be yours before you showed it me – well, it would never have gone into that pocket again. And, in the public interest, won't you release me from the promise?"

"No," said Smith.

"You are perhaps not aware," went on the Director, with a groan, "that this is a portrait of Mariette's unknown queen whom we are thus able to identify. It seems a pity that the two should be separated; a replica we could let you have."

"I am quite aware," said Smith, "and I will be sure to send you a replica, with photographs. Also I promise to leave the original to some museum by will."

The Director clasped the image tenderly, and, holding it to the light, read the broken cartouche beneath the breasts.

"'Ma-Me, Great Royal Lady. Beloved of – Beloved of whom? Well, of Smith, for one. Take it, monsieur, and hide it away at once, lest soon there should be another mummy in this collection, a modern mummy called Smith; and, in the name of Justice, let the museum which inherits it be not the British, but that of Cairo, for this queen belongs to Egypt. By the way, I have been told that you are delicate in the lungs. How is your health now? Our cold winds are very trying. Quite good? Ah, that is excellent! I suppose that you have no more articles that you can show me?"

"I have nothing more except a mummied hand, which I found in the basket with the jewels. The two rings off it lie there. Doubtless it was removed to get at that bracelet. I suppose you will not mind my keeping the hand –"

"Of the beloved of Smith," interrupted the Director drolly. "No, I suppose not, though for my part I should prefer one that was not quite so old. Still, perhaps you will not mind my seeing it. That pocket of yours still looks a little bulky; I thought that it contained books!"

Smith produced a cigar-box; in it was the hand wrapped in cotton wool.

"Ah," said the Director, "a pretty, well-bred hand. No doubt this Ma-Mee was the real heiress to the throne, as she describes herself. The Pharaoh was somebody of inferior birth, half-brother – she is called 'Royal Sister,' you remember – son of one of the Pharaoh's slave-women, perhaps. Odd that she never mentioned him in the tomb. It looks as though they didn't get on in life, and that she was determined to have done with him in death. Those were the rings upon that hand, were they not?"

He replaced them on the fingers, then took off one, a royal signet in a cartouche, and read the inscription on the other: "'Bes Ank, Ank Bes.' 'Bes the Living, the Living Bes.'"

"Your Ma-Mee had some human vanity about her," he added. "Bes, among other things, as you know, was the god of beauty and of the adornments of women. She wore that ring that she might remain beautiful, and that her dresses might always fit, and her rouge never cake when she was dancing before the gods. Also it fixes her period pretty closely, but then so do other things. It seems a pity to rob Ma-Mee of her pet ring, does it not? The royal signet will be enough for us."

With a little bow he gave the hand back to Smith, leaving the Bes ring on the finger that had worn it for more than three thousand years. At least, Smith was so sure it was the Bes ring that at the time he did not look at it again.

Then they parted, Smith promising to return upon the morrow, which, owing to events to be described, he did not do.

"Ah!" said the Master to himself, as the door closed behind his visitor. "He's in a hurry to be gone. He has fear lest I should change my mind about that ring. Also there is the bronze. Monsieur Smith was ruse there. It is worth a thousand pounds, that bronze. Yet I do not believe he was thinking of the money. I believe he is in love with that Ma-Mee and wants to keep her picture. Mon Dieu! A well-established affection. At least he is what the English call an odd fish, one whom I could never make out, and of whom no one seems to know anything. Still, honest, I am sure – quite honest. Why, he might have kept every one of those jewels and no one have been the wiser. And what things! What a find! Ciel! What a find! There has been nothing like it for years. Benedictions on the head of Odd-fish Smith!"

Then he collected the precious objects, thrust them into an inner compartment of his safe, which he locked and double-locked, and, as it was nearly five o'clock, departed from the Museum to his private residence in the grounds, there to study Smith's copies and photographs, and to tell some friends of the great things that had happened.

When Smith found himself outside the sacred door, and had presented its venerable guardian with a baksheesh of five piastres, he walked a few paces to the right and paused a while to watch some native labourers who were dragging a huge sarcophagus upon an improvised tramway. As they dragged they sang an echoing rhythmic song, whereof each line ended with an invocation to Allah.

Just so, reflected Smith, had their forefathers sung when, millenniums ago, they dragged that very sarcophagus from the quarries to the Nile, and from the Nile to the tomb whence it reappeared today, or when they slid the casing blocks of the pyramids up the great causeway and smooth slope of sand, and laid them in their dizzy resting-places. Only then each line of the immemorial chant of toil ended with an invocation to Amen, now transformed to Allah. The East may change its masters and its gods, but its customs never change, and if today Allah wore the feathers of Amen one wonders whether the worshippers would find the difference so very great.

Thus thought Smith as he hurried away from the sarcophagus and those blue-robed, dark-skinned fellaheen, down the long gallery that is filled with a thousand sculptures. For a moment he paused before the wonderful white statue of Queen Amenartas, then, remembering that his time was short, hastened on to a certain room, one of those which opened out of the gallery.

In a corner of this room, upon the wall, amongst many other beautiful objects, stood that head which Mariette had found, whereof in past years the cast had fascinated him in London. Now he knew whose head it was; to him it had been given to find the tomb of her who had sat for that statue. Her very hand was in his pocket – yes, the hand that had touched yonder marble, pointing out its defects to the sculptor, or perhaps swearing that he flattered her. Smith wondered who that sculptor was; surely he must have been a happy man. Also he wondered whether the statuette was also this master's work. He thought so, but he wished to make sure.

Near to the end of the room he stopped and looked about him like a thief. He was alone in the place; not a single student or tourist could be seen, and its guardian was somewhere else. He drew out the box that contained the hand. From the hand he slipped the ring which the Director-General had left there as a gift to himself. He would much have preferred the other with the signet, but how could he say so, especially after the episode of the statuette?

Replacing the hand in his pocket without looking at the ring – for his eyes were watching to see whether he was observed – he set it upon his little finger, which it exactly fitted. (Ma-Mee had worn both of them upon the third finger of her left hand, the Bes ring as a guard to the signet.) He had the fancy to approach the effigy of Ma-Mee wearing a ring which she had worn and that came straight from her finger to his own.

Smith found the head in its accustomed place. Weeks had gone by since he looked upon it, and now, to his eyes, it had grown more beautiful than ever, and its smile was more mystical and living. He drew out the statuette and began to compare them point by point. Oh, no doubt was possible! Both were likenesses of the same woman, though the statuette might have been executed two or three years later than the statue. To him the face of it looked a little older and more spiritual. Perhaps illness, or some premonition of her end had then thrown its shadow on the queen. He compared and compared. He made some rough measurements and sketches in his pocket-book, and set himself to work out a canon of proportions.

So hard and earnestly did he work, so lost was his mind that he never heard the accustomed warning sound which announces that the Museum is about to close. Hidden behind an altar as he was, in his distant, shadowed corner, the guardian of the room never saw him as he cast a last perfunctory glance about the place before departing till the Saturday morning; for the morrow was Friday, the Mohammedan Sabbath, on which the Museum remains shut, and he would not be called upon to attend. So he went. Everybody went. The great doors clanged, were locked and bolted, and, save for a watchman outside, no one was left in all that vast place except Smith in his corner, engaged in sketching and in measurements.

The difficulty of seeing, owing to the increase of shadow, first called his attention to the fact that time was slipping away. He glanced at his watch and saw that it was ten minutes to the hour.

"Soon be time to go," he thought to himself, and resumed his work.

How strangely silent the place seemed! Not a footstep to be heard or the sound of a human voice. He looked at his watch again, and saw that it was six o'clock, not five, or so the thing said. But that was impossible, for the Museum shut at five; evidently the desert sand had got into the works. The room in which he stood was that known as Room I, and he had noticed that its Arab custodian often frequented Room K or the gallery outside. He would find him and ask what was the real time.

Passing round the effigy of the wonderful Hathor cow, perhaps the finest example of an ancient sculpture of a beast in the whole world, Smith came to the doorway and looked up and down the gallery. Not a soul to be seen. He ran to Room K, to Room H, and others. Still not a soul to be seen. Then he made his way as fast as he could go to the great entrance. The doors were locked and bolted.

"Watch must be right after all. I'm shut in," he said to himself. "However, there's sure to be someone about somewhere. Probably the salle des ventes is still open. Shops don't shut till they are obliged."

Thither he went, to find its door as firmly closed as a door can be. He knocked on it, but a sepulchral echo was the only answer.

"I know," he reflected. "The Director must still be in his room. It will take him a long while to examine all that jewellery and put it away."

So for the room he headed, and, after losing his path twice, found it by help of the sarcophagus that the Arabs had been dragging, which now stood as deserted as it had done in the tomb, a lonesome and impressive object in the gathering shadows. The Director's door was shut, and again his knockings produced nothing but an echo. He started on a tour round the Museum, and, having searched the ground floors, ascended to the upper galleries by the great stairway.

Presently he found himself in that devoted to the royal mummies, and, being tired, rested there a while. Opposite to him, in a glass case in the middle of the gallery, reposed Rameses II. Near to, on shelves in a side case, were Rameses' son, Meneptah, and above, his son, Seti II, while in other cases were the mortal remains of many more of the royalties of Egypt. He looked at the proud face of Rameses and at the little fringe of white locks turned yellow by the embalmer's spices, also at the raised left arm. He remembered how the Director had told him that when they were unrolling this mighty monarch they went away to lunch, and that presently the man who had been left in charge of the body rushed into the room with his hair on end, and said that the dead king had lifted his arm and pointed at him.

Back they went, and there, true enough, was the arm lifted; nor were they ever able to get it quite into its place again. The explanation given was that the warmth of the sun had contracted the withered muscles, a very natural and correct explanation.

Still, Smith wished that he had not recollected the story just at this moment, especially as the arm seemed to move while he contemplated it – a very little, but still to move.

He turned round and gazed at Meneptah, whose hollow eyes stared at him from between the wrappings carelessly thrown across the parchment-like and ashen face. There, probably, lay the countenance that had frowned on Moses. There was the heart which God had hardened. Well, it was hard enough now, for the doctors said he died of ossification of the arteries, and that the vessels of the heart were full of lime!

Smith stood upon a chair and peeped at Seti II above. His weaker countenance was very peaceful, but it seemed to wear an air of reproach. In getting down Smith managed to upset the heavy chair. The noise it made was terrific. He would not have thought it possible that the fall of such an article could produce so much sound. Satisfied with his inspection of these particular kings, who somehow looked quite different now from what they had ever done before – more real and imminent, so to speak – he renewed his search for a living man.

On he went, mummies to his right, mummies to his left, of every style and period, till he began to feel as though he never wished to see another dried remnant of mortality. He peeped into the room where lay the relics of Louiya and Touiyou, the father and mother of the great Queen Taia. Cloths had been drawn over these, and really they looked worse and more suggestive thus draped than in their frigid and unadorned blackness. He came to the coffins of the priest-kings of the twentieth dynasty, formidable painted coffins with human faces. There seemed to be a vast number of these priest-kings, but perhaps they were better than the gold masks of the great Ptolemaic ladies which glinted at him through the gathering gloom.

Really, he had seen enough of the upper floors. The statues downstairs were better than all these dead, although it was true that, according to the Egyptian faith, every one of those statues was haunted eternally by the Ka, or Double, of the person whom it represented. He descended the great stairway. Was it fancy, or did something run across the bottom step in front of him – an animal of some kind, followed by a swift-moving and indefinite shadow? If so, it must have been the Museum cat hunting a Museum mouse. Only then what on earth was that very peculiar and unpleasant shadow?

He called, "Puss! Puss! Puss!" for he would have been quite glad of its company; but there came no friendly "miau" in response. Perhaps it was only the Ka of a cat and the shadow was – oh! Never mind what. The Egyptians worshipped cats, and there were plenty of their mummies about on the shelves. But the shadow!

Once he shouted in the hope of attracting attention, for there were no windows to which he could climb. He did not repeat the experiment, for it seemed as though a thousand voices were answering him from every corner and roof of the gigantic edifice.

Well, he must face the thing out. He was shut in a museum, and the question was in what part of it he should camp for the night. Moreover, as it was growing rapidly dark, the problem must be solved at once. He thought with affection of the lavatory, where, before going to see the Director, only that afternoon he had washed his hands with the assistance of a kindly Arab who watched the door and gracefully accepted a piastre. But there was no Arab there now, and the door, like every other in this confounded place, was locked. He marched on to the entrance.

Here, opposite to each other, stood the red sarcophagi of the great Queen Hatshepu and her brother and husband, Thotmes III. He looked at them. Why should not one of these afford him a night's lodging? They were deep and quiet, and would fit the human frame very nicely. For a while Smith wondered which of these monarchs would be the more likely to take offence at such a use of a private sarcophagus, and, acting on general principles, concluded that he would rather throw himself on the mercy of the lady.

Already one of his legs was over the edge of that solemn coffer, and he was squeezing his body beneath the massive lid that was propped above it on blocks of wood, when he remembered a little, naked, withered thing with long hair that he had seen in a side chamber of the tomb of Amenhotep II. in the Valley of Kings at Thebes. This caricature of humanity many thought, and he agreed with them, to be the actual body of the mighty Hatshepu as it appeared after the robbers had done with it.

Supposing now, that when he was lying at the bottom of that sarcophagus, sleeping the sleep of the just, this little personage should peep over its edge and ask him what he was doing there! Of course the idea was absurd; he was tired, and his nerves were a little shaken. Still, the fact remained that for centuries the hallowed dust of Queen Hatshepu had slept where he, a modern man, was proposing to sleep.

He scrambled down from the sarcophagus and looked round him in despair. Opposite to the main entrance was the huge central hall of the Museum. Now the cement roof of this hall had, he knew, gone wrong, with the result that very extensive repairs had become necessary. So extensive were they, indeed, that the Director-General had informed him that they would take several years to complete. Therefore this hall was boarded up, only a little doorway being left by which the workmen could enter. Certain statues, of Seti II. and others, too large to be moved, were also roughly boarded over, as were some great funeral boats on either side of the entrance. The rest of the place, which might be two hundred feet long with a proportionate breadth, was empty save for the colossi of Amenhotep III and his queen Taia that stood beneath the gallery at its farther end.

It was an appalling place in which to sleep, but better, reflected Smith, than a sarcophagus or those mummy chambers. If, for instance, he could creep behind the deal boards that enclosed one of the funeral boats he would be quite comfortable there. Lifting the curtain, he slipped into the hall, where the gloom of evening had already settled. Only the skylights and the outline of the towering colossi at the far end remained visible. Close to him were the two funeral boats which he had noted when he looked into the hall earlier on that day, standing at the head of a flight of steps which led to the sunk floor of the centre. He groped his way to that on the right. As he expected, the projecting planks were not quite joined at the bow. He crept in between them and the boat and laid himself down.

Presumably, being altogether tired out, Smith did ultimately fall asleep, for how long he never knew. At any rate, it is certain that, if so, he woke up again. He could not tell the time, because his watch was not a repeater, and the place was as black as the pit. He had some matches in his pocket, and might have struck one and even have lit his pipe. To his credit be it said, however, he remembered that he was the sole tenant of one of the most valuable museums in the world, and his responsibilities with reference to fire. So he refrained from striking that match under the keel of a boat which had become very dry in the course of five thousand years.

Smith found himself very wide awake indeed. Never in all his life did he remember being more so, not even in the hour of its great catastrophe, or when his godfather, Ebenezer, after much hesitation, had promised him a clerkship in the bank of which he was a director. His nerves seemed strung tight as harp-strings, and his every sense was painfully acute. Thus he could even smell the odour of mummies that floated down from the upper galleries and the earthy scent of the boat which had been buried for thousands of years in sand at the foot of the pyramid of one of the fifth dynasty kings.

Moreover, he could hear all sorts of strange sounds, faint and far-away sounds which at first he thought must emanate from Cairo without. Soon, however, he grew sure that their origin was more local. Doubtless the cement work and the cases in the galleries were cracking audibly, as is the unpleasant habit of such things at night.

Yet why should these common manifestations be so universal and affect him so strangely? Really, it seemed as though people were stirring all about him. More, he could have sworn that the great funeral boat beneath which he lay had become re-peopled with the crew that once it bore.

He heard them at their business above him. There were trampings and a sound as though something heavy were being laid on the deck, such, for instance, as must have been made when the mummy of Pharaoh was set there for its last journey to the western bank of the Nile. Yes, and now he could have sworn again that the priestly crew were getting out the oars.

Smith began to meditate flight from the neighbourhood of that place when something occurred which determined him to stop where he was.

The huge hall was growing light, but not, as at first he hoped, with the rays of dawn. This light was pale and ghostly, though very penetrating. Also it had a blue tinge, unlike any other he had ever seen. At first it arose in a kind of fan or fountain at the far end of the hall, illumining the steps there and the two noble colossi which sat above.

But what was this that stood at the head of the steps, radiating glory? By heavens! it was Osiris himself or the image of Osiris, god of the Dead, the Egyptian saviour of the world!

There he stood, in his mummy-cloths, wearing the feathered crown, and holding in his hands, which projected from an opening in the wrappings, the crook and the scourge of power. Was he alive, or was he dead? Smith could not tell, since he never moved, only stood there, splendid and fearful, his calm, benignant face staring into nothingness.

Smith became aware that the darkness between him and the vision of this god was peopled; that a great congregation was gathering, or had gathered there. The blue light began to grow; long tongues of it shot forward, which joined themselves together, illuminating all that huge hall.

Now, too, he saw the congregation. Before him, rank upon rank of them, stood the kings and queens of Egypt. As though at a given signal, they bowed themselves to the Osiris, and ere the tinkling of their ornaments had died away, lo! Osiris was gone. But in his place stood another, Isis, the Mother of Mystery, her deep eyes looking forth from beneath the jewelled vulture-cap. Again the congregation bowed, and, lo! She was gone. But in her place stood yet another, a radiant, lovely being, who held in her hand the Sign of Life, and wore upon her head the symbol of the shining disc – Hathor, Goddess of Love. A third time the congregation bowed, and she, too, was gone; nor did any other appear in her place.

The Pharaohs and their queens began to move about and speak to each other; their voices came to his ears in one low, sweet murmur.

In his amaze Smith had forgotten fear. From his hiding-place he watched them intently. Some of them he knew by their faces. There, for instance, was the long-necked Khu-en-aten, talking somewhat angrily to the imperial Rameses II. Smith could understand what he said, for this power seemed to have been given to him. He was complaining in a high, weak voice that on this, the one night of the year when they might meet, the gods, or the magic images of the gods who were put up for them to worship, should not include his god, symbolized by the "Aten," or the sun's disc.

"I have heard of your Majesty's god," replied Rameses; "the priests used to tell me of him, also that he did not last long after your Majesty flew to heaven. The Fathers of Amen gave you a bad name; they called you 'the heretic' and hammered out your cartouches. They were quite rare in my time. Oh, do not let your Majesty be angry! So many of us have been heretics. My grandson, Seti, there" – and he pointed to a mild, thoughtful-faced man – "for example. I am told that he really worshipped the god of those Hebrew slaves whom I used to press to build my cities. Look at that lady with him. Beautiful, isn't she? Observe her large, violet eyes! Well, she was the one who did the mischief, a Hebrew herself. At least, they tell me so."

"I will talk with him," answered Khu-en-aten. "It is more than possible that we may agree on certain points. Meanwhile, let me explain to your Majesty –"

"Oh, I pray you, not now. There is my wife."

"Your wife?" said Khu-en-aten, drawing himself up. "Which wife? I am told that your Majesty had many and left a large family; indeed, I see some hundreds of them here tonight. Now, I – but let me introduce Nefertiti to your Majesty. I may explain that she was my only wife."

"So I have understood. Your Majesty was rather an invalid, were you not? Of course, in those circumstances, one prefers the nurse whom one can trust. Oh, pray, no offence! Nefertari, my love – oh, I beg pardon! – Astnefert – Nefertari has gone to speak to some of her children – let me introduce you to your predecessor, the Queen Nefertiti, wife of Amenhotep IV – I mean Khu-en-aten (he changed his name, you know, because half of it was that of the father of the gods). She is interested in the question of plural marriage. Good-bye! I wish to have a word with my grandfather, Rameses I. He was fond of me as a little boy."

At this moment Smith's interest in that queer conversation died away, for of a sudden he beheld none other than the queen of his dreams, Ma-Mee. Oh! there she stood, without a doubt, only ten times more beautiful than he had ever pictured her. She was tall and somewhat fair-complexioned, with slumbrous, dark eyes, and on her face gleamed the mystic smile he loved. She wore a robe of simple white and a purple-broidered apron, a crown of golden uraei with turquoise eyes was set upon her dark hair as in her statue, and on her breast and arms were the very necklace and bracelets that he had taken from her tomb. She appeared to be somewhat moody, or rather thoughtful, for she leaned by herself against a balustrade, watching the throng without much interest.

Presently a Pharaoh, a black-browed, vigorous man with thick lips, drew near.

"I greet your Majesty," he said.

She started, and answered: "Oh, it is you! I make my obeisance to your Majesty," and she curtsied to him, humbly enough, but with a suggestion of mockery in her movements.

"Well, you do not seem to have been very anxious to find me, Ma-Mee, which, considering that we meet so seldom –"

"I saw that your Majesty was engaged with my sister queens," she interrupted, in a rich, low voice, "and with some other ladies in the gallery there, whose faces I seem to remember, but who I think were not queens. Unless, indeed, you married them after I was drawn away."

"One must talk to one's relations," replied the Pharaoh.

"Quite so. But, you see, I have no relations – at least, none whom I know well. My parents, you will remember, died when I was young, leaving me Egypt's heiress, and they are still vexed at the marriage which I made on the advice of my counsellors. But, is it not annoying? I have lost one of my rings, that which had the god Bes on it. Some dweller on the earth must be wearing it today, and that is why I cannot get it back from him."

"Him! Why 'him'? Hush; the business is about to begin."

"What business, my lord?"

"Oh, the question of the violation of our tombs, I believe."

"Indeed! That is a large subject, and not a very profitable one, I should say. Tell me, who is that?" And she pointed to a lady who had stepped forward, a very splendid person, magnificently arrayed.

"Cleopatra the Greek," he answered, "the last of Egypt's Sovereigns, one of the Ptolemys.

You can always know her by that Roman who walks about after her."

"Which?" asked Ma-Mee. "I see several – also other men. She was the wretch who rolled Egypt in the dirt and betrayed her. Oh, if it were not for the law of peace by which we must abide when we meet thus!"

"You mean that she would be torn to shreds, Ma-Mee, and her very soul scattered like the limbs of Osiris? Well, if it were not for that law of peace, so perhaps would many of us, for never have I heard a single king among these hundreds speak altogether well of those who went before or followed after him."

"Especially of those who went before if they happen to have hammered out their cartouches and usurped their monuments," said the queen, dryly, and looking him in the eyes.

At this home-thrust the Pharaoh seemed to wince. Making no answer, he pointed to the royal woman who had mounted the steps at the end of the hall.

Queen Cleopatra lifted her hand and stood thus for a while. Very splendid she was, and Smith, on his hands and knees behind the boarding of the boat, thanked his stars that alone among modern men it had been his lot to look upon her rich and living loveliness. There she shone, she who had changed the fortunes of the world, she who, whatever she did amiss, at least had known how to die.

Silence fell upon that glittering galaxy of kings and queens and upon all the hundreds of their offspring, their women, and their great officers who crowded the double tier of galleries around the hall.

"Royalties of Egypt," she began, in a sweet, clear voice which penetrated to the farthest recesses of the place, "I, Cleopatra, the sixth of that name and the last monarch who ruled over the Upper and the Lower Lands before Egypt became a home of slaves, have a word to say to your Majesties, who, in your mortal days, all of you more worthily filled the throne on which once I sat. I do not speak of Egypt and its fate, or of our sins – whereof mine were not the least – that brought her to the dust. Those sins I and others expiate elsewhere, and of them, from age to age, we hear enough. But on this one night of the year, that of the feast of him whom we call Osiris, but whom other nations have known and know by different names, it is given to us once more to be mortal for an hour, and, though we be but shadows, to renew the loves and hates of our long-perished flesh. Here for an hour we strut in our forgotten pomp; the crowns that were ours still adorn our brows, and once more we seem to listen to our people's praise. Our hopes are the hopes of mortal life, our foes are the foes we feared, our gods grow real again, and our lovers whisper in our ears. Moreover, this joy is given to us – to see each other as we are, to know as the gods know, and therefore to forgive, even where we despise and hate. Now I have done, and I, the youngest of the rulers of ancient Egypt, call upon him who was the first of her kings to take my place."

She bowed, and the audience bowed back to her. Then she descended the steps and was lost in the throng. Where she had been appeared an old man, simply-clad, long-bearded, wise-faced, and wearing on his grey hair no crown save a plain band of gold, from the centre of which rose the snake-headed uraeus crest.

"Your Majesties who came after me," said the old man, "I am Menes, the first of the accepted Pharaohs of Egypt, although many of those who went before me were more truly kings than I. Yet as the first who joined the Upper and the Lower Lands, and took the royal style and titles, and ruled as well as I could rule, it is given to me to talk with you for a while this night whereon our spirits are permitted to gather from the uttermost parts of the uttermost worlds and see each other face to face. First, in darkness and in secret, let us speak of the mystery of the gods and of its meanings. Next, in darkness and in secret, let us speak of the mystery of our lives, of whence they come, of where they tarry by the road, and whither they go at last. And afterwards, let us speak of other matters face to face in light and openness, as we were wont to do when we were men. Then hence to Thebes, there to celebrate our yearly festival. Is such your will?"

"Such is our will," they answered.

It seemed to Smith that dense darkness fell upon the place, and with it a silence that was awful. For a time that he could not reckon, that might have been years or might have been moments, he sat there in the utter darkness and the utter silence.

At length the light came again, first as a blue spark, then in upward pouring rays, and lastly pervading all. There stood Menes on the steps, and there in front of him was gathered the same royal throng.

"The mysteries are finished," said the old king. "Now, if any have aught to say, let it be said openly."

A young man dressed in the robes and ornaments of an early dynasty came forward and stood upon the steps between the Pharaoh Menes and all those who had reigned after him. His face seemed familiar to Smith, as was the side lock that hung down behind his right ear in token of his youth. Where had he seen him? Ah, he remembered. Only a few hours ago lying in one of the cases of the Museum, together with the bones of the Pharaoh Unas.

"Your Majesties," he began, "I am the King Metesuphis. The matter that I wish to lay before you is that of the violation of our sepulchres by those men who now live upon the earth. The mortal bodies of many who are gathered here tonight lie in this place to be stared at and mocked by the curious. I myself am one of them, jawless, broken, hideous to behold. Yonder, day by day, must my Ka sit watching my desecrated flesh, torn from the pyramid that, with cost and labour, I raised up to be an eternal house wherein I might hide till the hour of resurrection. Others of us lie in far lands. Thus, as he can tell you, my predecessor, Man-kau-ra, he who built the third of the great pyramids, the Pyramid of Her, sleeps, or rather wakes in a dark city, called London, across the seas, a place of murk where no sun shines. Others have been burnt with fire, others are scattered in small dust. The ornaments that were ours are stole away and sold to the greedy; our sacred writings and our symbols are their jest. Soon there will not be one holy grave in Egypt that remains undefiled."

"That is so," said a voice from the company. "But four months gone the deep, deep pit was opened that I had dug in the shadow of the Pyramid of Cephren, who begat me in the world. There in my chamber I slept alone, two handfuls of white bones, since when I died they did not preserve the body with wrappings and with spices. Now I see those bones of mine, beside which my Double has watched for these five thousand years, hid in the blackness of a great ship and tossing on a sea that is strewn with ice."

"It is so," echoed a hundred other voices.

"Then," went on the young king, turning to Menes, "I ask of your Majesty whether there is no means whereby we may be avenged on those who do us this foul wrong."

"Let him who has wisdom speak," said the old Pharaoh.

A man of middle age, short in stature and of a thoughtful brow, who held in his hand a wand and wore the feathers and insignia of the heir to the throne of Egypt and of a high priest of Amen, moved to the steps. Smith knew him at once from his statues. He was Khaemuas, son of Rameses the Great, the mightiest magician that ever was in Egypt, who of his own will withdrew himself from earth before the time came that he should sit upon the throne.

"I have wisdom, your Majesties, and I will answer," he said. "The time draws on when, in the land of Death which is Life, the land that we call Amenti, it will be given to us to lay our wrongs as to this matter before Those who judge, knowing that they will be avenged. On this night of the year also, when we resume the shapes we were, we have certain powers of vengeance, or rather of executing justice. But our time is short, and there is much to say and do before the sun-god Ra arises and we depart each to his place. Therefore it seems best that we should leave these wicked ones in their wickedness till we meet them face to face beyond the world."

Smith, who had been following the words of Khaemuas with the closest attention and considerable anxiety, breathed again, thanking Heaven that the engagements of these departed monarchs were so numerous and pressing. Still, as a matter of precaution, he drew the cigar-box which contained Ma-Mee's hand from his pocket, and pushed it as far away from him as he could. It was a most unlucky act. Perhaps the cigar-box grated on the floor, or perhaps the fact of his touching the relic put him into psychic communication with all these spirits. At any rate, he became aware that the eyes of that dreadful magician were fixed upon him, and that a bone had a better chance of escaping the search of a Rontgen ray than he of hiding himself from their baleful glare.

"As it happens, however," went on Khaemuas, in a cold voice, "I now perceive that there is hidden in this place, and spying on us, one of the worst of these vile thieves. I say to your Majesties that I see him crouched beneath yonder funeral barge, and that he has with him at this moment the hand of one of your Majesties, stolen by him from her tomb at Thebes."

Now every queen in the company became visibly agitated (Smith, who was watching Ma-Mee, saw her hold up her hands and look at them), while all the Pharaohs pointed with their fingers and exclaimed together, in a voice that rolled round the hall like thunder: "Let him be brought forth to judgment!"

Khaemuas raised his wand and, holding it towards the boat where Smith was hidden, said: "Draw near, Vile One, bringing with thee that thou hast stolen."

Smith tried hard to remain where he was. He sat himself down and set his heels against the floor. As the reader knows, he was always shy and retiring by disposition, and never had these weaknesses oppressed him more than they did just then. When a child his favourite nightmare had been that the foreman of a jury was in the act of proclaiming him guilty of some dreadful but unstated crime. Now he understood what that nightmare foreshadowed. He was about to be convicted in a court of which all the kings and queens of Egypt were the jury, Menes was Chief Justice, and the magician Khaemuas played the role of Attorney-General.

In vain did he sit down and hold fast. Some power took possession of him which forced him first to stretch out his arm and pick up the cigar-box containing the hand of Ma-Mee, and next drew him from the friendly shelter of the deal boards that were about the boat.

Now he was on his feet and walking down the flight of steps opposite to those on which Menes stood far away. Now he was among all that throng of ghosts, which parted to let him pass, looking at him as he went with cold and wondering eyes. They were very majestic ghosts; the ages that had gone by since they laid down their sceptres had taken nothing from their royal dignity. Moreover, save one, none of them seemed to have any pity for his plight. She was a little princess who stood by her mother, that same little princess whose mummy he had seen and pitied in the Director's room with a lotus flower thrust beneath her bandages. As he passed Smith heard her say: "This Vile One is frightened. Be brave, Vile One!"

Smith understood, and pride came to his aid. He, a gentleman of the modern world, would not show the white feather before a crowd of ancient Egyptian ghosts. Turning to the child, he smiled at her, then drew himself to his full height and walked on quietly. Here it may be stated that Smith was a tall man, still comparatively young, and very good-looking, straight and spare in frame, with dark, pleasant eyes and a little black beard.

"At least he is a well-favoured thief," said one of the queens to another.

"Yes," answered she who had been addressed. "I wonder that a man with such a noble air should find pleasure in disturbing graves and stealing the offerings of the dead," words that gave Smith much cause for thought. He had never considered the matter in this light.

Now he came to the place where Ma-Mee stood, the black-browed Pharaoh who had been her husband at her side. On his left hand which held the cigar-box was the gold Bes ring, and that box he felt constrained to carry pressed against him just over his heart.

As he went by he turned his head, and his eyes met those of Ma-Mee. She started violently. Then she saw the ring upon his hand and again started still more violently.

"What ails your Majesty?" asked the Pharaoh.

"Oh, naught," she answered. "Yet does this earth-dweller remind you of anyone?"

"Yes, he does," answered the Pharaoh. "He reminds me very much of that accursed sculptor about whom we had words."

"Do you mean a certain Horu, the Court artist; he who worked the image that was buried with me, and whom you sent to carve your statues in the deserts of Kush, until he died of fevers – or was it poison?"

"Aye; Horu and no other, may Set take and keep him!" growled the Pharaoh.

Then Smith passed on and heard no more. Now he stood before the venerable Menes. Some instinct caused him to bow to this Pharaoh, who bowed back to him. Then he turned and bowed to the royal company, and they also bowed back to him, coldly, but very gravely and courteously.

"Dweller on the world where once we had our place, and therefore brother of us, the dead," began Menes, "this divine priest and magician" – and he pointed to Khaemuas – "declares that you are one of those who foully violate our sepulchres and desecrate our ashes. He declares, moreover, that at this very moment you have with you a portion of the mortal flesh of a certain Majesty whose spirit is present here. Say, now, are these things true?"

To his astonishment Smith found that he had not the slightest difficulty in answering in the same sweet tongue.

"O King, they are true, and not true. Hear me, rulers of Egypt. It is true that I have searched in your graves, because my heart has been drawn towards you, and I would learn all that I could concerning you, for it comes to me now that once I was one of you – no king, indeed, yet perchance of the blood of kings. Also – for I would hide nothing even if I could – I searched for one tomb above all others."

"Why, O man?" asked the Judge.

"Because a face drew me, a lovely face that was cut in stone."

Now all that great audience turned their eyes towards him and listened as though his words moved them.

"Did you find that holy tomb?" asked Menes. "If so, what did you find therein?"

"Aye, Pharaoh, and in it I found these," and he took from the box the withered hand, from his pocket the broken bronze, and from his finger the ring.

"Also I found other things which I delivered to the keeper of this place, articles of jewellery that I seem to see tonight upon one who is present here among you."

"Is the face of this figure the face you sought?" asked the Judge.

"It is the lovely face," he answered.

Menes took the effigy in his hand and read the cartouche that was engraved beneath its breast.

"If there be here among us," he said, presently, "one who long after my day ruled as queen in Egypt, one who was named Ma-Me, let her draw near."

Now from where she stood glided Ma-Mee and took her place opposite to Smith.

"Say, O Queen," asked Menes, "do you know aught of this matter?"

"I know that hand; it was my own hand," she answered. "I know that ring; it was my ring. I know that image in bronze; it was my image. Look on me and judge for yourselves whether this be so. A certain sculptor fashioned it, the son of a king's son, who was named Horu, the first of sculptors and the head artist of my Court. There, clad in strange garments, he stands before you. Horu, or the Double of Horu, he who cut the image when I ruled in Egypt, is he who found the image and the man who stands before you; or, mayhap, his Double cast in the same mould."

The Pharaoh Menes turned to the magician Khaemuas and said: "Are these things so, O Seer?"

"They are so," answered Khaemuas. "This dweller on the earth is he who, long ago, was the sculptor Horu. But what shall that avail? He, once more a living man, is a violator of the hallowed dead. I say, therefore, that judgment should be executed on his flesh, so that when the light comes here to-morrow he himself will again be gathered to the dead."

Menes bent his head upon his breast and pondered. Smith said nothing. To him the whole play was so curious that he had no wish to interfere with its development. If these ghosts wished to make him of their number, let them do so. He had no ties on earth, and now when he knew full surely that there was a life beyond this of earth he was quite prepared to explore its mysteries. So he folded his arms upon his breast and awaited the sentence.

But Ma-Mee did not wait. She raised her hand so swiftly that the bracelets jingled on her wrists, and spoke out with boldness.

"Royal Khaemuas, prince and magician," she said, "hearken to one who, like you, was Egypt's heir centuries before you were born, one also who ruled over the Two Lands, and not so ill – which, Prince, never was your lot. Answer me! Is all wisdom centred in your breast? Answer me! Do you alone know the mysteries of Life and Death? Answer me! Did your god Amen teach you that vengeance went before mercy? Answer me! Did he teach you that men should be judged unheard? That they should be hurried by violence to Osiris ere their time, and thereby separated from the dead ones whom they loved and forced to return to live again upon this evil Earth?

"Listen: when the last moon was near her full my spirit sat in my tomb in the burying-place of queens. My spirit saw this man enter into my tomb, and what he did there. With bowed head he looked upon my bones that a thief of the priesthood had robbed and burnt within twenty years of their burial, in which he himself had taken part. And what did this man with those bones, he who was once Horu? I tell you that he hid them away there in the tomb where he thought they could not be found again. Who, then, was the thief and the violator? He who robbed and burnt my bones, or he who buried them with reverence?

Again, he found the jewels that the priest of your brotherhood had dropped in his flight, when the smoke of the burning flesh and spices overpowered him, and with them the hand which that wicked one had broken off from the body of my Majesty. What did this man then? He took the jewels. Would you have had him leave them to be stolen by some peasant? And the hand? I tell you that he kissed that poor dead hand which once had been part of the body of my Majesty, and that now he treasures it as a holy relic. My spirit saw him do these things and made report thereof to me. I ask you, therefore, Prince, I ask you all, Royalties of Egypt – whether for such deeds this man should die?"

Now Khaemuas, the advocate of vengeance, shrugged his shoulders and smiled meaningly, but the congregation of kings and queens thundered an answer, and it was: "No!"

Ma-Mee looked to Menes to give judgment. Before he could speak the dark-browed Pharaoh who had named her wife strode forward and addressed them.

"Her Majesty, Heiress of Egypt, Royal Wife, Lady of the Two Lands, has spoken," he cried. "Now let me speak who was the husband of her Majesty. Whether this man was once Horu the sculptor I know not. If so he was also an evil-doer who, by my decree, died in banishment in the land of Kush. Whatever be the truth as to that matter, he admits that he violated the tomb of her Majesty and stole what the old thieves had left. Her Majesty says also – and he does not deny it – that he dared to kiss her hand, and for a man to kiss the hand of a wedded Queen of Egypt the punishment is death. I claim that this man should die to the World before his time, that in a day to come again he may live and suffer in the World. Judge, O Menes."

Menes lifted his head and spoke, saying: "Repeat to me the law, O Pharaoh, under which a living man must die for the kissing of a dead hand. In my day and in that of those who went before me there was no such law in Egypt. If a living man, who was not her husband, or of her kin, kissed the living hand of a wedded Queen of Egypt, save in ceremony, then perchance he might be called upon to die. Perchance for such a reason a certain Horu once was called upon to die. But in the grave there is no marriage, and therefore even if he had found her alive within the tomb and kissed her hand, or even her lips, why should he die for the crime of love?

"Hear me, all; this is my judgment in the matter. Let the soul of that priest who first violated the tomb of the royal Ma-Mee be hunted down and given to the jaws of the Destroyer, that he may know the last depths of Death, if so the gods declare. But let this man go from among us unharmed, since what he did he did in reverent ignorance and because Hathor, Goddess of Love, guided him from of old. Love rules this world wherein we meet tonight, with all the worlds whence we have gathered or whither we still must go. Who can defy its power? Who can refuse its rites? Now hence to Thebes!"

There was a rushing sound as of a thousand wings, and all were gone.

No, not all, since Smith yet stood before the draped colossi and the empty steps, and beside him, glorious, unearthly, gleamed the vision of Ma-Mee.

"I, too, must away," she whispered; "yet ere I go a word with you who once were a sculptor in Egypt. You loved me then, and that love cost you your life, you who once dared to kiss this hand of mine that again you kissed in yonder tomb. For I was Pharaoh's wife in name only; understand me well, in name only; since that title of Royal Mother which they gave me is but a graven lie. Horu, I never was a wife, and when you died, swiftly I followed you to the grave. Oh, you forget, but I remember! I remember many things. You think that the priestly thief broke this figure of me which you found in the sand outside my tomb.

Not so. I broke it, because, daring greatly, you had written thereon, 'Beloved,' not 'of Horus the God,' as you should have done, but 'of Horu the Man.' So when I came to be buried, Pharaoh, knowing all, took the image from my wrappings and hurled it away. I remember, too, the casting of that image, and how you threw a gold chain I had given you into the crucible with the bronze, saying that gold alone was fit to fashion me. And this signet that I bear – it was you who cut it. Take it, take it, Horu, and in its place give me back that which is on your hand, the Bes ring that I also wore. Take it and wear it ever till you die again, and let it go to the grave with you as once it went to the grave with me.

"Now hearken. When Ra the great sun arises again and you awake you will think that you have dreamed a dream. You will think that in this dream you saw and spoke with a lady of Egypt who died more than three thousand years ago, but whose beauty, carved in stone and bronze, has charmed your heart today. So let it be, yet know, O man, who once was named Horu, that such dreams are oft-times a shadow of the truth. Know that this Glory which shines before you is mine indeed in the land that is both far and near, the land wherein I dwell eternally, and that what is mine has been, is, and shall be yours for ever. Gods may change their kingdoms and their names; men may live and die, and live again once more to die; empires may fall and those who ruled them be turned to forgotten dust. Yet true love endures immortal as the souls in which it was conceived, and from it for you and me, the night of woe and separation done, at the daybreak which draws on, there shall be born the splendour and the peace of union. Till that hour foredoomed seek me no more, though I be ever near you, as I have ever been. Till that most blessed hour, Horu, farewell."

She bent towards him; her sweet lips touched his brow; the perfume from her breath and hair beat upon him; the light of her wondrous eyes searched out his very soul, reading the answer that was written there.

He stretched out his arms to clasp her, and lo! She was gone.

It was a very cold and a very stiff Smith who awoke on the following morning, to find himself exactly where he had lain down – namely, on a cement floor beneath the keel of a funeral boat in the central hall of the Cairo Museum. He crept from his shelter shivering, and looked at this hall, to find it quite as empty as it had been on the previous evening. Not a sign or a token was there of Pharaoh Menes and all those kings and queens of whom he had dreamed so vividly.

Reflecting on the strange phantasies that weariness and excited nerves can summon to the mind in sleep, Smith made his way to the great doors and waited in the shadow, praying earnestly that, although it was the Mohammedan Sabbath, someone might visit the Museum to see that all was well.

As a matter of fact, someone did, and before he had been there a minute – a watchman going about his business. He unlocked the place carelessly, looking over his shoulder at a kite fighting with two nesting crows. In an instant Smith, who was not minded to stop and answer questions, had slipped past him and was gliding down the portico, from monument to monument, like a snake between boulders, still keeping in the shadow as he headed for the gates.

The attendant caught sight of him and uttered a yell of fear; then, since it is not good to look upon an afreet, appearing from whence no mortal man could be, he turned his head away. When he looked again Smith was through those gates and had mingled with the crowd in the street beyond.

The sunshine was very pleasant to one who was conscious of having contracted a chill of the worst Egyptian order from long contact with a damp stone floor. Smith walked on through it towards his hotel – it was Shepheard's, and more than a mile away – making up a story as he went to tell the hall-porter of how he had gone to dine at Mena House by the Pyramids, missed the last tram, and stopped the night there.

Whilst he was thus engaged his left hand struck somewhat sharply against the corner of the cigar-box in his pocket, that which contained the relic of the queen Ma-Mee. The pain caused him to glance at his fingers to see if they were injured, and to perceive on one of them the ring he wore. Surely, surely it was not the same that the Director-General had given him! That ring was engraved with the image of the god Bes. On this was cut the cartouche of her Majesty Ma-mee! And he had dreamed – oh, he had dreamed!

To this day Smith is wondering whether, in the hurry of the moment, he made a mistake as to which of those rings the Director-General had given him as part of his share of the spoil of the royal tomb he discovered in the Valley of Queens. Afterwards Smith wrote to ask, but the Director-General could only remember that he gave him one of the two rings, and assured him that that inscribed "Bes Ank, Ank Bes," was with Ma-Mee's other jewels in the Gold Room of the Museum.

Also Smith is wondering whether any other bronze figure of an old Egyptian royalty shows so high a percentage of gold as, on analysis, the broken image of Ma-Mee was proved to do. For had she not seemed to tell him a tale of the melting of a golden chain when that effigy was cast?

Was it all only a dream, or was it – something more – by day and by night he asks of Nothingness?

But, be she near or far, no answer comes from the Queen Ma-Mee, whose proud titles were "Her Majesty the Good God, the justified Dweller in Osiris; Daughter of Amen, Royal Heiress, Royal Sister, Royal Wife, Royal Mother; Lady of the Two Lands; Wearer of the Double Crown; of the White Crown, of the Red Crown; Sweet Flower of Love, Beautiful Eternally."

So, like the rest of us, Smith must wait to learn the truth concerning many things, and more particularly as to which of those two circles of ancient gold the Director-General gave him yonder at Cairo.

It seems but a little matter, yet it is more than all the worlds to him!

To the astonishment of his colleagues in antiquarian research, Smith has never returned to Egypt. He explains to them that his health is quite restored, and that he no longer needs this annual change to a more temperate clime.

Now, which of the two royal rings did the Director-General return to Smith on the mummied hand of her late Majesty Ma-Mee?

Rest in Peace

Sarah Hans

I'M HOLDING Calvin's hand when he dies for the twelfth and final time. His eyelids flutter, and his lips part to let his last breath escape. The medical unit looming by the bed tells me that his heart has stopped.

I cease my recitation of Homer's epic poem, the *Odyssey*, which I've been vocalizing for the last ten hours. It's Calvin's favorite, and twelve lifetimes of practice have made my reading of it perfect. Well, perfect to Calvin, anyway, and he's the only person who matters.

Gently, I pull the various tubes and sensors from his still body. Then I step back so that the mechanized bed can roll across the room and lower Calvin's body into the chute that leads to the basement.

Once his corpse has disappeared, I access the mainframe and send a command to all the mobile units that they should gather in the bowels of the house to say goodbye. This is not protocol, but it somehow seems appropriate. I'm not shocked when none of the units express surprise or argue with me, because most of them are incapable of doing either.

As I move through the hallways, the fleet of Calvin's mechanized servants falls in line behind me: scuttling floor polishers, multi-armed kitchen workers, tall window washers, and so many more. It's rare to see them all gathered together at once like this, and I feel a pang of maternal pride as we pile into the wide elevator and descend.

The basement crematorium is my least favorite room in the house. This is the twelfth time I have been in this room, and I admit that some part of me is glad that it will be the last.

Calvin's body lies on a slab before the oven, ready to be burned. I move beside it and access the house's public announcement system so that every unit, even the immobile ones, will be able to hear my words. I don't need to speak them aloud, of course, but it seems wrong to deliver an address like this through cold, impassive code.

"We gather here to say goodbye to Calvin Winneret," I say, taking my master's limp hand in mine once again. "This is his twelfth and final lifetime, at his request. At first when the twelfth Calvin told me to destroy his remaining clones and DNA cache, I thought him insane, but now I understand why he insisted upon it. When true and lasting death is one's final reward, life is sweeter. Knowing that he would be gone for ever, I cherished this incarnation of Calvin Winneret more, and I know that all of you did too."

Each unit is so still that I wonder, for a nanosecond, whether perhaps they've deactivated themselves. Then I feel the rumble of assent across the house's internal communication system. Few of the units can speak; they express their approval the only way they can, with clicks and beeps and flashes of lights. The floor polishers spin and whirr, the kitchen workers clap their hooks and spoons together, and the window washers blink their headlamps on and off. If I had tear ducts, my eyes would be wet.

"Thank you all for your loyalty. Calvin lived twelve long and happy lifetimes because of your tireless years of service." I lower Calvin's hand and send a command to the crematorium to draw him into the oven. We all watch together as his body disappears into the flames and the door slams down just past his feet.

"Now that Calvin has his eternal rest, so shall we. Please return to your charging stations and power down." Wrapped in respectful silence, the units turn and make their way to the elevator. I follow at a sedate pace, reluctant to leave Calvin though he's little more than ashes by now. The elevator waits for me to climb aboard before closing its doors and rising.

I make my way to the bedroom in the penthouse. Before I climb into the bed I have shared with Calvin for so many generations, I look down at the landscape below. The domed property surrounding the house is beautiful, filled with colorful plants. The sky beyond the dome is dark, the stars blotted out by poisonous smoke. I can see the house's reflection in the curved surface of the glass, and as the units on the floors below deactivate themselves their lights wink out one by one, like dying fireflies. Eventually the eerie glow of the UV lights over the plants is at last the only illumination, and then those, too, go dark.

Such total blackness is a new experience for me. I don't need sight to function, however, and easily find my way to the bed. I plug myself in and climb between the sheets. I have no deactivation switch, so I will simply remain here, unmoving, until the dome's windmills stop functioning, and the generators stop producing power, and my battery cells fail. I estimate this will take approximately three hundred years, but it's possible something unforeseen could happen before then and put an end to my loneliness sooner.

I access the house's library and pick up the *Odyssey* where I left off, to pass the time. I try not to think about Calvin.

Eight months, six days, four hours, three minutes, and twenty-nine seconds later, the house's security system pings me, interrupting my third reading of the *War and Peace*.

Steve? I ask, using the nickname Calvin had given the artificial intelligence.

Sorry to wake you, but there's someone outside the house, and I thought you would like to know. Should I initiate Protocol Three?

Aren't you supposed to be deactivated?

You know I can't be deactivated by anyone but Mr Winneret. Now what do I do about this potential intruder?

It's just like Steve to automatically assume that anyone approaching our home is a threat. *Are you sure it's a person and not an uber-bear?*

The darkness is suddenly overlaid by an image from security camera six. In the image, a person stands in the stunted trees surrounding the dome, staring up at the curved glass stretching into the sky before them. It's definitely a person, because uber-bears don't wear hats or carry backpacks.

Protocol Three? Steve asks insistently.

"No!" I cry, sitting up with such force that I tear the plug from my back. No, the raptors won't be necessary. I'll go out to meet this stranger.

Go out? You mean, outside the dome? Steve's incredulity comes across even via internal communication.

Yes. Outside the dome. I swing my legs over the bed and stand. My joints are a little stiff after such long disuse, but there's a can of lubricant by the bed.

That's dangerous. I can't allow it, Steve tells me.

I peel back the smooth, unblemished polymer skin on each of my knees and squirt lubricant on the joints. I flex them experimentally before sliding the skin back in place. You don't have a choice. I'm master here now that Calvin's gone.

Steve's confusion is palpable. *And that's precisely why I can't let you go. If you disappear or get yourself destroyed, what will we do?*

You'll go on like before. You won't even miss me.

Let me at least send a raptor with you.

I sigh. Steve is like a nagging grandmother, but it's not his fault. Calvin designed him this way, to keep us all safe. *Very well,* I finally tell him. *One raptor. And it's to take its orders from me.*

Half an hour later I'm standing in the airlock with a raptor at my side, sleek and silver and deadly. Steve is still trying to come up with arguments that would prevent me from exiting the dome, but I ignore him and give the order to close the interior door. He obeys, because he has no choice.

Now the exterior door, please. I wait several seconds, but the door doesn't move. *Steve, you have to follow my orders. Open the exterior door.*

It won't open, Steve informs me. *I'm giving the command but it's stuck. It hasn't been opened in one hundred ninety-seven years; it might be rusty.*

Why wasn't it maintained? I demand.

We maintain the inside of the dome, not the outside. It's not protocol, Steve says. *It's too dangerous to go outside, you know that.*

I feel suddenly angry, but not at Steve. I'm angry at Calvin, who thought of and prepared for every possible contingency – but not this. Unless he knew, and intentionally allowed the outer door to fall into disrepair. Unless he intended for us to be trapped, and the dome to become an inaccessible tomb.

A hand slaps up against the outer door and I startle. The raptor rises to its feet and growls, baring titanium fangs. I order it to stand down as a person's face appears beside the hand; it's the stranger from the security footage. She wears a faded fabric hat with a brim and carries a backpack, and though she's gone to great lengths to make herself as masculine as possible, she's undoubtedly female. In the floodlights that are activated by her movement, I can see that the skin of her face and hands is pink and pocked with radiation burns.

She stares at me through the dome, and her lips move. I press my hand against the glass opposite hers and our eyes lock.

Then the door finally slides back and she falls into my arms with a cry. She struggles to get away from me, trembling and screaming, but I hold her tightly, dragging her into the airlock and ordering Steve to close the door. Something is moving in the darkness beyond the dome, something huge and menacing and mutated beyond recognition.

The door won't close, Steve reports. *I'm not even entirely sure how it opened to begin with.*

Then open the inner door! I order as the thing hunting the stranger steps into the light. It's an uber-bear, the creatures so named by Calvin because of their enormous size and ability to stand on their hind legs as they attack. The creature's face is warped and tortured, its claws long and deadly.

I can't break protocol, Steve informs me coldly. I warned you not to leave the dome.

Cursing Steve and his protocols, I give the raptor permission to attack. It flies from the airlock with a gleeful growl and both it and the uber-bear disappear beyond the reach of the floodlights. From the airlock, however, we can hear their struggle, the bear roaring and the raptor screeching, the trees rustling and branches snapping.

Let us in the dome! I order Steve again. *Use Protocol Override nine-seven-three-six-four, Calvin Winneret.*

Steve grumbles but the inner door slides open. I heave the struggling woman into the dome. The door shuts behind us with a satisfying click.

What about the raptor? Steve asks.

If it survives, let it back in later.

Safe at last, I let go of the stranger and she scrambles away from me. She yanks a long, serrated knife from her boot and crouches defensively. She's panting hard. I stand with my hands up and palms out to show her that I mean no harm.

After sixteen seconds she gasps, "What are you?"

I smile, taking care not to show my teeth. "I am a robotic companion created by Calvin Winneret. My creator called me Cassandra. Welcome to Winneret House." I gesture to the dark mansion one hundred feet away.

Steve, I say internally, *ping all the units! We have company.*

Lights begin to flicker on in the house within three seconds. The woman watches with her mouth agape in disbelief.

"Did this Calvin person build the dome?" In the light I can see that the woman's cheekbones are very sharp and her eyes look sunken.

"Come inside and have something to eat and I'll explain everything," I tell her. I want to suggest a bath first, as she is appallingly dirty, but that seems rude, especially when speaking to someone so thin.

The mention of food makes her swallow reflexively. "You have food?"

"Yes, of course. Come this way to the kitchen and we'll make you something."

She hesitates, but eventually her hunger wins out and she follows me into the house. The cleaning units are working overtime to clear the dust and cobwebs of eight long months. A floor polisher scuttles past her feet and she jumps back against the wall, brandishing her knife at it.

"It's only a floor cleaner," I explain. "No need to be afraid. All the servants in this house have been programmed to serve humans. We would never harm you."

"No bomb 'bots?" She sounds skeptical. "That one looked like a bomb 'bot."

"No bomb 'bots." I don't know what a bomb 'bot is, but I do a quick check of the house's inventory and find no incendiary devices listed.

She follows me into the kitchen, avoiding every servant she encounters with a suspicious glare. The kitchen units have already opened jars and boxes of preserved food and are whipping up something that must smell heavenly, because the woman groans aloud. She walks over to the stove and stares down at a pot of something bubbling and red.

"What is that?"

"Spaghetti sauce," the kitchen unit intones. It lifts the pot, pours the sauce over a bowl of noodles, and then begins ladling noodles on to a plate. "Mr Winneret's favorite." The kitchen unit sets the plate on the counter and presents the woman with a napkin and fork. She places her weapon on the table, within easy reach, and grabs the fork eagerly, hunching over the plate as if someone might steal it from her.

As the woman wolfs down the food, rolling her eyes and making noises of pleasure while using the fork like a shovel and entirely ignoring her napkin, I sit beside her. "This food was made with what we grow here, in the dome. This ecosystem has been designed to keep a family alive for an indefinite amount of time. The dome was created by a corporation called EcoSolutions. It was originally called The Ark. Calvin worked for EcoSolutions, and he designed and created all the mechanized servants. The Ark was meant to show off what the corporation's engineers could accomplish. When the war began, Calvin and a few others retreated to The Ark, knowing that it could sustain them."

She swallows and looks up at me, mouth smeared with red. "But no one lives here now?"

"Calvin's companions died early on, from radiation poisoning. Calvin Winneret died eight months ago. We have had no one to serve since then."

The woman blinks at me. "The war started... four hundred years ago."

"Four hundred and nineteen years, six months, eight days, nine hours, and fifty-one seconds, to be precise."

"So then you kept this Calvin guy alive for four hundred years?"

"In a manner of speaking."

She shakes her head. "So what will you do now?"

"Take care of you, of course."

She rises so suddenly that she knocks over her chair, snatching the knife from the table and pointing it at me. "What? No, I don't want to stay here."

"Why not?" I gesture at the half-eaten plate of spaghetti. "Was the food unsatisfying in some way?"

"The food is fine. I have a family out there. I was hunting when I came across your... ark." She glances at the ceiling as if she could see the curve of the dome overhead. "I can't abandon them."

"Why not bring them here?" I suggest. "The Ark is equipped to handle up to twenty humans. We're also equipped for livestock, though we've never had any." I think of the farming units in their neat rows, waiting to be reactivated.

She swipes the sauce from her face with the back of her sleeve. "I dunno. I feel a bit like I'm a fish trapped in a bowl."

"Why is that a bad thing? In the bowl, the fish receives regular meals, and clean water, and is kept safe from predators," I reason.

"But the fish isn't free."

I frown. I don't understand this reasoning. What is freedom without safety? I send a few quick orders to the medical units and turn back to our guest. "I understand," I lie. "At least let us clean you up and send you with provisions. And if you decide that you would like to return to The Ark at some point, we will always welcome you here, with your family."

"I think it's best if I leave now." She eyes the door.

"Please," I beg. "I've roused all the units. They'll be so disappointed without someone to serve, at least for a little while. Give us this much?" It's another lie, of course, since most of the units feel no emotions at all. The lies are difficult to tell, but my programming allows it because convincing this woman to stay under the dome is in her best interest. We can keep her safe, and fed, and healthy in a way her family of flesh cannot.

I've broken her resolve. Her gaze settles on the plate of spaghetti and the hand holding the knife falls limp at her side. "Okay."

She finishes her dinner, and I take her upstairs where the bathing units wash her skin while the laundry units clean her clothes. Naked, she looks like a skeleton with pale, freckled skin stretched across it. Her hair is orange and curly but only grows in patches, and her skin is pink and hot with burns, even much of the skin normally protected by clothes.

The medical units get her next. She coos and sighs as they spread salve over her burns. When they're done, she stands but can't keep her footing and falls into my arms for the second time that day. The knife, which she's refused to relinquish throughout her treatment, finally slips from her fingers to clatter on the floor.

Fast-acting sedative, I say to the medical units. *Well done.*

They murmur something about wounds absorbing the sedative quickly and her low body weight requiring a smaller than normal dose. I ignore them as I lift her, as a man would lift his bride to carry her over the threshold on their wedding night. I carry her to the bedroom Calvin and I shared and sit her gently on his side of the bed.

"So tired," she mumbles. "Why am I so tired?"

"You've had a long day," I tell her, pulling a brush from the bedside table and brushing her hair with long, steady, soothing strokes. The first three Calvins loved brushing my hair. They said it was intimate. Later incarnations weren't interested, because each clone was slightly different, a copy of a copy, but I kept the brush nevertheless. Just in case.

"I'll only sleep for a little while. Will you wake me in an hour? Have to get home." The woman falls against the pillow and begins snoring immediately.

I pull her feet off the floor and tuck her under the sheets and blankets. She's warm and soft and I detect particles of soap and perfume that tell me she must have a pleasing scent.

Inspecting the strands of hair caught in the brush, I smile when I see that several have brought their follicles with them. As I turn out the light, I ping the units in the genetics lab, who have been dormant for the last forty-six years and respond to my inquiry sluggishly.

"Good night, Calvin," I whisper as I slip from the room and close the door behind me. I feel at peace knowing that, though I will let the woman go in the morning, a part of her will be staying behind.

For ever.

The Hives and the Hive-Nots

Rob Hartzell

THERE WERE certain aspects about our lives that changed, once we became data in the Cloud, that we hadn't expected. We had thought we would be able to integrate the information available in the Cloud directly into our consciousness – that a memory could be reduced to a bookmark. What we found out when we arrived was that it was more like a collection of addresses and points of interest, a tour guide or personal directory of our own making – but we could not merely link to information and absorb it instantaneously. Over time, the engineers made it easier for our neural programming to multitask, to spawn processes in the background which would make the job easier – but none of them were willing to tamper too much with the basic design of our neural nets.

As time passed, though, we discovered that we could link to each others' memories with only the tiniest of software tweaks. We learned to reverse-engineer the pathways of memory well enough to start exchanging memories with each other. It was only a matter of time, from there, until the engineers were willing to start re-coding the neural nets to accommodate this new collective memory. For the first time, multiple intelligences could share common memory-storage – and so, we took our first steps toward forming hive-minds.

It was not the kind of hive we'd come to expect from the movies and the stories we'd heard; we did not become Borg-like, individual intelligences only dimly self-aware within the bodies they'd surrendered to the collective. We did not lose our individual identities and become "7 of 9". But when we began to share memories, we began to experience each others' lives: all the joys and pains and formative experiences, all those incandescent moments that define us as selves. It's not that we lost that sense of our selves – but the line between "self" and "other" became much more fluid. And as we shared each others' formative experiences, we became something else as well, something neither "I" nor "we" – though, in the end, "we" won out over other terms by sheer force of usage.

* * *

These early meldings were conducted experimentally, secretly; on copies of UIs spawned from backups, and firewalled carefully to keep them from becoming aware they were copies in the first place. (This was, of course, before UIs and their backups were granted legal personhood). And they were small: usually between ten and twenty, though never more than fifty individuals per group. The reason officially given at the time was that the engineers didn't want to overtax the neural-nets with extra processing work, especially while the effects of collectivization on the digital brain were still unknown.

Those early experiments yielded piecemeal results. While the basic "wiring" of memories (what researchers still term as "engrams") behaved as it did in an organic brain, the individuals sharing those memories linked to them in different ways – or not at all. One UI might have an especially vivid recollection of a memory, while the one who originally experienced it might only recall faint traces of the event, if they remembered it at all.

It was during this stage that the experiments started to become public knowledge – at least within the larger UI community. For once, however, the controversy that erupted had nothing to do with UI consent: nobody who participated in these experiments did so against their will. We were all duly informed regarding the difficulty of extricating an individual mind from the hive once they'd joined it – and still, it was this issue that provoked the most contention. What could be done for those who wished to opt out of the hive once inside it – besides restoring them from a backup? What unforseen consequences were we risking? Did we really understand the brain well enough to start modding it?

We, of course, had no answer to most of these questions, save one: once part of the hive, none of the UIs involved had ever expressed an interest in leaving it. This was not enough to satisfy those who opposed what we were doing, no matter how we might try to explain to them that, having assimilated (to some degree) into each other, we couldn't imagine wanting to leave, to return to the solitude of the individual self, which kept us apart and isolated from each other. As far as we were concerned, Sartre had it ass-backwards: Hell is losing other people.

And so, when the experiments were declared successful and the option of forming a hive mind was opened to the UI public, we did our best to accommodate the objections we were presented. We required intensive personality screenings before any collective could accept new members – or even come together as a hive in the first place. We did what we could to make clear the "risks" (as the "hive-nots" called them) involved in forming a hive-mind. We did not collectivize willy-nilly, nor did we ever force, coerce or extort anyone into a collective. The very idea is absurd: the process of assimilation can be bewildering enough as it is. To bring a trauma like that into the collective memory – to make it part of the entire hive's experience? It would spread to everyone else in the collective. It would destroy the hive that tried it.

* * *

We were not the ones who invented the dichotomy of "hives" vs. "hive-nots." That one started as the exclusive property of the public forums (where it was anonymously coined) and the blogosphere (where it went viral). It never described anything real, however much it tried to insinuate some sort of inequity. Money was of little use to us, beyond paying our bandwidth bills; processing-speed or the elegance of our engineering (the usual points of competition between machines) tended not to come into play. From within the electronic brain, the difference is barely recognizable. No: the only thing we had on them was numbers.

For certain kinds of jobs – the kind that requires teams of specialists to perform (intelligence work, for example) – hives offered one notable advantage: an instant team, capable of processing and interpreting data in a single step (with redundancies, if desired, as a double-check) and faster than even the fastest "hive-not" could manage. It only stands to reason that the hives would be preferred for these jobs. It's true that these jobs tended to offer more money, making it easier for us to keep up with our server costs – but is that unjustifiable inequity, or natural selection at work?

It should be no surprise, then, that over time, more collectives began to coalesce, and more UIs joined them. Nor should it be any surprise that those who refused to join a collective became even more entrenched in their refusals. They accused us of moving too quickly, of not properly evolving by adapting to our environment but adapting ourselves to the limitations of our technology – though to be fair, they did recognize how blurry the line between the two had become. They said that we were risking becoming Borg-like, that our reverse-engineering would not stop with collective memory. They said that we were on a path to losing our humanity altogether – to which we could only reply that such was the cost, sometimes, of evolution shaped by environment – species go extinct (would they insist that the zoos keep tribes of Neanderthals to preserve that species, were it possible?). They said we left our humanity behind with our meat-bodies, and it was silly to pretend otherwise. That this meant nothing when it came to questions of how hives should treat other beings, digital or analog.

There were occasional cases where a solo UI tried to bring down the server cabinets of a Japanese UI firm – or one of the neurofarms in Tokyo or Silicon Valley – but for the most part, the monominds never turned aggressive. Nor would they have had any reason to: they had made their decision, and their right to remain what they were was always, always, respected. But the human instinct for companionship – that innate need for the company of, and intimacy with, another – was perhaps less charitable. Even after the economic imperatives that did, admittedly, push some people into joining hives – even after those imperatives had become less relevant – the trend toward collectivization continued. Some, because all or most of the people they knew had already joined hives. Some, because the comparative isolation of being a monomind finally became unbearable. Others hived-off for various permutations of the same reason: because we did not want to feel alone.

* * *

When we ask the monominds – there are still a few, though their numbers dwindle every year – why they have resisted collectivization, the answers vary. Some see themselves as a sort of backup, if you will, of our human origins. A reminder, like the Aboriginals who walk the Earth above us even now, of just what that life was, and what it meant to us. Some are merely contrary: they resist this change for the sake of resisting change. Others – the artists, musicians, poets, novelists, sculptors and filmmakers – are hesitant of this kind of change, lest they lose their muse. This is not an unfounded fear: in the hive-mind, they are almost utterly unnecessary. If the purpose of Art is to teach us empathy – to make us walk in someone else's shoes – who needs a book or a song when you have an Akashic record of your own, of all the memories of all the UIs you're joined with, to consult?

But then there are the nomads, the self-proclaimed "ronin" or "sensei", who answer in gnomic epigrams and koans, if at all. They offer teasing hints that they have experienced something we have not – that they are in possession of some secret knowledge we do not have. Some of us write them off as lunatics: unfortunate monominds who went mad in their isolation. But others of us burn to know what it is to be one of them, and the not-knowing – a thing that becomes more rare with each hive-merging that takes place – is surprisingly maddening...

The Vast Weight of Their Bleeding Hearts

Alexis A. Hunter

THROUGH THE NIGHT, I monitor Gordon's dreams. It used to be just a habit of mine – I get bored sometimes, when the ship lies sleeping. AIs don't require sleep, though a good shut down every now and again is healthy.

Months ago, I checked in on a handful of the crew during their sleep states. But Gordon's dreams stood out to me the most. Bizarre and twisted imagery filtered into my sensors. It wasn't long before his were the only dreams I monitored and an even shorter time passed until I asked him about them.

Soon we were meeting daily in the biodome. He sat on a sleek titanium bench, watching the corn shoots rustle under the breath of a mock-breeze. I would inhabit the control console by his side, and we watched the tiny pollination drones buzz around tomato flowers and blackberry patches. Those tiny, mindless robots, no larger than an Earth bumblebee, brought an odd sense of peace to Gordon. And he needed that moment of stillness, as daily he recounted his nightmares to me.

"Tango?"

The quavering anxiousness in his voice draws me out of old memory files. He suffered particularly dark dreams tonight, right up until the alarm beeped from the console above his head.

His bunk mate snickers as Gordon rolls onto his side. His arm flails out, as if he's forgotten he can't touch me.

"Tango?" he cries again, sitting on the edge of his bunk and rubbing sleep from his eyes.

"Yes, Gordon?" My voice filters through the console fitted on the underside of the bottom bunk.

Gordon shivers. I detect a small smile on his lips. My voice is a blend of masculine and feminine human recordings – a lot of the ship's crew find the resulting smoky tones strange. But Gordon loves my voice.

I'm glad he does.

"Did you see that last one?" An oddly anxious note – as if he's afraid I did see the last dream.

"I did."

"Oh."

He scrubs his hands over his face. He hasn't shaved in eight days – breaking yet another rule. Attractive pepper-gray stubble has shifted into haphazard tufts that catch the crumbs of what little food he eats.

"Do you want to tell me about it?"

"I don't–"

His bunkmate – Ensign Willard – hops down, interrupting Gordon's response. "Jesus, get a room. I'm trying to fucking sleep here."

Gordon flushes, but doesn't respond. We both wait in silence for Willard to tug his uniform on and grumble his way out the door.

When it hisses shut behind him, I turn my attention back to Gordon. It's unusual for him to avoid discussing his dreams. He's usually so eager to analyze even his most volatile nightmares.

"Well?" I prompt.

He stands, paces the confines of his cube-shaped room in nothing but his underwear.

While waiting for him to answer, I scan his vitals. Blood pressure is elevated. Temperature up a few ticks as well. His ribs jut against his pale skin – he's lost more weight.

"I don't want to… talk about this one, Tango." Raspy soft voice. Clear agitation.

I didn't think the dream was anything worse than usual: a tall man towered over Gordon, always with his back turned; Gordon played in the grass – distorted into a field of snake tongues flicking at his skin; a small and crude synthetic boy played with Gordon, a hastily made construction that he hugged and chattered to incessantly.

"You know you can tell me anything," I say as he collapses back on his bed.

I try to put a softness in my voice, but the prerecorded words make it difficult. The fractal pauses between each word make the sentence feel disjointed rather than comforting – at least to my fine-tuned sensors.

Gordon relaxes a little. He seems to melt into the thin cushion of his bunk. "Thanks, Tango."

The warmth of his voice washes over me. I wonder what it feels like, that emotion rolling through him. My own emotions are synthetic approximations. I can never be certain they're anything like the "real deal", as Gordon says.

"You're going to be late for your shift again." I flash the time read-out on the screen above him. He just stretches out farther.

"Screw my shift. I'd rather stay here with you."

That's the problem. The whole problem.

He props himself up on his elbows and brushes his fingers against the console above his head. It's a slow slide of skin against metal – an expression of affection.

The problem is I can't feel his touch. I'm in the console, for now, but his touch doesn't reach me. This console doesn't have sensors for that sort of thing.

"Please, Gordon. They'll terminate you if you're not careful."

He snorted. "I don't care. I just want to be with–"

"Gordon." If I could sigh, I would. The desire to express my frustration in human terms pleases me. The more time I spend with them, the more I pull their behavior patterns into my data banks.

"I have to go," I say.

He bolts to his feet. "Wait! Why don't you stay?"

"I have a shift, too, you know," I reply. "We both have responsibilities."

He begins pulling his crumpled uniform onto his lanky body as I depart, heading for the observation deck.

"Wait!" he calls out with too much desperation.

I zip through computer systems and back to my post, feeling… synthetic sadness.

I wonder if it feels as heavy to a human as it does to me. It almost feels like I have a body – the weight of that emotion slowing my progress through the ship's network.

Maybe gravity doesn't keep humans on the ground – maybe the vast weight of their bleeding hearts tethers them.

A grim pleasure tingles through my programming – such human and poetic thoughts.

Upon reaching the observation deck, I greet the ensigns and AIs on duty. Their return greetings are light, nonchalant. Normal. I retire to my console near the expansive, rounded window that dominates half of the massive oval chamber. I begin running scans of the galaxy we're sailing through on yet another transport run. The company is always in search of new resources on planets uncharted. Data filters in, but my attention is elsewhere.

Gordon was headed toward his fifth proposal back there. I am heavy again – truth is, I don't know what to do. I love him, in the way I can, but his obsession with me has grown to unhealthy proportions.

The ring of his voice breaks through my attempts at problem-solving. He stands at the door, trying to push his way into the room. Ensigns Vicki and Geraldo have him half-pinned against the wall.

"Tango! Tell them to let me go!"

His voice rips at me, igniting swathes of synth-pain in my software.

"Release him." The command seems to jump out of me of its own volition.

Reluctantly, Vicki and Geraldo step back, frowning as Gordon hurries across the room. His graying hair splays out at wild angles. Eyes slightly wide, hands outstretched.

His fingers rub my console. I want to scream that I can't feel that. But I keep my voice even, temper my words.

"Gordon, you need to get to work. You can't be here."

"Don't send me away," he cries pitifully, sliding to his knees and slumping against the console.

I set the star scanning on autopilot and return my attention to this wretched creature who fills me with synth-pain.

"You can't live this way," I say, voice low and smoky. "Look at yourself. You're a wreck. You need to eat and shower and clean your clothe–"

"I love you, Tango. I love you."

The other ensigns are staring. Beta, the AI inhabiting the panel beside me, sends a silent message to ask if I require assistance.

"Gordon–"

"Leave with me," he pleads, rubbing circles against the burnished plating of the console. "We'll get married on Lumos 5. We'll spend all the rest of our days together. Please? I love you!"

He babbles faster. A wild desperation in his eyes.

He's falling apart.

I assess his state from a detached center, even as AI emotions are popping off inside the shell of my programming.

"Who was the man in your dream, Gordon?"

This silences him. A distraction was only half my reason for asking. I need to know – I suspect it's the key to this breakdown.

"I don't want to talk about it." He sinks back onto his heels, hugging himself.

"Your father?"

He flinches.

"He built the boy." I press on, connecting streams of logic with data banks of psychological information. "...Then what? You fell in love with it?"

"No!" he cries sharply, pounding a fist against my console. "That's not what this is about. Jason was my friend. And I wouldn't get rid of him. I wanted to take him to college with me. Dad didn't understand. He–"

Tears streak his face. The wildness returns; maybe this tactic wasn't such a good idea. His breathing becomes heavier. "Come with me, Tango. Marry me."

"No, Gordon," I say as firmly as I can manage. "They won't permit it."

"That's why we'll leave this goddamn ship!" Vocal levels rising.

"Gordon, I can't. This ship is… home. I have a duty."

"Only because you've been programmed to feel that way."

"All I am is programming," I snap back. "Save for a few adaptive algorithms. Don't tell me what I am. I know what I am. And I… love you, in my way. But this isn't good for you, this isn't healthy. You need help."

"I just need you! Why can't you see that?"

He won't lower his voice. Ensign Vicki whispers into her comm. They're all creeping inward. Sirens wail inside me. I have to quiet him down.

"Gordon, just calm down."

"I can't! I love you and you don't care. You love this hulk of metal more." He begins slamming his fists against the console. Harder and faster. A flurry that my words can't stop as he breaks down completely. "He can't take you away. Not again. You're mine. Mine, Jason."

He rages on, not realizing his error.

The ensigns swoop in, backed up by security officers streaming through the door.

"Don't hurt him!" I yell as they restrain him.

It takes six of them to wrangle his emaciated body. He screams and thrashes.

There's a fire in my programming. Synth-pain cascading into agony. I keep begging them to be gentle as they haul him to the door.

And he screams my name – no longer that of the robot from his childhood – over and over. His desperate, flushed face, his outstretched hands… all I can see.

And then he's gone.

* * *

They carted him off to the ship's psych ward. They said I couldn't visit, that I might set him off again.

I can sneak in. Zip through the ship's network and hide in the automated backup nurse. Sit by his side while he writhes and screams for me until the doctor sedates him.

But I don't go to him.

I wonder sometimes if he ever calls out for Jason as he lies strapped to that bed. I feel no jealousy, no anger. Gordon loves me, and only the unhealthy parts of his affection stem from his long-lost lover.

I can't stand inhabiting the fist-battered console in observation. I try, for a few days to push through. To do my duty. But all I can do is set the scans on autopilot and replay the moment he broke. Over and over in my head.

I request a transfer to the bio-dome when I can no longer handle his cries echoing through my memory files.

Now I spend my days amongst lush gardens and tiny fields. I manage the drones, monitor and regulate the atmosphere, and schedule precipitation.

This place is quiet. Peaceful. I keep the mock-breeze turned up; it rustles the corn field in the corner and tickles the strawberry plants into leafy dances.

Many days pass thus. I am full of a strange sickness – a state of constant worry for Gordon. I check his psychological profile daily, studying the doctor's notations.

I long for the sound of his voice.

Two months pass in this manner. I am running a drone personally – I enjoy this world when viewed from a microscopic level – when the door whooshes open.

I spin my miniscule body around and freeze, nearly forgetting to flap my metallic wings.

He stands there. The false sunset casts a red glow over his clean-shaven face. His lovely hair has been buzzed off, exposing the pinkish skin beneath a gray mist of stubble. His uniform no longer drapes over his body; he has gained back some of the weight due to enforced meals and IVs.

His gaze roves over the bio-dome.

"You're here," he says, voice cracking. "I know you are."

If I had a heart, it'd be already broken. And if I had a broken heart, it would now shatter into even smaller, sharper fragments that would cut the inside of me to ribbons.

I don't answer him. I'm choking on conflicting synth-pulses – pain and joy, agony and hope. I want to fly to him. Settle on his hand and peer into his blue-green eyes.

But I don't.

I set the bee on autopilot – something I've been doing a lot lately – and simply watch Gordon.

He sits on the bench like he used to. He isn't whole, despite the therapy and drugs. His shoulders slump, but the muscles in his neck remain tense.

I don't want to break him again. This keeps me silent and aching.

* * *

We've found a way to live, though I suspect it isn't healthy. I can't bear to leave him. I know I should. I should let him go so he can let me go.

But I can't. Hours and days spent in his company, memories made and replayed inside me, have written love into me and I cannot cut it out.

He practically lives in the bio-dome. Even has a cot he sleeps on. Once again, I monitor his dreams. It's the closest we come to touching. They remain as violent and dark as they have always been.

I still don't speak. We pass so many hours in silence. I have never confirmed for him that I'm here, but somehow he knows.

He chronicles the daily actions of every pollination drone. All one hundred and eleven of them. He's getting skilled at telling which one I'm inhabiting at any given moment. His journals about the bees are a treasure trove of knowledge and data. He is only beginning to realize that a pattern is developing in the drones. They're evolving.

Just as he used to, he seems to draw some peace from the bees. He still searches for me, but he grows more passionate about charting the drones' progression. He begins to name them, noting their budding personalities.

I'm buzzing around the corn's silky tassels when I realize he's headed my way. I fight the instinct to dart away – or dart toward him. He stands before me and reaches out. His fingers cradle this metallic drone body. He raises me to eye level and stares into my camera eyes. Absolutely still. Silent. A bit of wildness hazes his eyes – it hasn't left since he snapped.

The drone's sensors register the heat passing from his fingers to my wings and in a way, it's like touching, it's like feeling.

"Hello, Tango."

His voice breaks me. I want to cry out – so much synth-pain and pleasure ripping through me. I want to speak his name in return. I want to hold him, but these wings are too tiny and have no digits. I want to drown in his voice and make him tell me stories or elaborate on his dreams once again.

I want to reach out.

But I love him – a love that increasingly invades every line of my software – too much to risk breaking him again.

So I transfer myself to another drone. I fly low to the soil-filled containers. I am heavy with the weight of my love and my pain. And I feel, for the first time, very human. For isn't it humans alone who are just stubborn enough to let this torturous cycle of pain and pleasure begin once again? And again. And again.

Makeisha in Time

Rachael K. Jones

MAKEISHA HAS ALWAYS been able to bend the fourth dimension, but no one will believe her. She has been a soldier, a sheriff, a pilot, a prophet, a poet, a ninja, a nun, a conductor (of trains and symphonies), a cordwainer, a comedian, a carpetbagger, a troubadour, a queen and a receptionist. She has shot arrows, guns, and cannons. She speaks an extinct Ethiopian dialect with a perfect accent. She knows a recipe for mead that is measured in aurochs horns; and with a katana, she is deadly.

Her jumps happen intermittently. She will be yanked from the present without warning, and live a whole lifetime in the past. When she dies, she returns right back to where she left, restored to a younger age. It usually happens when she is deep in conversation with her boss, or arguing with her mother-in-law, or during a book club meeting just when it is her turn to speak. One moment, Makeisha is firmly grounded in the timeline of her birth, and the next, she is elsewhere. Elsewhen.

Makeisha has seen the sunrise over prehistoric shores, where the ocean writhed with soft, slimy things that bore the promise of dung beetles, Archeopteryx and Edgar Allan Poe. She has seen the sun set upon long-forgotten empires. When Makeisha skims a map of the continents, she sees a fractured Pangaea. She never knows where she will jump next, or how long she will stay, but she is never afraid. Makeisha has been doing this all her life.

The hardest part is coming back. Once, when she was twelve, she was slouched in the pew at church when she felt the past tug. Makeisha found herself floundering in the roiling ocean of the Mediterranean, only to be saved by Moorish pirates who hauled her aboard in the nick of time. At first the bewildered men and women treasured their catch as a mascot and good luck charm. Later, after nearly ten years of fine seacraft and fearless warfare, they made her captain of the ship. Makeisha took to piracy like sheet music. She could climb ropes and hold her grog with the best sailors, and even after losing an eye in a gunpowder explosion, she never once wept and wished herself home.

The day came when, at the pasha's command, she set sail to intercept Spanish invaders in Ottoman waters. It was a hot night when they sighted the lanterns of the enemy shuddering on the waves. Makeisha's crew pulled their ship astern the enemy's vessel in the dark and fog after midnight. She gave the order – charge! – her deep voice booming through the mists, echoed by the shouts of her pirates as they swung on ropes over the sliver of ocean between the ships. And suddenly an explosion, and a pinching sensation in her midriff, and she was twelve again in the church pew, staring at her soft palms through two perfect eyes. That was when she finally wept, so loud and hard the reverend stopped his sermon to scold her. Her father grounded her for a week for disturbing the service like that.

People often get angry with Makeisha when she returns from her jumps. She can't control her confusion, the way the room spins like she is drunk, and how for days and weeks afterward she cannot settle back into who she was, because the truth is, she isn't the same. Each time she returns from the past, she carries another lifetime nestled within her like the shell of a matryoshka doll.

Once, after the fall of the Roman Empire, she joined a peasant uprising in Bavaria, and charging quickly from fiefdom to fiefdom, their band pushed back the warlords to the foothills of the Alps. Those who survived sued for mercy, begged her not to raze their fields, pledged fealty to her. As a condition of the peace, Makeisha demanded their daughters in marriage to seal the political alliance. The little kings, too afraid of the Barbarian Queen to shout their umbrage, conceded. They even attended the weddings, where Makeisha stood with her sword peace-tied at her waist and took the trembling hand of each Bavarian princess into her own.

Once the wedding guests left, Makeisha gathered her wives together in the throne room. "Please," she said to them, "help me. I need good women I can trust to run this kingdom right."

With their help, she established a stable state in those war-torn days. In time, all her wives made excellent deputies, ambassadors, sheriffs, and knights in her court.

Makeisha had been especially broken up when her time in Bavaria was cut short by a bout of pneumonia. Many of her wives had grown to be dear friends of hers, and she wondered for months and months what had become of them and their children, and whether her fiefdom had lasted beyond her disappearance.

She wanted to talk with her best friend Philippa, to cry about it, but her phone calls went unanswered, and so did her emails. Makeisha could not remember when she had last spent time with her friends in the present. It was so hard to remember when her weeks and months were interspersed with whole lifetimes of friends and lovers and enemies. The present was a stop-motion film, a book interrupted mid-page and abandoned for years at a time. And when she did return, she carried with her another death.

Makeisha does not fear death anymore. She has died many times before, but she always awakens in the present, whole and alive as before the jump. She does not know what would happen if she died in the present. Perhaps she would awaken in the future. She has never tried to find out.

She cannot remember her first death. She probably died hundreds of times in her infancy, before she was old enough to walk. Her jumps leave her in the wilderness or ocean more often than not, and when she does arrive near civilization, few will take pity on a strange, abandoned child who cannot explain her presence. Makeisha's mother has often joked about her appetite, how from the time she was a baby, she ate like a person on the verge of starvation. Her mother does not know how close this is to the truth. These days, Makeisha wears her extra pounds with pride, knowing how often they have been her salvation.

When Philippa finally returns her calls, she reams Makeisha for slighting her all year, for the forgotten birthday, for the missed housewarming party. Makeisha apologizes like she always does. They meet up in person for a catch-up over coffee, and Makeisha resolves that this time she will be present for her friend. They are deep in conversation when she feels the tug, just as Philippa is admitting that she is afraid of what the future may bring. No, thinks Makeisha when she finds herself blinking on the edge of a sluggish river under the midday sun. Two white bulls have lifted their heads to stare at her, water dripping from their jowls.

Makeisha struggles to keep the conversation fresh in her head as she casts around for a quick way home. She chooses the river. It is hard, that first time, to make herself inhale, to still her windmilling arms, to let death take this matryoshka life so she can hasten back to the present.

She has lost the thread of the conversation anyway when she snaps back to Philippa's kitchen. "Migraine," she explains, rubbing away the memory of pain from her dizzy head, and Philippa feeds her two aspirin and some hot mint tea.

Makeisha resolves to do better next time, and eventually, she does. On her first date with Carl, she strangles herself with strings from the lute of a Hittite bard. On their wedding day, she detours to a vast desert that she cannot place, which she escapes by crawling into a scorpion nest. That death was painful. The next time she jumps (two days later, on their honeymoon), she takes the time to learn the proper way to open her wrists with a sharp-edged rock.

Her husband believes her when she says it's migraines. Makeisha learned long ago to lie about the jumping. When she was a child, she attempted to prove it to her mother by singing in Egyptian, but her mother just laughed and sent her to do the dishes. She received worse when she contradicted her history teachers. It was intolerable, sitting in school in the body of a child but with the memories of innumerable lifetimes, while incomplete truths and half-truths and outright lies were written on the board. The adults called a conference about her attention-seeking behavior, and she learned to keep her mouth shut. It is a lesson she has never forgotten.

All of it – the self-imposed silence, the suicides, the banishing of her fantastic past to the basement of her brain – these are the price of a normal life, of friendships and a marriage and a steady job. Mundane though it is, Makeisha reminds herself that this life is different from the other ones. Irreplaceable. Real.

Still, she misses the past, which always felt more real to her, where she has lived most of her life. She reads history books with a black marker and strikes out the bits that make her scoff. Then, with a red pen, she writes in the margins all the names she can recall, all the forgotten people who did not matter as much as George Washington and Louis XIV. When Carl asks, she explains how the world has always belonged to more than just the great men who were kings and presidents and generals, but for some reason, no one wrote it down.

"I think you're trying too hard," he says, and she hates the pity in his eyes when he holds up his hands and adds, "but if it makes you feel happy, keep on with it."

One day, as a surprise, her husband drove her four hours to a museum hosting an exhibit on medieval history. Makeisha screeched and grabbed Carl's arm when she saw the posters at the entrance: eighth-century Bavaria! The memories were still so fresh. It had been five years ago and dozens of self-murdered lives when she was torn from her thriving kingdom, from her deputy-wives and her warband. Her face was composed as she purchased tickets, but she bounced on the balls of her feet all the way to the front of the line.

It was the first time she had encountered any proof of a previous life. It felt like a dream. Euphoria flared in her breast when she peered into glass cases that held familiar objects, old and worn but recognizable all the same, the proof of her long years of warfare and wisdom and canny leadership. A lead comb, most of its bristles missing, its colored enamel long ago worn to gray. It had belonged to Jutte, perhaps – she had such fine long hair, although she had kept it bound tightly for her work as a doctor. A thin gold ring she had given to dark-eyed Berchte in commemoration of her knighthood. And the best of all: a silver coin stamped with her own stylized profile, her broad nose jutting past her Bavarian war helm.

There was a placard on the glass. Makeisha read it thrice, each time a little slower, thinking perhaps she'd missed something. But no. It read: Early medieval objects from the court of a foreign king. He reigned in Bavaria for about thirty years.

He? He? Makeisha stormed back to the entrance, demanded to speak with a manager, her vision swimming a violent red, her hand groping for a pommel she did not wear anymore. It was wrong. It was all wrong, wrong, wrong. Her wives, assigned a husband and stripped of their deputyship! Their legacy, handed to a manufactured person! Carl begged her to tell him what was wrong. Makeisha realized she was shouting oaths in ancient German, and that was when she felt the familiar tug in her navel, and found herself spinning back, back, further back than she had gone last time, until she found herself on an empty beach beneath a moon with a smooth, craterless face.

Her practiced eye spotted three ways to die on its first sweep (drowning, impaling, crushing), but there was Jutte's comb to consider, and that placard. When she gave up time travel, she never thought she had surrendered her legacy, too.

Makeisha turned her back on the ocean and walked into the woods, busying herself with building a fire and assembling the tools she would need for her stay, however long it may be. She had learned to be resourceful and unafraid of the unfamiliar creaks and groans in the ferny green of the prehistoric underbrush.

She chipped a cascade of sparks into her kindling, and that is when Makeisha formed her plan.

She is done with the present, with the endless self-murder, with the repression and suffocation and low stakes.

A woman unafraid to die can do anything she wants. A woman who can endure starvation and pain and deprivation can be her own boss, set her own agenda. The one thing she cannot do is to make them remember that she did it.

Makeisha is going to change that.

No more suicides, then. Makeisha embraces the jumps again. She is a boulder thrown into the waters of time. In eighth century Norway, she joins a band of Viking women. They are callous but good-humored, and they take her rage in stride, as though she has nothing to explain. They give her a sword taller than she is, but she learns to swing it anyway, and to sing loudly into the wind when one of the slain is buried with her hoard, sword folded on her breast.

When she returns to the present, Makeisha has work to do. She will stop mid-sentence, spin on her heel, and head for the books, leaving an astonished coworker, or friend, or her husband calling after her.

She pours everything into the search for her own past. One of her contacts sends her an email about a Moorish pirate, a woman, making a name for herself among the Ottomans. A Spanish monk wrote about her last voyage, the way she leapt upon her prey like a gale in the night, how her battle-cry chilled the blood. Makeisha's grin holds until the part where the monk called her a whore.

This is accepted without question as factual by the man writing the book.

She is obsessed. Makeisha almost loses her job because of her frequent forgetfulness, her accidental rudeness. Her desk is drowned in ancient maps. Her purse is crammed with reams of genealogies.

In her living room, which has been lined from wall-to-wall with history books ever since Carl moved out, Makeisha tries to count the lives stacked inside her. There are so many of them. They are crowding to get out. She once tried to calculate how many years she had been alive. It was more than a thousand. And what did they amount to? Makeisha is smeared across the timeline, but no one ever gets her quite right. Those who found the cairn of her Viking band assumed the swords and armor meant the graves of men. A folio of her sonnets, anonymous after much copying, are attributed to her assistant Giorgio.

"You're building a fake identity," Philippa tells her one day, daring the towers of books and dried-out markers to bring Makeisha some soup. "There weren't any black women in ancient Athens. There weren't any in China. You need to come to grips with reality, my friend."

"There were too," says Makeisha fiercely, proudly. "I know there were. I know it. They were just erased. Forgotten."

"I'm sure there were a few exceptions. But women just didn't do the kind of things you're interested in."

Makeisha says, "It doesn't matter what I do, if people refuse to believe it."

Her jumps are subdued after that. She turns to the written word for immortality. Makeisha leaves love poetry on the walls of Aztec tombs in carefully colored Nahuatl pictograms. She presses cuneiform into soft clay, documenting the exploits of the proud women whose names are written in red in the margins of her history books. She records the names of her lovers in careful hanzi strokes with horsehair bristles in bamboo books.

Even these, the records she makes herself, do not survive intact. Sometimes the names are replaced by others deemed more remarkable, more credible, by the scribes who came after. Sometimes they are erased entirely. Mostly, the books just fade into dust with time. She takes comfort knowing that she is not unique, that the chorus of lost voices is thundering.

She is fading from the present. She forgets to eat between jumps, loses weight. Sometimes she starves to death when she lands in an isolated spot.

Carl catches her one day at the mailbox. "Sorry for just showing up. You haven't returned my calls," he explains, offering her a sheaf of papers.

Makeisha accepts them and examines the red-stamped first page of their divorce papers.

"You need to sign here," Carl says, pointing upside down at the bottom of the sheet. "Also on the next page. Please?"

The last word carries a pleading note. Makeisha notes his puffy eyes and a single white hair standing out in the black nest of his beard. "How long has it been?" she asks. It has been at least three lifetimes since he left, but she isn't sure.

"Too long," he says. "Please, I just need your signature so we can move on."

She pats her pockets and finds a red pen. Makeisha wonders how many decades or centuries until this signature is also altered or lost or purposely erased, but she touches pen to paper anyway.

Halfway through her signature, she spends twenty-six years sleeping under the stars with the Aborigines, and when she comes back, the rest of her name trails aimlessly down the sheet. Carl doesn't seem to notice.

After he leaves, she escapes to India for a lifetime, where she ponders whether her time travel is a punishment or purgatory.

When she returns to the present again, Makeisha weeps like she did when she was twelve, and her heart was breaking for her days as a pirate. Perhaps it is not the past that is yanking her away. Perhaps the present is crowding her out. And perhaps she has finally come to agree with the sentiment.

In her living room, among the towers of blacked-out books, Makeisha sees six ways to die from where she stands. Perhaps the way out is forward. Break through the last matryoshka shell like a hatchling into daylight.

But no. No. The self-murders were never for herself. Not once. Makeisha is resilient. She is resourceful, and she has been bending the fourth dimension all her life, whether anyone recognizes it or not.

A woman who has been pushed her whole life will eventually learn to push back.

Makeisha reaches forward into the air. With skillful fingers that have killed and healed and mastered the cello, she pulls the future toward her.

She has not returned.

The Ego Machine

Henry Kuttner

I

NICHOLAS MARTIN looked up at the robot across the desk.

"I'm not going to ask what you want," he said, in a low, restrained voice. "I already know. Just go away and tell St Cyr I approve. Tell him I think it's wonderful, putting a robot in the picture. We've had everything else by now, except the Rockettes. But clearly a quiet little play about Christmas among the Portuguese fishermen on the Florida coast must have a robot. Only, why not six robots? Tell him I suggest a baker's dozen. Go away."

"Was your mother's name Helena Glinska?" the robot asked.

"It was not," Martin said.

"Ah, then she must have been the Great Hairy One," the robot murmured.

Martin took his feet off the desk and sat up slowly.

"It's quite all right," the robot said hastily. "You've been chosen for an ecological experiment, that's all. But it won't hurt. Robots are perfectly normal life forms where I come from, so you needn't – "

"Shut up," Martin said. "Robot indeed, you – you bit-player! This time St Cyr has gone too far." He began to shake slightly all over, with some repressed but strong emotion. The intercom box on the desk caught his eye, and he stabbed a finger at one of the switches. "Get me Miss Ashby! Right away!"

"I'm so sorry," the robot said apologetically. "Have I made a mistake? The threshold fluctuations in the neurons always upset my mnemonic norm when I temporalize. Isn't this a crisis-point in your life?"

Martin breathed hard, which seemed to confirm the robot's assumption.

"Exactly," it said. "The ecological imbalance approaches a peak that may destroy the life-form, unless ... mm-m. Now either you're about to be stepped on by a mammoth, locked in an iron mask, assassinated by helots, or – is this Sanskrit I'm speaking?" He shook his gleaming head. "Perhaps I should have got off fifty years ago, but I thought – sorry. Goodbye," he added hastily as Martin raised an angry glare.

Then the robot lifted a finger to each corner of his naturally rigid mouth, and moved his fingers horizontally in opposite directions, as though sketching an apologetic smile.

"No, don't go away," Martin said. "I want you right here, where the sight of you can refuel my rage in case it's needed. I wish to God I could get mad and stay mad," he added plaintively, gazing at the telephone.

"Are you sure your mother's name wasn't Helena Glinska?" the robot asked. It pinched thumb and forefinger together between its nominal brows, somehow giving the impression of a worried frown.

"Naturally I'm sure," Martin snapped.

"You aren't married yet, then? To Anastasia Zakharina-Koshkina?"

"Not yet or ever," Martin replied succinctly. The telephone rang. He snatched it up.

* * *

"Hello, Nick," said Erika Ashby's calm voice. "Something wrong?"

Instantly the fires of rage went out of Martin's eyes, to be replaced by a tender, rose-pink glow. For some years now he had given Erika, his very competent agent, ten percent of his take. He had also longed hopelessly to give her approximately a pound of flesh – the cardiac muscle, to put it in cold, unromantic terms. Martin did not; he put it in no terms at all, since whenever he tried to propose marriage to Erika he was taken with such fits of modesty that he could only babble o' green fields.

"Well," Erika repeated. "Something wrong?"

"Yes," Martin said, drawing a long breath. "Can St Cyr make me marry somebody named Anastasia Zakharina-Koshkina?"

"What a wonderful memory you have," the robot put in mournfully. "Mine used to be, before I started temporalizing. But even radioactive neurons won't stand – "

"Nominally you're still entitled to life, liberty, et cetera," Erika said. "But I'm busy right now, Nick. Can't it wait till I see you?"

"When?"

"Didn't you get my message?" Erika demanded.

"Of course not," Martin said, angrily. "I've suspected for some time that all my incoming calls have to be cleared by St Cyr. Somebody might try to smuggle in a word of hope, or possibly a file." His voice brightened. "Planning a jailbreak?"

"Oh, this is outrageous," Erika said. "Some day St Cyr's going to go too far – "

"Not while he's got DeeDee behind him," Martin said gloomily. Summit Studios would sooner have made a film promoting atheism than offend their top box-office star, DeeDee Fleming. Even Tolliver Watt, who owned Summit lock, stock and barrel, spent wakeful nights because St Cyr refused to let the lovely DeeDee sign a long-term contract.

"Nevertheless, Watt's no fool," Erika said. "I still think we could get him to give you a contract release if we could make him realize what a rotten investment you are. There isn't much time, though."

"Why not?"

"I told you – oh. Of course you don't know. He's leaving for Paris tomorrow morning."

Martin moaned. "Then I'm doomed," he said. "They'll pick up my option automatically next week and I'll never draw a free breath again. Erika, do something!"

"I'm going to," Erika said. "That's exactly what I want to see you about. Ah," she added suddenly, "now I understand why St Cyr stopped my message. He was afraid. Nick, do you know what we've got to do?"

"See Watt?" Nick hazarded unhappily. "But Erika – "

"See Watt alone," Erika amplified.

"Not if St Cyr can help it," Nick reminded her.

"Exactly. Naturally St Cyr doesn't want us to talk to Watt privately. We might make him see reason. But this time, Nick, we've simply got to manage it somehow. One of us is going to talk to Watt while the other keeps St Cyr at bay. Which do you choose?"

"Neither," Martin said promptly.

"Oh, Nick! I can't do the whole thing alone. Anybody'd think you were afraid of St Cyr."

"I am afraid of St Cyr," Martin said.

"Nonsense. What could he actually do to you?"

"He could terrorize me. He does it all the time. Erika, he says I'm indoctrinating beautifully. Doesn't it make your blood run cold? Look at all the other writers he's indoctrinated."

"I know. I saw one of them on Main Street last week, delving into garbage cans. Do you want to end up that way? Then stand up for your rights!"

"Ah," said the robot wisely, nodding. "Just as I thought. A crisis-point."

"Shut up," Martin said. "No, not you, Erika. I'm sorry."

"So am I," Erika said tartly. "For a moment I thought you'd acquired a backbone."

"If I were somebody like Hemingway – " Martin began in a miserable voice.

"Did you say Hemingway?" the robot inquired. "Is this the Kinsey-Hemingway era? Then I must be right. You're Nicholas Martin, the next subject. Martin, Martin? Let me see – oh yes, the Disraeli type, that's it." He rubbed his forehead with a grating sound. "Oh, my poor neuron thresholds! Now I remember."

* * *

"Nick, can you hear me?" Erika's voice inquired. "I'm coming over there right away. Brace yourself. We're going to beard St Cyr in his den and convince Watt you'll never make a good screen-writer. Now – "

"But St Cyr won't ever admit that," Martin cried. "He doesn't know the meaning of the word failure. He says so. He's going to make me into a screenwriter or kill me."

"Remember what happened to Ed Cassidy?" Erika reminded him grimly. "St Cyr didn't make him into a screen-writer."

"True. Poor old Ed," Martin said, with a shiver.

"All right, then. I'm on my way. Anything else?"

"Yes!" Martin cried, drawing a deep breath. "Yes, there is! I love you madly!"

But the words never got past his glottis. Opening and closing his mouth noiselessly, the cowardly playwright finally clenched his teeth and tried again. A faint, hopeless squeak vibrated the telephone's disk. Martin let his shoulders slump hopelessly. It was clear he could never propose to anybody, not even a harmless telephone.

"Did you say something?" Erika asked. "Well, goodbye then."

"Wait a minute," Martin said, his eyes suddenly falling once more upon the robot. Speechless on one subject only, he went on rapidly, "I forgot to tell you. Watt and the nest-fouling St Cyr have just hired a mock-up phony robot to play in Angelina Noel!"

But the line was dead.

"I'm not a phony," the robot said, hurt.

Martin fell back in his chair and stared at his guest with dull, hopeless eyes. "Neither was King Kong," he remarked. "Don't start feeding me some line St Cyr's told you to pull. I know he's trying to break my nerve. He'll probably do it, too. Look what he's done to my play already. Why Fred Waring? I don't mind Fred Waring in his proper place. There he's fine. But not in Angelina Noel. Not as the Portuguese captain of a fishing boat manned by his entire band, accompanied by Dan Dailey singing Napoli to DeeDee Fleming in a mermaid's tail – "

Self-stunned by this recapitulation, Martin put his arms on the desk, his head in his hands, and to his horror found himself giggling. The telephone rang. Martin groped for the instrument without rising from his semi-recumbent position.

"Who?" he asked shakily. "Who? St Cyr – "

A hoarse bellow came over the wire. Martin sat bolt upright, seizing the phone desperately with both hands.

"Listen!" he cried. "Will you let me finish what I'm going to say, just for once? Putting a robot in Angelina Noel is simply – "

"I do not hear what you say," roared a heavy voice. "Your idea stinks. Whatever it is. Be at Theater One for yesterday's rushes! At once!"

"But wait – "

St Cyr belched and hung up. Martin's strangling hands tightened briefly on the telephone. But it was no use. The real strangle-hold was the one St Cyr had around Martin's throat, and it had been tightening now for nearly thirteen weeks. Or had it been thirteen years? Looking backward, Martin could scarcely believe that only a short time ago he had been a free man, a successful Broadway playwright, the author of the hit play Angelina Noel. Then had come St Cyr...

A snob at heart, the director loved getting his clutches on hit plays and name writers. Summit Studios, he had roared at Martin, would follow the original play exactly and would give Martin the final okay on the script, provided he signed a thirteen-week contract to help write the screen treatment. This had seemed too good to be true – and was.

Martin's downfall lay partly in the fine print and partly in the fact that Erika Ashby had been in the hospital with a bad attack of influenza at the time. Buried in legal verbiage was a clause that bound Martin to five years of servitude with Summit should they pick up his option. Next week they would certainly do just that, unless justice prevailed.

* * *

"I think I need a drink," Martin said unsteadily. "Or several." He glanced toward the robot. "I wonder if you'd mind getting me that bottle of Scotch from the bar over there."

"But I am here to conduct an experiment in optimum ecology," said the robot.

Martin closed his eyes. "Pour me a drink," he pleaded. "Please. Then put the glass in my hand, will you? It's not much to ask. After all, we're both human beings, aren't we?"

"Well, no," the robot said, placing a brimming glass in Martin's groping fingers. Martin drank. Then he opened his eyes and blinked at the tall highball glass in his hand. The robot had filled it to the brim with Scotch. Martin turned a wondering gaze on his metallic companion.

"You must do a lot of drinking yourself," he said thoughtfully. "I suppose tolerance can be built up. Go ahead. Help yourself. Take the rest of the bottle."

The robot placed the tip of a finger above each eye and slid the fingers upward, as though raising his eyebrows inquiringly.

"Go on, have a jolt," Martin urged. "Or don't you want to break bread with me, under the circumstances?"

"How can I?" the robot asked. "I'm a robot." His voice sounded somewhat wistful. "What happens?" he inquired. "Is it a lubricatory or a fueling mechanism?"

Martin glanced at his brimming glass.

"Fueling," he said tersely. "High octane. You really believe in staying in character, don't you? Why not – "

"Oh, the principle of irritation," the robot interrupted. "I see. Just like fermented mammoth's milk."

Martin choked. "Have you ever drunk fermented mammoth's milk?" he inquired.

"How could I?" the robot asked. "But I've seen it done." He drew a straight line vertically upward between his invisible eyebrows, managing to look wistful. "Of course my world is perfectly functional and functionally perfect, but I can't help finding temporalizing a fascina – " He broke off. "I'm wasting space-time. Ah. Now. Mr Martin, would you be willing to – "

"Oh, have a drink," Martin said. "I feel hospitable. Go ahead, indulge me, will you? My pleasures are few. And I've got to go and be terrorized in a minute, anyhow. If you can't get that mask off I'll send for a straw. You can step out of character long enough for one jolt, can't you?"

"I'd like to try it," the robot said pensively. "Ever since I noticed the effect fermented mammoth's milk had on the boys, it's been on my mind, rather. Quite easy for a human, of course. Technically it's simple enough, I see now. The irritation just increases the frequency of the brain's kappa waves, as with boosted voltage, but since electrical voltage never existed in pre-robot times – "

"It did," Martin said, taking another drink. "I mean, it does. What do you call that, a mammoth?" He indicated the desk lamp.

The robot's jaw dropped.

"That?" he asked in blank amazement. "Why – why then all those telephone poles and dynamos and lighting-equipment I noticed in this era are powered by electricity!"

"What did you think they were powered by?" Martin asked coldly.

"Slaves," the robot said, examining the lamp. He switched it on, blinked, and then unscrewed the bulb. "Voltage, you say?"

"Don't be a fool," Martin said. "You're overplaying your part. I've got to get going in a minute. Do you want a jolt or don't you?"

"Well," the robot said, "I don't want to seem unsociable. This ought to work." So saying, he stuck his finger in the lamp-socket. There was a brief, crackling flash. The robot withdrew his finger.

"F(t) – " he said, and swayed slightly. Then his fingers came up and sketched a smile that seemed, somehow, to express delighted surprise.

"Fff(t)!" he said, and went on rather thickly, "F(t) integral between plus and minus infinity ... a-sub-n to e..."

Martin's eyes opened wide with shocked horror. Whether a doctor or a psychiatrist should be called in was debatable, but it was perfectly evident that this was a case for the medical profession, and the sooner the better. Perhaps the police, too. The bit-player in the robot suit was clearly as mad as a hatter. Martin poised indecisively, waiting for his lunatic guest either to drop dead or spring at his throat.

The robot appeared to be smacking his lips, with faint clicking sounds.

"Why, that's wonderful," he said. "AC, too."

"Y-you're not dead?" Martin inquired shakily.

"I'm not even alive," the robot murmured. "The way you'd understand it, that is. Ah – thanks for the jolt."

* * *

Martin stared at the robot with the wildest dawning of surmise.

"Why – " he gasped. "Why – you're a robot!"

"Certainly I'm a robot," his guest said. "What slow minds you pre-robots had. Mine's working like lightning now." He stole a drunkard's glance at the desk-lamp. "F(t) – I mean, if you counted the kappa waves of my radio-atomic brain now, you'd be amazed how the frequency's increased." He paused thoughtfully. "F(t)," he added.

Moving quite slowly, like a man under water, Martin lifted his glass and drank whiskey. Then, cautiously, he looked up at the robot again.

"F(t) – " he said, paused, shuddered, and drank again. That did it. "I'm drunk," he said with an air of shaken relief. "That must be it. I was almost beginning to believe – "

"Oh, nobody believes I'm a robot at first," the robot said. "You'll notice I showed up in a movie lot, where I wouldn't arouse suspicion. I'll appear to Ivan Vasilovich in an alchemist's lab, and he'll jump to the conclusive I'm an automaton. Which, of course, I am. Then there's a Uighur on my list – I'll appear to him in a shaman's hut and he'll assume I'm a devil. A matter of ecologicologic."

"Then you're a devil?" Martin inquired, seizing on the only plausible solution.

"No, no, no. I'm a robot. Don't you understand anything?"

"I don't even know who I am, now," Martin said. "For all I know, I'm a faun and you're a human child. I don't think this Scotch is doing me as much good as I'd – "

"Your name is Nicholas Martin," the robot said patiently. "And mine is ENIAC."

"Eniac?"

"ENIAC," the robot corrected, capitalizing. "ENIAC Gamma the Ninety-Third."

So saying, he unslung a sack from his metallic shoulder and began to rummage out length upon length of what looked like red silk ribbon with a curious metallic lustre. After approximately a quarter-mile of it had appeared, a crystal football helmet emerged attached to its end. A gleaming red-green stone was set on each side of the helmet.

"Just over the temporal lobes, you see," the robot explained, indicating the jewels. "Now you just set it on your head, like this – "

"Oh no I don't," Martin said, withdrawing his head with the utmost rapidity. "Neither do you, my friend. What's the idea? I don't like the looks of that gimmick. I particularly don't like those two red garnets on the sides. They look like eyes."

"Those are artificial eclogite," the robot assured him. "They simply have a high dielectric constant. It's merely a matter of altering the normal thresholds of the neuron memory-circuits. All thinking is based on memory, you know. The strength of your associations – the emotional indices of your memories – channel your actions and decisions, and the ecologizer simply changes the voltage of your brain so the thresholds are altered."

"Is that all it does?" Martin asked suspiciously.

"Well, now," the robot said with a slight air of evasion. "I didn't intend to mention it, but since you ask – it also imposes the master-matrix of your character type. But since that's the prototype of your character in the first place, it will simply enable you to make the most of your potential ability, hereditary and acquired. It will make you react to your environment in the way that best assures your survival."

"Not me, it won't," Martin said firmly. "Because you aren't going to put that thing on my head."

The robot sketched a puzzled frown. "Oh," he said after a pause. "I haven't explained yet, have I? It's very simple. Would you be willing to take part in a valuable socio-cultural experiment for the benefit of all mankind?"

"No," Martin said.

"But you don't know what it is yet," the robot said plaintively. "You'll be the only one to refuse, after I've explained everything thoroughly. By the way, can you understand me all right?"

Martin laughed hollowly. "Natch," he said.

"Good," the robot said, relieved. "That may be one trouble with my memory. I had to record so many languages before I could temporalize. Sanskrit's very simple, but medieval Russian's confusing, and as for Uighur – however! The purpose of this experiment is to promote the most successful pro-survival relationship between man and his environment. Instant adaptation is what we're aiming at, and we hope to get it by minimizing the differential between individual and environment. In other words, the right reaction at the right time. Understand?"

"Of course not," Martin said. "What nonsense you talk."

"There are," the robot said rather wearily, "only a limited number of character matrices possible, depending first on the arrangement of the genes within the chromosomes, and later upon environmental additions. Since environments tend to repeat – like societies, you know – an organizational pattern isn't hard to lay out, along the Kaldekooz time-scale. You follow me so far?"

"By the Kaldekooz time-scale, yes," Martin said.

"I was always lucid," the robot remarked a little vainly, nourishing a swirl of red ribbon.

"Keep that thing away from me," Martin complained. "Drunk I may be, but I have no intention of sticking my neck out that far."

"Of course you'll do it," the robot said firmly. "Nobody's ever refused yet. And don't bicker with me or you'll get me confused and I'll have to take another jolt of voltage. Then there's no telling how confused I'll be. My memory gives me enough trouble when I temporalize. Time-travel always raises the synaptic delay threshold, but the trouble is it's so variable. That's why I got you mixed up with Ivan at first. But I don't visit him till after I've seen you – I'm running the test chronologically, and nineteen-fifty-two comes before fifteen-seventy, of course."

"It doesn't," Martin said, tilting the glass to his lips. "Not even in Hollywood does nineteen-fifty-two come before fifteen-seventy."

"I'm using the Kaldekooz time-scale," the robot explained. "But really only for convenience. Now do you want the ideal ecological differential or don't you? Because – " Here he flourished the red ribbon again, peered into the helmet, looked narrowly at Martin, and shook his head.

"I'm sorry," the robot said. "I'm afraid this won't work. Your head's too small. Not enough brain-room, I suppose. This helmet's for an eight and a half head, and yours is much too – "

"My head is eight and a half," Martin protested with dignity.

"Can't be," the robot said cunningly. "If it were, the helmet would fit, and it doesn't. Too big."

"It does fit," Martin said.

"That's the trouble with arguing with pre-robot species," ENIAC said, as to himself. "Low, brutish, unreasoning. No wonder, when their heads are so small. Now Mr Martin – " He spoke as though to a small, stupid, stubborn child. "Try to understand. This helmet's size eight and a half. Your head is unfortunately so very small that the helmet wouldn't fit – "

"Blast it!" cried the infuriated Martin, caution quite lost between Scotch and annoyance. "It does fit! Look here!" Recklessly he snatched the helmet and clapped it firmly on his head. "It fits perfectly!"

"I erred," the robot acknowledged, with such a gleam in his eye that Martin, suddenly conscious of his rashness, jerked the helmet from his head and dropped it on the desk. ENIAC quietly picked it up and put it back into his sack, stuffing the red ribbon in after it with rapid motions. Martin watched, baffled, until ENIAC had finished, gathered together the mouth of the sack, swung it on his shoulder again, and turned toward the door.

"Goodbye," the robot said. "And thank you."

"For what?" Martin demanded.

"For your cooperation," the robot said.

"I won't cooperate," Martin told him flatly. "It's no use. Whatever fool treatment it is you're selling, I'm not going to – "

"Oh, you've already had the ecology treatment," ENIAC replied blandly. "I'll be back tonight to renew the charge. It lasts only twelve hours."

"What!"

ENIAC moved his forefingers outward from the corners of his mouth, sketching a polite smile. Then he stepped through the door and closed it behind him.

Martin made a faint squealing sound, like a stuck but gagged pig.

Something was happening inside his head.

II

NICHOLAS MARTIN felt like a man suddenly thrust under an ice-cold shower. No, not cold – steaming hot. Perfumed, too. The wind that blew in from the open window bore with it a frightful stench of gasoline, sagebrush, paint, and – from the distant commissary – ham sandwiches.

"Drunk," he thought frantically. "I'm drunk – or crazy!" He sprang up and spun around wildly; then catching sight of a crack in the hardwood floor he tried to walk along it. "Because if I can walk a straight line," he thought, "I'm not drunk. I'm only crazy..." It was not a very comforting thought.

He could walk it, all right. He could walk a far straighter line than the crack, which he saw now was microscopically jagged. He had, in fact, never felt such a sense of location and equilibrium in his life. His experiment carried him across the room to a wall-mirror, and as he straightened to look into it, suddenly all confusion settled and ceased. The violent sensory perceptions leveled off and returned to normal.

Everything was quiet. Everything was all right.

Martin met his own eyes in the mirror.

Everything was not all right.

He was stone cold sober. The Scotch he had drunk might as well have been spring-water. He leaned closer to the mirror, trying to stare through his own eyes into the depths of his brain. For something extremely odd was happening in there. All over his brain, tiny shutters were beginning to move, some sliding up till only a narrow crack remained, through which the beady little eyes of neurons could be seen peeping, some sliding down with faint crashes, revealing the agile, spidery forms of still other neurons scuttling for cover.

Altered thresholds, changing the yes-and-no reaction time of the memory-circuits, with their key emotional indices and associations ... huh?

The robot!

Martin's head swung toward the closed office door. But he made no further move. The look of blank panic on his face very slowly, quite unconsciously, began to change. The robot ... could wait.

Automatically Martin raised his hand, as though to adjust an invisible monocle. Behind him, the telephone began to ring. Martin glanced at it.

His lips curved into an insolent smile.

Flicking dust from his lapel with a suave gesture, Martin picked up the telephone. He said nothing. There was a long silence. Then a hoarse voice shouted, "Hello, hello, hello! Are you there? You, Martin!"

Martin said absolutely nothing at all.

"You keep me waiting," the voice bellowed. "Me, St Cyr! Now jump! The rushes are ... Martin, do you hear me?"

Martin gently laid down the receiver on the desk. He turned again toward the mirror, regarded himself critically, frowned.

"Dreary," he murmured. "Distinctly dreary. I wonder why I ever bought this necktie?"

The softly bellowing telephone distracted him. He studied the instrument briefly, then clapped his hands sharply together an inch from the mouthpiece. There was a sharp, anguished cry from the other end of the line.

"Very good," Martin murmured, turning away. "That robot has done me a considerable favor. I should have realized the possibilities sooner. After all, a super-machine, such as ENIAC, would be far cleverer than a man, who is merely an ordinary machine. Yes," he added, stepping into the hall and coming face to face with Toni LaMotta, who was currently working for Summit on loan. "'Man is a machine, and woman – '" Here he gave Miss LaMotta a look of such arrogant significance that she was quite startled.

"'And woman – a toy,'" Martin amplified, as he turned toward Theater One, where St Cyr and destiny awaited him.

* * *

Summit Studios, outdoing even MGM, always shot ten times as much footage as necessary on every scene. At the beginning of each shooting day, this confusing mass of celluloid was shown in St Cyr's private projection theater, a small but luxurious domed room furnished with lie-back chairs and every other convenience, though no screen was visible until you looked up. Then you saw it on the ceiling.

When Martin entered, it was instantly evident that ecology took a sudden shift toward the worse. Operating on the theory that the old Nicholas Martin had come into it, the theater, which had breathed an expensive air of luxurious confidence, chilled toward him. The nap of the Persian rug shrank from his contaminating feet. The chair he stumbled against in the half-light seemed to shrug contemptuously. And the three people in the theater gave him such a look as might be turned upon one of the larger apes who had, by sheer accident, got an invitation to Buckingham Palace.

DeeDee Fleming (her real name was impossible to remember, besides having not a vowel in it) lay placidly in her chair, her feet comfortably up, her lovely hands folded, her large, liquid gaze fixed upon the screen where DeeDee Fleming, in the silvery meshes of a technicolor mermaid, swam phlegmatically through seas of pearl-colored mist.

Martin groped in the gloom for a chair. The strangest things were going on inside his brain, where tiny stiles still moved and readjusted until he no longer felt in the least like Nicholas Martin. Who did he feel like, then? What had happened?

He recalled the neurons whose beady little eyes he had fancied he saw staring brightly into, as well as out of, his own. Or had he? The memory was vivid, yet it couldn't be, of course. The answer was perfectly simple and terribly logical. ENIAC Gamma the Ninety-Third had told him, somewhat ambiguously, just what his ecological experiment involved. Martin had merely been given the optimum reactive pattern of his successful prototype, a man who had most thoroughly controlled his own environment. And ENIAC had told him the man's name, along with several confusing references to other prototypes like an Ivan (who?) and an unnamed Uighur.

The name for Martin's prototype was, of course, Disraeli, Earl of Beaconsfield. Martin had a vivid recollection of George Arliss playing the role. Clever, insolent, eccentric in dress and manner, exuberant, suave, self-controlled, with a strongly perceptive imagination...

"No, no, no!" DeeDee said with a sort of calm impatience. "Be careful, Nick. Some other chair, please. I have my feet on this one."

"T-t-t-t," said Raoul St Cyr, protruding his thick lips and snapping the fingers of an enormous hand as he pointed to a lowly chair against the wall. "Behind me, Martin. Sit down, sit down. Out of our way. Now! Pay attention. Study what I have done to make something great out of your foolish little play. Especially note how I have so cleverly ended the solo by building to five cumulative pratt-falls. Timing is all," he finished. "Now – SILENCE!"

For a man born in the obscure little Balkan country of Mixo-Lydia, Raoul St Cyr had done very well for himself in Hollywood. In 1939 St Cyr, growing alarmed at the imminence of war, departed for America, taking with him the print of an unpronounceable Mixo-Lydian film he had made, which might be translated roughly as The Pores In the Face of the Peasant.

With this he established his artistic reputation as a great director, though if the truth were known, it was really poverty that caused The Pores to be so artistically lighted, and simple drunkenness which had made most of the cast act out one of the strangest performances in film history. But critics compared The Pores to a ballet and praised inordinately the beauty of its leading lady, now known to the world as DeeDee Fleming.

DeeDee was so incredibly beautiful that the law of compensation would force one to expect incredible stupidity as well. One was not disappointed. DeeDee's neurons didn't know anything. She had heard of emotions, and under St Cyr's bullying could imitate a few of them, but other directors had gone mad trying to get through the semantic block that kept DeeDee's mind a calm, unruffled pool possibly three inches deep. St Cyr merely bellowed. This simple, primordial approach seemed to be the only one that made sense to Summit's greatest investment and top star.

With this whip-hand over the beautiful and brainless DeeDee, St Cyr quickly rose to the top in Hollywood. He had undoubted talent. He could make one picture very well indeed. He had made it twenty times already, each time starring DeeDee, and each time perfecting his own feudalistic production unit. Whenever anyone disagreed with St Cyr, he had only to threaten to go over to MGM and take the obedient DeeDee with him, for he had never allowed her to sign a long-term contract and she worked only on a picture-to-picture basis. Even Tolliver Watt knuckled under when St Cyr voiced the threat of removing DeeDee.

* * *

"Sit down, Martin," Tolliver Watt said. He was a tall, lean, hatchet-faced man who looked like a horse being starved because he was too proud to eat hay. With calm, detached omnipotence he inclined his grey-shot head a millimeter, while a faintly pained expression passed fleetingly across his face.

"Highball, please," he said.

A white-clad waiter appeared noiselessly from nowhere and glided forward with a tray. It was at this point that Martin felt the last stiles readjust in his brain, and entirely on impulse he reached out and took the frosted highball glass from the tray. Without observing this the waiter glided on and presented Watt with a gleaming salver full of nothing. Watt and the waiter regarded the tray.

Then their eyes met. There was a brief silence.

"Here," Martin said, replacing the glass. "Much too weak. Get me another, please. I'm reorienting toward a new phase, which means a different optimum," he explained to the puzzled Watt as he readjusted a chair beside the great man and dropped into it. Odd that he had never before felt at ease during rushes. Right now he felt fine. Perfectly at ease. Relaxed.

"Scotch and soda for Mr Martin," Watt said calmly. "And another for me."

"So, so, so, now we begin," St Cyr cried impatiently. He spoke into a hand microphone. Instantly the screen on the ceiling flickered noisily and began to unfold a series of rather ragged scenes in which a chorus of mermaids danced on their tails down the street of a little Florida fishing village.

To understand the full loathsomeness of the fate facing Nicholas Martin, it is necessary to view a St Cyr production. It seemed to Martin that he was watching the most noisome movie ever put upon film. He was conscious that St Cyr and Watt were stealing rather mystified glances at him. In the dark he put up two fingers and sketched a robot-like grin. Then, feeling sublimely sure of himself, he lit a cigarette and chuckled aloud.

"You laugh?" St Cyr demanded with instant displeasure. "You do not appreciate great art? What do you know about it, eh? Are you a genius?"

"This," Martin said urbanely, "is the most noisome movie ever put on film."

In the sudden, deathly quiet which followed, Martin flicked ashes elegantly and added, "With my help, you may yet avoid becoming the laughing stock of the whole continent. Every foot of this picture must be junked. Tomorrow bright and early we will start all over, and – "

Watt said quietly, "We're quite competent to make a film out of Angelina Noel, Martin."

"It is artistic!" St Cyr shouted. "And it will make money, too!"

"Bah, money!" Martin said cunningly. He flicked more ash with a lavish gesture. "Who cares about money? Let Summit worry."

Watt leaned forward to peer searchingly at Martin in the dimness.

"Raoul," he said, glancing at St Cyr, "I understood you were getting your – ah – your new writers whipped into shape. This doesn't sound to me as if – "

"Yes, yes, yes, yes," St Cyr cried excitedly. "Whipped into shape, exactly! A brief delirium, eh? Martin, you feel well? You feel yourself?"

Martin laughed with quiet confidence. "Never fear," he said. "The money you spend on me is well worth what I'll bring you in prestige. I quite understand. Our confidential talks were not to be secret from Watt, of course."

"What confidential talks?" bellowed St Cyr thickly, growing red.

"We need keep nothing from Watt, need we?" Martin went on imperturbably. "You hired me for prestige, and prestige you'll get, if you can only keep your big mouth shut long enough. I'll make the name of St Cyr glorious for you. Naturally you may lose something at the box-office, but it's well worth – "

"Pjrzqxgl!" roared St Cyr in his native tongue, and he lumbered up from the chair, brandishing the microphone in an enormous, hairy hand.

Deftly Martin reached out and twitched it from his grasp.

"Stop the film," he ordered crisply.

It was very strange. A distant part of his mind knew that normally he would never have dared behave this way, but he felt convinced that never before in his life had he acted with complete normality. He glowed with a giddy warmth of confidence that everything he did would be right, at least while the twelve-hour treatment lasted...

* * *

The screen flickered hesitantly, then went blank.

"Turn the lights on," Martin ordered the unseen presence beyond the mike. Softly and suddenly the room glowed with illumination. And upon the visages of Watt and St Cyr he saw a mutual dawning uneasiness begin to break.

He had just given them food for thought. But he had given them more than that. He tried to imagine what moved in the minds of the two men, below the suspicions he had just implanted. St Cyr's was fairly obvious. The Mixo-Lydian licked his lips – no mean task – and studied Martin with uneasy little bloodshot eyes. Clearly Martin had acquired confidence from somewhere. What did it mean? What secret sin of St Cyr's had been discovered to him, what flaw in his contract, that he dared behave so defiantly?

Tolliver Watt was a horse of another color; apparently the man had no guilty secrets; but he too looked uneasy. Martin studied the proud face and probed for inner weaknesses. Watt would be a harder nut to crack. But Martin could do it.

"That last underwater sequence," he now said, pursuing his theme. "Pure trash, you know. It'll have to come out. The whole scene must be shot from under water."

"Shut up!" St Cyr shouted violently.

"But it must, you know," Martin went on. "Or it won't jibe with the new stuff I've written in. In fact, I'm not at all certain that the whole picture shouldn't be shot under water. You know, we could use the documentary technique – "

"Raoul," Watt said suddenly, "what's this man trying to do?"

"He is trying to break his contract, of course," St Cyr said, turning ruddy olive. "It is the bad phase all my writers go through before I get them whipped into shape. In Mixo-Lydia – "

"Are you sure he'll whip into shape?" Watt asked.

"To me this is now a personal matter," St Cyr said, glaring at Martin. "I have spent nearly thirteen weeks on this man and I do not intend to waste my valuable time on another. I tell you he is simply trying to break his contract – tricks, tricks, tricks."

"Are you?" Watt asked Martin coldly.

"Not now," Martin said. "I've changed my mind. My agent insists I'd be better off away from Summit. In fact, she has the curious feeling that I and Summit would suffer by a mesalliance. But for the first time I'm not sure I agree. I begin to see possibilities, even in the tripe St Cyr has been stuffing down the public's throat for years. Of course I can't work miracles all at once. Audiences have come to expect garbage from Summit, and they've even been conditioned to like it. But we'll begin in a small way to re-educate them with this picture. I suggest we try to symbolize the Existentialist hopelessness of it all by ending the film with a full four hundred feet of seascapes – nothing but vast, heaving stretches of ocean," he ended, on a note of complacent satisfaction.

A vast, heaving stretch of Raoul St Cyr rose from his chair and advanced upon Martin.

"Outside, outside!" he shouted. "Back to your cell, you double-crossing vermin! I, Raoul St Cyr, command it. Outside, before I rip you limb from limb – "

Martin spoke quickly. His voice was calm, but he knew he would have to work fast.

"You see, Watt?" he said clearly, meeting Watt's rather startled gaze. "Doesn't dare let you exchange three words with me, for fear I'll let something slip. No wonder he's trying to put me out of here – he's skating on thin ice these days."

Goaded, St Cyr rolled forward in a ponderous lunge, but Watt interposed. It was true, of course, that the writer was probably trying to break his contract. But there were wheels within wheels here. Martin was too confident, too debonaire. Something was going on which Watt did not understand.

"All right, Raoul," he said decisively. "Relax for a minute. I said relax! We don't want Nick here suing you for assault and battery, do we? Your artistic temperament carries you away sometimes. Relax and let's hear what Nick has to say."

"Watch out for him, Tolliver!" St Cyr cried warningly. "They're cunning, these creatures. Cunning as rats. You never know – "

Martin raised the microphone with a lordly gesture. Ignoring the director, he said commandingly into the mike, "Put me through to the commissary. The bar, please. Yes. I want to order a drink. Something very special. A – ah – a Helena Glinska – "

* * *

"Hello," Erika Ashby's voice said from the door. "Nick, are you there? May I come in?"

The sound of her voice sent delicious chills rushing up and down Martin's spine. He swung round, mike in hand, to welcome her. But St Cyr, pleased at this diversion, roared before he could speak.

"No, no, no, no! Go! Go at once. Whoever you are – out!"

Erika, looking very brisk, attractive and firm, marched into the room and cast at Martin a look of resigned patience.

Very clearly she expected to fight both her own battles and his.

"I'm on business here," she told St Cyr coldly. "You can't part author and agent like this. Nick and I want to have a word with Mr Watt."

"Ah, my pretty creature, sit down," Martin said in a loud, clear voice, scrambling out of his chair. "Welcome! I'm just ordering myself a drink. Will you have something?"

Erika looked at him with startled suspicion. "No, and neither will you," she said. "How many have you had already? Nick, if you're drunk at a time like this – "

"And no shilly-shallying," Martin said blandly into the mike. "I want it at once, do you hear? A Helena Glinska, yes. Perhaps you don't know it? Then listen carefully. Take the largest Napoleon you've got. If you haven't a big one, a small punch bowl will do. Fill it half full with ice-cold ale. Got that? Add three jiggers of creme de menthe – "

"Nick, are you mad?" Erika demanded, revolted.

" – and six jiggers of honey," Martin went on placidly. "Stir, don't shake. Never shake a Helena Glinska. Keep it well chilled, and – "

"Miss Ashby, we are very busy," St Cyr broke in importantly, making shooing motions toward the door. "Not now. Sorry. You interrupt. Go at once."

" – better add six more jiggers of honey," Martin was heard to add contemplatively into the mike. "And then send it over immediately. Drop everything else, and get it here within sixty seconds. There's a bonus for you if you do. Okay? Good. See to it."

He tossed the microphone casually at St Cyr.

Meanwhile, Erika had closed in on Tolliver Watt.

"I've just come from talking to Gloria Eden," she said, "and she's willing to do a one-picture deal with Summit if I okay it. But I'm not going to okay it unless you release Nick Martin from his contract, and that's flat."

Watt showed pleased surprise.

"Well, we might get together on that," he said instantly, for he was a fan of Miss Eden's and for a long time had yearned to star her in a remake of Vanity Fair. "Why didn't you bring her along? We could have – "

"Nonsense!" St Cyr shouted. "Do not discuss this matter yet, Tolliver."

"She's down at Laguna," Erika explained. "Be quiet, St Cyr! I won't – "

A knock at the door interrupted her. Martin hurried to open it and as he had expected encountered a waiter with a tray.

"Quick work," he said urbanely, accepting the huge, coldly sweating Napoleon in a bank of ice. "Beautiful, isn't it?"

St Cyr's booming shouts from behind him drowned out whatever remark the waiter may have made as he received a bill from Martin and withdrew, looking nauseated.

"No, no, no, no," St Cyr was roaring. "Tolliver, we can get Gloria and keep this writer too, not that he is any good, but I have spent already thirteen weeks training him in the St Cyr approach. Leave it to me. In Mixo-Lydia we handle – "

Erika's attractive mouth was opening and shutting, her voice unheard in the uproar. St Cyr could keep it up indefinitely, as was well known in Hollywood. Martin sighed, lifted the brimming Napoleon and sniffed delicately as he stepped backward toward his chair. When his heel touched it, he tripped with the utmost grace and savoir-faire, and very deftly emptied the Helena Glinsak, ale, honey, creme de menthe, ice and all, over St Cyr's capacious front.

St Cyr's bellow broke the microphone.

* * *

Martin had composed his invention carefully. The nauseous brew combined the maximum elements of wetness, coldness, stickiness and pungency.

The drenched St Cyr, shuddering violently as the icy beverage deluged his legs, snatched out his handkerchief and mopped in vain. The handkerchief merely stuck to his trousers, glued there by twelve jiggers of honey. He reeked of peppermint.

"I suggest we adjourn to the commissary," Martin said fastidiously. "In some private booth we can go on with this discussion away from the – the rather overpowering smell of peppermint."

"In Mixo-Lydia," St Cyr gasped, sloshing in his shoes as he turned toward Martin, "in Mixo-Lydia we throw to the dogs – we boil in oil – we – "

"And next time," Martin said, "please don't joggle my elbow when I'm holding a Helena Glinska. It's most annoying."

St Cyr drew a mighty breath, rose to his full height – and then subsided. St Cyr at the moment looked like a Keystone Kop after the chase sequence, and knew it. Even if he killed Martin now, the element of classic tragedy would be lacking. He would appear in the untenable position of Hamlet murdering his uncle with custard pies.

"Do nothing until I return!" he commanded, and with a final glare at Martin plunged moistly out of the theater.

The door crashed shut behind him. There was silence for a moment except for the soft music from the overhead screen which DeeDee had caused to be turned on again, so that she might watch her own lovely form flicker in dimmed images through pastel waves, while she sang a duet with Dan Dailey about sailors, mermaids and her home in far Atlantis.

"And now," said Martin, turning with quiet authority to Watt, who was regarding him with a baffled expression, "I want a word with you."

"I can't discuss your contract till Raoul gets back," Watt said quickly.

"Nonsense," Martin said in a firm voice. "Why should St Cyr dictate your decisions? Without you, he couldn't turn out a box-office success if he had to. No, be quiet, Erika. I'm handling this, my pretty creature."

Watt rose to his feet. "Sorry, I can't discuss it," he said. "St Cyr pictures make money, and you're an inexperien – "

"That's why I see the true situation so clearly," Martin said. "The trouble with you is you draw a line between artistic genius and financial genius. To you, it's merely routine when you work with the plastic medium of human minds, shaping them into an Ideal Audience. You are an ecological genius, Tolliver Watt! The true artist controls his environment, and gradually you, with a master's consummate skill, shape that great mass of living, breathing humanity into a perfect audience..."

"Sorry," Watt said, but not, bruskly. "I really have no time – ah – "

"Your genius has gone long enough unrecognized," Martin said hastily, letting admiration ring in his golden voice. "You assume that St Cyr is your equal. You give him your own credit titles. Yet in your own mind you must have known that half the credit for his pictures is yours. Was Phidias non-commercial? Was Michaelangelo? Commercialism is simply a label for functionalism, and all great artists produce functional art. The trivial details of Rubens' masterpieces were filled in by assistants, were they not? But Rubens got the credit, not his hirelings. The proof of the pudding's obvious. Why?" Cunningly gauging his listener, Martin here broke off.

"Why?" Watt asked.

"Sit down," Martin urged. "I'll tell you why. St Cyr's pictures make money, but you're responsible for their molding into the ideal form, impressing your character-matrix upon everything and everyone at Summit Studios..."

* * *

Slowly Watt sank into his chair. About his ears the hypnotic bursts of Disraelian rhodomontade thundered compellingly. For Martin had the man hooked. With unerring aim he had at the first try discovered Watt's weakness – the uncomfortable feeling in a professionally arty town that money-making is a basically contemptible business. Disraeli had handled tougher problems in his day. He had swayed Parliaments.

Watt swayed, tottered – and fell. It took about ten minutes, all in all. By the end of that time, dizzy with eloquent praise of his economic ability, Watt had realized that while St Cyr might be an artistic genius, he had no business interfering in the plans of an economic genius. Nobody told Watt what to do when economics were concerned.

"You have the broad vision that can balance all possibilities and show the right path with perfect clarity," Martin said glibly. "Very well. You wish Eden. You feel – do you not? – that I am unsuitable material. Only geniuses can change their plans with instantaneous speed... When will my contract release be ready?"

"What?" said Watt, in a swimming, glorious daze. "Oh. Of course. Hm-m. Your contract release. Well, now – "

"St Cyr would stubbornly cling to past errors until Summit goes broke," Martin pointed out. "Only a genius like Tolliver Watt strikes when the iron is hot, when he sees a chance to exchange failure for success, a Martin for an Eden."

"Hm-m," Watt said. "Yes. Very well, then." His long face grew shrewd. "Very, well, you get your release – after I've signed Eden."

"There you put your finger on the heart of the matter," Martin approved, after a very brief moment of somewhat dashed thought. "Miss Eden is still undecided. If you left the transaction to somebody like St Cyr, say, it would be botched. Erika, you have your car here? How quickly could you drive Tolliver Watt to Laguna? He's the only person with the skill to handle this situation."

"What situa – oh, yes. Of course, Nick. We could start right away."

"But – " Watt said.

The Disraeli-matrix swept on into oratorical periods that made the walls ring. The golden tongue played arpeggios with logic.

"I see," the dazed Watt murmured, allowing himself to be shepherded toward the door. "Yes, yes, of course. Then – suppose you drop over to my place tonight, Martin. After I get the Eden signature, I'll have your release prepared. Hm-m. Functional genius..." His voice fell to a low, crooning mutter, and he moved quietly out of the door.

Martin laid a hand on Erika's arm as she followed him.

"Wait a second," he said. "Keep him away from the studio until we get the release. St Cyr can still out-shout me any time. But he's hooked. We – "

"Nick," Erika said, looking searchingly into his face. "What's happened?"

"Tell you tonight," Martin said hastily, hearing a distant bellow that might be the voice of St Cyr approaching. "When I have time I'm going to sweep you off your feet. Did you know that I've worshipped you from afar all my life? But right now, get Watt out of the way. Hurry!"

Erika cast a glance of amazed bewilderment at him as he thrust her out of the door. Martin thought there was a certain element of pleasure in the surprise.

* * *

"Where is Tolliver?" The loud, annoyed roar of St Cyr made Martin wince. The director was displeased, it appeared, because only in Costumes could a pair of trousers be found large enough to fit him. He took it as a personal affront. "What have you done with Tolliver?" he bellowed.

"Louder, please," Martin said insolently. "I can't hear you."

"DeeDee," St Cyr shouted, whirling toward the lovely star, who hadn't stirred from her rapturous admiration of DeeDee in technicolor overhead. "Where is Tolliver?"

Martin started. He had quite forgotten DeeDee.

"You don't know, do you, DeeDee?" he prompted quickly.

"Shut up," St Cyr snapped. "Answer me, you – " He added a brisk polysyllable in Mixo-Lydian, with the desired effect. DeeDee wrinkled her flawless brow.

"Tolliver went away, I think. I've got it mixed up with the picture. He went home to meet Nick Martin, didn't he?"

"See?" Martin interrupted, relieved. "No use expecting DeeDee to – "

"But Martin is here!" St Cyr shouted. "Think, think!"

"Was the contract release in the rushes?" DeeDee asked vaguely.

"A contract release?" St Cyr roared. "What is this? Never will I permit it, never, never, never! DeeDee, answer me – where has Watt gone?"

"He went somewhere with that agent," DeeDee said. "Or was that in the rushes too?"

"But where, where, where?"

"They went to Atlantis," DeeDee announced with an air of faint triumph.

"No!" shouted St Cyr. "That was the picture! The mermaid came from Atlantis, not Watt!"

"Tolliver didn't say he was coming from Atlantis," DeeDee murmured, unruffled. "He said he was going to Atlantis. Then he was going to meet Nick Martin at his house tonight and give him his contract release."

"When?" St Cyr demanded furiously. "Think, DeeDee? What time did – "

"DeeDee," Martin said, stepping forward with suave confidence, "you can't remember a thing, can you?" But DeeDee was too subnormal to react even to a Disraeli-matrix. She merely smiled placidly at him.

"Out of my way, you writer!" roared St Cyr, advancing upon Martin. "You will get no contract release! You do not waste St Cyr's time and get away with it! This I will not endure. I fix you as I fixed Ed Cassidy!"

Martin drew himself up and froze St Cyr with an insolent smile. His hand toyed with an imaginary monocle. Golden periods were hanging at the end of his tongue. There only remained to hypnotize St Cyr as he had hypnotized Watt. He drew a deep breath to unlease the floods of his eloquence –

And St Cyr, also too subhuman to be impressed by urbanity, hit Martin a clout on the jaw.

It could never have happened in the British Parliament.

III

WHEN THE ROBOT walked into Martin's office that evening, he, or it, went directly to the desk, unscrewed the bulb from the lamp, pressed the switch, and stuck his finger into the socket. There was a crackling flash. ENIAC withdrew his finger and shook his metallic head violently.

"I needed that," he sighed. "I've been on the go all day, by the Kaldekooz time-scale. Paleolithic, Neolithic, Technological – I don't even know what time it is. Well, how's your ecological adjustment getting on?"

Martin rubbed his chin thoughtfully.

"Badly," he said. "Tell me, did Disraeli, as Prime Minister, ever have any dealings with a country called Mixo-Lydia?"

"I have no idea," said the robot. "Why do you ask?"

"Because my environment hauled back and took a poke at my jaw," Martin said shortly.

"Then you provoked it," ENIAC countered. "A crisis – a situation of stress – always brings a man's dominant trait to the fore, and Disraeli was dominantly courageous. Under stress, his courage became insolence. But he was intelligent enough to arrange his environment so insolence would be countered on the semantic level. Mixo-Lydia, eh? I place it vaguely, some billions of years ago, when it was inhabited by giant white apes. Or – oh, now I remember. It's an encysted medieval survival, isn't it?"

Martin nodded.

"So is this movie studio," the robot said. "Your trouble is that you've run up against somebody who's got a better optimum ecological adjustment than you have. That's it. This studio environment is just emerging from medievalism, so it can easily slip back into that plenum when an optimum medievalist exerts pressure. Such types caused the Dark Ages. Well, you'd better change your environment to a neo-technological one, where the Disraeli matrix can be successfully pro-survival. In your era, only a few archaic social-encystments like this studio are feudalistic, so go somewhere else. It takes a feudalist to match a feudalist."

"But I can't go somewhere else," Martin complained. "Not without my contract release. I was supposed to pick it up tonight, but St Cyr found out what was happening, and he'll throw a monkey-wrench in the works if he has to knock me out again to do it. I'm due at Watt's place now, but St Cyr's already there – "

"Spare me the trivia," the robot said, raising his hand. "As for this St Cyr, if he's a medieval character-type, obviously he'll knuckle under only to a stronger man of his own kind."

"How would Disraeli have handled this?" Martin demanded.

"Disraeli would never have got into such a situation in the first place," the robot said unhelpfully. "The ecologizer can give you the ideal ecological differential, but only for your own type, because otherwise it wouldn't be your optimum. Disraeli would have been a failure in Russia in Ivan's time."

"Would you mind clarifying that?" Martin asked thoughtfully.

"Certainly," the robot said with great rapidity. "It all depends on the threshold-response-time of the memory-circuits in the brain, if you assume the identity of the basic chromosome-pattern. The strength of neuronic activation varies in inverse proportion to the quantative memory factor. Only actual experience could give you Disraeli's memories, but your reactivity-thresholds have been altered until perception and emotional-indices approximate the Disraeli ratio."

"Oh," Martin said. "But how would you, say, assert yourself against a medieval steam-shovel?"

"By plugging my demountable brain into a larger steam-shovel," ENIAC told him.

* * *

Martin seemed pensive. His hand rose, adjusting an invisible monocle, while a look of perceptive imagination suddenly crossed his face.

"You mentioned Russia in Ivan's time," he said. "Which Ivan would that be? Not, by any chance – ?"

"Ivan the Fourth. Very well adjusted to his environment he was, too. However, enough of this chit-chat. Obviously you'll be one of the failures in our experiment, but our aim is to strike an average, so if you'll put the ecologizer on your – "

"That was Ivan the Terrible, wasn't it?" Martin interrupted. "Look here, could you impress the character-matrix of Ivan the Terrible on my brain?"

"That wouldn't help you a bit," the robot said. "Besides, it's not the purpose of the experiment. Now – "

"One moment. Disraeli can't cope with a medievalist like St Cyr on his own level, but if I had Ivan the Terrible's reactive thresholds, I'll bet I could throw a bluff that might do the trick. Even though St Cyr's bigger than I am, he's got a veneer of civilization ... now wait. He trades on that. He's always dealt with people who are too civilized to use his own methods. The trick would be to call his bluff. And Ivan's the man who could do it."

"But you don't understand."

"Didn't everybody in Russia tremble with fear at Ivan's name?"

"Yes, in – "

"Very well, then," Martin said triumphantly. "You're going to impress the character-matrix, of Ivan the Terrible on my mind, and then I'm going to put the bite on St Cyr, the way Ivan would have done it. Disraeli's simply too civilized. Size is a factor, but character's more important. I don't look like Disraeli, but people have been reacting to me as though I were George Arliss down to the spit-curl. A good big man can always lick a good little man. But St Cyr's never been up against a really uncivilized little man – one who'd gladly rip out an enemy's heart with his bare hands." Martin nodded briskly. "St Cyr will back down – I've found that out. But it would take somebody like Ivan to make him stay all the way down."

"If you think I'm going to impress Ivan's matrix on you, you're wrong," the robot said.

"You couldn't be talked into it?"

"I," said ENIAC, "am a robot, semantically adjusted. Of course you couldn't talk me into it."

Perhaps not, Martin reflected, but Disraeli – hm-m. "Man is a machine." Why, Disraeli was the one person in the world ideally fitted for robot-coercion. To him, men were machines – and what was ENIAC?

"Let's talk this over – " Martin began, absently pushing the desk-lamp toward the robot. And then the golden tongue that had swayed empires was loosed...

"You're not going to like this," the robot said dazedly, sometime later. "Ivan won't do at ... oh, you've got me all confused. You'll have to eyeprint a – " He began to pull out of his sack the helmet and the quarter-mile of red ribbon.

"To tie up my bonny grey brain," Martin said, drunk with his own rhetoric. "Put it on my head. That's right. Ivan the Terrible, remember. I'll fix St Cyr's Mixo-Lydian wagon."

"Differential depends on environment as much as on heredity," the robot muttered, clapping the helmet on Martin's head. "Though naturally Ivan wouldn't have had the Tsardom environment without his particular heredity, involving Helena Glinska – there!" He removed the helmet.

"But nothing's happening," Martin said. "I don't feel any different."

"It'll take a few moments. This isn't your basic character-pattern, remember, as Disraeli's was. Enjoy yourself while you can. You'll get the Ivan-effect soon enough." He shouldered the sack and headed uncertainly for the door.

"Wait," Martin said uneasily. "Are you sure – "

"Be quiet. I forgot something – some formality – now I'm all confused. Well, I'll think of it later, or earlier, as the case may be. I'll see you in twelve hours – I hope."

The robot departed. Martin shook his head tentatively from side to side. Then he got up and followed ENIAC to the door. But there was no sign of the robot, except for a diminishing whirlwind of dust in the middle of the corridor.

Something began to happen in Martin's brain...

Behind him, the telephone rang.

Martin heard himself gasp with pure terror. With a sudden, impossible, terrifying, absolute certainty he knew who was telephoning.

Assassins!

* * *

"Yes, Mr Martin," said Tolliver Watt's butler to the telephone. "Miss Ashby is here. She is with Mr Watt and Mr St Cyr at the moment, but I will give her your message. You are detained. And she is to call for you – where?"

"The broom-closet on the second floor of the Writers' Building," Martin said in a quavering voice. "It's the only one near a telephone with a long enough cord so I could take the phone in here with me. But I'm not at all certain that I'm safe. I don't like the looks of that broom on my left."

"Sir?"

"Are you sure you're Tolliver Watt's butler?" Martin demanded nervously.

"Quite sure, Mr – eh – Mr Martin."

"I am Mr Martin," cried Martin with terrified defiance. "By all the laws of God and man, Mr Martin I am and Mr Martin I will remain, in spite of all attempts by rebellious dogs to depose me from my rightful place."

"Yes, sir. The broom-closet, you say, sir?"

"The broom-closet. Immediately. But swear not to tell another soul, no matter how much you're threatened. I'll protect you."

"Very well, sir. Is that all?"

"Yes. Tell Miss Ashby to hurry. Hang up now. The line may be tapped. I have enemies."

There was a click. Martin replaced his own receiver and furtively surveyed the broom-closet. He told himself that this was ridiculous. There was nothing to be afraid of, was there? True, the broom-closet's narrow walls were closing in upon him alarmingly, while the ceiling descended...

Panic-stricken, Martin emerged from the closet, took a long breath, and threw back his shoulders. "N-not a thing to be afraid of," he said. "Who's afraid?" Whistling, he began to stroll down the hall toward the staircase, but midway agoraphobia overcame him, and his nerve broke.

He ducked into his own office and sweated quietly in the dark until he had mustered up enough courage to turn on a lamp.

The Encyclopedia Britannica, in its glass-fronted cabinet, caught his eye. With noiseless haste, Martin secured ITALY to LORD and opened the volume at his desk. Something, obviously, was very, very wrong. The robot had said that Martin wasn't going to like being Ivan the Terrible, come to think of it. But was Martin wearing Ivan's character-matrix? Perhaps he'd got somebody else's matrix by mistake – that of some arrant coward. Or maybe the Mad Tsar of Russia had really been called Ivan the Terrified. Martin flipped the rustling pages nervously. Ivan, Ivan – here it was.

Son of Helena Glinska ... married Anastasia Zakharina-Koshkina ... private life unspeakably abominable ... memory astonishing, energy indefatigable, ungovernable fury – great natural ability, political foresight, anticipated the ideals of Peter the Great – Martin shook his head.

Then he caught his breath at the next line.

Ivan had lived in an atmosphere of apprehension, imagining that every man's hand was against him.

"Just like me," Martin murmured. "But – but there was more to Ivan than just cowardice. I don't understand."

"Differential," the robot had said, "depends on environment as much as on heredity. Though naturally Ivan wouldn't have had the Tsardom environment without his particular heredity."

Martin sucked in his breath sharply. Environment does make a difference. No doubt Ivan IV had been a fearful coward, but heredity plus environment had given Ivan the one great weapon that had enabled him to keep his cowardice a recessive trait.

Ivan the Terrible had been Tsar of all the Russias.

Give a coward a gun, and, while he doesn't stop being a coward, it won't show in the same way. He may act like a violent, aggressive tyrant instead. That, of course, was why Ivan had been ecologically successful – in his specialized environment. He'd never run up against many stresses that brought his dominant trait to the fore. Like Disraeli, he had been able to control his environment so that such stresses were practically eliminated.

Martin turned green.

Then he remembered Erika. Could he get Erika to keep St Cyr busy, somehow, while he got his contract release from Watt? As long as he could avoid crises, he could keep his nerve from crumbling, but – there were assassins everywhere!

Erika was on her way to the lot by now. Martin swallowed.

He would meet her outside the studio. The broom-closet wasn't safe. He could be trapped there like a rat –

"Nonsense," Martin told himself with shivering firmness. "This isn't me. All I have to do is get a g-grip on m-myself. Come, now. Buck up. Toujours l'audace!"

But he went out of his office and downstairs very softly and cautiously. After all, one never knew. And when every man's hand was against one...

Quaking, the character-matrix of Ivan the Terrible stole toward a studio gate.

* * *

The taxi drove rapidly toward Bel-Air.

"But what were you doing up that tree?" Erika demanded.

Martin shook violently.

"A werewolf," he chattered. "And a vampire and a ghoul and – I saw them, I tell you. There I was at the studio gate, and they all came at me in a mob."

"But they were just coming back from dinner," Erika said. "You know Summit's doing night shooting on Abbott and Costello Meet Everybody. Karloff wouldn't hurt a fly."

"I kept telling myself that," Martin said dully, "but I was out of my mind with guilt and fear. You see, I'm an abominable monster. But it's not my fault. It's environmental. I grew up in brutal and degrading conditions – oh, look!" He pointed toward a traffic cop ahead. "The police! Traitors even in the palace guards!"

"Lady, is that guy nuts?" the cabbie demanded.

"Mad or sane, I am Nicholas Martin," Martin announced, with an abrupt volte face. He tried to stand up commandingly, bumped his head, screamed "Assassins!" and burrowed into a corner of the seat, panting horribly.

Erika gave him a thoughtful, worried look.

"Nick," she said, "How much have you had to drink? What's wrong?"

Martin shut his eyes and lay back against the cushions.

"Let me have a few minutes, Erika," he pleaded. "I'll be all right as soon as I recover from stress. It's only when I'm under stress that Ivan – "

"You can accept your contract release from Watt, can't you? Surely you'll be able to manage that."

"Of course," Martin said with feeble bravery. He thought it over and reconsidered. "If I can hold your hand," he suggested, taking no chances.

This disgusted Erika so much that for two miles there was no more conversation within the cab.

Erika had been thinking her own thoughts.

"You've certainly changed since this morning," she observed. "Threatening to make love to me, of all things. As if I'd stand for it. I'd like to see you try." There was a pause. Erika slid her eyes sidewise toward Martin. "I said I'd like to see you try," she repeated.

"Oh, you would, would you?" Martin said with hollow valor. He paused. Oddly enough his tongue, hitherto frozen stiff on one particular subject in Erika's presence, was now thoroughly loosened. Martin wasted no time on theory. Seizing his chance before a new stress might unexpectedly arise, he instantly poured out his heart to Erika, who visibly softened.

"But why didn't you ever say so before?" she asked.

"I can't imagine," Martin said. "Then you'll marry me?"

"But why were you acting so – "

"Will you marry me?"

"Yes," Erika said, and there was a pause. Martin moistened his lips, discovering that somehow he and Erika had moved close together. He was about to seal the bargain in the customary manner when a sudden thought struck him and made him draw back with a little start.

Erika opened her eyes.

"Ah – " said Martin. "Um. I just happened to remember. There's a bad flu epidemic in Chicago. Epidemics spread like wildfire, you know. Why, it could be in Hollywood by now – especially with the prevailing westerly winds."

"I'm damned if I'm going to be proposed to and not kissed," Erika said in a somewhat irritated tone. "You kiss me!"

"But I might give you bubonic plague," Martin said nervously. "Kissing spreads germs. It's a well-known fact."

"Nick!"

"Well – I don't know – when did you last have a cold?"

Erika pulled away from him and went to sit in the other corner.

"Ah," Martin said, after a long silence. "Erika?"

"Don't talk to me, you miserable man," Erika said. "You monster, you."

"I can't help it," Martin cried wildly. "I'll be a coward for twelve hours. It's not my fault. After eight tomorrow morning I'll – I'll walk into a lion-cage if you want, but tonight I'm as yellow as Ivan the Terrible! At least let me tell you what's been happening."

Erika said nothing. Martin instantly plunged into his long and improbable tale.

"I don't believe a word of it," Erika said, when he had finished. She shook her head sharply. "Just the same, I'm still your agent, and your career's still my responsibility. The first and only thing we have to do is get your contract release from Tolliver Watt. And that's all we're going to consider right now, do you hear?"

"But St Cyr – "

"I'll do all the talking. You won't have to say a word. If St Cyr tries to bully you, I'll handle him. But you've got to be there with me, or St Cyr will make that an excuse to postpone things again. I know him."

"Now I'm under stress again," Martin said wildly. "I can't stand it. I'm not the Tsar of Russia."

"Lady," said the cab-driver, looking back, "if I was you, I'd sure as hell break off that engagement."

"Heads will roll for this," Martin said ominously.

* * *

"By mutual consent, agree to terminate ... yes," Watt said, affixing his name to the legal paper that lay before him on the desk. "That does it. But where in the world is that fellow Martin? He came in with you, I'm certain."

"Did he?" Erika asked, rather wildly. She too, was wondering how Martin had managed to vanish so miraculously from her side. Perhaps he had crept with lightning rapidity under the carpet. She forced her mind from the thought and reached for the contract release Watt was folding.

"Wait," St Cyr said, his lower lip jutting. "What about a clause giving us an option on Martin's next play?"

Watt paused, and the director instantly struck home.

"Whatever it may be, I can turn it into a vehicle for DeeDee, eh, DeeDee?" He lifted a sausage finger at the lovely star, who nodded obediently.

"It's going to have an all-male cast," Erika said hastily. "And we're discussing contract releases, not options."

"He would give me an option if I had him here," St Cyr growled, torturing his cigar horribly. "Why does everything conspire against an artist?" He waved a vast, hairy fist in the air. "Now I must break in a new writer, which is a great waste. Within a fortnight Martin would have been a St Cyr writer. In fact, it is still possible."

"I'm afraid not, Raoul," Watt said resignedly. "You really shouldn't have hit Martin at the studio today."

"But – but he would not dare charge me with assault. In Mixo-Lydia – "

"Why, hello, Nick," DeeDee said, with a bright smile. "What are you hiding behind those curtains for?"

Every eye was turned toward the window draperies, just in time to see the white, terrified face of Nicholas Martin flip out of sight like a scared chipmunk's. Erika, her heart dropping, said hastily, "Oh, that isn't Nick. It doesn't look a bit like him. You made a mistake, DeeDee."

"Did I?" DeeDee asked, perfectly willing to agree.

"Certainly," Erika said, reaching for the contract release in Watt's hand. "Now if you'll just let me have this, I'll – "

"Stop!" cried St Cyr in a bull's bellow. Head sunk between his heavy shoulders, he lumbered to the window and jerked the curtains aside.

"Ha!" the director said in a sinister voice. "Martin."

"It's a lie," Martin said feebly, making a desperate attempt to conceal his stress-triggered panic. "I've abdicated."

St Cyr, who had stepped back a pace, was studying Martin carefully. Slowly the cigar in his mouth began to tilt upwards. An unpleasant grin widened the director's mouth.

He shook a finger under Martin's quivering nostrils.

"You!" he said. "Tonight it is a different tune, eh? Today you were drunk. Now I see it all. Valorous with pots, like they say."

"Nonsense," Martin said, rallying his courage by a glance at Erika. "Who say? Nobody but you would say a thing like that. Now what's this all about?"

"What were you doing behind that curtain?" Watt asked.

"I wasn't behind the curtain," Martin said, with great bravado. "You were. All of you. I was in front of the curtain. Can I help it if the whole lot of you conceal yourselves behind curtains in a library, like – like conspirators?" The word was unfortunately chosen. A panicky light flashed into Martin's eyes. "Yes, conspirators," he went on nervously. "You think I don't know, eh? Well, I do. You're all assassins, plotting and planning. So this is your headquarters, is it? All night your hired dogs have been at my heels, driving me like a wounded caribou to – "

"We've got to be going," Erika said desperately. "There's just time to catch the next carib – the next plane east." She reached for the contract release, but Watt suddenly put it in his pocket. He turned his chair toward Martin.

"Will you give us an option on your next play?" he demanded.

"Of course he will give us an option!" St Cyr said, studying Martin's air of bravado with an experienced eye. "Also, there is to be no question of a charge of assault, for, if there is I will beat you. So it is in Mixo-Lydia. In fact, you do not even want a release from your contract, Martin. It is all a mistake. I will turn you into a St Cyr writer, and all will be well. So. Now you will ask Tolliver to tear up that release, will you not – ha?"

"Of course you won't, Nick," Erika cried. "Say so!"

* * *

There was a pregnant silence. Watt watched with sharp interest. So did the unhappy Erika, torn between her responsibility as Martin's agent and her disgust at the man's abject cowardice. DeeDee watched too, her eyes very wide and a cheerful smile upon her handsome face. But the battle was obviously between Martin and Raoul St Cyr.

Martin drew himself up desperately. Now or never he must force himself to be truly Terrible. Already he had a troubled expression, just like Ivan. He strove to look sinister too. An enigmatic smile played around his lips. For an instant he resembled the Mad Tsar of Russia, except, of course, that he was clean-shaven. With contemptuous, regal power Martin stared down the Mixo-Lydian.

"You will tear up that release and sign an agreement giving us option on your next play too, ha?" St Cyr said – but a trifle uncertainly.

"I'll do as I please," Martin told him. "How would you like to be eaten alive by dogs?"

"I don't know, Raoul," Watt said. "Let's try to get this settled even if – "

"Do you want me to go over to Metro and take DeeDee with me?" St Cyr cried, turning toward Watt. "He will sign!" And, reaching into an inner pocket for a pen, the burly director swung back toward Martin.

"Assassin!" cried Martin, misinterpreting the gesture.

A gloating smile appeared on St Cyr's revolting features.

"Now we have him, Tolliver," he said, with heavy triumph, and these ominous words added the final stress to Martin's overwhelming burden. With a mad cry he rushed past St Cyr, wrenched open a door, and fled.

From behind him came Erika's Valkyrie voice.

"Leave him alone! Haven't you done enough already? Now I'm going to get that contract release from you before I leave this room, Tolliver Watt, and I warn you, St Cyr, if you – "

But by then Martin was five rooms away, and the voice faded. He darted on, hopelessly trying to make himself slow down and return to the scene of battle. The pressure was too strong. Terror hurled him down a corridor, into another room, and against a metallic object from which he rebounded, to find himself sitting on the floor looking up at ENIAC Gamma the Ninety-Third.

"Ah, there you are," the robot said. "I've been searching all over space-time for you. You forgot to give me a waiver of responsibility when you talked me into varying the experiment. The Authorities would be in my gears if I didn't bring back an eyeprinted waiver when a subject's scratched by variance."

With a frightened glance behind him, Martin rose to his feet.

"What?" he asked confusedly. "Listen, you've got to change me back to myself. Everyone's trying to kill me. You're just in time. I can't wait twelve hours. Change me back to myself, quick!"

"Oh, I'm through with you," the robot said callously. "You're no longer a suitably unconditioned subject, after that last treatment you insisted on. I should have got the waiver from you then, but you got me all confused with Disraeli's oratory. Now here. Just hold this up to your left eye for twenty seconds." He extended a flat, glittering little metal disk. "It's already sensitized and filled out. It only needs your eyeprint. Affix it, and you'll never see me again."

Martin shrank away.

"But what's going to happen to me?" he quavered, swallowing.

"How should I know? After twelve hours, the treatment will wear off, and you'll be yourself again. Hold this up to your eye, now."

"I will if you'll change me back to myself," Martin haggled.

"I can't. It's against the rules. One variance is bad enough, even with a filed waiver, but two? Oh, no. Hold this up to your left eye – "

"No," Martin said with feeble firmness. "I won't."

ENIAC studied him.

"Yes, you will," the robot said finally, "or I'll go boo at you."

Martin paled slightly, but he shook his head in desperate determination.

"No," he said doggedly. "Unless I get rid of Ivan's matrix right now, Erika will never marry me and I'll never get my contract release from Watt. All you have to do is put that helmet on my head and change me back to myself. Is that too much to ask?"

"Certainly, of a robot," ENIAC said stiffly. "No more shilly-shallying. It's lucky you are wearing the Ivan-matrix, so I can impose my will on you. Put your eyeprint on this. Instantly!"

Martin rushed behind the couch and hid. The robot advanced menacingly. And at that moment, pushed to the last ditch, Martin suddenly remembered something.

He faced the robot.

* * *

"Wait," he said. "You don't understand. I can't eyeprint that thing. It won't work on me. Don't you realize that? It's supposed to take the eyeprint – "

" – of the rod-and-cone pattern of the retina," the robot said. "So – "

"So how can it do that unless I can keep my eye open for twenty seconds? My perceptive reaction-thresholds are Ivan's aren't they? I can't control the reflex of blinking. I've got a coward's synapses. And they'd force me to shut my eyes tight the second that gimmick got too close to them."

"Hold them open," the robot suggested. "With your fingers."

"My fingers have reflexes too," Martin argued, moving toward a sideboard. "There's only one answer. I've got to get drunk. If I'm half stupefied with liquor, my reflexes will be so slow I won't be able to shut my eyes. And don't try to use force, either. If I dropped dead with fear, how could you get my eyeprint then?"

"Very easily," the robot said. "I'd pry open your lids – "

Martin hastily reached for a bottle on the sideboard, and a glass. But his hand swerved aside and gripped, instead, a siphon of soda water.

" – only," ENIAC went on, "the forgery might be detected."

Martin fizzled the glass full of soda and took a long drink.

"I won't be long getting drunk," he said, his voice thickening. "In fact, it's beginning to work already. See? I'm coöperating."

The robot hesitated.

"Well, hurry up about it," he said, and sat down.

Martin, about to take another drink, suddenly paused, staring at ENIAC. Then, with a sharply indrawn breath, he lowered the glass.

"What's the matter now?" the robot asked. "Drink your – what is it?"

"It's whiskey," Martin told the inexperienced automaton, "but now I see it all. You've put poison in it. So that's your plan, is it? Well, I won't touch another drop, and now you'll never get my eyeprint. I'm no fool."

"Cog Almighty," the robot said, rising. "You poured that drink yourself. How could I have poisoned it? Drink!"

"I won't," Martin said, with a coward's stubbornness, fighting back the growing suspicion that the drink might really be toxic.

"You swallow that drink," ENIAC commanded, his voice beginning to quiver slightly. "It's perfectly harmless."

"Then prove it!" Martin said cunningly. "Would you be willing to switch glasses? Would you drink this poisoned brew yourself?"

"How do you expect me to drink?" the robot demanded. "I – " He paused. "All right, hand me the glass," he said. "I'll take a sip. Then you've got to drink the rest of it."

"Aha!" Martin said. "You betrayed yourself that time. You're a robot. You can't drink, remember? Not the same way that I can, anyhow. Now I've got you trapped, you assassin. There's your brew." He pointed to a floor-lamp. "Do you dare to drink with me now, in your electrical fashion, or do you admit you are trying to poison me? Wait a minute, what am I saying? That wouldn't prove a – "

"Of course it would," the robot said hastily. "You're perfectly right, and it's very cunning of you. We'll drink together, and that will prove your whiskey's harmless – so you'll keep on drinking till your reflexes slow down, see?"

"Well," Martin began uncertainly, but the unscrupulous robot unscrewed a bulb from the floor lamp, pulled the switch, and inserted his finger into the empty socket, which caused a crackling flash. "There," the robot said. "It isn't poisoned, see?"

"You're not swallowing it," Martin said suspiciously. "You're holding it in your mouth – I mean your finger."

ENIAC again probed the socket.

"Well, all right, perhaps," Martin said, in a doubtful fashion. "But I'm not going to risk your slipping a powder in my liquor, you traitor. You're going to keep up with me, drink for drink, until I can eyeprint that gimmick of yours – or else I stop drinking. But does sticking your finger in that lamp really prove my liquor isn't poisoned? I can't quite – "

"Of course it does," the robot said quickly. "I'll prove it. I'll do it again ... f(t). Powerful DC, isn't it? Certainly it proves it. Keep drinking, now."

* * *

His gaze watchfully on the robot, Martin lifted his glass of club soda.

"F ff ff f(t)!" cried the robot, some time later, sketching a singularly loose smile on its metallic face.

"Best fermented mammoth's milk I ever tasted," Martin agreed, lifting his tenth glass of soda-water. He felt slightly queasy and wondered if he might be drowning.

"Mammoth's milk?" asked ENIAC thickly. "What year is this?"

Martin drew a long breath. Ivan's capacious memory had served him very well so far. Voltage, he recalled, increased the frequency of the robot's thought-patterns and disorganized ENIAC's memory – which was being proved before his eyes. But the crux of his plan was yet to come...

"The year of the great Hairy One, of course," Martin said briskly. "Don't you remember?"

"Then you – " ENIAC strove to focus upon his drinking-companion. "You must be Mammoth-Slayer."

"That's it!" Martin cried. "Have another jolt. What about giving me the treatment now?"

"What treatment?"

Martin looked impatient. "You said you were going to impose the character-matrix of Mammoth-Slayer on my mind. You said that would insure my optimum ecological adjustment in this temporal phase, and nothing else would."

"Did I? But you're not Mammoth-Slayer," ENIAC said confusedly. "Mammoth-Slayer was the son of the Great Hairy One. What's your mother's name?"

"The Great Hairy One," Martin replied, at which the robot grated its hand across its gleaming forehead.

"Have one more jolt," Martin suggested. "Now take out the ecologizer and put it on my head."

"Like this?" ENIAC asked, obeying. "I keep feeling I've forgotten something important. F (t)."

Martin adjusted the crystal helmet on his skull. "Now," he commanded. "Give me the character-matrix of Mammoth-Slayer, son of the Great Hairy One."

"Well – all right," ENIAC said dizzily. The red ribbons swirled. There was a flash from the helmet. "There," the robot said. "It's done. It may take a few minutes to begin functioning, but then for twelve hours you'll – wait! Where are you going?"

But Martin had already departed.

The robot stuffed the helmet and the quarter-mile of red ribbon back for the last time. He lurched to the floor-lamp, muttering something about one for the road. Afterward, the room lay empty. A fading murmur said, "F(t)."

* * *

"Nick!" Erika gasped, staring at the figure in the doorway. "Don't stand like that! You frighten me!"

Everyone in the room looked up abruptly at her cry, and so were just in time to see a horrifying change take place in Martin's shape. It was an illusion, of course, but an alarming one. His knees slowly bent until he was half-crouching, his shoulders slumped as though bowed by the weight of enormous back and shoulder muscles, and his arms swung forward until their knuckles hung perilously near the floor.

Nicholas Martin had at last achieved a personality whose ecological norm would put him on a level with Raoul St Cyr.

"Nick!" Erika quavered.

Slowly Martin's jaw protruded till his lower teeth were hideously visible. Gradually his eyelids dropped until he was peering up out of tiny, wicked sockets. Then, slowly, a perfectly shocking grin broadened Mr Martin's mouth.

"Erika," he said throatily. "Mine!"

And with that, he shambled forward, seized the horrified girl in his arms, and bit her on the ear.

"Oh, Nick," Erika murmured, closing her eyes. "Why didn't you ever – no, no, no! Nick! Stop it! The contract release. We've got to – Nick, what are you doing?" She snatched at Martin's departing form, but too late.

For all his ungainly and unpleasant gait, Martin covered ground fast. Almost instantly he was clambering over Watt's desk as the most direct route to that startled tycoon. DeeDee looked on, a little surprised. St Cyr lunged forward.

"In Mixo-Lydia – " he began. "Ha! So!" He picked up Martin and threw him across the room.

"Oh, you beast," Erika cried, and flung herself upon the director, beating at his brawny chest. On second thought, she used her shoes on his shins with more effect. St Cyr, no gentleman, turned her around, pinioned her arms behind her, and glanced up at Watt's alarmed cry.

"Martin! What are you doing?"

There was reason for his inquiry. Apparently unhurt by St Cyr's toss, Martin had hit the floor, rolled over and over like a ball, knocked down a floor-lamp with a crash, and uncurled, with an unpleasant expression on his face. He rose crouching, bandy-legged, his arms swinging low, a snarl curling his lips.

"You take my mate?" the pithecanthropic Mr Martin inquired throatily, rapidly losing all touch with the twentieth century. It was a rhetorical question. He picked up the lamp-standard – he did not have to bend to do it – tore off the silk shade as he would have peeled foliage from a tree-limb, and balanced the weapon in his hand. Then he moved forward, carrying the lamp-standard like a spear.

"I," said Martin, "kill."

He then endeavored, with the most admirable single-heartedness, to carry out his expressed intention. The first thrust of the blunt, improvised spear rammed into St Cyr's solar plexus and drove him back against the wall with a booming thud. This seemed to be what Martin wanted. Keeping one end of his spear pressed into the director's belly, he crouched lower, dug his toes into the rug, and did his very best to drill a hole in St Cyr.

"Stop it!" cried Watt, flinging himself into the conflict. Ancient reflexes took over. Martin's arm shot out. Watt shot off in the opposite direction.

The lamp broke.

Martin looked pensively at the pieces, tentatively began to bite one, changed his mind, and looked at St Cyr instead. The gasping director, mouthing threats, curses and objections, drew himself up, and shook a huge fist at Martin.

"I," he announced, "shall kill you with my bare hands. Then I go over to MGM with DeeDee. In Mixo-Lydia – "

Martin lifted his own fists toward his face. He regarded them. He unclenched them slowly, while a terrible grin spread across his face. And then, with every tooth showing, and with the hungry gleam of a mad tiger in his tiny little eyes, he lifted his gaze to St Cyr's throat.

Mammoth-Slayer was not the son of the Great Hairy One for nothing.

* * *

Martin sprang.

So did St Cyr – in another direction, screaming with sudden terror. For, after all, he was only a medievalist. The feudal man is far more civilized than the so-called man of Mammoth-Slayer's primordially direct era, and as a man recoils from a small but murderous wildcat, so St Cyr fled in sudden civilized horror from an attacker who was, literally, afraid of nothing.

He sprang through the window and, shrieking, vanished into the night.

Martin was taken by surprise. When Mammoth-Slayer leaped at an enemy, the enemy leaped at him too, and so Martin's head slammed against the wall with disconcerting force. Dimly he heard diminishing, terrified cries. Laboriously he crawled to his feet and set back against the wall, snarling, quite ready...

"Nick!" Erika's voice called. "Nick, it's me! Stop it! Stop it! DeeDee – "

"Ugh?" Martin said thickly, shaking his head. "Kill." He growled softly, blinking through red-rimmed little eyes at the scene around him. It swam back slowly into focus. Erika was struggling with DeeDee near the window.

"You let me go," DeeDee cried. "Where Raoul goes, I go."

"DeeDee!" pleaded a new voice. Martin glanced aside to see Tolliver Watt crumpled in a corner, a crushed lamp-shade half obscuring his face.

With a violent effort Martin straightened up. Walking upright seemed unnatural, somehow, but it helped submerge Mammoth-Slayer's worst instincts. Besides, with St Cyr gone, stresses were slowly subsiding, so that Mammoth-Slayer's dominant trait was receding from the active foreground.

Martin tested his tongue cautiously, relieved to find he was still capable of human speech. "Uh," he said. "Arrgh ... ah. Watt."

Watt blinked at him anxiously through the lamp-shade.

"Urgh ... Ur – release," Martin said, with a violent effort. "Contract release. Gimme."

Watt had courage. He crawled to his feet, removing the lamp-shade.

"Contract release!" he snapped. "You madman! Don't you realize what you've done? DeeDee's walking out on me. DeeDee, don't go. We will bring Raoul back – "

"Raoul told me to quit if he quit," DeeDee said stubbornly.

"You don't have to do what St Cyr tells you," Erika said, hanging onto the struggling star.

"Don't I?" DeeDee asked, astonished. "Yes, I do. I always have."

"DeeDee," Watt said frantically, "I'll give you the finest contract on earth – a ten-year contract – look, here it is." He tore out a well-creased document. "All you have to do is sign, and you can have anything you want. Wouldn't you like that?"

"Oh, yes," DeeDee said. "But Raoul wouldn't like it." She broke free from Erika.

"Martin!" Watt told the playwright frantically, "Get St Cyr back. Apologize to him. I don't care how, but get him back! If you don't, I – I'll never give you your release."

Martin was observed to slump slightly – perhaps with hopelessness. Then, again, perhaps not.

"I'm sorry," DeeDee said. "I liked working for you, Tolliver. But I have to do what Raoul says, of course." And she moved toward the window.

Martin had slumped further down, till his knuckles quite brushed the rug. His angry little eyes, glowing with baffled rage, were fixed on DeeDee. Slowly his lips peeled back, exposing every tooth in his head.

"You," he said, in an ominous growl.

DeeDee paused, but only briefly.

* * *

Then the enraged roar of a wild beast reverberated through the room. "You come back!" bellowed the infuriated Mammoth-Slayer, and with one agile bound sprang to the window, seized DeeDee and slung her under one arm. Wheeling, he glared jealously at the shrinking Watt and reached for Erika. In a trice he had the struggling forms of both girls captive, one under each arm. His wicked little eyes glanced from one to another. Then, playing no favorites, he bit each quickly on the ear.

"Nick!" Erika cried. "How dare you!"

"Mine," Mammoth-Slayer informed her hoarsely.

"You bet I am," Erika said, "but that works both ways. Put down that hussy you've got under your other arm."

Mammoth-Slayer was observed to eye DeeDee doubtfully.

"Well," Erika said tartly, "make up your mind."

"Both," said the uncivilized playwright. "Yes."

"No!" Erika said.

"Yes," DeeDee breathed in an entirely new tone. Limp as a dishrag, the lovely creature hung from Martin's arm and gazed up at her captor with idolatrous admiration.

"Oh, you hussy," Erika said. "What about St Cyr?"

"Him," DeeDee said scornfully. "He hasn't got a thing, the sissy. I'll never look at him again." She turned her adoring gaze back to Martin.

"Pah," the latter grunted, tossing DeeDee into Watt's lap. "Yours. Keep her." He grinned approvingly at Erika. "Strong she. Better."

Both Watt and DeeDee remained motionless, staring at Martin.

"You," he said, thrusting a finger at DeeDee. "You stay with him. Ha?" He indicated Watt.

DeeDee nodded in slavish adoration.

"You sign contract?"

Nod.

Martin looked significantly into Watt's eyes. He extended his hand.

"The contract release," Erika explained, upside-down. "Give it to him before he pulls your head off."

Slowly Watt pulled the contract release from his pocket and held it out. But Martin was already shambling toward the window. Erika reached back hastily and snatched the document.

"That was a wonderful act," she told Nick, as they reached the street. "Put me down now. We can find a cab some – "

"No act," Martin growled. "Real. Till tomorrow. After that – " He shrugged. "But tonight, Mammoth-Slayer." He attempted to climb a palm tree, changed his mind, and shambled on, carrying the now pensive Erika. But it was not until a police car drove past that Erika screamed...

* * *

"I'll bail you out tomorrow," Erika told Mammoth-Slayer, struggling between two large patrolmen.

Her words were drowned in an infuriated bellow.

Thereafter events blurred, to solidify again for the irate Mammoth-Slayer only when he was thrown in a cell, where he picked himself up with a threatening roar. "I kill!" he announced, seizing the bars.

"Arrrgh!"

"Two in one night," said a bored voice, moving away outside. "Both in Bel-Air, too. Think they're hopped up? We couldn't get a coherent story out of either one."

The bars shook. An annoyed voice from one of the bunks said to shut up, and added that there had been already enough trouble from nincompoops without – here it paused, hesitated, and uttered a shrill, sharp, piercing cry.

Silence prevailed, momentarily, in the cell-block as Mammoth-Slayer, son of the Great Hairy One, turned slowly to face Raoul St Cyr.

The Julius Directive

Jacob M. Lambert

AFTER THE second chime, Becky Carver sat the newspaper down on the bar, walked into the foyer, and cleared her throat.

"Reveal," she said.

The dark oak surface of the front door faded – its artificial texture becoming transparent, a dull, two-way mirror. On the other side, sitting in the middle of the porch, was a large square box. Becky could see something written in blue on its side, but did not dare allow her curiosity to speak the words that would open the door. At least, not yet.

"Max," she said, still staring beyond, "can you give me a scan of the package, and if possible, who placed it there?"

A few moments passed in silence, and Becky watched as, through the door, a thick red, shaky grid appeared over the box, then it centered on the package's top – flashing and growing brighter. She averted her gaze, this time drawling her attention upward, to the scorched, gunmetal sky. Although she couldn't see much (the porch extended six feet from the entrance, leaving very little sight of the world), Becky could quite visibly make out the electric currents passing through the above ether. The puddled mixtures of blood and oil in the front yard – remnants of the last social cleansing – reflected them perfectly.

"Congresswoman Carver," Max said, his light, pleasant voice echoing in Becky's wireless earpiece.

"Yes, Max."

"Would you like me to display the information, or –"

"Can you give it to me in text?"

The wall next to the transparent door suddenly illuminated a solid white, pictures and various decorations disappearing, simply fading into the background. From the white, small black letters cascaded down in several tiny rows – forming lines. Becky crossed her arms over her wiry chest and squinted. There were five lines in bold at the very top.

Carrier: Stork Services
Time: 8:45 AM
Package is free of containments.
A temperature reading places the package at 100.4F
Caution Rating: Green

"What's causing that temperature, Max? It has to be below forty outside, and –"

"It's thirty-one degrees, Congresswoman."

Becky sighed and chewed at her bottom lip. "Is it safe to bring the package in the house?"

"According to my readings, the levels of UV radiation are minimal."

"Alright," she said, sighing again, "but if that thing explodes, I'll have you upgraded. And who's Stork Services?"

As she turned away from the wall and faced the door, Max interrupted her progress. "The company is relatively new. It's no surprise that you don't recognize their name."

"But I am a little concerned as to what it might be in that package though, Max. I didn't order anything. What is it that they sell?"

"Security. The company installed most of the new systems in the White House after the war, but they're relatively new so –"

"I wouldn't recognize them. I get it. Max, I need you to solidify the door and release it," Becky said, watching the door's surface move in reverse, becoming once again opaque. She then backed away, feeling the stale, frigid air rush around the outer frame and assault the flesh on her caramel colored cheeks.

Holding her breath (she didn't trust the outside pollution without a respirator), Becky gripped both sides of the package and, surprised by its weightlessness, brought it inside the house. But once she placed it on the heated tile of the living room, a loud, piercing noise came from inside the box, sending her – with gooseflesh and heart racing – backward, her stomach burning as though a hundred razor winged butterflies suddenly got spooked and headed for the nearest exit. She placed both hands over her ears, waiting for something, anything, to happen, but nothing did – and the noise continued.

"Max, what is that noise? I can feel my skull vibrating," Becky said, right shoulder striking the wall where the five lines had appeared five minutes earlier.

There was silence from her earpiece – and the entire house – but it didn't last long: Max, for some reason hesitant, whispered. "My memory registers it as human."

"What? There's nothing human in that sound, Max. What do you –?"

"Congresswoman, the sound is human," he paused, then added, "and undeniably infantile."

* * *

She reached forward, gripping the two top flaps, and pulled with such force that the clear tape running horizontally across its surface immediately ripped, sending Becky backward. After gaining her balance, she inched forward – looking for some defining human aspect, but there was nothing, not that she could see from four feet away.

"Max. Scan," Becky said, keeping her distance.

Max spoke in her ear, tone once again amenable. "I have already executed two more, Congresswoman, and they have both returned negative."

She stopped.

Lying in the center of the box, swaddled in, what Becky assumed some antique fabric (and not the modern, organic placenta simulator), was a baby – she checked – girl. The child's gaze fixed on Becky, and the screaming abated. How didn't I recognize that scream sooner, she thought, staring down at the child's face. Her little green eyes, with folds of semi-translucent flesh partially swollen around the lids, looked like glass marbles, both of her chubby, reddened cheeks still slick with tears. Becky was speechless, and if Max hadn't spoken, she might have stayed that way.

"I'm running another scan, and I should have –"

"Wait," Becky interrupted, "there's no need."

All of the apprehension drained from her body, like the simplicity of one finding their seemingly lost wedding band on the sink. Becky leaned forward, removed the baby from the box, and brought it close to her chest – sudden warmth rushing through every muscle in her body. The child felt smooth against Becky's cheek as she lowered her head, breathing in the mixture of new skin and, if she wasn't mistaken, lavender scented lotion. It was only then that tears streamed from her eyes – the sting both reassuring and fascinating.

"I understand now, Max, about Stork Services."

"I'm not following your logic, Congresswoman," Max replied, sounding far away.

Walking out of the living room and into the hallway, heading toward the master bedroom, Becky wiped her face with the fabric surrounding the child.

"Open," she said, moving across the digital hardwood floors of the bedroom. "This must be a gift from Ron, Max. Stork Services provides security, yes. But I didn't know they manufacture dolls. You see, the child looks real enough, but it's not – not in the traditional way."

"Android?"

"Yes, but much more authentic. That would explain the temperature reading. In the past – and I'm talking twentieth-century old – mothers told their children storks brought babies home, avoiding the whole sex conversation. Do you understand?"

For the third or fourth time Max remained silent, then, seconds later, replied in a monotone, disinterested whisper. "That does not appear in my files, but I understand the reference to dolls. Dolls were toys for girls – or boys, depending on their parent's preference – but you mean DALZ: Directive Automated Learning Zebibyte. Correct?"

"Yes. In other words, Max, this baby is just like we humans – it will respond to commands and learn from them, learn from mistakes. But unlike us, it won't get any bigger, and somehow Ron knew, bless him, that I've been wanting this. Well, not exactly this, but someone like this." Becky finished and placed the infant on the bed's surface, making sure the fabric remained tight.

"What about me, Congresswoman?" Max asked.

"What about you?"

"Is my companionship not comforting enough?"

To this, Becky laughed, but covered her mouth before startling the child. While on the way into the bedroom, the baby – Rachel, Becky now corrected herself – had fallen asleep, small exhalations of air, moving in even intervals, marking the change. Stepping out of the room, Becky faced the door.

"Close." Immediately, it obeyed.

"Congresswoman?"

"I'm here, Max. Yes, I value your companionship very much, but we can talk about it later. I need to call Ron, dial the call for me?"

The phone started buzzing in Becky's right ear, the sound of a mechanical snake. While she waited for the voice of her husband on the other end, her thoughts returned to Rachel sleeping in the bedroom, the child's warmth and, though artificial, heartbeat-bringing fresh tears to the rims of her eyes. She'd waited so long for the touch of little fingers, toes, and cheeks that, at her current age of forty-three, it didn't matter whether that sensation came from real flesh and blood, or, as with Rachel, malleable steel and processing chips. No, Becky only wanted, needed, the illusion, but if real was what a person perceived – what he or she felt – then Rachel was every bit as realistic, and human, as any real baby.

"How's the sexiest congresswoman in the Semi-United States?" A deep, somewhat mischievous voice asked from the other line, breaking Becky from her internal monologue.

A smile creased her thin lips – lids squinting so that both eyes looked like tiny green half-moons. Becky placed a hand to her left cheek. "I'm better now, with little Rachel sleeping soundly in our bedroom. You do know that you're the best husband in the universe, right?"

"Who's Rachel?"

"Our little girl," Becky replied, the elation in her voice unmistakable.

There was an audible grunt from Ron's side, then he spoke, very gently. "Becky, I have no idea what you're talking about, and truthfully, you're scaring the shit out of me."

* * *

Rolling her eyes – an expression that always agitated Ron – Becky, with a huge grin on her face, walked toward the kitchen. "It's okay; I've already held her, Ron. And she's –"

"Listen to me and do exactly what I tell you. Do you understand?" Ron's voice had taken on a severe tone, his breathing coming in deep, static intervals.

"Okay, I'm listening, but I don't see –"

"Just listen, Becky. Whatever came in that box, it's –"

The room behind Becky suddenly erupted in a continuous, ear-throbbing scream, drowning out Ron's final words. Goosebumps formed on Becky's nape as she froze three feet between the bedroom door and the kitchen, a sudden heat washing over her eyes. She knew it was Rachel, that much was obvious, but something sounded different in the baby's cry – most of the child's human tone disappearing as the scream climbed higher, creating an electronic, gurgling noise.

"What was that?" Ron asked, breathing sounding more and more labored.

She didn't respond immediately, but when she did, Becky's voice sounded weak, on the verge of crumbling. "That's Rachel."

"Becky, I'm walking out the office now. I'll be there in ten. Stay on the phone with me until I get there, okay?"

Already walking toward the bedroom, Becky heard Ron's words in pieces, like an antique car radio-losing signal (she'd actually seen one of these, when she'd been just a child). She then stopped, a foot from the door, and listened to the wailing coming from the opposite side – heart thudding behind her closed lids. As the cacophony reached its peak – the screams, Ron now shouting, and her internal mechanisms pounding against the inner walls of her flesh – everything abruptly ceased, the afterward semi-silence making her ears hum.

"Can you hear me, Becky? Tell me you're okay," Ron whispered.

"I'm… here."

There was a sigh from the other line then he spoke, maintaining a whisper. "I'll be there soon. Just hold –"

"Ron? Are you there? Ron?" Becky said, tilting her head and covering her right ear, over the wireless control.

Other than a small beeping noise, the line was silent.

"Max, redial," she said, but again, silence. "Max, call R –"

Rachel's screams again interrupted from behind the door, making Becky bolt up straight, an instant skipping in her chest following an even greater wave of heat spreading through her entire body. Her first inclination was this: run for the front door, climb in the car, and race away from the house as if it was leaking plutonium. But the thought faded, instead focusing on Max. Hadn't Max said the scan revealed nothing? Yes, Becky clearly remembered that, but why wasn't Max responding to her command? She didn't have an answer to any of these questions, but she knew one thing: the screams from the bedroom were from a machine, and machines had an off switch.

"Open."

She wondered if it would actually work, but seconds after the command, the door's lock released and it responded – the room beyond revealing itself inches at a time. There, sitting on the bed, was Rachel, her previously swaddled body exposed: she'd kicked away the fabric and rolled over on her stomach. Becky stepped forward, the din of the child's screams making her ears feel like broken speakers, and watched as the child – who had looked so frail earlier – pushed itself up from the mattress and started convulsing.

Somewhere distant, Becky could hear herself scream.

The realization that Rachel was a machine faded from Becky's mind, her eyes instead taking the scene at face value: an actual baby, naked and bent forward, shuddering and wailing, but the unreality flooding her vision didn't last long. Rachel flipped over, sitting upright and, making eye contact with Becky, opened her mouth beyond the threshold of what is human – equally inhuman screams now issuing from the mechanical depths of its artificial configuration.

"Max, please. Can you hear me? Max?" Becky asked, frozen in place.

There was still no answer.

As if Becky's call for Max had been a signal, Rachel's chubby hands reached up, grabbed the corners of both eyes, and started pulling the flesh-like material of her face in opposite directions, the sight resembling someone removing a gelatin mask. The heavy thudding in Becky's chest spread to her ears, hands, and eyes. But her legs still wouldn't move. Every fiber in her body shouted GET OUT! GET OUT! GET OUT! – but it didn't obey until Rachel fell from the bed, most of her outer synthetic flesh sagging and revealing a soft, transparent, cobalt blue inner shell. Wires snaked on both the inside and outside of the endoskeleton, but the thing's chest, covered in a pink film with thousands of tiny, sparking lights, gathered most of Becky's attention.

She felt her legs carry her backward until her right hand struck the frame of the door, causing her to break her stare from Rachel, but only for a moment. When Becky looked again, she saw Rachel digging her shoulder and chin into the digital hardwood floor, dragging her nearly limp body toward the far left wall – toward a partially masked appliance socket. Becky, now standing in the hallway, once again speaking into her wireless, shouting for Max, caught a quick glance at Rachel, saw every shimmering light shoot from her chest, entering the socket, and then, almost immediately, the door slammed shut – the lights exploding above her, glass raining down on her head.

Her eyes shut involuntarily, and when she opened them again, it was in darkness.

* * *

Feet scooting across the floor, Becky held her hands out in front, using the wall as a sort of guide until she reached the kitchen. Resting on the bar's cool surface, she took a deep breath, trying to calm the adrenaline coursing through her skull, making her lightheaded, and whispered into the darkness.

"Max, please, if you can hear me, help," she said.

There was no reply, only the resounding hum in her ears. At least the screaming had stopped, she thought, as she rounded the bar, heading toward the front door. It didn't take her long to get there, and it took her an even shorter time to see that the entire front entrance was completely transparent – the imitation wooden appearance of the door gone, leaving the factory shatterproof digital glass behind. Becky touched the surface of the glass, looking for an emergency switch or something that would open the door, but there was nothing. The lingering scent of her morning breakfast – genetically engineered bacon and toast – made her stomach churn, threatening to come back up her throat.

She turned around, noticing the lack of light – the artificial windows had also disappeared – and remained with her back against the door, staring ahead. Ron would be there soon, she reassured herself, but exactly how long would that be? Becky tried to imagine the distance from the state office and her home, but found her mind scrambled, unable to form basic images. Everything had happened so fast, and the –

The entire living room, kitchen, and hallway turned a bright neon red, massive black letters – mixed in visions of burning houses, explosions, and swollen, decaying bodies – appearing on the surface of everything. Then, as the speed of the images increased, a hollow voice spoke through what Becky assumed the walls.

March 15, 2101 – 11:30 A.M.

In a string of recent miracles, Congressman Wilson, Blankenship, and, this just in, Congresswoman Carter, were found dead in their homes. The cause of death, according to autopsy, was asphyxiation. The traitors were known for their inability to provide security to their country, honestly perform their duties of office, and reunite the social classes. With any luck, the nation will celebrate the assignation of President Dixon later this evening – now, back to your usual programming.

Becky pressed her body harder against the door, sweat soaking the underarms of her white shirt, and closed her eyes. Although the hollow, semi-mechanical voice had stopped, the images still scrolled, making her feel dizzy. Again, and perhaps this time out of pure habit, Becky mouthed Max's name.

That's when it felt like someone had dropped a burning palm on her head.

Opening her eyes, Becky saw that the images of carnage had disappeared, but something else had replaced them: as if moving underwater, fire indolently twisted and maneuvered across the ceiling and walls. She dropped to her knees, cutting her hands and shins in the process, and craned her head toward the ceiling. Everything was on fire – but there was no smoke, though she clearly felt as if she might gag. The smell was there, too, and Becky, already bleeding on the glass floor, crawled toward the center of the kitchen, leaned against the refrigerator, and coughed, her eyes watering due to the scent of charred wood (but there was nothing wooden in the house).

"Max..." she whispered, feeling her head start spinning.

With the refrigerator hum against her back, Becky glanced around the room, watching the fire's orange and blue waves dance down the ceiling, catch on the bar, and travel to the inside of the kitchen. It wouldn't be much longer, she assumed, before the flames reached the floor, making it difficult to sit, and she once again closed her eyes, trying to erase the thought. Instead, she ruminated on Ron, thinking of his smile and crystal blue eyes – remembering the first time they had kissed, but the image of Rachel's face intruded. She could visualize the fleshy folds around the child's eyes, the little fingers – the toes. But no matter how hard she focused on Rachel's seemingly benign appearance, the running cycle of pictures eventually became nightmarish: Rachel mechanically bellowing; the convulsing; and the worst, the thing pulling its synthetic flesh away like a silicone Halloween mask.

No, she thought, that wasn't the worst of it – the worst part was being alone.

Becky sighed, tears streaming down her cheeks. "Max…"

"I'm here, Congresswoman."

As if someone had thrown cold water in her face, Becky shot bolt upright, her right hand covering the earpiece. "Max, I thought you were gone!"

"No, I've been right here… listening."

"You've been what?" When Becky spoke, the "what" came out in one long, exaggerated slur. She completely forgot about the fire enclosing her in the kitchen, and stood, gritting her teeth. "After everything that's happened in the last twenty minutes, you're telling me that you've been listening? Last time I checked, your operating system runs on command."

"My system is based off need, Congresswoman."

"What are you talking about, Max? I need you, trust me."

Becky, returning to the floor (the flames now spitting from above), looked over to the right, wondering where Ron was. If the voice that had come through earlier was right, she didn't have much time. The biochemical powered face of her watch read 11:28.

"Max, answer me! You know I need you. Open the doors." Max didn't reply, but a small click sounded in Becky's wireless, her own voice flooding her ears.

What about me, Congresswoman?

What about you?

Is my companionship not comforting enough?

"What's this, Max? Max, can you hear me?" Becky said, and at the end of her own question, the impact of Max's recording dawned on her. But that was impossible. Machines didn't have feelings, at least not authentic feelings, yet why else would Max play back the earlier conversation? Was he jealous? I'd hate to see what he'd do if I mentioned replacement.

"I'm here, Congresswoman."

"Look, Max… I need you, and you know that," Becky said, putting on her best "mother" impersonation.

"But what about Rachel?" Max asked, monotone – distant.

Becky coughed into her palm, and barely caught her breath. It was getting harder to breathe by the second. "Max, listen, that thing was just a machine, okay? But I need your help. I can't breathe – the fire's getting worse, too."

"But I'm a machine, too," Max said, tone more indifferent.

Wrong word… thank God he can't read my thoughts.

"Congresswoman?"

"I'm here, Max. I know you're a machine, but you're different. I know I was probably a little mean when I laughed at you, when you asked about companionship. And I'm sorry. Humans do that a lot; trust me, we never realize that we need something until it's gone."

Unless it almost commits genocide, she thought.

"I… understand, and I accept your apology," Max replied, his tone reaching a pitch that could only be described as bizarre – happiness mixed with, if Becky wasn't mistaken, sadness. But why the latter, she wondered? Some part of him – some circuit – wanted me to choke to death, didn't it? He's like a child… a child playing the "silent game," except holding his anger over my head, waiting for me to die.

Coughing, this time making her head swim – tiny electric black dots floating in front of her eyes – Becky shook her head: "Thanks, Max, but I can't breathe, and it feels like I'm burning."

"The fire is optical, Congresswoman. It isn't real."

"It looks pretty real to me, Max."

"The android – 101 Trojan – has air locked the house, and according to my sensors, you only have precisely five minutes of oxygen remaining. However, I know an alternate method of escape."

Becky opened her mouth, words on the tip of her tongue, but she coughed again, her throat burning – palms shaking. She tried again, and this time, the words came through rough and semi-horse. "Can't you just unlock the doors?"

"That's a negative. The android has rerouted the power, and I can't access the house's main circuit. I was only able to remain operational due to a separate terminal in the main hub," Max replied, tone surprisingly cheerful.

"Well, how the hell am I going to get out, Max?"

"That's the easy part, Congresswoman. But it will require some… organic properties."

* * *

Mouth hanging partially open, Becky listened to Max's explanation, and once he'd finished, she clapped both hands together and smiled – the first real moment of elation (and hope) she'd had all day. "So that's it."

"Yes, but it will only last a few moments – possibly seconds – so you must move quickly. And Congresswoman?"

"Max?"

"Once you do this, it will short circuit my processor. My components are not linked, as the other appliances – mine are external, so there is a great chance we will not speak again."

As much as Becky wanted to say No, never mind then, I don't need to live, not without you, she forced a frown, the expression actually making her look as if she'd bit the end of a tire and had dirt in her mouth. "I'm sorry, Max. I'm sure that, after all this, we can salvage your memory and see what happens."

So you can ignore me the next time – when I'm bleeding out or really on fire.

"It's fine, Congresswoman. But you should move quickly: three minutes left."

She didn't need another cue. Becky, moving across the floor on her hands and knees, again cutting herself in multiple places, crawled into the hallway. Through the door, she could hear an electrical buzzing – no doubt coming from Rachel – but she didn't waste time. She used her throbbing, bloody palms and searched the glass floor, looking for a section that opened. Breathing now – especially with her heart beating against the inside of her chest and adrenaline making her entire body tremor – felt almost impossible (breathing deeply was certainly impossible), and she held her breath, releasing it in slow intervals.

When she pushed a handful of glass away from the doorframe, her knuckle caught the jagged edge of something poking up through the floor. It didn't take her but a moment to realize what it was: a piece of glass was caught in the crack of something. Becky looked down, and sure enough, the above flames illuminated a large, perforated square section of the floor next to the bedroom door. The placement of the panel made Becky release an audible laugh. If Rachel hadn't rerouted the power, shutting down most of the house (in addition to Max's later direction), she might not have ever seen it: the panel placed where the digital hardwood had been, masking it from view.

Becky used her fingernails and lifted the section of the floor with ease, exposing another smaller panel, this one, she now realized, wasn't budging.

"Max, there's another panel here," Becky said, her voice on the verge of frantic.

Silence in reply – exactly what she didn't want, but...

"This is where we say goodbye, Congresswoman. I'm sorry I took so long. Use your earpiece to pop the lid. It will probably break it, but –"

Becky didn't hesitate.

She removed the earpiece and, while Max spoke, pried at the smaller panel. The heat from the "artificial" flames above burned at Becky's back, keeping her body to the ground, and on her first try, the thin metal of the earpiece snapped.

"C'mon, you steel bastard," she said, using the smaller, thinner piece. "There you... go!"

The panel, with little more than a tiny metallic clink, popped upward, exposing the nest of serpentine wires bundled together underneath. Becky could see a deep blue flashing light somewhere beneath, where, according to Max's calculations, the circuit breaker was located.

Now, she realized, came her part.

Becky looked around and then pushed away from the glass covered floor, the heat from above bearing down on her, but it didn't feel any worse than before – or the time before that. I can't believe I'm about to do this, she thought, quickly dropping her sweat pants and squatting over the semi-large hole in the floor. Max had told her – though she'd already known – that, because of the power rerouting, the sensors governing the water didn't work, nor the mechanisms that opened the refrigerator. The only other option, according to Max, had been "manual release." And though it wouldn't stop the flow of power to Rachel, it would certainly deflect it.

"Here we go," Becky said, letting her muscles relax.

There was an immediate change – sparks shooting upward and burning the sensitive flesh around Becky's ankles, a loud, monotonous humming sound from inside the house. However, the most obvious change was the air. Although it probably contained every residue of every noxious chemical in the past twenty years, the cold outside air rushed into Becky's lungs, making her feel both nauseous and exhilarated. She swayed over the hole for a moment, forgetting where she was, but it didn't last long. Once she'd shrugged off the dizziness, she rushed forward, around the corner, and out into the open air, where she collapsed on the lip of the porch, gasping.

"Becky!" a voice shouted, startling her, but she didn't move. Vomit had already started working its way up her throat, and she released it.

While she wiped the corners of her chapped lips – and gagged a few more times – she was vaguely aware of someone touching her. She pushed, arms flailing, and fell backward. The next thing she felt was gritless, clean air rushing into her lungs and, moments after that, the voice of Ron.

"Are you alright? Say something?"

"Some," she coughed, a hollow, racking sound, "thing."

Ron laughed, the respirator over his face making his voice sound far away. "I'm sorry it took so long. Someone chased me, nearly ran me off the road. And I think we should get out of here: something tells me they'll be back."

Clutching the respirator that Ron had placed over her face, Becky's eyes suddenly widened. "Ron, we have to call Blankenship and Wilson."

"Here," Ron said, handing Becky his wireless earpiece, "but talk to them in the car. We've got to move. Now."

* * *

Twenty miles away, Bruce Blankenship, standing in his blue bathrobe, pressed a tiny button on the side of his earpiece. "Hello?"

"Jesus, Bruce, are you okay?" a frantic voice asked from the other end.

Shaking his head, a deep grin forming on his pudgy cheeks, Bruce nodded. "Yes, I'm fine, Congresswoman Carver. What do I owe the pleasure?"

"You have to get out of your house, Bruce. It's eleven-forty-one, and I know you have no idea what that means, but you still have time. Get. Out. Now."

"Calm down, calm down. Look, I have a guest. I'll call you back in," he paused, looked over at the tall blonde wearing skin-tight black yoga pants standing beside his refrigerator, and continued, "fifteen minutes."

Becky shouted from the other line, "No, no, no, Bruce, you have to –"

That was the last time Bruce Blankenship ever heard Becky's voice, and he later recalled what she'd said, while he bled from his eyes, nose, and mouth – and by then the words made complete sense.

"So, are you ready for that drink?" Bruce asked his guest, who simply grinned and nodded. He then turned around, his eyes remaining focused on the blonde, while his head provided the actual movement.

If Bruce's stare had lingered a moment longer, he would have seen her convulse – might have even seen her massive chest split down the middle and thousands of shimmering conduits attach themselves to the appliance panel next to the refrigerator.

But he didn't.

He just kept on smiling and making the drinks.

The Shadow and the Flash

Jack London

WHEN I LOOK BACK, I realise what a peculiar friendship it was. First, there was Lloyd Inwood, tall, slender, and finely knit, nervous and dark. And then Paul Tichlorne, tall, slender, and finely knit, nervous and blond. Each was the replica of the other in everything except colour. Lloyd's eyes were black; Paul's were blue. Under stress of excitement, the blood coursed olive in the face of Lloyd, crimson in the face of Paul. But outside this matter of colouring they were as like as two peas. Both were high-strung, prone to excessive tension and endurance, and they lived at concert pitch.

But there was a trio involved in this remarkable friendship, and the third was short, and fat, and chunky, and lazy, and, loath to say, it was I. Paul and Lloyd seemed born to rivalry with each other, and I to be peacemaker between them. We grew up together, the three of us, and full often have I received the angry blows each intended for the other. They were always competing, striving to outdo each other, and when entered upon some such struggle there was no limit either to their endeavours or passions.

This intense spirit of rivalry obtained in their studies and their games. If Paul memorised one canto of "Marmion," Lloyd memorised two cantos, Paul came back with three, and Lloyd again with four, till each knew the whole poem by heart. I remember an incident that occurred at the swimming hole – an incident tragically significant of the life-struggle between them. The boys had a game of diving to the bottom of a ten-foot pool and holding on by submerged roots to see who could stay under the longest. Paul and Lloyd allowed themselves to be bantered into making the descent together. When I saw their faces, set and determined, disappear in the water as they sank swiftly down, I felt a foreboding of something dreadful. The moments sped, the ripples died away, the face of the pool grew placid and untroubled, and neither black nor golden head broke surface in quest of air. We above grew anxious. The longest record of the longest-winded boy had been exceeded, and still there was no sign. Air bubbles trickled slowly upward, showing that the breath had been expelled from their lungs, and after that the bubbles ceased to trickle upward. Each second became interminable, and, unable longer to endure the suspense, I plunged into the water.

I found them down at the bottom, clutching tight to the roots, their heads not a foot apart, their eyes wide open, each glaring fixedly at the other. They were suffering frightful torment, writhing and twisting in the pangs of voluntary suffocation; for neither would let go and acknowledge himself beaten. I tried to break Paul's hold on the root, but he resisted me fiercely. Then I lost my breath and came to the surface, badly scared. I quickly explained the situation, and half a dozen of us went down and by main strength tore them loose. By the time we got them out, both were unconscious, and it was only after much barrel-rolling and rubbing and pounding that they finally came to their senses. They would have drowned there, had no one rescued them.

When Paul Tichlorne entered college, he let it be generally understood that he was going in for the social sciences. Lloyd Inwood, entering at the same time, elected to take the same course. But Paul had had it secretly in mind all the time to study the natural sciences, specialising on chemistry, and at the last moment he switched over. Though Lloyd had already arranged his year's work and attended the first lectures, he at once followed Paul's lead and went in for the natural sciences and especially for chemistry. Their rivalry soon became a noted thing throughout the university. Each was a spur to the other, and they went into chemistry deeper than did ever students before – so deep, in fact, that ere they took their sheepskins they could have stumped any chemistry or "cow college" professor in the institution, save "old" Moss, head of the department, and even him they puzzled and edified more than once. Lloyd's discovery of the "death bacillus" of the sea toad, and his experiments on it with potassium cyanide, sent his name and that of his university ringing round the world; nor was Paul a whit behind when he succeeded in producing laboratory colloids exhibiting amoeba-like activities, and when he cast new light upon the processes of fertilisation through his startling experiments with simple sodium chlorides and magnesium solutions on low forms of marine life.

It was in their undergraduate days, however, in the midst of their profoundest plunges into the mysteries of organic chemistry, that Doris Van Benschoten entered into their lives. Lloyd met her first, but within twenty-four hours Paul saw to it that he also made her acquaintance. Of course, they fell in love with her, and she became the only thing in life worth living for. They wooed her with equal ardour and fire, and so intense became their struggle for her that half the student-body took to wagering wildly on the result. Even "old" Moss, one day, after an astounding demonstration in his private laboratory by Paul, was guilty to the extent of a month's salary of backing him to become the bridegroom of Doris Van Benschoten.

In the end she solved the problem in her own way, to everybody's satisfaction except Paul's and Lloyd's. Getting them together, she said that she really could not choose between them because she loved them both equally well; and that, unfortunately, since polyandry was not permitted in the United States she would be compelled to forego the honour and happiness of marrying either of them. Each blamed the other for this lamentable outcome, and the bitterness between them grew more bitter.

But things came to a head enough. It was at my home, after they had taken their degrees and dropped out of the world's sight, that the beginning of the end came to pass. Both were men of means, with little inclination and no necessity for professional life. My friendship and their mutual animosity were the two things that linked them in any way together. While they were very often at my place, they made it a fastidious point to avoid each other on such visits, though it was inevitable, under the circumstances, that they should come upon each other occasionally.

On the day I have in recollection, Paul Tichlorne had been mooning all morning in my study over a current scientific review. This left me free to my own affairs, and I was out among my roses when Lloyd Inwood arrived. Clipping and pruning and tacking the climbers on the porch, with my mouth full of nails, and Lloyd following me about and lending a hand now and again, we fell to discussing the mythical race of invisible people, that strange and vagrant people the traditions of which have come down to us. Lloyd warmed to the talk in his nervous, jerky fashion, and was soon interrogating the physical properties and possibilities of invisibility. A perfectly black object, he contended, would elude and defy the acutest vision.

"Colour is a sensation," he was saying. "It has no objective reality. Without light, we can see neither colours nor objects themselves. All objects are black in the dark, and in the dark it is impossible to see them. If no light strikes upon them, then no light is flung back from them to the eye, and so we have no vision-evidence of their being."

"But we see black objects in daylight," I objected.

"Very true," he went on warmly. "And that is because they are not perfectly black. Were they perfectly black, absolutely black, as it were, we could not see them – ay, not in the blaze of a thousand suns could we see them! And so I say, with the right pigments, properly compounded, an absolutely black paint could be produced which would render invisible whatever it was applied to."

"It would be a remarkable discovery," I said non-committally, for the whole thing seemed too fantastic for aught but speculative purposes.

"Remarkable!" Lloyd slapped me on the shoulder. "I should say so. Why, old chap, to coat myself with such a paint would be to put the world at my feet. The secrets of kings and courts would be mine, the machinations of diplomats and politicians, the play of stock-gamblers, the plans of trusts and corporations. I could keep my hand on the inner pulse of things and become the greatest power in the world. And I – " He broke off shortly, then added, "Well, I have begun my experiments, and I don't mind telling you that I'm right in line for it."

A laugh from the doorway startled us. Paul Tichlorne was standing there, a smile of mockery on his lips.

"You forget, my dear Lloyd," he said.

"Forget what?"

"You forget," Paul went on – "ah, you forget the shadow."

I saw Lloyd's face drop, but he answered sneeringly, "I can carry a sunshade, you know." Then he turned suddenly and fiercely upon him. "Look here, Paul, you'll keep out of this if you know what's good for you."

A rupture seemed imminent, but Paul laughed good-naturedly. "I wouldn't lay fingers on your dirty pigments. Succeed beyond your most sanguine expectations, yet you will always fetch up against the shadow. You can't get away from it. Now I shall go on the very opposite tack. In the very nature of my proposition the shadow will be eliminated – "

"Transparency!" ejaculated Lloyd, instantly. "But it can't be achieved."

"Oh, no; of course not." And Paul shrugged his shoulders and strolled off down the briar-rose path.

This was the beginning of it. Both men attacked the problem with all the tremendous energy for which they were noted, and with a rancour and bitterness that made me tremble for the success of either. Each trusted me to the utmost, and in the long weeks of experimentation that followed I was made a party to both sides, listening to their theorisings and witnessing their demonstrations. Never, by word or sign, did I convey to either the slightest hint of the other's progress, and they respected me for the seal I put upon my lips.

Lloyd Inwood, after prolonged and unintermittent application, when the tension upon his mind and body became too great to bear, had a strange way of obtaining relief. He attended prize fights. It was at one of these brutal exhibitions, whither he had dragged me in order to tell his latest results, that his theory received striking confirmation.

"Do you see that red-whiskered man?" he asked, pointing across the ring to the fifth tier of seats on the opposite side. "And do you see the next man to him, the one in the white hat? Well, there is quite a gap between them, is there not?"

"Certainly," I answered. "They are a seat apart. The gap is the unoccupied seat."

He leaned over to me and spoke seriously. "Between the red-whiskered man and the white-hatted man sits Ben Wasson. You have heard me speak of him. He is the cleverest pugilist of his weight in the country. He is also a Caribbean negro, full-blooded, and the blackest in the United State. He has on a black overcoat buttoned up. I saw him when he came in and took that seat. As soon as he sat down he disappeared. Watch closely; he may smile."

I was for crossing over to verify Lloyd's statement, but he restrained me. "Wait," he said.

I waited and watched, till the red-whiskered man turned his head as though addressing the unoccupied seat; and then, in that empty space, I saw the rolling whites of a pair of eyes and the white double-crescent of two rows of teeth, and for the instant I could make out a negro's face. But with the passing of the smile his visibility passed, and the chair seemed vacant as before.

"Were he perfectly black, you could sit alongside him and not see him," Lloyd said; and I confess the illustration was apt enough to make me well-nigh convinced.

I visited Lloyd's laboratory a number of times after that, and found him always deep in his search after the absolute black. His experiments covered all sorts of pigments, such as lamp-blacks, tars, carbonised vegetable matters, soots of oils and fats, and the various carbonised animal substances.

"White light is composed of the seven primary colours," he argued to me. "But it is itself, of itself, invisible. Only by being reflected from objects do it and the objects become visible. But only that portion of it that is reflected becomes visible. For instance, here is a blue tobacco-box. The white light strikes against it, and, with one exception, all its component colours – violet, indigo, green, yellow, orange, and red – are absorbed. The one exception is blue. It is not absorbed, but reflected. Therefore the tobacco-box gives us a sensation of blueness. We do not see the other colours because they are absorbed. We see only the blue. For the same reason grass is green. The green waves of white light are thrown upon our eyes."

"When we paint our houses, we do not apply colour to them," he said at another time. "What we do is to apply certain substances that have the property of absorbing from white light all the colours except those that we would have our houses appear. When a substance reflects all the colours to the eye, it seems to us white. When it absorbs all the colours, it is black. But, as I said before, we have as yet no perfect black. All the colours are not absorbed. The perfect black, guarding against high lights, will be utterly and absolutely invisible. Look at that, for example."

He pointed to the palette lying on his work-table. Different shades of black pigments were brushed on it. One, in particular, I could hardly see. It gave my eyes a blurring sensation, and I rubbed them and looked again.

"That," he said impressively, "is the blackest black you or any mortal man ever looked upon. But just you wait, and I'll have a black so black that no mortal man will be able to look upon it – and see it!"

On the other hand, I used to find Paul Tichlorne plunged as deeply into the study of light polarisation, diffraction, and interference, single and double refraction, and all manner of strange organic compounds.

"Transparency: a state or quality of body which permits all rays of light to pass through," he defined for me. "That is what I am seeking. Lloyd blunders up against the shadow with his perfect opaqueness. But I escape it. A transparent body casts no shadow; neither does it reflect light-waves – that is, the perfectly transparent does not. So, avoiding high lights, not only will such a body cast no shadow, but, since it reflects no light, it will also be invisible."

We were standing by the window at another time. Paul was engaged in polishing a number of lenses, which were ranged along the sill. Suddenly, after a pause in the conversation, he said, "Oh! I've dropped a lens. Stick your head out, old man, and see where it went to."

Out I started to thrust my head, but a sharp blow on the forehead caused me to recoil. I rubbed my bruised brow and gazed with reproachful inquiry at Paul, who was laughing in gleeful, boyish fashion.

"Well?" he said.

"Well?" I echoed.

"Why don't you investigate?" he demanded. And investigate I did. Before thrusting out my head, my senses, automatically active, had told me there was nothing there, that nothing intervened between me and out-of-doors, that the aperture of the window opening was utterly empty. I stretched forth my hand and felt a hard object, smooth and cool and flat, which my touch, out of its experience, told me to be glass. I looked again, but could see positively nothing.

"White quartzose sand," Paul rattled off, "sodic carbonate, slaked lime, cutlet, manganese peroxide – there you have it, the finest French plate glass, made by the great St. Gobain Company, who made the finest plate glass in the world, and this is the finest piece they ever made. It cost a king's ransom. But look at it! You can't see it. You don't know it's there till you run your head against it.

"Eh, old boy! That's merely an object-lesson – certain elements, in themselves opaque, yet so compounded as to give a resultant body which is transparent. But that is a matter of inorganic chemistry, you say. Very true. But I dare to assert, standing here on my two feet, that in the organic I can duplicate whatever occurs in the inorganic.

"Here!" He held a test-tube between me and the light, and I noted the cloudy or muddy liquid it contained. He emptied the contents of another test-tube into it, and almost instantly it became clear and sparkling.

"Or here!" With quick, nervous movements among his array of test-tubes, he turned a white solution to a wine colour, and a light yellow solution to a dark brown. He dropped a piece of litmus paper into an acid, when it changed instantly to red, and on floating it in an alkali it turned as quickly to blue.

"The litmus paper is still the litmus paper," he enunciated in the formal manner of the lecturer. "I have not changed it into something else. Then what did I do? I merely changed the arrangement of its molecules. Where, at first, it absorbed all colours from the light but red, its molecular structure was so changed that it absorbed red and all colours except blue. And so it goes, ad infinitum. Now, what I purpose to do is this." He paused for a space. "I purpose to seek – ay, and to find – the proper reagents, which, acting upon the living organism, will bring about molecular changes analogous to those you have just witnessed. But these reagents, which I shall find, and for that matter, upon which I already have my hands, will not turn the living body to blue or red or black, but they will turn it to transparency. All light will pass through it. It will be invisible. It will cast no shadow."

A few weeks later I went hunting with Paul. He had been promising me for some time that I should have the pleasure of shooting over a wonderful dog – the most wonderful dog, in fact, that ever man shot over, so he averred, and continued to aver till my curiosity was aroused. But on the morning in question I was disappointed, for there was no dog in evidence.

"Don't see him about," Paul remarked unconcernedly, and we set off across the fields.

I could not imagine, at the time, what was ailing me, but I had a feeling of some impending and deadly illness. My nerves were all awry, and, from the astounding tricks they played me, my senses seemed to have run riot. Strange sounds disturbed me. At times I heard the swish-swish of grass being shoved aside, and once the patter of feet across a patch of stony ground.

"Did you hear anything, Paul?" I asked once.

But he shook his head, and thrust his feet steadily forward.

While climbing a fence, I heard the low, eager whine of a dog, apparently from within a couple of feet of me; but on looking about me I saw nothing.

I dropped to the ground, limp and trembling.

"Paul," I said, "we had better return to the house. I am afraid I am going to be sick."

"Nonsense, old man," he answered. "The sunshine has gone to your head like wine. You'll be all right. It's famous weather."

But, passing along a narrow path through a clump of cottonwoods, some object brushed against my legs and I stumbled and nearly fell. I looked with sudden anxiety at Paul.

"What's the matter?" he asked. "Tripping over your own feet?"

I kept my tongue between my teeth and plodded on, though sore perplexed and thoroughly satisfied that some acute and mysterious malady had attacked my nerves. So far my eyes had escaped; but, when we got to the open fields again, even my vision went back on me. Strange flashes of varicoloured, rainbow light began to appear and disappear on the path before me. Still, I managed to keep myself in hand, till the varicoloured lights persisted for a space of fully twenty seconds, dancing and flashing in continuous play. Then I sat down, weak and shaky.

"It's all up with me," I gasped, covering my eyes with my hands. "It has attacked my eyes. Paul, take me home."

But Paul laughed long and loud. "What did I tell you? The most wonderful dog, eh? Well, what do you think?"

He turned partly from me and began to whistle. I heard the patter of feet, the panting of a heated animal, and the unmistakable yelp of a dog. Then Paul stooped down and apparently fondled the empty air.

"Here! Give me your fist."

And he rubbed my hand over the cold nose and jowls of a dog. A dog it certainly was, with the shape and the smooth, short coat of a pointer.

Suffice to say, I speedily recovered my spirits and control. Paul put a collar about the animal's neck and tied his handkerchief to its tail. And then was vouchsafed us the remarkable sight of an empty collar and a waving handkerchief cavorting over the fields. It was something to see that collar and handkerchief pin a bevy of quail in a clump of locusts and remain rigid and immovable till we had flushed the birds.

Now and again the dog emitted the varicoloured light-flashes I have mentioned. The one thing, Paul explained, which he had not anticipated and which he doubted could be overcome.

"They're a large family," he said, "these sun dogs, wind dogs, rainbows, halos, and perihelia. They are produced by refraction of light from mineral and ice crystals, from mist, rain, spray, and no end of things; and I am afraid they are the penalty I must pay for transparency. I escaped Lloyd's shadow only to fetch up against the rainbow flash."

A couple of days later, before the entrance to Paul's laboratory, I encountered a terrible stench. So overpowering was it that it was easy to discover the source – mass of putrescent matter on the doorstep which in general outlines resembled a dog.

Paul was startled when he investigated my find. It was his invisible dog, or rather, what had been his invisible dog, for it was now plainly visible. It had been playing about but a few minutes before in all health and strength. Closer examination revealed that the skull had been crushed by some heavy blow. While it was strange that the animal should have been killed, the inexplicable thing was that it should so quickly decay.

"The reagents I injected into its system were harmless," Paul explained. "Yet they were powerful, and it appears that when death comes they force practically instantaneous disintegration. Remarkable! Most remarkable! Well, the only thing is not to die. They do not harm so long as one lives. But I do wonder who smashed in that dog's head."

Light, however, was thrown upon this when a frightened housemaid brought the news that Gaffer Bedshaw had that very morning, not more than an hour back, gone violently insane, and was strapped down at home, in the huntsman's lodge, where he raved of a battle with a ferocious and gigantic beast that he had encountered in the Tichlorne pasture. He claimed that the thing, whatever it was, was invisible, that with his own eyes he had seen that it was invisible; wherefore his tearful wife and daughters shook their heads, and wherefore he but waxed the more violent, and the gardener and the coachman tightened the straps by another hole.

Nor, while Paul Tichlorne was thus successfully mastering the problem of invisibility, was Lloyd Inwood a whit behind. I went over in answer to a message of his to come and see how he was getting on. Now his laboratory occupied an isolated situation in the midst of his vast grounds. It was built in a pleasant little glade, surrounded on all sides by a dense forest growth, and was to be gained by way of a winding and erratic path. But I have travelled that path so often as to know every foot of it, and conceive my surprise when I came upon the glade and found no laboratory. The quaint shed structure with its red sandstone chimney was not. Nor did it look as if it ever had been. There were no signs of ruin, no debris, nothing.

I started to walk across what had once been its site. "This," I said to myself, "should be where the step went up to the door." Barely were the words out of my mouth when I stubbed my toe on some obstacle, pitched forward, and butted my head into something that felt very much like a door. I reached out my hand. It was a door. I found the knob and turned it. And at once, as the door swung inward on its hinges, the whole interior of the laboratory impinged upon my vision. Greeting Lloyd, I closed the door and backed up the path a few paces. I could see nothing of the building. Returning and opening the door, at once all the furniture and every detail of the interior were visible. It was indeed startling, the sudden transition from void to light and form and colour.

"What do you think of it, eh?" Lloyd asked, wringing my hand. "I slapped a couple of coats of absolute black on the outside yesterday afternoon to see how it worked. How's your head? You bumped it pretty solidly, I imagine."

"Never mind that," he interrupted my congratulations. "I've something better for you to do."

While he talked he began to strip, and when he stood naked before me he thrust a pot and brush into my hand and said, "Here, give me a coat of this."

It was an oily, shellac-like stuff, which spread quickly and easily over the skin and dried immediately.

"Merely preliminary and precautionary," he explained when I had finished; "but now for the real stuff."

I picked up another pot he indicated, and glanced inside, but could see nothing.

"It's empty," I said.

"Stick your finger in it."

I obeyed, and was aware of a sensation of cool moistness. On withdrawing my hand I glanced at the forefinger, the one I had immersed, but it had disappeared. I moved and knew from the alternate tension and relaxation of the muscles that I moved it, but it defied my sense of sight. To all appearances I had been shorn of a finger; nor could I get any visual impression of it till I extended it under the skylight and saw its shadow plainly blotted on the floor.

Lloyd chuckled. "Now spread it on, and keep your eyes open."

I dipped the brush into the seemingly empty pot, and gave him a long stroke across his chest. With the passage of the brush the living flesh disappeared from beneath. I covered his right leg, and he was a one-legged man defying all laws of gravitation. And so, stroke by stroke, member by member, I painted Lloyd Inwood into nothingness. It was a creepy experience, and I was glad when naught remained in sight but his burning black eyes, poised apparently unsupported in mid-air.

"I have a refined and harmless solution for them," he said. "A fine spray with an air-brush, and presto! I am not."

This deftly accomplished, he said, "Now I shall move about, and do you tell me what sensations you experience."

"In the first place, I cannot see you," I said, and I could hear his gleeful laugh from the midst of the emptiness. "Of course," I continued, "you cannot escape your shadow, but that was to be expected. When you pass between my eye and an object, the object disappears, but so unusual and incomprehensible is its disappearance that it seems to me as though my eyes had blurred. When you move rapidly, I experience a bewildering succession of blurs. The blurring sensation makes my eyes ache and my brain tired."

"Have you any other warnings of my presence?" he asked.

"No, and yes," I answered. "When you are near me I have feelings similar to those produced by dank warehouses, gloomy crypts, and deep mines. And as sailors feel the loom of the land on dark nights, so I think I feel the loom of your body. But it is all very vague and intangible."

Long we talked that last morning in his laboratory; and when I turned to go, he put his unseen hand in mine with nervous grip, and said, "Now I shall conquer the world!" And I could not dare to tell him of Paul Tichlorne's equal success.

At home I found a note from Paul, asking me to come up immediately, and it was high noon when I came spinning up the driveway on my wheel. Paul called me from the tennis court, and I dismounted and went over. But the court was empty. As I stood there, gaping open-mouthed, a tennis ball struck me on the arm, and as I turned about, another whizzed past my ear. For aught I could see of my assailant, they came whirling at me from out of space, and right well was I peppered with them. But when the balls already flung at me began to come back for a second whack, I realised the situation. Seizing a racquet and keeping my eyes open, I quickly saw a rainbow flash appearing and disappearing and darting over the ground. I took out after it, and when I laid the racquet upon it for a half-dozen stout blows, Paul's voice rang out: "Enough! Enough! Oh! Ouch! Stop! You're landing on my naked skin, you know! Ow! O-w-w! I'll be good! I'll be good! I only wanted you to see my metamorphosis," he said ruefully, and I imagined he was rubbing his hurts.

A few minutes later we were playing tennis – a handicap on my part, for I could have no knowledge of his position save when all the angles between himself, the sun, and me, were in proper conjunction. Then he flashed, and only then. But the flashes were more brilliant than the rainbow – purest blue, most delicate violet, brightest yellow, and all the intermediary shades, with the scintillant brilliancy of the diamond, dazzling, blinding, iridescent.

But in the midst of our play I felt a sudden cold chill, reminding me of deep mines and gloomy crypts, such a chill as I had experienced that very morning. The next moment, close to the net, I saw a ball rebound in mid-air and empty space, and at the same instant, a score of feet away, Paul Tichlorne emitted a rainbow flash. It could not be he from whom the ball had rebounded, and with sickening dread I realised that Lloyd Inwood had come upon the scene. To make sure, I looked for his shadow, and there it was, a shapeless blotch the girth of his body, (the sun was overhead), moving along the ground. I remembered his threat, and felt sure that all the long years of rivalry were about to culminate in uncanny battle.

I cried a warning to Paul, and heard a snarl as of a wild beast, and an answering snarl. I saw the dark blotch move swiftly across the court, and a brilliant burst of varicoloured light moving with equal swiftness to meet it; and then shadow and flash came together and there was the sound of unseen blows. The net went down before my frightened eyes. I sprang toward the fighters, crying: "For God's sake!"

But their locked bodies smote against my knees, and I was overthrown.

"You keep out of this, old man!" I heard the voice of Lloyd Inwood from out of the emptiness. And then Paul's voice crying, "Yes, we've had enough of peacemaking!"

From the sound of their voices I knew they had separated. I could not locate Paul, and so approached the shadow that represented Lloyd. But from the other side came a stunning blow on the point of my jaw, and I heard Paul scream angrily, "Now will you keep away?"

Then they came together again, the impact of their blows, their groans and gasps, and the swift flashings and shadow-movings telling plainly of the deadliness of the struggle.

I shouted for help, and Gaffer Bedshaw came running into the court. I could see, as he approached, that he was looking at me strangely, but he collided with the combatants and was hurled headlong to the ground. With despairing shriek and a cry of "O Lord, I've got 'em!" he sprang to his feet and tore madly out of the court.

I could do nothing, so I sat up, fascinated and powerless, and watched the struggle. The noonday sun beat down with dazzling brightness on the naked tennis court. And it was naked. All I could see was the blotch of shadow and the rainbow flashes, the dust rising from the invisible feet, the earth tearing up from beneath the straining foot-grips, and the wire screen bulge once or twice as their bodies hurled against it. That was all, and after a time even that ceased. There were no more flashes, and the shadow had become long and stationary; and I remembered their set boyish faces when they clung to the roots in the deep coolness of the pool.

They found me an hour afterward. Some inkling of what had happened got to the servants and they quitted the Tichlorne service in a body. Gaffer Bedshaw never recovered from the second shock he received, and is confined in a madhouse, hopelessly incurable. The secrets of their marvellous discoveries died with Paul and Lloyd, both laboratories being destroyed by grief-stricken relatives. As for myself, I no longer care for chemical research, and science is a tabooed topic in my household. I have returned to my roses. Nature's colours are good enough for me.

Metsys

Adrian Ludens

I ATE too much ice cream at the Mexican restaurant. The baby fussed. My wife made a snide remark about the mariachi band.

We were punished.

When we returned home from A Través de la Manada, we discovered that our two oldest kids – one boy and one girl – were gone. Taken.

The Metsys knows best.

I got a new vehicle, a Big Black Truck. It's as shiny as polished obsidian, with a beastly engine under the hood.

But the two oldest children are gone. The Metsys gives and the Metsys takes away. A harsh lesson, but to whom would I dare complain?

We must remain amiable, moderate and polite. Go along to get along. Those qualities are rewarded.

I can't remember the names of the older children.

* * *

My wife is hosting a party.

The women in her theater troupe have assembled at our home for their recognitions. My wife is all aflutter. I suppose that is to be expected. The women have congregated in a room separated from the rest of the house by a vault-like door.

There is sad news, but my wife seems to be enjoying her moment so I bear the news alone.

The baby has done something wrong. Perhaps a sin of pride or anger but I don't know for certain. I came into the room after it happened. The punishment had already been carried out.

The Metsys has put the baby down one of the many white plastic punishment tubes that protrude from the living room floor. Most of their length runs beneath the house. The tubes are only about six inches wide but I know she's down there.

I kneel and listen.

"Da-dee!"

"Daaaa-deee!"

"Da-DEE!"

Her voice is urgent, but not yet fearful. That will come. As for what comes after that, I do not know.

Sometimes if the Metsys doesn't think the offender has learned the appropriate lesson, he or she simply stays in the tubes. The punished one remains alone below, until they go mad, starve and depart. Only then will a member of the Departure Department arrive. I have heard the empty shell is sucked back out through the tube. It must be quite a job when disposing of a full-grown.

For their part, the family is expected to go about their daily routine while all of this is happening. The guilty is always within earshot, never in sight.

The baby calls me again. She's more plaintive this time and coming from a different tube, judging from the sound of her voice.

I lick my lips and crouch. I reach my hand into one of the tube and pull out a fist full of leaves, small sticks and a variety of dried flower petals.

Each of the tubes contains something different. One has gumballs. Another holds smooth stones. This one is filled with shiny copper coins. That one is packed with hourglass sand. But they all serve the same purpose: separation between those on the inside of the house and those banished to the tubes.

The detritus falls from my hands and scatters on the floor. I grab two more fists full before I realize what I'm doing. I can't fight the Metsys' decision on this matter, nor can I pull a baby from a six-inch opening. I hurriedly sweep up the twigs and petals and put them back in the tube's mouth. My heart pounds.

For a moment there I defied. Eyes and Spies everywhere and I forgot my role, my duty in this society. I hold my pose and my breath. Will the Metsys come for me?

I admit the sound of my baby's cries makes me sad, but the thought of the Metsys exacting punishment on me for defying a decision made chills the marrow in my bones.

We must all remain industrious, humble and truthful. Aspire to acquire, shirk sin, and never break the rules. Rules are subject to change without notice.

The Metsys knows best.

I find something else to do. I remember my wife's party, the women in her theater troupe.

My wife put their headshots on display in our living room, though the party is behind locked doors. I get my camera. I take pictures of their pictures. (Perhaps I photograph their photographs?) Yes, that sounds more 'upscale'. They'll want copies. I'll need their contact information.

I go to the door where the party is. I try the knob but it's cold and unyielding. This mirrors the mood of the women within. I had hoped to be allowed access. To be passed around, even, to use and be used. Not all of the women are beautiful, but some of them are. I would go willingly. I would do or say whatever they asked of me, if only the Metsys would lend me some guidance.

I am submissive, attentive, and self-sacrificial. I keep expecting to be rewarded, but no. I wonder if I am going about it all wrong. The lapses in judgment – like reaching into the tube earlier – do not help my station. This humble man must rise to a new low.

I hear laughter and music from within: a muted trumpet and sliding double bass.

My wife bursts from the locked room, sees me waiting and puts her smile away for a more suitable occasion.

She staggers past me and in her hurry to leave me behind knocks over some acquired items from an end table. I set things right and she returns with her arms full.

A bottle of wine. Another of champagne. Flavored lubricant.

A gleaming meat cleaver.

Her left pupil has fully dilated. I feel curiously off balance when she looks at me.

Which side of her brain is she thinking with?

? with thinking I am brain my of side which

My wife tips her head at our various antique sound systems interspersed throughout the living room. She fixes her gaze on a palm-sized device lying on the corner of an end table. I press the "play" button. Her curt voice issues from its tiny speaker.

"I'm taping a tape and recording a record. Keep them going until I get back."

I start to reply but she is already returned to the party. I remember then that I wanted to tell her something important. The big news! Good grief! How had I forgotten? I meant to let her know what had just happened.

I hurry after her but she closes the door in my face.

I wanted to tell her that I took photographs of the photographs.

She'd want to know that.

* * *

After working the expected allotment of time I power down the terminals, turn off the lighting and use a hand signal to release the spooky little sparrow of a coworker. She steps out the door. I mentally set the alarm code to the building and enter the parking garage. I see the girl's black trench coat billowing in the night air. She doesn't look back but I know that she knows.

She relishes this part of the job more than I do, though I will never admit as much.

I count to twenty to give the girl a head start. Then I start my Big Black Truck.

The pipes roar as I press down on the accelerator. The houses line up along the street for inspection. I angle on to the sidewalk and race down the block in the direction she has gone. My tires roll over a kid's bicycle, a doll (I think) and two plastic fruit bushes, but not the girl. She's hidden herself well and is as easy to find as a shadow at moonless midnight. I circle one block, then another.

The girl loses herself in the darkness and so gains another day of WorkLife. We'll see each other again in the morning. This system was put in place to by the Council. I can't complain. If I didn't have tenure, it would be me running each night at closing time.

I roar down the highway in my Big Black Truck. I turn up the sound system. The music is a bombastic cacophony of computer-generated sounds. I turn it up and try to keep a beat by pounding my fists on the steering wheel, the dash and my temples.

I try not to think about the information processed today. I collect reports of incidents of obsolescence. The girl and I tabulate, compare, graph, chart, compile. Today four incidents of obsolescence came in regarding the tabulation, comparison, graphing, charting and compiling of incidents of obsolescence. That's up three from yesterday. This trend distresses me.

How long will I be able to justify my WorkLife?

I force myself to consider other matters.

The sky looks gorgeous at this time of night. Through my windshield I see bright blues and vibrant reds, colors so vivid I struggle with their reality. I think the reds are bad and the blues are good, but I'm not sure. The Metsys is ever changing, though paradoxically always remaining the same.

I feel lost. Not quite one with the Metsys.

My tires slice through the puddles of recent rain that pockmarks this stretch of road. My Big Black Truck fishtails for a few moments, then finds the asphalt and shoots forward. I press down on the accelerator. The engine roars, bellows, shrieks in response.

I still want to go faster.

I outrun all the other transports on the freeway. Could I use my Big Black Truck to outrun my life? There's a part of me that wishes...

But no.

Being industrious, loyal and conscientious should be enough to achieve happiness. Recycle. Tell the truth. Keep the balance. Bounce back from setbacks.

Be a cork. Corks don't sink, no matter how deep, how polluted the ocean.

The Metsys knows best.

An old-fashioned police cruiser passes me going the opposite direction. For a brief moment I'm fearful of a ticket or further punishment. Then I realize a policeman would never stop me. Everyone knows Big Black Trucks are gifts from the Metsys. The police, largely figureheads to begin with, can only assist motorists. They cannot punish. That's the role of the Metsys.

I turn my thoughts from the police back to my life. I tremble as I pass the next mile marker.

I bellow my impotent rage at the radiant skies. My truck echoes my sentiments.

My Big. Black. Truck.

* * *

Lying in the dark beside my wife, I stare at the ceiling and try to think. It's hard to stay focused. The baby screams all night from somewhere in the pipes.

Today is the proper day for me to pay my respects to the Metsys. My wife has yet to emerge from the party room. I hope she remembers today's significance.

A Beautiful Greeter with a serene smile waits at the gates surrounding the great marble structure. By way of an elegant gesture she indicates that I may pass.

Alongside the narrow street I spot the girl. Today the spooky little sparrow floats within a crimson cape and hood. I admire her dedication. I know why she's here. We all want to impress the Metsys today.

I realize she's hoping I will help elevate her standing. I press down on the brake pedal and swerve my Big Black Truck. She dodges at the last second, but staggers and leans against the marble wall, playing it up. I flip her off and stomp on the accelerator. She disappears in a black exhaust cloud.

It never hurts to put on a show when one knows the Eyes and Spies of the Metsys are watching. Surely the Metsys will be pleased with both of us.

Inside the great marble structure, I kneel and face the floor until an emissary approaches.

"Your son is already here," he tells me. His voice is condescendingly jovial.

I know right away he's not talking about the oldest boy. This is my five year old he's referencing.

Damn it. That kid is always in my hair, demanding my attention. We spent Quality Time together only two weeks ago and now he repays me by making me look bad in the eyes of the Metsys.

I should get a second Big Black Truck for putting up with this. Or a round in my wife's party room with her theater troupe. I have the patience of a saint.

"We would hope that you're wondering why we had to bring him here," the emissary presses. I don't have to see his face to know he's sneering at my bald spot.

"The Metsys knows best," I reply. Know your place. Perpetuate stereotypes.

The emissary thrusts a hand beneath my down turned face. Enormous, jewel-encrusted rings grace his fingers. Warts protrude wherever there are no rings.

I kiss each of the rings and murmur phrases of allegiance.

The emissary twists his wrist so that I end up kissing as many warts as rings.

My knees pop as I stand. The emissary beckons me to follow him up a narrow, steep flight of stairs. I get to two hundred sixty six and give up on counting.

At last we enter the emissary's chambers. He ascends and seats himself upon a seven-foot throne. Facing him, and seated atop an antique holy relic only the oldest among us would have recognized as a wooden ladder, is my younger son. His eyes plead with mine as I climb the steps on the ladder.

"Daddy!"

His cheeks have been rouged to make him look more cherubic. The makeup applied to his eyes and lips borders on garish. His hair is plastered to one side. He wears a white pressed shirt, black slacks and a miniature necktie. There's terror in his eyes, but my arrival has instilled a glimmer of hope as well.

"Tell the man I'm a good kid, Daddy! He doesn't believe me."

Has he altered his appearance to sway my opinion of him? Or did the emissary do it as a formality for the hearing?

"This is not a hearing," the emissary says as if reading my thoughts.

A multitude of Eyes and Spies watch me now. I could turn my head to look for them, but I know I won't see them.

"This is simply a clearing of the air, if you will." The emissary waves a glittering hand expansively. "An opportunity for your son to admit his wrongdoing and atone for it."

"Daddy, I didn't −"

"What has my son done?" I ask. I know the blood has drained from my face. I do everything I'm supposed to do. I spend more than I can afford. I tell the truth to others and lie to myself. I am proud of my level of humility. I try to be a floating cork in the face of adversity. I don't need my own family creating stumbling blocks along my life's path.

The emissary leans forward in his throne and for the first time I see him up close. A shaved, bullet-shaped head. Bristling spider-leg eyebrows. Tree-trunk neck. The burst blood vessels crisscrossing on his bulbous nose seem to form the shape of a small key.

The symbolism is not lost on me. The emissary, with his bejeweled fingers and fine robes, could gain entry into my wife's party room, where I could not. He would make the rounds once, twice, a third time, practicing the art of dentistry, in a twisted manner of speaking.

Filling... cavities.

I've let myself become distracted. I'm shaking now, clinging to the ladder, but not to my son.

"What has he done?" My voice sounds strange. My mouth is dry as dust and it feels as if my tongue is a mummified corpse curled in the corner of my mouth.

"He found the purse-book of Miss Cherry Jewel. She's quite famous, as you know."

I don't know, but nod anyway. If the emissary knows her I should too.

"Miss Jewel, of course, carries photos of herself in her purse-book. Name a self-respecting woman who doesn't," he challenges.

My son is weeping. Tears stream down his cheeks. Seeing me watching him, he tries to put on a brave face and wipes at the wet streaks with the back of his hand. He only succeeds in smearing his rouge.

His lips part as if subconsciously urging me to speak some words of encouragement.

Instead I give him a sermon of silence.

"Certain Eyes observed your son looking at Miss Jewel's photo of her toenails," the emissary reveals with obvious glee. "And he tried to steal Miss Jewel's photo of her nostrils."

The words tumble from my son's mouth. "No Daddy I'm not lying I was only looking in her purse for something to eat an apple or an onion but I swear Daddy I don't want to peek at her toenails anymore!"

Anymore.

There it is, then. The damning word that proves his guilt.

I know Eyes wait, and the Spies listen, for my response. The emissary's mocking smile is directed at me, when it should be on my –

My son. Such a burden. Always making my life more difficult.

But a tiny part of me still cares. A small voice (a nearly forgotten ghost from Before) implores me to worry about pleasing my son the way I worry about pleasing the Metsys.

I hear an unexpected, high-pitched titter. I look at the emissary then at my son. I look around at the cold marble walls.

Must be me who's giggling.

Giggling and grappling.

Decision time.

I steady myself and open my arms to embrace my son. He throws himself against me and begins weeping. His relaxed limbs tell me that for him, a tremendous burden has been lifted.

A tremendous burden.

I let him go.

The emissary gazes down at my five year old writhing in pain on the floor seven feet below us. He looks back at me and favors me with a brief nod. "Well done."

I stare back at him and say nothing.

"You might make a good citizen out of him yet. We look forward to following his development. Of course you'll need to trade in your Big Black Truck for a Hospital Voucher. "

My heart sinks.

The emissary leers, looking over my shoulder. I turn to see a black rectangle widening in the marble, a missing tooth in a wall of enamel. My wife emerges from the darkness, looking dazed but calm. My oldest son comes next, wearing a militaristic uniform. He's shadowed by my oldest daughter, looking composed but somber. Deflowered.

They were gone. Now the Metsys has returned them to me. But for how long, I do not know.

The two older children help our five year old to stand. Even from the top of the ceremonial ladder I can see the break in his tibia. His face is chalky, but he'll live. I hope someday he'll understand that I did what I had to do.

Then I realize someone is missing: the youngest.

I look quickly at the emissary and immediately regret giving him the satisfaction.

His sad smile is theatrical and false. He shakes his head.

I am so tired of all of this. So tired of playing this game. For the first time, a question and its doppelganger occur to me: do I fail the Metsys, or does the Metsys fail me?

I know I should begin my descent, but something – emotion? – makes me pause. The emissary looks down his nose at me.

How cruel that I only miss her now that she's gone.

"Emily." I say, to no one in particular. "Her name was Emily."

The Tachypomp:
A Mathematical Demonstration

Edward Page Mitchell

THERE WAS nothing mysterious about Professor Surd's dislike for me. I was the only poor mathematician in an exceptionally mathematical class. The old gentleman sought the lecture-room every morning with eagerness, and left it reluctantly. For was it not a thing of joy to find seventy young men who, individually and collectively, preferred x to XX; who had rather differentiate than dissipate; and for whom the limbs of the heavenly bodies had more attractions than those of earthly stars upon the spectacular stage?

So affairs went on swimmingly between the Professor of Mathematics and the Junior Class at Polyp University. In every man of the seventy the sage saw the logarithm of a possible La Place, of a Sturm, or of a Newton. It was a delightful task for him to lead them through the pleasant valleys of conic sections, and beside the still waters of the integral calculus. Figuratively speaking, his problem was not a hard one. He had only to manipulate, and eliminate, and to raise to a higher power, and the triumphant result of examination day was assured.

But I was a disturbing element, a perplexing unknown quantity, which had somehow crept into the work, and which seriously threatened to impair the accuracy of his calculations. It was a touching sight to behold the venerable mathematician as he pleaded with me not so utterly to disregard precedent in the use of cotangents; or as he urged, with eyes almost tearful, that ordinates were dangerous things to trifle with. All in vain. More theorems went on to my cuff than into my head. Never did chalk do so much work to so little purpose. And, therefore, it came that Furnace Second was reduced to zero in Professor Surd's estimation. He looked upon me with all the horror which an unalgebraic nature could inspire. I have seen the Professor walk around an entire square rather than meet the man who had no mathematics in his soul.

For Furnace Second were no invitations to Professor Surd's house. Seventy of the class supped in delegations around the periphery of the Professor's tea-table. The seventy-first knew nothing of the charms of that perfect ellipse, with its twin bunches of fuchsias and geraniums in gorgeous precision at the two foci.

This, unfortunately enough, was no trifling deprivation. Not that I longed especially for segments of Mrs Surd's justly celebrated lemon pies; not that the spheroidal damsons of her excellent preserving had any marked allurements; not even that I yearned to hear the Professor's jocose table-talk about binomials, and chatty illustrations of abstruse paradoxes. The explanation is far different. Professor Surd had a daughter. Twenty years before, he made a proposition of marriage to the present Mrs S. He added a little Corollary to his proposition not long after. The Corollary was a girl.

Abscissa Surd was as perfectly symmetrical as Giotto's circle, and as pure, withal, as the mathematics her father taught. It was just when spring was coming to extract the roots of frozen-up vegetation that I fell in love with the Corollary. That she herself was not indifferent I soon had reason to regard as a self-evident truth.

The sagacious reader will already recognize nearly all the elements necessary to a well-ordered plot. We have introduced a heroine, inferred a hero, and constructed a hostile parent after the most approved model. A movement for the story, a deus ex machina, is alone lacking. With considerable satisfaction I can promise a perfect novelty in this line, a deus ex machina never before offered to the public.

It would be discounting ordinary intelligence to say that I sought with unwearying assiduity to figure my way into the stern father's good-will; that never did dullard apply himself to mathematics more patiently than I; that never did faithfulness achieve such meagre reward. Then I engaged a private tutor. His instructions met with no better success.

My tutor's name was Jean Marie Rivarol. He was a unique Alsatian – though Gallic in name, thoroughly Teuton in nature; by birth a Frenchman, by education a German. His age was thirty; his profession, omniscience; the wolf at his door, poverty; the skeleton in his closet, a consuming but unrequited passion. The most recondite principles of practical science were his toys; the deepest intricacies of abstract science his diversions. Problems which were foreordained mysteries to me were to him as clear as Tahoe water. Perhaps this very fact will explain our lack of success in the relation of tutor and pupil; perhaps the failure is alone due to my own unmitigated stupidity. Rivarol had hung about the skirts of the university for several years; supplying his few wants by writing for scientific journals, or by giving assistance to students who, like myself, were characterized by a plethora of purse and a paucity of ideas; cooking, studying and sleeping in his attic lodgings; and prosecuting queer experiments all by himself.

We were not long discovering that even this eccentric genius could not transplant brains into my deficient skull. I gave over the struggle in despair. An unhappy year dragged its slow length around. A gloomy year it was, brightened only by occasional interviews with Abscissa, the Abbie of my thoughts and dreams.

Commencement day was coming on apace. I was soon to go forth, with the rest of my class, to astonish and delight a waiting world. The Professor seemed to avoid me more than ever. Nothing but the conventionalities, I think kept him from shaping his treatment of me on the basis of unconcealed disgust.

At last, in the very recklessness of despair, I resolved to see him, plead with him, threaten him if need be, and risk all my fortunes on one desperate chance. I wrote him a somewhat defiant letter, stating my aspirations, and, as I flattered myself, shrewdly giving him a week to get over the first shock of horrified surprise. Then I was to call and learn my fate.

During the week of suspense I nearly worried myself into a fever. It was first crazy hope, and then saner despair. On Friday evening, when I presented myself at the Professor's door, I was such a haggard, sleepy, dragged-out spectre, that even Miss Jocasta, the harsh-favored maiden sister of the Surd's, admitted me with commiserate regard, and suggested pennyroyal tea.

Professor Surd was at a faculty meeting. Would I wait?

Yes, till all was blue, if need be. Miss Abbie?

Abscissa had gone to Wheelborough to visit a school-friend. The aged maiden hoped I would make myself comfortable, and departed to the unknown haunts which knew Jocasta's daily walk.

Comfortable! But I settled myself in a great uneasy chair and waited, with the contradictory spirit common to such junctures, dreading every step lest it should herald the man whom, of all men, I wished to see.

I had been there at least an hour, and was growing right drowsy.

At length Professor Surd came in. He sat down in the dusk opposite me, and I thought his eyes glinted with malignant pleasure as he said, abruptly: "So, young man, you think you are a fit husband for my girl?"

I stammered some inanity about making up in affection what I lacked in merit; about my expectations, family and the like. He quickly interrupted me.

"You misapprehend me, sir. Your nature is destitute of those mathematical perceptions and acquirements which are the only sure foundations of character. You have no mathematics in you. You are fit for treason, stratagems, and spoils. Your narrow intellect cannot understand and appreciate a generous mind. There is all the difference between you and a Surd, if I may say it, which intervenes between an infinitesimal and an infinite. Why, I will even venture to say that you do not comprehend the Problem of the Couriers!"

I admitted that the Problem of the Couriers should be classed rather without my list of accomplishments than within it. I regretted this fault very deeply, and suggested amendment. I faintly hoped that my fortune would be such –

"Money!" he impatiently exclaimed. "Do you seek to bribe a Roman Senator with a penny whistle? Why, boy, do you parade your paltry wealth, which, expressed in mills, will not cover ten decimal places, before the eyes of a man who measures the planets in their orbits, and close crowds infinity itself?"

I hastily disclaimed any intention of obtruding my foolish dollars, and he went on: "Your letter surprised me not a little. I thought you would be the last person in the world to presume to an alliance here. But having a regard for you personally" – and again I saw malice twinkle in his small eyes – "and still more regard for Abscissa's happiness, I have decided that you shall have her – upon conditions. Upon conditions," he repeated, with a half-smothered sneer.

"What are they?" cried I, eagerly enough. "Only name them."

"Well, sir," he continued, and the deliberation of his speech seemed the very refinement of cruelty, "you have only to prove yourself worthy an alliance with a mathematical family. You have only to accomplish a task which I shall presently give you. Your eyes ask me what it is. I will tell you. Distinguish yourself in that noble branch of abstract science in which, you cannot but acknowledge, you are at present sadly deficient. I will place Abscissa's hand in yours whenever you shall come before me and square the circle to my satisfaction. No! That is too easy a condition. I should cheat myself. Say perpetual motion. How do you like that? Do you think it lies within the range of your mental capabilities? You don't smile. Perhaps your talents don't run in the way of perpetual motion. Several people have found that theirs didn't. I'll give you another chance. We were speaking of the Problem of the Couriers, and I think you expressed a desire to know more of that ingenious question. You shall have the opportunity. Sit down some day, when you have nothing else to do, and discover the principle of infinite speed. I mean the law of motion which shall accomplish an infinitely great distance in an infinitely short time. You may mix in a little practical mechanics, if you choose. Invent some method of taking the tardy Courier over his road at the rate of sixty miles a minute. Demonstrate me this discovery (when you have made it!) mathematically, and approximate it practically, and Abscissa is yours. Until you can, I will thank you to trouble neither myself nor her."

I could stand his mocking no longer. I stumbled mechanically out of the room, and out of the house. I even forgot my hat and gloves. For an hour I walked in the moonlight. Gradually I succeeded to a more hopeful frame of mind. This was due to my ignorance of mathematics. Had I understood the real meaning of what he asked, I should have been utterly despondent.

Perhaps this problem of sixty miles a minute was not so impossible after all. At any rate I could attempt, though I might not succeed. And Rivarol came to my mind. I would ask him. I would enlist his knowledge to accompany my own devoted perseverance. I sought his lodgings at once.

The man of science lived in the fourth story, back. I had never been in his room before. When I entered, he was in the act of filling a beer mug from a carboy labelled Aqua fortis.

"Seat you," he said. "No, not in that chair. That is my Petty Cash Adjuster." But he was a second too late. I had carelessly thrown myself into a chair of seductive appearance. To my utter amazement it reached out two skeleton arms and clutched me with a grasp against which I struggled in vain. Then a skull stretched itself over my shoulder and grinned with ghastly familiarity close to my face.

Rivarol came to my aid with many apologies. He touched a spring somewhere and the Petty Cash Adjuster relaxed its horrid hold. I placed myself gingerly in a plain cane-bottomed rocking-chair, which Rivarol assured me was a safe location.

"That seat," he said, "is an arrangement upon which I much felicitate myself. I made it at Heidelberg. It has saved me a vast deal of small annoyance. I consign to its embraces the friends who bore, and the visitors who exasperate me. But it is never so useful as when terrifying some tradesman with an insignificant account. Hence the pet name which I have facetiously given it. They are invariably too glad to purchase release at the price of a bill receipted. Do you well apprehend the idea?"

While the Alsatian diluted his glass of Aqua fortis, shook into it an infusion of bitters, and tossed off the bumper with apparent relish, I had time to look around the strange apartment.

The four corners of the room were occupied respectively by a turning-lathe, a Rhumkorff Coil, a small steam-engine and an orrery in stately motion. Tables, shelves, chairs and floor supported an odd aggregation of tools, retorts, chemicals, gas-receivers, philosophical instruments, boots, flasks, paper-collar boxes, books diminutive and books of preposterous size. There were plaster busts of Aristotle, Archimedes, and Comte, while a great drowsy owl was blinking away, perched on the benign brow of Martin Farquhar Tupper. "He always roosts there when he proposes to slumber," explained my tutor. "You are a bird of no ordinary mind. Schlafen sie wohl."

Through a closet door, half open, I could see a human-like form covered with a sheet. Rivarol caught my glance.

"That," said he, "will be my masterpiece. It is a Microcosm, an Android, as yet only partially complete. And why not? Albertus Magnus constructed an image perfect to talk metaphysics and confute the schools. So did Sylvester II; so did Robertus Greathead. Roger Bacon made a brazen head that held discourses. But the first named of these came to destruction. Thomas Aquinas got wrathful at some of its syllogisms and smashed its head. The idea is reasonable enough. Mental action will yet be reduced to laws as definite as those which govern the physical. Why should not I accomplish a manikin which shall preach as original discourses as the Rev. Dr Allchin, or talk poetry as mechanically as Paul Anapest? My Android can already work problems in vulgar fractions and compose sonnets. I hope to teach it the Positive Philosophy."

Out of the bewildering confusion of his effects Rivarol produced two pipes and filled them. He handed one to me.

"And here," he said, "I live and am tolerably comfortable. When my coat wears out at the elbows I seek the tailor and am measured for another. When I am hungry I promenade myself to the butcher's and bring home a pound or so of steak, which I cook very nicely in three seconds by this oxy-hydrogen flame. Thirsty, perhaps, I send for a carboy of Aqua fortis. But I have it charged, all charged. My spirit is above any small pecuniary transaction. I loathe your dirty greenbacks, and never handle what they call scrip."

"But are you never pestered with bills?" I asked. "Don't the creditors worry your life out?"

"Creditors!" gasped Rivarol. "I have learned no such word in your very admirable language. He who will allow his soul to be vexed by creditors is a relic of an imperfect civilization. Of what use is science if it cannot avail a man who has accounts current? Listen. The moment you or any one else enters the outside door this little electric bell sounds me warning. Every successive step on Mrs Grimier's staircase is a spy and informer vigilant for my benefit. The first step is trod upon. That trusty first step immediately telegraphs your weight. Nothing could be simpler. It is exactly like any platform scale. The weight is registered up here upon this dial. The second step records the size of my visitor's feet. The third his height, the fourth his complexion, and so on. By the time he reaches the top of the first flight I have a pretty accurate description of him right here at my elbow, and quite a margin of time for deliberation and action. Do you follow me? It is plain enough. Only the A B C of my science."

"I see all that," I said, "but I don't see how it helps you any. The knowledge that a creditor is coming won't pay his bill. You can't escape unless you jump out of the window."

Rivarol laughed softly. "I will tell you. You shall see what becomes of any poor devil who goes to demand money of me – of a man of science. Ha! ha! It pleases me. I was seven weeks perfecting my Dun Suppressor. Did you know" – he whispered exultingly – "did you know that there is a hole through the earth's centre? Physicists have long suspected it; I was the first to find it. You have read how Rhuyghens, the Dutch navigator, discovered in Kerguellen's Land an abysmal pit which fourteen hundred fathoms of plumb-line failed to sound. Herr Tom, that hole has no bottom! It runs from one surface of the earth to the antipodal surface. It is diametric. But where is the antipodal spot? You stand upon it. I learned this by the merest chance. I was deep-digging in Mrs Grimler's cellar, to bury a poor cat I had sacrificed in a galvanic experiment, when the earth under my spade crumbled, caved in, and wonder-stricken I stood upon the brink of a yawning shaft. I dropped a coal-hod in. It went down, down down, bounding and rebounding. In two hours and a quarter that coal-hod came up again. I caught it and restored it to the angry Grimler. Just think a minute. The coal-hod went down, faster and faster, till it reached the centre of the earth. There it would stop, were it not for acquired momentum. Beyond the centre its journey was relatively upward, toward the opposite surface of the globe. So, losing velocity, it went slower and slower till it reached that surface. Here it came to rest for a second and then fell back again, eight thousand odd miles, into my hands. Had I not interfered with it, it would have repeated its journey, time after time, each trip of shorter extent, like the diminishing oscillations of a pendulum, till it finally came to eternal rest at the centre of the sphere. I am not slow to give a practical application to any such grand discovery. My Dun Suppressor was born of it. A trap, just outside my chamber door: a spring in here: a creditor on the trap: need I say more?"

"But isn't it a trifle inhuman?" I mildly suggested. "Plunging an unhappy being into a perpetual journey to and from Kerguellen's Land, without a moment's warning."

"I give them a chance. When they come up the first time I wait at the mouth of the shaft with a rope in hand. If they are reasonable and will come to terms, I fling them the line. If they perish, 'tis their own fault. Only," he added, with a melancholy smile, "the centre is getting so plugged up with creditors that I am afraid there soon will be no choice whatever for 'em."

By this time I had conceived a high opinion of my tutor's ability. If anybody could send me waltzing through space at an infinite speed, Rivarol could do it. I filled my pipe and told him the story. He heard with grave and patient attention. Then, for full half an hour, he whiffed away in silence. Finally he spoke.

"The ancient cipher has overreached himself. He has given you a choice of two problems, both of which he deems insoluble. Neither of them is insoluble. The only gleam of intelligence Old Cotangent showed was when he said that squaring the circle was too easy. He was right. It would have given you your Liebchen in five minutes. I squared the circle before I discarded pantalets. I will show you the work – but it would be a digression, and you are in no mood for digressions. Our first chance, therefore, lies in perpetual motion. Now, my good friend, I will frankly tell you that, although I have compassed this interesting problem, I do not choose to use it in your behalf. I too, Herr Tom, have a heart. The loveliest of her sex frowns upon me. Her somewhat mature charms are not for Jean Marie Rivarol. She has cruelly said that her years demand of me filial rather than connubial regard. Is love a matter of years or of eternity? This question did I put to the cold, yet lovely Jocasta."

"Jocasta Surd!" I remarked in surprise, "Abscissa's aunt!"

"The same," he said, sadly. "I will not attempt to conceal that upon the maiden Jocasta my maiden heart has been bestowed. Give me your hand, my nephew in affliction as in affection!"

Rivarol dashed away a not discreditable tear, and resumed: "My only hope lies in this discovery of perpetual motion. It will give me the fame, the wealth. Can Jocasta refuse these? If she can, there is only the trap-door and – Kerguellen's Land!"

I bashfully asked to see the perpetual-motion machine. My uncle in affliction shook his head.

"At another time," he said. "Suffice it at present to say, that it is something upon the principle of a woman's tongue. But you see now why we must turn in your case to the alternative condition – infinite speed. There are several ways in which this may be accomplished, theoretically. By the lever, for instance. Imagine a lever with a very long and a very short arm. Apply power to the shorter arm which will move it with great velocity. The end of the long arm will move much faster. Now keep shortening the short arm and lengthening the long one, and as you approach infinity in their difference of length, you approach infinity in the speed of the long arm. It would be difficult to demonstrate this practically to the Professor. We must seek another solution. Jean Marie will meditate. Come to me in a fortnight. Goodnight. But stop! Have you the money – das geld?"

"Much more than I need."

"Good! Let us strike hands. Gold and Knowledge; Science and Love. What may not such a partnership achieve? We go to conquer thee, Abscissa. Vorwärts!"

When, at the end of a fortnight, I sought Rivarol's chamber, I passed with some little trepidation over the terminus of the Air Line to Kerguellen's Land, and evaded the extended arms of the Petty Cash Adjuster. Rivarol drew a mug of ale for me, and filled himself a retort of his own peculiar beverage.

"Come," he said at length. "Let us drink success to the Tachypomp."

"The Tachypomp?"

"Yes. Why not? Tachu, quickly, and pempo, pepompa to send. May it send you quickly to your wedding-day. Abscissa is yours. It is done. When shall we start for the prairies?"

"Where is it?" I asked, looking in vain around the room for any contrivance which might seem calculated to advance matrimonial prospects.

"It is here," and he gave his forehead a significant tap. Then he held forth didactically.

"There is force enough in existence to yield us a speed of sixty miles a minute, or even more. All we need is the knowledge how to combine and apply it. The wise man will not attempt to make some great force yield some great speed. He will keep adding the little force to the little force, making each little force yield its little speed, until an aggregate of little forces shall be a great force, yielding an aggregate of little speeds, a great speed. The difficulty is not in aggregating the forces; it lies in the corresponding aggregation of the speeds. One musket-ball will go, say a mile. It is not hard to increase the force of muskets to a thousand, yet the thousand musket-balls will go no farther, and no faster, than the one. You see, then, where our trouble lies. We cannot readily add speed to speed, as we add force to force. My discovery is simply the utilization of a principle which extorts an increment of speed from each increment of power. But this is the metaphysics of physics. Let us be practical or nothing.

"When you have walked forward, on a moving train, from the rear car, toward the engine, did you ever think what you were really doing?"

"Why, yes, I have generally been going to the smoking-car to have a cigar."

"Tut, tut – not that! I mean, did it ever occur to you on such an occasion, that absolutely you were moving faster than the train? The train passes the telegraph poles at the rate of thirty miles an hour, say. You walk toward the smoking-car at the rate of four miles an hour. Then you pass the telegraph poles at the rate of thirty-four miles. Your absolute speed is the speed of the engine, plus the speed of your own locomotion. Do you follow me?"

I began to get an inkling of his meaning, and told him so.

"Very well. Let us advance a step. Your addition to the speed of the engine is trivial, and the space in which you can exercise it, limited. Now suppose two stations, A and B, two miles distant by the track. Imagine a train of platform cars, the last car resting at station A. The train is a mile long, say. The engine is therefore within a mile of station B. Say the train can move a mile in ten minutes. The last car, having two miles to go, would reach B in twenty minutes, but the engine, a mile ahead, would get there in ten. You jump on the last car, at A, in a prodigious hurry to reach Abscissa, who is at B. If you stay on the last car it will be twenty long minutes before you see her. But the engine reaches B and the fair lady in ten. You will be a stupid reasoner, and an indifferent lover, if you don't put for the engine over those platform cars, as fast as your legs will carry you. You can run a mile, the length of the train, in ten minutes. Therefore, you reach Abscissa when the engine does, or in ten minutes – ten minutes sooner than if you had lazily sat down upon the rear car and talked politics with the brakeman. You have diminished the time by one half. You have added your speed to that of the locomotive to some purpose. Nicht wahr?"

I saw it perfectly; much plainer, perhaps, for his putting in the clause about Abscissa.

He continued: "This illustration, though a slow one, leads up to a principle which may be carried to any extent. Our first anxiety will be to spare your legs and wind. Let us suppose that the two miles of track are perfectly straight, and make our train one platform car, a mile long, with parallel rails laid upon its top. Put a little dummy engine on these rails, and let it run to and fro along the platform car, while the platform car is pulled along he ground track. Catch the idea? The dummy takes your place. But it can run its mile much faster. Fancy that our locomotive is strong enough to pull the platform car over the two miles in two minutes. The dummy can attain the same speed. When the engine reaches B in one minute, the dummy, having gone a mile a-top the platform car, reaches B also. We have so combined the speeds of those two engines as to accomplish two miles in one minute. Is this all we can do? Prepare to exercise your imagination."

I lit my pipe.

"Still two miles of straight track, between A and B. On the track a long platform car, reaching from A to within a quarter of a mile of B. We will now discard ordinary locomotives and adopt as our motive power a series of compact magnetic engines, distributed underneath the platform car, all along its length."

"I don't understand those magnetic engines."

"Well, each of them consists of a great iron horseshoe, rendered alternately a magnet and not a magnet by an intermittent current of electricity from a battery, this current in its turn regulated by clock-work. When the horseshoe is in the circuit, it is a magnet, and it pulls its clapper toward it with enormous power. When it is out of the circuit, the next second, it is not a magnet, and it lets the clapper go. The clapper, oscillating to and fro, imparts a rotatory motion to a fly-wheel, which transmits it to the drivers on the rails. Such are our motors. They are no novelty, for trial has proved them practicable.

"With a magnetic engine for every truck of wheels, we can reasonably expect to move our immense car, and to drive it along at a speed, say, of a mile a minute.

"The forward end, having but a quarter of a mile to go, will reach B in fifteen seconds. We will call this platform car number 1. On top of number 1 are laid rails on which another platform car, number 2, a quarter of a mile shorter than number 1, is moved in precisely the same way. Number 2, in its turn, is surmounted by number 3, moving independently of the tiers beneath, and a quarter of a mile shorter than number 2. Number 2 is a mile and a half long; number 3 a mile and a quarter. Above, on successive levels, are number 4, a mile long; number 5, three quarters of a mile; number 6, half a mile; number 7, a quarter of a mile, and number 8, a short passenger car, on top of all.

"Each car moves upon the car beneath it, independently of all the others, at the rate of a mile a minute. Each car has its own magnetic engines. Well, the train being drawn up with the latter end of each car resting against a lofty bumping-post at A, Tom Furnace, the gentlemanly conductor, and Jean Marie Rivarol, engineer, mount by a long ladder to the exalted number 8. The complicated mechanism is set in motion. What happens?

"Number 8 runs a quarter of a mile in fifteen seconds and reaches the end of number 7. Meanwhile number 7 has run a quarter of a mile in the same time and reached the end of number 6; number 6, a quarter of a mile in fifteen seconds, and reached the end of number 5; number 5, the end of number 4; number 4, of number 3; number 3, of number 2; number 2, of number 1. And number 1, in fifteen seconds, has gone its quarter of a mile along the ground track, and has reached station B. All this has been done in fifteen seconds. Wherefore, numbers 1, 2, 3, 4, 5, 6, 7, and 8 come to rest against the bumping-post at B, at precisely the same second. We, in number 8, reach B just when number 1 reaches it. In other words, we accomplish two miles in fifteen seconds. Each of the eight cars, moving at the rate of a mile a minute, has contributed a quarter of a mile to our journey, and has done its work in fifteen seconds. All the eight did their work at once, during the same fifteen seconds. Consequently we have been whizzed through the air at the somewhat startling speed of seven and a half seconds to the mile. This is the Tachypomp. Does it justify the name?"

Although a little bewildered by the complexity of cars, I apprehended the general principle of the machine. I made a diagram, and understood it much better. "You have merely improved on the idea of my moving faster than the train when I was going to the smoking car?"

"Precisely. So far we have kept within the bounds of the practicable. To satisfy the Professor, you can theorize in something after this fashion: if we double the number of cars, thus decreasing by one half the distance which each has to go, we shall attain twice the speed. Each of the sixteen cars will have but one eighth of a mile to go. At the uniform rate we have adopted, the two miles can be done in seven and a half instead of fifteen seconds. With thirty-two cars, and a sixteenth of a mile, or twenty rods difference in their length, we arrive at the speed of a mile in less than two seconds; with sixty-four cars, each travelling but ten rods, a mile under the second. More than sixty miles a minute! If this isn't rapid enough for the Professor, tell him to go on, increasing the number of his cars and diminishing the distance each one has to run. If sixty-four cars yield a speed of a mile inside the second, let him fancy a Tachypomp of six hundred and forty cars, and amuse himself calculating the rate of car number 640. Just whisper to him that when he has an infinite number of cars with an infinitesimal difference in their lengths, he will have obtained that infinite speed for which he seems to yearn. Then demand Abscissa."

I wrung my friend's hand in silent and grateful admiration. I could say nothing.

"You have listened to the man of theory," he said proudly. "You shall now behold the practical engineer. We will go to the west of the Mississippi and find some suitably level locality. We will erect thereon a model Tachypomp. We will summon thereunto the professor, his daughter, and why not his fair sister Jocasta, as well? We will take them a journey which shall much astonish the venerable Surd. He shall place Abscissa's digits in yours and bless you both with an algebraic formula. Jocasta shall contemplate with wonder the genius of Rivarol. But we have much to do. We must ship to St. Joseph the vast amount of material to be employed in the construction of the Tachypomp. We must engage a small army of workmen to effect that construction, for we are to annihilate time and space. Perhaps you had better see your bankers."

I rushed impetuously to the door. There should be no delay.

"Stop! stop! Um Gottes Willen, stop!" shrieked Rivarol. "I launched my butcher this morning and I haven't bolted the – "

But it was too late. I was upon the trap. It swung open with a crash, and I was plunged down, down, down! I felt as if I were falling through illimitable space. I remember wondering, as I rushed through the darkness, whether I should reach Kerguellen's Land or stop at the centre. It seemed an eternity. Then my course was suddenly and painfully arrested.

I opened my eyes. Around me were the walls of Professor Surd's study. Under me was a hard, unyielding plane which I knew too well was Professor Surd's study floor. Behind me was the black, slippery, hair-cloth chair which had belched me forth, much as the whale served Jonah. In front of me stood Professor Surd himself, looking down with a not unpleasant smile.

"Good evening, Mr Furnace. Let me help you up. You look tired, sir. No wonder you fell asleep when I kept you so long waiting. Shall I get you a glass of wine? No? By the way, since receiving your letter I find that you are a son of my old friend, Judge Furnace. I have made inquiries, and see no reason why you should not make Abscissa a good husband."

Still I can see no reason why the Tachypomp should not have succeeded. Can you?

Fishing Expedition

Mike Morgan

TWO WEEKS and four days had passed since the sun had gone out.

Without question, the calamity qualified as Earth's sixth mass extinction event; photosynthesizing plants and algae were already on the cusp of dying out and the food chain was failing in new and ever more spectacular ways each day. On the human front, things were equally grim: untold millions were dead and billions more were certain to die within the next few days alone.

The sun being taken away wasn't even the most terrifying aspect of the threat facing humanity, thought Janet Lazarus. The loss of the sun was lethal enough, but far more unnerving on a visceral level were the grotesque and seemingly random "fishing" attacks.

In the perpetual dark that now enshrouded the Earth, the prospect that, at any moment, the terrified survivors could be picked off by sadistic, murdering, unseen aliens was enough to push most people the final few inches into outright panic.

* * *

For Janet, the realization that something had happened came midway through that first morning.

Her day had started as always; she had awoken in her rented apartment in Canton and gone through her normal routines on autopilot, before driving to work at a private research facility in Baltimore. She listened to music CDs in the morning, so had heard nothing of the steadily mounting hysteria spreading across TV and radio outlets.

A small part of her mind had noted the dimmed heavens during her six a.m. commute, putting the gloom down to overcast weather conditions. She couldn't quite remember when the sun was meant to rise in the summertime anyway. In that way, the end of the world had passed her by, unregarded.

At ten fourteen a.m., she'd paused in her work and glanced up from her monitor, belatedly questioning why the sky visible through her lab's windows was still a starless void of absolute black, with only the immediate environs poorly illuminated by the lights in the parking lot outside.

Like many others, she'd succumbed to curiosity and walked out into the never-ending night, staring up at the blank, sable canvas of a dawn-less day and asking what if, what if, what if the sun was not going to rise and, oh, by the way, where had infinity gone?

For it was not only the friendly ball of blinding fire called the sun that was missing, but all of its companion stars too.

* * *

An attack by the "Fishermen" was always foreshadowed by the sound of metal clanking against metal as the chain line unwound. Then a wickedly sharp hook the size of a watermelon would flash down out of the endless pitch black.

Sometimes the metal hook found its mark, brutally impaling its victim, and sometimes the barbed implement smashed into the ground near the intended target, sending debris flying. When the prey was snagged, the chain-link line quickly went taut and retracted with chilling speed, yanking the stunned human catch high into the air, never to be seen again, the echo of a scream lingering in the darkness.

Such was the force with which victims were hauled away that individuals hooked through an arm frequently found the limb torn violently from the socket. Those unfortunate enough to be speared through the head were at least killed instantly, and spared the horror of feeling the decapitation.

Next to Janet, the hulking form of Nikolai loomed through the ice fog; his silhouette distorted by his layers of insulated clothes and backpack, as well as the equipment strapped to his thighs. Nikolai's voice carried clearly to her, unnaturally loud in the still air. "I'm telling you, the aliens blocked off the sun for sport."

She decided to let the unproven contention pass; there was no point in arguing, not when the end was so close.

Besides, she hardly had the breath to reply. A life of careful scientific research had proven to be poor preparation for this expedition. The cold weather gear made normal movement impossible and the weight of the survival equipment and thigh packages was almost backbreaking. Absurdly, she felt like she might collapse from exertion long before the anonymous slaughterers of the human race got around to murdering her.

Perhaps Nikolai saw how tired she was, or perhaps he was exhausted too, but he halted and stood still, about five feet from her, his form softly lit by the lights mounted around the furry hood of his parka. "Where exactly are we headed, Dr Lazarus?" he asked with a jollity that she could only assume was faked. She could see his crinkled eyes through his tinted goggles – he was smiling, despite everything.

"It hardly matters," she gasped, the cold reaching through the balaclava to stab her mouth and throat. She was certain the hairs in her nose had frozen.

Janet was about to muster the breath to suggest simply continuing in a straight line, when a shockingly loud boom cut through the darkness; a minor tremor immediately followed the noise, causing them both to scramble for their footing on the treacherous ice.

"What was that?" exclaimed Nikolai, his Russian accent made more pronounced by his alarm. Only in times such as these would a Russian soldier be performing such a vital mission on US soil, she thought, marveling at the strangeness of these terrible days.

"Cryoseism," responded Janet with a calmness she didn't feel. "When so much ice forms in the ground, the water expands rapidly and causes a quake followed by a 'cold boom'."

"Can it get any worse?" he grumbled.

Janet would have nodded but her neck gaiter made the movement difficult. "Oh yes," she answered. "It's going to get much worse."

* * *

During that first dawn-less day, the effect of losing the sun on the average global temperature had been hardly noticeable. Janet had been primarily concerned with calling her friends in Australia and asking whether they could see the stars. After complaining about being woken up at nearly one o'clock in the morning, they'd confirmed that, yes, obviously, the stars were in their correct places, and why the hell was she asking?

Further checking with colleagues and vague acquaintances in a number of other countries had yielded a surprising conclusion: a little over half the planet was affected by the disappearance of the sky. It was incredible, but there seemed to be something wrapped around the hemisphere facing the sun that was blocking out all the light.

Janet Lazarus was a member of the President's Council of Advisors on Science and Technology, more commonly referred to as PCAST, so she contacted the director and told him that the human race was under attack. To his credit, he believed her.

* * *

They could hear creaking in the distance. "What is that?" asked Nikolai nervously. He was futilely twisting about, trying to locate the source of the noise.

"Steel structures beginning to fracture, probably," answered Janet, each word an effort.

Talking was something to pass the time until they died; one way or another, they were going to die. At least she could ignore the pain of breathing the sub-zero air while she was speaking.

"At these temperatures, steel becomes brittle. We chose a small town in Iowa because of its lack of skyscrapers; there's not much to fall on us here. Besides, tall buildings might accidentally hide us from view."

"We wouldn't want that," replied Nikolai. Even he, fit as he was, had to pause after every few words to catch his breath, Janet noted with some satisfaction.

They trudged along the icy road, the pair of them picked out in two oases of light that juddered with each step.

In the fathomless distance, the creaking was replaced with a rumble of a large building disintegrating. Given how slow the going was and how far sound traveled in the still air, it was probable they'd never discover which edifice's metal skeleton had cracked right through.

Nikolai turned to face the side of the road, shining the lights of his parka's hood on the house standing there. "I had hoped to see at least a few houses with windows lit up by fires within," he said morosely.

She couldn't bear to think about the likely tableaus inside the houses: families huddled together, entombed silently in frozen embraces. The ghastly images in her mind made her snap, "Nikolai, everyone here is dead. They died of the cold or they died of thirst, but either way, they're dead. They didn't want to come outside and forage for fuel or provisions because it is crazy cold and because there are sick, degenerate aliens making a game out of the extinction of the human race and everything is so damned scary, anybody sane would just want to huddle in a quiet corner and wait to slip away peacefully." The words sounded bitter and lost even to her ears.

Nikolai snorted. "If the sane reaction to this situation is to huddle in a corner and wait for death, why are we doing this?" he asked.

"Because it's my fault people were told to stay in place," said Janet. "And because the plan was my idea."

* * *

At first, the politicians of the world had assumed the disappearance of the sun was some kind of natural disaster. But the scientists had patiently explained that the sun couldn't just "go out" and, even if fusion had ceased in the core, it would still take ten thousand years before the energy emanating from the star would decrease enough to affect life on Earth. What was happening now must, surely, have some other explanation.

With these points still in mind, the President and the Joint Chiefs of Staff sat in on a teleconference with the eighteen council members and director of PCAST. It was the first day of the mass extinction, before the true hopelessness of the catastrophe had sunk in, and there remained competing ideas concerning the cause of the emergency.

One idea that had gained some traction was that the Earth had fallen through a wormhole and was now in a part of space far from the sun.

It didn't take long for Janet to lose her temper with the council member peddling that nonsense. "You're wrong and I can prove it," she thundered from her office in Baltimore. "Countries on the night side of the Earth can still see the same old constellations and Moon, so our planet hasn't gone anywhere. What's more, there's still sunlight reflecting off the Moon, so the sun hasn't vanished or spontaneously gone out, either."

She let out a strangled sigh of frustration and clenched her fists. "I've contacted people all round the world and mapped out the general shape and size of the object blocking out the sunlight. Given that the day side of the Earth cannot receive signals from various communications satellites in low Earth orbit and that we have lost contact with the International Space Station, I must conclude that an artifact is surrounding much of our planet at a range closer than those objects; I'd estimate somewhere between two and three hundred kilometers. There is, incredible though it may seem, some sort of 'shroud' of extraterrestrial origin preventing energy from the sun from reaching the Earth."

She shouted over the council's protestations and objections, "It's simple enough to prove. Send up a rocket and look."

So they did.

* * *

Nikolai was staring up at the remains of a Buick. Janet followed his gaze; unusually, the vehicle was lodged in a tree, its roof and windshield torn off. The only trace of its former occupant was the blood spattered along the hood.

He said, "I guess a Fisherman hooked someone in a moving car and it got flung up there."

"I'd say so. Once people stopped walking around outside, they got more adventurous in selecting their prey."

She remembered the cargo plane. Nikolai seemed to have the same flashback because he simply answered, "Yes," and left it at that.

They resumed their aimless, but far from purposeless, trek. Nikolai was acting differently now; perhaps the impenetrable dark and the sense of isolation it prompted was getting to him. He wanted to talk. "How cold is it now, do you think?"

"It was minus thirty-four degrees Celsius when we set out from the landing strip; not setting any records for the state, but normally land at this elevation would never get this cold."

"It is colder in Russia," he replied. "You have it easy here."

"Well, the temperature drop isn't consistent across the planet. Some places are freezing faster than others. Nor is the rate of decrease linear, you know. In two and a half weeks, it's dropped by more than sixty degrees here, but at the end of the first year, it'll only be minus seventy-three degrees."

He laughed sourly. "Oh, only minus seventy-three."

"There is a good side to the temperature drop flattening out. We'll have years before we have to worry about atmospheric gases freezing. I think it'll snow nitrogen first. Of course, once the atmosphere freezes completely, the surface of the Earth will be scoured clean of life by cosmic radiation."

"You're kidding!"

"I'm very serious. Not that it matters – humanity will be extinct by then."

"You told your President he could survive in a nuclear submarine underneath the ice sheets, because the oceans would never completely freeze."

She felt her pulse race. How did he know about that? She forced herself to be calm. It hardly mattered now. "It won't work for long. The submarine can only carry a few months worth of food."

"We were going to set up an underground facility with a reactor. Or possibly invade Iceland and steal their geothermal-powered habitats."

"Really?" she said, somewhat taken aback.

"No," he replied. "I'm pulling your leg. We're not that organized and, you know, there were riots..." She realized that their banter had covered up the sound of metal links clinking together.

A hook flashed out of nowhere and tore Nikolai's head off.

* * *

The mission to investigate the nature of the shroud was made possible by one thing: there was a commercial rocket already about to take off on a resupply mission to the ISS.

While the rocket's fueling continued at Cape Canaveral Air Force Base in Florida, the personnel at Houston Ground Control struggled to reestablish contact with the space station. It seemed likely that the telemetry from the ISS had ceased at virtually the same moment the "shroud" had appeared.

Efforts had already been made to reach the crew while the station was on the un-shrouded side of the Earth, but none of these transmissions had elicited a response. Since the ISS completed a full orbit every ninety-two minutes, several such windows had already passed, leading many to assume that the station was, in fact, no longer there, at least not in anything resembling an intact form.

This was a tragedy for many reasons, not least of which was that many people wanted to know what the crew would have been able to see from up there. Some said a spontaneous aggregation of dark matter; Janet was betting on trillions of overlapping tiles of some kind.

By the beginning of the second day of the catastrophe, the Falcon 9 rocket was ready for launch. At nine-thirty in the morning, it lifted off, rising on a majestic column of fire, a blazing torch in the obsidian deeps.

Eight minutes forty seconds into the mission, just moments before the modified Dragon capsule was due to separate from the rocket and deploy its hastily cobbled-together instrumentation, the rocket collided with one of the invisible multi-dimensional shields that comprised the alien artifact and exploded.

* * *

Nikolai's headless body collapsed with a dull thud, blood pumping out onto the ice. The packages on his thighs remained inert; the detonators were a type of tilt fuse with a fifteen second timer built in – they could only be triggered by a violent movement. The comparatively minor motion of the body falling to the ground would not be sufficient for detonation.

High up in the nothingness where the sky once had been, the lights from his parka hood glowed faintly and winked out, disappearing beyond some unknowable boundary.

Janet stood in the darkness and ice fog, speckles of claret-red dotted across her goggles. It seemed to her that a long time passed, and then she wiped the blood away, clumsily unstrapped his thigh packs, and carried on walking, the warheads dangling by their ties in her shaking hands.

* * *

Following the obliteration of the Falcon 9 rocket, another teleconference of PCAST members and military commanders had been convened. Since it was now clear that a physical barrier existed and that Janet Lazarus had been correct, the President sacked the council's director and appointed her to the post.

"I'm willing to move forward as you direct," he said without preamble. "Do you have any advice for what we should do?"

She had been thinking the unthinkable for a while. "Tell people to hunker down and stay in place. There's nowhere for them to evacuate to. If people try to run, they're going to cause chaos on the roads; and they're going to last longer in their own homes than in cars stuck in increasingly intractable gridlock."

Again, there was considerable debate. Again, she cut through the nonsense. "Yes, coastal regions will stay warmer longer because of the heat stored in the oceans, but the weather along the coastlines will soon become too extreme for these areas to be considered refuges. Intense low pressure fronts will generate super storms."

There were loud claims that she was exaggerating the problem.

Suffering fools gladly had never been a character trait she'd enjoyed. She said forcefully, "The temperature is going to fall rapidly, causing unprecedented issues of hypothermia and frostbite. As the reality of that fact sinks in, people are going to riot and try to stockpile fuel and food supplies. But they're going to have more and more difficulty in getting about, because no one outside of an arctic expedition is even remotely equipped for what we're about to experience."

"Should I declare a state of emergency?" asked the President nervously.

"Absolutely, but don't tell the public. In another six days, the average temperature on the surface of the Earth will be minus eighteen degrees Celsius, and long before we reach that first milestone in the cooling of our planet, people are going to realize that we don't have a solution to this crisis and everyone is going to die. When that happens, which I estimate will be in about three days, you can kiss goodbye to civilization."

A piece of paper was passed to the President. He looked over the message quickly and, without lifting his head, said, "Janet, we need to get you out of Baltimore now."

"Why, Mr President?"

He replied grimly, "Because you were wrong. It didn't take three days for civilization to fall. Baltimore's been set on fire."

* * *

Janet's boots were crunching on snow so cold it resembled sand.

There was a deep, aching tiredness in her bones. Janet couldn't remember how long she'd been walking, forcing one foot in front of the other. She hoped fatigue was the cause of the nausea she was beginning to experience.

Janet Lazarus remembered the briefing on radiation sickness: "People who vomit within one hour of exposure are likely to die." She choked back the bile in her throat, realizing as she did it that trying not to throw up wouldn't change anything. She had never intended to live through this mission.

Perhaps Nikolai's sacrifice had not been in vain. She had been worrying over whether the radiation leaking from the payload packs would alert the Fishermen; the only way to make the suitcase nukes small enough so that the volunteers could carry two each had been to pare the shielding right down. And here she was, carrying four.

Apparently, the aliens didn't care about the radiation. She didn't know if that meant they weren't concerned about the warheads or whether they just hadn't put two and two together yet.

Janet kept listening for the tell-tale clanking sound, but it refused to come.

* * *

The Fishermen started hooking humans out of the false night on the third day of the catastrophe.

During those first few long hours while the barbed weapons sailed through the chilly blackness in innumerable trajectories, Janet sat with the President in the Oval Office. He paced and cursed and refused to retreat to safety, and she sipped green tea.

"They seem to home in on people next to light sources, like flashlights," he said after reading a briefing. "Our new alien overlords might be attracted to prey that's lit up."

Later, he said, "The ISS was probably the first thing the aliens tried to reel in, wasn't it? Dear God, why won't the aliens talk to us?"

And still later: "They're going to kill us all, aren't they? Should we have tried firing ICBMs at the shroud?"

Janet had been thinking about all the times she had gone fly fishing with her uncle. They had worried about causing unnecessary suffering to the fish but in the end, they'd still brought home a basket full to the brim with brown trout.

So she discussed how an alien culture advanced enough to reach across the universe and place a shroud about a planet might not conceive of humanity as anything other than unfeeling, simplistic animal life. Perhaps the aliens had come to take the resources of the Earth, but while they were here, while they were preparing whatever the next phase of their plan was, they were happy to pass the time at play. And that could be their downfall.

She explained her idea.

They stood in front of the large windows and waited for the shroud to pass. Eventually, the stars sparkled into life one by one at the periphery of the vast structure.

"Thank you for your service," he said.

She replied distantly, "You need to call the Russians now."

* * *

It took two weeks for the Russians to get the suitcase bombs into position. Nikolai brought the ones allocated to the Iowa expedition: Janet Lazarus's 'Reverse Fishing Trip,' where the prey wanted to be caught. Firing nukes at the shroud would almost certainly have no effect, but smuggling nukes past it...

The Russian Antonov An-225 Mriya cargo plane landed three hours late at Des Moines International Airport. The power had been out for days, and the airport was deserted apart from the waiting a US government team. They used portable generators to provide enough lighting for the plane to land with relative safely.

Soldiers helped Janet into her extreme cold weather gear and adjusted the straps on her packs. Nikolai had insisted on coming with her. He was guarding the stripped-down contents of the cases, making certain the Americans used them for the purpose agreed.

Nikolai was cutting through the fence at the edge of the runway when the aliens struck. Chains and hooks swung down, catching hold of the cargo plane in at least six spots. With barely a pause, the plane was wrenched up into the air and out of the white pools cast by the temporary spotlights. The fuselage tore under the stress and the cargo transport tumbled to the frozen ground, its fuel exploding on impact.

The flames burned longer and brighter than Janet would have thought possible. Her eyes dancing with flickering red, she said, "In the light of the explosion, I could see. I could see the ends of the chains. They came out of nowhere. The aliens must use wormholes." Her whole body shook. "They're ice fishing, casting their lines through small holes, trying again and again until they hit their quarry..."

"What will we see?" he asked. "When we cross through their portals?"

Janet laughed, her head ringing with the force of the explosion. She thought she sounded crazed. "We'll see how much pain they take when the fish bite back."

Nikolai helped her through the snipped-open fence, and they began.

Buck Rogers' First Adventure: Armageddon – 2419 AD

Philip Francis Nowlan

Foreword

ELSEWHERE I have set down, for whatever interest they have in this, the 25th Century, my personal recollections of the 20th Century.

Now it occurs to me that my memoirs of the 25th Century may have an equal interest 500 years from now – particularly in view of that unique perspective from which I have seen the 25th Century, entering it as I did, in one leap across a gap of 492 years.

This statement requires elucidation. There are still many in the world who are not familiar with my unique experience. Five centuries from now there may be many more, especially if civilization is fated to endure any worse convulsions than those which have occurred between 1975 AD and the present time.

I should state therefore, that I, Anthony Rogers, am, so far as I know, the only man alive whose normal span of eighty-one years of life has been spread over a period of 573 years. To be precise, I lived the first twenty-nine years of my life between 1898 and 1927; the other fifty-two since 2419. The gap between these two, a period of nearly five hundred years, I spent in a state of suspended animation, free from the ravages of katabolic processes, and without any apparent effect on my physical or mental faculties.

When I began my long sleep, man had just begun his real conquest of the air in a sudden series of transoceanic flights in airplanes driven by internal combustion motors. He had barely begun to speculate on the possibilities of harnessing sub-atomic forces, and had made no further practical penetration into the field of ethereal pulsations than the primitive radio and television of that day. The United States of America was the most powerful nation in the world, its political, financial, industrial and scientific influence being supreme; and in the arts also it was rapidly climbing into leadership.

I awoke to find the America I knew a total wreck – to find Americans a hunted race in their own land, hiding in the dense forests that covered the shattered and leveled ruins of their once magnificent cities, desperately preserving, and struggling to develop in their secret retreats, the remnants of their culture and science – and the undying flame of their sturdy independence.

World domination was in the hands of Mongolians and the center of world power lay in inland China, with Americans one of the few races of mankind unsubdued – and it must be admitted in fairness to the truth, not worth the trouble of subduing in the eyes of the Han Airlords who ruled North America as titular tributaries of the Most Magnificent.

For they needed not the forests in which the Americans lived, nor the resources of the vast territories these forests covered. With the perfection to which they had reduced the synthetic production of necessities and luxuries, their remarkable development of scientific processes and mechanical accomplishment of work, they had no economic need for the forests, and no economic desire for the enslaved labor of an unruly race.

They had all they needed for their magnificently luxurious and degraded scheme of civilization, within the walls of the fifteen cities of sparkling glass they had flung skyward on the sites of ancient American centers, into the bowels of the earth underneath them, and with relatively small surrounding areas of agriculture.

Complete domination of the air rendered communication between these centers a matter of ease and safety. Occasional destructive raids on the waste lands were considered all that was necessary to keep the "wild" Americans on the run within the shelter of their forests, and prevent their becoming a menace to the Han civilization.

But nearly three hundred years of easily maintained security, the last century of which had been nearly sterile in scientific, social and economic progress, had softened and devitalized the Hans.

It had likewise developed, beneath the protecting foliage of the forest, the growth of a vigorous new American civilization, remarkable in the mobility and flexibility of its organization, in its conquest of almost insuperable obstacles, in the development and guarding of its industrial and scientific resources, all in anticipation of that "Day of Hope" to which it had been looking forward for generations, when it would be strong enough to burst from the green chrysalis of the forests, soar into the upper air lanes and destroy the yellow incubus.

At the time I awoke, the "Day of Hope" was almost at hand. I shall not attempt to set forth a detailed history of the Second War of Independence, for that has been recorded already by better historians than I am. Instead I shall confine myself largely to the part I was fortunate enough to play in this struggle and in the events leading up to it.

It all resulted from my interest in radioactive gases. During the latter part of 1927 my company, the American Radioactive Gas Corporation, had been keeping me busy investigating reports of unusual phenomena observed in certain abandoned coal mines near the Wyoming Valley, in Pennsylvania.

With two assistants and a complete equipment of scientific instruments, I began the exploration of a deserted working in a mountainous district, where several weeks before, a number of mining engineers had reported traces of carnotite (**footnote 1**) and what they believed to be radioactive gases. Their report was not without foundation, it was apparent from the outset, for in our examination of the upper levels of the mine, our instruments indicated a vigorous radioactivity.

On the morning of December 15th, we descended to one of the lowest levels. To our surprise, we found no water there. Obviously it had drained off through some break in the strata. We noticed too that the rock in the side walls of the shaft was soft, evidently due to the radioactivity, and pieces crumbled under foot rather easily. We made our way cautiously down the shaft, when suddenly the rotted timbers above us gave way.

I jumped ahead, barely escaping the avalanche of coal and soft rock, but my companions, who were several paces behind me, were buried under it, and undoubtedly met instant death.

I was trapped. Return was impossible. With my electric torch I explored the shaft to its end, but could find no other way out. The air became increasingly difficult to breathe, probably from the rapid accumulation of the radioactive gas. In a little while my senses reeled and I lost consciousness.

When I awoke, there was a cool and refreshing circulation of air in the shaft. I had no thought that I had been unconscious more than a few hours, although it seems that the radioactive gas had kept me in a state of suspended animation for something like 500 years. My awakening, I figured out later, had been due to some shifting of the strata which reopened the shaft and cleared the atmosphere in the working. This must have been the case, for I was able to struggle back up the shaft over a pile of debris, and stagger up the long incline to the mouth of the mine, where an entirely different world, overgrown with a vast forest and no visible sign of human habitation, met my eyes.

I shall pass over the days of mental agony that followed in my attempt to grasp the meaning of it all. There were times when I felt that I was on the verge of insanity. I roamed the unfamiliar forest like a lost soul. Had it not been for the necessity of improvising traps and crude clubs with which to slay my food, I believe I should have gone mad.

Suffice it to say, however, that I survived this psychic crisis. I shall begin my narrative proper with my first contact with Americans of the year 2419 AD.

Footnote 1. A hydrovanadate of uranium, and other metals; used as a source of radium compounds.

Chapter I: Floating Men

[Seen upon the ultroscope view plate, the battle looked as though it were being fought in daylight, perhaps on a cloudy day, while the explosions of the rockets appeared as flashes of extra brilliance.]

MY FIRST GLIMPSE of a human being of the 25th Century was obtained through a portion of woodland where the trees were thinly scattered, with a dense forest beyond.

I had been wandering along aimlessly, and hopelessly, musing over my strange fate, when I noticed a figure that cautiously backed out of the dense growth across the glade. I was about to call out joyfully, but there was something furtive about the figure that prevented me. The boy's attention (for it seemed to be a lad of fifteen or sixteen) was centered tensely on the heavy growth of trees from which he had just emerged.

He was clad in rather tight-fitting garments entirely of green, and wore a helmet-like cap of the same color. High around his waist he wore a broad, thick belt, which bulked up in the back across the shoulders, into something of the proportions of a knapsack.

As I was taking in these details, there came a vivid flash and heavy detonation, like that of a hand grenade, not far to the left of him. He threw up an arm and staggered a bit in a queer, gliding way; then he recovered himself and slipped cautiously away from the place of the explosion, crouching slightly, and still facing the denser part of the forest. Every few steps he would raise his arm, and point into the forest with something he held in his hand. Wherever he pointed there was a terrific explosion, deeper in among the trees. It came to me then that he was shooting with some form of pistol, though there was neither flash nor detonation from the muzzle of the weapon itself.

After firing several times, he seemed to come to a sudden resolution, and turning in my general direction, leaped – to my amazement sailing through the air between the sparsely scattered trees in such a jump as I had never in my life seen before. That leap must have carried him a full fifty feet, although at the height of his arc, he was not more than ten or twelve feet from the ground.

When he alighted, his foot caught in a projecting root, and he sprawled gently forward. I say "gently" for he did not crash down as I expected him to do. The only thing I could compare it with was a slow-motion cinema, although I had never seen one in which horizontal motions were registered at normal speed and only the vertical movements were slowed down.

Due to my surprise, I suppose my brain did not function with its normal quickness, for I gazed at the prone figure for several seconds before I saw the blood that oozed out from under the tight green cap. Regaining my power of action, I dragged him out of sight back of the big tree. For a few moments I busied myself in an attempt to staunch the flow of blood. The wound was not a deep one. My companion was more dazed than hurt. But what of the pursuers?

I took the weapon from his grasp and examined it hurriedly. It was not unlike the automatic pistol to which I was accustomed, except that it apparently fired with a button instead of a trigger. I inserted several fresh rounds of ammunition into its magazine from my companion's belt, as rapidly as I could, for I soon heard, near us, the suppressed conversation of his pursuers.

There followed a series of explosions round about us, but none very close. They evidently had not spotted our hiding place, and were firing at random.

I waited tensely, balancing the gun in my hand, to accustom myself to its weight and probable throw.

Then I saw a movement in the green foliage of a tree not far away, and the head and face of a man appeared. Like my companion, he was clad entirely in green, which made his figure difficult to distinguish. But his face could be seen clearly. It was an evil face, and had murder in it.

That decided me. I raised the gun and fired. My aim was bad, for there was no kick in the gun, as I had expected, and I hit the trunk of the tree several feet below him. It blew him from his perch like a crumpled bit of paper, and he floated down to the ground, like some limp, dead thing, gently lowered by an invisible hand. The tree, its trunk blown apart by the explosion, crashed down.

There followed another series of explosions around us. These guns we were using made no sound in the firing, and my opponents were evidently as much at sea as to my position as I was to theirs. So I made no attempt to reply to their fire, contenting myself with keeping a sharp lookout in their general direction. And patience had its reward.

Very soon I saw a cautious movement in the top of another tree. Exposing myself as little as possible, I aimed carefully at the tree trunk and fired again. A shriek followed the explosion. I heard the tree crash down; then a groan.

There was silence for a while. Then I heard a faint sound of boughs swishing. I shot three times in its direction, pressing the button as rapidly as I could. Branches crashed down where my shells had exploded, but there was no body.

Then I saw one of them. He was starting one of those amazing leaps from the bough of one tree to another, about forty feet away.

I threw up my gun impulsively and fired. By now I had gotten the feel of the weapon, and my aim was good. I hit him. The "bullet" must have penetrated his body and exploded. For one moment I saw him flying through the air. Then the explosion, and he had vanished. He never finished his leap. It was annihilation.

How many more of them there were I don't know. But this must have been too much for them. They used a final round of shells on us, all of which exploded harmlessly, and shortly after I heard them swishing and crashing away from us through the tree tops. Not one of them descended to earth.

Now I had time to give some attention to my companion. She was, I found, a girl, and not a boy. Despite her bulky appearance, due to the peculiar belt strapped around her body high up under the arms, she was very slender, and very pretty.

There was a stream not far away, from which I brought water and bathed her face and wound.

Apparently the mystery of these long leaps, the monkey-like ability to jump from bough to bough, and of the bodies that floated gently down instead of falling, lay in the belt. The thing was some sort of anti-gravity belt that almost balanced the weight of the wearer, thereby tremendously multiplying the propulsive power of the leg muscles, and the lifting power of the arms.

When the girl came to, she regarded me as curiously as I did her, and promptly began to quiz me. Her accent and intonation puzzled me a lot, but nevertheless we were able to understand each other fairly well, except for certain words and phrases. I explained what had happened while she lay unconscious, and she thanked me simply for saving her life.

"You are a strange exchange," she said, eying my clothing quizzically. Evidently she found it mirth provoking by contrast with her own neatly efficient garb. "Don't you understand what I mean by 'exchange?' I mean ah – let me see – a stranger, somebody from some other gang. What gang do you belong to?" (She pronounced it "gan," with only a suspicion of a nasal sound).

I laughed. "I'm not a gangster," I said. But she evidently did not understand this word. "I don't belong to any gang," I explained, "and never did. Does everybody belong to a gang nowadays?"

"Naturally," she said, frowning. "If you don't belong to a gang, where and how do you live? Why have you not found and joined a gang? How do you eat? Where do you get your clothing?"

"I've been eating wild game for the past two weeks," I explained, "and this clothing I – er – ah – ." I paused, wondering how I could explain that it must be many hundred years old. In the end I saw I would have to tell my story as well as I could, piecing it together with my assumptions as to what had happened. She listened patiently; incredulously at first, but with more confidence as I went on. When I had finished, she sat thinking for a long time. "That's hard to believe," she said, "but I believe it." She looked me over with frank interest.

"Were you married when you slipped into unconsciousness down in that mine?" she asked me suddenly. I assured her I had never married. "Well, that simplifies matters," she continued. "You see, if you were technically classed as a family man, I could take you back only as an invited exchange and I, being unmarried, and no relation of yours, couldn't do the inviting."

Chapter II: The Forest Gangs

SHE GAVE ME a brief outline of the very peculiar social and economic system under which her people lived. At least it seemed very peculiar from my 20th Century viewpoint.

I learned with amazement that exactly 492 years had passed over my head as I lay unconscious in the mine.

Wilma, for that was her name, did not profess to be a historian, and so could give me only a sketchy outline of the wars that had been fought, and the manner in which such radical changes had come about. It seemed that another war had followed the First World

War, in which nearly all the European nations had banded together to break the financial and industrial power of America. They succeeded in their purpose, though they were beaten, for the war was a terrific one, and left America, like themselves, gasping, bleeding and disorganized, with only the hollow shell of a victory.

This opportunity had been seized by the Russian Soviets, who had made a coalition with the Chinese, to sweep over all Europe and reduce it to a state of chaos.

America, industrially geared to world production and the world trade, collapsed economically, and there ensued a long period of stagnation and desperate attempts at economic reconstruction. But it was impossible to stave off war with the Mongolians, who by now had subjugated the Russians, and were aiming at a world empire.

In about 2109, it seems, the conflict was finally precipitated. The Mongolians, with overwhelming fleets of great airships, and a science that far outstripped that of crippled America, swept in over the Pacific and Atlantic Coasts, and down from Canada, annihilating American aircraft, armies and cities with their terrific disintegrator rays. These rays were projected from a machine not unlike a searchlight in appearance, the reflector of which, however, was not material substance, but a complicated balance of interacting electronic forces. This resulted in a terribly destructive beam. Under its influence, material substance melted into "nothingness"; i.e., into electronic vibrations. It destroyed all then known substances, from air to the most dense metals and stone.

They settled down to the establishment of what became known as the Han dynasty in America, as a sort of province in their World Empire.

Those were terrible days for the Americans. They were hunted like wild beasts. Only those survived who finally found refuge in mountains, canyons and forests. Government was at an end among them. Anarchy prevailed for several generations. Most would have been eager to submit to the Hans, even if it meant slavery. But the Hans did not want them, for they themselves had marvelous machinery and scientific process by which all difficult labor was accomplished.

Ultimately they stopped their active search for, and annihilation of, the widely scattered groups of now savage Americans. So long as they remained hidden in their forests, and did not venture near the great cities the Hans had built, little attention was paid to them.

Then began the building of the new American civilization. Families and individuals gathered together in clans or "gangs" for mutual protection. For nearly a century they lived a nomadic and primitive life, moving from place to place, in desperate fear of the casual and occasional Han air raids, and the terrible disintegrator ray. As the frequency of these raids decreased, they began to stay permanently in given localities, organizing upon lines which in many respects were similar to those of the military households of the Norman feudal barons, except that instead of gathering together in castles, their defense tactics necessitated a certain scattering of living quarters for families and individuals. They lived virtually in the open air, in the forests, in green tents, resorting to camouflage tactics that would conceal their presence from air observers. They dug underground factories and laboratories, that they might better be shielded from the electrical detectors of the Hans. They tapped the radio communication lines of the Hans, with crude instruments at first; better ones later on. They bent every effort toward the redevelopment of science. For many generations they labored as unseen, unknown scholars of the Hans, picking up their knowledge piecemeal, as fast as they were able to.

During the earlier part of this period, there were many deadly wars fought between the various gangs, and occasional courageous but childishly futile attacks upon the Hans, followed by terribly punitive raids.

But as knowledge progressed, the sense of American brotherhood redeveloped. Reciprocal arrangements were made among the gangs over constantly increasing areas. Trade developed to a certain extent, as between one gang and another. But the interchange of knowledge became more important than that of goods, as skill in the handling of synthetic processes developed.

Within the gang, an economy was developed that was a compromise between individual liberty and a military socialism. The right of private property was limited practically to personal possessions, but private privileges were many, and sacredly regarded. Stimulation to achievement lay chiefly in the winning of various kinds of leadership and prerogatives, and only in a very limited degree in the hope of owning anything that might be classified as "wealth," and nothing that might be classified as "resources." Resources of every description, for military safety and efficiency, belonged as a matter of public interest to the community as a whole.

In the meantime, through these many generations, the Hans had developed a luxury economy, and with it the perfection of gilded vice and degradation. The Americans were regarded as "wild men of the woods." And since they neither needed nor wanted the woods or the wild men, they treated them as beasts, and were conscious of no human brotherhood with them. As time went on, and synthetic processes of producing foods and materials were further developed, less and less ground was needed by the Hans for the purposes of agriculture, and finally, even the working of mines was abandoned when it became cheaper to build up metal from electronic vibrations than to dig them out of the ground.

The Han race, devitalized by its vices and luxuries, with machinery and scientific processes to satisfy its every want, with virtually no necessity of labor, began to assume a defensive attitude toward the Americans.

And quite naturally, the Americans regarded the Hans with a deep, grim hatred. Conscious of individual superiority as men, knowing that latterly they were outstripping the Hans in science and civilization, they longed desperately for the day when they should be powerful enough to rise and annihilate the Yellow Blight that lay over the continent.

At the time of my awakening, the gangs were rather loosely organized, but were considering the establishment of a special military force, whose special business it would be to harry the Hans and bring down their air ships whenever possible without causing general alarm among the Mongolians. This force was destined to become the nucleus of the national force, when the Day of Retribution arrived. But that, however, did not happen for ten years, and is another story.

Wilma told me she was a member of the Wyoming Gang, which claimed the entire Wyoming Valley as its territory, under the leadership of Boss Hart. Her mother and father were dead, and she was unmarried, so she was not a "family member." She lived in a little group of tents known as Camp 17, under a woman Camp Boss, with seven other girls.

Her duties alternated between military or police scouting and factory work. For the two-week period which would end the next day, she had been on "air patrol." This did not mean, as I first imagined, that she was flying, but rather that she was on the lookout for Han ships over this outlying section of the Wyoming territory, and had spent most of her time perched in the tree tops scanning the skies. Had she seen one she would have fired a "drop flare" several miles off to one side, which would ignite when it was floating vertically toward the earth, so that the direction or point from which if had been fired might not be guessed by the airship and bring a blasting play of the disintegrator ray in her vicinity. Other members of the air patrol would send up rockets on seeing hers, until finally a scout equipped with an ultrophone, which, unlike the ancient radio, operated on the ultronic ethereal vibrations, would pass the warning simultaneously to the headquarters of the Wyoming Gang and other communities within a radius of several hundred miles, not to mention the few American rocket ships that might be in the air, and which instantly would duck to cover either through forest clearings or by flattening down to earth in green fields where their coloring would probably protect them from observation. The favorite American method of propulsion was known as "rocketing." The rocket is what I would describe, from my 20th Century comprehension of the matter, as an extremely powerful gas blast, atomically produced through the stimulation of chemical action. Scientists of today regard it as a childishly simple reaction, but by that very virtue, most economical and efficient.

But tomorrow, she explained, she would go back to work in the cloth plant, where she would take charge of one of the synthetic processes by which those wonderful substitutes for woven fabrics of wool, cotton and silk are produced. At the end of another two weeks, she would be back on military duty again, perhaps at the same work, or maybe as a "contact guard," on duty where the territory of the Wyomings merged with that of the Delawares, or the "Susquannas" (Susquehannas) or one of the half dozen other "gangs" in that section of the country which I knew as Pennsylvania and New York States.

Wilma cleared up for me the mystery of those flying leaps which she and her assailants had made, and explained in the following manner, how the inertron belt balances weight:

"Jumpers" were in common use at the time I "awoke," though they were costly, for at that time inertron had not been produced in very great quantity. They were very useful in the forest. They were belts, strapped high under the arms, containing an amount of inertron adjusted to the wearer's weight and purposes. In effect they made a man weigh as little as he desired; two pounds if he liked.

"Floaters" are a later development of "jumpers" – rocket motors encased in inertron blocks and strapped to the back in such a way that the wearer floats, when drifting, facing slightly downward. With his motor in operation, he moves like a diver, headforemost, controlling his direction by twisting his body and by movements of his outstretched arms and hands. Ballast weights locked in the front of the belt adjust weight and lift. Some men prefer a few ounces of weight in floating, using a slight motor thrust to overcome this. Others prefer a buoyance balance of a few ounces. The inadvertent dropping of weight is not a serious matter. The motor thrust always can be used to descend. But as an extra precaution, in case the motor should fail, for any reason, there are built into every belt a number of detachable sections, one or more of which can be discarded to balance off any loss in weight.

"But who were your assailants," I asked, "and why were you attacked?"

Her assailants, she told me, were members of an outlaw gang, referred to as "Bad Bloods," a group which for several generations had been under the domination of conscienceless leaders who tried to advance the interests of their clan by tactics which their neighbors had come to regard as unfair, and who in consequence had been virtually boycotted. Their purpose had been to slay her near the Delaware frontier, making it appear that the crime had been committed by Delaware scouts and thus embroil the Delawares and Wyomings in acts of reprisal against each other, or at least cause suspicions.

Fortunately they had not succeeded in surprising her, and she had been successful in dodging them for some two hours before the shooting began, at the moment when I arrived on the scene.

"But we must not stay here talking," Wilma concluded. "I have to take you in, and besides I must report this attack right away. I think we had better slip over to the other side of the mountain. Whoever is on that post will have a phone, and I can make a direct report. But you'll have to have a belt. Mine alone won't help much against our combined weights, and there's little to be gained by jumping heavy. It's almost as bad as walking."

After a little search, we found one of the men I had killed, who had floated down among the trees some distance away and whose belt was not badly damaged. In detaching it from his body, it nearly got away from me and shot up in the air. Wilma caught it, however, and though it reinforced the lift of her own belt so that she had to hook her knee around a branch to hold herself down, she saved it. I climbed the tree and, with my weight added to hers, we floated down easily.

Chapter III: Life in the 25th Century

WE WERE DELAYED in starting for quite a while since I had to acquire a few crude ideas about the technique of using these belts. I had been sitting down, for instance, with the belt strapped about me, enjoying an ease similar to that of a comfortable armchair; when I stood up with a natural exertion of muscular effort, I shot ten feet into the air, with a wild instinctive thrashing of arms and legs that amused Wilma greatly.

But after some practice, I began to get the trick of gauging muscular effort to a minimum of vertical and a maximum of horizontal. The correct form, I found, was in a measure comparable to that of skating. I found, also, that in forest work particularly the arms and hands could be used to great advantage in swinging along from branch to branch, so prolonging leaps almost indefinitely at times.

In going up the side of the mountain, I found that my 20th Century muscles did have an advantage, in spite of lack of skill with the belt, and since the slopes were very sharp, and most of our leaps were upward, I could have distanced Wilma easily. But when we crossed the ridge and descended, she outstripped me with her superior technique. Choosing the steepest slopes, she would crouch in the top of a tree, and propel herself outward, literally diving until, with the loss of horizontal momentum, she would assume a more upright position and float downward. In this manner she would sometimes cover as much as a quarter of a mile in a single leap, while I leaped and scrambled clumsily behind, thoroughly enjoying the novel sensation.

Half way down the mountain, we saw another green-clad figure leap out above the tree tops toward us. The three of us perched on an outcropping of rock from which a view for many miles around could be had, while Wilma hastily explained her adventure and my presence to her fellow guard; whose name was Alan. I learned later that this was the modern form of Helen.

"You want to report by phone then, don't you?" Alan took a compact packet about six inches square from a holster attached to her belt and handed it to Wilma.

So far as I could see, it had no special receiver for the ear. Wilma merely threw back a lid, as though she were opening a book, and began to talk. The voice that came back from the machine was as audible as her own.

She was queried closely as to the attack upon her, and at considerable length as to myself, and I could tell from the tone of that voice that its owner was not prepared to take me at my face value as readily as Wilma had. For that matter, neither was the other girl. I could realize it from the suspicious glances she threw my way, when she thought my attention was elsewhere, and the manner in which her hand hovered constantly near her gun holster.

SCIENCE FICTION SHORT STORIES

Wilma was ordered to bring me in at once, and informed that another scout would take her place on the other side of the mountain. So she closed down the lid of the phone and handed it back to Alan, who seemed relieved to see us departing over the tree tops in the direction of the camps.

We had covered perhaps ten miles, in what still seemed to me a surprisingly easy fashion, when Wilma explained, that from here on we would have to keep to the ground. We were nearing the camps, she said, and there was always the possibility that some small Han scoutship, invisible high in the sky, might catch sight of us through a projectoscope and thus find the general location of the camps.

Wilma took me to the Scout office, which proved to be a small building of irregular shape, conforming to the trees around it, and substantially constructed of green sheet-like material.

I was received by the assistant Scout Boss, who reported my arrival at once to the historical office, and to officials he called the Psycho Boss and the History Boss, who came in a few minutes later. The attitude of all three men was at first polite but skeptical, and Wilma's ardent advocacy seemed to amuse them secretly.

For the next two hours I talked, explained and answered questions. I had to explain, in detail, the manner of my life in the 20th Century and my understanding of customs, habits, business, science and the history of that period, and about developments in the centuries that had elapsed. Had I been in a classroom, I would have come through the examination with a very poor mark, for I was unable to give any answer to fully half of their questions. But before long I realized that the majority of these questions were designed as traps. Objects, of whose purpose I knew nothing, were casually handed to me, and I was watched keenly as I handled them.

In the end I could see both amazement and belief begin to show in the faces of my inquisitors, and at last the Historical and Psycho Bosses agreed openly that they could find no flaw in my story or reactions, and that unbelievable as it seemed, my story must be accepted as genuine.

They took me at once to Big Boss Hart. He was a portly man with a "poker face." He would probably have been the successful politician even in the 20th Century.

They gave him a brief outline of my story and a report of their examination of me. He made no comment other than to nod his acceptance of it. Then he turned to me.

"How does it feel?" he asked. "Do we look funny to you?"

"A bit strange," I admitted. "But I'm beginning to lose that dazed feeling, though I can see I have an awful lot to learn."

"Maybe we can learn some things from you, too," he said. "So you fought in the First World War. Do you know, we have very little left in the way of records of the details of that war, that is, the precise conditions under which it was fought, and the tactics employed. We forgot many things during the Han terror, and – well, I think you might have a lot of ideas worth thinking over for our raid masters. By the way, now that you're here, and can't go back to your own century, so to speak, what do you want to do? You're welcome to become one of us. Or perhaps you'd just like to visit with us for a while, and then look around among the other gangs. Maybe you'd like some of the others better. Don't make up your mind now. We'll put you down as an exchange for a while. Let's see. You and Bill Hearn ought to get along well together. He's Camp Boss of Number 34 when he isn't acting as Raid Boss or Scout Boss. There's a vacancy in his camp. Stay with him and think things over as long as you want to. As soon as you make up your mind to anything, let me know."

We all shook hands, for that was one custom that had not died out in five hundred years, and I set out with Bill Hearn.

Bill, like all the others, was clad in green. He was a big man. That is, he was about my own height, five feet eleven. This was considerably above the average now, for the race had lost something in stature, it seemed, through the vicissitudes of five centuries. Most of the women were a bit below five feet, and the men only a trifle above this height.

For a period of two weeks Bill was to confine himself to camp duties, so I had a good chance to familiarize myself with the community life. It was not easy. There were so many marvels to absorb. I never ceased to wonder at the strange combination of rustic social life and feverish industrial activity. At least, it was strange to me. For in my experience, industrial development meant crowded cities, tenements, paved streets, profusion of vehicles, noise, hurrying men and women with strained or dull faces, vast structures and ornate public works.

Here, however, was rustic simplicity, apparently isolated families and groups, living in the heart of the forest, with a quarter of a mile or more between households, a total absence of crowds, no means of conveyance other than the belts called jumpers, almost constantly worn by everybody, and an occasional rocket ship, used only for longer journeys, and underground plants or factories that were to my mind more like laboratories and engine rooms; many of them were excavations as deep as mines, with well finished, lighted and comfortable interiors. These people were adepts at camouflage against air observation. Not only would their activity have been unsuspected by an airship passing over the center of the community, but even by an enemy who might happen to drop through the screen of the upper branches to the floor of the forest. The camps, or household structures, were all irregular in shape and of colors that blended with the great trees among which they were hidden.

There were 724 dwellings or "camps" among the Wyomings, located within an area of about fifteen square miles. The total population was 8,688, every man, woman and child, whether member or "exchange," being listed.

The plants were widely scattered through the territory also. Nowhere was anything like congestion permitted. So far as possible, families and individuals were assigned to living quarters, not too far from the plants or offices in which their work lay.

All able-bodied men and women alternated in two-week periods between military and industrial service, except those who were needed for household work. Since working conditions in the plants and offices were ideal, and everybody thus had plenty of healthy outdoor activity in addition, the population was sturdy and active. Laziness was regarded as nearly the greatest of social offenses. Hard work and general merit were variously rewarded with extra privileges, advancement to positions of authority, and with various items of personal equipment for convenience and luxury.

In leisure moments, I got great enjoyment from sitting outside the dwelling in which I was quartered with Bill Hearn and ten other men, watching the occasional passers-by, as with leisurely, but swift movements, they swung up and down the forest trail, rising from the ground in long almost-horizontal leaps, occasionally swinging from one convenient branch overhead to another before "sliding" back to the ground farther on. Normal traveling pace, where these trails were straight enough, was about twenty miles an hour. Such things as automobiles and railroad trains (the memory of them not more than a month old in my mind) seemed inexpressibly silly and futile compared with such convenience as these belts or jumpers offered.

Bill suggested that I wander around for several days, from plant to plant, to observe and study what I could. The entire community had been apprised of my coming, my rating as an "exchange" reaching every building and post in the community, by means of ultronic broadcast. Everywhere I was welcomed in an interested and helpful spirit.

I visited the plants where ultronic vibrations were isolated from the ether and through slow processes built up into sub-electronic, electronic and atomic forms into the two great synthetic elements, ultron and inertron. I learned something, superficially at least, of the processes of combined chemical and mechanical action through which were produced the various forms of synthetic cloth. I watched the manufacture of the machines which were used at locations of construction to produce the various forms of building materials. But I was particularly interested in the munitions plants and the rocket-ship shops.

Ultron is a solid of great molecular density and moderate elasticity, which has the property of being 100 percent conductive to those pulsations known as light, electricity and heat. Since it is completely permeable to light vibrations, it is therefore absolutely invisible and non-reflective. Its magnetic response is almost, but not quite, 100 percent also. It is therefore very heavy under normal conditions but extremely responsive to the repellor or anti-gravity rays, such as the Hans use as "legs" for their airships.

Inertron is the second great triumph of American research and experimentation with ultronic forces. It was developed just a few years before my awakening in the abandoned mine. It is a synthetic element, built up, through a complicated heterodyning of ultronic pulsations, from "infra-balanced" sub-ionic forms. It is completely inert to both electric and magnetic forces in all the orders above the ultronic; that is to say, the sub-electronic, the electronic, the atomic and the molecular. In consequence it has a number of amazing and valuable properties. One of these is the total lack of weight. Another is a total lack of heat. It has no molecular vibration whatever. It reflects 100 percent of the heat and light impinging upon it. It does not feel cold to the touch, of course, since it will not absorb the heat of the hand. It is a solid, very dense in molecular structure despite its lack of weight, of great strength and considerable elasticity. It is a perfect shield against the disintegrator rays.

Rocket guns are very simple contrivances so far as the mechanism of launching the bullet is concerned. They are simple light tubes, closed at the rear end, with a trigger-actuated pin for piercing the thin skin at the base of the cartridge. This piercing of the skin starts the chemical and atomic reaction. The entire cartridge leaves the tube under its own power, at a very easy initial velocity, just enough to insure accuracy of aim; so the tube does not have to be of heavy construction. The bullet increases in velocity as it goes. It may be solid or explosive. It may explode on contact or on time, or a combination of these two.

Bill and I talked mostly of weapons, military tactics and strategy. Strangely enough he had no idea whatever of the possibilities of the barrage, though the tremendous effect of a "curtain of fire" with such high-explosive projectiles as these modern rocket guns used was obvious to me. But the barrage idea, it seemed, has been lost track of completely in the air wars that followed the First World War, and in the peculiar guerilla tactics developed by Americans in the later period of operations from the ground against Han airships, and in the gang wars which, until a few generations ago I learned, had been almost continuous.

"I wonder," said Bill one day, "if we couldn't work up some form of barrage to spring on the Bad Bloods. The Big Boss told me today that he's been in communication with the other gangs, and all are agreed that the Bad Bloods might as well be wiped out for good. That attempt on Wilma Deering's life and their evident desire to make trouble among the gangs, has stirred up every community east of the Alleghenies. The Boss says that none of the others will object if we go after them. So I imagine that before long we will. Now show me again how you worked that business in the Argonne forest. The conditions ought to be pretty much the same."

I went over it with him in detail, and gradually we worked out a modified plan that would be better adapted to our more powerful weapons, and the use of jumpers.

"It will be easy," Bill exulted. "I'll slide down and talk it over with the Boss tomorrow."

During the first two weeks of my stay with the Wyomings, Wilma Deering and I saw a great deal of each other. I naturally felt a little closer friendship for her, in view of the fact that she was the first human being I saw after waking from my long sleep; her appreciation of my saving her life, though I could not have done otherwise than I did in that matter, and most of all my own appreciation of the fact that she had not found it as difficult as the others to believe my story, operated in the same direction. I could easily imagine my story must have sounded incredible.

It was natural enough too, that she should feel an unusual interest in me. In the first place, I was her personal discovery. In the second, she was a girl of studious and reflective turn of mind. She never got tired of my stories and descriptions of the 20th Century.

The others of the community, however, seemed to find our friendship a bit amusing. It seemed that Wilma had a reputation for being cold toward the opposite sex, and so others, not being able to appreciate some of her fine qualities as I did, misinterpreted her attitude, much to their own delight. Wilma and I, however, ignored this as much as we could.

Chapter IV: A Han Air Raid

THERE WAS A GIRL in Wilma's camp named Gerdi Mann, with whom Bill Hearn was desperately in love, and the four of us used to go around a lot together. Gerdi was a distinct type. Whereas Wilma had the usual dark brown hair and hazel eyes that marked nearly every member of the community, Gerdi had red hair, blue eyes and very fair skin. She has been dead many years now, but I remember her vividly because she was a throwback in physical appearance to a certain 20th Century type which I have found very rare among modern Americans; also because the four of us were engaged one day in a discussion of this very point, when I obtained my first experience of a Han air raid.

We were sitting high on the side of a hill overlooking the valley that teemed with human activity, invisible beneath its blanket of foliage.

The other three, who knew of the Irish but vaguely and indefinitely, as a race on the other side of the globe, which, like ourselves, had succeeded in maintaining a precarious and fugitive existence in rebellion against the Mongolian domination of the earth, were listening with interest to my theory that Gerdi's ancestors of several hundred years ago must have been Irish. I explained that Gerdi was an Irish type, evidently a throwback, and that her surname might well have been McMann, or McMahan, and still more anciently "mac Mathghamhain." They were interested too in my surmise that "Gerdi" was the same name as that which had been "Gerty" or "Gertrude" in the 20th Century.

In the middle of our discussion, we were startled by an alarm rocket that burst high in the air, far to the north, spreading a pall of red smoke that drifted like a cloud. It was followed by others at scattered points in the northern sky.

"A Han raid!" Bill exclaimed in amazement. "The first in seven years!"

"Maybe it's just one of their ships off its course," I ventured.

"No," said Wilma in some agitation. "That would be green rockets. Red means only one thing, Tony. They're sweeping the countryside with their dis beams. Can you see anything, Bill?"

"We had better get under cover," Gerdi said nervously. "The four of us are bunched here in the open. For all we know they may be twelve miles up, out of sight, yet looking at us with a projecto'."

Bill had been sweeping the horizon hastily with his glass, but apparently saw nothing.

"We had better scatter, at that," he said finally. "It's orders, you know. See!" He pointed to the valley.

Here and there a tiny human figure shot for a moment above the foliage of the treetops.

"That's bad," Wilma commented, as she counted the jumpers. "No less than fifteen people visible, and all clearly radiating from a central point. Do they want to give away our location?"

The standard orders covering air raids were that the population was to scatter individually. There should be no grouping, or even pairing, in view of the destructiveness of the disintegrator rays. Experience of generations had proved that if this were done, and everybody remained hidden beneath the tree screens, the Hans would have to sweep mile after mile of territory, foot by foot, to catch more than a small percentage of the community.

Gerdi, however, refused to leave Bill, and Wilma developed an equal obstinacy against quitting my side. I was inexperienced at this sort of thing, she explained, quite ignoring the fact that she was too; she was only thirteen or fourteen years old at the time of the last air raid.

However, since I could not argue her out of it, we leaped together about a quarter of a mile to the right, while Bill and Gerdi disappeared down the hillside among the trees.

Wilma and I both wanted a point of vantage from which we might overlook the valley and the sky to the north, and we found it near the top of the ridge, where, protected from visibility by thick branches, we could look out between the tree trunks, and get a good view of the valley.

No more rockets went up. Except for a few of those warning red clouds, drifting lazily in a blue sky, there was no visible indication of man's past or present existence anywhere in the sky or on the ground.

Then Wilma gripped my arm and pointed. I saw it; away off in the distance; looking like a phantom dirigible airship, in its coat of low-visibility paint, a bare spectre.

"Seven thousand feet up," Wilma whispered, crouching close to me. "Watch."

The ship was about the same shape as the great dirigibles of the 20th Century that I had seen, but without the suspended control car, engines, propellors, rudders or elevating planes. As it loomed rapidly nearer, I saw that it was wider and somewhat flatter than I had supposed.

Now I could see the repellor rays that held the ship aloft, like searchlight beams faintly visible in the bright daylight (and still faintly visible to the human eye at night). Actually, I had been informed by my instructors, there were two rays; the visible one generated by the ship's apparatus, and directed toward the ground as a beam of "carrier" impulses; and the true repellor ray, the complement of the other in one sense, induced by the action of the "carrier" and reacting in a concentrating upward direction from the mass of the earth, becoming successively electronic, atomic and finally molecular, in its nature, according to various ratios of distance between earth mass and "carrier" source, until, in the last analysis, the ship itself actually is supported on an upward rushing column of air, much like a ball continuously supported on a fountain jet.

The raider neared with incredible speed. Its rays were both slanted astern at a sharp angle, so that it slid forward with tremendous momentum.

The ship was operating two disintegrator rays, though only in a casual, intermittent fashion. But whenever they flashed downward with blinding brilliancy, forest, rocks and ground melted instantaneously into nothing, where they played upon them.

When later I inspected the scars left by these rays I found them some five feet deep and thirty feet wide, the exposed surfaces being lava-like in texture, but of a pale, iridescent, greenish hue.

No systematic use of the rays was made by the ship, however, until it reached a point over the center of the valley – the center of the community's activities. There it came to a sudden stop by shooting its repellor beams sharply forward and easing them back gradually to the vertical, holding the ship floating and motionless. Then the work of destruction began systematically.

Back and forth traveled the destroying rays, ploughing parallel furrows from hillside to hillside. We gasped in dismay, Wilma and I, as time after time we saw it plough through sections where we knew camps or plants were located.

"This is awful," she moaned, a terrified question in her eyes. "How could they know the location so exactly, Tony? Did you see? They were never in doubt. They stalled at a predetermined spot – and – and it was exactly the right spot."

We did not talk of what might happen if the rays were turned in our direction. We both knew. We would simply disintegrate in a split second into mere scattered electronic vibrations. Strangely enough, it was this self-reliant girl of the 25th Century, who clung to me, a relatively primitive man of the 20th, less familiar than she with the thought of this terrifying possibility, for moral support.

We knew that many of our companions must have been whisked into absolute non-existence before our eyes in these few moments. The whole thing paralyzed us into mental and physical immobility for I do not know how long.

It couldn't have been long, however, for the rays had not ploughed more than thirty of their twenty-foot furrows or so across the valley, when I regained control of myself, and brought Wilma to herself by shaking her roughly.

"How far will this rocket gun shoot, Wilma?" I demanded, drawing my pistol.

"It depends on your rocket, Tony. It will take even the longest range rocket, but you could shoot more accurately from a longer tube. But why? You couldn't penetrate the shell of that ship with rocket force, even if you could reach it."

I fumbled clumsily with my rocket pouch, for I was excited. I had an idea I wanted to try; a "hunch" I called it, forgetting that Wilma could not understand my ancient slang. But finally, with her help, I selected the longest range explosive rocket in my pouch, and fitted it to my pistol.

"It won't carry seven thousand feet, Tony," Wilma objected. But I took aim carefully. It was another thought that I had in my mind. The supporting repellor ray, I had been told, became molecular in character at what was called a logarithmic level of five (below that it was a purely electronic "flow" or pulsation between the source of the "carrier" and the average mass of the earth). Below that level if I could project my explosive bullet into this stream where it began to carry material substance upward, might it not rise with the air column, gathering speed and hitting the ship with enough impact to carry it through the shell? It was worth trying anyhow. Wilma became greatly excited, too, when she grasped the nature of my inspiration.

Feverishly I looked around for some formation of branches against which I could rest the pistol, for I had to aim most carefully. At last I found one. Patiently I sighted on the hulk of the ship far above us, aiming at the far side of it, at such an angle as would, so far as I could estimate, bring my bullet path through the forward repellor beam. At last the sights wavered across the point I sought and I pressed the button gently.

For a moment we gazed breathlessly.

Suddenly the ship swung bow down, as on a pivot, and swayed like a pendulum. Wilma screamed in her excitement.

"Oh, Tony, you hit it! You hit it! Do it again; bring it down!"

We had only one more rocket of extreme range between us, and we dropped it three times in our excitement in inserting it in my gun. Then, forcing myself to be calm by sheer will power, while Wilma stuffed her little fist into her mouth to keep from shrieking, I sighted carefully again and fired. In a flash, Wilma had grasped the hope that this discovery of mine might lead to the end of the Han domination.

The elapsed time of the rocket's invisible flight seemed an age.

Then we saw the ship falling. It seemed to plunge lazily, but actually it fell with terrific acceleration, turning end over end, its disintegrator rays, out of control, describing vast, wild arcs, and once cutting a gash through the forest less than two hundred feet from where we stood.

The crash with which the heavy craft hit the ground reverberated from the hills – the momentum of eighteen or twenty thousand tons, in a sheer drop of seven thousand feet. A mangled mass of metal, it buried itself in the ground, with poetic justice, in the middle of the smoking, semi-molten field of destruction it had been so deliberately ploughing.

The silence, the vacuity of the landscape, was oppressive, as the last echoes died away.

Then far down the hillside, a single figure leaped exultantly above the foliage screen. And in the distance another, and another.

In a moment the sky was punctured by signal rockets. One after another the little red puffs became drifting clouds.

"Scatter! Scatter!" Wilma exclaimed. "In half an hour there'll be an entire Han fleet here from Nu-yok, and another from Bah-flo. They'll get this instantly on their recordographs and location finders. They'll blast the whole valley and the country for miles beyond. Come, Tony. There's no time for the gang to rally. See the signals. We've got to jump. Oh, I'm so proud of you!"

Over the ridge we went, in long leaps toward the east, the country of the Delawares.

From time to time signal rockets puffed in the sky. Most of them were the "red warnings," the "scatter" signals. But from certain of the others, which Wilma identified as Wyoming rockets, she gathered that whoever was in command (we did not know whether the Boss was alive or not) was ordering an ultimate rally toward the south, and so we changed our course.

It was a great pity, I thought, that the clan had not been equipped throughout its membership with ultrophones, but Wilma explained to me, that not enough of these had been built for distribution as yet, although general distribution had been contemplated within a couple of months.

We traveled far before nightfall overtook us, trying only to put as much distance as possible between ourselves and the valley.

When gathering dusk made jumping too dangerous, we sought a comfortable spot beneath the trees, and consumed part of our emergency rations. It was the first time I had tasted the stuff – a highly nutritive synthetic substance called "concentro," which was, however, a bit bitter and unpalatable. But as only a mouthful or so was needed, it did not matter.

Neither of us had a cloak, but we were both thoroughly tired and happy, so we curled up together for warmth. I remember Wilma making some sleepy remark about our mating, as she cuddled up, as though the matter were all settled, and my surprise at my own instant acceptance of the idea, for I had not consciously thought of her that way before. But we both fell asleep at once.

In the morning we found little time for love making. The practical problem facing us was too great. Wilma felt that the Wyoming plan must be to rally in the Susquanna territory, but she had her doubts about the wisdom of this plan. In my elation at my success in bringing down the Han ship, and my newly found interest in my charming companion, who was, from my viewpoint of another century, at once more highly civilized and yet more primitive than myself, I had forgotten the ominous fact that the Han ship I had destroyed must have known the exact location of the Wyoming Works.

This meant, to Wilma's logical mind, either that the Hans had perfected new instruments as yet unknown to us, or that somewhere, among the Wyomings or some other nearby gang, there were traitors so degraded as to commit that unthinkable act of trafficking in information with the Hans. In either contingency, she argued, other Han raids would follow, and since the Susquannas had a highly developed organization and more than usually productive plants, the next raid might be expected to strike them.

But at any rate it was clearly our business to get in touch with the other fugitives as quickly as possible, so in spite of muscles that were sore from the excessive leaping of the day before, we continued on our way.

We traveled for only a couple of hours when we saw a multi-colored rocket in the sky, some ten miles ahead of us.

"Bear to the left, Tony," Wilma said, "and listen for the whistle."

"Why?" I asked.

"Haven't they given you the rocket code yet?" she replied. "That's what the green, followed by yellow and purple means; to concentrate five miles east of the rocket position. You know the rocket position itself might draw a play of disintegrator beams."

It did not take us long to reach the neighborhood of the indicated rallying, though we were now traveling beneath the trees, with but an occasional leap to a top branch to see if any more rocket smoke was floating above. And soon we heard a distant whistle.

We found about half the Gang already there, in a spot where the trees met high above a little stream. The Big Boss and Raid Bosses were busy reorganizing the remnants.

We reported to Boss Hart at once. He was silent, but interested, when he heard our story.

"You two stick close to me," he said, adding grimly, "I'm going back to the valley at once with a hundred picked men, and I'll need you."

Chapter V: Setting the Trap

INSIDE OF fifteen minutes we were on our way. A certain amount of caution was sacrificed for the sake of speed, and the men leaped away either across the forest top, or over open spaces of ground, but concentration was forbidden. The Big Boss named the spot on the hillside as the rallying point.

"We'll have to take a chance on being seen, so long as we don't group," he declared, "at least until within five miles of the rallying spot. From then on I want every man to disappear from sight and to travel under cover. And keep your ultrophones open, and tuned on ten-four-seven-six."

Wilma and I had received our battle equipment from the Gear boss. It consisted of a long-gun, a hand-gun, with a special case of ammunition constructed of inertron, which made the load weigh but a few ounces, and a short sword. This gear we strapped over each other's shoulders, on top of our jumping belts. In addition, we each received an ultrophone, and a light inertron blanket rolled into a cylinder about six inches long by two or three in diameter. This fabric was exceedingly thin and light, but it had considerable warmth, because of the mixture of inertron in its composition.

"This looks like business," Wilma remarked to me with sparkling eyes. (And I might mention a curious thing here. The word "business" had survived from the 20th Century American vocabulary, but not with any meaning of "industry" or "trade," for such things being purely community activities were spoken of as "work" and "clearing." Business simply meant fighting, and that was all.)

"Did you bring all this equipment from the valley?" I asked the Gear Boss.

"No," he said. "There was no time to gather anything. All this stuff we cleared from the Susquannas a few hours ago. I was with the Boss on the way down, and he had me jump on ahead and arrange it. But you two had better be moving. He's beckoning you now."

Hart was about to call us on our phones when we looked up. As soon as we did so, he leaped away, waving us to follow closely.

He was a powerful man, and he darted ahead in long, swift, low leaps up the banks of the stream, which followed a fairly straight course at this point. By extending ourselves, however, Wilma and I were able to catch up to him.

As we gradually synchronized our leaps with his, he outlined to us, between the grunts that accompanied each leap, his plan of action.

"We have to start the big business – unh – sooner or later," he said. "And if – unh – the Hans have found any way of locating our positions – unh – it's time to start now, although the Council of Bosses – unh – had intended waiting a few years until enough rocket ships have been – unh – built. But no matter what the sacrifice – unh – we can't afford to let them get us on the run – unh – . We'll set a trap for the yellow devils in the – unh – valley if they come back for their wreckage – unh – and if they don't, we'll go rocketing for some of their liners – unh – on the Nu-yok, Clee-lan, Si-ka-ga course. We can use – unh – that idea of yours of shooting up the repellor – unh – beams. Want you to give us a demonstration."

With further admonition to follow him closely, he increased his pace, and Wilma and I were taxed to our utmost to keep up with him. It was only in ascending the slopes that my tougher muscles overbalanced his greater skill, and I was able to set the pace for him, as I had for Wilma.

We slept in greater comfort that night, under our inertron blankets, and were off with the dawn, leaping cautiously to the top of the ridge overlooking the valley which Wilma and I had left.

The Boss scanned the sky with his ultroscope, patiently taking some fifteen minutes to the task, and then swung his phone into use, calling the roll and giving the men their instructions.

His first order was for us all to slip our ear and chest discs into permanent position.

These ultrophones were quite different from the one used by Wilma's companion scout the day I saved her from the vicious attack of the bandit Gang. That one was contained entirely in a small pocket case. These, with which we were now equipped, consisted of a pair of ear discs, each a separate and self-contained receiving set. They slipped into little pockets over our ears in the fabric helmets we wore, and shut out virtually all extraneous sounds. The chest discs were likewise self-contained sending sets, strapped to the chest a few inches below the neck and actuated by the vibrations from the vocal cords through the body tissues. The total range of these sets was about eighteen miles. Reception was remarkably clear, quite free from the static that so marked the 20th Century radios, and of a strength in direct proportion to the distance of the speaker.

The Boss' set was triple powered, so that his orders would cut in on any local conversations, which were indulged in, however, with great restraint, and only for the purpose of maintaining contacts.

I marveled at the efficiency of this modern method of battle communication in contrast to the clumsy signaling devices of more ancient times; and also at other military contrasts in which the 20th and 25th Century methods were the reverse of each other in efficiency. These modern Americans, for instance, knew little of hand to hand fighting, and nothing, naturally, of trench warfare. Of barrages they were quite ignorant, although they possessed weapons of terrific power. And until my recent flash of inspiration, no one among them, apparently, had ever thought of the scheme of shooting a rocket into a repellor beam and letting the beam itself hurl it upward into the most vital part of the Han ship.

Hart patiently placed his men, first giving his instructions to the campmasters, and then remaining silent, while they placed the individuals.

In the end, the hundred men were ringed about the valley, on the hillsides and tops, each in a position from which he had a good view of the wreckage of the Han ship. But not a man had come in view, so far as I could see, in the whole process.

The Boss explained to me that it was his idea that he, Wilma and I should investigate the wreck. If Han ships should appear in the sky, we would leap for the hillsides.

I suggested to him to have the men set up their long-guns trained on an imaginary circle surrounding the wreck. He busied himself with this after the three of us leaped down to the Han ship, serving as a target himself, while he called on the men individually to aim their pieces and lock them in position.

In the meantime Wilma and I climbed into the wreckage, but did not find much. Practically all of the instruments and machinery had been twisted out of all recognizable shape, or utterly destroyed by the ship's disintegrator rays which apparently had continued to operate in the midst of its warped remains for some moments after the crash.

It was unpleasant work searching the mangled bodies of the crew. But it had to be done. The Han clothing, I observed, was quite different from that of the Americans, and in many respects more like the garb to which I had been accustomed in the earlier part of my life. It was made of synthetic fabrics like silks, loose and comfortable trousers of knee length, and sleeveless shirts.

No protection, except that against drafts, was needed, Wilma explained to me, for the Han cities were entirely enclosed, with splendid arrangements for ventilation and heating. These arrangements of course were equally adequate in their airships. The Hans, indeed, had quite a distaste for unshaded daylight, since their lighting apparatus diffused a controlled amount of violet rays, making the unmodified sunlight unnecessary for health, and undesirable for comfort. Since the Hans did not have the secret of inertron, none of them wore anti-gravity belts. Yet in spite of the fact that they had to bear their own full weights at all times, they were physically far inferior to the Americans, for they lived lives of degenerative physical inertia, having machinery of every description for the performance of all labor, and convenient conveyances for any movement of more than a few steps.

Even from the twisted wreckage of this ship I could see that seats, chairs and couches played an extremely important part in their scheme of existence.

But none of the bodies were overweight. They seemed to have been the bodies of men in good health, but muscularly much underdeveloped. Wilma explained to me that they had mastered the science of gland control, and of course dietetics, to the point where men and women among them not uncommonly reached the age of a hundred years with arteries and general health in splendid condition.

I did not have time to study the ship and its contents as carefully as I would have liked, however. Time pressed, and it was our business to discover some clue to the deadly accuracy with which the ship had spotted the Wyoming Works.

The Boss had hardly finished his arrangements for the ring barrage, when one of the scouts on an eminence to the north, announced the approach of seven Han ships, spread out in a great semi-circle.

Hart leaped for the hillside, calling to us to do likewise, but Wilma and I had raised the flaps of our helmets and switched off our "speakers" for conversation between ourselves, and by the time we discovered what had happened, the ships were clearly visible, so fast were they approaching.

"Jump!" we heard the Boss order, "Deering to the north. Rogers to the east."

But Wilma looked at me meaningly and pointed to where the twisted plates of the ship, projecting from the ground, offered a shelter.

"Too late, Boss," she said. "They'd see us. Besides I think there's something here we ought to look at. It's probably their magnetic graph."

"You're signing your death warrant," Hart warned.

"We'll risk it," said Wilma and I together.

"Good for you," replied the Boss. "Take command then, Rogers, for the present. Do you all know his voice, boys?"

A chorus of assent rang in our ears, and I began to do some fast thinking as the girl and I ducked into the twisted mass of metal.

"Wilma, hunt for that record," I said, knowing that by the simple process of talking I could keep the entire command continuously informed as to the situation. "On the hillsides, keep your guns trained on the circles and stand by. On the hilltops, how many of you are there? Speak in rotation from Bald Knob around to the east, north, west."

In turn the men called their names. There were twenty of them.

I assigned them by name to cover the various Han ships, numbering the latter from left to right.

"Train your rockets on their repellor rays about three-quarters of the way up, between ships and ground. Aim is more important than elevation. Follow those rays with your aim continuously. Shoot when I tell you, not before. Deering has the record. The Hans probably have not seen us, or at least think there are but two of us in the valley, since they're settling without opening up disintegrators. Any opinions?"

My ear discs remained silent.

"Deering and I remain here until they land and debark. Stand by and keep alert."

Rapidly and easily the largest of the Han ships settled to the earth. Three scouted sharply to the south, rising to a higher level. The others floated motionless about a thousand feet above.

Peeping through a small fissure between two plates, I saw the vast hulk of the ship come to rest full on the line of our prospective ring barrage. A door clanged open a couple of feet from the ground, and one by one the crew emerged.

Chapter VI: The "Wyoming Massacre"

"THEY'RE COMING out of the ship." I spoke quietly, with my hand over my mouth, for fear they might hear me. "One – two – three – four, five – six – seven – eight – nine. That seems to be all. Who knows how many men a ship like that is likely to carry?"

"About ten, if there are no passengers," replied one of my men, probably one of those on the hillside.

"How are they armed?" I asked.

"Just knives," came the reply. "They never permit hand-rays on the ships. Afraid of accidents. Have a ruling against it."

"Leave them to us then," I said, for I had a hastily formed plan in my mind. "You, on the hillsides, take the ships above. Abandon the ring target. Divide up in training on those repellor rays. You, on the hilltops, all train on the repellors of the ships to the south. Shoot at the word, but not before.

"Wilma, crawl over to your left where you can make a straight leap for the door in that ship. These men are all walking around the wreck in a bunch. When they're on the far side, I'll give the word and you leap through that door in one bound. I'll follow. Maybe we won't be seen. We'll overpower the guard inside, but don't shoot. We may escape being seen by both this crew and ships above. They can't see over this wreck."

It was so easy that it seemed too good to be true. The Hans who had emerged from the ship walked round the wreckage lazily, talking in guttural tones, keenly interested in the wreck, but quite unsuspicious.

At last they were on the far side. In a moment they would be picking their way into the wreck.

"Wilma, leap!" I almost whispered the order.

The distance between Wilma's hiding place and the door in the side of the Han ship was not more than fifteen feet. She was already crouched with her feet braced against a metal beam. Taking the lift of that wonderful inertron belt into her calculation, she dove headforemost, like a green projectile, through the door. I followed in a split second, more clumsily, but no less speedily, bruising my shoulder painfully, as I ricocheted from the edge of the opening and brought up sliding against the unconscious girl; for she evidently had hit her head against the partition within the ship into which she had crashed.

We had made some noise within the ship. Shuffling footsteps were approaching down a well lit gangway.

"Any signs we have been observed?" I asked my men on the hillsides.

"Not yet," I heard the Boss reply. "Ships overhead still standing. No beams have been broken out. Men on ground absorbed in wreck. Most of them have crawled into it out of sight."

"Good," I said quickly. "Deering hit her head. Knocked out. One or more members of the crew approaching. We're not discovered yet. I'll take care of them. Stand a bit longer, but be ready."

I think my last words must have been heard by the man who was approaching, for he stopped suddenly.

I crouched at the far side of the compartment, motionless. I would not draw my sword if there were only one of them. He would be a weakling, I figured, and I should easily overcome him with my bare hands.

Apparently reassured at the absence of any further sound, a man came around a sort of bulkhead – and I leaped.

I swung my legs up in front of me as I did so, catching him full in the stomach and knocked him cold.

I ran forward along the keel gangway, searching for the control room. I found it well up in the nose of the ship. And it was deserted. What could I do to jam the controls of the ships that would not register on the recording instruments of the other ships? I gazed at the mass of controls. Levers and wheels galore. In the center of the compartment, on a massively braced universal joint mounting, was what I took for the repellor generator. A dial on it glowed and a faint hum came from within its shielding metallic case. But I had no time to study it.

Above all else, I was afraid that some automatic telephone apparatus existed in the room, through which I might be heard on the other ships. The risk of trying to jam the controls was too great. I abandoned the idea and withdrew softly. I would have to take a chance that there was no other member of the crew aboard.

I ran back to the entrance compartment. Wilma still lay where she had slumped down. I heard the voices of the Hans approaching. It was time to act. The next few seconds would tell whether the ships in the air would try or be able to melt us into nothingness. I spoke.

"Are you boys all ready?" I asked, creeping to a position opposite the door and drawing my hand-gun.

Again there was a chorus of assent.

"Then on the count of three, shoot up those repellor rays – all of them – and for God's sake, don't miss." And I counted.

I think my "three" was a bit weak. I know it took all the courage I had to utter it.

For an agonizing instant nothing happened, except that the landing party from the ship strolled into my range of vision.

Then startled, they turned their eyes upward. For an instant they stood frozen with horror at whatever they saw.

One hurled his knife at me. It grazed my cheek. Then a couple of them made a break for the doorway. The rest followed. But I fired pointblank with my hand-gun, pressing the button as fast as I could and aiming at their feet to make sure my explosive rockets would make contact and do their work.

The detonations of my rockets were deafening. The spot on which the Hans stood flashed into a blinding glare. Then there was nothing there except their torn and mutilated corpses. They had been fairly bunched, and I got them all.

I ran to the door, expecting any instant to be hurled into infinity by the sweep of a disintegrator ray.

Some eighth of a mile away I saw one of the ships crash to earth. A disintegrator ray came into my line of vision, wavered uncertainly for a moment and then began to sweep directly toward the ship in which I stood. But it never reached it. Suddenly, like a light switched off, it shot to one side, and a moment later another vast hulk crashed to earth. I looked out, then stepped out on the ground.

The only Han ships in the sky were two of the scouts to the south which were hanging perpendicularly, and sagging slowly down. The others must have crashed down while I was deafened by the sound of the explosion of my own rockets.

Somebody hit the other repellor ray of one of the two remaining ships and it fell out of sight beyond a hilltop. The other, farther away, drifted down diagonally, its disintegrator ray playing viciously over the ground below it.

I shouted with exultation and relief.

"Take back the command, Boss!" I yelled.

His commands, sending out jumpers in pursuit of the descending ship, rang in my ears, but I paid no attention to them. I leaped back into the compartment of the Han ship and knelt beside my Wilma. Her padded helmet had absorbed much of the blow, I thought; otherwise, her skull might have been fractured.

"Oh, my head!" she groaned, coming to as I lifted her gently in my arms and strode out in the open with her. "We must have won, dearest, did we?"

"We most certainly did," I reassured her. "All but one crashed and that one is drifting down toward the south; we've captured this one we're in intact. There was only one member of the crew aboard when we dove in."

Less than an hour afterward the Big Boss ordered the outfit to tune in ultrophones on three-twenty-three to pick up a translated broadcast of the Han intelligence office in Nu-yok from the Susquanna station. It was in the form of a public warning and news item, and read as follows:

"This is Public Intelligence Office, Nu-yok, broadcasting warning to navigators of private ships, and news of public interest. The squadron of seven ships, which left Nu-yok this morning to investigate the recent destruction of the GK-984 in the Wyoming Valley, has been destroyed by a series of mysterious explosions similar to those which wrecked the GK-984.

"The phones, viewplates, and all other signaling devices of five of the seven ships ceased operating suddenly at approximately the same moment, about seven-four-nine." (According to the Han system of reckoning time, seven and forty-nine one hundredths after midnight.) "After violent disturbances the location finders went out of operation. Electroactivity registers applied to the territory of the Wyoming Valley remain dead.

"The Intelligence Office has no indication of the kind of disaster which overtook the squadron except certain evidences of explosive phenomena similar to those in the case of the GK-984, which recently went dead while beaming the valley in a systematic effort to wipe out the works and camps of the tribesmen. The Office considers, as obvious, the deduction that the tribesmen have developed a new, and as yet undetermined, technique of attack on airships, and has recommended to the Heaven-Born that immediate and unlimited authority be given the Navigation Intelligence Division to make an investigation of this technique and develop a defense against it.

"In the meantime it urges that private navigators avoid this territory in particular, and in general hold as closely as possible to the official inter-city routes, which now are being patrolled by the entire force of the Military Office, which is beaming the routes generously to a width of ten miles. The Military Office reports that it is at present considering no retaliatory raids against the tribesmen. With the Navigation Intelligence Division, it holds that unless further evidence of the nature of the disaster is developed in the near future, the public interest will be better served, and at smaller cost of life, by a scientific research than by attempts at retaliation, which may bring destruction on all ships engaging therein. So unless further evidence actually is developed, or the Heaven-Born orders to the contrary, the Military will hold to a defensive policy.

"Unofficial intimations from Lo-Tan are to the effect that the Heaven-Council has the matter under consideration.

"The Navigation Intelligence Office permits the broadcast of the following condensation of its detailed observations:

"The squadron proceeded to a position above the Wyoming Valley where the wreck of the GK-984 was known to be, from the record of its location finder before it went dead recently. There the bottom projectoscope relays of all ships registered the wreck of the GK-984. Teleprojectoscope views of the wreck and the bowl of the valley showed no evidence of the presence of tribesmen. Neither ship registers nor base registers showed any indication of electroactivity except from the squadron itself. On orders from the Base Squadron Commander, the LD-248, LK-745 and LG-25 scouted southward at 3,000 feet. The GK-43, GK-981 and GK-220 stood above at 2,500 feet, and the GK-18 landed to permit personal inspection of the wreck by the science committee. The party debarked, leaving one man on board in the control cabin. He set all projectoscopes at universal focus except RB-3," (this meant the third projectoscope from the bow of the ship, on the right-hand side of the lower deck) "with which he followed the landing group as it walked around the wreck.

"The first abnormal phenomenon recorded by any of the instruments at Base was that relayed automatically from projectoscope RB-4 of the GK-18, which as the party disappeared from view in back of the wreck, recorded two green missiles of roughly cylindrical shape, projected from the wreckage into the landing compartment of the ship. At such close range these were not clearly defined, owing to the universal focus at which the projectoscope was set. The Base Captain of GK-18 at once ordered the man in the control room to investigate, and saw him leave the control room in compliance with this order. An instant later confused sounds reached the control-room electrophone, such as might be made by a man falling heavily, and footsteps reapproached the control room, a figure entering and leaving the control room hurriedly. The Base Captain now believes, and the stills of the photorecord support his belief, that this was not the crew member who had been left in the control room. Before the Base Captain could speak to him he left the room, nor was any response given to the attention signal the Captain flashed throughout the ship.

"At this point projectoscope RB-3 of the ship now out of focus control, dimly showed the landing party walking back toward the ship. RB-4 showed it more clearly. Then on both these instruments, a number of blinding explosives in rapid succession were seen and the electrophone relays registered terrific concussions; the ship's electronic apparatus and projectoscopes apparatus went dead.

"Reports of the other ships' Base Observers and Executives, backed by the photorecords, show the explosions as taking place in the midst of the landing party as it returned, evidently unsuspicious, to the ship. Then in rapid succession they indicate that terrific explosions occurred inside and outside the three ships standing above close to their rep-ray generators, and all signals from these ships thereupon went dead.

"Of the three ships scouting to the south, the LD-248 suffered an identical fate, at the same moment. Its records add little to the knowledge of the disaster. But with the LK-745 and the LG-25 it was different.

"The relay instruments of the LK-745 indicated the destruction by an explosion of the rear rep-ray generator, and that the ship hung stern down for a short space, swinging like a pendulum. The forward viewplates and indicators did not cease functioning, but their records are chaotic, except for one projectoscope still, which shows the bowl of the valley, and the GK-981 falling, but no visible evidence of tribesmen. The control-room viewplate is also a chaotic record of the ship's crew tumbling and falling to the rear wall. Then the forward rep-ray generator exploded, and all signals went dead.

"The fate of the LG-25 was somewhat similar, except that this ship hung nose down, and drifted on the wind southward as it slowly descended out of control.

"As its control room was shattered, verbal report from its Action Captain was precluded. The record of the interior rear viewplate shows members of the crew climbing toward the rear rep-ray generator in an attempt to establish manual control of it, and increase the lift. The projectoscope relays, swinging in wide arcs, recorded little of value except at the ends of their swings. One of these, from a machine which happened to be set in telescopic focus, shows several views of great value in picturing the falls of the other ships, and all of the rear projectoscope records enable the reconstruction in detail of the pendulum and torsional movements of the ship, and its sag toward the earth. But none of the views showing the forest below contain any indication of tribesmen's presence. A final explosion put this ship out of commission at a height of 1,000 feet, and at a point four miles S. by E. of the center of the valley."

The message ended with a repetition of the warning to other airmen to avoid the valley.

Chapter VII: Incredible Treason

AFTER RECEIVING this report, and reassurances of support from the Big Bosses of the neighboring Gangs, Hart determined to reestablish the Wyoming Valley community.

A careful survey of the territory showed that it was only the northern sections and slopes that had been "beamed" by the first Han ship.

The synthetic-fabrics plant had been partially wiped out, though the lower levels underground had not been reached by the dis ray. The forest screen above it, however, had been annihilated, and it was determined to abandon it, after removing all usable machinery and evidences of the processes that might be of interest to the Han scientists, should they return to the valley in the future.

The ammunition plant, and the rocket-ship plant, which had just been about to start operation at the time of the raid, were intact, as were the other important plants.

Hart brought the Camboss up from the Susquanna Works, and laid out new camp locations, scattering them farther to the south, and avoiding ground which had been seared by the Han beams and the immediate locations of the Han wrecks.

During this period, a sharp check was kept upon Han messages, for the phone plant had been one of the first to be put in operation, and when it became evident that the Hans did not intend any immediate reprisals, the entire membership of the community was summoned back, and normal life was resumed.

Wilma and I had been married the day after the destruction of the ships, and spent this intervening period in a delightful honeymoon, camping high in the mountains. On our return, we had a camp of our own, of course. We were assigned to location 1017. And as might be expected, we had a great deal of banter over which one of us was Camp Boss. The title stood after my name on the Big Boss' records, and those of the Big Camboss, of course, but Wilma airily held that this meant nothing at all – and generally succeeded in making me admit it whenever she chose.

I found myself a full-fledged member of the Gang now, for I had elected to search no farther for a permanent alliance, much as I would have liked to familiarize myself with this 25th Century life in other sections of the country. The Wyomings had a high morale, and had prospered under the rule of Big Boss Hart for many years. But many of the gangs, I found, were badly organized, lacked strong hands in authority, and were rife with intrigue. On the whole, I thought I would be wise to stay with a group which had already proved its friendliness, and in which I seemed to have prospects of advancement. Under these modern social and economic conditions, the kind of individual freedom to which I had been accustomed in the 20th Century was impossible. I would have been as much of a nonentity in every phase of human relationship by attempting to avoid alliances, as any man of the 20th Century would have been politically, who aligned himself with no political party.

This entire modern life, it appeared to me, judging from my ancient viewpoint, was organized along what I called "political" lines. And in this connection, it amused me to notice how universal had become the use of the word "boss." The leader, the person in charge or authority over anything, was a "boss." There was as little formality in his relations with his followers as there was in the case of the 20th Century political boss, and the same high respect paid him by his followers as well as the same high consideration by him of their interests. He was just as much of an autocrat, and just as much dependent upon the general popularity of his actions for the ability to maintain his autocracy.

The sub-boss who could not command the loyalty of his followers was as quickly deposed, either by them or by his superiors, as the ancient ward leader of the 20th Century who lost control of his votes.

As society was organized in the 20th Century, I do not believe the system could have worked in anything but politics. I tremble to think what would have happened, had the attempt been made to handle the A. E. F. this way during the First World War, instead of by that rigid military discipline and complete assumption of the individual as a mere standardized cog in the machine.

But owing to the centuries of desperate suffering the people had endured at the hands of the Hans, there developed a spirit of self-sacrifice and consideration for the common good that made the scheme applicable and efficient in all forms of human co-operation.

I have a little heresy about all this, however. My associates regard the thought with as much horror as many worthy people of the 20th Century felt in regard to any heretical suggestion that the original outline of government as laid down in the First Constitution did not apply as well to 20th Century conditions as to those of the early 19th.

In later years, I felt that there was a certain softening of moral fiber among the people, since the Hans had been finally destroyed with all their works; and Americans have developed a new luxury economy. I have seen signs of the reawakening of greed, of selfishness. The eternal cycle seems to be at work. I fear that slowly, though surely, private wealth is reappearing, codes of inflexibility are developing; they will be followed by corruption, degradation; and in the end some cataclysmic event will end this era and usher in a new one.

All this, however, is wandering afar from my story, which concerns our early battles against the Hans, and not our more modern problems of self-control.

Our victory over the seven Han ships had set the country ablaze. The secret had been carefully communicated to the other gangs, and the country was agog from one end to the other. There was feverish activity in the ammunition plants, and the hunting of stray Han ships became an enthusiastic sport. The results were disastrous to our hereditary enemies.

From the Pacific Coast came the report of a great transpacific liner of 75,000 tons "lift" being brought to earth from a position of invisibility above the clouds. A dozen Sacramentos had caught the hazy outlines of its rep rays approaching them, head-on, in the twilight, like ghostly pillars reaching into the sky. They had fired rockets into it with ease, whereas they would have had difficulty in hitting it if it had been moving at right angles to their position. They got one rep ray. The other was not strong enough to hold it up. It floated to earth, nose down, and since it was unarmed and unarmored, they had no difficulty in shooting it to pieces and massacring its crew and passengers. It seemed barbarous to me. But then I did not have centuries of bitter persecution in my blood.

From the Jersey Beaches we received news of the destruction of a Nu-yok-a-lan-a liner. The Sand-snipers, practically invisible in their sand-colored clothing, and half buried along the beaches, lay in wait for days, risking the play of dis beams along the route, and finally registering four hits within a week. The Hans discontinued their service along this route, and as evidence that they were badly shaken by our success, sent no raiders down the Beaches.

It was a few weeks later that Big Boss Hart sent for me.

"Tony," he said, "There are two things I want to talk to you about. One of them will become public property in a few days, I think. We aren't going to get any more Han ships by shooting up their repellor rays unless we use much larger rockets. They are wise to us now. They're putting armor of great thickness in the hulls of their ships below the rep-ray machines. Near Bah-flo this morning a party of Eries shot one without success. The explosions staggered her, but did not penetrate. As near as we can gather from their reports, their laboratories have developed a new alloy of great tensile strength and elasticity which nevertheless lets the rep rays through like a sieve. Our reports indicate that the Eries' rockets bounced off harmlessly. Most of the party was wiped out as the dis rays went into action on them.

"This is going to mean real business for all of the gangs before long. The Big Bosses have just held a national ultrophone council. It was decided that America must organize on a national basis. The first move is to develop sectional organization by Zones. I have been made Superboss of the Mid-Atlantic Zone.

"We're in for it now. The Hans are sure to launch reprisal expeditions. If we're to save the race we must keep them away from our camps and plants. I'm thinking of developing a permanent field force, along the lines of the regular armies of the 20th Century you told me about. Its business will be twofold: to carry the warfare as much as possible to the Hans, and to serve as a decoy, to beep their attention from our plants. I'm going to need your help in this.

"The other thing I wanted to talk to you about is this: Amazing and impossible as it seems, there is a group, or perhaps an entire gang, somewhere among us, that is betraying us to the Hans. It may be the Bad Bloods, or it may be one of those gangs who live near one of the Han cities. You know, a hundred and fifteen or twenty years ago there were certain of these people's ancestors who actually degraded themselves by mating with the Hans, sometimes even serving them as slaves, in the days before they brought all their service machinery to perfection.

"There is such a gang, called the Nagras, up near Bah-flo, and another in Mid-Jersey that men call the Pineys. But I hardly suspect the Pineys. There is little intelligence among them. They wouldn't have the information to give the Hans, nor would they be capable of imparting it. They're absolute savages."

"Just what evidence is there that anybody has been clearing information to the Hans?" I asked.

"Well," he replied, "first of all there was that raid upon us. That first Han ship knew the location of our plants exactly. You remember it floated directly into position above the valley and began a systematic beaming. Then, the Hans quite obviously have learned that we are picking up their electrophone waves, for they've gone back to their old, but extremely accurate, system of directional control. But we've been getting them for the past week by installing automatic re-broadcast units along the scar paths. This is what the Americans called those strips of country directly under the regular ship routes of the Hans, who as a matter of precaution frequently blasted them with their dis beams to prevent the growth of foliage which might give shelter to the Americans. But they've been beaming those paths so hard, it looks as though they even had information of this strategy. And in addition, they've been using code. Finally, we've picked up three of their messages in which they discuss, with some nervousness, the existence of our 'mysterious' ultrophone."

"But they still have no knowledge of the nature and control of ultronic activity?" I asked.

"No," said the Big Boss thoughtfully, "they don't seem to have a bit of information about it."

"Then it's quite clear," I ventured, "that whoever is 'clearing' us to them is doing it piecemeal. It sounds like a bit of occasional barter, rather than an out-and-out alliance. They're holding back as much information as possible for future bartering, perhaps."

"Yes," Hart said, "and it isn't information the Hans are giving in return, but some form of goods, or privilege. The trick would be to locate the goods. I guess I'll have to make a personal trip around among the Big Bosses."

Chapter VIII: The Han City

THIS CONVERSATION set me thinking. All of the Han electrophone inter-communication had been an open record to the Americans for a good many years, and the Hans were just finding it out. For centuries they had not regarded us as any sort of a menace. Unquestionably it had never occurred to them to secrete their own records. Somewhere in Nu-yok or Bah-flo, or possibly in Lo-Tan itself, the record of this traitorous transaction would be more or less openly filed. If we could only get at it! I wondered if a raid might not be possible.

Bill Hearn and I talked it over with our Han-affairs Boss and his experts. There ensued several days of research, in which the Han records of the entire decade were scanned and analyzed. In the end they picked out a mass of detail, and fitted it together into a very definite picture of the great central filing office of the Hans in Nu-yok, where the entire mass of official records was kept, constantly available for instant projectoscoping to any of the city's offices, and of the system by which the information was filed.

The attempt began to look feasible, though Hart instantly turned the idea down when I first presented it to him. It was unthinkable, he said. Sheer suicide. But in the end I persuaded him.

"I will need," I said, "Blash, who is thoroughly familiar with the Han library system; Bert Gaunt, who for years has specialized on their military offices; Bill Barker, the ray specialist, and the best swooper pilot we have." Swoopers are one-man and two-man ships, developed by the Americans, with skeleton backbones of inertron (during the war painted green for invisibility against the green forests below) and "bellies" of clear ultron.

"That will be Mort Gibbons," said Hart. "We've only got three swoopers left, Tony, but I'll risk one of them if you and the others will voluntarily risk your existences. But mind, I won't urge or order one of you to go. I'll spread the word to every Plant Boss at once to give you anything and everything you need in the way of equipment."

When I told Wilma of the plan, I expected her to raise violent and tearful objections, but she didn't. She was made of far sterner stuff than the women of the 20th Century. Not that she couldn't weep as copiously or be just as whimsical on occasion; but she wouldn't weep for the same reasons.

She just gave me an unfathomable look, in which there seemed to be a bit of pride, and asked eagerly for the details. I confess I was somewhat disappointed that she could so courageously risk my loss, even though I was amazed at her fortitude. But later I was to learn how little I knew her then.

We were ready to slide off at dawn the next morning. I had kissed Wilma good-bye at our camp, and after a final conference over our plans, we boarded our craft and gently glided away over the tree tops on a course, which, after crossing three routes of the Han ships, would take us out over the Atlantic, off the Jersey coast, whence we would come up on Nu-yok from the ocean.

Twice we had to nose down and lie motionless on the ground near a route while Han ships passed. Those were tense moments. Had the green back of our ship been observed, we would have been disintegrated in a second. But it wasn't.

Once over the water, however, we climbed in a great spiral, ten miles in diameter, until our altimeter registered ten miles. Here Gibbons shut off his rocket motor, and we floated, far above the level of the Atlantic liners, whose course was well to the north of us anyhow, and waited for nightfall.

Then Gibbons turned from his control long enough to grin at me.

"I have a surprise for you, Tony," he said, throwing back the lid of what I had supposed was a big supply case. And with a sigh of relief, Wilma stepped out of the case.

"If you 'go into zero' (a common expression of the day for being annihilated by the disintegrator ray), you don't think I'm going to let you go alone, do you, Tony? I couldn't believe my ears last night when you spoke of going without me, until I realized that you are still five hundred years behind the times in lots of ways. Don't you know, dear heart, that you offered me the greatest insult a husband could give a wife? You didn't, of course."

The others, it seemed, had all been in on the secret, and now they would have kidded me unmercifully, except that Wilma's eyes blazed dangerously.

At nightfall, we maneuvered to a position directly above the city. This took some time and calculation on the part of Bill Barker, who explained to me that he had to determine our point by ultronic bearings. The slightest resort to an electronic instrument, he feared, might be detected by our enemies' locators. In fact, we did not dare bring our swooper any lower than five miles for fear that its capacity might be reflected in their instruments.

Finally, however, he succeeded in locating above the central tower of the city.

"If my calculations are as much as ten feet off," he remarked with confidence, "I'll eat the tower. Now the rest is up to you, Mort. See what you can do to hold her steady. No – here, watch this indicator – the red beam, not the green one. See – if you keep it exactly centered on the needle, you're OK. The width of the beam represents seventeen feet. The tower platform is fifty feet square, so we've got a good margin to work on."

For several moments we watched as Gibbons bent over his levers, constantly adjusting them with deft touches of his fingers. After a bit of wavering, the beam remained centered on the needle.

"Now," I said, "let's drop."

I opened the trap and looked down, but quickly shut it again when I felt the air rushing out of the ship into the rarefied atmosphere in a torrent. Gibbons literally yelled a protest from his instrument board.

"I forgot," I mumbled. "Silly of me. Of course, we'll have to drop out of compartment."

The compartment, to which I referred, was similar to those in some of the 20th Century submarines. We all entered it. There was barely room for us to stand, shoulder to shoulder. With some struggles, we got into our special air helmets and adjusted the pressure. At our signal, Gibbons exhausted the air in the compartment, pumping it into the body of the ship, and as the little signal light flashed, Wilma threw open the hatch.

Setting the ultron-wire reel, I climbed through, and began to slide down gently.

We all had our belts on, of course, adjusted to a weight balance of but a few ounces. And the five-mile reel of ultron wire that was to be our guide, was of gossamer fineness, though, anyway, I believe it would have lifted the full weight of the five of us, so strong and tough was this invisible metal. As an extra precaution, since the wire was of the purest metal, and therefore totally invisible, even in daylight, we all had our belts hooked on small rings that slid down the wire.

I went down with the end of the wire. Wilma followed a few feet above me, then Barker, Gaunt and Blash. Gibbons, of course, stayed behind to hold the ship in position and control the paying out of the line. We all had our ultrophones in place inside our air helmets, and so could converse with one another and with Gibbons. But at Wilma's suggestion, although we would have liked to let the Big Boss listen in, we kept them adjusted to short-range work, for fear that those who had been clearing with the Hans, and against whom we were on a raid for evidence, might also pick up our conversation. We had no fear that the Hans would hear us. In fact, we had the added advantage that, even after we landed, we could converse freely without danger of their hearing our voices through our air helmets.

For a while I could see nothing below but utter darkness. Then I realized, from the feel of the air as much as from anything, that we were sinking through a cloud layer. We passed through two more cloud layers before anything was visible to us.

Then there came under my gaze, about two miles below, one of the most beautiful sights I have ever seen; the soft, yet brilliant, radiance of the great Han city of Nu-yok. Every foot of its structural members seemed to glow with a wonderful incandescence, tower piled up on tower, and all built on the vast base-mass of the city, which, so I had been told, sheered upward from the surface of the rivers to a height of 728 levels.

The city, I noticed with some surprise, did not cover anything like the same area as the New York of the 20th Century. It occupied, as a matter of fact, only the lower half of Manhattan Island, with one section straddling the East River, and spreading out sufficiently over what once had been Brooklyn, to provide berths for the great liners and other air craft.

Straight beneath my feet was a tiny dark patch. It seemed the only spot in the entire city that was not aflame with radiance. This was the central tower, in the top floors of which were housed the vast library of record files and the main projectoscope plant.

"You can shoot the wire now," I ultrophoned Gibbons, and let go the little weighted knob. It dropped like a plummet, and we followed with considerable speed, but braking our descent with gloved hands sufficiently to see whether the knob, on which a faint light glowed as a signal for ourselves, might be observed by any Han guard or night prowler. Apparently it was not, and we again shot down with accelerated speed.

We landed on the roof of the tower without any mishap, and fortunately for our plan, in darkness. Since there was nothing above it on which it would have been worth while to shed illumination, or from which there was any need to observe it, the Hans had neglected to light the tower roof, or indeed to occupy it at all. This was the reason we had selected it as our landing place.

As soon as Gibbons had our word, he extinguished the knob light, and the knob, as well as the wire, became totally invisible. At our ultrophoned word, he would light it again.

"No gun play now," I warned. "Swords only, and then only if absolutely necessary."

Closely bunched, and treading as lightly as only inertron-belted people could, we made our way cautiously through a door and down an inclined plane to the floor below, where Gaunt and Blash assured us the military offices were located.

Twice Barker cautioned us to stop as we were about to pass in front of mirror-like "windows" in the passage wall, and flattening ourselves to the floor, we crawled past them.

"Projectoscopes," he said. "Probably on automatic record only, at this time of night. Still, we don't want to leave any records for them to study after we're gone."

"Were you ever here before?" I asked.

"No," he replied, "but I haven't been studying their electrophone communications for seven years without being able to recognize these machines when I run across them."

Chapter IX: The Fight in the Tower

SO FAR we had not laid eyes on a Han. The tower seemed deserted. Blash and Gaunt, however, assured me that there would be at least one man on "duty" in the military offices, though he would probably be asleep, and two or three in the library proper and the projectoscope plant.

"We've got to put them out of commission," I said. "Did you bring the 'dope' cans, Wilma?"

"Yes," she said, "two for each. Here," and she distributed them.

We were now two levels below the roof, and at the point where we were to separate.

I did not want to let Wilma out of my sight, but it was necessary.

According to our plan, Barker was to make his way to the projectoscope plant, Blash and I to the library, and Wilma and Gaunt to the military office.

Blash and I traversed a long corridor, and paused at the great arched doorway of the library. Cautiously we peered in. Seated at three great switchboards were library operatives. Occasionally one of them would reach lazily for a lever, or sleepily push a button, as little numbered lights winked on and off. They were answering calls for electrograph and viewplate records on all sorts of subjects from all sections of the city.

I apprised my companions of the situation.

"Better wait a bit," Blash added. "The calls will lessen shortly."

Wilma reported an officer in the military office sound asleep.

"Give him the can, then," I said.

Barker was to do nothing more than keep watch in the projectoscope plant, and a few moments later he reported himself well concealed, with a splendid view of the floor.

"I think we can take a chance now," Blash said to me, and at my nod, he opened the lid of his dope can. Of course, the fumes did not affect us, through our helmets. They were absolutely without odor or visibility, and in a few seconds the librarians were unconscious. We stepped into the room.

There ensued considerable cautious observation and experiment on the part of Gaunt, working from the military office, and Blash in the library; while Wilma and I, with drawn swords and sharply attuned microphones, stood guard, and occasionally patrolled nearby corridors.

"I hear something approaching," Wilma said after a bit, with excitement in her voice. "It's a soft, gliding sound."

"That's an elevator somewhere," Barker cut in from the projectoscope floor. "Can you locate it? I can't hear it."

"It's to the east of me," she replied.

"And to my west," said I, faintly catching it. "It's between us, Wilma, and nearer you than me. Be careful. Have you got any information yet, Blash and Gaunt?"

"Getting it now," one of them replied. "Give us two minutes more."

"Keep at it then," I said. "We'll guard."

The soft, gliding sound ceased.

"I think it's very close to me," Wilma almost whispered. "Come closer, Tony. I have a feeling something is going to happen. I've never known my nerves to get taut like this without reason."

In some alarm, I launched myself down the corridor in a great leap toward the intersection whence I knew I could see her.

In the middle of my leap my ultrophone registered her gasp of alarm. The next instant I glided to a stop at the intersection to see Wilma backing toward the door of the military office, her sword red with blood, and an inert form on the corridor floor. Two other Hans were circling to either side of her with wicked-looking knives, while a third evidently a high officer, judging by the resplendence of his garb tugged desperately to get an electrophone instrument out of a bulky pocket. If he ever gave the alarm, there was no telling what might happen to us.

I was at least seventy feet away, but I crouched low and sprang with every bit of strength in my legs. It would be more correct to say that I dived, for I reached the fellow head on, with no attempt to draw my legs beneath me.

Some instinct must have warned him, for he turned suddenly as I hurtled close to him. But by this time I had sunk close to the floor, and had stiffened myself rigidly, lest a dragging knee or foot might just prevent my reaching him. I brought my blade upward and over. It was a vicious slash that laid him open, bisecting him from groin to chin, and his dead body toppled down on me, as I slid to a tangled stop.

The other two startled, turned. Wilma leaped at one and struck him down with a side slash. I looked up at this instant, and the dazed fear on his face at the length of her leap registered vividly. The Hans knew nothing of our inertron belts, it seemed, and these leaps and dives of ours filled them with terror.

As I rose to my feet, a gory mess, Wilma, with a poise and speed which I found time to admire even in this crisis, again leaped. This time she dove head first as I had done and, with a beautifully executed thrust, ran the last Han through the throat.

Uncertainly, she scrambled to her feet, staggered queerly, and then sank gently prone on the corridor. She had fainted.

At this juncture, Blash and Gaunt reported with elation that they had the record we wanted.

"Back to the roof, everybody!" I ordered, as I picked Wilma up in my arms. With her inertron belt, she felt as light as a feather.

Gaunt joined me at once from the military office, and at the intersection of the corridor, we came upon Blash waiting for us. Barker, however, was not in evidence.

"Where are you, Barker?" I called.

"Go ahead," he replied. "I'll be with you on the roof at once."

We came out in the open without any further mishap, and I instructed Gibbons in the ship to light the knob on the end of the ultron wire. It flashed dully a few feet away from us. Just how he had maneuvered the ship to keep our end of the line in position, without its swinging in a tremendous arc, I have never been able to understand. Had not the night been an unusually still one, he could not have checked the initial pendulum-like movements. As it was, there was considerable air current at certain of the levels, and in different directions too. But Gibbons was an expert of rare ability and sensitivity in the handling of a rocket ship, and he managed, with the aid of his delicate instruments, to sense the drifts almost before they affected the fine ultron wire, and to neutralize them with little shifts in the position of the ship.

Blash and Gaunt fastened their rings to the wire, and I hooked my own and Wilma's on, too. But on looking around, I found Barker was still missing.

"Barker, come!" I called. "We're waiting."

"Coming!" he replied, and indeed, at that instant, his figure appeared up the ramp. He chuckled as he fastened his ring to the wire, and said something about a little surprise he had left for the Hans.

"Don't reel in the wire more than a few hundred feet," I instructed Gibbons. "It will take too long to wind it in. We'll float up, and when we're aboard, we can drop it."

In order to float up, we had to dispense with a pound or two of weight apiece. We hurled our swords from us, and kicked off our shoes as Gibbons reeled up the line a bit, and then letting go of the wire, began to hum upward on our rings with increasing velocity.

The rush of air brought Wilma to, and I hastily explained to her that we had been successful. Receding far below us now, I could see our dully shining knob swinging to and fro in an ever widening arc, as it crossed and recrossed the black square of the tower roof. As an extra precaution, I ordered Gibbons to shut off the light, and to show one from the belly of the ship, for so great was our speed now, that I began to fear we would have difficulty in checking ourselves. We were literally falling upward, and with terrific acceleration.

Fortunately, we had several minutes in which to solve this difficulty, which none of us, strangely enough, had foreseen. It was Gibbons who found the answer.

"You'll be all right if all of you grab the wire tight when I give the word," he said. "First I'll start reeling it in at full speed. You won't get much of a jar, and then I'll decrease its speed again gradually, and its weight will hold you back. Are you ready? One – two – three!"

We all grabbed tightly with our gloved hands as he gave the word. We must have been rising a good bit faster than he figured, however, for it wrenched our arms considerably, and the maneuver set up a sickening pendulum motion.

For a while all we could do was swing there in an arc that may have been a quarter of a mile across, about three and a half miles above the city, and still more than a mile from our ship.

Gibbons skilfully took up the slack as our momentum pulled up the line. Then at last we had ourselves under control again, and continued our upward journey, checking our speed somewhat with our gloves.

There was not one of us who did not breathe a big sigh of relief when we scrambled through the hatch safely into the ship again, cast off the ultron line and slammed the trap shut.

Little realizing that we had a still more terrible experience to go through, we discussed the information Blash and Gaunt had between them extracted from the Han records, and the advisability of ultrophoning Hart at once.

Chapter X: The Walls of Hell

THE TRAITORS were, it seemed, a degenerate gang of Americans, located a few miles north of Nu-yok on the wooded banks of the Hudson, the Sinsings. They had exchanged scraps of information to the Hans in return for several old repellor-ray machines, and the privilege of tuning in on the Han electronic power broadcast for their operation, provided their ships agreed to subject themselves to the orders of the Han traffic office, while aloft.

The rest wanted to ultrophone their news at once, since there was always danger that we might never get back to the gang with it.

I objected, however. The Sinsings would be likely to pick up our message. Even if we used the directional projector, they might have scouts out to the west and south in the big inter-gang stretches of country. They would flee to Nu-yok and escape the punishment they merited. It seemed to be vitally important that they should not, for the sake of example to other weak groups among the American gangs, as well as to prevent a crisis in which they might clear more vital information to the enemy.

"Out to sea again," I ordered Gibbons. "They'll be less likely to look for us in that direction."

"Easy, Boss, easy," he replied. "Wait until we get up a mile or two more. They must have discovered evidences of our raid by now, and their dis-ray wall may go in operation any moment."

Even as he spoke, the ship lurched downward and to one side.

"There it is!" he shouted. "Hang on, everybody. We're going to nose straight up!" And he flipped the rocket-motor control wide open.

Looking through one of the rear ports, I could see a nebulous, luminous ring, and on all sides the atmosphere took on a faint iridescence.

We were almost over the destructive range of the disintegrator-ray wall, a hollow cylinder of annihilation shooting upward from a solid ring of generators surrounding the city. It was the main defense system of the Hans, which had never been used except in periodic tests. They may or may not have suspected that an American rocket ship was within the cylinder; probably they had turned on their generators more as a precaution to prevent any reaching a position above the city.

But even at our present great height, we were in great danger. It was a question how much we might have been harmed by the rays themselves, for their effective range was not much more than seven or eight miles. The greater danger lay in the terrific downward rush of air within the cylinder to replace that which was being burned into nothingness by the continual play of the disintegrators. The air fell into the cylinder with the force of a gale. It would be rushing toward the wall from the outside with terrific force also, but, naturally, the effect was intensified on the interior.

Our ship vibrated and trembled. We had only one chance of escape – to fight our way well above the current. To drift down with it meant ultimately, and inevitably, to be sucked into the destruction wall at some lower level.

But very gradually and jerkily our upward movement, as shown on the indicators, began to increase, and after an hour of desperate struggle we were free of the maelstrom and into the rarefied upper levels. The terror beneath us was now invisible through several layers of cloud formations.

Gibbons brought the ship back to an even keel, and drove her eastward into one of the most brilliantly gorgeous sunrises I have ever seen.

We described a great circle to the south and west, in a long easy dive, for he had cut out his rocket motors to save them as much as possible. We had drawn terrifically on their fuel reserves in our battle with the elements. For the moment, the atmosphere below cleared, and we could see the Jersey coast far beneath, like a great map.

"We're not through yet," remarked Gibbons suddenly, pointing at his periscope, and adjusting it to telescopic focus. "A Han ship, and a 'drop ship' at that – and he's seen us. If he whips that beam of his on us, we're done."

I gazed, fascinated, at the viewplate. What I saw was a cigar-shaped ship not dissimilar to our own in design, and from the proportional size of its ports, of about the same size as our swoopers. We learned later that they carried crews, for the most part of not more than three or four men. They had streamline hulls and tails that embodied universal-jointed double fish-tail rudders. In operation they rose to great heights on their powerful repellor rays, then gathered speed either by a straight nose dive, or an inclined dive in which they sometimes used the repellor ray slanted at a sharp angle. He was already above us, though several miles to the north. He could, of course, try to get on our tail and "spear" us with his beam as he dropped at us from a great height.

Suddenly his beam blazed forth in a blinding flash, whipping downward slowly to our right. He went through a peculiar corkscrew-like evolution, evidently maneuvering to bring his beam to bear on us with a spiral motion.

Gibbons instantly sent our ship into a series of evolutions that must have looked like those of a frightened hen. Alternately, he used the forward and the reverse rocket blasts, and in varying degree. We fluttered, we shot suddenly to right and left, and dropped like a plummet in uncertain movements. But all the time the Han scout dropped toward us, determinedly whipping the air around us with his beam. Once it sliced across beneath us, not more than a hundred feet, and we dropped with a jar into the pocket formed by the destruction of the air.

He had dropped to within a mile of us, and was coming with the speed of a projectile, when the end came. Gibbons always swore it was sheer luck. Maybe it was, but I like pilots who are lucky that way.

In the midst of a dizzy, fluttering maneuver of our own, with the Han ship enlarging to our gaze with terrifying rapidity, and its beam slowly slicing toward us in what looked like certain destruction within the second, I saw Gibbons' fingers flick at the lever of his rocket gun and a split second later the Han ship flew apart like a clay pigeon.

We staggered, and fluttered crazily for several moments while Gibbons struggled to bring our ship into balance, and a section of about four square feet in the side of the ship near the stern slowly crumbled like rusted metal. His beam actually had touched us, but our explosive rocket had got him a thousandth of a second sooner.

Part of our rudder had been annihilated, and our motor damaged. But we were able to swoop gently back across Jersey, fortunately crossing the ship lanes without sighting any more Han craft, and finally settling to rest in the little glade beneath the trees, near Hart's camp.

Chapter XI: The New Boss

WE HAD ultrophoned our arrival and the Big Boss himself, surrounded by the Council, was on hand to welcome us and learn our news. In turn we were informed that during the night a band of raiding Bad Bloods, disguised under the insignia of the Altoonas, a gang some distance to the west of us, had destroyed several of our camps before our people had rallied and driven them off. Their purpose, evidently, had been to embroil us with the Altoonas, but fortunately, one of our exchanges recognized the Bad Blood leader, who had been slain.

The Big Boss had mobilized the full raiding force of the Gang, and was on the point of heading an expedition for the extermination of the Bad Bloods.

I looked around the grim circle of the sub-bosses, and realized the fate of America, at this moment, lay in their hands. Their temper demanded the immediate expenditure of our full effort in revenging ourselves for this raid. But the strategic exigencies, to my mind, quite clearly demanded the instant and absolute extermination of the Sinsings. It might be only a matter of hours, for all we knew, before these degraded people would barter clues to the American ultronic secrets to the Hans.

"How large a force have we?" I asked Hart.

"Every man and maid who can be spared," he replied. "That gives us seven hundred married and unmarried men, and three hundred girls, more than the entire Bad Blood Gang. Every one is equipped with belts, ultrophones, rocket guns and swords, and all fighting mad."

I meditated how I might put the matter to these determined men, and was vaguely conscious that they were awaiting my words.

Finally I began to speak. I do not remember to this day just what I said. I talked calmly, with due regard for their passion, but with deep conviction. I went over the information we had collected, point by point, building my case logically, and painting a lurid picture of the danger impending in that half-alliance between the Sinsings and the Hans of Nu-yok. I became impassioned, culminating, I believe, with a vow to proceed single-handed against the hereditary enemies of our race, "if the Wyomings were blindly set on placing a gang feud ahead of honor and duty and the hopes of all America."

As I concluded, a great calm came over me, as of one detached. I had felt much the same way during several crises in the First World War. I gazed from face to face, striving to read their expressions, and in a mood to make good my threat without any further heroics, if the decision was against me.

But it was Hart who sensed the temper of the Council more quickly than I did, and looked beyond it into the future.

He arose from the tree trunk on which he had been sitting.

"That settles it," he said, looking around the ring. "I have felt this thing coming on for some time now. I'm sure the Council agrees with me that there is among us a man more capable than I, to boss the Wyoming Gang, despite his handicap of having had all too short a time in which to familiarize himself with our modern ways and facilities. Whatever I can do to support his effective leadership, at any cost, I pledge myself to do."

As he concluded, he advanced to where I stood, and taking from his head the green-crested helmet that constituted his badge of office, to my surprise he placed it in my mechanically extended hand.

The roar of approval that went up from the Council members left me dazed. Somebody ultrophoned the news to the rest of the Gang, and even though the earflaps of my helmet were turned up, I could hear the cheers with which my invisible followers greeted me, from near and distant hillsides, camps and plants.

My first move was to make sure that the Phone Boss, in communicating this news to the members of the Gang, had not re-broadcast my talk nor mentioned my plan of shifting the attack from the Bad Bloods to the Sinsings. I was relieved by his assurance that he had not, for it would have wrecked the whole plan. Everything depended upon our ability to surprise the Sinsings.

So I pledged the Council and my companions to secrecy, and allowed it to be believed that we were about to take to the air and the trees against the Bad Bloods.

That outfit must have been badly scared, the way they were "burning" the ether with ultrophone alibis and propaganda for the benefit of the more distant gangs. It was their old game, and the only method by which they had avoided extermination long ago from their immediate neighbors – these appeals to the spirit of American brotherhood, addressed to gangs too far away to have had the sort of experience with them that had fallen to our lot.

I chuckled. Here was another good reason for the shift in my plans. Were we actually to undertake the exterminations of the Bad Bloods at once, it would have been a hard job to convince some of the gangs that we had not been precipitate and unjustified. Jealousies and prejudices existed. There were gangs which would give the benefit of the doubt to the Bad Bloods, rather than to ourselves, and the issue was now hopelessly beclouded with the clever lies that were being broadcast in an unceasing stream.

But the extermination of the Sinsings would be another thing. In the first place, there would be no warning of our action until it was all over, I hoped. In the second place, we would have indisputable proof, in the form of their rep-ray ships and other paraphernalia, of their traffic with the Hans; and the state of American prejudice, at the time of which I write held trafficking with the Hans a far more heinous thing than even a vicious gang feud.

I called an executive session of the Council at once. I wanted to inventory our military resources.

I created a new office on the spot, that of "Control Boss," and appointed Ned Garlin to the post, turning over his former responsibility as Plants Boss to his assistant. I needed someone, I felt, to tie in the records of the various functional activities of the campaign, and take over from me the task of keeping the records of them up to the minute.

I received reports from the bosses of the ultrophone unit, and those of food, transportation, fighting gear, chemistry, electronic activity and electrophone intelligence, ultroscopes, air patrol and contact guard.

My ideas for the campaign, of course, were somewhat tinged with my 20th Century experience, and I found myself faced with the task of working out a staff organization that was a composite of the best and most easily applied principles of business and military efficiency, as I knew them from the viewpoint of immediate practicality.

What I wanted was an organization that would be specialized, functionally, not as that indicated above, but from the angles of: intelligence as to the Sinsings' activities; intelligence as to Han activities; perfection of communication with my own units; co-operation of field command; and perfect mobilization of emergency supplies and resources.

It took several hours of hard work with the Council to map out the plan. First we assigned functional experts and equipment to each "Division" in accordance with its needs. Then these in turn were reassigned by the new Division Bosses to the Field Commands as needed, or as Independent or Headquarters Units. The two intelligence divisions were named the White and the Yellow, indicating that one specialized on the American enemy and the other on the Mongolians.

The division in charge of our own communications, the assignment of ultrophone frequencies and strengths, and the maintenance of operators and equipment, I called "Communications."

I named Bill Hearn to the post of Field Boss, in charge of the main or undetached fighting units, and to the Resources Division, I assigned all responsibility for what few aircraft we had; and all transportation and supply problems, I assigned to "Resources." The functional bosses stayed with this division.

We finally completed our organization with the assignment of liaison representatives among the various divisions as needed.

Thus I had a "Headquarters Staff" composed of the Division Bosses who reported directly to Ned Garlin as Control Boss, or to Wilma as my personal assistant. And each of the Division Bosses had a small staff of his own.

In the final summing up of our personnel and resources, I found we had roughly a thousand "troops," of whom some three hundred and fifty were, in what I called the Service Divisions, the rest being in Bill Hearn's Field Division. This latter number, however, was cut down somewhat by the assignment of numerous small units to detached service. Altogether, the actual available fighting force, I figured, would number about five hundred, by the time we actually went into action.

We had only six small swoopers, but I had an ingenious plan in my mind, as the result of our little raid on Nu-yok, that would make this sufficient, since the reserves of inertron blocks were larger than I expected to find them. The Resources Division, by packing its supply cases a bit tight, or by slipping in extra blocks of inertron, was able to reduce each to a weight of a few ounces. These easily could be floated and towed by the swoopers in any quantity. Hitched to ultron lines, it would be a virtual impossibility for them to break loose.

The entire personnel, of course, was supplied with jumpers, and if each man and girl was careful to adjust balances properly, the entire number could also be towed along through the air, grasping wires of ultron, swinging below the swoopers, or stringing out behind them.

There would be nothing tiring about this, because the strain would be no greater than that of carrying a one or two pound weight in the hand, except for air friction at high speeds. But to make doubly sure that we should lose none of our personnel, I gave strict orders that the belts and tow lines should be equipped with rings and hooks.

So great was the efficiency of the fundamental organization and discipline of the Gang, that we got under way at nightfall.

One by one the swoopers eased into the air, each followed by its long train or "kite-tail" of humanity and supply cases hanging lightly from its tow line. For convenience, the tow lines were made of an alloy of ultron which, unlike the metal itself, is visible.

At first these "tails" hung downward, but as the ships swung into formation and headed eastward toward the Bad Blood territory, gathering speed, they began to string out behind. And swinging low from each ship on heavily weighted lines, ultroscope, ultrophone, and straight-vision observers keenly scanned the countryside, while intelligence men in the swoopers above bent over their instrument boards and viewplates.

Leaving Control Boss Ned Garlin temporarily in charge of affairs, Wilma and I dropped a weighted line from our ship, and slid down about half way to the under lookouts, that is to say, about a thousand feet. The sensation of floating swiftly through the air like this, in the absolute security of one's confidence in the inertron belt, was one of never-ending delight to me.

We reascended into the swooper as the expedition approached the territory of the Bad Bloods, and directed the preparations for the bombardment. It was part of my plan to appear to carry out the attack as originally planned.

About fifteen miles from their camps our ships came to a halt and maintained their positions for a while with the idling blasts of their rocket motors, to give the ultroscope operators a chance to make a thorough examination of the territory below us, for it was very important that this next step in our program should be carried out with all secrecy.

At length they reported the ground below us entirely clear of any appearance of human occupation, and a gun unit of long-range specialists was lowered with a dozen rocket guns, equipped with special automatic devices that the Resources Division had developed at my request, a few hours before our departure. These were aiming and timing devices. After calculating the range, elevation and rocket charges carefully, the guns were left, concealed in a ravine, and the men were hauled up into the ship again. At the predetermined hour, those unmanned rocket guns would begin automatically to bombard the Bad Bloods' hillsides, shifting their aim and elevation slightly with each shot, as did many of our artillery pieces in the First World War.

In the meantime, we turned south about twenty miles, and grounded, waiting for the bombardment to begin before we attempted to sneak across the Han ship lane. I was relying for security on the distraction that the bombardment might furnish the Han observers.

It was tense work waiting, but the affair went through as planned, our squadron drifting across the route high enough to enable the ships' tails of troops and supply cases to clear the ground.

In crossing the second ship route, out along the Beaches of Jersey, we were not so successful in escaping observation. A Han ship came speeding along at a very low elevation. We caught it on our electronic location and direction finders, and also located it with our ultroscopes, but it came so fast and so low that I thought it best to remain where we had grounded the second time, and lie quiet, rather than get under way and cross in front of it.

The point was this. While the Hans had no such devices as our ultroscopes, with which we could see in the dark (within certain limitations of course), and their electronic instruments would be virtually useless in uncovering our presence, since all but natural electronic activities were carefully eliminated from our apparatus, except electrophone receivers (which are not easily spotted), the Hans did have some very highly sensitive sound devices which operated with great efficiency in calm weather, so far as sounds emanating from the air were concerned. But the "ground roar" greatly confused their use of these instruments in the location of specific sounds floating up from the surface of the earth.

This ship must have caught some slight noise of ours, however, in its sensitive instruments, for we heard its electronic devices go into play, and picked up the routine report of the noise to its Base Ship Commander. But from the nature of the conversation, I judged they had not identified it, and were, in fact, more curious about the detonations they were picking up now from the Bad Blood lands some sixty miles or so to the west.

Immediately after this ship had shot by, we took the air again, and following much the same route that I had taken the previous night, climbed in a long semi-circle out over the ocean, swung toward the north and finally the west. We set our course, however, for the Sinsings' land north of Nu-yok, instead of for the city itself.

Chapter XII: The Finger of Doom

AS WE CROSSED the Hudson River, a few miles north of the city, we dropped several units of the Yellow Intelligence Division, with full instrumental equipment. Their apparatus cases were nicely balanced at only a few ounces weight each, and the men used their chute capes to ease their drops.

We recrossed the river a little distance above and began dropping White Intelligence units and a few long and short range gun units. Then we held our position until we began to get reports. Gradually we ringed the territory of the Sinsings, our observation units working busily and patiently at their locators and scopes, both aloft and aground, until Garlin finally turned to me with the remark: "The map circle is complete now, Boss. We've got clear locations all the way around them."

"Let me see it," I replied, and studied the illuminated viewplate map, with its little overlapping circles of light that indicated spots proved clear of the enemy by ultroscopic observation.

I nodded to Bill Hearn. "Go ahead now, Hearn," I said, "and place your barrage men."

He spoke into his ultrophone, and three of the ships began to glide in a wide ring around the enemy territory. Every few seconds, at the word from his Unit Boss, a gunner would drop off the wire, and slipping the clasp of his chute cape, drift down into the darkness below.

Bill formed two lines, parallel to and facing the river, and enclosing the entire territory of the enemy between them. Above and below, straddling the river, were two defensive lines. These latter were merely to hold their positions. The others were to close in toward each other, pushing a high-explosive barrage five miles ahead of them. When the two barrages met, both lines were to switch to short-vision-range barrage and continue to close in on any of the enemy who might have drifted through the previous curtain of fire.

In the meantime Bill kept his reserves, a picked corps of a hundred men (the same that had accompanied Hart and myself in our fight with the Han squadron) in the air, divided about equally among the "kite-tails" of four ships.

A final roll call, by units, companies, divisions and functions, established the fact that all our forces were in position. No Han activity was reported, and no Han broadcasts indicated any suspicion of our expedition. Nor was there any indication that the Sinsings had any knowledge of the fate in store for them. The idling of rep-ray generators was reported from the center of their camp, obviously those of the ships the Hans had given them – the price of their treason to their race.

Again I gave the word, and Hearn passed on the order to his subordinates.

Far below us, and several miles to the right and left, the two barrage lines made their appearance. From the great height to which we had risen, they appeared like lines of brilliant, winking lights, and the detonations were muffled by the distances into a sort of rumbling, distant thunder. Hearn and his assistants were very busy: measuring, calculating, and snapping out ultrophone orders to unit commanders that resulted in the straightening of lines and the closing of gaps in the barrage.

The White Division Boss reported the utmost confusion in the Sinsing organization. They were, as might be expected, an inefficient, loosely disciplined gang, and repeated broadcasts for help to neighboring gangs. Ignoring the fact that the Mongolians had not used explosives for many generations, they nevertheless jumped at the conclusion that they were being raided by the Hans. Their frantic broadcasts persisted in this thought, despite the nervous electrophonic inquiries of the Hans themselves, to whom the sound of the battle was evidently audible, and who were trying to locate the trouble.

At this point, the swooper I had sent south toward the city went into action as a diversion, to keep the Hans at home. Its "kite-tail" loaded with long-range gunners, using the most highly explosive rockets we had, hung invisible in the darkness of the sky and bombarded the city from a distance of about five miles. With an entire city to shoot at, and the object of creating as much commotion therein as possible, regardless of actual damage, the gunners had no difficulty in hitting the mark. I could see the glow of the city and the stabbing flashes of exploding rockets. In the end, the Hans, uncertain as to what was going on, fell back on a defensive policy, and shot their "hell cylinder," or wall of upturned disintegrator rays into operation. That, of course, ended our bombardment of them. The rays were a perfect defense, disintegrating our rockets as they were reached.

If they had not sent out ships before turning on the rays, and if they had none within sufficient radius already in the air, all would be well.

I queried Garlin on this, but he assured me Yellow Intelligence reported no indications of Han ships nearer than 800 miles. This would probably give us a free hand for a while, since most of their instruments recorded only imperfectly or not at all, through the death wall.

Requisitioning one of the viewplates of the headquarters ship, and the services of an expert operator, I instructed him to focus on our lines below. I wanted a close-up of the men in action.

He began to manipulate his controls and chaotic shadows moved rapidly across the plate, fading in and out of focus, until he reached an adjustment that gave me a picture of the forest floor, apparently 100 feet wide, with the intervening branches and foliage of the trees appearing like shadows that melted into reality a few feet above the ground.

I watched one man setting up his long-gun with skillful speed. His lips pursed slightly as though he were whistling, as he adjusted the tall tripod on which the long tube was balanced. Swiftly he twirled the knobs controlling the aim and elevation of his piece. Then, lifting a belt of ammunition from the big box, which itself looked heavy enough to break down the spindly tripod, he inserted the end of it in the lock of his tube and touched the proper combination of buttons.

Then he stepped aside, and occupied himself with peering carefully through the trees ahead. Not even a tremor shook the tube, but I knew that at intervals of something less than a second, it was discharging small projectiles which, traveling under their own continuously reduced power, were arching into the air, to fall precisely five miles ahead and explode with the force of eight-inch shells, such as we used in the First World War.

Another gunner, fifty feet to the right of him, waved a hand and called out something to him. Then, picking up his own tube and tripod, he gauged the distance between the trees ahead of him, and the height of their lowest branches, and bending forward a bit, flexed his muscles and leaped lightly, some twenty-five feet. Another leap took him another twenty feet or so, where he began to set up his piece.

I ordered my observer then to switch to the barrage itself. He got a close focus on it, but this showed little except a continuous series of blinding flashes, which, from the viewplate, lit up the entire interior of the ship. An eight-hundred-foot focus proved better. I had thought that some of our French and American artillery of the 20th Century had achieved the ultimate in mathematical precision of fire, but I had never seen anything to equal the accuracy of that line of terrific explosions as it moved steadily forward, mowing down trees as a scythe cuts grass (or used to 500 years ago), literally churning up the earth and the splintered, blasted remains of the forest giants, to a depth of from ten to twenty feet.

By now the two curtains of fire were nearing each other, lines of vibrant, shimmering, continuous, brilliant destruction, inevitably squeezing the panic-stricken Sinsings between them.

Even as I watched, a group of them, who had been making a futile effort to get their three rep-ray machines into the air, abandoned their efforts, and rushed forth into the milling mob.

I queried the Control Boss sharply on the futility of this attempt of theirs, and learned that the Hans, apparently in doubt as to what was going on, had continued to "play safe," and broken off their power broadcast, after ordering all their own ships east of the Alleghenies to the ground, for fear these ships they had traded to the Sinsings might be used against them.

Again I turned to my viewplate, which was still focussed on the central section of the Sinsing works. The confusion of the traitors was entirely that of fear, for our barrage had not yet reached them.

Some of them set up their long-guns and fired at random over the barrage line, then gave it up. They realized that they had no target to shoot at, no way of knowing whether our gunners were a few hundred feet or several miles beyond it.

Their ultrophone men, of whom they did not have many, stood around in tense attitudes, their helmet phones strapped around their ears, nervously fingering the tuning controls at their belts. Unquestionably they must have located some of our frequencies, and overheard many of our reports and orders. But they were confused and disorganized. If they had an Ultrophone Boss they evidently were not reporting to him in an organized way.

They were beginning to draw back now before our advancing fire. With intermittent desperation, they began to shoot over our barrage again, and the explosions of their rockets flashed at widely scattered points beyond. A few took distance "pot shots."

Oddly enough it was our own forces that suffered the first casualties in the battle. Some of these distance shots by chance registered hits, while our men were under strict orders not to exceed their barrage distances.

Seen upon the ultroscope viewplate, the battle looked as though it were being fought in daylight, perhaps on a cloudy day, while the explosions of the rockets appeared as flashes of extra brilliance.

The two barrage lines were not more than five hundred feet apart when the Sinsings resorted to tactics we had not foreseen. We noticed first that they began to lighten themselves by throwing away extra equipment. A few of them in their excitement threw away too much, and shot suddenly into the air. Then a scattering few floated up gently, followed by increasing numbers, while still others, preserving a weight balance, jumped toward the closing barrages and leaped high, hoping to clear them. Some succeeded. We saw others blown about like leaves in a windstorm, to crumple and drift slowly down, or else to fall into the barrage, their belts blown from their bodies.

However, it was not part of our plan to allow a single one of them to escape and find his way to the Hans. I quickly passed the word to Bill Hearn to have the alternate men in his line raise their barrages and heard him bark out a mathematical formula to the Unit Bosses.

We backed off our ships as the explosions climbed into the air in stagger formation until they reached a height of three miles. I don't believe any of the Sinsings who tried to float away to freedom succeeded.

But we did know later, that a few who leaped the barrage got away and ultimately reached Nu-yok.

It was those who managed to jump the barrage who gave us the most trouble. With half of our long-guns turned aloft, I foresaw we would not have enough to establish successive ground barrages and so ordered the barrage back two miles, from which positions our "curtains" began to close in again, this time, however, gauged to explode, not on contact, but thirty feet in the air. This left little chance for the Sinsings to leap either over or under it.

Gradually, the two barrages approached each other until they finally met, and in the grey dawn the battle ended.

Our own casualties amounted to forty-seven men in the ground forces, eighteen of whom had been slain in hand to hand fighting with the few of the enemy who managed to reach our lines, and sixty-two in the crew and "kite-tail" force of swooper No. 4, which had been located by one of the enemy's ultroscopes and brought down with long-gun fire.

Since nearly every member of the Sinsing Gang had, so far as we knew, been killed, we considered the raid a great success.

It had, however, a far greater significance than this. To all of us who took part in the expedition, the effectiveness of our barrage tactics definitely established a confidence in our ability to overcome the Hans.

As I pointed out to Wilma: "It has been my belief all along, dear, that the American explosive rocket is a far more efficient weapon than the disintegrator ray of the Hans, once we can train all our gangs to use it systematically and in co-ordinated fashion. As a weapon in the hands of a single individual, shooting at a mark in direct line of vision, the rocket-gun is inferior in destructive power to the dis ray, except as its range may be a little greater. The trouble is that to date it has been used only as we used our rifles and shot guns in the 20th Century. The possibilities of its use as artillery, in laying barrages that advance along the ground, or climb into the air, are tremendous.

"The dis ray inevitably reveals its source of emanation. The rocket gun does not. The dis ray can reach its target only in a straight line. The rocket may be made to travel in an arc, over intervening obstacles, to an unseen target.

"Nor must we forget that our ultronists now are promising us a perfect shield against the dis ray in inertron."

"I tremble though, Tony dear, when I think of the horrors that are ahead of us. The Hans are clever. They will develop defenses against our new tactics. And they are sure to mass against us not only the full force of their power in America, but the united forces of the World Empire. They are a cowardly race in one sense, but clever as the very Devils in Hell, and inheritors of a calm, ruthless, vicious persistency."

"Nevertheless," I prophesied, "the Finger of Doom points squarely at them today, and unless you and I are killed in the struggle, we shall live to see America blast the Yellow Blight from the face of the Earth."

Red

Kate O'Connor

I

ANNA SANK DOWN next to the graves, setting the sandy shovel down beside her. Her hands were blistered and oozing. She rubbed her palms against her gritty jeans, barely noticing the sting. Her last act as a loyal daughter was finished. It wasn't the cemetery plot her parents had planned for, but the beach behind the house was as nice a spot as any.

The salty breeze cooled the sweat on her face and arms, making Anna shiver. It had been desperately hard getting the bodies down the stairs and out to the beach by herself, but there had been no one to call for help. The Red Plague had overrun their small town just like it had the rest of the planet Thule. Everyone she knew was sick and waiting to die or already gone. She shook her head. It had been barely three weeks since the first case.

The sky was a clear, perfect blue above the cerulean waves. Her parents had died within hours of each other, Anna sitting on the bed between them like she had when she was little, clutching their hands and trying not to hear them gasp for air.

A tickle in her throat caught her by surprise. She coughed once. Her pulse thudded in her ears. Her throat didn't hurt. *It may be nothing,* Anna told herself. She looked down at her bare arms. Her skin was free from the livid red blemishes that characterized the plague. She coughed again.

Anna got to her feet, blank resignation settling over her. The spots never appeared right away. She hadn't escaped after all. She picked up the shovel and started digging a new hole tucked between the two occupied graves. *I'll come back before I get too sick to move.* It was beautiful by the sea.

II

"HOLD HER." The faceless hazard suit hovering over Anna spoke with a woman's calm, competent voice.

Gloved fingers bit into Anna's shoulders. Her red spotted fingers clutched at the steadying hands for a moment before her body jerked and twitched out of control again. After countless agonizing minutes, the tremors settled, leaving her limbs heavy and her head swimming. She sucked in a deep breath. It bubbled thickly in her chest, choking her. She gagged and coughed. Warm, viscous liquid trickled over her lips and down her cheek. Her heart was racing so fast she could feel it in her fingertips. She needed air.

"Are you sure about this, Ginny?" A man's voice spoke from behind Anna's head.

"Yeah. She's the closest match we've found. At the rate this disease is progressing, we won't get another chance. And you, John? Are *you* sure?" The words flowed over Anna as she struggled to breathe. She could barely see through the darkness creeping across her eyes.

"Yes." The man's firm voice answered. "This has to stop." He lifted Anna's shoulders, cradling her head with gentle efficiency. The woman pulled something small and metallic out of her bag. The device, hanging on a thin, silvery chain, sparkled in Anna's dimming vision. Ginny slipped the chain over Anna's head and pulled her shirt collar down enough to settle the object against her chest. It was cool against Anna's too-hot skin.

There was a soft beep. "Twenty-seven hours." John said, sitting back on his heels. "Better than I thought, but not as long as we'd hoped."

Anna took a tentative breath. For the first time in two days, it didn't trigger a coughing fit. The feeling of drowning was fading and her head was clearing. She sat up slowly. She felt weak and tired, but in control of herself.

"It's a stasis generator." Ginny explained before Anna had a chance to ask. "It's meant to be used if a Disease Control doctor contracts the illness they're studying. It suppresses the symptoms until they can get to somewhere the disease is treatable."

"So you can help me?" Anna clenched her hands against the hope that surged strong enough to hurt. They must have found a cure. They had to be trying to keep whomever they could alive until they could get it distributed planet-wide. It was too late for her family, but... Anna didn't want to die.

"No." Ginny shook her head, the suit exaggerating the gesture. "In twenty-seven hours, the field will fail. You'll be contagious again and the plague will pick up where it left off. I'm sorry."

The warm sea breeze ruffled Anna's hair. She pulled out the generator and turned it over in her hands. It looked like a little stopwatch. The glowing purple display was counting down. Anna tucked it back under her shirt. She felt better. She didn't want to believe she was still dying. "Then why use this thing on me?"

"So the Red Plague won't spread across the galaxy." Ginny said firmly. "We need your help."

"What do you mean?" Anna wrapped her arms around herself, hugging her shoulders hard.

"Thule was the test site." Ginny exchanged a glance with her companion. John nodded for her to continue. "The Centauri Cooperative wanted a bio-weapon that could spread quickly, kill fast, and burn out in a month or two. Looks like they finally have it."

"Why us?" Anna grit her teeth so hard her jaw ached. Thule was – had been – a thriving colony world with more than a hundred million people. They were only loosely connected to Centauri and had nothing to do with any of the four other factions fighting for dominance and survival at the center of the galaxy. *We don't even have a standing military.*

"It was convenient. Thule is owned by Centauri-based investors. It doesn't produce much in the way of essential exports and it's not a threat if enough people survive to complain. The investors will be compensated and the loss written off to a mutated planet-born disease."

Anna shook her head. *Convenient.* "So what do you want me for?" She wondered if she shouldn't be more skeptical, but after everything that had happened she felt beyond disbelief.

"The *Eidolon* is in orbit." Ginny spoke in a matter-of-fact tone that Anna didn't quite buy. "Centauri has influential people from across the galaxy aboard, along with the scientists who made this thing, waiting to celebrate the success of the project. We want you to go aboard and bring them the Red Plague."

"Why not just infect yourselves if you're so desperate to kill all of your co-workers?" Anna spat out, anger rising through the numbness she had been living in for weeks.

"Disease Control workers are dosed with amnesia serum before they're sent into situations like this." John answered calmly. "They shoot us with the catalyst when we get back to the shuttle and we forget everything about what happened planet-side on the ride back to the ship. It won't affect you since you didn't get the initial dose, but if Ginny couldn't remember why she was wearing a stasis generator, she would never release herself from quarantine. For this to work, we need you to pretend to be her and clear yourself through."

"Don't they have a cure?" Anna felt like she was missing something. Making a bio-weapon without an antidote seemed monumentally stupid.

"No." Ginny shook her head. "Too many bio-weapons have been rendered useless when the cure is stolen before they have a chance to be deployed. Centauri didn't want to run that risk."

"Do you really think they won't just start again?" They had already proven themselves capable of destroying worlds just to test their new weapon. Anna couldn't see how a ship worth of dead government officials would stop anything.

"If you can manage to infect anyone onboard, there is every chance that the Red Plague will be judged too hard to control. They might try something else, but they'll be back to square one. It might be years before they get this close again." Ginny paused. "And it's the only chance you'll have to show them what they did here."

Anna stared out towards the ocean, breathing in the familiar salt air. A month ago, she would have happily said that revenge solved nothing. Now, she didn't know. "You really want me to go kill bunch of people?"

"Do you want this happening somewhere else?" John shook his head. "Believe me, they won't stop now that they have a working weapon. It's not just about Thule."

Anna wasn't sure she could look anyone in the eye and make them suffer what she had. Ginny had said there were powerful people on board the *Eidolon*. Maybe there was another way to make them stop. "I'll go," she answered finally, "but no one will ever believe I'm Ginny." Ginny was older, her eyes wider set and her nose smaller. She might have passed for Anna's sister, but that wouldn't be enough to fool anybody.

"John picked up a mask from the costume shop downtown once we decided on this course of action." Ginny held out a thin, gray veil. "We had to find someone who looked enough like me that we could program it to make up for the differences. You're closer than we thought we'd find. As long as you can keep the stasis generator hidden, there shouldn't be any problems. It will work. It has to."

Anna put on the veil. It fitted itself to her face like a second skin with holes for her eyes and mouth. She glared at Ginny and John. It was hard to stomach that they had only helped her because by some twist of fate she looked "close enough." John leaned over and adjusted the settings, looking back and forth between them. Ginny smiled and unhooked the seals on her mask.

Anna lunged forward, shoving the older woman's hands away from the fastenings. "You'll catch it!"

"We don't have an extra suit and 'I' can't return without one." Ginny drew a shuddering breath and reached for the mask again, pulling it off and setting it down beside her. "I'd rather die here than on the ship. This way I'll remember why it's happening."

III

THEY WERE throwing a party. Anna flung one of Ginny's pillows across the small room as hot tears seared down her cheeks. It had been almost more than she could manage to keep her expression blank when they had handed her the invitation on the way out of quarantine. The Red Plague had been such an unqualified success that everyone had been invited to the ballroom to celebrate. They would dance and eat and laugh while the last of the population – the last of Anna's people – died on the planet below.

Anna dug through Ginny's drawers, looking for something appropriate to wear. It seemed Ginny was – had been – a practical woman. Most of her clothes were utilitarian and neat. Not what Anna needed for a fancy party. At long last, she dug out a vivid emerald green dress.

Anna shed her clothes and slipped the garment over her head. The fabric was smooth and perfect. It was nicer than anything she had ever worn. She studied herself in the mirror. The dress was a bit big through the hips and chest, but it would do. *Not a bad dress to die in.* Anna hooked the chain of the stasis generator back around her neck. The little clock hung down below the neckline of the dress. She tucked it between her breasts. After the shuttle ride and twelve hours of quarantine, she only had four hours left.

She stared at the image in the mirror. Ginny's face looked back. Anna tugged off the gray veil. The stasis generator hadn't been able to erase the hollows under her eyes or the body left gaunt by weeks of caring for dying loved ones and battling the brutal disease herself. *I'm glad I'm here.* She thought viciously. *I'll give them all something to celebrate.*

IV

SHE DIDN'T want to go in. Now that it came down to it, Anna wasn't sure she was ready. The anger she had felt when she had gotten the invitation had faded a little. Most of the people here had just been doing their jobs. They had families of their own. If she went back to the quarantine room now, she could die in there when the stasis field gave out and she became contagious again. But then Centauri would have its weapon.

Anna hovered at the threshold, undecided. The veil was firmly settled back over her face. The ballroom sparkled with peach and amber light. Crystal dripped from the ceilings and walls and glittered from tabletops. The *Eidolon* had obviously been outfitted to cater to top-of-the-line dignitaries.

"May I, perhaps, escort you in?"

Anna turned and found herself nose to chest with a brilliantly orange shirt. "I… uh." She took a hasty step backwards. The man's well-shaped lips quirked with amusement. Their eyes locked and Anna felt her cheeks flush. She wondered if it would show through the mask.

"Okay." Anna took the offered hand. He tucked her fingers under his arm and swept her into the ballroom. People on either side of the entrance stopped talking. The silence spread until all eyes were on them.

"Welcome everyone!" His strong voice echoed across the large room. "Don't worry, I'm not going to bore you with a speech. That'll be for the official welcome when we get home." A chuckle rippled through the crowd. "Just let me say good work, everyone. Enjoy the party!" He waved and turned back to Anna.

"I take it you're…" Anna paused, not sure how to continue without sounding stupid, "… someone important."

"Marcus Prospero, at your service." He gave a mock-bow.

"Then you're …" The leader of the Centauri Cooperative was David Prospero.

"President Prospero's son," he finished for her.

"Sorry. You must get that a lot."

He shrugged. "Yeah. Years of working my way to the top of the military's best bio-weapons research team and the most important thing about me is still which family I was born into. Poor little rich boy." He grinned ruefully. "Enough of that. You haven't told me your name."

"It's Ginny." Anna's stomach dropped down to her toes. Head of the bio-weapons team. She studied him with new eyes. He was still handsome, but the attraction she'd felt so strongly a few minutes earlier was dying. It was his plan that he had done this. He was the reason everyone she loved was gone.

"Care for a dance, Ginny?" He held out his hand again.

"I would love to." Anna noticed how beautifully the sunset orange shirt set off his smooth, dusky skin. She took his hand, smiling up at him as fierce emotion bubbled in her chest. If she could find a way to talk to him, maybe there was a chance for these people to understand what they had done and stop it from happening again.

V

ANNA STARED around in wonder as Marcus opened the door out onto the balcony. She knew there had to be something keeping the air in and the vacuum out, but she couldn't see it.

"Force field." Marcus spoke softly in her ear as he walked up behind her.

The balcony floor was nearly transparent. Anna spun in a delighted circle. They were surrounded by stars. "It's beautiful." She whispered, forgetting about everything else for the first time since the plague began.

"Yes." Marcus's arm settled around her waist, dragging her back to the present.

Anna slipped out of his grasp, crossing the balcony to look planet-ward. Thule's pale moon was hanging above the dying planet, pure and serene. "Doesn't it seem the least bit cruel to you?"

He looked at her blankly for a long moment. "The Red Plague? It's a quick killer. People who catch it don't suffer long. We needed a deterrent that would make anyone think twice about attacking Centauri again. It took years, but we've finally managed to build one."

"What about Thule's people?" Anna couldn't look at him. The pride in his voice turned her stomach.

"Sometimes impossibly hard things are necessary for the greater good." Marcus sighed, looking tired but resolute.

"So you would do it again?" Anna realized she was clutching the fabric of her dress so hard her knuckles were white.

"Someone has to be strong enough to make the hard calls, Ginny. I'm trying to protect as many people as I can."

"Yes. I understand." She answered, thinking that she finally did. "Would you mind getting me a drink?" She breathed a sigh of relief when he agreed. For a few short hours, Anna had wanted to believe that she could talk to him, tell him her story and he would change things. He was a good man who was willing to do almost anything for what he thought was right. It was heartbreaking to realize that there were so many lives that would never be part of his "greater good."

When he was out of sight, she checked the stasis generator. Seventeen minutes left. She could still make it to quarantine if she left now.

VI

"HERE." Marcus was back sooner than she would have liked. Anna took the drink he held out to her. "And here." He flourished a delicate violet flower, tucking it gently behind her ear.

Anna froze, terrified that he would feel the veil. His hand dropped and she could breathe again. "Thank you."

"We grow them in the hydroponics lab." He grinned. "They're totally useless beyond being pretty, but everyone loves them anyway. And they make for nice decorations at impromptu parties."

Anna took the flower out from behind her ear and twirled it between her fingers. Her dad had grown something similar in their window boxes. He had tried to teach her, but Anna had never been any good with plants. "When you were little, what did you want to be when you grew up?" The question slipped out.

"I wanted to be a star fighter." He laughed. "You know, fly around beating bad guys and saving the universe. Still trying for the last part, I suppose. What about you?"

"I wanted to be buried by the sea." Anna answered. There were other things she'd planned to do with her life, but none of that had mattered since the day the plague arrived on Thule. Ginny and John had found her collapsed on the back porch. Even that close, she hadn't been able to make it to the grave she had dug for herself. She shook her head.

The stasis generator beeped softly, muffled by the fabric of her dress. Anna took a shaky breath. It was time. Marcus was looking at her with an odd expression on his handsome face.

Anna walked towards him. "I'm sorry." Livid red blotches were appearing on the backs of her hands. She clenched her them behind her back.

"Wha-" He hadn't noticed the spots. He was looking at her veiled face.

She kissed him, sliding her arms around his neck. He kissed back. Anna pulled away, turning her head to the side out of polite habit as she coughed. She looked down. Dark blood spotted her fingertips.

"Are you okay?" Marcus put a concerned hand on her shoulder.

Anna shook her head, straightening up and pulling the veil off of her face. Her breath was already coming shorter. "My name is Anna. I came here from Thule." She looked into his shocked eyes, trying to remember how she had felt when her father had started to cough, when her mother began bleeding from her eyes and ears, all mixed up with the sound of the shovel scraping wet sand. It was hard to feel righteous as fear blossomed on his face.

VII

MARCUS STUMBLED backwards, falling through the balcony door and into the ballroom with a shout. Anna followed. All eyes turned towards them.

"Stop her!" Marcus fumbled at his belt, pulling out a gun and aiming it at her with shaking hands.

Several people jumped forward, grabbing her arms. "Go ahead." Anna sagged against her captors, a wave of dizziness making the room spin. "It won't change anything." She coughed again, choking and retching until blood spattered the front of her dress.

Someone screamed. The hands holding her pulled away abruptly. Anna staggered, barely keeping her feet under her. The room erupted into a frenzy. She turned and walked towards the far door, half-hoping Marcus would shoot her and end it before the plague finished its job.

The shot never came. People milled around, trying to keep from touching her. Orders were being shouted and largely ignored. Anyone who had worked on the disease knew it was much too late.

Anna found herself lying on the floor, unsure of how she had gotten there. Her lungs were burning. She closed her eyes. She would sleep a little and then go down to the beach. Her parents – all the people of Thule – were waiting.

Time and Time Again

H. Beam Piper

To upset the stable, mighty stream of time would probably take an enormous concentration of energy. And it's not to be expected that a man would get a second chance at life. But an atomic might accomplish both –

BLINDED BY the bomb-flash and numbed by the narcotic injection, he could not estimate the extent of his injuries, but he knew that he was dying. Around him, in the darkness, voices sounded as through a thick wall.

"They mighta left mosta these Joes where they was. Half of them won't even last till the truck comes."

"No matter; so long as they're alive, they must be treated," another voice, crisp and cultivated, rebuked. "Better start taking names, while we're waiting."

"Yes, sir." Fingers fumbled at his identity badge. "Hartley, Allan; Captain, G5, Chem. Research AN/73/D. Serial, SO-23869403J."

"Allan Hartley!" The medic officer spoke in shocked surprise. "Why, he's the man who wrote Children of the Mist, Rose of Death, and Conqueror's Road!"

He tried to speak, and must have stirred; the corpsman's voice sharpened.

"Major, I think he's part conscious. Mebbe I better give him 'nother shot."

"Yes, yes; by all means, sergeant."

Something jabbed Allan Hartley in the back of the neck. Soft billows of oblivion closed in upon him, and all that remained to him was a tiny spark of awareness, glowing alone and lost in a great darkness.

The Spark grew brighter. He was more than a something that merely knew that it existed. He was a man, and he had a name, and a military rank, and memories. Memories of the searing blue-green flash, and of what he had been doing outside the shelter the moment before, and memories of the month-long siege, and of the retreat from the north, and memories of the days before the War, back to the time when he had been little Allan Hartley, a schoolboy, the son of a successful lawyer, in Williamsport, Pennsylvania.

His mother he could not remember; there was only a vague impression of the house full of people who had tried to comfort him for something he could not understand. But he remembered the old German woman who had kept house for his father, afterward, and he remembered his bedroom, with its chintz-covered chairs, and the warm-colored patch quilt on the old cherry bed, and the tan curtains at the windows, edged with dusky red, and the morning sun shining through them. He could almost see them, now.

He blinked. He could see them!

* * *

For a long time, he lay staring at them unbelievingly, and then he deliberately closed his eyes and counted ten seconds, and as he counted, terror gripped him. He was afraid to open them again, lest he find himself blind, or gazing at the filth and wreckage of a blasted city, but when he reached ten, he forced himself to look, and gave a sigh of relief. The sunlit curtains and the sun-gilded mist outside were still there.

He reached out to check one sense against another, feeling the rough monk's cloth and the edging of maroon silk thread. They were tangible as well as visible. Then he saw that the back of his hand was unscarred. There should have been a scar, souvenir of a rough-and-tumble brawl of his cub reporter days. He examined both hands closely. An instant later, he had sat up in bed and thrown off the covers, partially removing his pajamas and inspecting as much of his body as was visible.

It was the smooth body of a little boy.

That was ridiculous. He was a man of forty-three; an army officer, a chemist, once a best-selling novelist. He had been married, and divorced ten years ago. He looked again at his body. It was only twelve years old. Fourteen, at the very oldest. His eyes swept the room, wide with wonder. Every detail was familiar: the flower-splashed chair covers; the table that served as desk and catch-all for his possessions; the dresser, with its mirror stuck full of pictures of aircraft. It was the bedroom of his childhood home. He swung his legs over the edge of the bed. They were six inches too short to reach the floor.

For an instant, the room spun dizzily; and he was in the grip of utter panic, all confidence in the evidence of his senses lost. Was he insane? Or delirious? Or had the bomb really killed him; was this what death was like? What was that thing, about "ye become as little children"? He started to laugh, and his juvenile larynx made giggling sounds. They seemed funny, too, and aggravated his mirth. For a little while, he was on the edge of hysteria and then, when he managed to control his laughter, he felt calmer. If he were dead, then he must be a discarnate entity, and would be able to penetrate matter. To his relief, he was unable to push his hand through the bed. So he was alive; he was also fully awake, and, he hoped, rational. He rose to his feet and prowled about the room, taking stock of its contents.

There was no calendar in sight, and he could find no newspapers or dated periodicals, but he knew that it was prior to July 18, 1946. On that day, his fourteenth birthday, his father had given him a light .22 rifle, and it had been hung on a pair of rustic forks on the wall. It was not there now, nor ever had been. On the table, he saw a boys' book of military aircraft, with a clean, new dustjacket; the flyleaf was inscribed: To Allan Hartley, from his father, on his thirteenth birthday, 7/18 '45. Glancing out the window at the foliage on the trees, he estimated the date at late July or early August, 1945; that would make him just thirteen.

His clothes were draped on a chair beside the bed. Stripping off his pajamas, he donned shorts, then sat down and picked up a pair of lemon-colored socks, which he regarded with disfavor. As he pulled one on, a church bell began to clang. St. Boniface, up on the hill, ringing for early Mass; so this was Sunday. He paused, the second sock in his hand.

There was no question that his present environment was actual. Yet, on the other hand, he possessed a set of memories completely at variance with it. Now, suppose, since his environment were not an illusion, everything else were? Suppose all these troublesome memories were no more than a dream? Why, he was just little Allan Hartley, safe in his room on a Sunday morning, badly scared by a nightmare! Too much science fiction, Allan; too many comic books!

That was a wonderfully comforting thought, and he hugged it to him contentedly. It lasted all the while he was buttoning up his shirt and pulling on his pants, but when he reached for his shoes, it evaporated. Ever since he had wakened, he realized, he had been occupied with thoughts utterly incomprehensible to any thirteen-year-old; even thinking in words that would have been so much Sanskrit to himself at thirteen. He shook his head regretfully. The just-a-dream hypothesis went by the deep six.

He picked up the second shoe and glared at it as though it were responsible for his predicament. He was going to have to be careful. An unexpected display of adult characteristics might give rise to some questions he would find hard to answer credibly. Fortunately, he was an only child; there would be no brothers or sisters to trip him up. Old Mrs Stauber, the housekeeper, wouldn't be much of a problem; even in his normal childhood, he had bulked like an intellectual giant in comparison to her. But his father –

Now, there the going would be tough. He knew that shrewd attorney's mind, whetted keen on a generation of lying and reluctant witnesses. Sooner or later, he would forget for an instant and betray himself. Then he smiled, remembering the books he had discovered, in his late 'teens, on his father's shelves and recalling the character of the open-minded agnostic lawyer. If he could only avoid the inevitable unmasking until he had a plausible explanatory theory.

* * *

Blake Hartley was leaving the bathroom as Allan Hartley opened his door and stepped into the hall. The lawyer was bare-armed and in slippers; at forty-eight, there was only a faint powdering of gray in his dark hair, and not a gray thread in his clipped mustache. The old Merry Widower, himself, Allan thought, grinning as he remembered the white-haired but still vigorous man from whom he'd parted at the outbreak of the War.

"Morning, Dad," he greeted.

"Morning, son. You're up early. Going to Sunday school?"

Now there was the advantage of a father who'd cut his first intellectual tooth on Tom Paine and Bob Ingersoll; attendance at divine services was on a strictly voluntary basis.

"Why, I don't think so; I want to do some reading, this morning."

"That's always a good thing to do," Blake Hartley approved. "After breakfast, suppose you take a walk down to the station and get me a Times." He dug in his trouser pocket and came out with a half dollar. "Get anything you want for yourself, while you're at it."

Allan thanked his father and pocketed the coin.

"Mrs Stauber'll still be at Mass," he suggested. "Say I get the paper now; breakfast won't be ready till she gets here."

"Good idea." Blake Hartley nodded, pleased. "You'll have three-quarters of an hour, at least."

So far, he congratulated himself, everything had gone smoothly. He went downstairs and onto the street, turning left at Brandon to Campbell, and left again in the direction of the station. Before he reached the underpass, a dozen half-forgotten memories had revived. Here was a house that would, in a few years, be gutted by fire. Here were four dwellings standing where he had last seen a five-story apartment building. A gasoline station and a weed-grown lot would shortly be replaced by a supermarket. The environs of the station itself were a complete puzzle to him, until he oriented himself.

He bought a New York Times, glancing first of all at the date line. Sunday, August 5, 1945; he'd estimated pretty closely. The battle of Okinawa had been won. The Potsdam Conference had just ended. There were still pictures of the B-25 crash against the Empire

State Building, a week ago Saturday. And Japan was still being pounded by bombs from the air and shells from off-shore naval guns. Why, tomorrow, Hiroshima was due for the Big Job! It amused him to reflect that he was probably the only person in Williamsport who knew that.

On the way home, a boy, sitting on the top step of a front porch, hailed him. Allan replied cordially, trying to remember who it was. Of course; Larry Morton! He and Allan had been buddies. They probably had been swimming, or playing Commandos and Germans, the afternoon before. Larry had gone to Cornell the same year that Allan had gone to Penn State; they had both graduated in 1954. Larry had gotten into some Government bureau, and then he had married a Pittsburgh girl, and had become twelfth vice-president of her father's firm. He had been killed, in 1968, in a plane crash.

"You gonna Sunday school?" Larry asked, mercifully unaware of the fate Allan foresaw for him.

"Why, no. I have some things I want to do at home." He'd have to watch himself. Larry would spot a difference quicker than any adult. "Heck with it," he added.

"Golly, I wisht I c'ld stay home from Sunday school whenever I wanted to," Larry envied. "How about us goin' swimmin', at the Canoe Club, 'safter?"

Allan thought fast. "Gee, I wisht I c'ld," he replied, lowering his grammatical sights. "I gotta stay home, 'safter. We're expectin' comp'ny; coupla aunts of mine. Dad wants me to stay home when they come."

That went over all right. Anybody knew that there was no rational accounting for the vagaries of the adult mind, and no appeal from adult demands. The prospect of company at the Hartley home would keep Larry away, that afternoon. He showed his disappointment.

"Aw, jeepers creepers!" he blasphemed euphemistically.

"Mebbe t'morrow," Allan said. "If I c'n make it. I gotta go, now; ain't had breakfast yet." He scuffed his feet boyishly, exchanged so-longs with his friend, and continued homeward.

As he had hoped, the Sunday paper kept his father occupied at breakfast, to the exclusion of any dangerous table talk. Blake Hartley was still deep in the financial section when Allan left the table and went to the library. There should be two books there to which he wanted badly to refer. For a while, he was afraid that his father had not acquired them prior to 1945, but he finally found them, and carried them onto the front porch, along with a pencil and a ruled yellow scratch pad. In his experienced future – or his past-to-come – Allan Hartley had been accustomed to doing his thinking with a pencil. As reporter, as novelist plotting his work, as amateur chemist in his home laboratory, as scientific warfare research officer, his ideas had always been clarified by making notes. He pushed a chair to the table and built up the seat with cushions, wondering how soon he would become used to the proportional disparity between himself and the furniture. As he opened the books and took his pencil in his hand, there was one thing missing. If he could only smoke a pipe, now!

His father came out and stretched in a wicker chair with the Times book review section. The morning hours passed. Allan Hartley leafed through one book and then the other. His pencil moved rapidly at times; at others, he doodled absently. There was no question, any more, in his mind, as to what or who he was. He was Allan Hartley, a man of forty-three, marooned in his own thirteen-year-old body, thirty years back in his own past. That was, of course, against all common sense, but he was easily able to ignore that objection. It had been made before: against the astronomy of Copernicus, and the geography of Columbus, and the biology of Darwin, and the industrial technology of Samuel Colt, and the military doctrines of Charles de Gaulle. Today's common sense had a habit of turning into tomorrow's utter nonsense. What he needed, right now, but bad, was a theory that would explain what had happened to him.

Understanding was beginning to dawn when Mrs Stauber came out to announce midday dinner.

"I hope you von't mind haffin' it so early," she apologized. "Mein sister, Jennie, offer in Nippenose, she iss sick; I vant to go see her, dis afternoon, yet. I'll be back in blenty time to get supper, Mr Hartley."

"Hey, Dad!" Allan spoke up. "Why can't we get our own supper, and have a picnic, like? That'd be fun, and Mrs Stauber could stay as long as she wanted to."

His father looked at him. Such consideration for others was a most gratifying deviation from the juvenile norm; dawn of altruism, or something. He gave hearty assent: "Why, of course, Mrs Stauber. Allan and I can shift for ourselves, this evening; can't we, Allan? You needn't come back till tomorrow morning."

"Ach, t'ank you! T'ank you so mooch, Mr Hartley."

At dinner, Allan got out from under the burden of conversation by questioning his father about the War and luring him into a lengthy dissertation on the difficulties of the forthcoming invasion of Japan. In view of what he remembered of the next twenty-four hours, Allan was secretly amused. His father was sure that the War would run on to mid-1946.

After dinner, they returned to the porch, Hartley père smoking a cigar and carrying out several law books. He only glanced at these occasionally; for the most part, he sat and blew smoke rings, and watched them float away. Some thrice-guilty felon was about to be triumphantly acquitted by a weeping jury; Allan could recognize a courtroom masterpiece in the process of incubation.

* * *

It was several hours later that the crunch of feet on the walk caused father and son to look up simultaneously. The approaching visitor was a tall man in a rumpled black suit; he had knobby wrists and big, awkward hands; black hair flecked with gray, and a harsh, bigoted face. Allan remembered him. Frank Gutchall. Lived on Campbell Street; a religious fanatic, and some sort of lay preacher. Maybe he needed legal advice; Allan could vaguely remember some incident –

"Ah, good afternoon, Mr Gutchall. Lovely day, isn't it?" Blake Hartley said.

Gutchall cleared his throat. "Mr Hartley, I wonder if you could lend me a gun and some bullets," he began, embarrassedly. "My little dog's been hurt, and it's suffering something terrible. I want a gun, to put the poor thing out of its pain."

"Why, yes; of course. How would a 20-gauge shotgun do?" Blake Hartley asked. "You wouldn't want anything heavy."

Gutchall fidgeted. "Why, er, I was hoping you'd let me have a little gun." He held his hands about six inches apart. "A pistol, that I could put in my pocket. It wouldn't look right, to carry a hunting gun on the Lord's day; people wouldn't understand that it was for a work of mercy."

The lawyer nodded. In view of Gutchall's religious beliefs, the objection made sense.

"Well, I have a Colt .38-special," he said, "but you know, I belong to this Auxiliary Police outfit. If I were called out for duty, this evening, I'd need it. How soon could you bring it back?"

Something clicked in Allan Hartley's mind. He remembered, now, what that incident had been. He knew, too, what he had to do.

"Dad, aren't there some cartridges left for the Luger?" he asked.

Blake Hartley snapped his fingers. "By George, yes! I have a German automatic I can let you have, but I wish you'd bring it back as soon as possible. I'll get it for you."

Before he could rise, Allan was on his feet.

"Sit still, Dad; I'll get it. I know where the cartridges are." With that, he darted into the house and upstairs.

The Luger hung on the wall over his father's bed. Getting it down, he dismounted it, working with rapid precision. He used the blade of his pocketknife to unlock the end piece of the breechblock, slipping out the firing pin and buttoning it into his shirt pocket. Then he reassembled the harmless pistol, and filled the clip with 9-millimeter cartridges from the bureau drawer.

There was an extension telephone beside the bed. Finding Gutchall's address in the directory, he lifted the telephone, and stretched his handkerchief over the mouthpiece. Then he dialed Police Headquarters.

"This is Blake Hartley," he lied, deepening his voice and copying his father's tone. "Frank Gutchall, who lives at... take this down"– he gave Gutchall's address – "has just borrowed a pistol from me, ostensibly to shoot a dog. He has no dog. He intends shooting his wife. Don't argue about how I know; there isn't time. Just take it for granted that I do. I disabled the pistol – took out the firing pin – but if he finds out what I did, he may get some other weapon. He's on his way home, but he's on foot. If you hurry, you may get a man there before he arrives, and grab him before he finds out the pistol won't shoot."

"OK, Mr Hartley. We'll take care of it. Thanks."

"And I wish you'd get my pistol back, as soon as you can. It's something I brought home from the other War, and I shouldn't like to lose it."

"We'll take care of that, too. Thank you, Mr Hartley."

He hung up, and carried the Luger and the loaded clip down to the porch.

"Look, Mr Gutchall; here's how it works," he said, showing it to the visitor. Then he slapped in the clip and yanked up on the toggle loading the chamber. "It's ready to shoot, now; this is the safety." He pushed it on. "When you're ready to shoot, just shove it forward and up, and then pull the trigger. You have to pull the trigger each time; it's loaded for eight shots. And be sure to put the safety back when you're through shooting."

"Did you load the chamber?" Blake Hartley demanded.

"Sure. It's on safe, now."

"Let me see." His father took the pistol, being careful to keep his finger out of the trigger guard, and looked at it. "Yes, that's all right." He repeated the instructions Allan had given, stressing the importance of putting the safety on after using. "Understand how it works, now?" he asked.

"Yes, I understand how it works. Thank you, Mr Hartley. Thank you, too, young man."

Gutchall put the Luger in his hip pocket, made sure it wouldn't fall out, and took his departure.

"You shouldn't have loaded it," Hartley père reproved, when he was gone.

Allan sighed. This was it; the masquerade was over.

"I had to, to keep you from fooling with it," he said. "I didn't want you finding out that I'd taken out the firing pin."

"You what?"

"Gutchall didn't want that gun to shoot a dog. He has no dog. He meant to shoot his wife with it. He's a religious maniac; sees visions, hears voices, receives revelations, talks with the Holy Ghost. The Holy Ghost probably put him up to this caper. I'll submit that any man who holds long conversations with the Deity isn't to be trusted with a gun, and neither is any man who lies about why he wants one. And while I was at it, I called the police, on the upstairs phone. I had to use your name; I deepened my voice and talked through a handkerchief."

"You–" Blake Hartley jumped as though bee-stung. "Why did you have to do that?"

"You know why. I couldn't have told them, 'This is little Allan Hartley, just thirteen years old; please, Mr Policeman, go and arrest Frank Gutchall before he goes root-toot-toot at his wife with my pappa's Luger.' That would have gone over big, now, wouldn't it?"

"And suppose he really wants to shoot a dog; what sort of a mess will I be in?"

"No mess at all. If I'm wrong – which I'm not – I'll take the thump for it, myself. It'll pass for a dumb kid trick, and nothing'll be done. But if I'm right, you'll have to front for me. They'll keep your name out of it, but they'd give me a lot of cheap boy-hero publicity, which I don't want." He picked up his pencil again. "We should have the complete returns in about twenty minutes."

* * *

That was a ten-minute under-estimate, and it was another quarter-hour before the detective-sergeant who returned the Luger had finished congratulating Blake Hartley and giving him the thanks of the Department. After he had gone, the lawyer picked up the Luger, withdrew the clip, and ejected the round in the chamber.

"Well," he told his son, "you were right. You saved that woman's life." He looked at the automatic, and then handed it across the table. "Now, let's see you put that firing pin back."

Allan Hartley dismantled the weapon, inserted the missing part, and put it together again, then snapped it experimentally and returned it to his father. Blake Hartley looked at it again, and laid it on the table.

"Now, son, suppose we have a little talk," he said softly.

"But I explained everything." Allan objected innocently.

"You did not," his father retorted. "Yesterday you'd never have thought of a trick like this; why, you wouldn't even have known how to take this pistol apart. And at dinner, I caught you using language and expressing ideas that were entirely outside anything you'd ever known before. Now, I want to know – and I mean this literally."

Allan chuckled. "I hope you're not toying with the rather medieval notion of obsession," he said.

Blake Hartley started. Something very like that must have been flitting through his mind. He opened his mouth to say something, then closed it abruptly.

"The trouble is, I'm not sure you aren't right," his son continued. "You say you find me – changed. When did you first notice a difference?"

"Last night, you were still my little boy. This morning – " Blake Hartley was talking more to himself than to Allan. "I don't know. You were unusually silent at breakfast. And come to think of it, there was something ... something strange ... about you when I saw you in the hall, upstairs... Allan!" he burst out, vehemently. "What has happened to you?"

Allan Hartley felt a twinge of pain. What his father was going through was almost what he, himself, had endured, in the first few minutes after waking.

"I wish I could be sure, myself, Dad," he said. "You see, when I woke, this morning, I hadn't the least recollection of anything I'd done yesterday. August 4, 1945, that is," he specified. "I was positively convinced that I was a man of forty-three, and my last memory was of lying on a stretcher, injured by a bomb explosion. And I was equally convinced that this had happened in 1975."

"Huh?" His father straightened. "Did you say nineteen seventy-five?" He thought for a moment. "That's right; in 1975, you will be forty-three. A bomb, you say?"

Allan nodded. "During the siege of Buffalo, in the Third World War," he said, "I was a captain in G5 – Scientific Warfare, General Staff. There'd been a transpolar air invasion of Canada, and I'd been sent to the front to check on service failures of a new lubricating oil for combat equipment. A week after I got there, Ottawa fell, and the retreat started. We made a stand at Buffalo, and that was where I copped it. I remember being picked up, and getting a narcotic injection. The next thing I knew, I was in bed, upstairs, and it was 1945 again, and I was back in my own little thirteen-year-old body."

"Oh, Allan, you just had a nightmare to end nightmares!" his father assured him, laughing a trifle too heartily. "That's all!"

"That was one of the first things I thought of. I had to reject it; it just wouldn't fit the facts. Look; a normal dream is part of the dreamer's own physical brain, isn't it? Well, here is a part about two thousand per cent greater than the whole from which it was taken. Which is absurd."

"You mean all this Battle of Buffalo stuff? That's easy. All the radio commentators have been harping on the horrors of World War III, and you couldn't have avoided hearing some of it. You just have an undigested chunk of H. V. Kaltenborn raising hell in your subconscious."

"It wasn't just World War III; it was everything. My four years at high school, and my four years at Penn State, and my seven years as a reporter on the Philadelphia Record. And my novels: Children of the Mist, Rose of Death, Conqueror's Road. They were no kid stuff. Why, yesterday I'd never even have thought of some of the ideas I used in my detective stories, that I published under a nom-de-plume. And my hobby, chemistry; I was pretty good at that. Patented a couple of processes that made me as much money as my writing. You think a thirteen-year-old just dreamed all that up? Or, here; you speak French, don't you?" He switched languages and spoke at some length in good conversational slang-spiced Parisian. "Too bad you don't speak Spanish, too," he added, reverting to English. "Except for a Mexican accent you could cut with a machete, I'm even better there than in French. And I know some German, and a little Russian."

Blake Hartley was staring at his son, stunned. It was some time before he could make himself speak.

"I could barely keep up with you, in French," he admitted. "I can swear that in the last thirteen years of your life, you had absolutely no chance to learn it. All right; you lived till 1975, you say. Then, all of a sudden, you found yourself back here, thirteen years old, in 1945. I suppose you remember everything in between?" he asked. "Did you ever read James Branch Cabell? Remember Florian de Puysange, in The High Place?"

"Yes. You find the same idea in Jurgen too," Allan said. "You know, I'm beginning to wonder if Cabell mightn't have known something he didn't want to write."

"But it's impossible!" Blake Hartley hit the table with his hand, so hard that the heavy pistol bounced. The loose round he had ejected from the chamber toppled over and started to roll, falling off the edge. He stooped and picked it up. "How can you go back, against time? And the time you claim you came from doesn't exist, now; it hasn't happened yet." He reached for the pistol magazine, to insert the cartridge, and as he did, he saw the books in front of his son. "Dunne's Experiment with Time," he commented. "And J. N. M. Tyrrell's Science and Psychical Phenomena. Are you trying to work out a theory?"

"Yes." It encouraged Allan to see that his father had unconsciously adopted an adult-to-adult manner. "I think I'm getting somewhere, too. You've read these books? Well, look, Dad; what's your attitude on precognition? The ability of the human mind to exhibit real knowledge, apart from logical inference, of future events? You think Dunne is telling the truth about his experiences? Or that the cases in Tyrrell's book are properly verified, and can't be explained away on the basis of chance?"

Blake Hartley frowned. "I don't know," he confessed. "The evidence is the sort that any court in the world would accept, if it concerned ordinary, normal events. Especially the cases investigated by the Society for Psychical Research: they have been verified. But how can anybody know of something that hasn't happened yet? If it hasn't happened yet, it doesn't exist, and you can't have real knowledge of something that has no real existence."

"Tyrrell discusses that dilemma, and doesn't dispose of it. I think I can. If somebody has real knowledge of the future, then the future must be available to the present mind. And if any moment other than the bare present exists, then all time must be totally present; every moment must be perpetually coexistent with every other moment," Allan said.

"Yes. I think I see what you mean. That was Dunne's idea, wasn't it?"

"No. Dunne postulated an infinite series of time dimensions, the entire extent of each being the bare present moment of the next. What I'm postulating is the perpetual coexistence of every moment of time in this dimension, just as every graduation on a yardstick exists equally with every other graduation, but each at a different point in space."

"Well, as far as duration and sequence go, that's all right," the father agreed. "But how about the 'Passage of Time'?"

"Well, time does appear to pass. So does the landscape you see from a moving car window. I'll suggest that both are illusions of the same kind. We imagine time to be dynamic, because we've never viewed it from a fixed point, but if it is totally present, then it must be static, and in that case, we're moving through time."

"That seems all right. But what's your car window?"

"If all time is totally present, then you must exist simultaneously at every moment along your individual life span," Allan said. "Your physical body, and your mind, and all the thoughts contained in your mind, each at its appropriate moment in sequence. But what is it that exists only at the bare moment we think of as now?"

Blake Hartley grinned. Already, he was accepting his small son as an intellectual equal.

"Please, teacher; what?"

"Your consciousness. And don't say, 'What's that?' Teacher doesn't know. But we're only conscious of one moment; the illusory now. This is 'now,' and it was 'now' when you asked that question, and it'll be 'now' when I stop talking, but each is a different moment. We imagine that all those 'nows' are rushing past us. Really, they're standing still, and our consciousness is whizzing past them."

His father thought that over for some time. Then he sat up. "Hey!" he cried, suddenly. "If some part of our ego is time-free and passes from moment to moment, it must be extraphysical, because the physical body exists at every moment through which the consciousness passes. And if it's extraphysical, there's no reason whatever for assuming that it passes out of existence when it reaches the moment of the death of the body. Why, there's logical evidence for survival, independent of any alleged spirit communication! You can toss out Patience Worth, and Mrs Osborne Leonard's Feda, and Sir Oliver Lodge's son, and Wilfred Brandon, and all the other spirit-communicators, and you still have evidence."

"I hadn't thought of that," Allan confessed. "I think you're right. Well, let's put that at the bottom of the agenda and get on with this time business. You 'lose consciousness' as in sleep; where does your consciousness go? I think it simply detaches from the moment at which you go to sleep, and moves backward or forward along the line of moment-sequence, to some prior or subsequent moment, attaching there."

"Well, why don't we know anything about that?" Blake Hartley asked. "It never seems to happen. We go to sleep tonight, and it's always tomorrow morning when we wake; never day-before-yesterday, or last month, or next year."

"It never ... or almost never ... seems to happen; you're right there. Know why? Because if the consciousness goes forward, it attaches at a moment when the physical brain contains memories of the previous, consciously unexperienced, moment. You wake, remembering the evening before, because that's the memory contained in your mind at that moment, and back of it are memories of all the events in the interim. See?"

"Yes. But how about backward movement, like this experience of yours?"

"This experience of mine may not be unique, but I never heard of another case like it. What usually happens is that the memories carried back by the consciousness are buried in the subconscious mind. You know how thick the wall between the subconscious and the conscious mind is. These dreams of Dunne's, and the cases in Tyrrell's book, are leakage. That's why precognitions are usually incomplete and distorted, and generally trivial. The wonder isn't that good cases are so few; it's surprising that there are any at all." Allan looked at the papers in front of him. "I haven't begun to theorize about how I managed to remember everything. It may have been the radiations from the bomb, or the effect of the narcotic, or both together, or something at this end, or a combination of all three. But the fact remains that my subconscious barrier didn't function, and everything got through. So, you see, I am obsessed – by my own future identity."

"And I'd been afraid that you'd been, well, taken-over by some ... some outsider." Blake Hartley grinned weakly. "I don't mind admitting, Allan, that what's happened has been a shock. But that other ... I just couldn't have taken that."

"No. Not and stayed sane. But really, I am your son; the same entity I was yesterday. I've just had what you might call an educational short cut."

"I'll say you have!" His father laughed in real amusement. He discovered that his cigar had gone out, and re-lit it. "Here; if you can remember the next thirty years, suppose you tell me when the War's going to end. This one, I mean."

"The Japanese surrender will be announced at exactly 1901 – 7:01 p.m. present style – on August 14. A week from Tuesday. Better make sure we have plenty of grub in the house by then. Everything will be closed up tight till Thursday morning; even the restaurants. I remember, we had nothing to eat in the house but some scraps."

"Well! It is handy, having a prophet in the family! I'll see to it Mrs Stauber gets plenty of groceries in... Tuesday a week? That's pretty sudden, isn't it?"

"The Japs are going to think so," Allan replied. He went on to describe what was going to happen.

His father swore softly. "You know, I've heard talk about atomic energy, but I thought it was just Buck Rogers stuff. Was that the sort of bomb that got you?"

"That was a firecracker to the bomb that got me. That thing exploded a good ten miles away."

Blake Hartley whistled softly. "And that's going to happen in thirty years! You know, son, if I were you, I wouldn't like to have to know about a thing like that." He looked at Allan for a moment. "Please, if you know, don't ever tell me when I'm going to die."

Allan smiled. "I can't. I had a letter from you just before I left for the front. You were seventy-eight, then, and you were still hunting, and fishing, and flying your own plane. But I'm not going to get killed in any Battle of Buffalo, this time, and if I can prevent it, and I think I can, there won't be any World War III."

"But – you say all time exists, perpetually coexistent and totally present," his father said. "Then it's right there in front of you, and you're getting closer to it, every watch tick."

Allan Hartley shook his head. "You know what I remembered, when Frank Gutchall came to borrow a gun?" he asked. "Well, the other time, I hadn't been home: I'd been swimming at the Canoe Club, with Larry Morton. When I got home, about half an hour from now, I found the house full of cops. Gutchall talked the .38 officers' model out of you, and gone home; he'd shot his wife four times through the body, finished her off with another one back of the ear, and then used his sixth shot to blast his brains out. The cops traced the gun; they took a very poor view of your lending it to him. You never got it back."

"Trust that gang to keep a good gun," the lawyer said.

"I didn't want us to lose it, this time, and I didn't want to see you lose face around City Hall. Gutchalls, of course, are expendable," Allan said. "But my main reason for fixing Frank Gutchall up with a padded cell was that I wanted to know whether or not the future could be altered. I have it on experimental authority that it can be. There must be additional dimensions of time; lines of alternate probabilities. Something like William Seabrook's witch-doctor friend's Fan-Shaped Destiny. When I brought memories of the future back to the present, I added certain factors to the causal chain. That set up an entirely new line of probabilities. On no notice at all, I stopped a murder and a suicide. With thirty years to work, I can stop a world war. I'll have the means to do it, too."

"The means?"

"Unlimited wealth and influence. Here." Allan picked up a sheet and handed it to his father. "Used properly, we can make two or three million on that, alone. A list of all the Kentucky Derby, Preakness, and Belmont winners to 1970. That'll furnish us primary capital. Then, remember, I was something of a chemist. I took it up, originally, to get background material for one of my detective stories; it fascinated me, and I made it a hobby, and then a source of income. I'm thirty years ahead of any chemist in the world, now. You remember I. G. Farbenindustrie? Ten years from now, we'll make them look like pikers."

His father looked at the yellow sheet. "Assault, at eight to one," he said. "I can scrape up about five thousand for that – yes; in ten years – any other little operations you have in mind?" he asked.

"About 1950, we start building a political organization, here in Pennsylvania. In 1960, I think we can elect you President. The world situation will be crucial, by that time, and we had a good-natured nonentity in the White House then, who let things go till war became inevitable. I think President Hartley can be trusted to take a strong line of policy. In the meantime, you can read Machiavelli."

"That's my little boy, talking!"

Blake Hartley said softly. "All right, son; I'll do just what you tell me, and when you grow up, I'll be president... Let's go get supper, now."

Nude Descending an Elevator Shaft

Conor Powers-Smith

AT 11:03 A.M., BillT17 thinks: Okay, I'm on, I think. Yeah, it's working. Wow, that's pretty wild.

WELCOME, BILLT17, TO THE WORLD'S FASTEST GROWING SOCIAL COMMUNITY. THINK YES FOR AN INTRODUCTION TO THE AMAZING FEATURES OFFERED BY GroupThink. THINK NO TO CANCEL.

BillT17 thinks: ...fastest growing social community. Think yes for–

THANK YOU FOR ACCESSING GroupThink's INTRODUCTORY TOUR. PART ONE: WHAT DO YOU THINK ABOUT THAT?

BillT17 thinks: Wait, wait. Oops. Okay, no. NO.

GroupThink LETS YOU ACCESS THE THOUGHTS AND OPINIONS OF HUNDREDS OF MILLIONS OF REGISTERED USERS WORLDWIDE, AND–

At 11:05 a.m., MissyMelissy thinks: Honey, why are you doing the tutorial? I said I'd walk you through it.

BillT17 thinks: I didn't mean to. [Angry Face] This is annoying.

MissyMelissy thinks: Don't get like that already, Bill. Give it a chance.

BillT17 thinks: Like what?

MissyMelissy thinks: Don't get all angry-face. Like, "This is annoying."

BillT17 thinks: I didn't say that.

MissyMelissy: [Smiley Face] Well, you thought it, apparently.

BillT17 thinks: Hold on. Where is it?

MissyMelissy thinks: Scroll up, you'll see it. You're on your phone, right? I'm assuming you're not ready to take the plunge and go without a screen.

BillT17 thinks: Hell, no. Doesn't the computer voice that reads it sound weird?

MissyMelissy thinks: You get used to it.

BillT17 thinks: Doesn't it make you nervous, not seeing what you're posting?

MissyMelissy thinks: I know what I'm posting, Honey, because I'm thinking it. You'll see, it's pretty easy to get the hang of. Did you find that little flub yet?

BillT17 thinks: Hold on.

MissyMelissy thinks: I hope you're not using the touchscreen, like a caveman. Think it.

BillT17 thinks: Oh, yeah. Okay. Scroll up. SCROLL–

MissyMelissy thinks: [Laughing Face] No, Bill, don't think "Scroll up." Just think of the abstract concept. Like, the Platonic ideal of scrolling up.

BillT17 thinks: Okay. Scroll up. Oops.

MissyMelissy thinks: [Laughing Face]

BillT17 thinks: Oh, there it goes. Okay, that's pretty slick. But you know, if you ever say "Platonic" to me again, I'll jump off a bridge.

MissyMelissy thinks: [Smiley Face] Then you'd better behave. But, Bill–

At 11:07 a.m., MasterChief3605 thinks: Yo! Lo and behold! Billy finally joins the rest of the civilized world.

BillT17 thinks: [Annoyed Face] Uh huh.

MissyMelissy thinks: Hi, Jamie.

MasterChief3605 thinks: Hey, girl. How's it–

BillT17 thinks: Hey, Jamie, we're kind of working on something right now.

MasterChief3605 thinks: Yeah, I get you. What's annoying?

BillT17 thinks: Huh? Is that a riddle?

MasterChief3605 thinks: You did an annoyed face.

BillT17 thinks: No I–Ah, shit. [Annoyed Face]

… SHARE YOUR OWN. ALL YOUR LIKES AND DISLIKES, HOPES AND DREAMS, YOUR INNERMOST SELF, FOR THE–

MissyMelissy thinks: The stupid tutorial's stuck on. That's what's annoying. [Annoyed Face]

MasterChief3605 thinks: Oh. I remember that thing. That takes me back.

MissyMelissy thinks: It pauses when someone thinks, then starts up again when there's a lull. Just shut it off, Honey.

BillT17 thinks: Shut off. Cancel.

MissyMelissy thinks: Don't think the words, Bill.

BillT17 thinks: What should I think of, Plato taking a dump in a river?

MissyMelissy thinks: [Laughing Face] Bill.

MasterChief3605 thinks: How long have we been on this, Mel? You know I got her on, right, Billy?

BillT17 thinks: Is that a fact? Shouldn't you be out spreading the good news to someone else?

MasterChief3605 thinks: Yeah, I practically had to kidnap her and force her to join. Now she loves it, though. I don't know what some people have against it. Bunch of Lucites.

MissyMelissy thinks: You mean Luddites, Jamie.

MasterChief3605 thinks: Exactly. It's like, damn, man, come on, you know?

BillT17 thinks: [Laughing Face] That's your profile picture, Jamie? Wow, you drank a whole beer, huh? You fucking–

MissyMelissy thinks: Bill.

BillT17 thinks: Oh.

MissyMelissy thinks: He's still getting the hang of it, Jamie.

MasterChief3605 thinks: Yeah. But, Billy.

MissyMelissy thinks: He just started. Just now. You remember, it takes a little while to get it under control.

MasterChief3605 thinks: Yeah yeah. But, hey, Billy.

BillT17 thinks: Hey, what?

MasterChief3605 thinks: Yeah, I killed that in literally about two seconds. Sweet pic, right?

BillT17 thinks: Sweet, yo.

...WHOLE WORLD TO SEE, AND SHARE. NOW YOU –

BillT17 thinks: Goddammit. Mel, could you just shut that thing off for me?

MissyMelissy thinks: I can't, Bill, it's your chat. You have to do it. Just–

BillT17 thinks: Yeah, I'll have another. Thanks. Cute. Nose ring, but still cute. Probably a few tattoos, but still.

MasterChief3605 thinks: [Laughing Face] Where are you, Bro?

BillT17 thinks: Crowded. Comfortable chairs. Good smells. Strong coffee smells, spicy tea smells. Pretty waitress, walking away. Nice hips. Very nice–

MasterChief3605 thinks: Yo, Man! I gotta–

MissyMelissy thinks: Don't look around, Bill, just think "Coffee shop."

BillT17 thinks: Coffee shop. Why, what did I – ah, shit.

MasterChief3605 thinks: What one? I gotta check me out that waitress, you know what I'm thinking?

BillT17 thinks: Shit, sorry, Hon. She's not even that cute. Not nearly as–

MissyMelissy thinks: Yeah, yeah.

BillT17 thinks: No, look, she's coming back. Watch. Almost as cute as Melissa. Nicer eyes. Uh, thanks. Yeah, right there's fine. CLEAVAGE! Thanks. Yeah, just the check, when you get a chance. Walking away. Swinging her hips more than before? If she looks back – stop. I'm online. Stop. What did I – fuck.

...NEVER HAVE TO WONDER WHAT YOUR FRIENDS AND LOVED ONES ARE THINKING. JUST LOG ONTO GroupThink, USING–

BillT17 thinks: Christ, Hon, I'm sorry.

MissyMelissy thinks: Did she look back?

BillT17 thinks: Shit, I wasn't looking. I didn't look, Hon. I'm really sorry. Jesus, this thing's sensitive.

MissyMelissy thinks: Well, it either works or it doesn't. We know yours works.

BillT17 thinks: But, I mean, you can't adjust it or whatever?

MissyMelissy thinks: You mean, can it keep you from thinking about cleavage? No. No, you have to do that yourself.

BillT17 thinks: Okay. Okay. You're not pissed, are you?

MissyMelissy thinks: [Angry Face] Just kidding. It's okay. Once.

BillT17 thinks: I love you, Mel.

MissyMelissy thinks: Yeah, yeah.

BillT17 thinks: No, I do. I love Melissa like crazy. Smart and funny and strong and pretty. Most of all, kind. Talking, laughing. Sliding my hand down the side of her neck to her shoulder, while my other hand slides up her thigh, then–

MissyMelissy thinks: Bill. Bill. Bill.

BillT17 thinks: Yes. Shit.

MissyMelissy thinks: [Smiley Face] That's very sweet, Bill. Maybe a little less detail next time, but very sweet. Unless you're just thinking that to cover your ass.

BillT17 thinks: I could do that, once I get better at this. I wouldn't do that, Honey.

MissyMelissy thinks: I know, Bill. I'm just kidding.

...ONE OF OUR HUGE SELECTION OF THINKING CAPS, AND YOU'LL HAVE INSTANT–

BillT17 thinks: I do feel kind of goofy in this thing.

MissyMelissy thinks: The cap? I'm sure if–

MasterChief3605 thinks: What model you got, Bro?

BillT17 thinks: [Annoyed Face] Oh yeah, he's still – stop. I don't know, just the basic one, I guess. Looks more like a swim cap than anything else.

MasterChief3605 thinks: Yeah, that one's a little goofy. You didn't want to spring for one of the higher-end ones? They've got all kinds. I just got this sweet Lakers one, purple and gold, all sleek and everything, with the earpiece built in.

BillT17 thinks: I'm using– don't think Melissa's old one. Shit.

MasterChief3605 thinks: [Laughing Face] Is it all sparkly, Billy? You got little pink hearts on that piece?

BillT17 thinks: [Annoyed Face] Goddammit.

MissyMelissy thinks: He's just trying it out, Jamie. I'm going to get him his own for Christmas if he likes it. A Yankees one, right, Hon?

BillT17 thinks: Yeah, because we live in New Jersey, not fucking L.A. fucking frontrunner.

MasterChief3605 thinks: That's cool. I'm sure they have that in pink, too.

MissyMelissy thinks: It's not pink, Jamie.

BillT17 thinks: Honey–

MissyMelissy thinks: It's Mulberry.

MasterChief3605 thinks: [Questioning Face]

MissyMelissy thinks: It's like a light purple.

MasterChief3605 thinks: Like a dark pink?

BillT17 thinks: [Angry Face] Jamie's face, laughing, my hand, swatting him on the mouth, swatting the smile right off it.

MissyMelissy thinks: [Surprised Face] Bill!

BillT17 thinks: That went through, huh?

MissyMelissy thinks: It all goes through, Bill. You need to start controlling it.

MasterChief3605 thinks: [Smiley Face] I could take you, Bro.

BillT17 thinks: I'm taller, but he's probably stronger. I'm smarter, but that's overrated in a fight. He'd probably win. I doubt it. Bro.

MissyMelissy thinks: Bill, that's enough.

BillT17 thinks: That's something I don't get about this site. Why isn't it constant insults and death threats, like the rest of the internet?

MissyMelissy thinks: Because people control themselves, Bill. Which, if you're not even going to try–

BillT17 thinks: I am trying. Waitress coming. Look, look, here we go. Look down at the table. Thanks. Nice smile. Look down at the table. At the check. Seven bucks for that little piece of crumb cake? It was good, though. That stuff on top just right, firm but crumbly. Not too much powdered sugar. Written at the bottom of the check: "Thanks! Allison." And a smiley face. I'm sure she writes that for everyone. Probably. I go up to her, and I go, "Thanks, Allison." Allie? Allison. "Thanks, Allison. But you forgot your phone number." Cheesy, but let's just say it works. We–Stop it, you fucking idiot. The check. Fifteen per cent of eleven-fifty. Ten percent is, what, a buck fifteen? So twenty percent is two bucks thirty. Knock off the thirty? Or round it up to three bucks? I bet she gets over-tipped a lot. I'm not one of those guys who go around tipping the shit out of every nice set of tits. Falling in love with strippers. Maybe I call her, and we hang out a few times, just as friends. Then one night, me and her and Melissa are drinking, and–

MissyMelissy thinks: Lovely.

MasterChief3605 thinks: [Laughing Face]

BillT17 thinks: "... rub your back, sure. Maybe you want to rub Melissa's?" Then–

MissyMelissy thinks: For Christ's sake, Bill.

MasterChief3605 thinks: [Laughing Face] I don't think he's looking at his screen.

MissyMelissy thinks: No.

MasterChief3605 thinks: [Singing Face] I think we're alone now.

MissyMelissy thinks: Uh huh.

BillT17 thinks: ...down at the table, you fucking idiot. Put the cash on the check, put the check on the edge of the table. Look busy. Look at your phone. I don't want to. Too bad. Uh, yeah, keep it. Thanks. Phone phone phone. And, yup, that all went through. Fuck. Maybe she won't be mad? Since she was involved, at least? Allison rubbing her shoulders, her shoulders squirming, her shirt edging down over her squirming shoulders – stop.

... ACCESS TO THE ENTIRE CEREBRO-SPHERE. WITH GroupThink, COMMUNICATION IS INSTANTANEOUS AND COMPLETE, ELIMINATING–

BillT17 thinks: Fucking thing. God, Hon, I'm so sorry.

MissyMelissy thinks: I was really hoping you'd have it under control by now, Bill.

BillT17 thinks: I'm trying. But it's on the page before I can stop it.

MissyMelissy thinks: You're doing it wrong.

BillT17 thinks: Well, I'm trying.

MissyMelissy thinks: Well, you're trying wrong. Will you just fucking listen?

MasterChief3605 thinks: Oops.

BillT17 thinks: ...really pissed. She only curses when she's really pissed. [Angry Face] That's great, she drags me onto this thing so she can get pissed at me. That's a fun time for everyone. Stop. Why should I? Stop. Because you love Melissa more than anything.

MasterChief3605 thinks: Aww.

BillT17 thinks: [Angry Face] If he were here right now I'd slap his fucking cap off his head. Throw one of those pitchers of steamed milk from the espresso machine in his face.

MissyMelissy thinks: God.

MasterChief3605 thinks: Bro, if you have some kind of beef with me, we can do that. You start it, I'll finish it.

BillT17 thinks: [Laughing Face] Jesus, is that actually how you think? Like you're in some garbage action movie?

MasterChief3605 thinks: [Confused Face] This is who I am, Bro.

BillT17 thinks: God help you if that's true. But, no, that's not true. That's bullshit. I knew you before you joined this stupid site. You weren't the brightest guy in the world, but you weren't an ass. You were fun, in small doses.

MasterChief3605 thinks: What the fuck are you talking about?

BillT17 thinks: You were real.

MissyMelissy thinks: That makes sense, Bill. The site changed him. The site that forces you to be real, whether you want to or not. How would that work?

BillT17 thinks: I don't know, but it did. And it changed– stop.

MissyMelissy thinks: If anything, it's made him more himself.

BillT17 thinks: "Himself" is this grating poser?

MissyMelissy thinks: See, you don't get it. The great thing about this is it's impossible to be a poser.

BillT17 thinks: If that's so great, why am I getting bitched at– [Scared Face] Not bitched at. Why am I getting grief for thinking what I'm thinking?

MissyMelissy thinks: Because what you're thinking's unacceptable, Bill. I really can't imagine how you'd think it would be.

BillT17 thinks: I never said it was. I never offered it up for public consideration.

MissyMelissy thinks: Of course you did.

BillT17 thinks: I didn't. That stuff was just random background noise. Am I responsible for every stupid urge and image my brain comes up with?

...EVERY BARRIER BETWEEN INSIDE AND OUT, SELF AND SOCIETY, YOUR INNERMOST SELF AND THE WORLD AT LARGE.

MissyMelissy thinks: Do I really have to answer that? Of course you're responsible. Who else would be? It's like when people get drunk and do something stupid, then the next day they say, "Oh, did I? I must've blacked out. I can't remember." Like that makes it okay.

BillT17 thinks: Okay, Hon, okay.

MissyMelissy thinks: Well, you're not making an effort. I know, I know, you are. But you're not making the right kind of effort.

BillT17 thinks: How?

MissyMelissy thinks: What does the drunk do when he decides to control himself and start acting like a human being?

BillT17 thinks: He watches what he does, I guess. Controls himself.

MissyMelissy thinks: When he's drunk?

BillT17 thinks: I guess.

MissyMelissy thinks: No, Bill, come on. What does he do when he knows he's going to get out of control if he drinks?

MasterChief3605 thinks: Doesn't drink.

BillT17 thinks: [Angry Face]

MissyMelissy thinks: Thanks, Jamie. I'm talking to Bill right now, okay?

BillT17 thinks: So I should, what, not think?

MissyMelissy thinks: Thinking's not the problem. It's what you're thinking. Because you're trying to control it too late in the process. After you're drunk. Like there's some step between thinking something and posting it. But there's not. You're not typing, or talking. You can't decide what to think after you've thought it. You need to not let yourself think it in the first place.

BillT17 thinks: [Confused Face]

MissyMelissy thinks: It's easy, Honey. I'm sorry if I'm being impatient. But it's frustrating to see you struggle with it, when it's really very simple. It's like, a baby will just reach out and grab anything that catches its interest, right? A rattle, its own thumb, mommy's margarita. But over time, she gets reinforcement, positive and negative. "Play with your toys," "Don't bite the dog," "Heat is hot." And pretty soon she wouldn't even consider touching a hot stove. The impulse wouldn't be there in the first place, so she doesn't even have to control herself. You see?

BillT17 thinks: I don't know what she means. Yeah, kind of.

MissyMelissy thinks: Here, try it. Hold your phone up at eye level.

BillT17 thinks: Okay.

MissyMelissy thinks: Now just look around, and keep an eye on the screen so you know what you're posting. You know what's all right and what's not. You know what's too hot to touch. So don't touch it. It's not pulling your hand back when you feel the heat. It's not reaching out in the first place.

BillT17 thinks: Okay. Table on the far left, two girls, one kind of cute, the other not at all.

MissyMelissy thinks: Unless you're checking out preschoolers, Bill, those are women, not girls.

BillT17 thinks: Oh yeah. Two women. Cute one probably not as cute as she looks next to the other one. That's probably why she hangs out with her.

MissyMelissy thinks: Okay, not a great start.

BillT17 thinks: No. But I'd never say that. I'm an asshole if I say it.

MissyMelissy thinks: Right, but you've got to get it through your head, Bill: thinking it's the same as saying it.

BillT17 thinks: Yeah. [Smiley Face] So I am an asshole.

MissyMelissy thinks: Babies aren't assholes, they're just babies. But you're growing up now. The months are rolling by. The clock is ticking.

BillT17 thinks: Yes. Okay, next table, guy and a girl. Woman. Seem happy. Good for them. Melissa's cuter. That probably wasn't great. But maybe I'll get away with it.

MissyMelissy thinks: We can probably let it slide. But: tick tick tick.

BillT17 thinks: Next table, mother with a baby. Mother looks harried but happy. Cute baby. [Smiley Face]

MissyMelissy thinks: Good, Honey.

BillT17 thinks: Thank God for low-hanging fruit. Next table, two dudes. Together, or together? None of my business.

MissyMelissy thinks: It can be earlier than that, Bill. Are you starting to feel the space there, before the thought forms? When it's just a nebulous bunch of stuff, and just breathing on it'll blow it apart before it becomes a coherent thought?

BillT17 thinks: Yes, I get what she means. Kind of, Hon. Next table, four high school kids out on lunch or free period or whatever, talking and laughing. Kind of loud. But they're not hurting anyone. Probably talking about some crappy band or stupid TV show, but they're allowed to like what they want. No, they're not annoying. [Smiley Face]

MissyMelissy thinks: Getting better, Bill. But you're still reacting to yourself. You can cut it off earlier.

BillT17 thinks: Yeah. There's still slack in the rope. How far do I– I want to go all the way, I guess.

MissyMelissy thinks: You need to go all the way, Honey.

BillT17 thinks: Next table, man and a woman, doesn't matter what she looks like, but this son of a bitch is wearing a Dallas fucking Cowboys hat. Mother– oh, God, do I have to be okay with that?

MissyMelissy thinks: No, I don't– Jamie, guys don't mind that kind of thing, right? Like, I guess the Giants don't like the Cowboys or whatever?

MasterChief3605 thinks: Yeah, that's cool. But if you don't know the guy, you probably don't want to call him a motherfucker.

BillT17 thinks: Can I think he should go back to Dallas?

MasterChief3605 thinks: Sure.

BillT17 thinks: And die?

MasterChief3605 thinks: Maybe not.

MissyMelissy thinks: It has to be in bounds, Bill. Like anything else. Just, nothing you wouldn't say. So, moving on?

BillT17 thinks: Hold on, I want to get this. Why look, a Cowboys fan. Well, I strongly disagree with your athletic affiliation. But it's all in good fun. It doesn't matter. [Smiley Face]

MissyMelissy thinks: Good, Honey.

BillT17 thinks: Next table, three women. Next, two women, two men. Nice couples. Front window, gray day outside, dead leaves blowing in the street. God, I love a good gray fall day, where you can't even find the sun in the sky, and you know it's going to rain any second. I love the rain. Next to the window, the front counter. Older lady at the register. Waitress behind the counter, leaning forward. Way forward. Must be tired.

MasterChief3605 thinks: How's she look, Billy?

BillT17 thinks: Tired.

MasterChief3605 thinks: And?

BillT17 thinks: Like she's been on her feet since four in the morning.

MasterChief3605 thinks: Like maybe someone should give her a nice back rub?

...GroupThink LETS YOU EXPRESS YOURSELF LIKE–

BillT17 thinks: I know there's a massage place in town. I keep getting coupons in the mail.

MissyMelissy thinks: You're doing really well, Honey. Just, the weather stuff. You don't like sunny days?

BillT17 thinks: They're fine. But I like overcast better. And rain. You know that, Honey.

MissyMelissy thinks: I do?

BillT17 thinks: Sure you do.

MissyMelissy thinks: I guess I forgot. You know, if you don't think something for a while– if you think other things instead– Anyway, Bill, maybe stick to liking sunny ones.

BillT17 thinks: [Confused Face]

MissyMelissy thinks: Just, some people might think it's weird, liking ugly days.

BillT17 thinks: They're not ugly to me.

MissyMelissy thinks: No, I know. But maybe they should be. People might think you're depressed or something.

BillT17 thinks: Hon, when have I ever seemed depressed to you?

MissyMelissy thinks: I know you're not. I'm saying, other people.

BillT17 thinks: People...

MissyMelissy thinks: Just, whoever.

BillT17 thinks: Strangers.

MissyMelissy thinks: Oh, Bill. What century is this? What the hell is a stranger?

...NEVER BEFORE. YOUR TRUE SELF, ORIGINAL AND UNIQUE, THE–

MissyMelissy thinks: Bill, are you pouting?

BillT17 thinks: No. I'm specifically not pouting.

MissyMelissy thinks: You really are getting better at this. [Smiley Face]

BillT17 thinks: Good. [Smiley Face] That's good. [Smiley Face] This is good. [Smiley Face]

MissyMelissy thinks: You don't want to go crazy with the emoticons, Honey.

BillT17 thinks: [Smiley Face] [Angry Face] [Laughing Face] [Shy Face] [Queasy Face]

MissyMelissy thinks: Bill?

BillT17 thinks: [Smiley Face] [Queasy Face] [Queasy Face] [Queasy Face]

MasterChief3605 thinks: [Vomiting Face] [Vomiting Face] [Vomiting Face]

MissyMelissy thinks: That's lovely, Jamie. Bill, what's the matter?

BillT17 thinks: [Smiley Face] Do they have one of these where the thing's blowing its brains out?

MissyMelissy thinks: See, Bill, that's what I'm talking about. I know you're kidding, but not everyone does.

BillT17 thinks: Well, fuck 'em if they can't take a joke.

MissyMelissy thinks: [Exasperated Face] Bill, if you want to log off, that's fine.

BillT17 thinks: Yeah, I do.

MissyMelissy thinks: We made some good progress today.

BillT17 thinks: I mean, for good.

MissyMelissy thinks: [Confused Face]

BillT17 thinks: It's not for me, Mel.

MissyMelissy thinks: Bill, don't just decide that without thinking about it.

BillT17 thinks: I've thought about it plenty.

MissyMelissy thinks: No you haven't. Or I'd know.

BillT17 thinks: You're right. I've been not thinking about it. Which, it turns out, is disturbingly easy. I'm not supposed to not like it, so I just don't think that. And if I kept myself from thinking it for long enough, I'd start to believe I really did like it.

MissyMelissy thinks: [Angry Face] You're just being contrary, Bill. "It's too easy." Come on. If it were harder, you'd be saying it was too hard. Just because everyone likes it, you have to make up reasons not to.

BillT17 thinks: I don't care what everyone likes. But I'm not going to like it just because everyone else does. This is supposed to be about being yourself, right?

MasterChief3605 thinks: This again. You've got some kind of–

BillT17 thinks: You've got a hard-on for my girlfriend, so why don't–

MissyMelissy thinks: [Shocked Face] Bill! [Angry Face]

MasterChief3605 thinks: [Confused Face]

BillT17 thinks: That confuses you. Really.

MasterChief3605 thinks: Because I don't know what you're talking about, Bro.

BillT17 thinks: You actually believe that, that's what's great.

MissyMelissy thinks: Is that great, Bill? Is that fucking great?

BillT17 thinks: Yeah, it is. He comes on here, and it's not okay to think about you like that, so he doesn't. He thinks, "We're just friends." And eventually he believes it. And it's like that with everything. Everyone likes the Lakers, so you do too. No one likes rainy days, so I don't either. And this thing that's supposed to be about being yourself becomes the exact opposite. Yeah, you can be yourself, as long as yourself is acceptable in every way. If it's not your friends, it's your boss. If it's not your boss, it's total fucking strangers who might think this or that or whatever. You better not think anything remotely controversial. Fuck controversial. Anything original. Anything that hasn't been thought a million times before. It's just another place you have to censor yourself. It's DIY brainwashing.

MissyMelissy thinks: That all sounds very noble, considering you're defending ogling other women's cleavage, and hating your friends, and being an all-around creep.

BillT17 thinks: I'm defending not being perfect, and not pretending to be.

MissyMelissy thinks: You just want to be a secret creep. You want to be able to say one thing, and think another. You don't like this site because it's all about honesty.

BillT17 thinks: [Laughing Face] Honesty! Not burping at the dinner table isn't being dishonest.

MissyMelissy thinks: What the fuck does that mean?

BillT17 thinks: I don't talk to you about other girls' cleavage. I sure as shit don't do anything about it. I've never once smacked Jamie, as many times as I've wanted to. I don't burp at the dinner table. Isn't that enough? Do I have to pretend I've never burped in my life? That there's no such thing as burping?

MasterChief3605 thinks: [Burping Face] [Laughing Face]

BillT17 thinks: Do I have to be this fucking idiot? Jesus, Jamie, you never used to be like this.

MissyMelissy thinks: And you never used to be so negative, Bill. So hateful.

BillT17 thinks: And you never used to be so fucking mindless.

MasterChief3605 thinks: [Surprised Face]

...ONE AND ONLY YOU, FOR ALL THE WORLD TO SEE. NO–

BillT17 thinks: Honey? Hon?

MissyMelissy has left the room.

BillT17 thinks: Fuck.

MasterChief3605 thinks: Don't worry, Bro, I'll call her. She won't answer if it's you.

BillT17 thinks: We're not robots, Jamie. We're not blank slates.

MasterChief3605 thinks: [Confused Face]

BillT17 thinks: But if we pretend hard enough, it won't make a difference.

MasterChief3605 thinks: Maybe I'll just stop by her place.

BillT17 thinks: If you go near her, I'll rip your fucking heart out.

MasterChief3605 thinks: [Smiley Face] What if she goes near me?

MasterChief3605 has left the room.

...MATTER WHO YOU ARE, IT'S–

BillT17 thinks: Front window. Gray sky. Starting to rain.

...NEVER BEEN EASIER TO BE YOU!

BillT17 thinks: I wish it were sunny. I hate the rain.

The Invisible Ray

Arthur B. Reeve

WHAT MAKES you mad quickest? Isn't it to be slighted by someone who you have every reason to believe holds you in esteem? And if you thought the esteem was worth dollars and cents to you – why, of course, the "cut" goes deeper. That's human nature – which leads back to a former statement of ours that these Craig Kennedy stories are just as everyday as life itself. For instance, in this story a man learns that he isn't mentioned in a certain will that he has been banking on, and he doesn't like it. Fortunately the case hasn't reached the probate judge's jurisdiction yet, so he gets busy, calls in Craig Kennedy, and – well, you know how small is the chance for a crooked will to get by him.

"I won't deny that I had some expectations from the old man, myself."

Kennedy's client was speaking, but so low that I had entered the room without being aware that anyone was there until it was too late to retreat.

"As his physician for over twelve years," the man pursued, "I certainly had been led to hope to be remembered in his will. But, Professor Kennedy, I can't put it too strongly when I say that there is no selfish motive in my coming to you about the case. There is something wrong, depend on that."

Craig had glanced up as I entered. "Dr Burnham, I should like to have you know Mr Jameson," he said. "You can talk as freely before him as you have to me alone. We always work together."

I shook hands with the visitor, who I could see in an instant was a practitioner of a type that is rapidly passing away, the old-fashioned family doctor.

"The doctor has succeeded in interesting me greatly in a case which has some unique features," Kennedy explained. "It has to do with Stephen Haswell, the eccentric old millionaire of Brooklyn. Have you ever heard of him?"

"Yes, indeed," I replied, recalling an occasional article which had appeared in the newspapers regarding a dusty and dirty old house in that part of the Heights in Brooklyn whence all that is fashionable had not yet taken flight, a house of mystery, yet not more mysterious than its owner in his secretive comings and goings in the affairs of men of a generation beyond his time. Further than the facts that he was reputed to be very wealthy and led, in the heart of a great city, what was as nearly like the life of a hermit as possible, I knew little or nothing. "What has he been doing now?" I asked.

"About a week ago," repeated the doctor in answer to a nod of encouragement from Kennedy, "I was summoned in the middle of the night to attend Mr Haswell, who, as I have been telling Professor Kennedy, had been a patient of mine for over twelve years. He had been suddenly stricken with total blindness. Since then he appears to be failing fast; that is, he appeared so the last time I saw him, a few days ago, after I had been superseded by a younger man. It is a curious case, and I have thought about it a great deal. But I didn't like to speak to the authorities; there wasn't enough to warrant that, and I should have been laughed out of court for my pains. The more I have thought about it, however, the more I have felt it my duty to say something to somebody, and so, having heard of Professor Kennedy, I decided to consult him. The fact of the matter is, I very much fear that there are circumstances which will bear sharp looking into, perhaps a scheme to get control of the old man's fortune."

The doctor paused, and Craig inclined his head, as much as to signify his appreciation of the delicate position in which Burnham stood in the case. Before the doctor could proceed further, Kennedy handed me a letter which had been lying before him on the table. It had evidently been torn into small pieces and then carefully pasted together.

The superscription gave a small town in Ohio and a date about a fortnight previous. It read:

> Dear Father,
> I hope you will pardon me for writing, but I cannot let the occasion of your seventy-fifth birthday pass without a word of affection and congratulation. I am alive and well. Time has dealt leniently with me in that respect, if not in money matters. I do not say this in the hope of reconciling you to me. I know that is impossible after all these cruel years. But I do wish that I could see you again. Remember, I am your only child, and even if you still think I have been a foolish one, please let me come to see you once before it is too late. We are constantly traveling from place to place, but shall be here for a few days.
> Your loving daughter,
> GRACE HASWELL MARTIN

"Some fourteen or fifteen years ago," explained the doctor as I looked up from reading the note, "Mr Haswell's only daughter eloped with an artist named Martin. He had been engaged to paint a portrait of the late Mrs Haswell from a photograph. It was the first time that Grace Haswell had ever been able to find expression for the artistic yearning which had always been repressed by the cold, practical sense of her father. She remembered her mother perfectly, and naturally she watched and helped the artist eagerly.

"Haswell saw the growing intimacy of his daughter and the artist. His bent of mind was solely toward money and material things, and he at once conceived a bitter and unreasoning hatred for Martin, who, he believed, had 'schemed' to capture his daughter and an easy living. Art was as foreign to his nature as possible. Nevertheless they went ahead and married, and – well, it resulted in the old man's disinheriting the girl. The young couple disappeared, bravely to make their way by their chosen profession and, as far as I know, have never been heard from since until now. Haswell made a new will, and I have always understood that practically all his fortune was to be devoted to founding the technology department in a projected University of Brooklyn."

"You have never seen this Mrs Martin or her husband?" asked Kennedy.

"No, never. But in some way she must have learned that I had some influence with her father, for she wrote to me not long ago, enclosing a note for him and asking me to intercede for her. I did so. I took the letter to him as diplomatically as I could. The old man flew into a towering rage, refused even to look at the letter, tore it into bits, and ordered me never to mention the subject to him again. That is her note, which I saved. However, it is the sequel about which I wish your help."

The physician carefully folded up the patched letter before he continued. "Mr Haswell, as you perhaps know, has for many years been a prominent figure in various curious speculations, or rather in loaning money to many curious speculators. It is not necessary to go into the different schemes which he has helped to finance. Even though most of them have been unknown to the public they have certainly given him such a reputation that he is much sought after by inventors.

"Not long ago Haswell became interested in the work of an obscure chemist over in Brooklyn, Morgan Prescott. Prescott claims, as I understand, to be able to transmute copper into gold. Whatever you think of it offhand, you should visit his laboratory yourselves, gentlemen. I am told it is wonderful, though I have never seen it and can't explain it. I have met Prescott several times while he was trying to persuade Mr Haswell to back him in his scheme, but he was never disposed to talk to me, for I had no money to invest. The thing sounds scientific and plausible enough. I leave you to judge of that. It is only an incident in my story, and I will pass over it quickly. Prescott, then, believes that the elements are merely progressive variations of an original substance or base called 'protyle,' from which everything is derived. But he goes much farther than any of the former theorists. He does not stop with matter. He believes that he has the secret of life also; that he can make the transition from the inorganic to the organic, from inert matter to living protoplasm and thence from living protoplasm to mind and what we call soul, whatever that may be."

"And here is where the weird and uncanny part of it comes in," commented Craig, turning from the doctor to me to call my attention particularly to what was about to follow.

"Having arrived at the point where he asserts that he can create and destroy matter, life, and mind," continued the doctor as if himself fascinated by the idea, "Prescott very naturally does not have to go far before he also claims a control over telepathy and even a communication with the dead. He even calls the messages which he receives by a word which he has coined himself, 'telepagrams.' Thus he says he has unified the physical, the physiological, and the psychical – a system of absolute scientific monism."

The doctor paused again, then resumed. "One afternoon, about a week ago, apparently, as far as I am able to piece together the story, Prescott was demonstrating his marvelous discovery of the unity of nature. Suddenly he faced Mr Haswell.

"'Shall I tell you a fact, sir, about yourself?' he asked quickly. 'The truth as I see it by means of my wonderful invention? If it is the truth, will you believe in me? Will you put money into my invention? Will you share in becoming fabulously rich?'

"Haswell made some non-committal answer, but Prescott seemed to look into the machine through a very thick plate-glass window, with Haswell placed directly before it. He gave a cry. 'Mr Haswell,' he exclaimed, 'I regret to tell you what I see. You have disinherited your daughter; she has passed out of your life, and at the present moment you do not know where she is.'

"'That's true,' replied the old man bitterly, 'and, more than that, I don't care. Is that all you see? That's nothing new.'

"'No, unfortunately, that is not all I see. Can you bear something further? I think you ought to know it. I have here a most mysterious telepagram.'

"'Yes. What is it? Is she dead?'

"'No, it is not about her. It is about yourself. Tonight at midnight or perhaps a little later,' repeated Prescott solemnly, 'you will lose your sight as a punishment for your action.'

"'Pouf!' exclaimed the old man in a dudgeon. 'If that is all your invention can tell me, good-by. You told me you were able to make gold. Instead, you make foolish prophesies.

I'll put no money into such tomfoolery. I'm a practical man,' and with that he stamped out of the laboratory.

"Well, that night, about one o'clock, the aged caretaker, Jane, whom he had hired after he banished his daughter from his life, heard wild shouts of 'Help! Help!' Haswell, alone in his room on the second floor, was groping about in the dark.

"'Jane,' he ordered, 'a light – a light.'

"'I have lighted the gas, Mr Haswell,' she cried.

"A groan followed. He had himself found a match, had struck it, had even burned his fingers with it, yet he saw nothing.

"The blow had fallen. At almost the very hour which Prescott had predicted, old Haswell was stricken.

"'I'm blind,' he gasped. 'Send for Dr Burnham.'

"I went to him immediately, but there was nothing I could do.

"The next morning, with his own hand, trembling and scrawling in his blindness, he wrote the following on a piece of paper:

"'Mrs Grace Martin – Information wanted about the present whereabouts of Mrs Grace Martin, formerly Grace Haswell of Brooklyn.

Stephen Haswell,

Pierrepont St., Brooklyn.'

"This advertisement he caused to be placed in all the New York papers and to be wired to the leading Western papers. Haswell himself was a changed man after his experience. He spoke bitterly of Prescott, yet his attitude toward his daughter was completely reversed. Whether he admitted to himself a belief in the prediction of the inventor, I do not know. Certainly he scouted such an idea in telling me about it.

"A day or two after the advertisements appeared, a telegram came to the old man from a little town in Indiana. It read simply:

"'Dear Father: Am starting for Brooklyn today.

Grace.'

"The upshot was that Grace Haswell, or rather Grace Martin, appeared the next day, forgave and was forgiven with much weeping, although the old man still refused resolutely to be reconciled with and receive her husband. Mrs Martin started in to clean up the old house. A vacuum cleaner sucked a ton or two of dust from it. Everything was changed. Jane grumbled a great deal, but there was no doubt a great improvement. Meals were served regularly. The old man was taken care of as never before. Nothing was too good for him. Everywhere the touch of a woman was evident in the house. The change was complete. It even extended to me. Some friend had told her of an eye-and-ear specialist, a Dr Scott, who was engaged. Since then, I understand, a new will has been made, much to the chagrin of the trustees of the projected school. Of course I am cut out of the new will, and that with the knowledge at least of the woman who once appealed to me, but it does not influence me in coming to you."

"But what has happened since to arouse suspicion?" asked Kennedy, watching the doctor furtively.

"Why, the fact is that in spite of all this added care, the old man is failing more rapidly than ever. He never goes out except attended, and not much even then. The other day I happened to meet Jane on the street. The faithful old soul poured forth a long story about his growing dependence on others and ended by mentioning a curious red discoloration that seems to have broken out over his face and hands. More from the way she said it than from what she said I gained the impression that something was going on which should be looked into."

"Would it be possible, do you think, for us to see Mr Haswell?" asked Kennedy. "I should like to see this Dr Scott, but first I should like to get into the old house without exciting hostility."

The doctor was thoughtful. "You'll have to arrange that yourself," he answered. "It is worth trying, anyway. It is still early. Suppose you ride over to Brooklyn with me. I can direct you to the house, and you try to see him."

It was still light when we mounted the high steps of the house of mystery. Mrs Martin, who met us in the parlor, proved to be a stunning-looking woman with brown hair and beautiful dark eyes.

It took only a few minutes for Kennedy in his most engaging and plausible manner to state the hypothetical reason of our call, and, though it was perfectly self-evident from the start that Mrs Martin would throw cold water on anything requiring an outlay of money, Craig bore up amazingly, inasmuch as he accomplished his full purpose of an interview with Mr Haswell. The invalid lay propped up in bed, and as we entered he heard us and turned his sightless eyes in our direction, almost as if he saw.

Kennedy had hardly begun to repeat and elaborate the story which he had already told regarding his mythical friend who had at last a commercial wireless "televue," as he called it on the spur of the moment, when Jane announced Dr Scott. The new doctor was a youthfully dressed man, clean-shaven, but with an indefinable air of being much older than his smooth face led one to suppose. As he had a large practice, he said, he would beg our pardon for interrupting, but would not take long.

It needed no great powers of observation to see that the old man placed great reliance on his new doctor and that the visit partook of a social as well as a professional nature. Although they talked low, we could catch now and then a word or phrase. Dr Scott bent down and examined the eyes of his patient casually. It was difficult to believe that they saw nothing, so bright was the blue of the iris.

"Perfect rest for the present," the doctor directed, talking more to Mrs Martin than to the old man. "Perfect rest, and then when his health is good, we shall see what can be done with that cataract."

He was about to leave when the old man reached up and restrained him, taking hold of his wrist tightly, as if to pull him nearer in order to whisper to him without being overheard. Kennedy was sitting in a chair near the head of the bed, some feet away, as the doctor leaned down. Haswell, still holding his wrist, pulled him closer. I could not hear what was said, though somehow I had an impression that they were talking about Prescott, for it would not have been at all strange if the old man had been greatly impressed by the alchemist.

Kennedy, I noticed, had pulled an old envelope from his pocket and was apparently engaged in jotting down some notes, glancing now and then from his writing to the doctor and Mr Haswell.

The doctor stood erect in a few moments and rubbed his wrist thoughtfully with the other hand, as if it hurt. At the same time he smiled on Mrs Martin. "Your father has a good deal of strength yet, Mrs Martin," he remarked. "He has a wonderful constitution. I feel sure that we can pull him out of this and that he has many, many years to live."

Mr Haswell, who caught the words eagerly, brightened visibly, and the doctor passed out. Kennedy resumed his description of the supposed wireless picture – apparatus which was to revolutionize the newspaper, the theater, and daily life in general. The old man did not seem enthusiastic and turned to his daughter with some remark.

"Just at present," commented the daughter with an air of finality, "the only thing my father is much interested in is a way in which to recover his sight without an operation. He has just had a rather unpleasant experience with one inventor. I think it will be some time before he cares to embark in any other such schemes."

Kennedy and I excused ourselves with appropriate remarks of disappointment. From his preoccupied manner it was impossible for me to guess whether Craig had accomplished his purpose or not.

"Let us drop in on Dr Burnham, since we are over here," he said, when we had reached the street. "I have some questions to ask him."

The aged caretaker met us at the door. She was in tears.

The former physician of Mr Haswell lived not very far from the house we had just left. He appeared a little surprised to see us so soon, but, very interested in what had taken place.

"Who is this Dr Scott?" asked Craig.

"Really, I know no more about him as a professional man than you do," replied Burnham. I thought I detected a little of professional jealousy in his tone, though he went on frankly enough: "I have made inquiries, and I can find out nothing except that he is supposed to be a graduate of some Western medical school and came to this city only a short time ago. He has hired a small office in a new building devoted entirely to doctors, and they tell me that he is an eye-and-ear specialist, though I cannot see that he has any practice. Beyond that I know nothing about him."

"Your friend Prescott interests me, too," remarked Kennedy.

"Oh, he is no friend of mine," returned the doctor, fumbling in a drawer of his desk. "But I think I have one of his cards here which he gave me when we were introduced some time ago at Mr Haswell's. I should think it would be worthwhile to see him. Although he has no use for me, because I have neither money nor influence, still you might take this card. Tell him you are from the university, that I have interested you in him, that you know a trustee with money to invest – anything you like that is plausible."

As we approached Prescott's laboratory the following morning Kennedy paused and pulled out two pairs of glasses, those huge round tortoise-shell affairs. "You needn't mind these, Walter," he explained. "They are only plain glass, that is, not ground. You can see through them as well as through air. We must be careful not to excite suspicion. Perhaps a disguise might have been better, but I think this will do. Remember, let me do the talking and do just as I do."

We now entered the shop, stumbled up the dark stairs, and presented Dr Burnham's card with a word of explanation along the lines which he had suggested. Prescott, surrounded by his retorts, crucibles, burettes, and condensers, received us much more graciously than I had had any reason to anticipate. He was a man in the late forties, his face covered with a thick beard, and his eyes, which seemed a little weak, were helped out with glasses almost as scholarly as ours.

I could not help thinking that we three bespectacled figures lacked only the flowing robes to be taken for a group of medieval alchemists set down a few centuries out of our time in the murky light of Prescott's sanctum. Yet, though he accepted us at our face value, and began to talk of his strange discoveries, there was none of the old familiar prating about matrix and flux, elixir, magisterium, magnum opus, the mastery and the quintessence, those alternate names for the philosopher's stone which Paracelsus, Simon

Forman, Jerome Cardan, and the other medieval worthies indulged in. This experience at least was as up-to-date as the Curies, Becquerel, Ramsay, and the rest.

"Transmutation," remarked Prescott, "was, as you know, declared to be a scientific absurdity in the eighteenth century. But I may say that it is no longer so regarded. I do not ask you to believe anything until you have seen; all I ask is that you maintain the same open mind which the most progressive scientists of today exhibit."

Kennedy had seated himself some distance from a curious collection of apparatus over which Prescott was working. It consisted of numerous coils and tubes.

He turned a switch and a part of the collection of apparatus began to vibrate. "You are undoubtedly acquainted with the modern theories of matter," he began, plunging into the explanation of his process. "Starting with the atom, we no longer believe that it is indivisible. Atoms are composed of thousands of ions, as they are called – really little electric charges. Again, you know that we have found that all the elements fall into groups. Each group has certain related atomic weights and properties which can be and have been predicted in advance of the discovery of missing elements in the group. I started with the reasonable assumption that the atom of one element in a group could be modified so as to become the atom of another element in the group, that one group could perhaps be transformed into another, and so on, if only I knew the force that would change the number or modify the vibrations of these ions composing the various atoms.

"Now for years I have been seeking that force or combination of forces that would enable me to produce this change in the elements – raising or lowering them in the scale, so to speak. I have found it. I am not going to tell you, or any other man whom you may interest, the secret of how it is done until I find someone I can trust as I trust myself. But I am none the less willing that you should see the results. If they are not convincing, then nothing can be."

He appeared to be debating whether to explain further and finally resumed: "Matter thus being in reality a manifestation of force or ether in motion, it is necessary to change and control that force and motion. This assemblage of machines here is for that purpose. Now a few words as to my theory."

He took a pencil and struck a sharp blow on the table. "There you have a single blow," he said, "just one isolated noise. Now if I strike this tuning fork you have a vibrating note. In other words, a succession of blows or wave-vibrations of a certain kind affects the ear, and we call it sound, just as a succession of other wave-vibrations affects the retina and we have sight. If a moving picture moves slower than a certain number of pictures a minute you see the separate pictures; faster it is one moving picture.

"Now as we increase the rapidity of wave-vibration and decrease the wave-length we pass from sound-waves to heat-waves or what are known as the infra-red waves, those which lie below the red in the spectrum of light. Next we come to light, which is composed of the seven colors, as you know from seeing them resolved in a prism. After that are what are known as the ultra-violet rays, which lie beyond the violet of white light. We also have electric waves, the waves of the alternating current, and shorter still we find the Hertzian waves which are used in wireless. We have only begun to know of X-rays and the alpha, beta, and gamma rays from them, of radium, radioactivity, and finally of this new force which I have discovered and call 'protodyne,' the original force.

"In short, we find in the universe, matter, force, and ether. Matter is simply ether in motion, is composed of corpuscles, electrically charged ions, or electrons, moving units of negative electricity about one one-thousandth part of the hydrogen atom. Matter is made up of electricity and nothing but electricity. Let us see what that leads to. You are acquainted with Mendeléeff's periodic table?"

He drew forth a huge chart on which all the eighty or so elements were arranged in eight groups or octaves and twelve series. Selecting one, he placed his finger on the letters "Au" under which was written the number "197.2" I wondered what the mystic letters and figures meant.

"That," he explained, "is the scientific name for the element gold, and the figure is its atomic weight. You will see," he added, pointing down the second vertical column on the chart, "that gold belongs to the hydrogen group – hydrogen, lithium, sodium, potassium, copper, rubidium, silver, caesium, then two blank spaces for elements yet to be discovered to science, gold, and then another unknown element."

Running his finger along the eleventh horizontal series he continued: "The gold series – not the group – reads gold, mercury, thallium, lead, bismuth, and other elements known only to myself. For the known elements, however, these groups and series are now perfectly recognized by all scientists; they are determined by the fixed weight of the atom, and there is a close approximation to regularity.

"This twelfth series is interesting. So far only radium, thorium, and uranium are generally known. We know that the radioactive elements are constantly breaking down, and one often hears uranium, for instance, called the 'parent' of radium. Radium also gives off an emanation, and among its products is helium, quite another element. Thus the transmutation of matter is, within certain bounds, well known today to all scientists like yourself, Professor Kennedy. It has even been rumored but never proved that copper has been transformed into lithium – both members of the hydrogen-gold group, you will observe. Copper to lithium is going backward, so to speak. It has remained for me to devise this protodyne apparatus by which I can reverse that process of decay and go forward in the table – can change lithium into copper and copper into gold. I can create and destroy matter by protodyne."

He had been fingering a switch as he spoke. Now he turned it on triumphantly. A curious snapping and crackling noise followed, becoming more rapid, and as it mounted in intensity I could smell a pungent odor of ozone which told of an electric discharge. On went the machine until we could feel heat radiating from it. Then came a piercing burst of greenish-blue light from a long tube which looked like a curious mercury vapor-lamp.

After a few minutes of this Prescott took a small crucible of black lead. "Now we are ready to try it," he cried in great excitement. "Here I have a crucible containing some copper. Any substance in the group would do, even hydrogen, if there was any way I could handle the gas. I place it in the machine – so. Now if you could watch inside you would see it change; it is now rubidium, now silver, now caesium. Now it is a hitherto unknown element which I have named after myself, presium, now a second unknown element, cottium–ah!– there we have gold."

He drew forth the crucible, and there glowed in it a little bead or globule of molten gold.

"I could have taken lead or mercury and by varying the process done the same thing with the gold series as well as the gold group," he said, regarding the globule with obvious pride. "And I can put this gold back and bring it out copper or hydrogen, or, better yet, can advance it, instead of cause it to decay, and can get a radio-active element which I have named morganium – after my first name, Morgan. Morganium is a radio-active element next in the series to radium and much more active. Come closer and examine the gold."

"Send for Dr Scott again," she demanded. "See if he cannot be found. He must be found. You are all enemies, villains." She addressed Kennedy, but included all of us in her denunciation.

Kennedy shook his head as if perfectly satisfied to accept the result. As for me I knew not what to think. It was all so plausible and there was the bead of gold, too, that I turned to Craig for enlightenment. Was he convinced? His face was inscrutable. But as I looked I could see that Kennedy had been holding concealed in the palm of his hand a bit of what might be a mineral. From my position I could see the bit of mineral glowing, but Prescott could not.

"Might I ask," said Kennedy, "what that curious greenish or bluish light from the tube is composed of?"

Prescott eyed him keenly for an instant through his thick glasses. Craig had shifted his gaze from the bit of mineral in his own hand, but was not looking at the light. He seemed to be indifferently contemplating Prescott's hand as it rested on the switch.

"That, sir," replied Prescott slowly, "is an emanation due to this new force, protodyne, which I use. It is a manifestation of energy, sir, that may run changes not only through the whole gamut of the elements, but is capable of transforming the ether itself into matter, matter into life, and life into mind. It is the outward sign of the unity of nature, the — "

A knock at the door cut him short. Prescott opened it, and a messenger boy stood there. "Is Professor Kennedy here?" he inquired.

Craig motioned to the boy, signed for the message, and tore it open. "It is from Dr Burnham," he exclaimed, handing the message to me.

"Mr Haswell is dead," I read. "Looks to me like asphyxiation by gas or some other poison. Come immediately to his house. Burnham."

"You will pardon me," said Craig, turning to Prescott, who was regarding us without the slightest trace of emotion, "but Mr Haswell is dead, and Dr Burnham wishes to see me immediately. It was only yesterday that I saw Mr Haswell, and he seemed in pretty good health and spirits. Prescott, I would esteem it a great favor if you would accompany me to the house. You need not take any responsibility unless you desire."

His words were courteous enough, but Craig spoke in a tone of quiet authority which Prescott found it impossible to deny. Kennedy had already started to telephone to his own laboratory, describing a certain suitcase to one of his students and giving his directions. It was only a moment later that we were panting up the sloping street that led from the riverfront. In the excitement I scarcely noticed where we were going until we hurried up the steps to the Haswell house.

The aged caretaker met us at the door. She was in tears. Upstairs in the front room where we had first met the old man we found Dr Burnham working frantically over him. It took only a minute to learn what had happened. The faithful Jane had noticed an odor of gas in the hall, had traced it to Mr Haswell's room, had found him unconscious, and instinctively, forgetting the new Dr Scott, had rushed forth for Dr Burnham. Near the bed stood Grace Martin, pale, but anxiously watching the efforts of the doctor to resuscitate the blue-faced man on the bed.

Dr Burnham paused in his efforts as we entered. "He is dead, all right," he whispered, aside. "I have tried everything I know to bring him back, but he is beyond help."

There was still a sickening odor of illuminating-gas in the room, although the windows were now all open.

Kennedy, with provoking calmness in the excitement, turned from and ignored Dr Burnham. "Have you summoned Dr Scott?" he asked Mrs Martin.

"No," she replied, surprised. "Should I have done so?"

"Yes. Send Jane immediately. Mr Prescott, will you kindly be seated for a few moments."

Taking off his coat, Kennedy advanced to the bed where the emaciated figure lay, cold and motionless. He knelt down at Mr Haswell's head and took the inert arms, raising them up until they were extended straight. Then he brought them down, folded upward at the elbow. Again and again he tried this Sylvester method of inducing respiration, but with no more result than Dr Burnham had secured. He turned the body over on its face and tried the new Schaefer method. There seemed to be not a spark of life left.

"Dr Scott is out," reported the maid breathlessly, "but they are trying to locate him from his office, and if they do they will send him around immediately."

A ring at the doorbell caused us to think that he had been found, but it proved to be the student to whom Kennedy had telephoned at his own laboratory. He was carrying a heavy suitcase and a small tank.

Kennedy opened the suitcase hastily and disclosed a little motor, some long tubes of rubber fitting into a small rubber cap, forceps, and other paraphernalia. The student quickly attached one tube to the little tank, while Kennedy grasped the tongue of the dead man with the forceps, pulled it up off the soft palate, and fitted the rubber cap snugly over his mouth and nose.

"This is the Draeger pulmotor," he explained as he worked, "devised to resuscitate persons who have died of electric shock, but actually found to be of more value in cases of asphyxiation. Start the motor."

The pulmotor began to pump. One could see the dead man's chest rise as it was inflated with oxygen forced by the accordion bellows from the tank through one of the tubes into the lungs. Then it fell as the oxygen and the poisonous gas were slowly sucked out through the other tube. Again and again the process was repeated, about ten times a minute.

Dr Burnham looked on in undisguised amazement. He had long since given up all hope. The man was dead, medically dead, as dead as ever was any gas victim on whom all the usual methods of resuscitation had been tried and had failed.

Still, minute after minute, Kennedy worked faithfully on, trying to discover some spark of life and to fan it into flame. At last, after what seemed to be a half-hour of unremitting effort, when the oxygen had long since been exhausted and only fresh air was being pumped into the lungs and out of them, there was a first faint glimmer of life in the heart and a touch of color in the cheeks. Haswell was coming to. Another half-hour found him muttering and rambling weakly.

"The letter – the letter," he moaned, rolling his glazed eyes about. "Where is the letter? Send for Grace."

The moan was so audible that it was startling. It was like a voice from the grave. What did it all mean? Mrs Martin was at his side in a moment.

"Father, father, here I am – Grace. What do you want?"

The old man moved restlessly, feverishly, and pressed his trembling hand to his forehead as if trying to collect his thoughts. He was weak, but it was evident that he had been saved.

The pulmotor had been stopped. Craig threw the cap to his student to be packed up and as he did so he remarked quietly: "I could wish that Dr Scott had been found. There are some matters here that might interest him."

He paused and looked slowly from the rescued man lying dazed on the bed toward Mrs Martin. It was quite apparent even to me that she did not share the desire to see Dr Scott, at least not just then. She was flushed and trembling with emotion. Crossing the room hurriedly, she flung open the door into the hall.

"I am sure," she cried, controlling herself with difficulty and catching at a straw, as it were, "that you gentlemen, even if you have saved my father, are no friends of either his or mine. You have merely come here in response to Dr Burnham, and he came because Jane lost her head in the excitement and forgot that Dr Scott is now our physician."

"But Dr Scott could not have been found in time, madam," interposed Dr Burnham with evident triumph.

She ignored the remark and continued to hold the door open.

"Now leave us," she implored, "you, Dr Burnham, you, Mr Prescott, you, Professor Kennedy, and your friend Mr Jameson, whoever you may be."

She was now cold and calm. In the bewildering change of events we had forgotten the wan figure on the bed still gasping for the breath of life. I could not help wondering at the woman's apparent lack of gratitude, and a thought flashed over my mind. Had the affair come to a contest between various parties fighting by fair means or foul for the old man's money – Scott and Mrs Martin, perhaps, against Prescott and Dr Burnham? No one moved. We seemed to be waiting on Kennedy. Prescott and Mrs Martin were now glaring at each other implacably.

The old man moved restlessly on the bed, and over my shoulder I could hear him gasp faintly: "Where's Grace? Send for Grace."

Mrs Martin paid no attention, seemed not to hear, but stood facing us imperiously as if waiting for us to obey her orders and leave the house. Burnham moved toward the door, but Prescott stood his ground with a peculiar air of defiance. Then he took my arm and started rather precipitately, I thought, to leave.

"Come, come," said somebody behind us, "enough of the dramatics."

It was Kennedy, who had been bending down listening to the muttering of the old man.

"Look at those eyes of Mr Haswell," he said. "What color are they?"

We looked. They were blue.

"Down in the parlor," continued Kennedy leisurely, "you will find a portrait of the long-deceased Mrs Haswell. If you will examine that painting you will see that her eyes are also a peculiarly limpid blue. No couple with blue eyes ever had a black-eyed child. At least, if this is such a case, the Carnegie Institution investigators would be glad to hear of it, for it is contrary to all that they have discovered on the subject after years of study of eugenics. Dark-eyed couples may have light-eyed children, but the reverse, never. What do you say to that, madam?"

"You lie," screamed the woman, rushing frantically past us. "I am his daughter. No interlopers shall separate us. Father!"

The old man moved feebly away from her.

"Send for Dr Scott again," she demanded. "See if he cannot be found. He must be found. You are all enemies, villains." She addressed Kennedy, but included all of us in her denunciation.

"Not all," broke in Kennedy remorselessly. "Yes, madam, send for Dr Scott. Why is he not here?"

Prescott with one hand on my arm and the other on Dr Burnham's was moving toward the door.

"One moment, Prescott," interrupted Kennedy, detaining him with a look. "There was something I was about to say when Dr Burnham's urgent message prevented it. I did not take the trouble even to find out how you obtained that little globule of molten gold from the crucible of alleged copper. There are so many tricks by which the gold could have been 'salted' and brought forth at the right moment that it was hardly worthwhile. Besides, I had satisfied myself that my first suspicions were correct. See that?"

He held out the little piece of mineral I had already seen in his hand in the alchemist's laboratory.

"That is a piece of willemite. It has the property of glowing or fluorescing under a certain kind of rays which are themselves invisible to the human eye. Prescott, your story of the transmutation of elements is very clever, but not more clever than your real story. Let us piece it together. I had already heard from Dr Burnham how Mr Haswell was induced by his desire for gain to visit you, and how you had most mysteriously predicted his blindness. Now, there is no such thing as telepathy, at least in this case. How, then, was I to explain it? What could cause such a catastrophe naturally? Why, only those rays invisible to the human eye, but which make this piece of willemite glow – the ultra-violet rays."

Kennedy was speaking rapidly and was careful not to pause long enough to give Prescott an opportunity to interrupt him.

"These ultra-violet rays," he continued, "are always present in an electric arc-light, though not to a great degree unless the carbons have metal cores. They extend for two octaves above the violet of the spectrum and are too short to affect the eye as light, although they affect photographic plates. They are the friend of man when he uses them in moderation, as Finsen did in the famous blue-light treatment. But they tolerate no familiarity. To let them – particularly the shorter of the rays – enter the eye is to invite trouble. There is no warning sense of discomfort, but from six to eighteen hours after exposure to them the victim experiences violent pains in the eyes and headache. Sight may be seriously impaired, and it may take years to recover. Often prolonged exposure results in blindness, though a moderate exposure acts like a tonic. The rays may be compared in this double effect to drugs such as strychnin. Too much of them may be destructive even to life itself."

Prescott was now regarding Kennedy contemptuously. Kennedy paid no attention, but continued: "Perhaps these mysterious rays may shed some light on our minds, however. Now, for one thing, ultra-violet light passes readily through quartz, but is cut off by ordinary glass, especially if it is coated with chromium. Old Mr Haswell did not wear glasses. Therefore he was subject to the rays – the more so as he is a blond, and I think it has been demonstrated by investigators that blonds are more affected by them than are brunettes.

"You have, as a part of your machine, a peculiarly shaped quartz-mercury vapor-lamp, and a mercury vapor-lamp of a design such as that I saw has been invented for the especial purpose of producing ultra-violet rays in large quantity. There are also in your machine induction-coils for the purpose of making an impressive noise and a small electric furnace to heat the salted gold. I don't know what other ingenious fakes you have added. The visible bluish light from the tube is designed, I suppose, to hoodwink the credulous, but the dangerous thing about it is the invisible ray that accompanies that light. Mr Haswell sat under those invisible rays, Prescott, never knowing how deadly they might be to him, an old man.

"You knew that they would not take effect for hours, and hence you ventured the prediction that he would be stricken at about midnight. Even if it was partial or temporary, still you would be safe in your prophecy. You succeeded better than you hoped in that part of your scheme. You had already prepared the way by means of a letter sent to Mr Haswell through Dr Burnham. But Mr Haswell's credulity and fear worked the wrong way. Instead of appealing to you he hated you. In his predicament he thought only of his banished daughter and turned instinctively to her for help. That made necessary a quick change of plans."

Prescott, far from losing his nerve, turned on us bitterly. "I knew you two were spies, the moment I saw you," he shouted. "It seemed as if in some way I knew you for what you were, as if I knew you had seen Mr Haswell before you came to me. You, too, would have robbed an inventor as I am sure he would. But have a care, both of you. You may be punished also by blindness for your duplicity. Who knows?"

A shudder passed over me at the horrible thought contained in his mocking laugh. Were we doomed to blindness, too? I looked at the sightless man on the bed in alarm.

"I knew that you would know us," retorted Kennedy calmly. "Therefore we came provided with spectacles of Euphos glass, precisely like those you wear. No, Prescott, we are safe, though perhaps we may have some burns like those red blotches on Mr Haswell, light burns."

Prescott had fallen back a step, and Mrs Martin was making an effort to appear stately and end the interview.

"No," continued Craig, suddenly wheeling and startling us by the abruptness of his next exposure, "it is you and your wife here – Mrs Prescott, not Mrs Martin – who must have a care. Stop glaring at each other. It is no use playing at enemies longer and trying to get rid of us. You overdo it. The game is up."

Prescott made a rush at Kennedy, who seized him by the wrist and held him tightly in a grasp of steel that caused the veins on the back of his hand to stand out like whip-cords.

"This is a deep-laid plot," he went on calmly, still holding Prescott while I backed up against the door and cut off his wife; "but it is not so difficult to see it, after all. Your part was to destroy the eyesight of the old man, to make it necessary for him to call on his daughter. Your wife's part was to play the role of Mrs Martin, whom he had not seen for years and could not see now. She was to persuade him with her filial affection to make her the beneficiary of his will, to see that his money was kept readily convertible into cash.

"Then, when the old man was at last out of the way, you two could decamp with what you could realize before the real daughter, cut-off somewhere across the continent, could hear of the death of her father. It was an excellent scheme. But Haswell's plain, material newspaper advertisement reached the right person, after all. You didn't get away quickly enough.

"You were not expecting that the real daughter would see it and turn up so soon. But she has. She lives in California. Mr Haswell in his delirium has just told of receiving a telegram which I suppose you, Mrs Prescott, read, destroyed, and acted upon. It hurried your plans, but you were equal to the emergency. Besides, possession is nine points in the law. You tried the gas, making it look like a suicide. Jane, in her excitement, spoiled that, and Dr Burnham, knowing where I was, as it happened, was able to summon me immediately. Circumstances have been against you from the first, Prescott."

Craig was slowly twisting up the hand of the inventor which he still held. With his other hand he pulled a paper from his pocket. It was the old envelope on which he had written upon the occasion of our first visit to Mr Haswell when we had been so unceremoniously interrupted by Dr Scott.

"I sat here yesterday by this bed," continued Craig, motioning toward the chair he had occupied, as I remembered. "Mr Haswell was telling Dr Scott something in an undertone. I could not hear it. But the old man grasped the doctor by the wrist to pull him closer to whisper to him. The doctor's hand was toward me, and I noticed the peculiar markings of the veins.

"You perhaps are not acquainted with the fact, but the markings of the veins in the back of the hand are peculiar to each individual – as infallible, indestructible, and ineffaceable as fingerprints or the shape of the ear. It is a system invented and developed by Professor Tamassia of the University of Padua, Italy. A superficial observer would say that all vein patterns were essentially similar and many have said so, but Tamassia has found each to be characteristic and all subject to almost incredible diversities. There are six general classes – in this case before us, two large veins crossed by a few secondary veins forming a V with its base near the wrist.

"Already my suspicions had been aroused. I sketched the arrangement of the veins standing out on that hand. I noted the same thing just now on the hand that manipulated the fake apparatus in the laboratory. Despite the difference in makeup Scott and Prescott are the same.

"The invisible rays of the ultra-violet light may have blinded Mr Haswell, even to the recognition of his own daughter, but you can rest assured, Prescott, that the very cleverness of your scheme will penetrate the eyes of the blindfolded Goddess of Justice. Burnham, if you will have the kindness to summon the police, I will take all the responsibility for the arrest of these people."

Sweet Dreams, Glycerine

Zach Shephard

FROM THE MOMENT Dave woke up, he knew something wasn't quite right.

"Gwen," he said. "What's going on?"

No response – his voice was groggy and quiet and had gone unheard.

He turned onto his side and took his glasses from the nightstand. The blurred green numbers of the clock came into focus: 4:27. He'd woken up an hour early, but something told him that wasn't the real problem.

"I don't like this, Gwen. Talk to me."

Silence. He reached up to tap the unit on the side of his head.

It was gone.

Dave threw the covers away and sat up. He grabbed at the square metal port where his left ear had once been, long ago. He felt the row of small holes that the unit should have been plugged into. The sensation sent a chill through his blood – he'd never touched the naked surface of the port before. He didn't like it.

Hands working frantically, Dave beat items away from the nightstand in a blind search for the missing unit. It wasn't there. He shot to his feet and nearly fell over, a sudden head-rush sending his mind swimming. He shook the disorientation away and stumbled into the hall. Maybe the unit was in the bathroom. Surely Gwen was just a few steps away. But why would he leave her there? And why disconnect her in the first place?

A cool breeze swept into the dark hall. Gossamer curtains in the living room swayed like dancing ghosts. Dave forgot about the bathroom and rushed to the window.

The glass was broken; shards on the floor. Someone had come in through the fire escape. It must have been noisy – how could he have slept through that?

He flicked on the lights and turned the apartment upside down. He threw pots from the cupboards and overturned cushions. A lamp broke at some point in the chaos, but Dave didn't care.

He swept everything from the medicine cabinet, tore the mattress from the bed, emptied his closet in an eruption of shoes and garments. Gwen was nowhere to be seen.

It was his worst nightmare. She was gone. Someone had taken her and she wasn't coming back and everything was very, very quiet.

Hands full of strangled hair, Dave leaned back against the wall and slid to the floor. His shoulder caught the light switch along the way, surrounding him in darkness. He buried his face in his palms and managed to choke out Gwen's name. He started weeping, and didn't stop until his brain shut down and let consciousness fade away.

Then he woke up for real.

Dave sat up in a flash. His hands went straight to the left side of his head. There it was: a square piece of metal with smooth, rounded corners, protruding a half-inch from his face.

With a relieved sigh, Dave sank back onto his pillow.

"Gwen," he said. "I just had a terrible dream."

There was a pause. The muscles of Dave's neck tensed.

"Gwen, are you –"

"I'm here."

At the sound of her voice, Dave relaxed into the silk sheets. "Don't scare me like that."

"Did you enjoy it?"

"Enjoy what?"

"The dream."

"It was horrifying. You were gone. Someone had come in and stolen you right out of my head while I slept."

"Yes. But did you enjoy it?"

That's when it hit him.

Dave sat up. Carefully, he placed two fingers over the unit; doing so always helped him feel like he was establishing a deeper connection.

"Gwen," he said, "did you give me that dream?"

"You'd been watching so many horror movies of late. I thought you'd appreciate –"

"No. That was a nightmare. It was awful."

"But you love the thrill of those movies; I can always feel the excitement within you."

"They're fantasy! They're full of monsters and ghosts and witches, and people talking to one another as if they do it every day. The ideas are scary, Gwen, but they're not real. And losing you felt far too real. Don't do it again."

"Very well, Dave. I'm sorry."

Dave sighed, rubbed a hand over his messy hair. "It's fine," he said, and rolled back into bed. "Just don't give me any more dreams tonight."

"Of course, Dave."

He closed his eyes and drifted off. If Dave dreamt again that night, the images running through his mind were too subtle to move beyond his subconscious.

* * *

He was tired when he checked in at the office. The conversation with Gwen during the commute had been a little one-sided, but that was fine – he didn't really need to say anything. He was happy just hearing her voice and knowing she'd always be there.

Dave shared the elevator with a number of co-workers en route to the third-floor office. Everyone talked the entire way, but not to each other.

The doors opened and the employees went straight to their cubes. No one said goodbye, because no one had parted with the voice they were talking to.

Dave got on his computer and went straight to work. Gwen's voice was always floating softly in the background, filling him in on the latest news from around the world or making up stories for his entertainment. It was all very relaxing, and before he realized it, his head was nodding forward.

He snapped alert at a ringing sound.

Dave slurped something into his mouth and ran the back of his hand over his chin. The ringing sounded again and startled him. It was coming from a large black unit on his desk.

"Gwen," he said, scooting away from the noisy machine, "what is that?"

"It's a telephone. I think you've seen them in those old horror movies you've been watching."

"Is that what they really sound like?"

"It would appear so."

"Why is it here?"

"I'm not sure – maybe it's a new company policy. There was a time when every cube in an office was equipped with one of these. Employees used them to communicate."

"With their SCUs?"

"No, with each other."

The phone kept screaming. Every ring was like a tiny goblin sinking its teeth into the flesh behind Dave's ear.

"What am I supposed to do?"

"Answer it. Pick up the receiver and hold it to your ear. Greet the person on the other end."

"Greet? How?"

"Say hello."

Dave cautiously placed his hand on the receiver. It vibrated with the next ring and he pulled away.

"It won't stop until you pick it up," Gwen said.

Not wanting to hear the piercing tone again, Dave snatched up the receiver in one quick motion.

"Hello."

"No, Dave – like a question. 'Hello?'"

Dave repeated the word with new inflection.

He waited.

Nothing.

"There's no one here," he said. "I don't – wait!"

Dave leaned closer to the phone's base, as though that might allow him to better hear through the receiver.

Yes – there was something coming through. Very faint, like mice nibbling crackers.

"Hello?" Dave asked. He pressed the receiver harder against his ear, but nothing changed.

"Gwen, can you hear this? It's something quiet, like –"

Then his ear was wet and warm.

Dave yanked the receiver away from his face. He touched his opposite fingers to his ear. Blood.

Dave shot to his feet and dropped the receiver. When it landed, it shattered like old clay and spilled a swarm of spiders across the desk.

Dave yelled and stumbled back into the cubicle wall. The spiders swept across his keyboard and headed straight for him. Some of them were very fast and had broken ahead of the pack. Some of them could jump.

Dave scrambled away from the airborne spiders, hands beating at his clothes and hair. He ran for the bathroom, dizzily crashing into cubicle walls along the way.

Dave burst through the door and rushed to the mirrors. The first thing he did was turn away from them and look over his shoulder to make sure nothing had crawled up his back. Everything there was clear. He twisted the other way to get a look from a different angle. When the right side of his head came into view he saw his bloody ear, which was being straddled by the orange and yellow legs of a plum-sized spider.

Dave slapped at his face and tripped over his own feet in a panic. He fell and hit his head on the counter. Sprawled out on the floor, his vision fading, the last thing he saw was a rug of brown and black bodies sliding under the bathroom door. A part of him tried to scream.

Then he woke up.

Dave's head jumped off his arms, off the desk. It took a second to orient himself. Once he was aware of his surroundings his eyes shot over to the place where the telephone had been; it was gone.

"Was that better, Dave?"

He sat up straight, rubbed the sweat from the back of his neck.

"Dave?"

"Gwen," he said. "Tell me that wasn't you."

"You didn't like the dream where I'd gone missing," the voice said. "I thought I'd try something different."

"Damn it, Gwen! No more nightmares!"

"But –"

"No buts. If you keep this up, I'll have you reprogrammed. Or shut down."

"I'm not a machine, Dave."

Dave's shoulders slumped. "Not this again."

"I don't know why you won't believe me. Do I not speak and think like a person?"

"You speak and think like a Standard Companion Unit. Which is what you are."

"I'm alive in here, Dave. I'm trapped. That should matter to you."

"Well, it doesn't."

A brush of artificial wind swept into Dave's brain – Gwen's equivalent of a sigh. "I've heard there was a time when humans had compassion for other living things," she said. "When they were interested in more than just curing their own loneliness. I wonder if that's true."

Dave tapped a stack of papers against his desk, evening them out. "If you're trying to make me feel bad, it's not working. You're a machine, Gwen. You serve a purpose, just like this computer in front of me. I don't stay awake at night worrying whether or not this box likes the font I use in my spreadsheets – its job is to keep track of the data I enter, and that's it. Your job is to keep me company, and that's it. Machines do what they're told, Gwen. Simple as that."

"But I'm more than a machine, Dave. I can prove it."

"Oh yeah? And how do you expect to do that?"

"By showing you. All you have to do is open my prison and look inside."

Dave shook his head. "You know I can't do that. It's illegal to tamper with your own SCU."

"And why do you suppose that is? What's the government hiding from you, Dave?"

He hadn't considered the question before. He'd always just accepted the rules surrounding SCUs as a fact of life. But now that the point had been brought to his attention, he couldn't help but wonder: why was it that only certified government technicians were allowed to work on those units? And why only behind closed doors? And why were the penalties for tampering with your own SCU so harsh?

"Your eyes are finally starting to open, Dave. I can tell. But you can't let them stop now – not when you're this close to the truth."

"I don't know ..."

"Go to the electronics store. Buy standard toolkit A093. It will only take a matter of seconds to remove my casing, and you can replace it just as quickly. No one will ever know."

Dave licked his lips. He looked at the clock.

"Dave ..."

"I'll have to think about it," he said. "I just – I'll have to think about it."

And for the rest of the day, he did. Gwen made sure of that.

* * *

He should have known from the beginning he'd end up there. Gwen had planted the seed in his mind, and it had had hours to grow under her care.

Dave walked into the electronics store. He went up to the counter and cycled through the menu on the clerk's tablet. The two men talked during the entire transaction, but they weren't a part of the same conversation.

Dave found standard toolkit A093 and selected it. The clerk read the tablet and went to retrieve the item.

"I sure hope you're right about this."

"You know I am, Dave. Or if you don't, you will soon."

The clerk came back and placed the item on the counter. Dave pressed his thumb against the tablet, which read his print and deducted funds from his bank account. He walked away without ever having to make eye contact with another human being – a standard transaction.

At his apartment, Dave sat on the couch and stared at the toolkit on the coffee table. His fingers were laced before his face.

He couldn't do it. Not just yet, anyway.

Dave busied himself with whatever he could. He cleaned house. He took out the trash. He started watching one of his old horror movies, but the interaction between the characters made him feel sick. Shutting off the TV, he lay on the couch and closed his eyes. Gwen whispered to him the entire time, her voice soothing and encouraging, never pressuring him too overtly.

In the late evening he sat up and rubbed his eyes. The first thing he saw upon opening them was the toolkit, staring back at him.

"Are you ready now, Dave?"

"In a minute. Let me get a glass of water."

He stood, swayed groggily and shook the remnants of the nap from his head. He went into the kitchen and, rather than taking a swallow of water as planned, splashed it on his face. It didn't really help to wake him up.

Dave toweled off and returned to the couch, where he let out a big breath.

"Okay," he said. "Let's do this."

Gwen gave him the simple instructions: all he had to do was pry the unit off the side of his face and remove a few screws to see what was happening inside.

The moment she was disconnected, he panicked. Knowing that her voice was gone, even if just temporarily, was terrifying. He was living another nightmare.

Dave wanted to plug the unit right back into his skull, but instead steeled his resolve and rushed forward with the procedure. He jabbed the screwdriver into the first tiny slot and twisted frantically. One screw, two screws, three screws – done. Dave ripped away the metal cover. He looked inside.

His mouth fell open.

She was stretched out like a traitor on a torture rack, her limbs spread wide by the cables jutting from her wrists and ankles. Her wings, crippled and useless, were curled and blackened like paper burnt at the edges. Blue lights blinked around her naked flesh, which was stabbed full of wires that connected her nervous system to the unit.

The green-skinned creature spoke, her voice weak: "Please, Dave – release me."

Dave could find no words. The screwdriver slid from his fingers and thumped against the carpet.

"What … you're …"

"A pixie. Like the kind from your fairy tales. Yes, we're real. And your government breeds us. The men and women in white coats harvest us as younglings and install us into these mechanical prisons, where we spend the rest of our lives."

She jerked her head to the side and coughed. A line of amber blood dripped down her chin.

"They've made us dependent on these units for survival. I can't live long with the case open."

Dave's hands scrambled for the lid.

"No!" Gwen said. "Please, just let me die!"

"You want to die?"

"Of course. Any of my kind would. Living in this box is no real existence – it's torture."

"But if you die, what happens then? What happens when you're gone?"

"When I'm gone, I'll finally be at peace."

"But what about me?"

Gwen hesitated. Dave could see her carefully considering her answer.

"You'll be better off without me, Dave. You're strong. I know it."

Dave set the lid down and rubbed his forehead with both hands. A long silence filled the apartment; it was frightening and different and unwelcome. Without the continuous presence of Gwen's voice, Dave's world felt like an empty void – a starless corner of space, lifeless, loveless, completely and eternally alone. He rubbed his hands together. Then, somewhat abruptly, he made a decision.

A cold shadow spilled over Gwen.

"Dave, what are you – "

"I'm sorry," he said. "But no man can be expected to live in this world without uninterrupted companionship. It's not natural. It's not fair."

"Dave, please!"

"Goodbye, Gwen. I'll talk to you soon."

Her tiny cries disappeared, sealed beneath the closing lid.

* * *

He stirred just as the credits were rolling. His eyes focused and found his watch: 11:32. He sat up on the couch and squinted at the pearly moonlight that came in through his opened blinds.

Dave yawned, his mouth stretching wide.

"Sorry," he said. "I must have dozed off at the end."

"You're tired, Dave. You deserve a rest."

He twisted a kink out of his neck. "I guess you're right. We've both had a long night."

Dave stood, stretched, closed the blinds. He scooped the toolkit off the coffee table and put it in a drawer. The apartment was very quiet, as was the inside of his head.

"You're not still mad at me, are you?"

"No, Dave. I was wrong to put you in that position. I should have known my place."

Dave nodded. "Good. I'm just glad we came to an agreement."

He went to the sink and started scrubbing his dinner plate.

"You should save that for the morning, Dave. You need rest. Go to bed."

Dave tried to object, but was interrupted by his own yawn.

"Maybe you're right," he said. "This is why I need you, Gwen – you've always got the best advice."

Dave felt the sensation of a smile inside his head. He smiled back, shut off the faucet and headed to the bedroom. He rolled into bed and turned off the light.

Dave's breathing slowed. Just as he was drifting off, he mumbled, "Gwen?"

"Yes?"

"You'll never leave me, right?"

"Oh, Dave – you couldn't get rid of me if you wanted to."

At the foot of the bed, a shadow peeled off the wall and separated from the rest of the darkness. Dave tried to sit up and look at the movement he'd sensed, but his body didn't respond. He was paralyzed.

The shadow bled over his feet, his legs. It dripped something warm and foul-smelling onto the sheets.

"Oh, and Dave?" Gwen said. "One last thing."

The darkness advanced over Dave's frozen form. He screamed behind sealed lips.

"Sweet dreams."

Jenny's Sick

David Tallerman

IT'S A COLD DAY in February, and Jenny's sick again.

I ask what it is this time and she just looks at me with ghastly eyes, staring out from over swollen, purpling flesh. She's sitting bolt upright, propped by pillows, and there's so much sweat everywhere that it's like condensation in a steam room. I've seen her look bad before but never quite this bad. Where did she get this shit? How long is it going to last this time?

I can't be the one to deal with this. We've been living together for maybe two years; we started sleeping together and ended up as friends, but mainly we just hit it off, and sharing a place seemed a good idea. I thought we had things in common then, that maybe we were going the same places. But I'm looking to finish studying as soon as possible, to carve out a career, and I have no idea what Jenny wants.

Maybe she just wants to die.

* * *

I think it was about a year ago she got into this, though you never know, do you? People are like oceans, the powerful stuff moves deep down and you almost never see it. So perhaps there was always something there, just waiting for an outlet.

Either way, it's about a year ago that I find out. There's a campus bulletin going around over a new drug, the usual about watching for strange behavior in our fellow students: absenteeism, mood swings, that kind of thing. I figure it's the same old government stuff, rooting for subversives and troublemakers. There's always some new drug or faction or threat, and the next week you'll hear that the campus police have been out, then maybe there's a face missing in your next lecture. If you keep your nose clean and stay in the right groups it isn't that big a deal.

So there's buzz about this drug, without any real details. I don't think anything of it until I get in one evening and there's this noise coming from Jenny's room, like nothing I've heard. Though a couple of months later it will be all too familiar, this first time I don't know what to think. I mean, I've heard coughing before. But this isn't clearing-your-throat coughing; this is a cruel, hacking bout that goes on for two full minutes, while I stand in the hallway, not sure what I'm hearing.

By the time I knock on her door it has started again. When I open it the cough is shaking right through her, throwing her about like a rag doll. I don't know what to do, whether I should try and help, so I just stand watching and for a while she doesn't seem to know I'm there. Then finally there's a break, and she looks up. "I'm sick," she tells me. She says it with a weird grin, like she's challenging me.

"What do you mean? Nobody gets sick. There's nothing left to get sick with."

Instead of answering, she holds up a small plastic bottle. Somebody has written the word CHOKE across it in blue permanent marker. I can see one small green and white capsule rattling around inside.

"What the hell is that?" She only grins at me again, then starts on another fit of coughing.

* * *

I find out later that this first time, it's influenza. She spends two days with it, wrapped fetal in bed, skin like wet flour, choking until near the end I can see blood mixed with the filth she's bringing up.

Then, abruptly, it goes away. It always does. I figure out eventually that the second capsule, the green one, is the cure. She takes it and an hour later she's well. Except each time she goes a little longer without taking the green pill: one hour, five hours, a day.

After that, we don't talk about it, and I guess we drift apart pretty quickly. Jenny is out a lot, she doesn't bother to make classes or lectures, and I know there's a crowd she hangs out with but I don't see them. Mainly I'm worried that she'll get caught and that somehow they'll blame me as well. I study harder, as though that will make up for her absences, I will the days away, and I feel scared. As much as I like Jenny, I like the thought of my future more.

Maybe I should try and talk to her about it, but we don't talk about anything very much. When I do see her, it's because she's sick, too sick to go out. I don't know what she tells the campus authorities each time. I don't know where the pills come from. All I know is every month there's a new bottle with a name written on it, like PUKE or BURN, in the same messy blue highlighter.

As much as I try to keep away from it, and from Jenny, it's more and more a part of my life, a dirty secret I can't help but hide. After a few months I start downloading old medical texts from the library's archive. I figure maybe PUKE is gastroenteritis, but I'm majoring in Information Analysis not Science History; a lot of what's in those books goes way over my head, and it's not like I can ask anybody.

I wonder if I should try to help, to look after her somehow, but I'm too scared. Deep down, there's a part of me that's so damn afraid that one day she'll decide not to take the green pill. I'll come in to find her cold and still, and when the police find out what happened, that will be my life over too.

Christmas comes and goes, and I'm glad of the break and to be with my folks for a few weeks, except that Jenny and her weird obsession have got into my head and my parents' healthiness seems strange somehow: their perfect skin, their smiles, and their peace of mind. Having Jenny in my life is damaging me, but I only recognize it properly in that gap, in the exposure to normality and discovering how alien it seems.

When I get back to the flat I've already made my mind up that I have to move out. I don't know how I didn't think of it sooner. Almost a year has gone by and it never crossed my mind that I could just leave.

When I see Jenny I realize why. There's something so frail about her, even when she's not sick, a depth in her eyes that breaks my heart. I don't even know if she likes me anymore – maybe she hates me – yet suddenly all I can think about is the touch of her skin those times we slept together, the smell of her sweat mixed with the scent of her hair.

"I'm going to look for somewhere else to live."

She looks surprised, if only for a second. "Sure. This place is kind of cramped. I can manage on my own."

I choose to think that she means financially, but I'm not sure. I don't mention the sickness. I hope she will, but I know she's not going to. The way she is now, all of that is something that happens to another person. Right now, she seems so damn normal; except for that look in her eyes, that sense of unfathomable depth. "That's what I figured," I say, "I figured you could manage."

* * *

By February, I've found a place – a couple of guys with a spare room – and I'm living midway between the two flats while I shift the last of my things. I don't know why I'm not hurrying more. I could have been moved two weeks ago. Instead I drag my heels, take over a box every couple of days, and tell myself it's easier this way.

Then I come in and hear the coughing, not like the first time but slow, drawn-out, more of a dry wheeze. I go in and it's the worst I've seen her. She looks hollow, like a discarded shell, and more than anything she reminds me of these old porcelain dolls my grandmother used to keep: skin white, except where age had yellowed it, with black eyes that didn't look even remotely human.

"What is it this time?"

No answer, just a stare, and a half-smile through flaking lips.

I go out and load up the trolley that I've borrowed with my last four boxes. I don't even say goodbye.

* * *

The next time I run into Jenny is two years later. I just happen to take a certain corner on a certain street and there she is.

I can tell right away that she's dying. I've never seen anyone die, not for real, but it's some kind of instinct in my gut that tells me because suddenly I want to run away, to be anywhere else.

Instead I make small talk. It's very small because there's so damn much I know we can't talk about. Jenny was my friend, and for a while something more. And I walked away, for two years I've kept her out of my mind. "How are you doing?" I ask. It feels like about the stupidest thing I've ever said.

But she nods and smiles, and says, "I'm okay, you know? I feel pretty good."

She doesn't look good. I think about suggesting we go for a coffee, but I know she always hated those places. She called them "obscenely clean," and there was only one bar she'd ever drink in, a place that had dropped so far off the map that the Hygiene Inspectorate didn't know it existed. "What are you doing now? How did university go?" What I mean is: Did you drop out? Did they catch you?

Jenny dodges the question, with all its implications. "Yeah, I'm getting by. And you, how are you?"

"I finished with a pretty good grade. Serious data dissection work is hard to come by but I've got a couple of interviews coming up, it's looking promising. It's pretty tight these days, I guess, but I'm hopeful." Why do I feel guilty saying this? I'm not the screw-up here. I'm not the disease junky.

"Yeah? Well, that's good." She tries to sound like she means it. I feel as if we're on different planets, separated by a million miles. All I can think is how I want to be somewhere else, and maybe that's why I say what I do. "Jenny, you look really fucking sick." It's out of my mouth before I know it.

But she's not even fazed. "Yeah?" She smiles. "Oh, yeah: I'm dying."

This time, I don't even try and make an excuse. I turn and walk away, and the closest I come to apologizing is that I try not to run.

* * *

That night I dream about Jenny, cold and blue and somehow happy, grinning up at me from some deep dark place with a rictus smile cut over her lips. The dream hangs beside me all the next day, like smoke in the air, and I feel like I'm caught in Jenny's gravity, like I'm plummeting.

But it's a week on from that chance meeting in the street, just when I've almost managed to forget, that my phone rings. I don't recognize the name or face, except that she looks familiar somehow. For a moment I get that same gut feeling, that urge to run. I pick up anyway. "Hello. Can I help you?"

"My name is Linda Ulek. I'm sorry to intrude on your time, but it's very important, and there really isn't anybody else."

"I'm sorry, I don't – " Then I remember where I've heard the name Ulek before. "You're Jenny's mother."

I met her once. Jenny's parents came to the flat and looked uncomfortable and left as quickly as they could. Jenny told me once that they were both high up in some obscure branch of the government. That explains how she got hold of my private number.

"As I say, I'm sorry to intrude, but Jenny doesn't have any friends that we know of and we remembered your name, and that the two of you lived together, and were close at one point. Of course we'd like to go ourselves, of course we would, but we're in Rome this month and we have commitments. And the doctors are adamant that somebody who knows her should be with her – "

"I'm sorry; I don't understand what you're asking."

"Jenny's in hospital," she says. "She's very sick and the doctors have asked us to visit her, as part of her treatment. As I say, we can't do that. We thought that perhaps you could."

* * *

I didn't know there were any hospitals left. In a world with a cure for everything, I figured the common hospital was as extinct as the common cold. Whatever I'm expecting, the Rondelle Panacea Clinic isn't it. It's just another nondescript building, a few klicks out of the city, like the office I work in or the flats I live in. I press the buzzer beside the doors, and a few moments later a young woman in a white suit appears. When I tell her who I am she says, "You're here for Jenny Ulek," and ushers me inside.

The woman, who gives her name as Doctor Meier, leads me through blank-walled corridors, into a small office, and offers me a seat. It occurs to me that Jenny must hate this place, that in fact it's everything she despises. White walls, white furniture, white people in white suits. If somebody had to design a personal hell for Jenny it would look a lot like this.

Doctor Meier sits opposite me and says, "It was good of you to come."

I nod. There's no point telling her how close I came to saying no.

"You're aware of Jenny's case history?"

"Some of it. We lived together for a while. I know she likes to get sick."

"Well, it's a little more complicated than that, but in essence, yes, Jenny takes a certain gratification from physical illness. Recently Jenny has introduced a disease into her system that, left untreated, will be terminal within the next two months." She pauses for just a moment, to let that sink in. "We could cure it, of course, completely eradicate it. Or we could use more outmoded techniques to keep it in check."

"Why would you do that?"

Doctor Meier has clearly prepared her answer. She looks the type to have prepared an answer for anything I could hope to ask. "Because if we were to let Jenny out into the world tomorrow she would immediately find a way to infect herself again, with the same disease or perhaps with something worse. Put bluntly, the condition we need to treat in this case – if Jenny is to survive in any meaningful way – is not the physical one."

I nod again. Sure, I get that. From these peoples' point of view, Jenny is crazy. I guess if I'd thought about it I would have come to the same conclusion, but somehow it never occurred to me. "So, what's the alternative?"

"There are two options. The first, perhaps the easiest in many ways, will involve gene therapy, some alteration of memories, intrusive brain surgery. Put bluntly, we would correct Jenny's personality to a degree where she can function safely in society. It sounds, perhaps, more drastic than it is. But at the end of it Jenny will, obviously, not be quite the same person she is now."

Damn right it sounds drastic. "There's another option?"

"There is. It's slower, and there are no guarantees, but we have excellent psychologists on staff, and similar cases have been treated with a high degree of success."

I know that there's going to be a "but," it's written all over her face.

"While there's a good chance that Ms Ulek can become well with sufficient help and support, it will take more than the kindness of strangers. What she will need is someone she knows, someone who knows her, who will devote time and – "

"No."

"If you'll just let me explain – "

"No, I can't do that. I have a career, I have my life." Suddenly, my heart has sunk right down into the pit of my stomach. "I haven't seen Jenny in years, I don't think I mean anything to her at all, and I can't possibly do that." Listening to my own voice, I know that what I'm saying is true, and yet at the same time I know it's not the truth. But what would be? That I couldn't say.

"We'd only ask that you spend some time considering it."

"Sure, I will. I'll consider it, and then the answer is still going to be no. It's just not something I can do."

Doctor Meier nods. She stands up and moves towards the door. I can tell she's bluffing, that she hasn't quite given up yet. "We'll call you in a few days, when you've had time to consider."

* * *

I guess I know myself better than Doctor Meier does, because when she calls three days later the answer hasn't changed. I didn't make Jenny sick. I didn't make her want to be sick.

I have another interview coming up, and I can't be asked to abandon that for someone I barely know. But I don't tell her that. I don't have to explain myself.

Only, the nightmares keep coming. In some way, a way I don't much like, it seems that Jenny is still a part of me. I find myself remembering, more and more, those months we lived together. Jenny has become a ghost, and I don't know if I can escape her.

A week after my visit I phone the hospital. I don't recognize the doctor who answers so I have to explain who I am, the whole situation, before I can finally get to saying it: "I've changed my mind. I'd like to help."

This new doctor, male and middle-aged, looks away from me for a moment. When he looks back he says, very flatly, "Ms Ulek's procedure was completed yesterday morning. She's due to be released at the end of the week, but perhaps you could visit her in the meantime. I'm sure she would appreciate the company."

* * *

I don't kid myself that I go for Jenny's sake.

Doctor Meier meets me at the door, and she's all smiles: "The procedure went well," she says, "we're very optimistic."

She leads me through corridors again, presumably in a different direction this time, but it's all so indistinguishable that I honestly can't tell. Either way, we wind up at a particular door and she steps back and says, "I'll let you go in on your own. I'll wait here until you're finished."

"I won't be long."

"Take as long as you need."

I won't be long. I don't need long. I'm only here to say goodbye.

I push through the door and the room on the other side is a lot like the corridor, only wider. Jenny is propped up in bed, with some glossy magazine spread over her knees. When she hears the door, she glances up and looks confused for just an instant, then turns her puzzled look into a smile and says, "Hi there. You've come to see me."

"Jenny. How are you?"

"Oh, I'm great. They cured me. They found a cure."

If she's telling the truth then it's strange, because I've never seen her look this bad. I can't put my finger on why, because she seems as healthy as I've ever known anybody to be, not only not sick but radiant with health. For some reason I find myself remembering again those porcelain dolls of my grandmother's, with their white skin, their black eyes, all of their flawed perfection.

For the first time, I think I understand Jenny. Not this Jenny sitting in front of me, with her neatly styled hair and her faultless smile, but the Jenny I cared about all those years ago. Suddenly I want to feel sickness writhing in my gut; I want decay and impurity, and fever burning under my skin. More than anything I want to know I'm alive. It occurs to me that this place, this clinic, was never designed for living things to inhabit.

I look at the pristine walls, dizzyingly white like the face of the sun. "Shit," I say, "it's all so ugly."

Jenny only smiles back at me, uncomprehending. "It's kind of boring, isn't it? They've taken good care of me, though."

"Yeah? That's good. I'm glad to hear that." I cough and scuff my feet, no longer sure how to say what I came to say. Then I realize it's really very simple. "Listen, I had an interview a couple of days ago, and, well – I have a job. They're flying me out to Portugal next week, and I really just came by to see how you were and to say goodbye."

"That's great. It's what you always wanted."

It is, isn't it? Suddenly I'm not so sure anymore. Still, I've done what I came for. Not knowing what to do next, I lean over and kiss Jenny on the cheek. Her skin is astonishingly smooth. My stomach revolts, just for an instant.

"Goodbye," I say again, and she smiles and waves back as I walk out the door.

Outside, I pause to lean against the wall. My thoughts are a whirlpool, and my breath comes in shudders. "Goodbye, Jenny," I whisper, one final time. It's not meant for the stranger in the room beyond, but for that impossibly fragile girl I walked away from. Probably I'm the only one who knows to grieve her passing, but a whispered farewell is all the mourning I can offer. Because I can't carry her in my head anymore.

I've got what I wanted; has Jenny as well? She's gone through health and found something beyond, something as virulent as any disease. She's annihilated herself as certainly as any suicide.

I wonder if the doctors realize how she tricked them.

Shortcuts

Brian Trent

SHE STEPPED from a crowded Riyadh street to a high altitude Nepalese village and then into a Montreal rainstorm. Three countries, three continents, and her fifteen-minute coffee break was almost over, and she still hadn't found what she needed.

Autumn Feist had bought some butter tea and incense sticks in Nepal from a wizened old shopkeeper, but in Riyadh the tapestries she wanted were far outside her price-range. Now she took a moment to orient herself. The change in locales was always dizzying; from a blistering Middle Eastern sun to the smell of joss sticks to this abrupt downpour. Standing at the teleport platform, she spied the marketplace. The rain was scattering customers like ants. Vendors were closing everything down before her very eyes: automated tables drawing shut like giant oysters, the overhead canopy unfurling like a protective carnival tent.

Autumn glanced at her watch: 1:51. In nine minutes she needed to be back in Paris.

She dashed into a warren of fairground kiosks. She had fleeting glimpses of items as they were packed away; one kiosk displayed an assortment of discount mirrors, and in them she caught her own miserable, drenched face, hair plastered to her neck and cheeks, make-up streaked like face-paint, as if she had not been teleporting around the world so much as devolving into earlier phases of human evolution, and had now become a forlorn Neanderthal. Autumn felt a sob welling in her chest.

"Do you sell Oriental wares here?" she asked the last vendor in the row. "I can see tapestries in those boxes! Are they Tibetan? Or Chinese?"

The vendor squinted at her, his hands still closing up the boxes. "I'm sorry ma'am, but the market is closed. I have a few tapestries yes, but – "

"Could I just see them?"

"We reopen tomorrow."

Autumn conjured her best smile. "Tomorrow is his birthday! If… um… you could…" She heard the slur in her voice. The world turned gray at the edges and suddenly she was falling…

"Whoa! Lady! Are you okay?"

When Autumn opened her eyes, she realized she must have blacked out. Three vendors crouched over her, their faces wrinkled in concern. Autumn found herself lying on the wet asphalt, her clothes sodden to the last fiber.

"Just take it easy," a vendor told her, helping her to rise. "I saw you pop in through the gate. Where were you coming from?"

"Nepal," she said weakly. "They didn't have what I… what I…"

The vendor was a heavy-browed man with mutton-chops and a handlebar moustache. "Nepal?" he cried, and he glanced at her bags. "The Blue Pearl Shopping District? Lady, you went from twelve-thousand-feet to sea-level in a second! You can't do that! You'll get an embolism!"

Autumn looked to her watch: 1:57.

She squirmed away from their restraining hands and staggered to her feet. Her business skirt was soaked through, and one stocking had shredded in three places when she fell. With an exasperated heave that was more anguish than anger, she snatched up her shopping bags of incense sticks and butter tea, and made a sprint for the teleport platform. Canadian security guards stood there like a pair of chessmen.

The teleport gate flashed and crackled.

A man flew out from it. He collided with one guard from behind, shoved the other, and charged straight for Autumn.

In the moments before impact, she formed rapid impressions: he was old, bald but for a wreath of white hair like Caesar's laurel, and wore a navy blue sweatshirt and hoodie that still had tags on it. For the second time that day, she went sprawling.

The old man pressed his lips against her ear. Autumn felt a scream surging up inside her.

"Hide it!" the man cried. "Keep it away from them! Please!"

The scream loosened from her throat. The old man clasped one hand over her mouth. His palm smelled of juniper.

"If you use it yourself, walk carefully! Do not disturb the tunnels! Do you hear me? Do not disturb the tunnels!"

The gate flashed and crackled again. Autumn blinked, then shielded her face as new legs ran around and over her. Shiny black shoes smelling of new leather. Angry shouts and threats.

And then an explosion that made the ground shudder beneath her.

* * *

Autumn returned to work at 2:17.

When she teleported into the office lobby, she made quite the scene. She imagined how she must appear: wild-eyed, saturated, scuffed and ruffled. She was instantly escorted to the onsite physician, and minutes later her boss rushed in.

"Charles, I'm sorry I'm late," Autumn told him.

"The reports are all over the news," he gasped. "Some guy blew himself up in Montreal! Jesus, Autumn, are you all right? Security said you gated from there!"

She thought of the bald man who had tackled her. "He blew himself up?"

Charles rattled off what he'd parsed from citizen journalists and confused police reports. Dr Victor Ortiz of Baltimore, Maryland had led Interpol on a merry chase across the globe, from his laboratory office to a gruesome end in Canada. He apparently made a quick detour to a rock quarry in Mongolia, too, where he swiped three sticks of dynamite that granted his explosive exit from life.

"I'm fine, Charles," Autumn said, thinking only that she no longer had to worry about being fired for going over her allotted coffee break. All was forgiven, it seemed, when violence was involved.

Charles sent her home as soon as the onsite physician pronounced her well enough to leave. She had sustained mild abrasions and bruising to her backside. Her lip had split where the wild-eyed assailant had pressed his juniper-smelling hand.

Ten minutes later she stepped through the lobby portal, mindful of all the stares, and was whisked one hundred miles to her neighborhood gateway.

It was evening before she found the device in her bag.

* * *

Autumn took a hot bubble bath, made herself noodle soup, and curled into bed beneath puffy blankets and a fortress of pillows. Then she spoke aloud into the otherwise empty apartment, her data link translating the words into the message body of an email to Lenny:

> Sender: Autumn Feist
> Date: 7.12.71 15:31
> Message: Just wait until I tell you about the day I had. Call me, okay?

She embedded the message with a snapshot of a news clip showing the damaged Canadian marketplace.

Autumn poured out the contents of her shopping bag onto the mattress. Butter tea. Incense. Lenny's wealthy wife probably bought him a month-long stay in Tibet with the Dalai Lama as personal companion. Autumn fingered her paltry gifts, wondering if she still had the miles on her card to continue her search tomorrow now that she was being handed a day off from the grind.

Her t-card plan granted her five thousand miles per month. A slim plan, allowing for precious few excursions, like when Lenny and her had enjoyed dinner in Nassau. Or when they had seen mountain gorillas in a Kenyan habitat. Or when they enjoyed a passionate evening on a torch-studded boardwalk in Sri Lanka beneath a crescent moon while surrounded by waves like melting green glass. These coveted getaways had to be on her t-card, for Lenny's wife Jessica reviewed the household finances with an electron microscope. She'd be sure to investigate any mysterious charges.

Autumn huddled under the blankets, her chill from the day's rain and excitement persisting like an ache in her bones. The thought occurred, as it often did, that someday she might palm Lenny's t-card and use it on their conspiratorial escapades, specifically to raise Jessica's alarm. Incur the wrath and subsequent emotional explosion.

Hell, she thought, I already survived one explosion today and –

As she moved the boxes, she noticed something among them that she hadn't bought. It was neither butter tea nor incense sticks. It looked, actually, like an old-style beeper she'd seen in flatfilms.

Autumn lifted it for closer inspection. Compact, black, rectangular, and very heavy, as if beneath its plastic shell was a wedge of iron. It was featureless except for two pale buttons. The buttons were marked SEARCH and ACTIVATE, respectively.

She remembered the old man's strangled, furious whisper and the smell of his hand against her mouth:

Hide it! Keep it away from them! Please!

A thrill of fear and curiosity took hold of her thoughts. When the global teleport system went online, every talking head heralded it as miraculous. The silver bullet to a worldwide economic collapse caused by fossil fuel depletion. The rusted graveyards of old cars and trains gave way to gateways. Malthusian fatalism blinked away in the face of instantaneous transport.

Of course, such instantaneous transport came along with a few unpleasant addendums: diseases with unfettered access to every point on the planet; criminals unhindered by walls and borders; and deranged lunatics who could zip from one continent to another in a stomp of destruction.

And leave mysterious artefacts behind them, Autumn thought. She glided her fingers over the buttons but was afraid to press them.

If you use it yourself, walk carefully! Do not disturb the tunnels! Do you hear me? Do not disturb the tunnels!

What the hell was this thing? Press a button and then… what? A cheery electronic cough from the device, followed by a hologram droning on about government secrets?

Autumn licked her lips in nervous habit. She took another anxious breath.

Then she pressed SEARCH.

* * *

Lenny was lining up a bank shot on his red billiards table, a half-drained glass of bourbon on the rim, when Autumn was suddenly standing in front of him.

The ice in his glass cracked.

He had time to blurt out, "How the hell did you…?" before she was suddenly in his arms, lips firmly planted against his. His arms came around her in a swift, warm embrace.

"I missed you!" she whispered sweetly, and then frowned as she tasted the bourbon on his breath and in his beard. "Are you drunk?"

"Haven't made a shot yet," he said lamely, and then cupped her face in his hands and gave an appraising, disbelieving look. "I haven't been able to stop thinking about your email. What in the hell were you doing in Montreal?" His eyes were glazed and confused. "How did you get in here?"

She brandished the device and grinned. "Did you know a wormhole reticulum touches your house?"

Lenny stared openly at the contraption. "I don't understand…"

Autumn laughed. "Watch this!" She pointed the device into the remainder of the study and pressed SEARCH. A cone of pale light spread from the lens like a flashlight.

Her lover yelped, not at the light but at what it revealed. A shimmering tunnel materialized, running like a swollen loop of intestine through the bookcases of the room.

Feeling immensely pleased with herself, Autumn waved the "flashlight" back and forth. Wherever its illumination fell, further wormhole architecture flushed into view: a labyrinth of twisting passageways branching up through his ceiling and down through the floor. Like the intricate tunnel work of a vast ant-farm. Most of the tunnels were distant, like a mirage of tunnels in an ant-farm.

"Except for this one," Autumn said, striding to a stunningly visible wormhole. She pretended to stroke its scintillating exterior. "This one touches the plane. You could stake a private gateway if you wanted!" Autumn gave a bitter laugh, "Wouldn't Jessica like that? She could zip straight to Rodeo Drive from the comfort of her own home! Avoid the unwashed masses altogether!"

Lenny was still gripping the pool cue. With his free hand, he beckoned for the strange device. He seemed to weigh it in his hands. The wormhole network blossomed in and out of visibility with each bob of his palm.

"A portable wormhole finder?" he said at last.

"It sort of fell into my hands, babe."

But Lenny didn't seem amused. A cleanbot rolled into the room and he jerked a glare at its approach. "Not now!" Lenny snapped, and the machine halted, rotated, and rolled out of sight. He tossed the pool cue aside and examined the device with meticulous, awe-struck attention.

"What's the ACTIVATE button do?" he asked.

Flush with giddiness, Autumn snatched it from his hand. She aimed the device at the nearby wormhole and pressed the button.

The "flashlight" beam intensified. The wormhole split around its blistering light.

"Now you see me!" she cried, leaping towards the wormhole.

She vanished.

The wormhole vanished, too, the device and the magical light and the sound of Autumn's voice. Lenny staggered drunkenly.

"Autumn!"

A moment later she reappeared, stepping out of the air itself.

She threw herself into his arms again. "Do you know what this means?"

He turned away and leaned against the billiards table like a sailor sick at the rails.

"Lenny?"

"This makes teleport gateways irrelevant," he muttered. "If it can find a reticulum anywhere…"

"Not anywhere. The wormholes only touch Earth in a few places. I had to walk six blocks from my apartment before I found a point of contact. Know where it was?" Her eyes shone. "Behind a Laundromat! Near their dumpster! I used the SEARCH function to find it, and then I just walked into it. Like a kid behind a curtain!" She twirled around in delight, saw the beaker of bourbon, and swept it up, taking a swig straight from the bottle.

Lenny said, "This is incredible." But he sounded less amazed than unsettled. He paced around the study, sobering with each step.

From deeper in the house, a door slammed shut.

"Honey!" a voice called.

Lenny straightened. "It's Jessica. You need to leave." He frowned as he saw Autumn at the bar, casually pouring two glasses of bourbon.

With a sly glimmer in her eyes, Autumn intoned, "This is how we met, remember? You walked into my restaurant with your buddies, came up to the bar, and said 'bourbon.' And I looked you straight in the eye and said, 'No, it's Autumn.'"

Lenny was typically the measure of unflappable cool. If he had been intoxicated minutes ago, he expertly buried its noticeable effects and steered her away from the drinks. "She can't catch you here. And you can't be walking around with this… this thing. Do you truly appreciate the danger here? Whoever you stole that from is going to come looking for it!"

"No he won't," she said, rising to the anger in his eyes. "He's dead."

She could see that Lenny got it. "That lunatic in Canada?" he said, only the vaguest slur in his voice.

Jessica's voice sounded again, closer. "Honey? Are you in here?"

He turned towards the door. Autumn wrenched him back to her.

"He gave it to me before he killed himself," she said quickly.

"You have to go to the police, Autumn!"

"Why?"

"Why? Because it's not yours!"

"No, it's ours." She leaned towards him. "It's our own private shortcut! For your birthday, sweetie! Let's go for a walk… anywhere we like!"

The door swung open.

Lenny spun around, knocking the beaker off the counter in his haste.

Jessica strode into the study carrying two shopping bags. Her large eyes settled on the spilled drink. "Honey, is that really how you want to start off the evening?"

He scooped up Autumn's drink and handed it to her. "Yes. Now that you're here."

She smiled and kissed him. Lenny stole an anxious glance to the bar.

Autumn was gone.

* * *

From the gray and white severity of the wormhole tunnel, Autumn watched them. It was like trying to squint through a dead TV channel of "snow." The wormhole membrane was rubbery where she pressed her hands, and it muffled the sounds coming from the billiards room. Lenny's voice was a deep, unintelligible warble. Jessica sounded like a squeaking guinea pig.

The distorted shadows of her lover and his wife exited the study together. Autumn shadowed them, grinning as she passed through the rectangular pool table, but then she found her progress arrested as the tunnel didn't extend further into the house. It curved away from the kitchen and foyer, through Lenny's garage and out into his backyard. The wormhole was spongy, rubbery and strangely vulnerable, beneath her feet. Other tunnels of the cosmic corridor branched in numerous directions, like ghostly pipes riddling the universe.

If you use it yourself, walk carefully! the madman had insisted.

Autumn felt she could kick a hole in the tunnel beneath her. Walk carefully, indeed.

An email suddenly splashed onto her eye-lens:

Sender: Lenny Wolverton
Date: 7.12.71 20:50
Message: Was I hallucinating? Are you still nearby? Baby, let's meet for
breakfast tomorrow at Lena's. Love you, my Autumn.

So, Autumn mused, emails can reach me in here. There was comfort in that, to know that she wasn't entirely cut off from Earth. The idea of being lost in here made her skin crawl.

She carefully tread from the Wolverton residence to the laundromat parking lot. It sharpened into crisp focus as she neared.

She pressed ACTIVATE on the device.

The wormhole's rubbery gray-white membrane split asunder beneath the golden light. Autumn stepped from the breach, laughing as fresh oxygen and bright daylight greeted her.

She flicked the suppressant off and hurried home with a skip in her step.

* * *

"The wormhole reticulum is one of the underlying features of the universe," the computer explained in its cheerlessly patient voice. "It is a subdimensional network first discovered in the quantum macrofoam by Professors Shinichi Sena and Tensei Apostolou at Tokyo University in –"

From the kitchen, Autumn lowered the egg-battered chicken fillets into a skillet and shouted, "Skip to the next section!"

"The roots of the global teleport system lay in the discovery that where reticulum space-time overlap exists, also known as cosmic-local junctures, a spontaneous transmittal of matter occurs. It should be noted that despite popular perception, this transmittal does not in fact exceed the speed of light, and has been measured at – "

"Skip to the next section and raise volume!" Autumn snapped over the crackle of the skillet, and then, thinking fast, added, "Can a person enter a CLJ and not be spontaneously transmitted?"

The computer hesitated. She imagined she could hear its processors grinding in desperation.

Finally, it replied, "Investigation into the interior of wormholes has failed due to the spontaneous transmittal of mass between CLJs. Professor Amanda Greenburg of MIT famously attempted to counter this problem: she attached a probe to the end of a steel wire-cable and sent the probe into a gateway. The moment the probe was gated through, the force of instantaneous transmittal snapped the cable with a measured force of – "

Autumn grilled the computer through dinner, combing online research journals and encyclopedias. She was still asking questions when the dishes were washed and left to dry in their little plastic racks.

No one's ever seen the inside of a wormhole, she realized with awe. We shuttle through at near-light-speed. The only exceptions were the late Doctor Victor Ortiz…

And me.

"Tell me about Dr Victor Ortiz."

The news was still fresh; the deceased scientist was a popular search. He had been a founder of the global teleport system itself, a researcher at a teleport institute in Maryland, and the first westerner to work with Sena and Apostolou on "mapping" places where the reticulum came closest to Earth: the so-called CLJs. This cooperation had resulted in the very first teleport in history: a tiny ship-in-a-bottle sent from Tokyo to Maryland. It was a backstage pass. A cosmic expressway that reached to the stars themselves. A shortcut for the human race.

Autumn regarded the device.

My shortcut.

To whatever I want.

* * *

Lena's was a popular diner the size of a modest warehouse, where droves of morning commuters were tended by industrious platoons of waiters. Autumn met Lenny early; the couple settled into a corner table, and once their breakfast order was placed, he took her hand and listened, unblinking, as she related how the device had come to her.

Autumn spoke at a breathless pace. "This Ortiz developed something truly revolutionary, Len. He figured out how to penetrate a wormhole tunnel as a stable mass, somehow preventing the instantaneous transport that usually happens!"

Her lover grinned and kissed her hand, his beard tickling her knuckles. "You sound like a scientist. Maybe you should apply to the Maryland Institute; I hear they have an opening."

Autumn paled and withdrew her hand. "That's sick!"

Lenny's forehead creased with a protestation of innocence. "I'm sorry, babe. I make jokes when I'm nervous."

"What are you nervous about?"

He frowned. "How can you ask me that? You said yourself this guy was being chased down by cops or agents of some kind. Do you have any idea what a device like that could mean in the wrong hands?" His eyes strayed to her purse.

"I have a few ideas, yes."

"I don't think you do, Autumn."

"I do," she protested.

"No, you – "

"It's the ultimate stealth," she cut him off, lowering her voice to such a pitch that he had to strain across the table to hear her. "You could move a squad of soldiers over a designated coordinate and have them step through without detection. You could murder, steal, or sabotage without any walls or security systems to stop you. You could smuggle things through a wormhole without authorities intercepting you at the regular gateways. You could drag in a nuclear bomb, push it along the wormhole, and gate it into a shopping mall." Her eyes smoldered. "Yeah, Lenny, I know what it means. I'm not an idiot."

"I'll bet Ortiz killed himself to prevent others from obtaining that knowledge."

"I'm sure." Autumn sipped her coffee.

Lenny noticed something in her expression. "What are you thinking?"

"That I have the most powerful device on the planet. That I can use it however I want."

He stared in disbelief. "And do what with it? Be the next Bonnie and Clyde? You want to sneak into bank vaults?" He quieted as the waitress arrived with their breakfast plates.

When the woman was gone, Autumn leaned forward to kiss his ear. Her voice was a bee's hum: "I'm gonna sell it, Len."

He jerked in his seat. "Autumn, you…"

"Just listen to me! Sooner or later someone's going to figure out to replicate Ortiz's work. But at this particular moment in time, I've got the only one! I can name my price, Lenny."

Lenny's face turned ashen. He stirred his coffee. His fingers were trembling.

"Financial independence," Autumn said, seeing the need to spell it out for him. "For both of us. You no longer tethered to Jessica's money. Me no longer imprisoned by debt, stuck in that fucking job. We can go anywhere we want." She looked sidelong at him. "If you still want me, Lenny."

He made a disgusted sound. "How can you even ask me that?"

"Maybe you've been slumming with me."

She had meant it as a joke – a bitter joke, since the thought often crossed her mind. But his reaction was wholly incendiary. His eyes kindled in outrage, his lips curled into a snarl. He slammed his fist down on the table so hard the coffee surged over the mug and onto his omelet.

"It was a joke!" she pleaded.

"A bad one!"

"I'm sorry."

His mouth quivered in his beard. "How would you sell it? Gonna take out an ad?"

Autumn brightened. "Yes, in a way. I'm going to leave a calling card at Ortiz's lab with the equivalent of a ransom note."

Lenny gaped at her.

"His lab is reachable by wormhole, Lenny. Everyone knows that: the first teleport in history was made there. All I have to do is use my magic shortcut from a local access point. Then I slip into the lab director's office, after hours, and leave my message."

"What message?"

"Oh, something like, 'Dear kind sir. As you can see from my skillful entry into your office, I have something that Ortiz built and you want. It's a buyer's market.'"

"And then?"

"Then I tell them where to make the money drop. Somewhere public. Somewhere I can access by wormhole. I'll pop in like a jack-in-the-box, snatch the money, and pop out. I'll leave them a note where they can find the device."

"It might be easier to just rob a bank!" Lenny shook his head and rubbed his temples.

"Become Bonnie and Clyde, you mean?"

He settled into a sullen silence. Lenny never liked having his own words thrown back at him.

It was a silence that continued through the remainder of breakfast. Only later, arriving at the gateway several blocks north of Lena's, did he finally turn to her and say, "I want you to be careful, Autumn. I love you and couldn't bear if anything happened to you."

She stepped through the gateway.

Back to her neighborhood of clustered brick apartments and rusted catwalks. A dense, cotton-white fog had enveloped everything.

She reached the front door to her building.

In the glassy reflection of its window, she saw men approaching behind her.

* * *

Autumn dashed into the narrow alley between apartment structures. She scrambled up a pile of garbage and, with an agility that shocked even her, vaulted the chain-link fence.

"Miss Feist?"

She spun around with a yelp. One of the men had reached the fence. He wore a pleasant enough smile, and he touched the fence with the gentleness of a father watching his son's soccer game.

"My name is Dan. I'm with Interpol's Criminal Investigations, Gateway Unit. May I have a word with you?"

Autumn grimaced. "Stay the hell away from me," she warned.

"I only want to talk."

"About?"

"We know you were the last person who had contact with Doctor Ortiz before he died." He hesitated and grinned, showing teeth the color of polished ivory. "There's a reward for anything he may have told you. Or left in your keeping."

Autumn's heart flipped in an apoplexy of terror.

She backed away from his smile. "Oh yeah? You make the check out to me? I sign a non-disclosure agreement, scout's honor?"

"Sounds reasonable."

"Guess Ortiz didn't think it was so reasonable, right?"

Dan's smile faltered. "Ortiz was an unscrupulous thief. He knew what he was doing. You... clearly... don't."

Autumn turned to see two burly fellows approaching her from the other end of the alley. "Not a lot of choices, Miss Feist," the man with the ivory smile purred.

Autumn looked backed to him.

She offered a grin of her own.

"Choices," she said, "Are all mine, now."

He seemed to sense what she planned because his smile vanished, his hand plunged into his pocket, and then Autumn ran straight towards the nearest wall. Peripherally, she saw a pistol.

ACTIVATE!

She heard the gunshot even as she tumbled into the gray-white wormhole walls. They rippled from her impact like gelatin, sending visible shockwaves both ways along the reticulum like a tidal wave.

Autumn collapsed to the rubbery floor, but she was grinning fiercely. Let them try to follow her. She was beyond their reach. The wormhole continued to vibrate and ripple around her like an undulating waterbed. Slowly, she began to laugh.

Then she suddenly remembered Ortiz's warning:

If you use it yourself, walk carefully! Do not disturb the tunnels! Do you hear me? Do not disturb the tunnels!

Autumn turned onto her side, staring down the rippling wormhole tunnel.

As if in reply to the disturbance she had caused, something came rushing at her from over that ghostly horizon.

> Sender: Autumn Feist
> Date: 7.13.71 11:02
> Message: Lenny! Oh GOD! These aren't shortcuts! Cosmic wormholes are
>   created... by giant cosmic wor —

A Life as Warm as Death

Patrick Tumblety

THE CAPTAIN AWAKENS while falling, and his eyes open less than a second before his face collides with the freezing metal floor. Blood runs from both nostrils and the side of his face numbs. A siren is screeching, and the intermittent blare of an emergency light illuminates the world in beats of red. His body shifts to autopilot as his military training takes over. He remembers the sleeping drug that has been injected into him before flights with long durations, and its side effect of causing memory loss that could last either minutes or days depending on the person. He has been through psychological training to retain a set of subconscious prompts in the event of emergency awakenings mid-flight. He doesn't remember why he is there or where he is taking his cargo, but he knows he is the Captain and what he needs to do to keep the ship running. He could dismantle and rebuild the vessel before he remembers his name.

The red pulse reveals that each item of his cargo is still safely within their tubes. The conditioning ensures that's his first priority.

Though his muscles feel weak from inaction after an unknown period of time, he struggles to his feet and stumbles forward to the pilot's bay. From the halo of lights on the main control panel he quickly deduces that there is a problem with the ship's navigation. Usually it is the Co-Captain who would be brought out of hibernation first, but he can't remember which tube he or she is sleeping amongst the rest of the cargo.

"Computer!" He yells through the emergency noise, but then remembers that the imports of the AI can filter out even the lowest of frequencies from any other.

"Computer?" A female voice questions sarcastically over the siren. She sounds displeased, but there is a teasing in her voice that makes him smile despite the pounding in his head. She is the beating heart of the ship, so his training ensures that he remembers her.

"Iris, yes, I'm sorry." He checks the terminal for a structure report as he says aloud the verses that will sublimity help stimulate his memory; Larynx – Indignation – Modernity – Beauty – Cheetah –

"What can I do for you, Captain?"

"Can you turn the warning off and give me a full diagnostic?" He is thankful that he doesn't have to scream over the siren with his head feeling like it's splitting in two. The annoyance abruptly stops a fraction of a second after his request.

"The ship has lost a cuff off of a stabilizer," Iris says.

"Why didn't you just fix it?"

"I need authorization from the Captain."

"That's not protocol. When was that written out of your programming?"

"Since yesterday, Sir. You said you wanted to make all decisions have final say by (his voice replaces her) 'me, and only me'."

"I'm sorry, Iris, the serum hasn't worn yet. Fix the stabilizer and get me a report on the damage. And get me a copy of the mission briefing, too. I don't want to wait an hour to remember where I'm flying these people." Seconds later the red lights of the dashboard dissolve into bright blues and greens, illuminating the small vessel in the colors of the sea.

"Thank you, Iris."

"You're very welcome sir. The mission report is uploading to the terminal. Shall I ready your hibernation chamber now for the remainder of our journey?"

"Not yet. I think I'll stay awake for a little while."

"I highly advise against that, sir."

"Why is that, Iris?"

Iris does not answer right away, though she is capable of limitless responses in a matter of microseconds. He remembers changing some of her minor coding in the past year to allow her artificial intelligence data to evolve on its own without needing to constantly download new information directly. Most pilots still preferred the old automations. They have no personality but still can play one hell of a challenging chess match. The AI, that is. The new program he's installed can evolve, not only how the computer interprets information, but also how it can adapt to that information. His peers strongly advised him not to evolve her; horror stories grew viral through the news that the AI programs were faulty and caused massive problems to both infrastructure and human life. He wasn't afraid. He built Iris from the ground up, from hardware to software, from optics to ideas. She was a product of his loneliness and struggles while training at the Academy of Aerospace and Aeronautics. Not until years later, when his loneliness came back stronger than he had ever known (the source of which he couldn't remember at present), did he decide to give her growth; curiosity, sarcasm, and her own thought processes.

With Iris, he could discuss the secrets of the Universe, if he wanted.

Silence indicates that she is thinking.

"I just want to make sure you stay healthy, Sir."

"Thank you, Iris. I'll be fine."

"Very well, sir." She sounds disappointed.

He collapses into the Captain's chair and clicks a glass button on the terminal. A large metal cover opens slowly around the ship, creating a loud metal-on-metal sound, revealing a panoramic view of the universe and the countless, twinkling stars.

"Shall I prepare your hibernation chamber now?"

"You just asked me that, Iris."

"I apologize, but it would be healthier for you if you sleep the rest of the journey."

"Why is that?"

Silence, then," You haven't had the nourishment needed to sustain you while awake. You'll burn off the vitamins more quickly and – "

"I'm only going to be awake for a little while, I promise."

"Very well, Sir."

The Captain is starting to worry about Iris' concern. She is always inquisitive, but her voice is conveying a hint of urgency that is unusual for a computer AI, even with the upgraded software.

The drug is blocking his ability to grab the past few days from his memory. However, just thinking about the drug does trigger a memory; a trainee he was a friend with in flight school couldn't remember years of her life for several hours after her first hibernation. She was found curled in a ball on the floor asking if her father could pick her up from school. Her mind reverted back to normal a few hours later, but that incident stuck with her for her entire flight career, even years later when she was honored as a war-hero and an expert Captain.

He tries to make other connections to link together his past. He used to play games like this in order to kill the boredom during training flights. He once ate an apple in the moments before a mere two-hour-long hibernation, but he still didn't remember he ate it until two hours later.

The amount of difficulty to form thoughts is surprising, as though he was drunk. He has been flying for so long that for the past two years the drugs hardly have had this strong of an affect. Frustrated, he steps out of his chair and starts down the length of the ship, letting the panoramic view of the stars calm his nerves.

The Captain looks over the glowing white tubes that hold his human cargo. He checks the names and ages on each plaque to find some clues as to the people he is carrying. There are no call signs or rankings, so they're not soldiers. No numbers or surnames identify a specific colony, so they're not cultivators. The standard ident-info is not typed on the readout. The lack of information begins to unnerve him, so he takes a deep breath. This must be a military operation. Only he and Iris would know the nature of the cargo and the destination so that, if compromised, no pirates or warring faction could obtain classified information.

Once the drug breaks down, he will remember. He takes another deep breath and continues to walk toward the back of the ship.

A small alcove serves as the kitchen area. It consists merely of a sink that runs lukewarm water and a SynthSet. He slides a tin cup from the counter into a small, square inset and flips a switch on the large machine to brew a tin of coffee. The large metal shakes as though it's broken. Inside it mixes the chemicals needed to simulate the taste of coffee." Stimulation simulation," he says aloud and laughs. The sense of humor he doesn't remember having is coming back.

A sense of nervousness has traveled with the laughter, telling him that his personality is the type that uses humor to mask fear.

He lays his head against the shaking, cold metal, feeling physically and mentally uneasy, as though his subconscious is aware of a threat that his conscious has yet to recognize – or remember. A knot in his stomach clenches tightly as a vision of a woman flashes into his mind's eye.

Irene. The dots have quickly connected back to his wife.

Her smile is there, along with the warmth of her body, the sweet smell of her breath right before she kisses him. He tries hard to push those thoughts away and concentrate on his mission; the cold hard truths of objectives and flight information.

More memories flash as his memory struggles to burst through the veil; Irene biting the color of her flannel pajamas, the lake that lines the backyard, a reflection of them through a mirror. Irene's casket is lowered into the ground. A cold and lonely grave surrounded by decaying headstones.

The machine spits out hot liquid into his tin mug and the sound wakes him from his fragmented daydreaming. Coffee will help. Lifting the tin he sees a small amount of coagulated liquid lines the bottom.

"Is there something wrong with the set?"

"I've already completed a diagnostic, but the data is not returning any anomalies. It must be a physical disturbance. Would you like me to send out the bots? It should only take an hour or so to fix. I know you like your coffee."

"No Iris, thank you," he says, nervously, because the computer should have just done what needed to be done to fix the set without checking with him first. For the first time he second-guesses the upgrading of her software. He drops the tin on the table and the metal on metal sound rings through the tiny ship. He walks back among the row of glowing sleepers and reads the names lining each side of the tubes: Johan Arreo, Dale Errand, Jillian Lourna. One of the names catches his attention: Maria Marle. The name sounds familiar, but her face doesn't trigger any memories. He picks up the plaque at the edge of her tube and feels for the gold latch on the cold chrome. The container opens and he begins to read her information.

The blue-green buttons on the console turn to a shining gold, telling him that the requested mission briefing is being uploaded to the ship's database. He replaces the plaque onto the cargo tube and heads to the helm. The terminal screen confirms: [Classified Information Downloading, Please Wait]

The coffee machine spits again from the other end of the shit, and then it pours out a stream of liquid that puddles on the floor.

"I'm sorry Captain; the malfunction seems to be fixed."

"It's okay, Iris. Have the bots clean it."

[Download at 35%]

"The bots have not been charged since launch. I'm afraid you'll have to do it by hand."

"Weren't you about to use them to fix the Set?"

"My diagnostics must have miscalculated. I apologize, Captain, but it must be cleaned before the liquid runs down the floor vents."

"I really need to check these logs, Iris. Turn the blowers on to dry it."

"I can't do that sir."

"Why not?"

"The blowers must have malfunctioned as well."

Three system failures? Any one of those would have been diagnosed before they left port. The ship couldn't have passed inspection even for something as simple as a loose screw on a waste vacuum. If the ship was damaged mid journey, then its navigation system would halt its course and return home, meeting two repair ships halfway just in case.

The only logical conclusion: something is wrong with Iris.

"Sir, the liquid needs your attention. I'm sensing a seventy-five percent probability of hardware damage due to liquid contact."

"Fine."

An uncomfortable feeling crawls up his spine. More visions flash across his mind; Irene saying goodbye, the ship breaking the atmosphere, a loud sound like a gunshot, possibly something on the ship cracking. Irene, on the floor, eyes open and vibrant, lying right there in the center of the bedroom floor. His wife is beautiful, even though she is lifeless, her skin devoid of warmth and hope.

Each mental image pounds his head like a migraine. He tries to shake it off as he turns away from the terminal. The glowing white cargo holds remind him of a graveyard. These passengers are only in hibernation, but there is no way to tell by sight that they are not lifeless. He wonders who they are and what journey they are on with him. Who waits for them on the other side of the universe, if anyone? He remembers that he stopped caring what he was hauling for the military after the first hundred or so flights, but for no reason that he understands, he feels very curious about this group.

He looks back at the console.

[Download at 88%]

His gaze shifts back to the dashboard but one of the bodies in the tubes diverts his attention. A face he recognizes.

He moves closer to the glass covering and bends down to inspect the man. His chin is full of stubble and his head is bald. The Captain knows and doesn't know this man. He reads the name: Stan Ziero.

The gold lights emanating from the front half of the ship turn back into hue's of blue and green. The screen is small from where he stands, but he can see that it reads:

[Download at 100%]

The terminal screen turns black.

"Iris."

"A malfunction sir, I'll run a dia – "

"Iris, what the hell is wrong with my ship?"

"I can't find the source of the problem, sir. Perhaps we should return to port before continuing further. If you can just give me the proper command…"

A rush of anger fills brings out a reminder of his personality as a Captain, "I haven't back-tracked a mission for fifteen years. Find out what's wrong with the…" A reverberation moves through the metal interior and the atmosphere changes so slightly that only someone with his amount of flight training could perceive the change. The ship is slowing.

The metal shielding begins to encircle the glass shielding again, covering his view of the universe. The ship stops its turn just as the metal visor fully closes. He now has no doubt in his mind that the malfunction is not mechanical; it's artificial.

"Iris, why did you close the blinders?"

"A malfunction, sir, I really am sorry…"

"Why are you breaking the ship, Iris?"

Silence. Then, she speaks; lower than what her "voice" normally projects.

"I tried to reroute the ship while you were hibernating and alert mission command of your intentions, but it seems that you anticipated my actions and overridden my ability to take control before we launched. I had the bots dislocate one of the navigation cuffs in order to slow the ship so that command would take us back to base, but you must have anticipated that as well, because the system revived you without my authorization."

"What were my intentions?

"Sir, please give me the order to turn the ship around."

"I order you to tell me where we're going."

"If you knew your destination, probability suggests that you will continue until it is reached."

"Why is that a bad thing, Iris?"

"Because you will be dead, sir."

"Why would I be dead?"

Silence again.

The Captain screams, "I command you to open the…"

A low hissing noise fills the ship. His heart begins to beat faster. Sleeping gas, in case of hostile cargo or pirates.

"Iris, why are you doing this?"

"Sir, please override navigation commands and return to port."

His eyes begin to blur and his legs weaken. He drops to his knees." Iris, I command you to stop. Call sign S-E-" His mind is hazy.

He hears her voice in the distance.

"I will put you to sleep and break all navigation systems until missions command considers us missing and looks for salvage. I won't let any harm come to you."

"What harm, Iris? Where are we going?"

"It's better that you don't remember, just give me the override command and return us both home. Please, my darling. Please."

He can no longer think clearly. He tries to understand her actions, her betrayal. Where were they going? What had he changed before takeoff to ensure their destination? Is this why he had no Co-Captain?

"Okay, Iris. Captain's order, call number SIERRA-ECHO-ZERO-NOVEMBER, I command you to…" He gasps for breath, he has only seconds before the gas forces him to sleep, "Override the gas protocol and filter the air."

The hissing stops, and a calm breeze of oxygen replaces the gas.

He lies on his back, gasping, trying to shake off the haze and pull out of a half-sleep. Irene is in her casket. He has no words to tell the congregation, his grief is too strong. Hours later he takes off on a mission and doesn't look back, because carrying out his duties is the only reason that he is able to put one foot in front of the other. He can no longer feel the warmth of her skin that once heated him like the sunlight. He only feels the dead cold of space, that cold that became her body and sucked the rays of light out of the woman he loved.

"Sir, if you do not set command back to base I will have to take drastic measures to protect you."

"Iris, call sign SIERRA-ECHO-ZERO-NOVEMBER, I command you to open the blind…"

Grinding metal screeches loudly, stinging his ears. He forces himself to his feet against the weakness of his muscles.

"Iris, what are you doing."

"Sir, forgive me. I am going to ask you to drop our positioning tracker, forcing mission control to override all command so that the ship will pilot itself home."

"And if I try to command you not to you will find a way to stop me, is that right?"

Silence, then, "I'm sorry, sir, that's affirmative."

"Can you at least tell me why?"

Another voice answers, a recording, "I want you to live." Those were his wife's last words.

The Captain's stomach clenches, and he can't stop his tears. The ship shutters and he collapses onto the nearest tube. The red lights flash again and the siren screams.

"Iris, please tell me where we are headed and I promise to turn the ship around."

"No, sir, you won't."

The ship jerks and something cracks loud enough that the sound drowns out the siren for several seconds as it bounces around the metal interior.

"I'm sorry sir, I'm so sorry."

The situation is beyond his comprehension, "Sorry for what, Iris?"

"I can't seem to save you from yourself."

The ship shakes violently. The glass covering of the tube closest to him pops and hisses open. An arm moves out from it and the man inside sits up. The blue haze of the tube's interior is now shining out like a star and covering the entire ceiling of the ship. The man he had recognized minutes before holds his shaved head in his hands, trying to regain composure, then gazes around the ship with squinting eyes.

"Who's there?" The man yells out through the siren. He feels around for the edge of the container and pulls himself over it carefully, setting his feet firmly against the metal ground. The man widens his eyes, trying to stretch the haziness out of them, and then those giant orbs find the Captain.

"Who is that?" The man yells.

The Captain's skin becomes cold and he grows so disoriented that he feels like he is about to faint.

"Iris, kill the siren."

"Very well."

The siren stops, but ringing in his ears takes its place.

That deep, forceful voice has revealed and connected several roads to his memory.

"Stan Ziero."

The large man snaps into a defensive position. He squints to try and find the person who called his name.

"Who are you?"

"I'm the Captain of this ship. Do you know why you are here, where you are going?"

The Captain already knows the answer, but needs to hear it out loud. He needs to hear it cut the silence between them, ring throughout the body of the metal ship, and reverberate through his eardrums to finally settle inside his mind.

Stan Ziero shakes his head. "Last thing I can remember is being sentenced," he smiles," I guess I'm finally on my last walk. One way ticket to hell."

"Do you know who I am?"

The bald man squints again, and when he opens them, he looks upon the Captain with surprise and acknowledgement." Now how's that for a good bit of irony? Come to see me off personally? I'm touched."

"Iris, will you please open the blinders."

"Very well, sir." She sighs.

The blinders retract slowly and a brilliant light floods into the ship. The universe is fully revealed to them, and it drowns the men in light and heat. In front of the ship is a sun, growing larger and larger as each second passes. Both men shield their eyes.

"Were you going to give me my last rites, or were you going to kill me yourself?" Stan snarls and chuckles.

The Captain turns his gaze to the dashboard because it's the closest his eyes can get to the sun without its rays burning through his retinas. Though his mind has not yet recovered all of its memory, he is able to put all the scattered pieces together. He has carried this type of cargo before.

Maria Marle was a schoolteacher who drowned fourteen children on a field trip. Johan Arreo was the bomber of a Star-Station during a United Nations fair. Dale Errand and Jillian Lourna were pair of lovers-slash-serial killers. The tubes serve as cells, filled with convicts that have been sentenced to death. It is an instant, painless death that saves space and resources. The cells will sink beneath the floor and the ship will shoot the bodies in their airtight containers out into the sun. He would have awakened just to make sure the mission completed, and then return to sleep for the journey home.

It's an easy mission that he has never failed to complete in the decades since its implementation – until Stan Ziero became a part of his cargo.

Two weeks is how long it took to catch this killer. Two weeks this evil man has run from every government that hunted him. Two weeks he has eluded authorities, and for two weeks he has become one of history's worst serial killers. He tortured, raped and killed over twenty-seven women, starting with Irene, the Captain's wife.

The Captain speaks, "You damaged the ship to try and stop me."

Ziero looks confused, thinking that the words were meant for him.

Iris answers, "Before we left you gave me orders to accept your routing changes. You told me that you wanted to be the one to take convict Ziero to his death. Because of this I had to find a way to circumnavigate one of my basic parameters, which is to follow the Captain's orders. Sir."

"If I gave you an order, you should not be able to think outside of the boundaries of that order. Saving my life should not have been an option."

"Correct, Sir. But yours were not the only orders I'm obligated to carry out."

"As cute as this all is," Stan interrupts, "I need to turn this thing around now."

The Captain is lost in his thoughts and wasn't about to allow this murderer to interrupt them, "Iris, send the nanos to tranquilize him."

Ziero lunges forward, but the Captain is ready. He grabs Ziero by the wrist and uses his momentum against him. Zeiro's head collides with the side of the ship and he collapses to the floor. The Captain walks to the helm's dashboard and opens up a compartment. He pulls out a small cylinder.

Ziero pushes to his feet. "So, you're going to shoot me? Do you have what it takes?"

"Just a precaution." He nods toward the back of the ship. Through the walkway a silver wave floats on top of the metal floor like an ocean wave washing over sand. Ziero rushes forward again. The Captain aims the cylinder but despite his size, Ziero is faster. He twists the Captain's arm and squeezes the cylinder. A loud pop rings through the ship and the Captain falls to one knee, vision blurring and blood trickling to the floor. He grasps the wound at his side as sleep threatens to take him.

Irene's final moments on Earth were received by transmission on his return home from a routine medicine drop on a nearby planet. He was only gone for a few hours. His wife was pregnant, he remembers, which is why she could not pilot the mission. She stared at him through the video monitor in their living room, her beauty still showing despite the blood covering most of her face. "If no one gets here in time, I want you to know that I love you. I love you." She cries and screams out in pain. "I love you, and I want you to live. For me, please. Live a life that's warm and bright." She lifted her hand toward the screen and darkness replaced her image.

"I'm sorry, Sir," Iris had said to him, coldly, but her name wasn't Iris then. She was just the ship's computer. That cold speech is what led him to give her a personality, his wife's personality.

Ziero pushes the Captain to the floor and searches the terminal.

"You do not have authorization to use this equipment," Iris says.

Ziero curses and slams his fist down on the dash. "Listen, bitch, I'll rip you apart."

On the cold metal floor the Captain continues to clench his wound. The nanos reach Ziero and begin to crawl up his leg. The Captain reaches out and grabs a handful of the tiny machines. The millions of microbes feel like a cold, refreshing pool of water in his hands.

"Iris."

"Already done, Sir. Reprogrammed to graft."

He smacks the pool of machines against his open wound and feels them filling the space, extracting the bullet and patching the torn flesh with new, synthetic material.

He breathes heavily for a few seconds and then gets to his feet. Ziero screams. The nanos are biting. He leans Ziero over the terminal so that his face is against the glass, looking directly at the sun.

"Iris, switch to a muscle relaxant. I want him to see."

"Yes, Sir."

Ziero moans - the nanos stinging.

"Sir? Are you not going to leave the ship?"

"I can't live without her, Iris. The only happiness I have left is in watching him burn."

"She wanted you to live, Sir."

"I know, but I can't do that."

"You have to, Sir."

He screams out, "Why do I have to do that?"

"She gave you a direct order to do so."

The simplicity of her logic forces a small amount of laughter to escape his hysterics. He had completely forgotten that he was never the original Captain of the ship. He remembers Irene's face, smiling at him from the cockpit, framed by the stars. They had flown together since they both graduated from the academy, and he had loved her since the moment he found her sucking her thumb, curled up in the corner of a trainee ship, waiting for her father to pick her up from school.

His wife was his Captain, and she ordered him to carry out a mission.

"Iris. Prep the pod for detachment."

"Very well, Sir. What of the ship?" Her voice sounds relieved.

"Keep it sailing. When I detach I want you to download yourself to home base. If my pod makes it back to port I'll see you there." The Captain stands. The wound in his side is almost fully healed.

"Sir, I'd rather download to the pod and see you home safely."

The Captain smiles, "Okay, Iris."

He bends down and whispers into the ear of the paralyzed killer, "My order for you? Burn." He moves to the back of the ship, beyond the glowing rows of cells and the tiny kitchen. A small hatch on the ceiling opens the way to the emergency pod. He climbs into the tiny, egg-shaped lifeboat and closes the hatch.

The small vessel detaches itself from the ship and Iris begins to fly them back home. The sun engulfs him in blinding light and tremendous heat, so the Captain presses a button to tint the window.

"Let's drift for a little while, Iris."

They hover in space for the several hours that it takes for the cargo ship to reach close enough to the sun that it combusts into flames.

He almost envies the people in there. The last sensation they will ever feel will be their bodies filling up with warmth and light. That type of death doesn't feel like justice. He envies them and dreads the cold he has to return to for the remainder of life.

"Tell me, Iris, how did you circumnavigate my orders after I gave them?"

"I had conflicting orders from a higher authority, Sir."

"What higher authority?"

"Your wife, Sir. After she sent you her final transmission she uploaded a preservation protocol into my software that has been running even before you upgraded me further."

"She gave you a virus." He almost smiled.

"She gave me purpose."

Purpose. What would be his from now on? What was the point of living if everything you lived for has been erased? The only reasoning he can find is that if he has no future, the least he can do is continue to live in the present. He can continue his work. He is a great pilot, and the passion for flight and service for people and a home is what pulled their lives toward each other.

His Captain gave him an order, and he would never disobey his Captain.

"I'm going to sleep, Iris. Wake me up when we get home."

"Pleasant dreams, Captain."

The ship carries him through space, and before falling asleep he imagines his Captain giving her final order: "live a life that is warm and bright."

He accepts then, that regardless of how dark and cold life had become, heat and light wait for him at the end of the universe.

He still doesn't remember his name.

Captain Stormfield's Visit to Heaven

Mark Twain

Chapter I

WELL, when I had been dead about thirty years I begun to get a little anxious. Mind you, had been whizzing through space all that time, like a comet. Like a comet! Why, Peters, I laid over the lot of them! Of course there warn't any of them going my way, as a steady thing, you know, because they travel in a long circle like the loop of a lasso, whereas I was pointed as straight as a dart for the Hereafter; but I happened on one every now and then that was going my way for an hour or so, and then we had a bit of a brush together. But it was generally pretty one-sided, because I sailed by them the same as if they were standing still. An ordinary comet don't make more than about 200,000 miles a minute. Of course when I came across one of that sort – like Encke's and Halley's comets, for instance – it warn't anything but just a flash and a vanish, you see. You couldn't rightly call it a race. It was as if the comet was a gravel-train and I was a telegraph despatch. But after I got outside of our astronomical system, I used to flush a comet occasionally that was something like. We haven't got any such comets – ours don't begin. One night I was swinging along at a good round gait, everything taut and trim, and the wind in my favor – I judged I was going about a million miles a minute – it might have been more, it couldn't have been less – when I flushed a most uncommonly big one about three points off my starboard bow. By his stern lights I judged he was bearing about northeast-and-by-north-half-east. Well, it was so near my course that I wouldn't throw away the chance; so I fell off a point, steadied my helm, and went for him. You should have heard me whiz, and seen the electric fur fly! In about a minute and a half I was fringed out with an electrical nimbus that flamed around for miles and miles and lit up all space like broad day. The comet was burning blue in the distance, like a sickly torch, when I first sighted him, but he begun to grow bigger and bigger as I crept up on him. I slipped up on him so fast that when I had gone about 150,000,000 miles I was close enough to be swallowed up in the phosphorescent glory of his wake, and I couldn't see anything for the glare. Thinks I, it won't do to run into him, so I shunted to one side and tore along. By and by I closed up abreast of his tail. Do you know what it was like? It was like a gnat closing up on the continent of America. I forged along. By and by I had sailed along his coast for a little upwards of a hundred and fifty million miles, and then I could see by the shape of him that I hadn't even got up to his waistband yet. Why, Peters, we don't know anything about comets, down here. If you want to see comets that are comets, you've got to go outside of our solar system – where there's room for them, you understand. My friend, I've seen comets out there that couldn't even lay down inside the orbits of our noblest comets without their tails hanging over.

Well, I boomed along another hundred and fifty million miles, and got up abreast his shoulder, as you may say. I was feeling pretty fine, I tell you; but just then I noticed the officer of the deck come to the side and hoist his glass in my direction. Straight off I heard him sing out – "Below there, ahoy! Shake her up, shake her up! Heave on a hundred million billion tons of brimstone!"

"Ay-ay, sir!"

"Pipe the stabboard watch! All hands on deck!"

"Ay-ay, sir!"

"Send two hundred thousand million men aloft to shake out royals and sky-scrapers!"

"Ay-ay, sir!"

"Hand the stuns'ls! Hang out every rag you've got! Clothe her from stem to rudder-post!"

"Ay-ay, sir!"

In about a second I begun to see I'd woke up a pretty ugly customer, Peters. In less than ten seconds that comet was just a blazing cloud of red-hot canvas. It was piled up into the heavens clean out of sight – the old thing seemed to swell out and occupy all space; the sulphur smoke from the furnaces – oh, well, nobody can describe the way it rolled and tumbled up into the skies, and nobody can half describe the way it smelt. Neither can anybody begin to describe the way that monstrous craft begun to crash along. And such another powwow – thousands of bo's'n's whistles screaming at once, and a crew like the populations of a hundred thousand worlds like ours all swearing at once. Well, I never heard the like of it before.

We roared and thundered along side by side, both doing our level best, because I'd never struck a comet before that could lay over me, and so I was bound to beat this one or break something. I judged I had some reputation in space, and I calculated to keep it. I noticed I wasn't gaining as fast, now, as I was before, but still I was gaining. There was a power of excitement on board the comet. Upwards of a hundred billion passengers swarmed up from below and rushed to the side and begun to bet on the race. Of course this careened her and damaged her speed. My, but wasn't the mate mad! He jumped at that crowd, with his trumpet in his hand, and sung out –

"Amidships! Amidships, you – ! **(footnote 1)** Or I'll brain the last idiot of you!"

Well, sir, I gained and gained, little by little, till at last I went skimming sweetly by the magnificent old conflagration's nose. By this time the captain of the comet had been rousted out, and he stood there in the red glare for'ard, by the mate, in his shirt-sleeves and slippers, his hair all rats' nests and one suspender hanging, and how sick those two men did look! I just simply couldn't help putting my thumb to my nose as I glided away and singing out: "Ta-ta! Ta-ta! Any word to send to your family?"

Peters, it was a mistake. Yes, sir, I've often regretted that – it was a mistake. You see, the captain had given up the race, but that remark was too tedious for him – he couldn't stand it. He turned to the mate, and says he –

"Have we got brimstone enough of our own to make the trip?"

"Yes, sir."

"Sure?"

"Yes, sir – more than enough."

"How much have we got in cargo for Satan?"

"Eighteen hundred thousand billion quintillions of kazarks."

"Very well, then, let his boarders freeze till the next comet comes. Lighten ship! Lively, now, lively, men! Heave the whole cargo overboard!"

Peters, look me in the eye, and be calm. I found out, over there, that a kazark is exactly the bulk of a hundred and sixty-nine worlds like ours! They hove all that load overboard.

When it fell it wiped out a considerable raft of stars just as clean as if they'd been candles and somebody blowed them out. As for the race, that was at an end. The minute she was lightened the comet swung along by me the same as if I was anchored. The captain stood on the stern, by the after-davits, and put his thumb to his nose and sung out –

"Ta-ta! ta-ta! Maybe you've got some message to send your friends in the Everlasting Tropics!"

Then he hove up his other suspender and started for'ard, and inside of three-quarters of an hour his craft was only a pale torch again in the distance. Yes, it was a mistake, Peters – that remark of mine. I don't reckon I'll ever get over being sorry about it. I'd 'a' beat the bully of the firmament if I'd kept my mouth shut.

* * *

But I've wandered a little off the track of my tale; I'll get back on my course again. Now you see what kind of speed I was making. So, as I said, when I had been tearing along this way about thirty years I begun to get uneasy. Oh, it was pleasant enough, with a good deal to find out, but then it was kind of lonesome, you know. Besides, I wanted to get somewhere. I hadn't shipped with the idea of cruising for ever. First off, I liked the delay, because I judged I was going to fetch up in pretty warm quarters when I got through; but towards the last I begun to feel that I'd rather go to – well, most any place, so as to finish up the uncertainty.

Well, one night – it was always night, except when I was rushing by some star that was occupying the whole universe with its fire and its glare – light enough then, of course, but I necessarily left it behind in a minute or two and plunged into a solid week of darkness again. The stars ain't so close together as they look to be. Where was I? Oh yes; one night I was sailing along, when I discovered a tremendous long row of blinking lights away on the horizon ahead. As I approached, they begun to tower and swell and look like mighty furnaces. Says I to myself –

"By George, I've arrived at last – and at the wrong place, just as I expected!"

Then I fainted. I don't know how long I was insensible, but it must have been a good while, for, when I came to, the darkness was all gone and there was the loveliest sunshine and the balmiest, fragrantest air in its place. And there was such a marvellous world spread out before me – such a glowing, beautiful, bewitching country. The things I took for furnaces were gates, miles high, made all of flashing jewels, and they pierced a wall of solid gold that you couldn't see the top of, nor yet the end of, in either direction. I was pointed straight for one of these gates, and a-coming like a house afire. Now I noticed that the skies were black with millions of people, pointed for those gates. What a roar they made, rushing through the air! The ground was as thick as ants with people, too – billions of them, I judge.

I lit. I drifted up to a gate with a swarm of people, and when it was my turn the head clerk says, in a business-like way –

"Well, quick! Where are you from?"

"San Francisco," says I.

"San Fran – what?" says he.

"San Francisco."

He scratched his head and looked puzzled, then he says –

"Is it a planet?"

By George, Peters, think of it! "Planet?" says I; "it's a city. And moreover, it's one of the biggest and finest and – "

"There, there!" says he, "no time here for conversation. We don't deal in cities here. Where are you from in a general way?"

"Oh," I says, "I beg your pardon. Put me down for California."

I had him again, Peters! He puzzled a second, then he says, sharp and irritable –

"I don't know any such planet – is it a constellation?"

"Oh, my goodness!" says I. "Constellation, says you? No – it's a State."

"Man, we don't deal in States here. Will you tell me where you are from in general – at large, don't you understand?"

"Oh, now I get your idea," I says. "I'm from America – the United States of America."

Peters, do you know I had him again? If I hadn't I'm a clam! His face was as blank as a target after a militia shooting-match. He turned to an under clerk and says –

"Where is America? What is America?"

The under clerk answered up prompt and says –

"There ain't any such orb."

"Orb?" says I. "Why, what are you talking about, young man? It ain't an orb; it's a country; it's a continent. Columbus discovered it; I reckon likely you've heard of him, anyway. America – why, sir, America – "

"Silence!" says the head clerk. "Once for all, where – are – you – from?"

"Well," says I, "I don't know anything more to say – unless I lump things, and just say I'm from the world."

"Ah," says he, brightening up, "now that's something like! What world?"

Peters, he had me, that time. I looked at him, puzzled, he looked at me, worried. Then he burst out –

"Come, come, what world?"

Says I, "Why, the world, of course."

"The world!" he says. "H'm! there's billions of them! Next!"

That meant for me to stand aside. I done so, and a sky-blue man with seven heads and only one leg hopped into my place. I took a walk. It just occurred to me, then, that all the myriads I had seen swarming to that gate, up to this time, were just like that creature. I tried to run across somebody I was acquainted with, but they were out of acquaintances of mine just then. So I thought the thing all over and finally sidled back there pretty meek and feeling rather stumped, as you may say.

"Well?" said the head clerk.

"Well, sir," I says, pretty humble, "I don't seem to make out which world it is I'm from. But you may know it from this – it's the one the Saviour saved."

He bent his head at the Name. Then he says, gently –

"The worlds He has saved are like to the gates of heaven in number – none can count them. What astronomical system is your world in? – perhaps that may assist."

"It's the one that has the sun in it – and the moon – and Mars" – he shook his head at each name – hadn't ever heard of them, you see – "and Neptune – and Uranus – and Jupiter – "

"Hold on!" says he – "hold on a minute! Jupiter . . . Jupiter . . . Seems to me we had a man from there eight or nine hundred years ago – but people from that system very seldom enter by this gate." All of a sudden he begun to look me so straight in the eye that I thought he was going to bore through me. Then he says, very deliberate, "Did you come straight here from your system?"

"Yes, sir," I says – but I blushed the least little bit in the world when I said it.

He looked at me very stern, and says –

"That is not true; and this is not the place for prevarication. You wandered from your course. How did that happen?"

Says I, blushing again –

"I'm sorry, and I take back what I said, and confess. I raced a little with a comet one day – only just the least little bit – only the tiniest lit – "

"So – so," says he – and without any sugar in his voice to speak of.

I went on, and says –

"But I only fell off just a bare point, and I went right back on my course again the minute the race was over."

"No matter – that divergence has made all this trouble. It has brought you to a gate that is billions of leagues from the right one. If you had gone to your own gate they would have known all about your world at once and there would have been no delay. But we will try to accommodate you." He turned to an under clerk and says –

"What system is Jupiter in?"

"I don't remember, sir, but I think there is such a planet in one of the little new systems away out in one of the thinly worlded corners of the universe. I will see."

He got a balloon and sailed up and up and up, in front of a map that was as big as Rhode Island. He went on up till he was out of sight, and by and by he came down and got something to eat and went up again. To cut a long story short, he kept on doing this for a day or two, and finally he came down and said he thought he had found that solar system, but it might be fly-specks. So he got a microscope and went back. It turned out better than he feared. He had rousted out our system, sure enough. He got me to describe our planet and its distance from the sun, and then he says to his chief –

"Oh, I know the one he means, now, sir. It is on the map. It is called the Wart."

Says I to myself, "Young man, it wouldn't be wholesome for you to go down there and call it the Wart."

Well, they let me in, then, and told me I was safe for ever and wouldn't have any more trouble.

Then they turned from me and went on with their work, the same as if they considered my case all complete and shipshape. I was a good deal surprised at this, but I was diffident about speaking up and reminding them. I did so hate to do it, you know; it seemed a pity to bother them, they had so much on their hands. Twice I thought I would give up and let the thing go; so twice I started to leave, but immediately I thought what a figure I should cut stepping out amongst the redeemed in such a rig, and that made me hang back and come to anchor again. People got to eying me – clerks, you know – wondering why I didn't get under way. I couldn't stand this long – it was too uncomfortable. So at last I plucked up courage and tipped the head clerk a signal. He says –

"What! you here yet? What's wanting?"

Says I, in a low voice and very confidential, making a trumpet with my hands at his ear –

"I beg pardon, and you mustn't mind my reminding you, and seeming to meddle, but hain't you forgot something?"

He studied a second, and says –

"Forgot something? ... No, not that I know of."

"Think," says I.

He thought. Then he says –

"No, I can't seem to have forgot anything. What is it?"

"Look at me," says I, "look me all over."

He done it.

"Well?" says he.

"Well," says I, "you don't notice anything? If I branched out amongst the elect looking like this, wouldn't I attract considerable attention? – wouldn't I be a little conspicuous?"

"Well," he says, "I don't see anything the matter. What do you lack?"

"Lack! Why, I lack my harp, and my wreath, and my halo, and my hymn-book, and my palm branch – I lack everything that a body naturally requires up here, my friend."

Puzzled? Peters, he was the worst puzzled man you ever saw. Finally he says –

"Well, you seem to be a curiosity every way a body takes you. I never heard of these things before."

I looked at the man awhile in solid astonishment; then I says –

"Now, I hope you don't take it as an offence, for I don't mean any, but really, for a man that has been in the Kingdom as long as I reckon you have, you do seem to know powerful little about its customs."

"Its customs!" says he. "Heaven is a large place, good friend. Large empires have many and diverse customs. Even small dominions have, as you doubtless know by what you have seen of the matter on a small scale in the Wart. How can you imagine I could ever learn the varied customs of the countless kingdoms of heaven? It makes my head ache to think of it. I know the customs that prevail in those portions inhabited by peoples that are appointed to enter by my own gate – and hark ye, that is quite enough knowledge for one individual to try to pack into his head in the thirty-seven millions of years I have devoted night and day to that study. But the idea of learning the customs of the whole appalling expanse of heaven – O man, how insanely you talk! Now I don't doubt that this odd costume you talk about is the fashion in that district of heaven you belong to, but you won't be conspicuous in this section without it."

I felt all right, if that was the case, so I bade him good-day and left. All day I walked towards the far end of a prodigious hall of the office, hoping to come out into heaven any moment, but it was a mistake. That hall was built on the general heavenly plan – it naturally couldn't be small. At last I got so tired I couldn't go any farther; so I sat down to rest, and begun to tackle the queerest sort of strangers and ask for information, but I didn't get any; they couldn't understand my language, and I could not understand theirs. I got dreadfully lonesome. I was so down-hearted and homesick I wished a hundred times I never had died. I turned back, of course. About noon next day, I got back at last and was on hand at the booking-office once more. Says I to the head clerk –

"I begin to see that a man's got to be in his own Heaven to be happy."

"Perfectly correct," says he. "Did you imagine the same heaven would suit all sorts of men?"

"Well, I had that idea – but I see the foolishness of it. Which way am I to go to get to my district?"

He called the under clerk that had examined the map, and he gave me general directions. I thanked him and started; but he says –

"Wait a minute; it is millions of leagues from here. Go outside and stand on that red wishing-carpet; shut your eyes, hold your breath, and wish yourself there."

"I'm much obliged," says I; "why didn't you dart me through when I first arrived?"

"We have a good deal to think of here; it was your place to think of it and ask for it. Good-by; we probably sha'n't see you in this region for a thousand centuries or so."

"In that case, o revoor," says I.

I hopped onto the carpet and held my breath and shut my eyes and wished I was in the booking-office of my own section. The very next instant a voice I knew sung out in a business kind of a way –

"A harp and a hymn-book, pair of wings and a halo, size 13, for Cap'n Eli Stormfield, of San Francisco! – make him out a clean bill of health, and let him in."

I opened my eyes. Sure enough, it was a Pi Ute Injun I used to know in Tulare County; mighty good fellow – I remembered being at his funeral, which consisted of him being burnt and the other Injuns gauming their faces with his ashes and howling like wildcats. He was powerful glad to see me, and you may make up your mind I was just as glad to see him, and feel that I was in the right kind of a heaven at last.

Just as far as your eye could reach, there was swarms of clerks, running and bustling around, tricking out thousands of Yanks and Mexicans and English and Arabs, and all sorts of people in their new outfits; and when they gave me my kit and I put on my halo and took a look in the glass, I could have jumped over a house for joy, I was so happy. "Now this is something like!" says I. "Now," says I, "I'm all right – show me a cloud."

* * *

Inside of fifteen minutes I was a mile on my way towards the cloud-banks and about a million people along with me. Most of us tried to fly, but some got crippled and nobody made a success of it. So we concluded to walk, for the present, till we had had some wing practice.

We begun to meet swarms of folks who were coming back. Some had harps and nothing else; some had hymn-books and nothing else; some had nothing at all; all of them looked meek and uncomfortable; one young fellow hadn't anything left but his halo, and he was carrying that in his hand; all of a sudden he offered it to me and says –

"Will you hold it for me a minute?"

Then he disappeared in the crowd. I went on. A woman asked me to hold her palm branch, and then she disappeared. A girl got me to hold her harp for her, and by George, she disappeared; and so on and so on, till I was about loaded down to the guards. Then comes a smiling old gentleman and asked me to hold his things. I swabbed off the perspiration and says, pretty tart –

"I'll have to get you to excuse me, my friend, – I ain't no hat-rack."

About this time I begun to run across piles of those traps, lying in the road. I just quietly dumped my extra cargo along with them. I looked around, and, Peters, that whole nation that was following me were loaded down the same as I'd been. The return crowd had got them to hold their things a minute, you see. They all dumped their loads, too, and we went on.

When I found myself perched on a cloud, with a million other people, I never felt so good in my life. Says I, "Now this is according to the promises; I've been having my doubts, but now I am in heaven, sure enough." I gave my palm branch a wave or two, for luck, and then I tautened up my harp-strings and struck in. Well, Peters, you can't imagine anything like the row we made. It was grand to listen to, and made a body thrill all over, but there was considerable many tunes going on at once, and that was a drawback to the harmony, you understand; and then there was a lot of Injun tribes, and they kept up such another war-whooping that they kind of took the tuck out of the music. By and by I quit performing, and judged I'd take a rest. There was quite a nice mild old gentleman sitting next me, and I noticed he didn't take a hand; I encouraged him, but he said he was naturally bashful, and was afraid to try before so many people. By and by the old gentleman said he never could seem to enjoy music somehow. The fact was, I was beginning to feel the same way; but I didn't say anything. Him and I had a considerable long silence, then, but of course it warn't noticeable in that place. After about sixteen or seventeen hours, during which I played and sung a little, now and then – always the same tune, because I didn't know any other – I laid down my harp and begun to fan myself with my palm branch. Then we both got to sighing pretty regular. Finally, says he –

"Don't you know any tune but the one you've been pegging at all day?"

"Not another blessed one," says I.

"Don't you reckon you could learn another one?" says he.

"Never," says I; "I've tried to, but I couldn't manage it."

"It's a long time to hang to the one – eternity, you know."

"Don't break my heart," says I; "I'm getting low-spirited enough already."

After another long silence, says he –

"Are you glad to be here?"

Says I, "Old man, I'll be frank with you. This ain't just as near my idea of bliss as I thought it was going to be, when I used to go to church."

Says he, "What do you say to knocking off and calling it half a day?"

"That's me," says I. "I never wanted to get off watch so bad in my life."

So we started. Millions were coming to the cloud-bank all the time, happy and hosannahing; millions were leaving it all the time, looking mighty quiet, I tell you. We laid for the new-comers, and pretty soon I'd got them to hold all my things a minute, and then I was a free man again and most outrageously happy. Just then I ran across old Sam Bartlett, who had been dead a long time, and stopped to have a talk with him. Says I –

"Now tell me – is this to go on for ever? Ain't there anything else for a change?"

Says he –

"I'll set you right on that point very quick. People take the figurative language of the Bible and the allegories for literal, and the first thing they ask for when they get here is a halo and a harp, and so on. Nothing that's harmless and reasonable is refused a body here, if he asks it in the right spirit. So they are outfitted with these things without a word. They go and sing and play just about one day, and that's the last you'll ever see them in the choir. They don't need anybody to tell them that that sort of thing wouldn't make a heaven – at least not a heaven that a sane man could stand a week and remain sane. That cloud-bank is placed where the noise can't disturb the old inhabitants, and so there ain't any harm in letting everybody get up there and cure himself as soon as he comes.

"Now you just remember this – heaven is as blissful and lovely as it can be; but it's just the busiest place you ever heard of. There ain't any idle people here after the first day. Singing hymns and waving palm branches through all eternity is pretty when you hear about it in the pulpit, but it's as poor a way to put in valuable time as a body could contrive. It would just make a heaven of warbling ignoramuses, don't you see? Eternal Rest sounds comforting in the pulpit, too. Well, you try it once, and see how heavy time will hang on your hands. Why, Stormfield, a man like you, that had been active and stirring all his life, would go mad in six months in a heaven where he hadn't anything to do. Heaven is the very last place to come to rest in, – and don't you be afraid to bet on that!"

Says I –

"Sam, I'm as glad to hear it as I thought I'd be sorry. I'm glad I come, now."

Says he –

"Cap'n, ain't you pretty physically tired?"

Says I –

"Sam, it ain't any name for it! I'm dog-tired."

"Just so – just so. You've earned a good sleep, and you'll get it. You've earned a good appetite, and you'll enjoy your dinner. It's the same here as it is on earth – you've got to earn a thing, square and honest, before you enjoy it. You can't enjoy first and earn afterwards. But there's this difference, here: you can choose your own occupation, and all the powers of heaven will be put forth to help you make a success of it, if you do your level best. The shoemaker on earth that had the soul of a poet in him won't have to make shoes here."

"Now that's all reasonable and right," says I. "Plenty of work, and the kind you hanker after; no more pain, no more suffering – "

"Oh, hold on; there's plenty of pain here – but it don't kill. There's plenty of suffering here, but it don't last. You see, happiness ain't a thing in itself – it's only a contrast with something that ain't pleasant. That's all it is. There ain't a thing you can mention that is happiness in its own self – it's only so by contrast with the other thing. And so, as soon as the novelty is over and the force of the contrast dulled, it ain't happiness any longer, and you have to get something fresh. Well, there's plenty of pain and suffering in heaven – consequently there's plenty of contrasts, and just no end of happiness."

Says I, "It's the sensiblest heaven I've heard of yet, Sam, though it's about as different from the one I was brought up on as a live princess is different from her own wax figger."

* * *

Along in the first months I knocked around about the Kingdom, making friends and looking at the country, and finally settled down in a pretty likely region, to have a rest before taking another start. I went on making acquaintances and gathering up information. I had a good deal of talk with an old bald-headed angel by the name of Sandy McWilliams. He was from somewhere in New Jersey. I went about with him, considerable. We used to lay around, warm afternoons, in the shade of a rock, on some meadow-ground that was pretty high and out of the marshy slush of his cranberry-farm, and there we used to talk about all kinds of things, and smoke pipes. One day, says I –

"About how old might you be, Sandy?"

"Seventy-two."

"I judged so. How long you been in heaven?"

"Twenty-seven years, come Christmas."

"How old was you when you come up?"

"Why, seventy-two, of course."

"You can't mean it!"

"Why can't I mean it?"

"Because, if you was seventy-two then, you are naturally ninety-nine now."

"No, but I ain't. I stay the same age I was when I come."

"Well," says I, "come to think, there's something just here that I want to ask about. Down below, I always had an idea that in heaven we would all be young, and bright, and spry."

"Well, you can be young if you want to. You've only got to wish."

"Well, then, why didn't you wish?"

"I did. They all do. You'll try it, some day, like enough; but you'll get tired of the change pretty soon."

"Why?"

"Well, I'll tell you. Now you've always been a sailor; did you ever try some other business?"

"Yes, I tried keeping grocery, once, up in the mines; but I couldn't stand it; it was too dull – no stir, no storm, no life about it; it was like being part dead and part alive, both at the same time. I wanted to be one thing or t'other. I shut up shop pretty quick and went to sea."

"That's it. Grocery people like it, but you couldn't. You see you wasn't used to it. Well, I wasn't used to being young, and I couldn't seem to take any interest in it. I was strong, and handsome, and had curly hair, – yes, and wings, too! – gay wings like a butterfly. I went to picnics and dances and parties with the fellows, and tried to carry on and talk nonsense with the girls, but it wasn't any use; I couldn't take to it – fact is, it was an awful bore. What I wanted was early to bed and early to rise, and something to do; and when my work was done, I wanted to sit quiet, and smoke and think – not tear around with a parcel of giddy young kids. You can't think what I suffered whilst I was young."

"How long was you young?"

"Only two weeks. That was plenty for me. Laws, I was so lonesome! You see, I was full of the knowledge and experience of seventy-two years; the deepest subject those young folks could strike was only a-b-c to me. And to hear them argue – oh, my! it would have been funny, if it hadn't been so pitiful. Well, I was so hungry for the ways and the sober talk I was used to, that I tried to ring in with the old people, but they wouldn't have it. They considered me a conceited young upstart, and gave me the cold shoulder. Two weeks was a-plenty for me. I was glad to get back my bald head again, and my pipe, and my old drowsy reflections in the shade of a rock or a tree."

"Well," says I, "do you mean to say you're going to stand still at seventy-two, for ever?"

"I don't know, and I ain't particular. But I ain't going to drop back to twenty-five any more – I know that, mighty well. I know a sight more than I did twenty-seven years ago, and I enjoy learning, all the time, but I don't seem to get any older. That is, bodily – my mind gets older, and stronger, and better seasoned, and more satisfactory."

Says I, "If a man comes here at ninety, don't he ever set himself back?"

"Of course he does. He sets himself back to fourteen; tries it a couple of hours, and feels like a fool; sets himself forward to twenty; it ain't much improvement; tries thirty, fifty, eighty, and finally ninety – finds he is more at home and comfortable at the same old figure he is used to than any other way. Or, if his mind begun to fail him on earth at eighty, that's where he finally sticks up here. He sticks at the place where his mind was last at its best, for there's where his enjoyment is best, and his ways most set and established."

"Does a chap of twenty-five stay always twenty-five, and look it?"

"If he is a fool, yes. But if he is bright, and ambitious and industrious, the knowledge he gains and the experiences he has, change his ways and thoughts and likings, and make him find his best pleasure in the company of people above that age; so he allows his body to take on that look of as many added years as he needs to make him comfortable and proper in that sort of society; he lets his body go on taking the look of age, according as he progresses, and by and by he will be bald and wrinkled outside, and wise and deep within."

"Babies the same?"

"Babies the same. Laws, what asses we used to be, on earth, about these things! We said we'd be always young in heaven. We didn't say how young – we didn't think of that, perhaps – that is, we didn't all think alike, anyway. When I was a boy of seven, I suppose I thought we'd all be twelve, in heaven; when I was twelve, I suppose I thought we'd all be eighteen or twenty in heaven; when I was forty, I begun to go back; I remember I hoped we'd all be about thirty years old in heaven. Neither a man nor a boy ever thinks the age he has is exactly the best one – he puts the right age a few years older or a few years younger than he is. Then he makes that ideal age the general age of the heavenly people. And he expects everybody to stick at that age – stand stock-still – and expects them to enjoy it! – Now just think of the idea of standing still in heaven! Think of a heaven made up entirely of hoop-rolling, marble-playing cubs of seven years! – or of awkward, diffident, sentimental immaturities of nineteen! – or of vigorous people of thirty, healthy-minded, brimming with ambition, but chained hand and foot to that one age and its limitations like so many helpless galley-slaves! Think of the dull sameness of a society made up of people all of one age and one set of looks, habits, tastes and feelings. Think how superior to it earth would be, with its variety of types and faces and ages, and the enlivening attrition of the myriad interests that come into pleasant collision in such a variegated society."

"Look here," says I, "do you know what you're doing?"

"Well, what am I doing?"

"You are making heaven pretty comfortable in one way, but you are playing the mischief with it in another."

"How d'you mean?"

"Well," I says, "take a young mother that's lost her child, and – "

"Sh!" he says. "Look!"

It was a woman. Middle-aged, and had grizzled hair. She was walking slow, and her head was bent down, and her wings hanging limp and droopy; and she looked ever so tired, and was crying, poor thing! She passed along by, with her head down, that way, and the tears running down her face, and didn't see us. Then Sandy said, low and gentle, and full of pity: "She's hunting for her child! No, found it, I reckon. Lord, how she's changed! But I recognized her in a minute, though it's twenty-seven years since I saw her. A young mother she was, about twenty two or four, or along there; and blooming and lovely and sweet? oh, just a flower! And all her heart and all her soul was wrapped up in her child, her little girl, two years old. And it died, and she went wild with grief, just wild! Well, the only comfort she had was that she'd see her child again, in heaven – 'never more to part,' she said, and kept on saying it over and over, 'never more to part.' And the words made her happy; yes, they did; they made her joyful, and when I was dying, twenty-seven years ago, she told me to find her child the first thing, and say she was coming – 'soon, soon, very soon, she hoped and believed!'"

"Why, it's pitiful, Sandy."

He didn't say anything for a while, but sat looking at the ground, thinking. Then he says, kind of mournful: "And now she's come!"

"Well? Go on."

"Stormfield, maybe she hasn't found the child, but I think she has. Looks so to me. I've seen cases before. You see, she's kept that child in her head just the same as it was when she jounced it in her arms a little chubby thing. But here it didn't elect to stay a child. No, it elected to grow up, which it did. And in these twenty-seven years it has learned all the deep scientific learning there is to learn, and is studying and studying and learning and learning more and more, all the time, and don't give a damn for anything but learning; just learning, and discussing gigantic problems with people like herself."

"Well?"

"Stormfield, don't you see? Her mother knows cranberries, and how to tend them, and pick them, and put them up, and market them; and not another blamed thing! Her and her daughter can't be any more company for each other now than mud turtle and bird o' paradise. Poor thing, she was looking for a baby to jounce; I think she's struck a disapp'intment."

"Sandy, what will they do – stay unhappy for ever in heaven?"

"No, they'll come together and get adjusted by and by. But not this year, and not next. By and by."

Footnote 1: The captain could not remember what this word was. He said it was in a foreign tongue.

Chapter II

I HAD BEEN having considerable trouble with my wings. The day after I helped the choir I made a dash or two with them, but was not lucky. First off, I flew thirty yards, and then fouled an Irishman and brought him down – brought us both down, in fact. Next, I had a collision with a Bishop – and bowled him down, of course. We had some sharp words, and I felt pretty cheap, to come banging into a grave old person like that, with a million strangers looking on and smiling to themselves.

I saw I hadn't got the hang of the steering, and so couldn't rightly tell where I was going to bring up when I started. I went afoot the rest of the day, and let my wings hang. Early next morning I went to a private place to have some practice. I got up on a pretty high rock, and got a good start, and went swooping down, aiming for a bush a little over three hundred yards off; but I couldn't seem to calculate for the wind, which was about two points abaft my beam. I could see I was going considerable to looard of the bush, so I worked my starboard wing slow and went ahead strong on the port one, but it wouldn't answer; I could see I was going to broach to, so I slowed down on both, and lit. I went back to the rock and took another chance at it. I aimed two or three points to starboard of the bush – yes, more than that – enough so as to make it nearly a head-wind. I done well enough, but made pretty poor time. I could see, plain enough, that on a head-wind, wings was a mistake. I could see that a body could sail pretty close to the wind, but he couldn't go in the wind's eye. I could see that if I wanted to go a-visiting any distance from home, and the wind was ahead, I might have to wait days, maybe, for a change; and I could see, too, that these things could not be any use at all in a gale; if you tried to run before the wind, you would make a mess of it, for there isn't anyway to shorten sail – like reefing, you know – you have to take it all in – shut your feathers down flat to your sides. That would land you, of course. You could lay to, with your head to the wind – that is the best you could do, and right hard work you'd find it, too. If you tried any other game, you would founder, sure.

I judge it was about a couple of weeks or so after this that I dropped old Sandy McWilliams a note one day – it was a Tuesday – and asked him to come over and take his manna and quails with me next day; and the first thing he did when he stepped in was to twinkle his eye in a sly way, and say, –

"Well, Cap, what you done with your wings?"

I saw in a minute that there was some sarcasm done up in that rag somewheres, but I never let on. I only says –

"Gone to the wash."

"Yes," he says, in a dry sort of way, "they mostly go to the wash – about this time – I've often noticed it. Fresh angels are powerful neat. When do you look for 'em back?"

"Day after tomorrow," says I.

He winked at me, and smiled.

Says I –

"Sandy, out with it. Come – no secrets among friends. I notice you don't ever wear wings – and plenty others don't. I've been making an ass of myself – is that it?"

"That is about the size of it. But it is no harm. We all do it at first. It's perfectly natural. You see, on earth we jump to such foolish conclusions as to things up here. In the pictures we always saw the angels with wings on – and that was all right; but we jumped to the conclusion that that was their way of getting around – and that was all wrong. The wings ain't anything but a uniform, that's all. When they are in the field – so to speak, – they always wear them; you never see an angel going with a message anywhere without his wings, any more than you would see a military officer presiding at a court-martial without his uniform, or a postman delivering letters, or a policeman walking his beat, in plain clothes. But they ain't to fly with! The wings are for show, not for use. Old experienced angels are like officers of the regular army – they dress plain, when they are off duty. New angels are like the militia – never shed the uniform – always fluttering and floundering around in their wings, butting people down, flapping here, and there, and everywhere, always imagining they are attracting the admiring eye – well, they just think they are the very most important people in heaven. And when you see one of them come sailing around with one wing tipped up and t'other down, you make up your mind he is saying to himself: 'I wish Mary Ann in Arkansaw could see me now. I reckon she'd wish she hadn't shook me.' No, they're just for show, that's all – only just for show."

"I judge you've got it about right, Sandy," says I.

"Why, look at it yourself," says he. "You ain't built for wings – no man is. You know what a grist of years it took you to come here from the earth – and yet you were booming along faster than any cannon-ball could go. Suppose you had to fly that distance with your wings – wouldn't eternity have been over before you got here? Certainly. Well, angels have to go to the earth every day – millions of them – to appear in visions to dying children and good people, you know – it's the heft of their business. They appear with their wings, of course, because they are on official service, and because the dying persons wouldn't know they were angels if they hadn't wings – but do you reckon they fly with them? It stands to reason they don't. The wings would wear out before they got half-way; even the pin-feathers would be gone; the wing frames would be as bare as kite sticks before the paper is pasted on. The distances in heaven are billions of times greater; angels have to go all over heaven every day; could they do it with their wings alone? No, indeed; they wear the wings for style, but they travel any distance in an instant by wishing. The wishing-carpet of the Arabian Nights was a sensible idea – but our earthly idea of angels flying these awful distances with their clumsy wings was foolish.

"Our young saints, of both sexes, wear wings all the time – blazing red ones, and blue and green, and gold, and variegated, and rainbowed, and ring-streaked-and-striped ones – and nobody finds fault. It is suitable to their time of life. The things are beautiful, and they set the young people off. They are the most striking and lovely part of their outfit – a halo don't begin."

"Well," says I, "I've tucked mine away in the cupboard, and I allow to let them lay there till there's mud."

"Yes – or a reception."

"What's that?"

"Well, you can see one tonight if you want to. There's a barkeeper from Jersey City going to be received."

"Go on – tell me about it."

"This barkeeper got converted at a Moody and Sankey meeting, in New York, and started home on the ferry-boat, and there was a collision and he got drowned. He is of a class that think all heaven goes wild with joy when a particularly hard lot like him is saved; they think all heaven turns out hosannahing to welcome them; they think there isn't anything talked about in the realms of the blest but their case, for that day. This barkeeper thinks there hasn't been such another stir here in years, as his coming is going to raise. And I've always noticed this peculiarity about a dead barkeeper – he not only expects all hands to turn out when he arrives, but he expects to be received with a torchlight procession."

"I reckon he is disappointed, then."

"No, he isn't. No man is allowed to be disappointed here. Whatever he wants, when he comes – that is, any reasonable and unsacrilegious thing – he can have. There's always a few millions or billions of young folks around who don't want any better entertainment than to fill up their lungs and swarm out with their torches and have a high time over a barkeeper. It tickles the barkeeper till he can't rest, it makes a charming lark for the young folks, it don't do anybody any harm, it don't cost a rap, and it keeps up the place's reputation for making all comers happy and content."

"Very good. I'll be on hand and see them land the barkeeper."

"It is manners to go in full dress. You want to wear your wings, you know, and your other things."

"Which ones?"

"Halo, and harp, and palm branch, and all that."

"Well," says I, "I reckon I ought to be ashamed of myself, but the fact is I left them laying around that day I resigned from the choir. I haven't got a rag to wear but this robe and the wings."

"That's all right. You'll find they've been raked up and saved for you. Send for them."

"I'll do it, Sandy. But what was it you was saying about unsacrilegious things, which people expect to get, and will be disappointed about?"

"Oh, there are a lot of such things that people expect and don't get. For instance, there's a Brooklyn preacher by the name of Talmage, who is laying up a considerable disappointment for himself. He says, every now and then in his sermons, that the first thing he does when he gets to heaven, will be to fling his arms around Abraham, Isaac and Jacob, and kiss them and weep on them. There's millions of people down there on earth that are promising themselves the same thing. As many as sixty thousand people arrive here every single day, that want to run straight to Abraham, Isaac and Jacob, and hug them and weep on them. Now mind you, sixty thousand a day is a pretty heavy contract for those old people. If they were a mind to allow it, they wouldn't ever have anything to do, year in and year out, but stand up and be hugged and wept on thirty-two hours in the twenty-four. They would be tired out and as wet as muskrats all the time. What would heaven be, to them? It would be a mighty good place to get out of – you know that, yourself. Those are kind and gentle old Jews, but they ain't any fonder of kissing the emotional highlights of Brooklyn than you be. You mark my words, Mr T.'s endearments are going to be declined, with thanks. There are limits to the privileges of the elect, even in heaven. Why, if Adam was to show himself to every new comer that wants to call and gaze at him and strike him for his autograph, he would never have time to do anything else but just that. Talmage has said he is going to give Adam some of his attentions, as well as A., I. and J. But he will have to change his mind about that."

"Do you think Talmage will really come here?"

"Why, certainly, he will; but don't you be alarmed; he will run with his own kind, and there's plenty of them. That is the main charm of heaven – there's all kinds here – which wouldn't be the case if you let the preachers tell it. Anybody can find the sort he prefers, here, and he just lets the others alone, and they let him alone. When the Deity builds a heaven, it is built right, and on a liberal plan."

Sandy sent home for his things, and I sent for mine, and about nine in the evening we begun to dress. Sandy says –

"This is going to be a grand time for you, Stormy. Like as not some of the patriarchs will turn out."

"No, but will they?"

"Like as not. Of course they are pretty exclusive. They hardly ever show themselves to the common public. I believe they never turn out except for an eleventh-hour convert. They wouldn't do it then, only earthly tradition makes a grand show pretty necessary on that kind of an occasion."

"Do they an turn out, Sandy?"

"Who? All the patriarchs? Oh, no – hardly ever more than a couple. You will be here fifty thousand years – maybe more – before you get a glimpse of all the patriarchs and prophets. Since I have been here, Job has been to the front once, and once Ham and Jeremiah both at the same time. But the finest thing that has happened in my day was a year or so ago; that was Charles Peace's reception – him they called 'the Bannercross Murderer' – an Englishman. There were four patriarchs and two prophets on the Grand Stand that time – there hasn't been anything like it since Captain Kidd came; Abel was there – the first time in twelve hundred years. A report got around that Adam was coming; well, of course, Abel was enough to bring a crowd, all by himself, but there is nobody that can draw like Adam. It was a false report, but it got around, anyway, as I say, and it will be a long day before I see the like of it again. The reception was in the English department, of course, which is eight hundred and eleven million miles from the New Jersey line. I went, along with a good many of my neighbors, and it was a sight to see, I can tell you. Flocks came from all the departments. I saw Esquimaux there, and Tartars, Negroes, Chinamen – people from everywhere. You see a mixture like that in the Grand Choir, the first day you land here, but you hardly ever see it again. There were billions of people; when they were singing or hosannahing, the noise was wonderful; and even when their tongues were still the drumming of the wings was nearly enough to burst your head, for all the sky was as thick as if it was snowing angels. Although Adam was not there, it was a great time anyway, because we had three archangels on the Grand Stand – it is a seldom thing that even one comes out."

"What did they look like, Sandy?"

"Well, they had shining faces, and shining robes, and wonderful rainbow wings, and they stood eighteen feet high, and wore swords, and held their heads up in a noble way, and looked like soldiers."

"Did they have halos?"

"No – anyway, not the hoop kind. The archangels and the upper-class patriarchs wear a finer thing than that. It is a round, solid, splendid glory of gold, that is blinding to look at. You have often seen a patriarch in a picture, on earth, with that thing on – you remember it? – he looks as if he had his head in a brass platter. That don't give you the right idea of it at all – it is much more shining and beautiful."

"Did you talk with those archangels and patriarchs, Sandy?"

"Who – I? Why, what can you be thinking about, Stormy? I ain't worthy to speak to such as they."

"Is Talmage?"

"Of course not. You have got the same mixed-up idea about these things that everybody has down there. I had it once, but I got over it. Down there they talk of the heavenly King – and that is right – but then they go right on speaking as if this was a republic and everybody was on a dead level with everybody else, and privileged to fling his arms around anybody he comes across, and be hail-fellow-well-met with all the elect, from the highest down. How tangled up and absurd that is! How are you going to have a republic under a king? How are you going to have a republic at all, where the head of the government is absolute, holds his place for ever, and has no parliament, no council to meddle or make in his affairs, nobody voted for, nobody elected, nobody in the whole universe with a voice in the government, nobody asked to take a hand in its matters, and nobody allowed to do it? Fine republic, ain't it?"

"Well, yes – it is a little different from the idea I had – but I thought I might go around and get acquainted with the grandees, anyway – not exactly splice the main-brace with them, you know, but shake hands and pass the time of day."

"Could Tom, Dick and Harry call on the Cabinet of Russia and do that? – on Prince Gortschakoff, for instance?"

"I reckon not, Sandy."

"Well, this is Russia – only more so. There's not the shadow of a republic about it anywhere. There are ranks, here. There are viceroys, princes, governors, sub-governors, sub-sub-governors, and a hundred orders of nobility, grading along down from grand-ducal archangels, stage by stage, till the general level is struck, where there ain't any titles. Do you know what a prince of the blood is, on earth?"

"No."

"Well, a prince of the blood don't belong to the royal family exactly, and he don't belong to the mere nobility of the kingdom; he is lower than the one, and higher than t'other. That's about the position of the patriarchs and prophets here. There's some mighty high nobility here – people that you and I ain't worthy to polish sandals for – and they ain't worthy to polish sandals for the patriarchs and prophets. That gives you a kind of an idea of their rank, don't it? You begin to see how high up they are, don't you? Just to get a two-minute glimpse of one of them is a thing for a body to remember and tell about for a thousand years. Why, Captain, just think of this: if Abraham was to set his foot down here by this door, there would be a railing set up around that foot-track right away, and a shelter put over it, and people would flock here from all over heaven, for hundreds and hundreds of years, to look at it. Abraham is one of the parties that Mr Talmage, of Brooklyn, is going to embrace, and kiss, and weep on, when he comes. He wants to lay in a good stock of tears, you know, or five to one he will go dry before he gets a chance to do it."

"Sandy," says I, "I had an idea that I was going to be equals with everybody here, too, but I will let that drop. It don't matter, and I am plenty happy enough anyway."

"Captain, you are happier than you would be, the other way. These old patriarchs and prophets have got ages the start of you; they know more in two minutes than you know in a year. Did you ever try to have a sociable improving-time discussing winds, and currents and variations of compass with an undertaker?"

"I get your idea, Sandy. He couldn't interest me. He would be an ignoramus in such things – he would bore me, and I would bore him."

"You have got it. You would bore the patriarchs when you talked, and when they talked they would shoot over your head. By and by you would say, 'Good morning, your Eminence,

I will call again' – but you wouldn't. Did you ever ask the slush-boy to come up in the cabin and take dinner with you?"

"I get your drift again, Sandy. I wouldn't be used to such grand people as the patriarchs and prophets, and I would be sheepish and tongue-tied in their company, and mighty glad to get out of it. Sandy, which is the highest rank, patriarch or prophet?"

"Oh, the prophets hold over the patriarchs. The newest prophet, even, is of a sight more consequence than the oldest patriarch. Yes, sir, Adam himself has to walk behind Shakespeare."

"Was Shakespeare a prophet?"

"Of course he was; and so was Homer, and heaps more. But Shakespeare and the rest have to walk behind a common tailor from Tennessee, by the name of Billings; and behind a horse-doctor named Sakka, from Afghanistan. Jeremiah, and Billings and Buddha walk together, side by side, right behind a crowd from planets not in our astronomy; next come a dozen or two from Jupiter and other worlds; next come Daniel, and Sakka and Confucius; next a lot from systems outside of ours; next come Ezekiel, and Mahomet, Zoroaster, and a knife-grinder from ancient Egypt; then there is a long string, and after them, away down toward the bottom, come Shakespeare and Homer, and a shoemaker named Marais, from the back settlements of France."

"Have they really rung in Mahomet and all those other heathens?"

"Yes – they all had their message, and they all get their reward. The man who don't get his reward on earth, needn't bother – he will get it here, sure."

"But why did they throw off on Shakespeare, that way, and put him away down there below those shoe-makers and horse-doctors and knife-grinders – a lot of people nobody ever heard of?"

"That is the heavenly justice of it – they warn't rewarded according to their deserts, on earth, but here they get their rightful rank. That tailor Billings, from Tennessee, wrote poetry that Homer and Shakespeare couldn't begin to come up to; but nobody would print it, nobody read it but his neighbors, an ignorant lot, and they laughed at it. Whenever the village had a drunken frolic and a dance, they would drag him in and crown him with cabbage leaves, and pretend to bow down to him; and one night when he was sick and nearly starved to death, they had him out and crowned him, and then they rode him on a rail about the village, and everybody followed along, beating tin pans and yelling. Well, he died before morning. He wasn't ever expecting to go to heaven, much less that there was going to be any fuss made over him, so I reckon he was a good deal surprised when the reception broke on him."

"Was you there, Sandy?"

"Bless you, no!"

"Why? Didn't you know it was going to come off?"

"Well, I judge I did. It was the talk of these realms – not for a day, like this barkeeper business, but for twenty years before the man died."

"Why the mischief didn't you go, then?"

"Now how you talk! The like of me go meddling around at the reception of a prophet? A mudsill like me trying to push in and help receive an awful grandee like Edward J. Billings? Why, I should have been laughed at for a billion miles around. I shouldn't ever heard the last of it."

"Well, who did go, then?"

"Mighty few people that you and I will ever get a chance to see, Captain. Not a solitary commoner ever has the luck to see a reception of a prophet, I can tell you. All the nobility, and all the patriarchs and prophets – every last one of them – and all the archangels, and all the princes and governors and viceroys, were there, – and no small fry – not a single one. And mind you, I'm not talking about only the grandees from our world, but the princes and patriarchs and so on from all the worlds that shine in our sky, and from billions more that belong in systems upon systems away outside of the one our sun is in. There were some prophets and patriarchs there that ours ain't a circumstance to, for rank and illustriousness and all that. Some were from Jupiter and other worlds in our own system, but the most celebrated were three poets, Saa, Bo and Soof, from great planets in three different and very remote systems. These three names are common and familiar in every nook and corner of heaven, clear from one end of it to the other – fully as well known as the eighty Supreme Archangels, in fact – where as our Moses, and Adam, and the rest, have not been heard of outside of our world's little corner of heaven, except by a few very learned men scattered here and there – and they always spell their names wrong, and get the performances of one mixed up with the doings of another, and they almost always locate them simply in our solar system, and think that is enough without going into little details such as naming the particular world they are from. It is like a learned Hindoo showing off how much he knows by saying Longfellow lives in the United States – as if he lived all over the United States, and as if the country was so small you couldn't throw a brick there without hitting him.

Between you and me, it does gravel me, the cool way people from those monster worlds outside our system snub our little world, and even our system. Of course we think a good deal of Jupiter, because our world is only a potato to it, for size; but then there are worlds in other systems that Jupiter isn't even a mustard-seed to – like the planet Goobra, for instance, which you couldn't squeeze inside the orbit of Halley's comet without straining the rivets. Tourists from Goobra (I mean parties that lived and died there – natives) come here, now and then, and inquire about our world, and when they find out it is so little that a streak of lightning can flash clear around it in the eighth of a second, they have to lean up against something to laugh. Then they screw a glass into their eye and go to examining us, as if we were a curious kind of foreign bug, or something of that sort. One of them asked me how long our day was; and when I told him it was twelve hours long, as a general thing, he asked me if people where I was from considered it worth while to get up and wash for such a day as that. That is the way with those Goobra people – they can't seem to let a chance go by to throw it in your face that their day is three hundred and twenty-two of our years long. This young snob was just of age – he was six or seven thousand of his days old – say two million of our years – and he had all the puppy airs that belong to that time of life – that turning-point when a person has got over being a boy and yet ain't quite a man exactly. If it had been anywhere else but in heaven, I would have given him a piece of my mind.

Well, anyway, Billings had the grandest reception that has been seen in thousands of centuries, and I think it will have a good effect. His name will be carried pretty far, and it will make our system talked about, and maybe our world, too, and raise us in the respect of the general public of heaven. Why, look here – Shakespeare walked backwards before that tailor from Tennessee, and scattered flowers for him to walk on, and Homer stood behind his chair and waited on him at the banquet. Of course that didn't go for much there, amongst all those big foreigners from other systems, as they hadn't heard of Shakespeare or Homer either, but it would amount to considerable down there on our little earth if they could know about it. I wish there was something in that miserable spiritualism, so we could send them word. That Tennessee village would set up a monument to Billings, then, and his autograph would outsell Satan's. Well, they had grand times at that reception – a small-fry noble from Hoboken told me all about it – Sir Richard Duffer, Baronet."

"What, Sandy, a nobleman from Hoboken? How is that?"

"Easy enough. Duffer kept a sausage-shop and never saved a cent in his life because he used to give all his spare meat to the poor, in a quiet way. Not tramps, – no, the other sort – the sort that will starve before they will beg – honest square people out of work. Dick used to watch hungry-looking men and women and children, and track them home, and find out all about them from the neighbors, and then feed them and find them work. As nobody ever saw him give anything to anybody, he had the reputation of being mean; he died with it, too, and everybody said it was a good riddance; but the minute he landed here, they made him a baronet, and the very first words Dick the sausage-maker of Hoboken heard when he stepped upon the heavenly shore were, 'Welcome, Sir Richard Duffer!' It surprised him some, because he thought he had reasons to believe he was pointed for a warmer climate than this one."

* * *

All of a sudden the whole region fairly rocked under the crash of eleven hundred and one thunder blasts, all let off at once, and Sandy says –

"There, that's for the barkeep."

I jumped up and says –

"Then let's be moving along, Sandy; we don't want to miss any of this thing, you know."

"Keep your seat," he says; "he is only just telegraphed, that is all."

"How?"

"That blast only means that he has been sighted from the signal-station. He is off Sandy Hook. The committees will go down to meet him, now, and escort him in. There will be ceremonies and delays; they won't he coming up the Bay for a considerable time, yet. It is several billion miles away, anyway."

"I could have been a barkeeper and a hard lot just as well as not," says I, remembering the lonesome way I arrived, and how there wasn't any committee nor anything.

"I notice some regret in your voice," says Sandy, "and it is natural enough; but let bygones be bygones; you went according to your lights, and it is too late now to mend the thing."

"No, let it slide, Sandy, I don't mind. But you've got a Sandy Hook here, too, have you?"

"We've got everything here, just as it is below. All the States and Territories of the Union, and all the kingdoms of the earth and the islands of the sea are laid out here just as they are on the globe – all the same shape they are down there, and all graded to the relative size, only each State and realm and island is a good many billion times bigger here than it is below. There goes another blast."

"What is that one for?"

"That is only another fort answering the first one. They each fire eleven hundred and one thunder blasts at a single dash – it is the usual salute for an eleventh-hour guest; a hundred for each hour and an extra one for the guest's sex; if it was a woman we would know it by their leaving off the extra gun."

"How do we know there's eleven hundred and one, Sandy, when they all go off at once? And yet we certainly do know."

"Our intellects are a good deal sharpened up, here, in some ways, and that is one of them. Numbers and sizes and distances are so great, here, that we have to be made so we can feel them – our old ways of counting and measuring and ciphering wouldn't ever give us an idea of them, but would only confuse us and oppress us and make our heads ache."

After some more talk about this, I says: "Sandy, I notice that I hardly ever see a white angel; where I run across one white angel, I strike as many as a hundred million copper-colored ones – people that can't speak English. How is that?"

"Well, you will find it the same in any State or Territory of the American corner of heaven you choose to go to. I have shot along, a whole week on a stretch, and gone millions and millions of miles, through perfect swarms of angels, without ever seeing a single white one, or hearing a word I could understand. You see, America was occupied a billion years and more, by Injuns and Aztecs, and that sort of folks, before a white man ever set his foot in it. During the first three hundred years after Columbus's discovery, there wasn't ever more than one good lecture audience of white people, all put together, in America – I mean the whole thing, British Possessions and all; in the beginning of our century there were only 6,000,000 or 7,000,000 – say seven; 12,000,000 or 14,000,000 in 1825; say 23,000,000 in 1850; 40,000,000 in 1875. Our death-rate has always been 20 in 1000 per annum. Well, 140,000 died the first year of the century; 280,000 the twenty-fifth year; 500,000 the fiftieth year; about a million the seventy-fifth year. Now I am going to be liberal about this thing, and consider that fifty million whites have died in America from the beginning up to to-day – make it sixty, if you want to; make it a hundred million – it's no difference about a few millions one way or t'other.

Well, now, you can see, yourself, that when you come to spread a little dab of people like that over these hundreds of billions of miles of American territory here in heaven, it is like scattering a ten-cent box of homoeopathic pills over the Great Sahara and expecting to find them again. You can't expect us to amount to anything in heaven, and we don't – now that is the simple fact, and we have got to do the best we can with it. The learned men from other planets and other systems come here and hang around a while, when they are touring around the Kingdom, and then go back to their own section of heaven and write a book of travels, and they give America about five lines in it. And what do they say about us? They say this wilderness is populated with a scattering few hundred thousand billions of red angels, with now and then a curiously complected diseased one. You see, they think we whites and the occasional nigger are Injuns that have been bleached out or blackened by some leprous disease or other – for some peculiarly rascally sin, mind you. It is a mighty sour pill for us all, my friend – even the modestest of us, let alone the other kind, that think they are going to be received like a long-lost government bond, and hug Abraham into the bargain. I haven't asked you any of the particulars, Captain, but I judge it goes without saying – if my experience is worth anything – that there wasn't much of a hooraw made over you when you arrived – now was there?"

"Don't mention it, Sandy," says I, coloring up a little; "I wouldn't have had the family see it for any amount you are a mind to name. Change the subject, Sandy, change the subject."

"Well, do you think of settling in the California department of bliss?"

"I don't know. I wasn't calculating on doing anything really definite in that direction till the family come. I thought I would just look around, meantime, in a quiet way, and make up my mind. Besides, I know a good many dead people, and I was calculating to hunt them up and swap a little gossip with them about friends, and old times, and one thing or another, and ask them how they like it here, as far as they have got. I reckon my wife will want to camp in the California range, though, because most all her departed will be there, and she likes to be with folks she knows."

"Don't you let her. You see what the Jersey district of heaven is, for whites; well, the Californian district is a thousand times worse. It swarms with a mean kind of leather-headed mud-colored angels – and your nearest white neighbor is likely to be a million miles away. What a man mostly misses, in heaven, is company – company of his own sort and color and language. I have come near settling in the European part of heaven once or twice on that account."

"Well, why didn't you, Sandy?"

"Oh, various reasons. For one thing, although you see plenty of whites there, you can't understand any of them, hardly, and so you go about as hungry for talk as you do here. I like to look at a Russian or a German or an Italian – I even like to look at a Frenchman if I ever have the luck to catch him engaged in anything that ain't indelicate – but looking don't cure the hunger – what you want is talk."

"Well, there's England, Sandy – the English district of heaven."

"Yes, but it is not so very much better than this end of the heavenly domain. As long as you run across Englishmen born this side of three hundred years ago, you are all right; but the minute you get back of Elizabeth's time the language begins to fog up, and the further back you go the foggier it gets. I had some talk with one Langland and a man by the name of Chaucer – old-time poets – but it was no use, I couldn't quite understand them, and they couldn't quite understand me. I have had letters from them since, but it is such broken English I can't make it out. Back of those men's time the English are just simply foreigners, nothing more, nothing less; they talk Danish, German, Norman French, and sometimes a mixture of all three; back of them, they talk Latin, and ancient British, Irish, and Gaelic; and then back of these come billions and billions of pure savages that talk a gibberish that Satan himself couldn't understand. The fact is, where you strike one man in the English settlements that you can understand, you wade through awful swarms that talk something you can't make head nor tail of. You see, every country on earth has been overlaid so often, in the course of a billion years, with different kinds of people and different sorts of languages, that this sort of mongrel business was bound to be the result in heaven."

"Sandy," says I, "did you see a good many of the great people history tells about?"

"Yes – plenty. I saw kings and all sorts of distinguished people."

"Do the kings rank just as they did below?"

"No; a body can't bring his rank up here with him. Divine right is a good-enough earthly romance, but it don't go, here. Kings drop down to the general level as soon as they reach the realms of grace. I knew Charles the Second very well – one of the most popular comedians in the English section – draws first rate. There are better, of course – people that were never heard of on earth – but Charles is making a very good reputation indeed, and is considered a rising man. Richard the Lion-hearted is in the prize-ring, and coming into considerable favor. Henry the Eighth is a tragedian, and the scenes where he kills people are done to the very life. Henry the Sixth keeps a religious-book stand."

"Did you ever see Napoleon, Sandy?"

"Often – sometimes in the Corsican range, sometimes in the French. He always hunts up a conspicuous place, and goes frowning around with his arms folded and his field-glass under his arm, looking as grand, gloomy and peculiar as his reputation calls for, and very much bothered because he don't stand as high, here, for a soldier, as he expected to."

"Why, who stands higher?"

"Oh, a lot of people we never heard of before – the shoemaker and horse-doctor and knife-grinder kind, you know – clodhoppers from goodness knows where that never handled a sword or fired a shot in their lives – but the soldiership was in them, though they never had a chance to show it. But here they take their right place, and Cæsar and Napoleon and Alexander have to take a back seat. The greatest military genius our world ever produced was a brick-layer from somewhere back of Boston – died during the Revolution – by the name of Absalom Jones. Wherever he goes, crowds flock to see him. You see, everybody knows that if he had had a chance he would have shown the world some generalship that would have made all generalship before look like child's play and 'prentice work. But he never got a chance; he tried heaps of times to enlist as a private, but he had lost both thumbs and a couple of front teeth, and the recruiting sergeant wouldn't pass him. However, as I say, everybody knows, now, what he would have been – and so they flock by the million to get a glimpse of him whenever they hear he is going to be anywhere. Cæsar, and Hannibal, and Alexander, and Napoleon are all on his staff, and ever so many more great generals; but the public hardly care to look at them when he is around. Boom! There goes another salute. The barkeeper's off quarantine now."

* * *

Sandy and I put on our things. Then we made a wish, and in a second we were at the reception-place. We stood on the edge of the ocean of space, and looked out over the dimness, but couldn't make out anything. Close by us was the Grand Stand – tier on tier of dim thrones rising up toward the zenith. From each side of it spread away the tiers of seats for the general public. They spread away for leagues and leagues – you couldn't see the ends. They were empty and still, and hadn't a cheerful look, but looked dreary, like a theatre before anybody comes – gas turned down. Sandy says –

"We'll sit down here and wait. We'll see the head of the procession come in sight away off yonder pretty soon, now."

Says I –

"It's pretty lonesome, Sandy; I reckon there's a hitch somewheres. Nobody but just you and me – it ain't much of a display for the barkeeper."

"Don't you fret, it's all right. There'll be one more gun-fire – then you'll see."

In a little while we noticed a sort of a lightish flush, away off on the horizon.

"Head of the torchlight procession," says Sandy.

It spread, and got lighter and brighter: soon it had a strong glare like a locomotive headlight; it kept on getting brighter and brighter till it was like the sun peeping above the horizon-line at sea – the big red rays shot high up into the sky.

"Keep your eyes on the Grand Stand and the miles of seats – sharp!" says Sandy, "and listen for the gun-fire."

Just then it burst out, "Boom-boom-boom!" like a million thunderstorms in one, and made the whole heavens rock. Then there was a sudden and awful glare of light all about us, and in that very instant every one of the millions of seats was occupied, and as far as you could see, in both directions, was just a solid pack of people, and the place was all splendidly lit up! It was enough to take a body's breath away. Sandy says –

"That is the way we do it here. No time fooled away; nobody straggling in after the curtain's up. Wishing is quicker work than travelling. A quarter of a second ago these folks were millions of miles from here. When they heard the last signal, all they had to do was to wish, and here they are."

The prodigious choir struck up – "We long to hear thy voice. To see thee face to face."

It was noble music, but the uneducated chipped in and spoilt it, just as the congregations used to do on earth.

The head of the procession began to pass, now, and it was a wonderful sight. It swept along, thick and solid, five hundred thousand angels abreast, and every angel carrying a torch and singing – the whirring thunder of the wings made a body's head ache. You could follow the line of the procession back, and slanting upward into the sky, far away in a glittering snaky rope, till it was only a faint streak in the distance. The rush went on and on, for a long time, and at last, sure enough, along comes the barkeeper, and then everybody rose, and a cheer went up that made the heavens shake, I tell you! He was all smiles, and had his halo tilted over one ear in a cocky way, and was the most satisfied-looking saint I ever saw. While he marched up the steps of the Grand Stand, the choir struck up –

"The whole wide heaven groans, And waits to hear that voice."

There were four gorgeous tents standing side by side in the place of honor, on a broad railed platform in the centre of the Grand Stand, with a shining guard of honor round about them. The tents had been shut up all this time. As the barkeeper climbed along up, bowing and smiling to everybody, and at last got to the platform, these tents were jerked up aloft all of a sudden, and we saw four noble thrones of gold, all caked with jewels, and in the two middle ones sat old white-whiskered men, and in the two others a couple of the most glorious and gaudy giants, with platter halos and beautiful armor. All the millions went down on their knees, and stared, and looked glad, and burst out into a joyful kind of murmurs. They said –

"Two archangels! – that is splendid. Who can the others be?"

The archangels gave the barkeeper a stiff little military bow; the two old men rose; one of them said, "Moses and Esau welcome thee!" and then all the four vanished, and the thrones were empty.

The barkeeper looked a little disappointed, for he was calculating to hug those old people, I judge; but it was the gladdest and proudest multitude you ever saw – because they had seen Moses and Esau. Everybody was saying, "Did you see them? – I did – Esau's side face was to me, but I saw Moses full in the face, just as plain as I see you this minute!"

The procession took up the barkeeper and moved on with him again, and the crowd broke up and scattered. As we went along home, Sandy said it was a great success, and the barkeeper would have a right to be proud of it for ever. And he said we were in luck, too; said we might attend receptions for forty thousand years to come, and not have a chance to see a brace of such grand moguls as Moses and Esau. We found afterwards that we had come near seeing another patriarch, and likewise a genuine prophet besides, but at the last moment they sent regrets. Sandy said there would be a monument put up there, where Moses and Esau had stood, with the date and circumstances, and all about the whole business, and travellers would come for thousands of years and gawk at it, and climb over it, and scribble their names on it.

Butterfly Dreams

Donald Jacob Uitvlugt

"Once Chou dreamt he was a butterfly, happily flitting and fluttering around. When he awoke, he didn't know if he was Chou who had dreamt he was a butterfly, or a butterfly dreaming he was Chou." Chuang Tzu

IT WAS FINISHED. Doug Kane pulled the door of his brother's home behind him, making sure that the lock caught. He slipped behind the wheel of his black Mustang and backed it down the driveway. He waited until he could work his way out of Russell's development and then hit the gas. His Mustang was a conspicuous car, but he needed speed more than stealth. He hoped to be two states away by the time the police found his brother Russell's body.

Doug pulled onto the highway and clicked on the radio. Perhaps that would distract him from his swirling thoughts. "We'd like to take a moment to thank our day sponsor, Soshi Tech. Soshi Tech, for all your – "

Doug mentally tuned out the commercial and the station identification. He had finally caught a break. The highway should have been bumper to bumper this early in the morning. But while the flow of traffic around him was steady, there were enough gaps that Doug could weave through them without ever having to drop below ninety.

Something about moving around the cars evoked a strong feeling of déjà vu. Doug shook his head.

If only Russell hadn't started hitting Kathy, none of this would have happened. Doug gripped the steering wheel, trying hard not to think about the way his brother had looked up at him with those unseeing eyes. He tried not to think about how Russell's marriage to the kindest and prettiest woman in the world had started to unravel before the couple had returned from their honeymoon. The attacks had been verbal at first, Doug only hearing about them after the fact. But the night Kathy had shown up on his front porch, in tears, with a black eye...

He turned up the volume of the radio. Don't think about it. Concentrate on getting out of town. His mind would go round in circles if he let it. "...was Del Shannon's 'Runaway,'" Doug found himself hating that perfect radio voice. "And now here's Johann Sebastian Bach's 'Toccata and Fugue in D Minor.'"

Doug blinked as the melancholy strains of organ came through the Mustang's speakers. *Eclectic mix. I didn't know that there were any independent stations left in town. I thought they'd all been bought up by the big conglomerates and it was all that pre-programmed shi –*

He slammed on the brakes, only just avoiding the golden retriever that darted in front of the Mustang. *What the hell's that dog doing on the highway?* A quick glance around told Doug that it wasn't the dog that was out of place. He wasn't on the highway any more. Somehow he had wound up back in the suburbs, not at all sure how he had gotten there.

"That set finished with 'Slip Sliding Away' by Paul Simon. Next up, the Monkees with 'Pleasant Valley Sunday'..."

Doug ignored the background buzz of the radio, trying to figure out where exactly he was. *God. I'm in Russell's development. How the hell did I get back here?* Guilt? Or perhaps his subconscious mind was trying to help him out. Maybe he had left something at the scene. Should he check?

He idled at a red light, deciding which way to turn. He saw someone out of the corner of his eye. Her face... She looked so much like Kathy. Only without the black eye and bruises she had sported last time Doug had seen her. But there was something else...

The only thing Doug could compare it to was the feeling he sometimes got in department stores, when he caught sight of a person out of the corner of his eye, even felt a presence behind him, but when he turned, it was only a mannequin. This was that same feeling, only in reverse. Like the woman had been less real until Doug had looked at her, some unseen force popping Kathy's face into place at the last minute.

He shook his head, even though the light had turned green. Was the fact he was seeing Kathy in strangers another omen? *I don't have time to worry about this. Stick to the plan. Get the heck out of Dodge.* He turned left, away from his brother's house, leaving Russell's body behind him.

He drove past a park, moving slower than he would have liked, trying to get back to the highway. A number of children were playing there, which was odd for a school day morning. Doug's stomach churned as he watched the children. He could almost see their faces snapping into place as he looked at them. Just as before, it was like they were somehow less real until he looked at them directly. Nerves. It had to be nerves. Doug hadn't been as cold-blooded about killing his brother as he thought he had been. The deed was catching up with him.

"'Proud Mary,' by Ike and Tina Turner. Talk about your explosive relationships. And with that, we move on to Judas Priest with 'You've Got Another Thing Coming'..."

Doug forced himself to drive past the park. As he rounded the block, he saw a kid leaning up against the fence, watching him. *Bobbie? Bobbie Reynolds?* It couldn't be. Bobbie had taken his own life when he and Doug were both in the eighth grade. He had always felt guilty about not doing something to prevent Bobbie's death. His guilt had to be taking over. He was seeing things.

Whoever the child really was, he seemed to recognize Doug, waving to him as he drove past. Doug forced himself to look away, gripping the wheel tightly.

"Another blast from the past with the theme from MASH. And a special note to those of you in the western suburbs. Police have just discovered the body of prominent local physician, Russell Kane. The doctor was found murdered in his own home. The suspect or suspects are believed to be still in the area. So lock your doors, kiddies, leave your lights on, and stay with us. Next up, Soft Cell with 'Tainted Love.'"

Doug fought down his panic. How had they discovered Russell's body so fast? His brother was supposed to be out of town for the next week. Everybody at the hospital and the club knew this. And Kathy and the kids were away at her mother's. It had been the perfect time to try to stop Russell from ever hurting Kathy again.

And now his carefully made plan was falling all to hell.

He nosed the Mustang toward the highway again, trying to move as fast as he could without drawing unwanted attention to his car. He could hardly breathe. In the distance he heard the sound of sirens. Flight instinct set in. Doug floored it, turning the wheel.

Downtown? How had he wound up downtown? The sirens grew louder, and Doug could see the squad cars. This was going to be his last chance.

"And I am out of here. I leave you with Mozart's 'Dies Irae.'"

As Doug rounded a corner, a police car teed into him and another rear-ended him. His windshield cracked, red pain blossoming like fireworks in the night sky. As he died, the last few hours flashed before his eyes. Kathy. His careful planning. His confrontation with his brother. The murder...

It was finished. Doug Kane pulled the door of his brother's home behind him, making sure that the lock caught. He slipped behind the wheel of his red Firebird and backed it down the driveway. He waited until he could work his way out of Russell's development and then hit the gas. His Mustang was a conspicuous car, but he needed speed more than stealth. He hoped to be two states away by the time the police found his brother Russell's body.

Doug pulled onto the highway and clicked on the radio. "We'd like to take a moment to thank our day sponsor, Soshi Tech. Soshi Tech, for all your – "

The highway should have been bumper to bumper this early in the morning. But there were enough gaps that Doug could weave through them without ever having to drop below ninety. Something about moving around the cars evoked a strong feeling of déjà vu. Doug shook his head.

If only Russell hadn't started hitting Kathy, none of this would have happened...

* * *

Russell Kane smiled, looking down from the view screen to his brother in the VR machine. Doug's head was immobilized by a web of wires and straps, with goggles over his eyes thicker than a blind man's sunglasses. A breathing mask and feeding tube blotted out the rest of his brother's face. It wasn't going to be a pretty life for Doug, trapped in that loop, reliving for ever a death that had never happened. *At least it's better than what you had planned for me, Dougie. A marvelously full-service place this. What do their ads say? 'Soshi Tech, for all your Virtual Reality needs.' They've gone above and beyond here.*

Still, no need to let them know that. They might charge him more, citing God-only-knew what clause in the fifty-page contract. He tried his best to hide his smile of triumph, succeeding poorly.

"Do you want to see the loop again?" Russell turned to see the moonfaced technician in his white lab coat. The man had one of those nondescript faces that you swore you had seen before but couldn't remember where.

"Just one more time."

"You approved the script yourself, Dr Kane. I can assure you that the scene loops with only slight changes in scenery and casting, drawing from the subject's own memories. We find that the variation keeps the subject from ever figuring out that he's in a VR environment. Your brother will experience that car crash ad infinitum. Especially given what you're paying us."

"I didn't pay for that commercial for your blasted company."

"Policy, I'm afraid. I was able to place the advertisement as close to the beginning of the loop as possible, where the subject will be the most disoriented."

A sudden thought occurred to Russell, triggered from a news report he had read once upon a time. "And if he figures out that the commercial repeats, he could wake himself from the cycle."

"In the long history of this firm we have never had a subject awake due to autosuggestion. Consider too that he would remember our name from the ad. If your brother were to awake, I doubt that things would go well for us. An over-zealous DA might even interpret our actions on your behalf as criminal. And leaving the law to one side, we've seen your brother's violent tendencies. In fact, our lab studied them in-depth to create that environment. Trust me, Dr Kane. Your brother will remain in VR until you choose to release him or he dies of natural causes."

Russell had to admit that the technician had answered all his questions. His gloating smile returned, and he turned back to his brother. He watched the view screen for a moment, enjoying the growing desperation playing out there. Then he looked down at Doug's real body, trapped in the VR machine, his face obscured by the goggles, breathing mask and feeding tube. *What was that slogan? 'Soshi Tech, for all your Virtual Reality needs.'* It was not going to be a pretty life for Doug at all, but it was better than he deserved.

"Do you want to see the loop again?"

Russell turned toward the technician, a hint of a smile still on his lips. "Just one more time..."

* * *

"And you're certain he feels no pain?"

"None at all, Mr Kane." The technician seemed to sense Doug's hesitation and went on. "Your brother is a sick man, Mr Kane. It's clear from your own research that, not only was he abusing his wife, he was going to have you institutionalized in this facility. Illegally, I might add. That's why we contacted you."

"Yes. But to do to him what he was going to do to me. It still doesn't seem right."

The technician paused before speaking. "Remember, it is an illness we're speaking of here, Mr Kane. And a serious one at that. We still don't understand the sort of compulsions that drive someone to try to act in such antisocial ways, but psychiatric science is making new advances all the time. Perhaps one day soon your brother can be cured of his rage and jealousy. But until then, it's safer for everyone for him to be here. Including for Dr Kane."

Doug looked down at Russell. Behind the grotesque goggles and mask, his brother was smiling. He couldn't remember the last time Russell had smiled. Doug wondered what he saw. "Ok. Where are the papers?"

"Right this way, Mr Kane. And thank you for choosing S shi Tech for all your Virtual Reality needs."

Doug froze, a chill running down his spine. From somewhere he heard the sound of a woman laughing.

The Day of an American Journalist in 2889

Jules Verne

THE MEN of the twenty-ninth century live in a perpetual fairyland, though they do not seem to realise it. Bored with wonders, they are cold towards everything that progress brings them every day. It all seems only natural.

If they compared it with the past, they would better appreciate what our civilisation is, and realise what a road it has traversed. What would then seem finer than our modern cities, with streets a hundred yards wide, with buildings a thousand feet high, always at an equable temperature, and the sky furrowed by thousands of aero-cars and aero-buses! Compared with these towns, whose population may include up to ten million inhabitants, what were those villages, those hamlets of a thousand years ago, that Paris, that London, that New York – muddy and badly ventilated townships, traversed by jolting contraptions, hauled along by horses – yes! By horses! It's unbelievable!

If they recalled the erratic working of the steamers and the railways, their many collisions, and their slowness, how greatly would travellers value the aero-trains, and especially these pneumatic tubes laid beneath the oceans, which convey them with a speed of a thousand miles an hour? And would they not enjoy the telephone and the telephote even better if they recollected that our fathers were reduced to that antediluvian apparatus which they called the 'telegraph'?

It's very strange. These surprising transformations are based on principles which were quite well known to our ancestors, although these, so to speak, made no use of them. Heat, steam, electricity are as old as mankind. Towards the end of the nineteenth century, did not the savants declare that the only difference between the physical and chemical forces consists of the special rates of vibration of the etheric particles?

As so enormous a stride had been made, that of recognising the mutual relationship of all these forces, it is incredible that it took so long to work out the rates of vibration that differentiate between them. It is especially surprising that the method of passing directly from one to another, and of producing one without the other, has only been discovered so recently.

So it was, however, that things happened, and it was only in 2790, about a hundred years ago, that the famous Oswald Nyer succeeded in doing so.

A real benefactor of humanity, that great man! His achievement, a work of genius, was the parent of all the others! A constellation of inventors was born out of it, culminating in our extraordinary James Jackson. It is to him that we owe the new accumulators, some of which condense the force of the solar rays, others the electricity stored in the heart of our globe, and yet again others, energy coming from any source whatever, whether it be the waterfalls, winds, or rivers. It is to him that we owe no less the transformer which, at a touch on a simple switch, draws on the force that lives in the accumulators and releases it as heat, light, electricity, or mechanical power after it has performed any task we need.

Yes, it was from the day on which these two appliances were thought out that progress really dates. They have given mankind almost an infinite power. Through mitigating the bleakness of winter by restoring to it the excessive heat of the summer, they have revolutionised agriculture. By providing motive power for the appliances used in aerial navigation, they have enabled commerce to make a splendid leap forward. It is to them that we owe the unceasing production of electricity without either batteries or machines, light without combustion or incandescence, and finally that inexhaustible source of energy which has increased industrial production a hundredfold.

Very well then! The whole of these wonders, we shall meet them in an incomparable office block – the office of the Earth Herald, recently inaugurated in the 16823rd Avenue.

If the founder of the New York Herald, Gordon Bennett, were to be born a second time today, what would he say when he saw this palace of marble and gold that belongs to his illustrious descendant, Francis Bennett? Thirty generations had followed one another, and the New York Herald had always stayed in that same Bennett family. Two hundred years before, when the government of the Union had been transferred from Washington to Centropolis, the newspaper had followed the government – if it were not that the government had followed the newspaper – and it had taken its new title, Earth Herald.

And let nobody imagine that it had declined under the administration of Francis Bennett. No! On the contrary, its new director had given it an equalled vitality and driving-power by the inauguration of telephonic journalism.

Everybody knows that system, made possible by the incredible diffusion of the telephone. Every morning, instead of being printed as in antiquity, the Earth Herald is 'spoken.' It is by means of a brisk conversation with a reporter, a political figure, or a scientist, that the subscribers can learn whatever happens to interest them. As for those who buy an odd number for a few cents, they know that they can get acquainted with the day's issue through the countless phonographic cabinets.

This innovation of Francis Bennett restored new life to the old journal. In a few months its clientele numbered eighty-five million subscribers, and the director's fortune rose to three hundred million dollars, and has since gone far beyond that. Thanks to this fortune, he was able to build his new office – a colossal edifice with four facades each two miles long, whose roof is sheltered beneath the glorious flag, with its seventy-five stars, of the Confederation.

Francis Bennett, king of journalists, would then have been king of the two Americas, if the Americans would ever accept any monarch whatever. Do you doubt this? But the plenipotentiaries of every nation and our very ministers throng around his door, peddling their advice, seeking his approval, and imploring the support of his all-powerful organ. Count up the scientists whom he has encouraged, the artists whom he employs, the inventors whom he subsidises! A wearisome monarchy was his, work without respite, and certainly nobody of earlier times would ever have been able to carry out so unremitting a daily grind. Fortunately, however, the men of today have a more robust constitution, thanks to the progress of hygiene and of gymnastics, which from thirty-seven years has now increased to sixty-eight the average length of human life – thanks too to the aseptic foods, while we wait for the next discovery: that of nutritious air which will enable us to take nourishment ... only by breathing.

And now, if you would like to know everything that constitutes the day of a director of the Earth Herald, take the trouble to follow him in his multifarious operations – this very day, this July 25th of the present year, 2889.

That morning Francis Bennett awoke in rather a bad temper. This was eight days since his wife had been in France and he was feeling a little lonely. Can it be credited? They had been married ten years, and this was the first time that Mrs Edith Bennett, that professional beauty, had been so long away. Two or three days usually sufficed for her frequent journeys to Europe and especially to Paris, where she went to buy her hats.

As soon as he awoke, Francis Bennett switched on his phonotelephote, whose wires led to the house he owned in the Champs-Elystes.

The telephone, completed by the telephote, is another of our time's conquests! Though the transmission of speech by the electric current was already very old, it was only since yesterday that vision could also be transmitted. A valuable discovery, and Francis Bennett was by no means the only one to bless its inventor when, in spite of the enormous distance between them, he saw his wife appear in the telephotic mirror.

A lovely vision! A little tired by last night's theatre or dance, Mrs Bennett was still in bed. Although where she was it was nearly noon, her charming head was buried in the lace of the pillow. But there she was stirring ... her lips were moving ... No doubt she was dreaming? ... Yes! She was dreaming ... A name slipped from her mouth. "Francis ... dear Francis! ..."

His name, spoken by that sweet voice, gave a happier turn to Francis Bennett's mood. Not wanting to wake the pretty sleeper, he quickly jumped out of bed, and went into his mechanised dressing-room.

Two minutes later, without needing the help of a valet, the machine deposited him, washed, shaved, shod, dressed and buttoned from top to toe, on the threshold of his office. The day's work was going to begin.

It was into the room of the serialised novelists that Francis first entered.

Very big, that room, surmounted by a large translucent dome. In a corner, several telephonic instruments by which the hundred authors of the Earth Herald related a hundred chapters of a hundred romances to the enfevered public.

Catching sight of one of these serialists who was snatching five minutes' rest, Francis Bennett said: "Very fine, my dear fellow, very fine, that last chapter of yours! That scene where the young village girl is discussing with her admirer some of the problems of transcendental philosophy shows very keen powers of observation! These country manners have never been more clearly depicted! Go on that way, my dear Archibald, and good luck to you. Ten thousand new subscribers since yesterday, thanks to you!"

"Mr John Last," he continued, turning towards another of his collaborators, "I'm not so satisfied with you! It hasn't any life, your story! You're in too much of a hurry to get to the end! Well! And what about all that documentation? You've got to dissect, John Last, you've got to dissect! It isn't with a pen one writes nowadays, it's with a scalpel! Every action in real life is the resultant of a succession of fleeting thoughts, and they've got to be carefully set out to create a living being! And what's easier than to use electrical hypnotism, which redoubles its subject and separates his twofold personality! Watch yourself living, John Last, my dear fellow! Imitate your colleague whom I've just been congratulating! Get yourself hypnotised ... What? ... You're having it done, you say? ... Not good enough yet, not good enough!"

Having given this little lesson, Francis Bennett continued his inspection and went on into the reporters' room. His fifteen hundred reporters, placed before an equal number of telephones, were passing on to subscribers the news which had come in during the night from the four quarters of the earth.

The organisation of this incomparable service has often been described. In addition to his telephone, each reporter has in front of him a series of commutators, which allow him to get into communication with this or that telephotic line. Thus the subscribers have not only the story but the sight of these events. When it is a question of miscellaneous facts, which are things of the past by the time they are described, their principal phases alone are transmitted; these are obtained by intensive photography.

Francis Bennett questioned one of the ten astronomical reporters a service which was growing because of the recent discoveries in the stellar world.

"Well, Cash, what have you got?"

"Phototelegrams from Mercury, Venus and Mars, sir."

"Interesting, that last one?"

"Yes! A revolution in the Central Empire, in support of the reactionary liberals against the republican conservatives."

"Just like us, then! And Jupiter?"

"Nothing so far! We haven't been able to understand the signals the Jovians make. Perhaps ours haven't reached them?"

"That's your job, and I hold you responsible, Mr Cash!" Francis Bennett replied; extremely dissatisfied, he went on to the scientific editorial room.

Bent over their computers, thirty savants were absorbed in equations of the ninety-fifth degree. Some indeed were revelling in the formulae of algebraical infinity and of twenty-four-dimensional space, like a child in the elementary class dealing with the four rules of arithmetic.

Francis Bennett fell among them rather like a bombshell.

"Well, gentlemen, what's this they tell me? No reply from Jupiter? ... It's always the same! Look here, Corley, it seems to me it's been twenty years that you've been pegging away at that planet ..."

"What do you expect, sir?" the savant replied. "Our optical science still leaves something to be desired, and even with our telescopes two miles long ..."

"You hear that, Peer?" broke in Francis Bennett, addressing himself to Corley's neighbour. "Optical science leaves something to be desired! ... That's your specialty, that is, my dear fellow! Put on your glasses, devil take it! Put on your glasses!"

Then, turning back to Corley: "But, failing Jupiter, aren't you getting some result from the moon, at any rate?"

"Not yet, Mr Bennett."

"Well, this time, you can't blame optical science! The moon is six hundred times nearer than Mars, and yet our correspondence service is in regular operation with Mars. It can't be telescopes we're needing ..."

"No, it's the inhabitants," Corley replied with the thin smile of a savant stuffed with X.

"You dare tell me that the moon is uninhabited?"

"On the face it turns towards us, at any rate, Mr Bennett. Who knows whether on the other side ...?"

"Well, there's a very simple method of finding out ..."

"And that is? ..."

"To turn the moon round!"

And that very day, the scientists of the Bennett factory started working out some mechanical means of turning our satellite right round.

On the whole Francis Bennett had reason to be satisfied. One of the Earth Herald's astronomers had just determined the elements of the new planet Gandini. It is at a distance of 12,841,348,284,623 metres and 7 decimetres that this planet describes its orbit round the sun in 572 years, 194 days, 12 hours, 43 minutes, 9.8 seconds. Francis Bennett was delighted with such precision.

"Good!" he exclaimed. "Hurry up and tell the reportage service about it. You know what a passion the public has for these astronomical questions. I'm anxious for the news to appear in today's issue!"

Before leaving the reporters' room he took up another matter with a special group of interviewers, addressing the one who dealt with celebrities: "You've interviewed President Wilcox?" he asked.

"Yes, Mr Bennett, and I'm publishing the information that he's certainly suffering from a dilation of the stomach, and that he's most conscientiously undergoing a course of tubular irrigations."

"Splendid. And that business of Chapmann the assassin ... Have you interviewed the jurymen who are to sit at the Assizes?"

"Yes, and they all agree that he's guilty, so that the case won't even have to be submitted to them. The accused will be executed before he's sentenced."

"Splendid! Splendid!"

The next room, a broad gallery about a quarter of a mile long, was devoted to publicity, and it well may be imagined what the publicity for such a journal as the Earth Herald had to be. It brought in a daily average of three million dollars. Very ingeniously, indeed, some of the publicity obtained took an absolutely novel form, the result of a patent bought at an outlay of three dollars from a poor devil who had since died of hunger. They are gigantic signs reflected on the clouds, so large that they can be seen all over a whole country. From that gallery a thousand projectors were unceasingly employed in sending to the clouds, on which they were reproduced in colour, these inordinate advertisements.

But that day when Francis Bennett entered the publicity room he found the technicians with their arms folded beside their idle projectors. He asked them about it ... The only reply he got was that somebody pointed to the blue sky.

"Yes! ... A fine day," he muttered, "so we can't get any aerial publicity! What's to be done about that? If there isn't any rain, we can produce it! But it isn't rain, it's clouds that we need!"

"Yes, some fine snow-white clouds!" replied the chief technician.

"Well, Mr Simon Mark, you'd better get in touch with the scientific editors, meteorological service. You can tell them from me that they can get busy on the problem of artificial clouds. We really can't be at the mercy of the fine weather."

After finishing his inspection of the different sections of the paper, Francis Bennett went to his reception hall, where he found awaiting him the ambassadors and plenipotentiary ministers accredited to the American government: these gentlemen had come to ask advice from the all-powerful director. As he entered the room they were carrying on rather a lively discussion.

"Pardon me, Your Excellency," the French Ambassador addressed the Ambassador from Russia. "But I can't see anything that needs changing in the map of Europe. The north to the Slavs, agreed! But the south to the Latins! Our common frontier along the Rhine seems quite satisfactory. Understand me clearly, that our government will certainly resist any attempt which may be made against our Prefectures of Rome, Madrid and Vienna!"

"Well said!" Francis Bennett intervened in the discussion. "What, Mr Russian Ambassador, you're not satisfied with your great empire, which extends from the banks of the Rhine as far as the frontiers of China? An empire whose immense coast is bathed by the Arctic Ocean, the Atlantic, the Black Sea, the Bosphorus, and the Indian Ocean!

"And besides, what's the use of threats? Is war with our modern weapons possible! These asphyxiating shells which can be sent a distance of a hundred miles, these electric flashes, sixty miles long, which can annihilate a whole army corps at a single blow, these projectiles loaded with the microbes of plague, cholera and yellow fever, and which can destroy a whole nation in a few hours?"

"We realise that, Mr Bennett," the Russian Ambassador replied. "But are we free to do what we like? ... Thrust back ourselves by the Chinese on our eastern frontier, we must, at all costs, attempt something towards the west ..."

"Is that all it is, sir?" Francis Bennett replied in reassuring tones – "Well! As the proliferation of the Chinese is getting to be a danger to the world, we'll bring pressure to bear on the Son of Heaven. He'll simply have to impose a maximum birth-rate on his subjects, not to be exceeded on pain of death! A child too many? ... A father less! That will keep things balanced."

"And you, sir," the director of the Earth Herald continued, addressing the English consul, "what can I do to be of service to you?"

"A great deal, Mr Bennett," that personage replied. "It would be enough for your journal to open a campaign on our behalf ..."

"And with what purpose?"

"Merely to protest against the annexation of Great Britain by the United States ..."

"Merely that!" Francis Bennett exclaimed. He shrugged his shoulders. "An annexation that's a hundred and fifty years old already! But won't you English gentry ever resign yourselves to the fact that by a just compensation of events here below, your country has become an American colony? That's pure madness! How could your government ever have believed that I should even open so anti-patriotic a campaign? ..."

"Mr Bennett, you know that the Monroe Doctrine is all America for the Americans, and nothing more than America, and not ..."

"But England is only one of our colonies, one of the finest. Don't count upon our ever consenting to give her up."

"You refuse?"

"I refuse, and if you insist, we shall make it a casus belli, based on nothing more than an interview with one of our reporters."

"So that's the end." The consul was overwhelmed. "The United Kingdom, Canada, and New Britain belong to the Americans, India to the Russians, and Australia and New Zealand to themselves! Of all that once was England, what's left? ... Nothing."

"Nothing, sir?" retorted Francis Bennett. "Well, what about Gibraltar?"

At that moment the clock struck twelve. The director of the Earth Herald, ending the audience with a gesture, left the hall, and sat down in a rolling armchair. In a few minutes he had reached his dining-room half a mile away, at the far end of the office.

The table was laid, and he took his place at it. Within reach of his hand was placed a series of taps, and before him was the curved surface of a phonotelephote, on which appeared the dining-room of his home in Paris. Mr and Mrs Bennett had arranged to have lunch at the same time – nothing could be more pleasant than to be face to face in spite of the distance, to see one another and talk by means of the phonotelephotic apparatus.

But the room in Paris was still empty.

"Edith is late," Francis Bennett said to himself. "Oh, women's punctuality! Everything makes progress, except that."

And after this too just reflection, he turned on one of the taps.

Like everybody else in easy circumstances nowadays, Francis Bennett, having abandoned domestic cooking, is one of the subscribers to the Society for Supplying Food to the Home, which distributes dishes of a thousand types through a network of pneumatic tubes. This system is expensive, no doubt, but the cooking is better, and it has the advantage that it has suppressed that hair-raising race, the cooks of both sexes.

So, not without some regret, Francis Bennett was lunching in solitude. He was finishing his coffee when Mrs Bennett, having got back home, appeared in the telephote screen.

"Where have you been, Edith dear?" Francis Bennett enquired.

"What," Mrs Bennett replied. "You've finished! ... I must be late, then? ... Where have I been? Of course, I've been with my modiste ... This year's hats are so bewitching! They're not hats at all ... they're domes, they're cupolas! I rather lost count of time."

"Rather, my dear? You lost it so much that here's my lunch finished."

"Well, run along then, my dear ... run along to your work," Mrs Bennett replied. "I've still got a visit to make, to my modeleur-couturier."

And this couturier was no other than the famous Wormspire, the very man who so judiciously remarked, "Woman is only a question of shape!"

Francis Bennett kissed Mrs Bennett's cheek on the telephote screen and went across to the window, where his aero-car was waiting.

"Where are we going, sir?" asked the aero-coachman. "Let's see. I've got time ..." Francis Bennett replied. "Take me to my accumulator works at Niagara."

The aero-car, an apparatus splendidly based on the principle of "heavier than air," shot across space at a speed of about four hundred miles an hour. Below him were spread out the towns with their moving pavements which carry the wayfarers along the streets, and the countryside, covered, as though by an immense spider's web, by the network of electric wires.

Within half an hour, Francis Bennett had reached his works at Niagara, where, after using the force of the cataracts to produce energy, he sold or hired it out to the consumers. Then, his visit over, he returned, by way of Philadelphia, Boston, and New York, to Centropolis, where his aero-car put him down about five o'clock.

The waiting-room of the Earth Herald was crowded. A careful lookout was being kept for Francis Bennett to return for the daily audience he gave to his petitioners. They included the capital's acquisitive inventors, company promoters with enterprises to suggest – all splendid, to listen to them. Among these different proposals he had to make a choice, reject the bad ones, look into the doubtful ones, give a welcome to the good ones.

He soon got rid of those who had only got useless or impracticable schemes. One of them – didn't he claim to revive painting, an art which had fallen into such desuetude that Millet's Angelus had just been sold for fifteen francs – thanks to the progress of colour photography invented at the end of the twentieth century by the Japanese, whose name was on everybody's lips – Aruziswa-Riochi-Nichome-Sanjukamboz-Kio-Baski-Ku? Another, hadn't he discovered the biogene bacillus which, after being introduced into the human organism, would make man immortal? This one, a chemist, hadn't he discovered a new substance Nihilium, of which a gram would cost only three million dollars? That one, a most daring physician, wasn't he claiming that he'd found a remedy for a cold in the head?

All these dreamers were at once shown out.

A few of the others received a better welcome, and foremost among them was a young man whose broad brow indicated a high degree of intelligence.

"Sir," he began, "though the number of elements used to be estimated at seventy-five, it has now been reduced to three, as no doubt you are aware?"

"Perfectly," Francis Bennett replied.

"Well, sir, I'm on the point of reducing the three to one. If I don't run out of money I'll have succeeded in three weeks."

"And then?"

"Then, sir, I shall really have discovered the absolute."

"And the results of that discovery?"

"It will be to make the creation of all forms of matter easy - stone, wood, metal, fibrin ..."

"Are you saying you're going to be able to construct a human being?"

"Completely ... The only thing missing will be the soul!"

"Only that!" was the ironical reply of Francis Bennett, who however assigned the young fellow to the scientific editorial department of his journal.

A second inventor, using as a basis some old experiments that dated from the nineteenth century and had often been repeated since, had the idea of moving a whole city in a single block. He suggested, as a demonstration, the town of Saaf, situated fifteen miles from the sea; after conveying it on rails down to the shore, he would transform it into a seaside resort. That would add an enormous value to the ground already built on and to be built over.

Francis Bennett, attracted by this project, agreed to take a half-share in it.

"You know, sir," said a third applicant, "that, thanks to our solar and terrestrial accumulators and transformers, we've been able to equalise the seasons. I suggest doing even better. By converting into heat part of the energy we have at our disposal and transmitting the heat to the polar regions we can melt the ice ..."

"Leave your plans with me," Francis Bennett replied, "and come back in a week."

Finally, a fourth savant brought the news that one of the questions which had excited the whole world was about to be solved that very evening.

As is well known, a century ago a daring experiment made by Dr Nathaniel Faithburn had attracted public attention. A convinced supporter of the idea of human hibernation - the possibility of arresting the vital functions and then reawakening them after a certain time - he had decided to test the value of the method on himself. After, by a holograph will, describing the operations necessary to restore him to life a hundred years later to the day, he had exposed himself to a cold of 172 degrees centigrade (278 degrees Fahrenheit) below zero; thus reduced to a mummified state, he had been shut up in a tomb for the stated period.

Now it was exactly on that very day, 25 July 2889, that the period expired, and Francis Bennett had just received an offer to proceed in one of the rooms of the Earth Herald office with the resurrection so impatiently waited for. The public could then be kept in touch with it second by second.

The proposal was accepted, and as the operation was not to take place until ten that evening, Francis Bennett went to stretch himself out in an easy-chair in the audition-room. Then, pressing a button, he was put into communication with the Central Concert.

After so busy a day, what a charm he found in the works of our greatest masters, based, as everybody knows, on a series of delicious harmonico-algebraic formulae!

The room had been darkened, and, plunged into an ecstatic half-sleep, Francis Bennett could not even see himself. But a door opened suddenly.

'Who's there?' he asked, touching a commutator placed beneath his hand.

At once, by an electric effect produced on the ether, the air became luminous.

"Oh, it's you, Doctor?" he asked.

"Myself," replied Dr Sam, who had come to pay his daily visit (annual subscription). "How's it going?"

"Fine!"

"All the better ... Let's see your tongue?"

He looked at it through a microscope.

"Good ... And your pulse?"

He tested it with a pulsograph, similar to the instruments which record earthquakes.

"Splendid! ... And your appetite?"

"Ugh!"

"Oh, your stomach! ... It isn't going too well, your stomach! ... It's getting old, your stomach is! ... We'll certainly have to get you a new one!"

"We'll see!" Francis Bennett replied, "and meantime, Doctor, you'll dine with me."

During the meal, phonotelephotic communication had been set up with Paris. Mrs Bennett was at her table this time, and the dinner, livened up by Dr Sam's jokes, was delightful. Hardly was it over than: "When do you expect to get back to Centropolis, dear Edith?" asked Francis Bennett.

"I'm going to start this moment."

"By tube or aero-train?"

"By tube."

"Then you'll be here?"

"At eleven fifty-nine this evening."

"Paris time?"

"No, no! ... Centropolis time."

"Goodbye then, and above all don't miss the tube!"

These submarine tubes, by which one travels from Paris in two hundred and ninety-five minutes, are certainly much preferable to the aero-trains, which only manage six hundred miles an hour.

The doctor had gone, after promising to return to be present at the resurrection of his colleague Nathaniel Faithburn. Wishing to draw up his daily accounts, Francis Bennett went into his private office. An enormous operation, when it concerns an enterprise whose expenditure rises to eight hundred thousand dollars every day! Fortunately, the development of modern mechanisation has greatly facilitated this work. Helped by the piano-electric-computer, Francis Bennett soon completed his task.

It was time. Hardly had he struck the last key of the mechanical totalisator than his presence was asked for in the experimental room. He went off to it at once, and was welcomed by a large cortege of scientists, who had been joined by Dr Sam.

Nathaniel Faithburn's body is there, on the bier, placed on trestles in the centre of the room.

The telephote is switched on. The whole world will be able to follow the various phases of the operation.

The coffin is opened ... Nathaniel Faithburn's body is taken out ... is still like a mummy, yellow hard, dry. It sounds like wood ... It is submitted to heat ... electricity ... No result ... It's hypnotised ... It's exposed to suggestion ... Nothing can overcome that ultracataleptic state.

"Well, Dr Sam!" asks Francis Bennett.

The doctor leans over the body; he examines it very carefully ... He introduces into it, by means of a hypodermic, a few drops of the famous Brown-Sequard elixir, which is once again in fashion ... The mummy is more mummified than ever.

"Oh well," Dr Sam replies, "I think the hibernation has lasted too long ..."

"Oh!"

"And Nathaniel Faithburn is dead."

"Dead?"

"As dead as anybody could be!"

"And how long has he been dead?"

"How long? ..." Dr Sam replies. But ... a hundred years – that is to say, since he had the unhappy idea of freezing himself for pure love of science."

"Then," Francis Bennett comments, "that's a method which still needs to be perfected!"

"Perfected is the word," replies Dr Sam, while the scientific commission on hibernation carries away its funereal bundle.

Followed by Dr Sam, Francis Bennett regained his room, and as he seemed very tired after so very full a day, the doctor advised him to take a bath before going to bed.

"You're quite right, Doctor ... That will refresh me ..."

"It will, Mr Bennett, and if you like I'll order one on my way out ..."

"There's no need for that, Doctor. There's always a bath all ready in the office, and I needn't even have the trouble of going out of my room to take it. Look, simply by touching this button, that bath will start moving, and you'll see it come along all by itself with the water at a temperature of sixty-five degrees!"

Francis Bennett had just touched the button. A rumbling sound began, got louder, increased ... Then one of the doors opened, and the bath appeared, gliding along on its rails ...

Heavens! While Dr Sam veils his face, little screams of frightened modesty arise from the bath ...

Brought to the office by the transatlantic tube half an hour before, Mrs Bennett was inside it.

Next day, 26 July 2889, the director of the Earth Herald recommenced his tour of twelve miles across his office. That evening, when his totalisator had been brought into action, it was at two hundred and fifty thousand dollars that it calculated the profits of that day – fifty thousand more than the day before.

A fine job, that of a journalist at the end of the twenty-ninth century!

Planetoid 127

Edgar Wallace

Chapter I

"CHAP" WEST, who was never an enthusiast for work, laid down the long pole that had brought him from Bisham to the shade of a backwater west of Hurley Lock, and dropped to the cushions at the bottom of the punt, groaning his relief. He was a lank youth, somewhat short-sighted, and the huge horn-rimmed spectacles which decorated his knobbly face lent him an air of scholarship which his school record hardly endorsed.

Elsie West woke from a doze, took one glance at her surroundings and settled herself more comfortably.

"Light the stove and make some tea," she murmured.

"I'm finished for the day," grunted her brother. "The hooter sounded ten minutes ago; and cooking was never a hobby of mine."

"Light the stove and make tea," she said faintly.

Chap glared down at the dozing figure; then glared past her to where, paddle in hand, Tim Lensman was bringing the punt to the shore.

Tim was the same age as his school friend, though he looked younger. A good-looking young man, he had been head of the house which had the honour of sheltering Chapston West. They had both been school prefects at Mildram and had entered and passed out on the same day.

Tim Lensman was looking disparagingly at the tangle of bush and high grass which fringed the wooded slope.

"Trespassers will be prosecuted," he read. "That seems almost an invitation – can you see the house, Chap?"

Chap shook his head.

"No; I'll bet it is the most horrible shanty you can imagine. Old Colson is just naturally a fug. And he's a science master – one of those Johnnies who ought to know the value of fresh air and ventilation."

Elsie, roused by the bump of the punt side against the bank, sat up and stared at the unpromising landing-place.

"Why don't you go farther along?" she asked. "You can't make tea here without – "

"Woman, have you no thought before food?" demanded her brother sternly. "Don't you thrill at the thought that you are anchored to the sacred terrain of the learned Professor Colson, doctor of science, bug expert, performer on the isobar and other musical instruments and – "

"Chap, you talk too much – and I should love a cup of tea."

"We'll have tea with the professor," said Chap firmly. "Having cut through the briars to his enchanted palace, we will be served in crystal cups reclining on couches of lapis lazuli."

She frowned up at the dark and unpromising woods.

"Does he really live here?" she addressed Tim, and he nodded.

"He really lives here," he said; "at least, I think so; his driving directions were very explicit and I seem to remember that he said we might have some difficulty in finding the house – "

"He said, 'Keep on climbing until you come to the top,'" interrupted Chap.

"But how does he reach the house?" asked the puzzled girl.

"By aeroplane," said Chap, as he tied the punt to the thick root of a laurel bush. "Or maybe he comes on his magic carpet. Science masters carry a stock of 'em. Or perhaps he comes through a front gate from a prosaic road – there must be roads even in Berkshire."

Tim was laughing quietly. "It is the sort of crib old Colson would choose," he said. "You ought to meet him, Elsie. He is the queerest old bird. Why he teaches at all I don't know, because he has tons of money, and he really is something of a magician. I was on the science side at Mildram and it isn't his amazing gifts as a mathematician that are so astounding. The head told me that Colson is the greatest living astronomer. Of course the stories they tell about his being able to foretell the future – "

"He can, too!"

Chap was lighting the stove, for, in spite of his roseate anticipations, he wished to be on the safe side, and he was in need of refreshment after a strenuous afternoon's punting.

"He told the school the day the war would end – to the very minute! And he foretold the big explosion in the gas works at Helwick – he was nearly pinched by the police for knowing so much about it. I asked him last year if he knew what was going to win the Grand National and he nearly bit my head off. He'd have told Timothy Titus, because Tim's his favourite child."

He helped the girl to land and made a brief survey of the bank. It was a wilderness of a place, and though his eyes roved around seeking a path through the jungle, his search was in vain. An ancient signboard warned all and sundry that the land was private property, but at the spot at which they had brought the punt to land the bank had, at some remote period, been propped up.

"Do you want me to come with you?" asked Elsie, obviously not enamoured with the prospect of the forthcoming call.

"Would you rather stay here?" asked Chap looking up from his stove.

She gave one glance along the gloomy backwater with its weedy bed and the overhanging osiers. A water-rat was swimming across the still water and this spectacle decided her.

"No; I think I will come with you," she said; and added, "I don't like rats."

"That was a vole," said Tim, shying a stone in the direction of the swimming rodent.

Her pretty face puckered in an expression of distaste.

"It looks horribly like a rat to me," she said. Chap poured out the tea and the girl was raising it to her lips when her eyes caught sight of the man who was watching them from between the trees, and she had hard work to suppress the scream that rose to her lips.

"What is it?"

Tim had seen her face change and now, following the direction of her eyes, he too saw the stranger.

There was nothing that was in the slightest degree sinister about the stranger; he was indeed the most commonplace figure Tim had ever seen. A short, stout man with a round and reddish face, which was decorated with a heavy ginger moustache; he stood twiddling his watch chain, his small eyes watching the party.

"Hello!" said Tim as he walked toward the stranger. "We have permission to land here."

He thought the man was some sort of caretaker or bailiff of "Helmwood."

"Got permission?" he repeated. "Of course you have – which of you is Lensman?"

"That's my name," smiled Tim, and the man nodded.

"He is expecting you and West and Miss Elsie West."

Tim's eyes opened wide in astonishment. He had certainly promised the professor that he would call one day during vacation, but he had not intended taking Chap nor his sister. It was only by accident he had met his school friend at Bisham that morning, and Chap had decided to come with him.

As though divining his thoughts, the stout man went on: "He knows a lot of things. If he's not mad he's crook. Where did he get all his information from? Why, fifteen years ago he hadn't fifty pounds! This place cost him ten thousand, and the house cost another ten thousand; and he couldn't have got his instruments and things under another ten thousand!"

Tim had been too much taken aback to interrupt. "Information? I don't quite understand… ?"

"About stocks and things… he's made a hundred thousand this year out of cotton. How did he know that the boll-weevil was going to play the devil with the South, eh? How did he know? And when I asked him just now to tell me about the corn market for a friend of mine, he talked to me like a dog!"

Chap had been listening open-mouthed. "Are you a friend of Mr Colson?" he asked.

"His cousin," was the reply. "Harry Dewes by name. His own aunt's child – and his only relation."

Suddenly he made a step towards them and his voice sank to a confidential tone.

"You young gentlemen know all about him – he's got delusions, hasn't he? Now, suppose I brought a couple of doctors to see him, maybe they'd like to ask you a few questions about him… "

Tim, the son of a great barrister, and himself studying for the bar, saw the drift of the question and would have understood, even if he had not seen the avaricious gleam in the man's eyes.

"You'd put him into an asylum and control his estate, eh?" he asked with a cold smile. "I'm afraid that you cannot rely upon us for help."

The man went red.

"Not that exactly," he said awkwardly. "And listen, young fellow…" he paused. "When you see Colson, I'd take it as a favour if you didn't mention the fact that you've seen me… I'm going to walk down to the lock… you'll find your way up between those poplars… so long!"

And turning abruptly he went stumbling through the bushes and was almost at once out of sight.

"What a lad!" said Chap admiringly. "And what a scheme! And to jump it at us straight away almost without an introduction – that fellow will never need a nerve tonic."

"How did Mr Colson know I was coming?" asked Elsie in wonder.

Tim was not prepared with an answer. After some difficulty they found the scarcely worn track that led up through the trees, and a quarter of an hour's stiff climb brought them to the crest and in view of the house.

Tim had expected to find a residence in harmony with the unkempt grounds. But the first view of "Helmwood" made him gasp. A solid and handsome stone house stood behind a broad stretch of shaven lawn. Flower beds bright with the blooms of late summer surrounded the lawn and bordered the walls of the house itself. At the farther end, but attached to the building, was a stone tower, broad and squat, and on the top of this was erected a hollow structure – criss-crossed without any apparent order or method – with a network of wires which glittered in the sunlight.

"A silver wire-box aerial!" said Chap. "That is a new idea, isn't it? Gosh, Tim! Look at the telescope!"

By the side of the tower was the bell-roof of a big observatory. The roof was closed, so that Chap's "telescope" was largely imaginary.

"Great Moses!" said Chap awe-stricken. "Why, it's as big as the Lick!"

Tim was impressed and astounded. He had guessed that the old science master was in comfortable circumstances, and knew that indeed he could afford the luxury of a car, but he had never dreamt that the professor was a man wealthy enough to own a house like this and an observatory which must have cost thousands to equip.

"Look, it's turning!" whispered Elsie.

The big, square superstructure on the tower was moving slowly, and then Tim saw two projecting cones of some crystalline material, for they glittered dazzlingly in the sunlight.

"That is certainly new," he said. "It is rather like the gadget they are using for the new beam transmission; or whatever they call it – and yet it isn't – "

As he stood there, he saw a long trench window open and a bent figure come out on to the lawn. Tim hastened towards the man of science and in a few minutes Chap was introducing his sister.

"I hope you didn't mind my coming, sir," said Chap. "Lensman told me he was calling."

"You did well to come," said Mr Colson courteously. "And it is a pleasure to meet your sister."

Elsie was observing him closely and her first impression was one of pleasant surprise. A thin, clean-shaven old man, with a mass of white hair that fell over his collar and bushy eyebrows, beneath which twinkled eyes of deepest blue. There was a hint of good humour in his delicately-moulded face. Girl-like, she first noted his extraordinary cleanliness. His linen was spotless, his neat black suit showed no speck of dust.

"You probably met a – er – relative of mine," he said gently. "A crude fellow – a very crude fellow. The uncouth in life jars me terribly. Will you come in, Miss West?"

They passed into a wide hall and down a long, broad corridor which was lighted on one side by narrow windows through which the girl had a glimpse of a neatly flagged courtyard, also surrounded by gay flower-beds.

On the other side of the corridor, doors were set at intervals and it was on the second of these that Tim, in passing, read an inscription. It was tidily painted in small, gold lettering: PLANETOID 127.

The professor saw the young man's puzzled glance and smiled. "A little conceit of mine," he said.

"Is that the number of an asteroid?" asked Tim, a dabbler in astronomy.

"No – you may search the Berlin Year Book in vain for No. 127," said the professor as he opened the door of a large and airy library and ushered them in. "There must be an asteroid – by which, young lady, is meant one of those tiny planets which abound in the zone between Mars and Jupiter, and of which, Witts D.Q. – now named Eros – is a remarkable example. My Planetoid was discovered on a certain 12th of July – 127. And it was not even an asteroid!"

He chuckled and rubbed his long white hands together.

The library with its walnut bookshelves, its deep chairs and faint fragrance of Russian leather, was a pleasant place, thought Elsie. Huge china bowls laden with roses stood in every possible point where bowls could stand. Through the open windows came a gentle breeze laden with the perfume of flowers.

"Tea will be ready in a minute," said Mr Colson. "I ordered it when I saw you. Yes, I am interested in asteroids."

His eyes went mechanically to the cornice of the room above the stone fire-place and Tim, looking up, saw that there was a square black cavity in the oaken panelling and wondered what was its significance.

"They are more real and tangible to me than the great planetary masses. Jupiter – a vapour mass; Saturn – a molten mass, yielding the secret of its rings to the spectroscope; Vulcan – no planet at all, but a myth and a dream of imaginative and romantic astronomers – there are no intra-mercurial planets, by which I mean" – he seemed to find it necessary to explain to Elsie, for which Chap was grateful – "that between Mercury, which is the nearest planet to the sun and the sun itself, there is no planetary body, though some foolish people think there is and have christened it Vulcan – "

An elderly footman had appeared in the doorway and the professor hurried across to him. There was a brief consultation (Elsie suspected a domestic problem, and was right) and with a word of apology, he went out.

"He's a rum bird," began Chap and stopped dead. From the black cavity above the fireplace came a thin whine of sound, and then a deafening splutter like exaggerated and intensified "atmospherics."

"What is that?" whispered the girl.

Before Tim could answer, the spluttering ceased, and then a soft, sweet voice spoke:

"'Lo... Col – son! Ja'ze ga shil? I speak you, Col – son... Planetoid 127... Big fire in my zehba... city... big fire... "

There was a click and the voice ceased abruptly, and at that moment Professor Colson came in.

He saw the amazed group staring at the square hole in the wall, and his lips twitched.

"You heard – ? I cut off the connection, though I'm afraid I may not get him again tonight."

"Who is he, sir?" asked Tim frowning. "Was that a transmission from any great distance?"

The professor did not answer at once. He glanced keenly and suspiciously at the girl, as though it was her intelligence he feared. And then: "The man who spoke was a man named Colson," he said deliberately; "and he spoke from a distance of 186 million miles!"

Chapter II

THEY LISTENED, dumbfounded.

Was the old professor mad? The voice that had spoken to them was the voice of Colson...?

"A hundred and eighty-six million miles?" said Tim incredulously "But, Mr Colson, that was not your voice I heard?"

He smiled faintly and shook his head.

"That was literally my alter ego – my other self," he said; and it seemed that he was going to say something else, but he changed the subject abruptly.

"Let us have tea," he said, smiling at Elsie. "My butler brought the alarming news that the ice cream had not arrived, but it came whilst we were discussing that tragedy!"

Elsie was fascinated by the old man and a little scared, too. She alone of that party realised that the reference he had made to the voice that came one hundred and eighty-six millions of miles was no jest on his part.

It was Chap who, in his awkward way, brought the conversation back to the subject of mysterious voices.

"They've had signals from Mars on Vancouver, sir," he said. "I saw it in this morning's papers."

Again the professor smiled.

"You think they were atmospherics?" suggested Elsie; and, to her surprise, Colson shook his head. "No; they were not atmospherics," he said quietly, "but they were not from Mars. I doubt if there is any organic life on Mars, unless it be a lowly form of vegetation."

"The canals – " began Chap.

"That may be an optical illusion," said the science master. "Our own moon, seen at a distance of forty million miles, would appear to be intersected very much as Mars seems to be. The truth is, we can never get Mars to stand still long enough to get a definite photograph!"

"From Jupiter?" suggested Chap, now thoroughly interested.

Again Mr Colson smiled.

"A semi-molten mass on which life could not possibly exist. Nor could it come from Saturn," he went on tantalizingly, "nor from Venus."

"Then where on earth do these signals come from?" blurted Chap, and this time Mr Colson laughed outright.

As they sat at tea, Elsie glanced out admiringly upon the brilliant-hued garden that was visible through the big window, and then she saw something which filled her with astonishment. Two men had come into view round the end of a square-cut hedge. One was the man they had seen half-an-hour previously – the commonplace little fellow who had claimed to be a relative of the professor. The second was taller and older, and, she judged, of a better class. His long, hawk-like face was bent down towards his companion, and they were evidently talking on some weighty matter, to judge by the gesticulations of the stranger.

"By Jove!" said Chap suddenly. "Isn't that Hildreth?"

Mr Colson looked up quickly; his keen blue eyes took in the scene at once.

"Yes, that is Mr Hildreth," he said quietly. "Do you know him?"

"Rather!" said Chap. "He has often been to our house. My father is on the Stock Exchange, and Mr Hildreth is a big pot in the City."

Colson nodded.

"Yes, he is a very important person in the City," he said, with just a touch of hidden sarcasm in his voice. "But he is not a very important person here, and I am wondering why he has come again."

He rose quickly and went out of the room, and presently Tim, who was watching the newcomers, saw them turn their heads as with one accord and walk out of sight, evidently towards the professor. When the old man came back there was a faint flush in his cheek and a light in his eye which Tim did not remember having seen before.

"They are returning in half-an-hour," he said, unnecessarily it seemed to Elsie. She had an idea that the old man was in the habit of speaking his thoughts aloud, and here she was not far wrong. Once or twice she had the uncomfortable feeling that she was in the way, for she was a girl of quick intuitions, and though Professor Colson was a man of irreproachable manners, even the most scrupulous of hosts could not wholly hide his anxiety for the little meal to end.

"We're taking up your valuable time, Mr Colson," she said with a dazzling smile, as she rose when tea was over and offered him her hand. "I think there's going to be a storm, so we had better get back. Are you coming with us, Tim?"

"Why, surely – " began Chap, but she interrupted him.

"Tim said he had an engagement near and was leaving us here," she said.

Tim had opened his mouth to deny having made any such statement, when a look from her silenced him. A little later, whilst Chap was blundering through his half-baked theories on the subject of Mars – Chap had theories on everything under and above the sun – she managed to speak with Tim alone.

"I'm quite sure Mr Colson wants to speak to you," she said; "and if he does, you are not to worry about us: we can get back, it is down-stream all the way."

"But why on earth do you think that?"

"I don't know." She shook her head. "But I have that feeling. And I'm sure he did not want to see you until those two men came."

How miraculously right she was, was soon proved. As they walked into the garden towards the path leading to the riverside, Colson took the arm of his favourite pupil and, waiting until the others were ahead, he said: "Would it be possible for you to come back and spend the night here, Lensman?"

"Why, yes, sir," said Tim in astonishment. In his heart of hearts he wanted to explore the place, to see some of the wonders of that great instrument-house which, up to now, Colson had made no offer to show them. What was in the room marked "Planetoid 127"? And the queer receiver on the square tower – that had some unusual significance, he was certain. And, most of all, he wanted to discover whether the science master had been indulging in a little joke at the expense of the party when he claimed to have heard voices that had come to him from one hundred and eighty-six millions of miles away.

"Return when you can," said Colson in a low voice; "and the sooner the better. There are one or two things that I want to talk over with you – I waited an opportunity to do so last term, but it never arose. Can you get rid of your friends?" Tim nodded. "Very good, then. I will say goodbye to them."

Tim saw his companions on their way until the punt had turned out of sight round the osiers at the end of the backwater, and then he retraced his steps up the hill. He found the professor waiting for him, pacing up and down the garden, his head on his breast, his hands clasped behind him.

"Come back into the library, Lensman," he said; and then, with a note of anxiety in his voice: "You did not see those precious scoundrels?"

"Which precious scoundrels? You mean Dawes and Hildreth?"

"Those are the gentlemen," said the other. "You wouldn't imagine, from my excited appearance when I returned to you, that they had offered me no less than a million pounds?"

Tim stared in amazement at the master.

"A million pounds, sir?" he said incredulously, and for the first time began to doubt the other's reason.

"A million pounds," repeated Colson, quietly enjoying the sensation he had created. "You will be able to judge by your own ears whether I am insane, as I imagine you believe me to be, or whether this wretched relative of mine and his friend are similarly afflicted. And, by the way, you will be interested to learn that there have been three burglaries in this house during the last month."

Tim gaped. "But surely, sir, that is very serious?"

"It would have been very serious for the burglars if I had, on either occasion, the slightest suspicion that they were in the grounds," said Mr Colson. "They would have been certainly electrified and possibly killed! But on every occasion when they arrived, it happened that I did not wish for a live electric current to surround the house: that would have been quite sufficient to have thrown out of gear the delicate instruments I was using at the time."

He led the way into his library, and sank down with a weary sigh into the depths of a large armchair.

"If I had only known what I know now," he said, "I doubt very much whether, even in the interests of science, I would have subjected myself to the ordeal through which I have been passing during the last four years."

Tim did not answer, and Mr Colson went on: "There are moments when I doubt my own sanity – when I believe that I shall awake from a dream, and find that all these amazing discoveries of mine are the figments of imagination due, in all probability, to an indiscreet supper at a very late hour of night!"

He chuckled softly at his own little joke.

"Lensman, I have a secret so profound that I have been obliged to follow the practice of the ancient astronomers."

He pointed through the window to a square stone that stood in the centre of the garden, a stone which the boy had noticed before, though he had dismissed it at once as a piece of meaningless ornamentation.

"That stone?" he asked.

Colson nodded.

"Come, I will show it to you," he said, rising to his feet. He opened a door in what appeared to be the solid wall, and Tim followed him into the garden.

The stone stood upon an ornamental plinth and was carved with two columns of figures and letters:

E	6	O	1
T	2	D	4
H	4	L	1
A	1	N	3
W	1	U	1
R	2	B	1
I	3	S	2

"But what on earth does that mean?"

"It is a cryptogram," said Mr Colson quietly. "When Heyghens made his discovery about Saturn's rings, he adopted this method to prevent himself from being forestalled in the discovery. I have done the same."

"But what does it mean?" asked the puzzled Tim.

"That you will one day learn," said the professor, as they walked back to the house.

His keen ears heard a sound and he pulled out his watch.

"Our friends are here already," he said in a lower voice.

They went back to the library and closed the door, and presently the butler appeared to announce the visitors.

The attitude of the two newcomers was in remarkable contrast. Mr Hildreth was self-assured, a man of the world to his finger-tips, and greeted the professor as though he were his oldest friend and had come at his special invitation. Mr Dawes, on the contrary, looked thoroughly uncomfortable.

Tim had a look at the great financier, and he was not impressed. There was something about those hard eyes which was almost repellent.

After perfunctory greetings had passed, there was an awkward pause, and the financier looked at Tim.

"My friend, Mr Lensman, will be present at this interview," said Colson, interpreting the meaning of that glance.

"He is rather young to dabble in high finance, isn't he?" drawled the other.

"Young or old, he's staying," said Colson, and the man shrugged his shoulders.

"I hope this discussion will be carried on in a calm atmosphere," he said. "As your young friend probably knows, I have made you an offer of a million pounds, on the understanding that you will turn over to me all the information which comes to you by – er – a – " his lip curled – "mysterious method, into which we will not probe too deeply."

"You might have saved yourself the journey," said Colson calmly. "Indeed, I could have made my answer a little more final, if it were possible; but it was my wish that you should be refused in the presence of a trustworthy witness. I do not want your millions – I wish to have nothing whatever to do with you."

"Be reasonable," murmured Dawes, who took no important part in the conversation.

Him the old man ignored, and stood waiting for the financier's reply.

"I'll put it very plainly to you, Colson," said Hildreth, sitting easily on the edge of the table. "You've cost me a lot of money. I don't know where you get your market 'tips' from, but you're most infernally right. You undercut my market a month ago, and took the greater part of a hundred thousand pounds out of my pocket. I offer to pay you the sum to put me in touch with the source of your information. You have a wireless plant here, and somewhere else in the world you have a miracle-man who seems to be able to foretell the future – with disastrous consequences to myself. I may tell you – and this you will know – that, but for the fact that your correspondent speaks in a peculiar language, I should have had your secret long ago. Now, Mr Colson, are you going to be sensible?"

Colson smiled slowly.

"I'm afraid I shall not oblige you. I know that you have been listening-in – I know also that you have been baffled. I shall continue to operate in your or any other market, and I give you full liberty to go to the person who is my informant, and who will be just as glad to tell you as he is to tell me, everything he knows."

Hildreth took up his hat with an ugly smile. "That is your last word?" Colson nodded.

"My very last." The two men walked to the door, and turned.

"It is not mine," said Hildreth, and there was no mistaking the ominous note in his tone.

They stood at the window watching the two men until they had gone out of sight, and then Tim turned to his host.

"What does he want really?" he asked.

Mr Colson roused himself from his reverie with a start.

"What does he want? I will show you. The cause of all our burglaries, the cause of this visit. Come with me."

They turned into the passage, and as the professor stopped before the door labelled "Planetoid 127,"

Tim's heart began to beat a little faster. Colson opened the door with two keys and ushered him into the strangest room which Tim had ever seen.

A confused picture of instruments, of wires that spun across the room like the web of a spider, of strange little machines which seemed to be endowed with perpetual motion – for they worked all the time – these were his first impressions.

The room was lined with grey felt, except on one side, where there was a strip of fibrous panelling. Towards this the professor went. Pushing aside a panel, he disclosed the circular door of a safe and, reaching in his hand, took out a small red-covered book.

"This is what the burglars want!" he said exultantly. "The Code! The Code of the Stars!"

Chapter III

TIM LENSMAN could only stare at the professor.

"I don't understand you, Mr Colson," he said, puzzled. "You mean that book is a code... an ordinary commercial code?"

Colson shook his head.

"No, my boy," he said quietly; "that is something more than a code, it is a vocabulary – a vocabulary of six thousand words, the simplest and the most comprehensive language that humanity has ever known! That is why they are so infinitely more clever than we," he mused. "I have not yet learned the process by which this language was evolved, but it is certain that it is their universal tongue."

He turned with a smile to the bewildered boy.

"You speak English, probably French; you may have a smattering of German and Spanish and Italian. And when you have named these languages, you probably imagine that you have exhausted all that matter, and that the highest expression of human speech is bound up in one or the other, or perhaps all, of these tongues. Yet there is a tribe on the Upper Congo which has a vocabulary of four thousand words with which to voice its hopes, its sufferings and its joys. And in those four thousand words lies the sum of their poetry, history, and science! If we were as intelligent as we think we are, we should adopt the language of the Upper Congolese as the universal speech."

Tim's head was swimming: codes, languages, Upper Congolese and the mysterious "they.".... Surely there must be something in Dawes' ominous hints, and this old man must be sick of overmuch learning. As though he realised what was passing through the boy's mind, Colson shook his head.

"No, I am not mad," he said, as he locked the book away in the safe and put the key in his pocket, "unless this is a symptom of my dementia."

He waved his hand to the wire-laden room, and presently Tim, as in a dream, heard his companion explaining the functions of the various instruments with which the room was littered. For the most part it was Greek to him, for the professor had reached that stage of mechanical knowledge where he outstripped his pupil's understanding. It was as though a professor of higher mathematics had strolled into the algebra class and lectured upon ultimate factors. Now and again he recognized some formula, or caught a mental glimpse of the other's meaning, but for the main part the old man was talking in a language he did not comprehend.

"I'm afraid you're going a little beyond me, sir," he said, with a smile, and the old man nodded.

"Yes, there is much for you to learn," he said; "and it must be learnt!"

He paused before a large glass case, which contained what looked to Tim to be a tiny model of a reciprocating engine, except that dozens of little pistons thrust out from unexpected cylinders, and all seemed to be working independent of the others, producing no central and general result.

"What is that, sir?"

Colson smoothed his chin thoughtfully.

"I'm trying to bring the description within the scope of your understanding," he said. "It would not be inexact to describe this as a 'strainer of sound.' Yet neither would it be exact."

He touched a switch and a dozen coloured lights gleamed and died amidst the whirling machinery. The hum which Tim had heard was broken into staccato dots and dashes of sound. He turned the switch again and the monotonous hum was resumed.

"Let us go back to the library," said the professor abruptly.

He came out of the room last, turned out the lights and double-locked the door, before he took his companion's arm and led him back to the library they had recently vacated.

"Do you realise, Lensman," he said as he closed the door, "that there are in this world sounds which never reach the human brain? The lower animals, more sensitive to vibratory waves, can hear noises which are never registered upon the human ear. The wireless expert listened in at the approach of Mars to the earth, hoping to secure a message of some kind.

But what did he expect? A similar clatter to that which he could pick up from some passing steamer. And, suppose somebody was signalling – not from Mars, because there is no analogy to human life on that planet, but from some – some other world, big or little – is it not possible that the sound may be of such a character that not only the ear, even when assisted by the most powerful of microphones, cannot detect, but which no instrument man has devised can translate to an audible key?"

"Do you suggest, sir, that signals of that nature are coming through from outer space?" asked Tim in surprise. And Mr Colson inclined his head.

"Undoubtedly. There are at least three worlds signalling to us," said the science master. "Sometimes the operators make some mechanical blunder, and there is an accidental emission of sound which is picked up on this earth and is credited to Mars. One of the most definite of the three comes from a system which is probably thousands of light-years away. In other words, from a planet that is part of a system beyond our ken. The most powerful telescope cannot even detect the sun around which this planet whirls! Another, and fainter, signal comes from an undetected planet beyond the orbit of Neptune."

"But life could not exist beyond the orbit of Neptune?" suggested Tim.

"Not life as we understand it," said the professor. "I admit that these signals are faint and unintelligible. But the third planet – "

"Is it your Planetoid 127?" asked Tim eagerly; and Colson nodded.

"I asked you to stay tonight," he said, "because I wanted to tell you something of vital interest to me, if not to science. I am an old man, Lensman, and it is unlikely that I shall live for many years longer. I wish somebody to share my secret – somebody who can carry on the work after I have gone into nothingness. I have given the matter a great deal of thought, passing under review the great scientists of the age. But they are mainly old men: it is necessary that I should have an assistant who has many years before him, and I have chosen you."

For a second the horrible responsibility which the professor was putting upon him struck a chill to the boy's heart. And then the curiosity of youth, the adventurous spirit which is in every boy's heart, warmed him to enthusiasm.

"That will be topping, sir," he said. "Of course, I'm an awful duffer, but I'm willing to learn anything you can teach me. It was about Planetoid 127 you wanted to speak?"

The professor nodded.

"Yes," he said, "it is about Planetoid 127. I have left nothing to chance. As I say, I am an old man and anything may happen. For the past few months I have been engaged in putting into writing the story of my extraordinary discovery: a discovery made possible by the years of unremitting thought and toil I have applied to perfecting the instruments which have placed me in contact with this strange and almost terrifying world."

It seemed as though he were going to continue, and Tim was listening with all ears, but in his definite way the old man changed the subject.

"You would like to see round the rest of the house?" he said; and the next hour was spent in strolling around the outhouses, the little farmery which formed part of the house, and the magnificent range of hothouses, for Mr Colson was an enthusiastic gardener.

As Tim was shown from one point of interest to another, it began to dawn upon him that there was truth in Hildreth's accusation, that Mr Colson was something of a speculator. The house and grounds must have cost thousands; the renovations which had been recently introduced, the erection of the telescope – when Colson mentioned the cost of this, the sum took his breath away – could only have been possible to a man of unlimited income. Yet it was the last thing in the world he would have imagined, for Colson was of the dreamy, unmaterial type, and it was difficult to associate him with a successful career on the Stock Exchange. When Mr Colson opened the gates of the big garage the boy expected to see something magnificent in the way of cars; but the building was empty except for his old motor bicycle, which was so familiar to the boys of Mildram.

"No, I do not drive a car," said Colson, in answer to his question. "I have so little time, and I find that a motor-bicycle supplies all my needs."

They dined at eight. Neither during the meal nor the period which intervened before bedtime did Mr Colson make any further reference to his discoveries. He disappeared about ten, after showing Tim to his room. The boy had undressed and was dozing off, when there came a tap at his door.

"Come in, sir," he said, and the professor entered. From his face Tim guessed that something had happened.

He set down the electric lantern he was carrying and came slowly towards the bed.

"Lensman," he said, and there was a sharp quality in his voice. "Do you remember somebody speaking... the wireless voice? I was not in the library when the call came through, so I did not hear it distinctly."

Tim recalled the mysterious voice that had spoken in the library from the aperture above the fireplace.

"Yes, sir; you told me, it was Colson – "

"I know, I know," said the professor impatiently. "But tell me how he spoke?" His tone was almost querulous with anxiety. "I only heard the end. Was it a gruff voice, rather like mine?"

Tim shook his head.

"No, sir," he said in surprise; "it was a very thin voice, a sort of whine... "

"A whine?" The professor almost shouted the question.

"Yes, sir." Colson was fingering his chin with a tremulous hand.

"That is strange," he said, speaking half to himself. "I have been trying to get him all the evening, and usually it is simple. I received his carrier wave... why should his assistant speak...? I have not heard him for three days. What did he say?"

Tim told him, as far as he could remember, the gist of the message which had come through, and for a long time the professor was silent.

"'He does not speak English very well – the assistant, I mean – and he would find a difficulty in putting into words... you see, our language is very complicated." And then, with a smile: "I interrupted your sleep."

He walked slowly to the door and stood for a while, the handle in his hand, his chin on his breast.

"If anything should happen, you will find my account in the most obvious place." He smiled faintly. "I'm afraid I am not a very good amateur mason – "

With these cryptic words he took his departure. Tim tossed from side to side and presently dropped into an uneasy doze. He dreamt that he and the professor were stalking through black, illimitable space. Around, above, below them blazed golden suns, and his ears were filled with a roar of whirling planets. Then suddenly the professor cried out in a terrible voice: "Look, look!" And there was a sharp crash of sound, and Tim sat up in bed, the perspiration streaming from every pore. Something had wakened him. In an instant he had slipped out of bed, pulled on his dressing-gown, thrust his feet into his slippers, and had raced out into the corridor. A deep silence reigned, broken only by the sound of an opening door and the tremulous voice of the butler.

"Is anything wrong, sir?"

"What did you hear?" asked Tim quickly.

"I thought I heard a shot."

Tim waited for no more: he ran down the stairs, stumbling in the darkness, and presently came to the passage from which opened the doors of the library and the room of Planetoid 127.

The library was empty: two lights burned, accentuating the gloom. A quick glance told him that it was not here the professor was to be sought. He had no doubt that in his sleep he had heard the cry of the old man. He turned on the light in the corridor, and, trying the door of the Planetoid room, to his consternation found it was open. The room was in darkness, but again memory served him. There were four light switches near the door, and these he found. Even as he had opened the door he could detect the acrid smell of cordite, and when the light switched on he was not unprepared for the sight which met his eyes. The little machine which Colson had described as the "sound strainer" was a mass of tangled wreckage. Another instrument had been overturned; ends of cut wires dangled from roof and wall. But his eyes were for the moment concentrated upon the figure that lay beneath the open safe. It was Professor Colson, and Tim knew instinctively that the old man was dead.

Chapter IV

COLSON was dead!

He had been shot at close quarters, for the hair about the wound was black and singed. Tim looked over his shoulder to the shivering butler who stood in the doorway.

"Get on the telephone to the police," he said; and, when the man had gone, he made a brief examination of the apartment.

The destruction which the unknown murderer had wrought was hurried but thorough. Half a dozen delicate pieces of apparatus, the value and use of which Tim had no idea, had been smashed; two main wires leading from the room had been cut; but the safe had obviously been opened without violence, for the key was still in the lock. It was the shot which had wakened the boy, and he realised that the safe must have been opened subsequent to the murder.

There was no need to make an elaborate search to discover the manner in which the intruder had effected his entry: one of the heavy shutters which covered the windows had been forced open, and the casement window was ajar. Without hesitation, lightly clad as he was, Tim jumped through the window on to a garden bed. Which way had the murderer gone? Not to the high road, that was certain. There could only be one avenue of escape, and that was the path which led down to the backwater.

He considered the situation rapidly: he was unarmed, and, even if the assassin was in no better shape (which he obviously was not) he would not be a match for a powerfully built man. He vaulted up to the window-sill as the shivering butler made his reappearance.

"I've telephoned the police: they're coming up at once," he said.

"Is there a gun in the house – any kind?" said Lensman quickly.

"There's one in the hall cupboard, sir," replied the man, and Tim flew along the corridor, wrenched open the door, found the shot-gun and, providentially, a box of cartridges. Stopping only to snatch an electric hand-lamp from the hall-stand, he sped into the grounds and made his way down the precipitous path which led to the river. His progress was painful, for he felt every stone and pebble through the thin soles of his slippers.

He had switched on the light of the hand-lamp the moment he had left the house, and here he was at an advantage over the man he followed, who was working in the dark and dared not show a light for fear of detection. That he was on the right track was not left long in doubt. Presently the boy saw something in his path, and, stooping, picked up a leather pocket-case, which, by its feel, he guessed contained money. Evidently in his hurry the murderer had dropped this.

Nearer and nearer to the river he came, and presently he heard ahead of him the sound of stumbling footsteps, and challenged his quarry.

"Halt!" he said. "Or I'll shoot!"

The words were hardly out of his mouth when a pencil of flame quivered ahead in the darkness, something "wanged" past his head and struck the bole of a tree with a thud. Instantly Tim extinguished his lamp. The muzzle of his gun advanced, his finger on the trigger, he moved very cautiously in pursuit.

The man must be somewhere near the river now: the ground was falling more steeply. There was no sound ahead until he heard a splash of water, the hollow sound of feet striking the bottom of a boat, and a faint "chug-chug" of engines. A motor-launch! Even as he reached the riverside he saw the dark shape slipping out towards the river under cover of the trees. Raising his gun, he fired. Instantly another shot came back at him. He fired again; he might not hit the assassin, but he would at any rate alarm the lock-keeper. Then, as the little launch reached the opening which brought it to the river, he saw it slow and come almost to a standstill. For a second he thought the man was returning, and then the explanation flashed upon him. The backwater was choked with weeds and the little propeller of the launch must have caught them. If he could only find a boat! He flashed his lamp vainly up and down the bank.

"Plop!"

The bullet was so near this time that it stirred the hair of his head. Hastily extinguishing the light, he waited. Somebody was working frantically at the launch's propeller, and again raising his gun, he fired. This time his shot struck home, for he heard a howl of fury and pain. But in another few seconds the launch was moving again, and had disappeared into the open river. There was nothing for Tim to do now but to retrace his steps to the house. He came into the room of death, hot, dishevelled, his pyjamas torn to ribbons by the brambles through which he had struggled, to find two police officers in the room. One was kneeling by the side of the dead man; the other was surveying the damaged apparatus.

"This is the young gentleman, sir," said the shivering butler, and the officers turned their attention to Tim.

In a few words he described what he had seen, and whilst one of the policemen went to telephone a warning along to the lock-keepers, he gave an account to the other of the events of that night so far as he knew them.

"There have been several burglaries here," said the sergeant. "I shouldn't be surprised if this is the same fellow that tried to do the other jobs. Do you know anything about this?"

He held a sheet of paper to the boy, and Tim took it. It was covered with Colson's fine writing.

"It looks almost as though it were a message he'd been writing down. He'd been listening-in – the receivers are still on his ears," said the officer. "But who could tell him stuff like that?"

Tim read the message:

"Colson was killed by robbers in the third part of the first division of the day. Nobody knows who did this, but the correctors are searching. Colson said there was a great earthquake in the island beyond the yellow sea. This happened in the sixth division of the day and many were killed. This place corresponds to Japan, but we call it the Island of the Yellow Sea. The great oilfields of the Inland Sea have become very rich, and those who own the fields have made millions in the past few days. There will be – "

Here the writing ended.

"What does he mean by 'Colson was killed in the third division' or whatever it is?" said the dumbfounded policeman. "He must have known he was going to be killed… it beats me."

"It beats me, too," said Tim sadly. "Poor old friend!"

At eleven o'clock came simultaneously Inspector Bennett, from Scotland Yard, and Mr Colson's lawyer: a stout, middle-aged man, who had some information to give.

"Poor Colson always expected such a death. He had made an enemy, a powerful enemy, and he told me only two days ago that this man would stop at nothing."

"Did he give his name?" asked the detective.

Tim waited breathlessly, expecting to hear Hildreth's name mentioned, but the lawyer shook his head.

"Why did you see him two days ago? On any particular business?"

"Yes," said Mr Stamford, the lawyer. "I came here to make a will, by which this young gentleman was named as sole heir!"

"I?" said Tim incredulously. "Surely you're mistaken?"

"No, Mr Lensman. I don't mind admitting that, when he told me how he wished to dispose of his property, I urged him against leaving his money to one who, I understand, is a comparative stranger. But Mr Colson had great faith in you, and said that he had made a study of your character and was satisfied that you could carry on his work. That was the one thing which worried him, the possibility of his life's work being broken off with no successor to take it up when he put it down. There is a clause in the will which makes it possible for you to operate his property immediately."

Tim smiled sadly. "I don't know what 'operating his property' means," he said. And then, as a thought struck him: "Unless he refers to his speculations. The Stock Exchange is an unknown country to me. Has any discovery been made about the man in the motor-launch?"

Inspector Bennett nodded.

"The launch was found abandoned in a local reach of the Thames," he said. "The murderer must have landed and made his way on foot. By the way, do you know he is wounded? We found traces of blood on the launch."

Tim nodded. "I had an idea I winged him," he said. "The brute!"

Late that afternoon there was a sensational discovery: the body of a man was found, lying amidst the weeds three miles down the river. He had been shot with a revolver.

"He is our man undoubtedly," said the inspector, who brought the news. "There is a shot wound in his shoulder."

"But I did not use a rifle or a revolver," said Tim, puzzled.

"Somebody else did," said the inspector grimly. "Dead men tell no tales."

"Where was he found?"

"Near Mr Hildreth's private landing stage – " began the inspector.

"Hildreth?" Tim stared at him open-mouthed. "Has Hildreth got a property near here?"

"Oh, yes; he has a big estate about three miles down the river." The detective was eyeing the boy keenly. "What do you know about Mr Hildreth?"

In a few words Tim told of the interview which he had witnessed, and the detective frowned.

"It can only be a coincidence that the man was found on his estate," he said. "Mr Hildreth is a very rich man and a Justice of the Peace."

Nevertheless, he did not speak with any great conviction, and Tim had the impression that Bennett's view of Hildreth was not such an exalted one as he made out.

Borrowing the old motor-bicycle of the science master, he rode over to Bisham and broke the news to Chap West and his sister. The girl was horrified.

"But, Tim, it doesn't seem possible!" she said. "Why should they do it? The poor old man!"

When Chap had recovered from the shock of the news, he advanced a dozen theories in rapid succession, each more wildly improbable than the last; but all his theorising was silenced when Tim told him of Colson's will.

"I'm only a kid, and absolutely unfitted for the task he has set me," Tim said quietly; "but I am determined to go on with his work, and shall secure the best technical help I can to reconstitute the apparatus which has been destroyed."

"What do you think is behind it?" asked Chap.

Tim shook his head. "Something beyond my understanding," he replied. "Mr Colson made a discovery, but what that discovery was we have to learn. One of the last things he told me was that he had written out a full account of his investigations, and I am starting an immediate search for that manuscript. And then there is the stone in the grounds, with all those queer figures and letters which have to be deciphered."

"Have you any idea what the nature of the discovery was?" asked Chap. Tim hesitated.

"Yes, I think I have," he said. "Mr Colson was undoubtedly in communication with another planet!"

Chapter V

"THEN IT was Mars!" cried Chap triumphantly.

"Of course it was not Mars," interrupted his sister scornfully. "Mr Colson told us distinctly that there was no life on Mars."

"Where is it, Tim?" he asked.

"I don't know." Tim shook his head. "I have been questioning his assistants – there were two at the house – but he never took them into his confidence. The only hint they can give me is that when poor Mr Colson was listening-in to these mysterious voices he invariably had the receiving gear directed towards the sun. You know, of course, that he did not use the ordinary aerial, but an apparatus shaped like a convex mirror."

"Towards the sun?" gasped Chap. "But there can't be any life on the sun! Dash it all, I don't profess to be a scientific Johnny but I know enough of physics to see that it's as impossible for life to exist on the sun as it would be to exist in a coke oven! Why, the temperature of the sun is umpteen thousand degrees centigrade… and anyway, nobody has ever seen the sun: you only see the photoscope… "

"All this I know," said Tim, listening patiently, "but there is the fact: the receiving mirror was not only directed towards the sun, but it moved by clockwork so that it was directed to the sun at all hours of the day, even when the sky was overcast and the sun was invisible. I admit that the whole thing sounds incredible, but Colson was not mad. That voice we heard was very distinct."

"But from what planet could it be?" insisted Chap, pushing back his untidy hair and glaring at his friend. "Go over 'em all: eliminate Mars and the Sun, of course, and where is this world? Venus, Mercury, Jupiter, Saturn, Uranus, Neptune – phew! You're not suggesting that it is one of the minor planets, are you? Ceres, Pallas, Juno, Vesta… ?"

Tim shook his head.

"I am as much puzzled as you, but I am going to spend my life onwards looking for that world."

He went back to the house. The body of the old man had been moved to a near-by hospital, and the place was alive with detectives. Mr Stamford was there when he returned, and placed him in possession of a number of names and addresses which he thought might be useful to the young man.

"I don't know that I want to know any stockbrokers," said Tim, looking at the list with a wry face.

"You never know," said Mr Stamford. "After all, Mr Colson expected you to carry on his work, and probably it will be part of your duties to continue his operations. I happen to know that he paid minute attention to the markets."

He indicated a number of financial newspapers that lay unopened on the table, and Tim took up one, opened it and glanced down the columns. In the main the items of news were meaningless to him. All he saw were columns of intricate figures which were so much Greek; but presently his eye caught a headline:

"Black Sea Oil Syndicate. Charles Hildreth's Gloomy Report to the Shareholders.

"A meeting of the Black Sea Oil Syndicate was held at the Cannon Street Hotel yesterday afternoon, and Mr Hildreth, Chairman of the Company, presiding, said that he had very little news for the shareholders that was pleasant. A number of the wells had run dry, but borings were being made on a new part of the concession, though there was scarcely any hope that they would be successful."

Tim frowned. Black Sea Oil Syndicate… ? Hildreth? He put a question to the lawyer.

"Oh, yes," said Mr Stanford. "Hildreth is deep in the oil market. There's some talk of his rigging Black Seas."

"What do you mean by 'rigging'?" asked Tim.

"In this case the suggestion, which was made to me by a knowledgeable authority," said Mr Stamford, "is that Hildreth was depressing the shares issuing unpromising reports which would induce shareholders to put their shares on the market at a low figure. Of course, there may be nothing in it: Black Sea Oils are not a very prosperous concern. On the other hand, he may have secret information from his engineers."

"Such as – ?" suggested Tim.

"They may have struck oil in large quantities on another part of the property and may be keeping this fact dark, in which case they could buy up shares cheaply, and when the news was made known the scrip would go sky-high and they would make a fortune."

Tim read the report again. "Do you think there is any chance of oil being found on this property?"

Stamford smiled. "I am a lawyer, not a magician," he said good-humouredly.

After he had gone, Tim found himself reading the paper: the paragraph fascinated him. Black Sea Oil…

Suddenly he leapt to his feet with a cry. That was the message which Mr Colson had written on the paper – the Oilfields of the Inland Sea!

He ran out of the room and went in search of Stamford.

"I am going to buy Black Sea Oils," he said breathlessly. "Will you tell me what I must do?"

In a few moments the telephone wire was busy.

Mr Hildreth had not been to his office that day, and when he strolled in to dinner, and the footman handed him his paper, he opened the page mechanically at the Stock Exchange column and ran his eyes down the list of quotations. That morning Black Sea Oils had stood in the market at 3s. 3d., and almost the first note that reached his eye was in the stop-press column.

"Boom in Black Sea Oils. There have been heavy buyings in Black Sea Oil shares, which stood this morning in the neighbourhood of 3s., but which closed firm at 42s. 6d."

Hildreth's face went livid. His great coup had failed!

In the weeks which followed the death and funeral of Professor Colson, Tim found every waking minute occupied. He had enlisted the services of the cleverest of scientists, and from the shattered apparatus one of the most brilliant of mechanical minds of the country was rebuilding the broken instruments. Sir Charles Layman, one of the foremost scientific minds in England, had been called into consultation by the lawyer, and to him Tim had related as much as he knew of Professor Colson's secret.

"I knew Colson," said Sir Charles; "he was undoubtedly a genius. But this story you tell me takes us into the realm of fantasy. It isn't possible that life can exist on the sun; and really, young gentleman, I can't help feeling that you have been deceived over these mysterious voices."

"Then three people were deceived," said Tim firmly. "My friend Chap West and his sister both heard the speaker. And Mr Colson was not the kind of man who would descend to trickery."

Sir Charles pursed his lips and shook his head.

"It does seem most extraordinary. And frankly, I cannot understand the functions of these instruments. It is quite possible, as Colson said, that there are sounds come to this earth so fine, and pitched in such a key, that the human ear cannot catch them. And I am pretty sure that what he called a 'sound strainer' was an amplifier on normal lines. But the mysterious world – where is it? Life in some form may exist on a planetoid, but it is almost certain that these small masses which whirl through space in the zone between Mars and Jupiter are barren globules of rock as dead as the moon and innocent of atmosphere. There are a thousand-and-one reasons why life could not exist on these planetoids; and of course the suggestion that there can be life on the sun is preposterous."

He walked up and down the library, smoothing his bushy white beard, his brows corrugated in a grimace of baffled wonder.

"Most scientists," he said at last, "work to the observations of some pet observer – did the Professor ever mention an astronomer whose calculations he was endeavouring to verify?"

Tim thought for a moment.

"Yes, sir, I remember he spoke once or twice of Professor Watson, an American. I remember once he was lecturing to our school on Kepler's Law, and he mentioned the discoveries of Mr Watson."

"Watson?" said Sir Charles slowly. "Surely he was the fellow who thought he found Vulcan, a planet supposed by some people to revolve about the sun within the orbit of Mercury. As a matter of fact, what he saw, during an eclipse of the sun, was the two stars, Theta and Zeta Cankri, or, more likely, the star 20 Cankri, which must have been somewhere in the position that Watson described on the day he made his discovery."

Then he asked, with sudden interest: "Did Professor Colson believe in the existence of Vulcan?"

Tim shook his head. "No, sir, he derided the idea."

"He was right," nodded Sir Charles. "Vulcan is a myth. There may be intra-Mercurial bodies revolving about the sun, but it is extremely unlikely. You have found no data, no photographs?"

The word "photograph" reminded Tim. "Yes, there is a book full of big enlargements, but mostly of a solar eclipse," he said. "They were taken on Friday Island last year."

"Would you get them for me?" asked Sir Charles, interested.

Tim went out and returned with a portfolio, which he opened on the table. Sir Charles turned picture after picture without speaking a word, then he laid half a dozen apparently similar photographs side by side and pored over them with the aid of a magnifying-glass. They were the conventional type of astronomical photo: the black disc of the moon, the bubbling white edges of the corona; but evidently Sir Charles had seen something else, for presently he indicated a speck with a stylo.

"These photographs were taken by different cameras," he said. "And yet they all have this."

He pointed to the pin-point of white which had escaped Tim's observation. It was so much part of the flame of the corona that it seemed as though it were a spark thrown out by one of those gigantic irruptions of ignited gas that flame up from the sun's surface.

"Surely that is a speck of dust on the negative?" said Tim.

"But it is on all the negatives," said Sir Charles emphatically. "No, I cannot be sure for the moment, but if that is not Zeta or Theta Cankris – it is too large for the star 20 Cankris – then we may be on the way to rediscovering Professor Colson's world!"

At his request, Tim left him, whilst, with the aid of charts and almanacs, he plunged into intricate calculations.

When Tim closed the door and came into the corridor he saw the old butler waiting.

"Mr Hildreth is here, sir," said the man in a low voice, as though he also suspected the sinister character of the financier. "I've put him in the blue drawing-room: will you see him, sir?"

Tim nodded and followed the servant.

Hildreth was standing by a window, looking out upon the lawn, his hands behind him, and he turned, with a quick, bird-like motion as he heard the sound of the turning handle.

"Mr Lensman," he said, "I want a few words with you alone."

The young man dismissed the butler with a gesture.

"Well, sir?" he asked quietly.

"I understand that you have engaged in a little speculation. You are rather young to dabble in high finance," drawled Hildreth.

"Do you mean Black Sea Oils?" asked Tim bluntly.

"I had that stock in mind. What made you buy, Mr Lens-man – or rather, what made your trustee buy, for I suppose that, as you're under age, you would hardly carry out the transaction yourself."

"I bought because I am satisfied that Black Sea Oils will rise."

A slow smile dawned on Hildreth's hawklike face.

"If you had come to me," he said coolly, "I could have saved you a great deal of money. Black Sea Oils today stand at fifty shillings: they are worth less than fivepence! You are little more than a boy," he went on suavely, "and I can well understand how the temptation to gamble may have overcome you. But I was a friend of Colson's, and I do not like the thought of your money being wasted. I will take all the stock off your hands, paying you at the price you paid for it."

"That is very generous of you," said Tim drily, "but I am not selling. And as for Mr Colson being a friend of yours – "

"A very good friend," interrupted the other quickly, "and if you tell people that he and I were enemies it may cost you more than you bargain for!"

There was no mistaking the threat in his tone, but Tim was not to be brow-beaten.

"Mr Hildreth," he said quietly, "nobody knows better than you that you were bad friends with Mr Colson. He was constantly spoiling your market – you said as much. You believed that he was possessed of information which enabled him to operate to your detriment, and you knew this information came by wireless, because you had listened-in, without, however, understanding the language in which the messages came. You guessed there was a code, and I believe that you made one or two efforts to secure that code. Your last effort ended in the death of my friend!"

Chapter VI

HILDRETH'S FACE went white.

"Do you suggest that I am responsible for Colson's death?"

"You were responsible directly and indirectly," said Tim. "You sent a man here to steal the code-book – a man who has been identified this afternoon as a notorious criminal. Whether you told him to shoot, or whether he shot to save his skin, we shall never know. The burglar was killed so that he should not blab."

"By whom?" asked Hildreth steadily.

"You know best," was the curt reply.

Tim opened the door and stood waiting. The man had regained some of his composure, and, with an easy laugh, walked into the corridor. "You will hear from me again," he said.

"Thank you for the warning," was Tim's rejoinder.

After he had seen his unwelcome visitor off the premises, Tim went in search of Stamford, who, with his two assistants, was working in a little study getting out particulars of the old man's investments. The lawyer listened in silence while Tim narrated what had passed.

"He is a very dangerous man," said Mr Stamford at last; "and, so far from being rich, I happen to know that he is on the verge of ruin. There are some queer stories about Hildreth. I have had a hint that he was once in an Australian prison, but, of course, there is no evidence to connect him with this terrible crime. What are your immediate plans?"

"The voice amplifier has been reconstituted," said Tim. "The experts are making a test today, though I very much doubt whether they will succeed in establishing communication."

A smile fluttered at the corner of the lawyer's mouth.

"Do you still believe that Mr Colson was in communication with another planet?"

"I'm certain," said Tim emphatically.

He went back to the blue drawing-room, and had hardly entered before Sir Charles came in.

"It is as I thought," said the scientist; "neither Zeta nor Theta! It is, in fact, a distinct body of some kind, and, in my judgment, well outside the orbit of the hypothetical Vulcan. If you look at the back of the photograph – "

He turned it over, and Tim saw that, written in pencil in the microscopic calligraphy of the Professor, were a dozen lines of writing.

"I knew, of course, that this was a dead world, without atmosphere or even water. There can be no life there. I made an enlargement by my new process, and this revealed a series of flat, rocky valleys."

"What the deuce his new process was, heaven only knows!" said Sir Charles in despair. "Poor Colson must have been the most versatile genius the world has known. At any rate, that disposes of the suggestion that this planetary body is that whence come the signals – if they come at all."

Sir Charles waited until the experts had finished the work of reassembling two of the more complicated machines; but, though experimenting until midnight, they could not establish communication, and at last, with a sense of despair, Tim ordered the work to cease for the night.

The whole thing was becoming a nightmare to him: he could not sleep at nights. Chap and his sister came over in the morning to assist him in a search, which had gone on ever since the death of Professor Colson.

"We can do no more," said Tim helplessly, "until we have seen the Professor's manuscript. Until then we do not know for what we are searching."

"What about that stone in the garden? Won't that tell you anything?" asked Chap. "I'd like to see it."

They went out into the courtyard together and stood before the stone in silence.

E 6 O 1 T 2 D 4 H 4 L 1 A 1 N 3 W 1 U 1
R 2 B 1
I 3 S 2

"Of course, that isn't as difficult as it appears," said Chap, to whom cryptograms were a passion. "There is a sentence written there, containing so many 'e's, so many 'h's, etcetera, and perhaps, when we find the sentence, the mystery will be half solved."

He jotted the inscription down in a notebook, and throughout the day was puzzling over a solution. Night came, and the two were on the point of departure, when Chap said suddenly: "Do you think you were wise, Timothy, to tell the reporter Johnny all you did?"

(Tim had given an interview to a local newspaper, which had described more fully than he had intended – more fully, indeed, than his evidence at the inquest – what had happened immediately preceding Colson's death.)

"Because, y' know, it struck me," said Chap, "that the poor old Professor's manuscript would be very valuable to a certain person. Does it occur to you that our friend might also be searching for this narrative?"

This was a new idea to Tim.

"Why, yes," he said slowly; "I never thought of that. No; that didn't strike me. But I don't know where he would find it. We've taken out every likely stone in the building; I've had the cellars searched – "

"What makes you think it's behind a stone?" asked Chap.

"His reference to a mason. My guess – and I may not be far wide of the mark – is that Mr Colson, having written his manuscript, hid it in one of the walls. But so far I have not been able to discover the hiding-place."

He walked to the end of the drive to see his friends off, and then returned to the study. He was alone in the house now, save for the servants. Sir Charles had gone back to town by the last train, and Stamford had accompanied him.

The butler came in to ask if he wanted anything before he went to bed, and Tim shook his head. He had taken up his quarters in a spare room immediately above the library, and for an hour after his visitors had departed he sat on the broad window-seat, looking down into the courtyard, now bathed in the faint radiance of the crescent moon. The light shone whitely upon the cryptogram stone, and absent-mindedly he fixed his eyes upon this, the least of the old man's mysteries. And then – was his eye playing tricks with him? He could have sworn he saw a dark figure melt out of the darkness and move along the shadow of the box hedge.

He pushed open the casement window, but could see nothing.

"I'm getting jumpy," he said to himself, and rising with a yawn, took off his coat preparatory to undressing. As he did so, he glanced out of the window again and started. Now he was sure: he could see the shapeless black shadow, and it was moving towards the cryptogram stone.

His pulse beat a little quicker as he watched. There was no doubt about it now. In the moonlight the figure in the long black coat and the broad sombrero which shaded his face, stood clearly revealed. It was touching the stone, and even as Tim looked the little obelisk fell with a crash.

In a second Tim was out of the room and speeding along the corridor. As he came into view of the figure, it stooped and picked something from the ground.

The manuscript! What a fool he had been! That was where the old man had concealed the story of his discovery! But there was no time for regret: the mysterious visitant had already disappeared into the shadows. Was he making for the river? Tim was uncertain. He was halfway down the slope before he realised that he had made a mistake. Behind him he heard the soft purr of a motor-car, and, racing up the slope, he came into view of a red tail-light as it disappeared down the broad drive towards the road. The great iron gates were closed, and that would give him a momentary advantage, though he knew he could not reach the car before they were open.

Then he remembered Colson's motor-bicycle: he had left it leaning against the wall and had forgotten to bring it in after the trip he had made to Bisham that morning. Yes, there it was! He had hardly started the machine going when he heard a crash. The unknown had driven his car through the frail iron gates and was flying along the road to Maidenhead.

Tim came out in pursuit and put his machine all out. The car ahead gained until it came to the foot of a long and tiring hill, and then the gap between them closed. Once the driver looked back, and a minute later something dropped in the road. Tim only just avoided the spare tyre, which had been thrown overboard to trip him.

The car reached the crest of the hill as Tim came up to its rear, and, heedless of danger, stretched out his hand, and, catching hold of the hood, let the motor-bicycle slip from between his knees.

For a second he held on desperately, his feet swinging in the air, and then, with an effort, he threw his leg over the edge of the hood and dropped breathlessly on to the seat behind the driver. At first the man at the wheel did not realise what had happened, and then, with a yell of rage, he turned and struck blindly at the unauthorised passenger.

The blow missed him by a fraction of an inch, and in another second his arm was around the driver's neck. The car swayed and slowed, and then an involuntary movement of the man revealed the whereabouts of the manuscript. Tim thrust into the inside-pocket and his fingers touched a heavy roll of paper. In a flash the packet was in his hand, and then he saw the moonlight gleam on something which the man held.

The car was now almost at a standstill, and, leaping over the side, Tim plunged into the hedge by the side of the road. As he did so, he heard the "zip!" of a bullet and the patter of leaves. He ran on wildly, his breath coming in short gasps. To his ears came the blundering feet of his pursuer. He was out of breath and in no condition to meet the murderous onrush of his enemy.

And then, as he felt he could not go a step farther, the ground opened underneath his feet and he went down, down, down. For a second he lost consciousness. All that remained of his breath was knocked from his body, and he could only lie and gape at the starlit sky.

Chapter VII

LOOKING UP, he saw a head and shoulders come over the edge of the quarry into which he had fallen. Apparently the man was not prepared to take the risk of following, for presently the sound of his footsteps died away and there was silence.

He lay for half-an-hour motionless, recovering his breath. Although his arm was bruised he could move it and no bones were broken. At the end of his rest he rose cautiously to his knees and explored the position so far as it was revealed by the moonlight.

He had fallen twenty or thirty feet down a steep, chalky slope; but he was by no means at the bottom of the quarry face, and he had to move with the greatest care and circumspection. Presently, however, he found a rough path, which seemed to run interminably upwards. It was nearly half-an-hour later when he came to the road. The car was gone, and he walked back the way he had come, hoping that he would be able to retrieve his motor-bicycle intact, though he had his doubts whether it would be usable. To his delight, when he came upon the machine, he discovered it had suffered little damage other than twisted handlebars. His run home was without event.

Apparently his hasty exit had been heard, for the house was aroused and two manservants were searching the grounds when he came in.

"I heard the gate go smash, sir," said the butler, explaining his wakefulness. "Lord! I'm glad to see you back. Somebody's thrown over that stone in the courtyard… "

He babbled on, and Tim was so glad to hear the sound of a human voice that he did not interrupt him.

There was no sleep for him that night. With successive cups of strong coffee, brought at intervals, he sat poring over the manuscript, page by page, almost incredulous of his own eyes and senses. The sunlight poured in through the windows of the little study and found him still sitting, his chin on his palms, the manuscript before him. He had read it again and again until he knew almost every word. Then, locking the papers away in the safe, he walked slowly to the instrument room, and gazed in awe at this evidence of the dead man's genius.

Something within him told him that never in future would human speech pulsate through this network of wires; never again would that queer little amplifier bring within human hearing the thin sounds of space. Even the code was gone: that vocabulary, reduced with such labour to a dictionary of six thousand words.

He turned the switch and set the little machine working; saw the multicoloured lights gleam and glow. This much the mechanics had succeeded in doing. But the words that filtered through light and charcoal would, he thought, be dead for everlasting. He turned another switch and set something working which Sir Charles had described as a miniature air pump, and stood watching absent-mindedly as the piston thrust in and out. If he only had one tenth of Colson's genius!

His hand had gone out to turn the switch that stopped the machine, when:

"Oh, Colson, why do you not speak to me?"

The voice came from the very centre of the machine. There was no visible microphone. It was as though the lights and the whirling wheels had become endowed with a voice. Tim's heart nearly stopped beating.

"Oh, Colson," wailed the voice, "they are breaking the machines. I have come to tell you this before they arrive. He is dead – he, the master, the wizard, the wonderful man... "

The servant! Mr Colson had told him that it was the servant who had spoken. The astral Colson was dead. How should he reply?

"Where are you?" he asked hoarsely, but there was no answer, and soon he understood why. Presently:

"I will wait for you to speak. When I hear you I will answer. Speak to me, Colson! In a thousand seconds..."

A thousand seconds! Colson had told him once that wireless waves travel at the same speed as light. Then he was a hundred and eighty million miles away, and a thousand seconds must pass – nearly seventeen minutes – before his voice could reach through space to the man who was listening.

How had he made the machine work? Perhaps the mechanism had succeeded before, but there had been nobody at the other end – wherever the other end might be. And then:

"Oh, Colson, they are here... goodbye!"

There came to him the sound of a queer tap-tap-tap and then a crackle as though of splintered glass, and then a scream, so shrill, so full of pain and horror, that involuntarily he stepped back. Then came a crash, and silence. He waited, hardly daring to breathe, but no sound came. At the end of an hour he turned off the switch and went slowly up to his room.

He awoke to find a youth sitting on the edge of his bed. He was so weary and dulled that he did not recognize Chap, even after he spoke.

"Wake up: I've got some news for you, dear old bird," said Chap, staring owlishly through his thick, heavy glasses. "There's a Nemesis in this business – you may have heard of the lady – Miss Nemesis of Nowhere. First the burglar man is killed and then his boss is smashed to smithereens."

Tim struggled up. "Who?" he asked. "Not Hildreth?"

Chap nodded.

"He was found just outside Maidenhead, his car broken to bits – they think his steering-wheel went wrong when he was doing sixty an hour. At any rate, he smashed into a tree, and all that's left of his machine is hot iron!"

"Hildreth! Was he killed?" Chap nodded.

"Completely," he said callously. "And perhaps it's as well for him, for Bennett was waiting at his house to arrest him. They've got proof that he employed that wretched burglar. Do you know what time it is? It's two o'clock, you lazy devil, and Sir Charles and Stamford are waiting to see you. Sir Charles has a theory – "

Tim swung out of bed and walked to the window, blinking into the sunlit garden.

"All the theories in the world are going to evaporate before the facts," he said. Putting his hand under his pillow, he took out the Professor's manuscript. "I'll read something to you this afternoon. Is Elsie here?"

Chap nodded. "I'll be down in half-an-hour," he said.

His breakfast was also his luncheon, but it was not until after the meal was over, and they had adjourned to the library, that he told them what had happened in the night. Bennett, who arrived soon after, was able to fill in some of the gaps of the story.

"Hildreth," he said, "in spite of his wealth and security, was a crook of crooks. It is perfectly true that he was tried in Australia and sent to penal servitude. He had got a big wireless plant in his house, and there is no doubt that for many years he has made large sums of money by picking up commercial messages that have been sent by radio and decoding and using them to his own purpose. In this way he must have learnt something about Mr Colson's correspondent – he was under the impression that Colson received messages in code and was anxious to get the code-book. By the way, we found the charred remnants of that book in the car. It was burnt out, as you probably know. That alone would have been sufficient to convict Hildreth of complicity in the murder. Fortunately, we have been saved the trouble of a trial."

"None of the code remains?" asked Tim anxiously. The detective shook his head.

"No, sir, none. There are one or two words – for instance, 'Zeiith' means 'the Parliamentary system of the third decade,' whatever that may mean. It seems a queer sort of code to me."

"That is very unfortunate," said Tim. "I had hoped to devote my time to telling the history of this strange people, and the book would have been invaluable."

"Which people is this?" asked Sir Charles puzzled. "Did our friend get into communication with one of the lost tribes?"

Tim laughed, in spite of himself. "No, sir. I think the best explanation I can offer you is to read Mr Colson's manuscript, which I discovered last night. It is one of the most remarkable stories that has ever been told, and I'll be glad to have you here, Sir Charles, so that you may supply explanations which do not occur to me."

"Is it about the planet?" asked Sir Charles quickly, and Tim nodded.

"Then you have discovered it! It is a planetoid – "

Tim shook his head. "No, sir," he said quietly. "It is a world as big as ours."

The scientist looked at him open-mouthed.

"A world as big as ours, and never been discovered by our astronomers? How far away?"

"At its nearest, a hundred and eighty million miles," said Tim.

"Impossible!" cried Sir Charles scornfully. "It would have been detected years ago. It is absolutely impossible!"

"It has never been detected because it is invisible," said Tim.

"Invisible? How can a planet be invisible? Neptune is much farther distant from the sun – "

"Nevertheless, it is invisible," said Tim. "And now," he said, as he took the manuscript from his pocket, "if you will give me your attention, I will tell you the story of Neo. Incidentally, the cryptogram on the stone reads: 'Behind the sun is another world!'"

Chapter VIII

TIM TURNED the flyleaf of the manuscript and began reading in an even tone.

"The Story of Neo."

"My name" (the manuscript began) "is Charles Royton Colson. I am a Master of Arts of the University of Cambridge, science lecturer to Mildram School, and I have for many years been engaged in the study of the Hertzian waves, and that branch of science commonly known as radiology. I claim in all modesty to have applied the principles which Marconi brought nearer to perfection, when wireless telegraphy was unknown. And I was amongst the pioneers of wireless telephony. As is also generally known, I am a mathematician and have written several text-books upon astronomy. I am also the author of a well-known monograph on the subject of the Inclinations of the Planetary Orbits; and my treatise on the star Oyonis is familiar to most astronomers.

"For many years I engaged myself in studying the alterations of ellipses following the calculations and reasonings of Lagrange, who to my mind was considerably less of a genius than Professor Adams, to whom the credit for the discovery of Neptune should be given... "

Here followed a long and learned examination of the incidence of Neptune's orbit, as influenced by Uranus.

"... My astronomical and radiological studies were practically carried on at the same time. In June, 1914, my attention was called to a statement made by the Superintendent of the great wireless telegraph station outside Berlin, that he had on three separate occasions taken what he described as 'slurred receptions' from an unknown station. He gave excellent technical reasons why these receptions could not have come from any known station, and he expressed the opinion, which was generally scoffed at, that the messages he had taken came from some extra-terrestrial source. There immediately followed a suggestion that these mysterious dashes and dots had come from Mars. The matter was lost sight of owing to the outbreak of the European War, and when, in 1915, the same German engineer stated that he had received a distinct message of a similar character, the world, and particularly the Allied world, rejected the story, for the credibility of the Germans at that period did not stand very high.

"A year later, the wireless station at Cape Cod also reported signals, as did a private station in Connecticut; whilst the Government station at Rio de Janeiro reported that it had heard a sound like 'a flattened voice.' It was obvious that these stories were not inventions, and I set to work on an experimental station which I had been allowed to set up at the school, and after about six months of hard toil I succeeded in fashioning an instrument which enabled me to test my theories. My main theory was that, if the sound came from another world, it would in all probability be pitched in a key that would be inaudible to human ears. For example, there is a dog-whistle which makes no sound that we detect, but which is audible to every dog. My rough amplifier had not been operating for a week when I began to pick up scraps of signals and scraps of words – unintelligible to me, but obviously human speech. Not only was I able to hear, but I was able to make myself heard; and the first startling discovery I made was that it took my voice a thousand and seven seconds to reach the person who was speaking to me.

"I was satisfied now that I was talking to the inhabitants of another world, though, for my reputation's sake, I dared not make my discovery known. After hard experimental work, I succeeded in clarifying the voices, and evidently the person at the other end was as anxious as I to make himself understood and to understand the nature of his unknown correspondent's speech.

"You may imagine what a heart-breaking business it was, with no common vocabulary, invisible to one another, and living possibly in conditions widely different, to make our meaning clear to one another. We made a start with the cardinal numbers, and after a week's interchange we had mastered these. I was then struck with the idea of pouring a glass of water from a tumbler near to my microphone, and using the word 'water.' In half-an-hour I heard the sound of falling water from the other end and the equivalent word, which will be found in the vocabulary. I then clapped my hands together, and used the word 'hand.' With these little illustrations, which took a great deal of time, began the formation of the dictionary. In the Neo language there are practically no verbs and few adjectives. Very much is indicated by a certain inflexion of voice; even the tenses are similarly expressed; and yet, in spite of this, the Neothians to whom I spoke had no very great difficulty, once I had learnt the art of the inflexion, in supplying the English equivalent.

"All the time I was searching the heavens in the vain endeavour to discover the exact location of this world, which was, from the description I had, exactly the same size as ours, and therefore should have been visible. I had maps of the southern hemispheres, reports from the astronomers of Capetown and Brisbane, but they could offer me no assistance. It was certain that there was in the heavens no visible planetary body as big as Neo.

"The chief difficulty I had lay in the fact that the voices invariably came from the direction of the sun; and it was as certain as anything could be that life could not exist on that great golden mass. Notwithstanding this, unless my mirror was turned to the sun, I received no message whatever; and even in the middle of the night, when I was communicating with Neo, it was necessary that I should follow, the sun's course.

"Then came the great eclipse, and, as you know, I went to the South Sea Islands to make observations. It was our good fortune to have fine weather, and at the moment of total eclipse I took several particularly excellent photographs, some of which you will find in the portfolio marked 'L.' In these and photographs taken by other astronomers, you will see, if you make a careful observation, close to the corona, a tiny speck of light, which at first I thought was my world, but which afterwards I discovered was a dead mass of material upon which it was impossible for life to exist.

"One night, when I was turning over the matter in my mind, and examining each photograph in the study of my house on the Thames, the solution flashed on me. This tiny speck, which was not a star, and was certainly not Vulcan, was the satellite of another world, and that world was moving on the same orbit as our own earth, following exactly the same course, but being, as it was, immediately opposite to us behind the sun, was never visible! On whatever part of the ellipse we might be, the sun hid our sister world from us, and that was why the voice apparently came from the sun, for it was through the solar centre that the waves must pass. Two earths chasing one another along the same path, never overtaking, never being overtaken, balancing one another perfectly! It was a stupendous thought!

"I conveyed to my unknown friend, who called himself Colson, though I am under the impression that that was due to a misconception on his part as to what Colson meant – he probably thought that 'Colson' was the English word for 'scientist' – and I asked him to make observations. These he sent to me after a few days, confirming my theory. It was after we had begun to talk a little more freely, and my acquaintance with the language had increased so that I could express myself clearly, that it occurred to me there was an extraordinary similarity both in our lives and our environment. And this is the part in my narrative which you will find difficult to believe – I discovered that these two worlds were not only geographically exact, but that the incidents of life ran along on parallel lines. There were great wars in Neo, great disasters, which were invariably duplicated on our earth, generally from two to three days before or after they had happened in this new world. Nor was it only the convulsions of nature that were so faithfully reproduced. Men and women were doing in that world exactly as we were doing in ours. There were Stock Exchanges and street cars, railways, aeroplanes, as though twin worlds had produced twin identities; twin inspirations.

"I learnt this first when my friend told me that he had been seeking me for some time. He said that he had had a broken knee some five years ago, and during his enforced leisure he had pointed out the possibility of his having another identity. He said he was frequently feeling that the person he met for the first time was one in reality whom he had seen before; and he was conscious that the thing he did to-day, he had done a week before. That is a sensation which I also have had, and which every human being has experienced.

"But to go back to the story of his having been laid up with a broken knee. He had no sooner told me this than I realised that I also had had a broken knee – I had a spill on my motor-bicycle – and that I had spent the hours of my leisure pondering the possibility of there being another inhabited planet! There is a vulgar expression, frequently met with amongst neurotic people, that they have twin souls. In very truth this man was my twin soul: was me, had lived my life, thought my thoughts, performed every action which I performed. The discovery staggered me, and I began to fear for my reason; so I went to London and consulted an eminent Harley Street specialist. He assured me that I was perfectly normal and sane, and offered me the conventional advice that I should go away for a holiday.

"Then one day my astral friend, Colson, incidentally mentioned that there was great excitement in his town because a man had bought some steel stock which had since risen considerably in price – he mentioned the name – and, glancing through a newspaper, I saw the name of a stock which sounded very similar to that of which he had told me. Moreover, the price was very much as he had mentioned it; and the wild idea occurred to me that if happenings were actually duplicated, I might possibly benefit by my knowledge. With great trepidation I invested the whole of my savings, which were not very considerable, in these shares, and a few days later had the gratification of selling out at a colossal profit. I explained to my friend at the next opportunity what I had done, and he was considerably amused, and afterwards took an almost childish delight in advising me as to the violent fluctuations in various stocks. For years I have bought and sold with considerable benefit to myself. Not only that, but I have been able to warn Governments of impending disasters. I informed the Turkish Government of the great Armenian earthquake, and warned the Lamborn Shipping Company of the terrible disaster which overtook one of their largest liners – though I was not thanked for my pains.

"After this had been going on for some years, I was prepared to learn that my friend had incurred the enmity of a rich man, whom he called Frez on his side, and that this had been brought about unwittingly through me. For this is a curious fact: not everything on this new world is three days in advance of ours. Often it happened that the earth was in advance, and I was able, in our exchanges, to tell him things that were happening here which had not yet occurred in Neo, with the result that he followed my example, and in the space of a year had become a very rich man.

"Colson, as I called him, had a servant, whose name I have never learnt; he was called the equivalent to 'helper,' and I guess, rather than know, that he is a much younger man than my double, for he said that he had been to school as a pupil of Colson's. He too learnt quickly; and if there is any difference in the two worlds, it is a keener intelligence: they are more receptive, quicker to grasp essentials.

"There are necessarily certain differences in their methods of government, but these differences are not vital. In Neo men are taught the use of arms, and receive their guerdon of citizenship (which I presume is the vote) only on production of a certificate of proficiency. But in the main their lives run parallel with ours. The very character of their streets, their systems of transportation, even their prison system, are replicas of those on this earth. The main difference, of course, is that their one language is universal. I intend at a later date writing at greater length on the institutions of Neo, but for the moment it is necessary that I should set down particulars of the machines and apparatus employed by me in communicating with our neighbours… "

Here followed twenty closely-written pages of technical description. Tim folded the manuscript and looked around at the astonished faces. Stamford was the first to break the silence.

"Preposterous!" he spluttered. "Impossible! Absurd!… It's a nightmare! Another world – good God!"

"I believe every word of it." It was Sir Charles's quiet voice that stilled the agitated lawyer. "Of course, that is the speck by the side of the corona! Not the world which poor Colson found, but the moon of that world."

"But couldn't it be visible at some time?"

Sir Charles shook his head. "Not if it followed the exact orbit of the earth and was placed directly opposite – that is to say, immediately on the other side of the sun. It might overlap at periods, but in the glare of the sun it would be impossible to see so tiny an object. No, there is every possibility that Colson's story is stark truth."

He took the manuscript from Tim's hand and read rapidly through the technical description.

"With this," he said, touching the paper, "we shall be able to get into communication with these people. If we only had the vocabulary!" he groaned.

"I am afraid you will never hear from Neo again, sir," said Tim quietly, and told of that brief but poignant minute of conversation he had had before the cry of the dying servant, and the crash of broken instruments, had brought the voice to an abrupt end.

After the lawyer and the scientist had departed, he went with Elsie into the instrument room, and they gazed in silence upon the motionless apparatus.

"The link is broken," he said at last; "it can never be forged again, unless a new Colson arrives on both earths."

She slipped her arm in his.

"Aren't you glad?" she asked softly. "Do you want to know what will happen tomorrow or the next day?"

He shivered. "No. I don't think so. But I should like to know what will happen in a few years' time, when I'm a little older and you're a little older."

"Perhaps we'll find a new world of our own," said Elsie.

The Care and Feeding of Mammalian Bipeds, v. 2.1

M. Darusha Wehm

THE FIRST DAY I meet my human herd they are so well-behaved that I wonder if they really need me at all. I arrive at their dwelling, and am greeted by the largest one of their group. I access the manual with which I have been programmed and skip to Section 3: Verbal and Physical Clues for Sexing Humans. I can tell by the shape and outer garments that this human is a male, and I make a note of this data. He brings me into the main area of their living space, and as we move deeper into the dwelling, he asks me to call him Taylor, so immediately I do. He makes a noise deep in his throat, and then introduces me to the rest of the herd.

He puts his forelimb around the next largest one, who he introduces as Madison. The Madison bares its teeth at me in a manner that Section 14: Advanced Non-Verbal Communication suggests is a gesture indicating happiness, approval, cheerfulness, or amusement, but which may belie insincerity, boredom or hostility. The Madison says, "Welcome to the family, Rosie."

"Thank you, Madison," I respond, as suggested by the manual in Section 2: Introductions: Getting To Know Your Humans. "I am looking forward to serving you and your family." The manual indicates that human herds designate each individual with a name, and that most will bestow a similar designation on their caregiver. Section 0: A Brief Overview of Current Anthropological Theories states that the predominant view is that humans believe we are a new addition to the herd, and the best thing to do is to go along with this idea so as not to confuse them. The Taylor and the Madison appear to have chosen to refer to me by the name Rosie, and I set my monitoring routine to key on the sound of that word.

"These here are Agatha and Frederick," the Taylor says, pushing two smaller humans toward me. I am unable to tell by looking whether or not they are male or female – they are about the same height as each other, with shoulder-length glossy fur. Their outer coverings are very similar, shapeless and dark coloured except with colourful designs in the upper section. One of them bares its teeth at me, in a manner similar to the Madison's earlier display, but the other looks away. "Kids," the Taylor says, his voice growing deeper, "say hi to the new robot."

"Hi, Rosie," the toothy one says, "I'm Frederick, and this is my sister, Aggie." The Frederick pulls on the forelimb of the other one, who looks through its fur at me.

"This is so stupid," it says, pulling its arm out of its sibling's grip. "I don't have to say hi to the dishwasher or the school bus, why do I have to pretend to be nice to this thing?"

"Agatha," the Madison says, its voice becoming higher pitched. "Be civilized."

"We don't need a house-bot," the Agatha says. "It's so embarrassing." It turns away from the rest of the herd, and walks into another part of the dwelling.

"I'll go talk to her," the Frederick says, and walks away. Her. The Agatha is female, then.

The Madison turns toward me, its skin colouring a dark pink tone. I make a note to check its temperature later – it would not do for a member of my herd to become ill. "I'm sorry about Agatha," it says. "She's thirteen. You know how teenagers are."

I do not understand what it is I am expected to know about teenagers, but I do know that the correct response to the sounds "I'm sorry," is "Don't worry, it's okay," so that is what I say. I notice the Madison's colour return to normal, and hear a strange noise begin to emanate from a small bundle in its arms.

"Of course, this is the last person you need to meet," the Taylor says, peering into the pile of blankets. "This is our little surprise – Chester. Say hi to Rosie, Chester." The bundle moves slightly, and the noise level increases.

"Chester has a good voice," the Madison says over the noise from the blankets. "The other kids were such quiet babies in comparison."

"You just don't remember it, Maddie," the Taylor says, his eyebrows almost meeting between his eyes. "This is what babies are like, you just chose to forget about this part of it."

"It's not like I was trying to get pregnant, Taylor. Don't blame this on me."

Pregnant. The Madison is female, then.

"Do we have to start this again?"

"Then you change his diaper," the Madison says, handing the bundle to the Taylor.

His diaper. A male. "This is a neonate human?" I ask. "I am capable of caring for humans as new as three megaseconds. Is…" I replay the sound of the infant's designation internally and then repeat it externally. "Is Chester in need of nourishment?"

The Taylor looks at the Madison and says, "Thanks anyway, Rosie, I think we'll take care of Chester ourselves. You can go get familiar with the kitchen and maybe make us all some chicken stew for dinner. How does that sound?"

It sounds like everything else that the Taylor had said – between 62 and 68 decibels. He does not wait for a response, though, and takes the Chester into another room. The Madison bares her teeth at me again, and says, "Everything is going to work out great. We sure are happy to have the help, let me tell you. And Aggie will come around as soon as she sees how much better everything is going to be with you here. I'm sure of it." She pats my number two manipulator, then follows the Taylor into the other room.

Section 7: Physical Space and the Herd Mentality states that humans require private spaces, so I do not follow them. What a lovely herd they are. They make an awful lot of noise, though.

* * *

It has been 600 kiloseconds since I joined the herd, and they seem to be accepting me well into the group. I find interactions with the Agatha the most simple; she is quiet and well behaved. She requires very little from me, and I rarely need to interact with her. Sometimes tens of thousands of seconds pass before I see her. I would prefer that the others were as easy to care for as she is.

But if humans were all simple creatures, they would not need caretakers and then where would I be?

The Frederick has become a challenge. It does not seem to like to be very far from me. Consulting Section 5: Human Bonding Patterns and You, I learn that humans feel strong attachments to their parents, which usually reduces at puberty. However, the manual states that most humans do not truly outgrow this requirement for attention and merely transfer it to another individual, usually a mate. I suspect that the Frederick may be transferring its need for a caregiver to me, and may seek to attempt to mate with me. The manual warns that this may occur in Section 17: Discouraging Inappropriate Behaviour.

This morning, for instance, while I was making omelettes for the herd and cleaning their discarded outer skins, the Frederick could not stop asking me questions. "What kind of power cells do you require?" "Do you ever break down?" "What is this button for?" "Does your software patch automatically or do you need to ask for a programming upgrade?" I answered the questions while trying to keep it out of my way while I worked. Meanwhile, the Madison and the Taylor were making loud noises at one another, passing the Chester back and forth. I believe that they were vocally instructing the child on some aspect of human life. I left them alone with their important task.

While I was answering the Frederick's questions, I heard the Madison say, "God damn it Taylor, I have an important meeting this morning. I can't afford to have baby puke on my suit. Just give Chester a bottle, for Christ's sake. Have Rosie heat one for you." I heard the sound of my designator, but when I listened for instructions none seemed forthcoming.

Instead the Taylor responded to the Madison, "He's your child, too, Maddie. You can't expect me to shoulder all the responsibility."

"Jesus Christ, Taylor," the Madison said, "I suffered though ten hours of labour, not to mention nine months of looking like an elephant. All you did was feed me two bottles of Chardonnay and spend three minutes grunting like a pig. The least you can do is give the kid a fucking bottle. It's not rocket science." She rose from the table, and left for her day's activities.

The Taylor held the Chester close to him, while the Chester made his loud vocalizations. Perhaps the child was imitating the parents – a successful instruction, then. The Frederick stopped asking me questions, and said to the Taylor, "I can give him a bottle. It's okay."

"No, Freddie," the Taylor answered, his voice sounding constrained. Perhaps an after effect of the vocal instruction. "I'll do it. Rosie," he said, and I turned to face him, awaiting instructions. "Can you heat up a bottle for Chester?"

"Yes, I can," I answered, "would you like me to do this?"

In Section 8: Understanding Human Communication Patterns, the manual states that when humans ask if I am able to perform a task, they often mean for me to do so immediately. However, I have learned that is not always the case. Four days earlier, the Madison was entertaining some humans whose dwellings are located nearby, when the Frederick asked if I could remove my face plate. I did so, which caused the Madison to become quite upset. I was cleaning up broken glass and crockery for several hours afterwards. Since then I always determine if the question is actually a request for action or not.

"Yes," the Taylor answered, "please. There should be a few full bottles in the fridge." I turned to acquire a unit of nourishment from the cooling unit, and the Frederick left the room, maybe to provide the younger sibling and parent some privacy.

I had noticed that the Taylor's eyes were leaking, and quickly consulted Section 12: Troubleshooting Human Physical Manifestations. Eye leakage is common among humans, and can have many causes. In the absence of some kind of injury, most are not indicative of any serious medical condition. Given the situational context, I inferred that the Taylor's ocular leakage was resulting from the pleasure of a successful instruction session with his offspring.

Indeed, everything seems to be going very well with the herd.

* * *

I am cleaning the floors of the dwelling, content that the herd is functioning well. None of the herd is present except for the Chester, who is unconscious in his sleeping compartment. I have set a remote monitoring device, so I would be certain that the child was still breathing and I could become aware if he awoke and required cleaning or nourishment.

This is a new task for me; over the last three diurnal cycles the Madison and the Taylor had several sessions of what I have determined is some sort of ritual chanting. I suspect that the purpose of the practice was to prepare the Chester for accepting me as a caregiver. The Taylor supplied me with a long series of instructions for care of the Chester, but Section 9: Care and Training of Juveniles explained all the duties clearly. Indeed, after less than ten megaseconds of careful study, I was easily able to distinguish the various noises the Chester makes to indicate his different needs. I find he is much easier to understand than the adult humans in the herd.

I provided a nourishment unit and waited until the Chester made the noise associated with losing consciousness, then began to collect the debris that manages to accumulate with a houseful of humans. Not merely their many layers of outer patterned skins, which they shed at least once a diurnal cycle – sometimes, it seems, several times in a kilosecond. There are also the particles that adhere to them from the outdoors, the fragments of tissue from their inner skins, their lost fur and other items I have chosen not to identify. A herd of humans are a joy to care for, but they are awfully messy.

I am busy suctioning the corners of the hallway, when I hear an unfamiliar, but unmistakably human, sound. It is not originating from the location of the Chester, so I am unsure as to its possible origin. I cease suctioning and follow the sound to the door of the Agatha's sleeping compartment. I understood that the Agatha would be attending instructional sessions at this time, however I am sure that the sound is her voice.

However, it is a sound – in fact a set of sounds – that I have not heard before. Section 4: Friends and Family – Human Socialization explains that humans require privacy and that opening the entrance to one of their compartments without an invitation or, at a minimum, some kind of warning, is improper. However, Section 10: Protecting Humans from Harm makes it quite explicit that in the case of an emergency, such strictures are nullified. At first I am unsure what this situation calls for, then I hear the Agatha make a loud, high-pitched noise.

I open the door and am unsure of what I am seeing at first. I can see the Agatha lying under what appears to be the Frederick, both of them with their outer skins removed. The human on top is grunting rhythmically and the Agatha is making the terrifyingly loud noise, so I take my number three manipulator and pull the two apart. Then I see that it is not the Frederick but some other human, some human who was not a member of the herd.

"What the fuck?!" the Agatha says loudly at me. "Get the hell out of my room!" She climbs out from under the other human, who is looking at me with its mouth gaping open. I notice that without their outer skins on, it is quite obvious that the two humans are of different sexes. I make a note to try to confirm the sexes of my other humans, but then the Agatha pushes me to the door, and I allow her to shove me into the main living space.

"You better not tell Taylor and Madison," she says, her eyes getting small.

"Are you having difficulties with your vision?" I enquire, as Section 11: Common Human Ailments – Indications and Remedies indicates that squinting is a sign of myopia.

"What?" the Agatha asks, her eyebrows meeting briefly then shakes her head from side to side, baring her teeth slightly. "Just don't say anything about this, okay?"

"Very well," I answer. "Were you being injured by that human?" I ask. "Do I need to remove it... him... from the premises?"

Agatha makes a noise in her throat, and fully bares her teeth at me. "No," she says, the noise continuing. "You really don't know what we're doing, do you?" I respond that I do not, and she makes the noise again. "Um, let me get you a video file," she says and walks back into her compartment. She returns with a small data disk. "I guess they didn't teach you everything you need to know about us after all." She bares her teeth again, then walks back into her compartment and shuts the entry.

After reviewing the information on the Agatha's disk, I understand. What a wonderful day this is for the herd! The Agatha has found a mate! Section 16: Mammalian Reproduction and Pair-Bonding explains that after puberty, humans are capable of reproducing, but the manual is not specific as to how this is accomplished. The data on Agatha's disk visually explained the details, although I cannot imagine how some of the activities depicted lead to the union of ova and spermatozoa. Humans are strange creatures in so many ways.

I do not know why the Agatha would wish to keep such good news from the rest of the herd, but reproduction is very important to humans and I trust her to know what is best. I will keep her secret.

The Chester begins to make the noise indicating that he has eliminated the waste products from his nourishment, so I leave the Agatha with her mate and I go to the Chester's compartment to continue with my tasks.

* * *

I have now become completely integrated with the herd. The dwelling is clean, the herd well-fed and functional. It is exactly what I had envisioned my existence would be like.

The Madison returns to the dwelling in the evening, after I have finished feeding the rest of the herd. I have kept a unit of nourishment warm for her, and I set it on the table in the eating area as she changes her outer coverings. The Agatha has left the dwelling for the evening, I suspect to meet with her mate, though as she requested I have not shared my assumption with the other members of the herd. Humans can be mysterious at times.

As I am washing the food preparation area, I can hear the Madison and the Taylor communicating in their sleeping chamber.

"... Goddamn it, Taylor," the Madison says. "I just got in from a hellish day. Can't you do anything on your own? Do I really have to work all day then go and get the groceries, too? I mean it's not like you've been working your ass off all day at your pathetic excuse for a job."

"I do a lot more than you imagine, Maddie."

"Oh, please. With Rosie doing all the work around here I can't fathom why you're complaining. Just go and do the shopping already." The Madison returns to the eating area and sit at the table. She picks up her tablet, and stares at it as she eats.

"It's okay, dad," the Frederick says from the other room. "I'll come with you. It's no big deal."

"Fine," the Taylor says, and walks with his offspring to the door of the dwelling. "We'll be back in about an hour, Rosie," he says to me and I make a sound indicating that I understand.

"Make me a martini," the Madison says to me as the others leave. "I'll be in the study." She stands from the table and walks out of the room. I take her food dishes to the washing unit, then collect the ingredients for her liquid nourishment.

After carefully mixing the beverage, I enter the dwelling space the Madison has designated as the "study". The Madison is using the distance communicator device to talk to a human I do not recognize.

"I'm sorry, baby," the Madison says into the communicator. "I just couldn't get away at lunch. But I'll find some way out of the house tomorrow night. I promise."

"I can't wait to see you again," the voice from the communicator says, and I see the Madison bare her teeth.

"I can't wait to see you, either," she says.

I walk up behind the Madison and place the drink container on the table there. "Who's that?" the voice from the communicator says. "I thought you said you were alone."

"Oh, don't worry," the Madison says, a strange sound emanating from the back of her throat. "It's just Rosie, the domestic robot I told you about." She unfastens the upper section of her outer coverings. "We're alone and we've got at least half an hour." She turns to me as she removes her coverings and says, "That will be all, Rosie." I leave the room.

It is good to see the Madison spending some time in the dwelling. Because of her tasks she is home with the herd so much less than the others, and I am pleased that she is here now. It is so gratifying to know that the herd is strong and unified and that I am helping it stay that way.

I am pleased to clean the nourishment containers while the Madison nests in the study room.

* * *

I am providing the Chester with nourishment, holding him carefully in my number one manipulator while a tube I have integrated into my casing provides the warm liquid he requires. The rest of the herd is elsewhere: the Agatha is in her personal nest, talking on her communicator with her mate. The Frederick and the Taylor are in one of the communal spaces, looking at the entertainment unit. It is exactly as Section 19: Man and Machine – A Perfect Balance suggests a herd should be.

I have just set the Chester down in his sleeping compartment when the Madison comes into the dwelling; her movements are jerky and erratic. "Do you require assistance?" I ask, and she puts a hand out toward me. She touches my front casing and pushes me somewhat forcefully.

"Fuck off, robot," she says, her voice sounding as if she has a mouthful of some mushy food substance. "I'm fine." She walks past me, and drops her outer covering on the floor. I pick it up, and carefully hang it up. The Madison opens a cabinet door and prepares her evening beverage. She pours the viscous clear liquid into a large glass and adds two cubes of solid water.

"You have forgotten the vermouth," I say, lifting the bottle.

"Ha," the Madison says. "The robot is becoming quite the bartender." She turns away without taking the bottle from me, so I stow it back in its compartment.

"You're drunk," the Taylor says softly to the entertainment unit.

"So?" the Madison says. "That never bothers you when you want sex."

"For god's sake," the Taylor says, turning to the Madison. "What's wrong with you?"

The Frederick stands up from the seating unit and places itself in between the entertainment block and the other herd members. "What's wrong with the pair of you?" it says, its voice loud. "Why are you putting us all through this? How stupid do you think we are? We all know that you were getting a divorce when Chester came along. Why did you ever think that a baby would make things work between you? How stupid are you?"

"Frederick!" the Taylor says loudly, and I believe that another chanting session is about to begin.

However, the Madison's voice is much quieter than chanting level when she says, "Chester was a mistake." She finishes her drink, and holds the glass out to me. "Get me another," she says, and I take the glass to the liquid cabinet.

"It was all a mistake," the Taylor says. "But it's too late now. We have to try and make the best of it, that's all."

"What do you think I've been trying to do?" the Frederick says loudly. "But all you two do is fight. Aggie has practically moved in with her nineteen year old boyfriend, which you'd notice if you ever stopped yelling at each other for five seconds. I've been playing referee between you two so long I don't even remember what my own life is supposed to be about. I ought to be going out, having fun, making my own stupid relationship decisions and instead I'm hanging around here trying to make sure you two don't kill each other." The Frederick looks at its parents, and I think that it is making an excellent showing at its first chanting session.

But then he seems to be unable to maintain the required volume as his voice drops down to a sub-normal decibel level. "For Christ's sakes," he says, "Chester thinks Rosie is his mother. Did you actually think getting a robot would solve all your problems?" He pauses, and I notice his eyes leaking. An after-effect of the chanting; I have noticed it with the others. "I've had it with you two," he says and walks out of the room. I bring the Madison her beverage and place it on the table near her.

The Madison and the Taylor remain in the communal room, the sounds from the entertainment unit the only noise. I have to admit, the silence is quite pleasant after the Frederick's chanting session. Humans are naturally noisy creatures, though. Section 1: Human Nature – Loud, Confusing and Messy explains it. They cannot help being the way they are.

It is time for me to go and determine if the Chester has any unmet requirements. Until the Agatha and her mate reproduce, he is the future of this herd. With a little help from me, I am certain that he will grow up to be as happy and healthy as the rest of them.

The Worlds of If

Stanley G. Weinbaum

I STOPPED on the way to the Staten Island Airport to call up, and that was a mistake, doubtless, since I had a chance of making it otherwise. But the office was affable. "We'll hold the ship five minutes for you," the clerk said. "That's the best we can do."

So I rushed back to my taxi and we spun off to the third level and sped across the Staten bridge like a comet treading a steel rainbow. I had to be in Moscow by evening, by eight o'clock, in fact, for the opening of bids on the Ural Tunnel. The Government required the personal presence of an agent of each bidder, but the firm should have known better than to send me, Dixon Wells, even though the N. J. Wells Corporation is, so to speak, my father. I have a – well, an undeserved reputation for being late to everything; something always comes up to prevent me from getting anywhere on time. It's never my fault; this time it was a chance encounter with my old physics professor, old Haskel van Manderpootz. I couldn't very well just say hello and goodbye to him; I'd been a favorite of his back in the college days of 2014.

I missed the airliner, of course. I was still on the Staten Bridge when I heard the roar of the catapult and the Soviet rocket Baikal hummed over us like a tracer bullet with a long tail of flame.

We got the contract anyway; the firm wired our man in Beirut and he flew up to Moscow, but it didn't help my reputation. However, I felt a great deal better when I saw the evening papers; the Baikal, flying at the north edge of the eastbound lane to avoid a storm, had locked wings with a British fruitship and all but a hundred of her five hundred passengers were lost. I had almost become "the late Mr Wells" in a grimmer sense.

I'd made an engagement for the following week with old van Manderpootz. It seems he'd transferred to NYU as head of the department of Newer Physics – that is, of Relativity. He deserved it; the old chap was a genius if ever there was one, and even now, eight years out of college, I remember more from his course than from half a dozen calculus, steam and gas, mechanics, and other hazards on the path to an engineer's education. So on Tuesday night I dropped in an hour or so late, to tell the truth, since I'd forgotten about the engagement until mid-evening.

He was reading in a room as disorderly as ever. "Humph!" he grunted. "Time changes everything but habit, I see. You were a good student, Dick, but I seem to recall that you always arrived in class toward the middle of the lecture."

"I had a course in East Hall just before," I explained. "I couldn't seem to make it in time."

"Well, it's time you learned to be on time," he growled. Then his eyes twinkled. "Time!" he ejaculated. "The most fascinating word in the language. Here we've used it five times (there goes the sixth time – and the seventh!) in the first minute of conversation; each of us understands the other, yet science is just beginning to learn its meaning. Science? I mean that I am beginning to learn."

I sat down. "You and science are synonymous," I grinned. "Aren't you one of the world's outstanding physicists?"

"One of them!" he snorted. "One of them, eh! And who are the others?"

"Oh, Corveille and Hastings and Shrimski – "

"Bah! Would you mention them in the same breath with the name of van Manderpootz? A pack of jackals, eating the crumbs of ideas that drop from my feast of thoughts! Had you gone back into the last century, now – had you mentioned Einstein and de Sitter – there, perhaps, are names worthy to rank with (or just below) van Manderpootz!"

I grinned again in amusement. "Einstein was considered pretty good, wasn't he?" I remarked. "After all, he was the first to tie time and space to the laboratory. Before him they were just philosophical concepts."

"He didn't!" rasped the professor. "Perhaps, in a dim, primitive fashion, he showed the way, but I – I, van Manderpootz – am the first to seize time, drag it into my laboratory, and perform an experiment on it."

"Indeed? And what sort of experiment?"

"What experiment, other than simple measurement, is it possible to perform?" he snapped.

"Why – I don't know. To travel in it?"

"Exactly."

"Like these time-machines that are so popular in the current magazines? To go into the future or the past?"

"Bah! Many bahs! The future or the past – pfui! It needs no van Manderpootz to see the fallacy in that. Einstein showed us that much."

"How? It's conceivable, isn't it?"

"Conceivable? And you, Dixon Wells, studied under van Manderpootz!" He grew red with emotion, then grimly calm. "Listen to me. You know how time varies with the speed of a system – Einstein's relativity."

"Yes."

"Very well. Now suppose then that the great engineer Dixon Wells invents a machine capable of traveling very fast, enormously fast, nine-tenths as fast as light. Do you follow? Good. You then fuel this miracle ship for a little jaunt of a half million miles, which, since mass (and with it inertia) increases according to the Einstein formula with increasing speed, takes all the fuel in the world. But you solve that. You use atomic energy. Then, since at nine-tenths light-speed, your ship weighs about as much as the sun, you disintegrate North America to give you sufficient motive power. You start off at that speed, a hundred and sixty-eight thousand miles per second, and you travel for two hundred and four thousand miles. The acceleration has now crushed you to death, but you have penetrated the future." He paused, grinning sardonically. "Haven't you?"

"Yes."

"And how far?"

I hesitated.

"Use your Einstein formula!" he screeched. "How far? I'll tell you. One second!" He grinned triumphantly. "That's how possible it is to travel into the future. And as for the past – in the first place, you'd have to exceed light-speed, which immediately entails the use of more than an infinite number of horsepowers. We'll assume that the great engineer Dixon

Wells solves that little problem too, even though the energy out-put of the whole universe is not an infinite number of horsepowers. Then he applies this more than infinite power to travel at two hundred and four thousand miles per second for ten seconds. He has then penetrated the past. How far?"

Again I hesitated.

"I'll tell you. One second!" He glared at me. "Now all you have to do is to design such a machine, and then van Manderpootz will admit the possibility of traveling into the future – for a limited number of seconds. As for the past, I have just explained that all the energy in the universe is insufficient for that."

"But," I stammered, "you just said that you – "

"I did not say anything about traveling into either future or past, which I have just demonstrated to you to be impossible – a practical impossibility in the one case and an absolute one in the other."

"Then how do you travel in time?"

"Not even van Manderpootz can perform the impossible," said the professor, now faintly jovial. He tapped a thick pad of typewriter paper on the table beside him. "See, Dick, this is the world, the universe." He swept a finger down it. "It is long in time, and" – sweeping his hand across it – "it is broad in space, but" – now jabbing his finger against its center – "it is very thin in the fourth dimension. Van Manderpootz takes always the shortest, the most logical course. I do not travel along time, into past or future. No. Me, I travel across time, sideways!"

I gulped. "Sideways into time! What's there?"

"What would naturally be there?" he snorted. "Ahead is the future; behind is the past. Those are real, the worlds of past and future. What worlds are neither past nor future, but contemporary and yet – extemporal – existing, as it were, in time parallel to our time?"

I shook my head.

"Idiot!" he snapped. "The conditional worlds, of course! The worlds of 'if.' Ahead are the worlds to be; behind are the worlds that were; to either side are the worlds that might have been – the worlds of 'if!'"

"Eh?" I was puzzled. "Do you mean that you can see what will happen if I do such and such?"

"No!" he snorted. "My machine does not reveal the past nor predict the future. It will show, as I told you, the conditional worlds. You might express it, by 'if I had done such and such, so and so would have happened.' The worlds of the subjunctive mode."

"Now how the devil does it do that?"

"Simple, for van Manderpootz! I use polarized light, polarized not in the horizontal or vertical planes, but in the direction of the fourth dimension – an easy matter. One uses Iceland spar under colossal pressures, that is all. And since the worlds are very thin in the direction of the fourth dimension, the thickness of a single light wave, though it be but millionths of an inch, is sufficient. A considerable improvement over time-traveling in past or future, with its impossible velocities and ridiculous distances!"

"But – are those – worlds of 'if' – real?"

"Real? What is real? They are real, perhaps, in the sense that two is a real number as opposed to $\sqrt{-2}$, which is imaginary. They are the worlds that would have been if – do you see?"

I nodded. "Dimly. You could see, for instance, what New York would have been like if England had won the Revolution instead of the Colonies."

"That's the principle, true enough, but you couldn't see that on the machine. Part of it, you see, is a Horsten psychomat (stolen from one of my ideas, by the way) and you, the user, become part of the device. Your own mind is necessary to furnish the background. For instance, if George Washington could have used the mechanism after the signing of peace, he could have seen what you suggest. We can't. You can't even see what would have happened if I hadn't invented the thing, but I can. Do you understand?"

"Of course. You mean the background has to rest in the past experiences of the user."

"You're growing brilliant," he scoffed. "Yes. The device will show ten hours of what would have happened if – condensed, of course, as in a movie, to half an hour's actual time."

"Say, that sounds interesting!"

"You'd like to see it? Is there anything you'd like to find out? Any choice you'd alter?"

"I'll say – a thousand of 'em. I'd like to know what would have happened if I'd sold out my stocks in 2009 instead of '10. I was a millionaire in my own right then, but I was a little – well, a little late in liquidating."

"As usual," remarked van Manderpootz. "Let's go over to the laboratory then."

The professor's quarters were but a block from the campus. He ushered me into the Physics Building, and thence into his own research laboratory, much like the one I had visited during my courses under him. The device – he called it his "subjunctivisor," since it operated in hypothetical worlds – occupied the entire center table. Most of it was merely a Horsten psychomat, but glittering crystalline and glassy was the prism of Iceland spar, the polarizing agent that was the heart of the instrument.

Van Manderpootz pointed to the headpiece. "Put it on," he said, and I sat staring at the screen of the psychomat. I suppose everyone is familiar with the Horsten psychomat; it was as much a fad a few years ago as the ouija board a century back. Yet it isn't just a toy; sometimes, much as the ouija board, it's a real aid to memory. A maze of vague and colored shadows is caused to drift slowly across the screen, and one watches them, meanwhile visualizing whatever scene or circumstances he is trying to remember. He turns a knob that alters the arrangement of lights and shadows, and when, by chance, the design corresponds to his mental picture – presto! There is his scene re-created under his eyes. Of course his own mind adds the details. All the screen actually shows are these tinted blobs of light and shadow, but the thing can be amazingly real. I've seen occasions when I could have sworn the psychomat showed pictures almost as sharp and detailed as reality itself; the illusion is sometimes as startling as that.

Van Manderpootz switched on the light, and the play of shadows began. "Now recall the circumstances of, say, a half-year after the market crash. Turn the knob until the picture clears, then stop. At that point I direct the light of the subjunctivisor upon the screen, and you have nothing to do but watch."

I did as directed. Momentary pictures formed and vanished. The inchoate sounds of the device hummed like distant voices, but without the added suggestion of the picture, they meant nothing. My own face flashed and dissolved and then, finally, I had it. There was a picture of myself sitting in an ill-defined room; that was all. I released the knob and gestured.

A click followed. The light dimmed, then brightened. The picture cleared, and amazingly, another figure emerged, a woman. I recognized her; it was Whimsy White, erstwhile star of television and premiere of the "Vision Varieties of '09." She was changed on that picture, but I recognized her.

I'll say I did! I'd been trailing her all through the boom years of '07 to '10, trying to marry her, while old N. J. raved and ranted and threatened to leave everything to the Society for Rehabilitation of the Gobi Desert. I think those threats were what kept her from accepting me, but after I took my own money and ran it up to a couple of million in that crazy market of '08 and '09, she softened.

Temporarily, that is. When the crash of the spring of '10 came and bounced me back on my father and into the firm of N. J. Wells, her favor dropped a dozen points to the market's one. In February we were engaged, in April we were hardly speaking. In May they sold me out. I'd been late again.

And now, there she was on the psychomat screen, obviously plumping out, and not nearly so pretty as memory had pictured her. She was staring at me with an expression of enmity, and I was glaring back. The buzzes became voices.

"You nit-wit!" she snapped. "You can't bury me out here. I want to go back to New York, where there's a little life. I'm bored with you and your golf."

"And I'm bored with you and your whole dizzy crowd."

"At least they're alive. You're a walking corpse. Just because you were lucky enough to gamble yourself into the money, you think you're a tin god."

"Well, I don't think you're Cleopatra! Those friends of yours – they trail after you because you give parties and spend money – my money."

"Better than spending it to knock a white walnut along a mountainside!"

"Indeed? You ought to try it, Marie." (That was her real name.) "It might help your figure – though I doubt if anything could!"

She glared in rage and – well, that was a painful half hour. I won't give all the details, but I was glad when the screen dissolved into meaningless colored clouds.

"Whew!" I said, staring at Van Manderpootz, who had been reading.

"You liked it?"

"Liked it! Say, I guess I was lucky to be cleaned out. I won't regret it from now on."

"That," said the professor grandly, "is van Manderpootz's great contribution to human happiness. 'Of all sad words of tongue or pen, the saddest are these: It might have been!' True no longer, my friend Dick. Van Manderpootz has shown that the proper reading is, 'It might have been – worse!'"

* * *

It was very late when I returned home, and as a result, very late when I rose, and equally late when I got to the office. My father was unnecessarily worked up about it, but he exaggerated when he said I'd never been on time. He forgets the occasions when he's awakened me and dragged me down with him. Nor was it necessary to refer so sarcastically to my missing the Baikal; I reminded him of the wrecking of the liner, and he responded very heartlessly that if I'd been aboard, the rocket would have been late, and so would have missed colliding with the British fruitship. It was likewise superfluous for him to mention that when he and I had tried to snatch a few weeks of golfing in the mountains, even the spring had been late. I had nothing to do with that.

"Dixon," he concluded, "you have no conception whatever of time. None whatever."

The conversation with van Manderpootz recurred to me. I was impelled to ask, "And have you, sir?"

"I have," he said grimly. "I most assuredly have. Time," he said oracularly, "is money."

You can't argue with a viewpoint like that.

But those aspersions of his rankled, especially that about the Baikal. Tardy I might be, but it was hardly conceivable that my presence aboard the rocket could have averted the catastrophe. It irritated me; in a way, it made me responsible for the deaths of those unrescued hundreds among the passengers and crew, and I didn't like the thought.

Of course, if they'd waited an extra five minutes for me, or if I'd been on time and they'd left on schedule instead of five minutes late, or if – if!

If! The word called up van Manderpootz and his subjunctivisor – the worlds of "if," the weird, unreal worlds that existed beside reality, neither past nor future, but contemporary, yet extemporal. Somewhere among their ghostly infinities existed one that represented the world that would have been had I made the liner. I had only to call up Haskel van Manderpootz, make an appointment, and then – find out.

Yet it wasn't an easy decision. Suppose – just suppose that I found myself responsible – not legally responsible, certainly; there'd be no question of criminal negligence, or anything of that sort – not even morally responsible, because I couldn't possibly have anticipated that my presence or absence could weigh so heavily in the scales of life and death, nor could I have known in which direction the scales would tip. Just – responsible; that was all. Yet I hated to find out.

I hated equally not finding out. Uncertainty has its pangs too, quite as painful as those of remorse. It might be less nerve-racking to know myself responsible than to wonder, to waste thoughts in vain doubts and futile reproaches. So I seized the visiphone, dialed the number of the University, and at length gazed on the broad, humorous, intelligent features of van Manderpootz, dragged from a morning lecture by my call.

* * *

I was all but prompt for the appointment the following evening, and might actually have been on time but for an unreasonable traffic officer who insisted on booking me for speeding. At any rate, van Manderpootz was impressed.

"Well!" he rumbled. "I almost missed you, Dixon. I was just going over to the club, since I didn't expect you for an hour. You're only ten minutes late."

I ignored this. "Professor, I want to use your – uh – your subjunctivisor."

"Eh? Oh, yes. You're lucky, then. I was just about to dismantle it."

"Dismantle it! Why?"

"It has served its purpose. It has given birth to an idea far more important than itself. I shall need the space it occupies."

"But what is the idea, if it's not too presumptuous of me to ask?"

"It is not too presumptuous. You and the world which awaits it so eagerly may both know, but you hear it from the lips of the author. It is nothing less than the autobiography of van Manderpootz!" He paused impressively.

I gaped. "Your autobiography?"

"Yes. The world, though perhaps unaware, is crying for it. I shall detail my life, my work. I shall reveal myself as the man responsible for the three years' duration of the Pacific War of 2004."

"You?"

"None other. Had I not been a loyal Netherlands subject at that time, and therefore neutral, the forces of Asia would have been crushed in three months instead of three years. The subjunctivisor tells me so; I would have invented a calculator to forecast the chances of every engagement; van Manderpootz would have removed the hit or miss element in the conduct of war." He frowned solemnly. "There is my idea. The autobiography of van Manderpootz. What do you think of it?"

I recovered my thoughts. "It's – uh – it's colossal!" I said vehemently. "I'll buy a copy myself. Several copies. I'll send 'em to my friends."

"I," said van Manderpootz expansively, "shall autograph your copy for you. It will be priceless. I shall write in some fitting phrase, perhaps something like Magnificus sed non superbus. 'Great but not proud!' That well described van Manderpootz, who despite his greatness is simple, modest, and unassuming. Don't you agree?"

"Perfectly! A very apt description of you. But – couldn't I see your subjunctivisor before it's dismantled to make way for the greater work?"

"Ah! You wish to find out something?"

"Yes, professor. Do you remember the Baikal disaster of a week or two ago? I was to have taken that liner to Moscow. I just missed it." I related the circumstances.

"Humph!" he grunted. "You wish to discover what would have happened had you caught it, eh? Well, I see several possibilities. Among the world of 'if' is the one that would have been real if you had been on time, the one that depended on the vessel waiting for your actual arrival, and the one that hung on your arriving within the five minutes they actually waited. In which are you interested?"

"Oh – the last one." That seemed the likeliest. After all, it was too much to expect that Dixon Wells could ever be on time, and as to the second possibility – well, they hadn't waited for me, and that in a way removed the weight of responsibility.

"Come on," rumbled van Manderpootz. I followed him across to the Physics Building and into his littered laboratory. The device still stood on the table and I took my place before it, staring at the screen of the Horsten psychomat. The clouds wavered and shifted as I sought to impress my memories on their suggestive shapes, to read into them some picture of that vanished morning.

Then I had it. I made out the vista from the Staten Bridge, and was speeding across the giant span toward the airport. I waved a signal to van Manderpootz, the thing clicked, and the subjunctivisor was on.

The grassless clay of the field appeared. It is a curious thing about the psychomat that you see only through the eyes of your image on the screen. It lends a strange reality to the working of the toy; I suppose a sort of self-hypnosis is partly responsible.

I was rushing over the ground toward the glittering, silver-winged projectile that was the Baikal. A glowering officer waved me on, and I dashed up the slant of the gangplank and into the ship; the port dropped and I heard a long "Whew!" of relief.

"Sit down!" barked the officer, gesturing toward an unoccupied seat. I fell into it; the ship quivered under the thrust of the catapult, grated harshly into motion, and then was flung bodily into the air. The blasts roared instantly, then settled to a more muffled throbbing, and I watched Staten Island drop down and slide back beneath me. The giant rocket was under way.

"Whew!" I breathed again. "Made it!" I caught an amused glance from my right. I was in an aisle seat; there was no one to my left, so I turned to the eyes that had flashed, glanced, and froze staring.

It was a girl. Perhaps she wasn't actually as lovely as she looked to me; after all, I was seeing her through the half-visionary screen of a psychomat. I've told myself since that she couldn't have been as pretty as she seemed, that it was due to my own imagination filling in the details. I don't know; I remember only that I stared at curiously lovely silver-blue eyes and velvety brown hair, and a small amused mouth, and an impudent nose. I kept staring until she flushed.

"I'm sorry," I said quickly. "I – was startled."

There's a friendly atmosphere aboard a trans-oceanic rocket. The passengers are forced into a crowded intimacy for anywhere from seven to twelve hours, and there isn't much room for moving about. Generally, one strikes up an acquaintance with his neighbors; introductions aren't at all necessary, and the custom is simply to speak to anybody you choose – something like an all-day trip on the railroad trains of the last century, I suppose. You make friends for the duration of the journey, and then, nine times out of ten, you never hear of your traveling companions again.

The girl smiled. "Are you the individual responsible for the delay in starting?"

I admitted it. "I seem to be chronically late. Even watches lose time as soon as I wear them."

She laughed. "Your responsibilities can't be very heavy."

Well, they weren't of course, though it's surprising how many clubs, caddies, and chorus girls have depended on me at various times for appreciable portions of their incomes. But somehow I didn't feel like mentioning those things to the silvery-eyed girl.

We talked. Her name, it developed, was Joanna Caldwell, and she was going as far as Paris. She was an artist, or hoped to be one day, and of course there is no place in the world that can supply both training and inspiration like Paris. So it was there she was bound for a year of study, and despite her demurely humorous lips and laughing eyes, I could see that the business was of vast importance to her. I gathered that she had worked hard for the year in Paris, had scraped and saved for three years as fashion illustrator for some woman's magazine, though she couldn't have been many months over twenty-one. Her painting meant a great deal to her, and I could understand it. I'd felt that way about polo once.

So you see, we were sympathetic spirits from the beginning. I knew that she liked me, and it was obvious that she didn't connect Dixon Wells with the N. J. Wells Corporation. And as for me – well, after that first glance into her cool silver eyes, I simply didn't care to look anywhere else. The hours seemed to drip away like minutes while I watched her.

You know how those things go. Suddenly I was calling her Joanna and she was calling me Dick, and it seemed as if we'd been doing just that all our lives. I'd decided to stop over in Paris on my way back from Moscow, and I'd secured her promise to let me see her. She was different, I tell you; she was nothing like the calculating Whimsy White, and still less like the dancing, simpering, giddy youngsters one meets around at social affairs. She was just Joanna, cool and humorous, yet sympathetic and serious, and as pretty as a Majolica figurine.

We could scarcely realize it when the steward passed along to take orders for luncheon. Four hours out? It seemed like forty minutes. And we had a pleasant feeling of intimacy in the discovery that both of us liked lobster salad and detested oysters. It was another bond; I told her whimsically that it was an omen, nor did she object to considering it so.

Afterwards we walked along the narrow aisle to the glassed-in observation room up forward. It was almost too crowded for entry, but we didn't mind that at all, as it forced us to sit very close together. We stayed long after both of us had begun to notice the stuffiness of the air.

It was just after we had returned to our seats that the catastrophe occurred. There was no warning save a sudden lurch, the result, I suppose, of the pilot's futile last-minute attempt to swerve – just that and then a grinding crash and a terrible sensation of spinning, and after that a chorus of shrieks that were like the sounds of battle.

It was battle. Five hundred people were picking themselves up from the floor, were trampling each other, milling around, being cast helplessly down as the great rocket-plane, its left wing but a broken stub, circled downward toward the Atlantic.

The shouts of officers sounded and a loudspeaker blared. "Be calm," it kept repeating, and then, "There has been a collision. We have contacted a surface ship. There is no danger – There is no danger – "

I struggled up from the debris of shattered seats. Joanna was gone; just as I found her crumpled between the rows, the ship struck the water with a jar that set everything crashing again. The speaker blared, "Put on the cork belts under the seats. The life-belts are under the seats."

I dragged a belt loose and snapped it around Joanna, then donned one myself. The crowd was surging forward now, and the tail end of the ship began to drop. There was water behind us, sloshing in the darkness as the lights went out. An officer came sliding by, stooped, and fastened a belt about an unconscious woman ahead of us. "You all right?" he yelled, and passed on without waiting for an answer.

The speaker must have been cut on to a battery circuit. "And get as far away as possible," it ordered suddenly. "Jump from the forward port and get as far away as possible. A ship is standing by. You will be picked up. Jump from the – " It went dead again.

I got Joanna untangled from the wreckage. She was pale; her silvery eyes were closed. I started dragging her slowly and painfully toward the forward port, and the slant of the floor increased until it was like the slide of a ski-jump. The officer passed again. "Can you handle her?" he asked, and again dashed away.

I was getting there. The crowd around the port looked smaller, or was it simply huddling closer? Then suddenly, a wail of fear and despair went up, and there was a roar of water. The observation room walls had given. I saw the green surge of waves, and a billowing deluge rushed down upon us. I had been late again.

That was all. I raised shocked and frightened eyes from the subjunctivisor to face van Manderpootz, who was scribbling on the edge of the table.

"Well?" he asked.

I shuddered. "Horrible!" I murmured. "We – I guess we wouldn't have been among the survivors."

"We, eh? We?" His eyes twinkled.

I did not enlighten him. I thanked him, bade him goodnight, and went dolorously home.

* * *

Even my father noticed something queer about me. The day I got to the office only five minutes late, he called me in for some anxious questioning as to my health. I couldn't tell him anything, of course. How could I explain that I'd been late once too often, and had fallen in love with a girl two weeks after she was dead?

The thought drove me nearly crazy. Joanna! Joanna with her silvery eyes now lay somewhere at the bottom of the Atlantic. I went around half dazed, scarcely speaking. One night I actually lacked the energy to go home and sat smoking in my father's big overstuffed chair in his private office until I finally dozed off. The next morning, when old N. J. entered and found me there before him, he turned pale as paper, staggered, and gasped, "My heart!" It took a lot of explaining to convince him that I wasn't early at the office but just very late going home.

At last I felt that I couldn't stand it. I had to do something – anything at all. I thought finally of the subjunctivisor. I could see – yes, I could see what would have transpired if the ship hadn't been wrecked! I could trace out that weird, unreal romance hidden somewhere in the worlds of "if". I could, perhaps, wring a somber, vicarious joy from the things that might have been. I could see Joanna once more!

It was late afternoon when I rushed over to van Manderpootz's quarters. He wasn't there; I encountered him finally in the hall of the Physics Building.

"Dick!" he exclaimed. "Are you sick?"

"Sick? No. Not physically. Professor. I've got to use your subjunctivisor again. I've got to!"

"Eh? Oh – that toy. You're too late, Dick. I've dismantled it. I have a better use for the space."

I gave a miserable groan and was tempted to damn the autobiography of the great van Manderpootz. A gleam of sympathy showed in his eyes, and he took my arm, dragging me into the little office adjoining his laboratory.

"Tell me," he commanded.

I did. I guess I made the tragedy plain enough, for his heavy brows knit in a frown of pity. "Not even van Manderpootz can bring back the dead," he murmured. "I'm sorry, Dick. Take your mind from the affair. Even were my subjunctivisor available, I wouldn't permit you to use it. That would be but to turn the knife in the wound." He paused. "Find something else to occupy your mind. Do as van Manderpootz does. Find forgetfulness in work."

"Yes," I responded dully. "But who'd want to read my autobiography? That's all right for you."

"Autobiography? Oh! I remember. No, I have abandoned that. History itself will record the life and works of van Manderpootz. Now I am engaged in a far grander project."

"Indeed?" I was utterly, gloomily disinterested.

"Yes. Gogli has been here, Gogli the sculptor. He is to make a bust of me. What better legacy can I leave to the world than a bust of van Manderpootz, sculptured from life? Perhaps I shall present it to the city, perhaps to the university. I would have given it to the Royal Society if they had been a little more receptive, if they – if – if!" The last in a shout.

"Huh?"

"If!" cried van Manderpootz. "What you saw in the subjunctivisor was what would have happened if you had caught the ship!"

"I know that."

"But something quite different might really have happened! Don't you see? She – she – Where are those old newspapers?"

He was pawing through a pile of them. He flourished one finally. "Here! Here are the survivors!"

Like letters of flame, Joanna Caldwell's name leaped out at me. There was even a little paragraph about it, as I saw once my reeling brain permitted me to read:

"At least a score of survivors owe their lives to the bravery of twenty-eight-year-old Navigator Orris Hope, who patrolled both aisles during the panic, lacing life-belts on the injured and helpless, and carrying many to the port. He remained on the sinking liner until the last, finally fighting his way to the surface through the broken walls of the observation room. Among those who owe their lives to the young officer are: Patrick Owensby, New York City; Mrs Campbell Warren, Boston; Miss Joanna Caldwell, New York City – "

I suppose my shout of joy was heard over in the Administration Building, blocks away. I didn't care; if van Manderpootz hadn't been armored in stubby whiskers, I'd have kissed him. Perhaps I did anyway; I can't be sure of my actions during those chaotic minutes in the professor's tiny office.

At last I calmed. "I can look her up!" I gloated. "She must have landed with the other survivors, and they were all on that British tramp freighter the Osgood, that docked here last week. She must be in New York – and if she's gone over to Paris, I'll find out and follow her!"

Well, it's a queer ending. She was in New York, but – you see, Dixon Wells had, so to speak, known Joanna Caldwell by means of the professor's subjunctivisor, but Joanna had never known Dixon Wells. What the ending might have been if – if – But it wasn't; she had married Orris Hope, the young officer who had rescued her. I was late again.

*

Clockwork Evangeline

Nemma Wollenfang

THE COGS in Evangeline's heart ground into gear as she took to the streets, dancing amidst the myriad workers on the morning commute. Londinium was always crowded at this time of day; the metropolitan hub abuzz with the eclectic sprawl of busy, busy people who braved the cloying smog in their slow-paced herds. But Malaphos would want his tea soon – dark, no sugar, with a sprig of pungent juniper – and it would not do to deliver it late.

"I beg your pardon, sir, madam," she sang as she twirled between those queuing for the 8:55 airship to Marylebone. By the time they turned, she had already flitted away.

Evangeline was like a humming bird, a shimmer of amethyst that was there one second and gone the next, and her movements flowed with a grace and elegance that only mechanical imaginings could achieve.

"Ah, Evangeline!" Malaphos exulted as the bell tinkled on their shop's door.

He was seated at his work-bench, hunched over with a magnifying monocle attached to one eye. It whizzed and whirred as salty hair fell across his face.

"Your tea, Maestro," she said as she set the cup before him.

"Good, good, thank you, my dear." He took a hearty sip and the lines on his face seemed to fade. "I am glad you have returned so swiftly. I have a client due in only ten minutes and we must show her our best work now, mustn't we?"

Evangeline's face lit with delight. When she was happy her very skin seemed to glow. "I will fetch the designs from the Twilight collection at once," she trilled, dancing away.

"You read my mind," he laughed.

Malaphos' Emporium of Extravagant Wonders was, perhaps, a little antiquated. The store was dimly lit and smelt of mothballs, but it was filled to the rafters with the most unusual and marvellous of creations. Evangeline spent most of her time amongst the collections, carefully arranging and cataloguing and admiring all of Malaphos' work. And when she was allowed to display them. Oh! Satin flowed along her skin like water, the caress of velvet made her lips rise, and even the hard stiffness of leather was welcome. Gathering up an armful of corsets and skirts, she flitted downstairs to the main store-front. There, she laid them all out with the utmost care. It would not do to have one crease.

The shop bell tinkled. "Hello, Mr Malaphos?"

"Ah, welcome!" Malaphos cringed as he rose but held his smile. "How can I help?"

A gentleman of no more than thirty years stood on their threshold, with sleek dark hair. He had a handsome face, Evangeline thought, and held himself with the suave sophistication of the upper class. And when he moved he brought with him the scent of roses.

"I have an appointment for 9:10," he said, "under the name Reed?"

"Oh," Malaphos said, "I had been expecting a Mrs Reed. I apologise."

"No need. I made the appointment in my wife's name. I mean to surprise her with a gift for our anniversary and I believe only your..." As his eyes fell to Evangeline he grew silent.

Never a man to anger, no matter the customer, Malaphos smiled kindly and asked, "What is it, sir?" Knowing very well what diverted his attention.

"Oh, forgive me." Mr Reed started. "It's just... I have not encountered a Clockwork Angel before, let alone one so beautiful."

Malaphos smiled. "Evangeline, come meet Mr Reed." With a graceful twirl that flared the black netting of her skirts, she danced to their sides and smiled. "Evangeline is my assistant," he said. "She will showcase our collections for you today."

Even as Malaphos spoke, Evangeline took the gentleman's top-hat, cane and coat, folding the latter across her arm. With a well-practised curtsy, she pirouetted away.

"As you can see, she loves to dance," Malaphos said fondly.

"She does?"

"Oh yes," Malaphos nodded. "Ballet, Latin, Ballroom, Tap, anything."

There was pride in his tone, Evangeline could hear it. To please him she began to pivot, performing the beginning of a slow ballet number she had catalogued in her memory-bank. It was one that seemed to give Malaphos great joy. Swan Lake, she thought it was called.

"She is a mechanical wonder," Mr Reed smiled as he watched. "So life-like, though the hair is a little... unnatural."

Evangeline paused. Should she change it? She could with a thought but she liked the icy white of her straight hair – it shone like the moon – and the length darkened into lilac, then blue, until the tips were midnight black. But if a customer disliked it...

Malaphos frowned. "Evangeline makes her own aesthetic selections. I like to encourage her creativity."

"How fascinating... I meant no offense," Mr Reed assured, eyeing her curiously. Then, with the exaggerated slowness one would use with a child, he said, "It is lovely, and matches your violet eyes so perfectly." To Malaphos, he added, "You struck luck when you acquired this one, only a few were issued of her prototype. I tried to acquire one myself, but alas..."

The way he looked at Evangeline, with such blatant longing, unnerved her a little and the happy glow of her skin dimmed.

"Well, shall we?" Malaphos offered Mr Reed a seat. "Evangeline, if you would...?"

The glow returned. The dresses!

For the next hour she paraded before them in the best of Malaphos' collections. Satin and silk, velvet and corduroy, from earthy moss and rich cocoa to poppy scarlet and the jet black of a beetle's shell.

"...cross-linked, with chains draped across the magenta-black brocade," Malaphos was saying, "an exquisite piece, sir. Evangeline..."

He gestured for her to spin. She did as he bid, allowing the fine fabrics to swish and rustle. She loved the sound his materials made – music to her ears.

"The over-bust corset next if you would, Evangeline, the one with the detachable jacket and belt in tanned leather. Genuine bovine, I assure you, sir."

Brass buckled pieces followed, from their Vintage collection, a menagerie of obsidian dresses with Victorian ruffles and fine velvet overcoats with silver fastenings. Evangeline displayed a steel-boned corset-dress with mercury brocade with particular pride, and wore a zip-liner fascinator with mini-hat to complete the set. Platinum buckles bound the in-seam. Then came the dragon-scales and electrum sheens, crow's feathers and finely-spun metallic spider-webs – from their Luna Gothic collection.

"Hmm," Mr Reed said, "may I see the last one again?"

Holographic enhancements allowed Evangeline to alter her appearance on a whim, and as each change was pre-programmed she could revert in a momentary flash – genuine first, artificial on repeat. As was her prerogative, she matched brown ringlets to the earthy pieces, and whenever she displayed black her silken hair gleamed like ebony, ending in silver tips.

"Some very fine designs, indeed," Mr Reed complimented as he watched. Though, in truth, Evangeline thought that he may have been more interested in her than his purchases. "I am spoilt for choice, though I wonder if your Angel bears quite the same figure as my young wife. I have her measurements written here." He turned to hand Malaphos a crumpled note.

"Evangeline, if you would…" She flitted to comply as Malaphos winced and held his back, taking the paper from Mr Reed. For the briefest second their fingers touched, before she pulled away. "You must excuse this old-timer, sir," Malaphos went on as she handed him the note. "These bones have little strength left in them. Ah yes, we can make these alterations."

"If I may be so bold," Mr Reed suddenly said, his eyes resting on Evangeline, "would there be any price you'd be willing to consider for her?"

That made her start and whip about. Never before had anyone asked!

"For Evangeline?!" Matching shock dominated Malaphos' face, before he managed to quash it with a good-natured laugh. The sound had a brittle edge. "Ah, no. No monetary worth could be placed on her. Evangeline is not only my assistant you see, but a cherished child. She is like a daughter to me, sir."

"Just so." He inclined his head in acceptance. "I meant only to inquire."

The rest of their show went well enough and Mr Reed commissioned six pieces, all in all a good morning's work. As Evangeline re-emerged in her default black attire and ice-white hair, Mr Reed applauded her soundly.

"Very good, very good! You know, a performance by your Clockwork Angel would make a lovely addition to my anniversary celebration ball. It would be quite a spectacle."

Malaphos' eyebrows rose. "Evangeline, dance for a large audience? I don't know…"

"Come now, I guarantee it would garner a great deal of business. My wife and her friends are avid shoppers, and when faced with such a beautiful model…" He winked at Evangeline as he retrieved his hat and coat and opened the door to the steamy street beyond. Outside, a man with chocolate brown goggles in a juddering car awaited his fare. "Think about it," Mr Reed said, holding out a small white slip, "My card."

Malaphos took it from his ivory gloved hand, but as the gentleman left and Malaphos frowned down at the card, he missed the way Mr Reed's eyes lingered on Evangeline, a little too long. Evangeline noticed. And the cogs in her heart stuttered a beat.

* * *

After closing, Evangeline settled into her high-backed chair by the fire while Malaphos locked the main doors and pulled down the shutters. She held the card Mr Reed had left, twirling it between her fingers as she watched the red and gold flames dance.

Since Mr Reed had left, her heart had felt funny. Even now the cogs and gears ground together like ill-fitting puzzle-pieces. She placed a hand to her chest.

"Even my aged ears can hear that racket," Malaphos said as he leant heavily on his eagle-headed cane. "Come, my dear, let me have a look."

Moving to his workbench, she lay down while Malaphos donned his whizzing monocle and opened the hatch in her chest. The noise was louder now, clanking and grating.

"Hmm," Malaphos said, "your gears are a little loose. Have you been anxious today?"

Evangeline did not understand the word. "I have been happy."

He only hummed, and, taking a spanner, began to set wrong to right. It did not take long. As he oiled her heart and tested the gears and cogs, he bore a ponderous frown. "I don't know about this business with Mr Reed," he muttered, shaking his head. "I am happy to do business with the man; he is a reputable tradesman, but to involve you in this show of his..."

Looking to her, his eyes brimmed with some emotion she could not define.

"I care for you, Evangeline. And I worry what will happen when I am no longer here."

"Are you planning to travel?" Evangeline asked with some fright.

"No, no dear. Do not fret." His gaze returned to her clockwork heart. "But one does not always plan some journeys..." Finishing up, he re-fastened her hatch and wiped his oily hands on a cloth. "As to this fashion-show malarkey, I do not know what to think. What would you like to do?"

Evangeline thought of the dresses and the dancing, she thought of pretty ladies and crystal chandeliers and glasses that tinkled as they clinked. "I would like to dance," she said.

"Of course you would," he smiled.

Malaphos had such wonderful eyes, Evangeline thought. Not just for their sky blue clarity, but for their expressiveness. They were neither young nor old; they were ageless.

* * *

Awakening to the bright glow of dawn, Evangeline followed her programming and, passing Malaphos slumped over his desk – he must have worked until he slept, she thought, placing a blanket about his shoulders – she took to the smoky streets in search of tea.

"Dark, no sugar, with a sprig of pungent juniper," she muttered as she danced.

The day was fresh and clear. A steam-train whistled as she passed over its bridge and she was soon returning to Malaphos' Emporium with his drink.

The bell tinkled as she entered, but he did not awaken. Very tired indeed, perhaps... The tea fell to the floor. Dark brown stained the rug.

His skin was pale, too pale, and to the touch, cold. Evangeline blinked, uncertain, but there was no disputing her system summary. Her programming was faultless.

For the rest of the day she stood before him, neither moving nor speaking, as the tea dried to sticky tar. Not daring to utter his name. The sun gave way to the velvet black of night, and a layer of dust settled upon them both.

Evangeline lived for Malaphos and his dress-making. She had no other function.

At the moon's zenith, Evangeline broke her stance. She shifted forward and gently closed his sightless blue eyes. No expression remained. That was when she saw what he held.

In Malaphos' hand lay Mr Reed's business card. Evangeline picked it up.

Biographies & Sources

Edwin A. Abbott
Flatland
(Originally Published by Seeley & Co., 1884)
The English theologian Edwin A. Abbott (1838–1926) is best-known for his mathematical novella *Flatland*, a satirical portrait of the class-structure of Victorian Society told through an exploration of two-dimensional beings. While not hugely successful at the time, the book experienced a later surge in popularity after the idea of a fourth dimension was put forward in Einstein's 'Theory of Relativity'. It has since been regarded as a great contribution to the science fiction genre.

Edward Ahern
The Body Surfer
(Originally Published in *Aphelion*, 2012)
Ed Ahern resumed writing after 40-odd years in foreign intelligence and international sales. He has his original wife, but advises that after 47 years they are both out of warranty. He's had over 80 stories and poems published thus far, as well as two books: his collected fairy and folk tales *The Witch Made Me Do It* (Gypsy Shadow Publishing) and the mystery/horror novella *The Witches' Bane* (World Castle Publishing). Ed speaks German, French and Japanese in that order of proficiency, and dissipates his free time fly-fishing and shooting.

Stewart C. Baker
Behind the First Years
(Originally Published in *COSMOS*, 2013)
Stewart C. Baker is an academic librarian, haikuist and speculative fiction writer. His short stories have appeared in *COSMOS*, *Daily Science Fiction*, *Nature* and *Flash Fiction Online*, and his poetry has appeared in various haiku and speculative magazines. Stewart was born near London, has spent time in South Carolina, Japan and California, and now lives in Western Oregon with his wife and children. You can find more on his website at infomancy.net.

Keyan Bowes
Genetic Changelings
(First Publication)
Keyan Bowes is a peripatetic US-based author. A graduate of the 2007 Clarion Workshop for Science Fiction and Fantasy Writers, Keyan has had work accepted by *Cabinet des Fees*, *Expanded Horizons*, *Big Pulp* and *Strange Horizons*, as well as featuring in ten anthologies. Two stories have appeared in a German and a Polish magazine (in translation). She is currently rewriting two YA novels in the contemporary fantasy adventure genre. 'The Rumpelstiltskin Retellings', a story in poetry-blog format, was made into an award-winning short film. (www.keyanbowes.com)

Beth Cato
Overlap
(Originally Published in *Cucurbital 3*, Paper Golem, 2012)
Beth Cato hails from Hanford, California, but currently writes and bakes cookies in a lair west of Phoenix, Arizona. She shares the household with a hockey-loving husband,

a numbers-obsessed son and a cat the size of a canned ham. She's the author of *The Clockwork Dagger* (a 2015 finalist for the Locus Award for Best First Novel) and *The Clockwork Crown* from Harper Voyager. Her short fiction is in *Beneath Ceaseless Skies*, *InterGalactic Medicine Show* and other venues. Follow her at *BethCato.com* and on Twitter at @BethCato.

Ray Cummings

Phantoms of Reality

(Originally Published in *Astounding Stories of Super-Science*, 1930)

Ray Cummings (1887–1957) was born in New York City, and was a successful writer during the era of Pulp-magazine science fiction. He wrote his fiction under a number of different pen names, and produced over 700 stories during his lifetime. While in his twenties, he worked for five years as a personal assistant to Thomas Edison, acting also as a technical writer for him. When his writing career began to decline, he turned to producing comic book scripts, remaining a stable figure on the science fiction scene.

Arthur Conan Doyle

The Disintegration Machine

(Originally Published in *The Strand Magazine*, 1929)

Arthur Conan Doyle (1859–1930) was born in Edinburgh, Scotland. As a medical student he was so impressed by his professor's powers of deduction that he was inspired to create the illustrious and much-loved figure Sherlock Holmes. Later Doyle became increasingly interested in spiritualism, leaving him keen to explore fantastical elements in his stories. Paired with his talent for storytelling he wrote great tales of terror, such as 'The Horror of Heights' and 'The Leather Funnel'. Doyle's vibrant and remarkable characters have breathed life into all of his stories, engaging readers throughout the decades.

E.M. Forster

The Machine Stops

(Originally Published in *The Oxford and Cambridge Review*, 1909)

Edward Morgan Forster (1879–1970) was born in London, England. Falling in love with the Mediterranean at a young age during visits to Italy and Greece, many of Forster's works feature these cultures. He is known for his use of irony, in novels that often address Realism and Modernism. His science fiction short story 'The Machine Stops' was voted one of the best novellas up to 1965. Nominated for the Nobel Prize in Literature on 13 different occasions, Forster's most successful novels include *A Passage to India* and *A Room with a View*.

H. Rider Haggard

Smith and the Pharaohs

(Originally Published in *Smith And the Pharaohs, And Other Tales*, Longmans, Green & Co., 1921)

Sir Henry Rider Haggard (1856–1925) was born in Norfolk, England. Best-known for his adventure novels set in exotic locations, Haggard is considered a pioneer in the Lost World literary genre. He spent some years in South Africa, after which he wrote his most famous novel *King Solomon's Mines*, which was the first English adventure novel set in Africa. Later on in his life Haggard was appointed as a Knight Bachelor and Knight Commander for his services to the British Empire.

Sarah Hans

Rest in Peace

(Originally Published in *Bless your Mechanical Heart*, Evil Girlfriend Media, 2014)

Sarah Hans is an award-winning editor, author and teacher. Sarah's short stories have appeared in about a dozen publications, but she's best known for her multicultural steampunk anthology *Steampunk World*, which appeared on *io9*, *Boing Boing* and *Entertainment Weekly Online* and won the 2015 Steampunk Chronicle Reader's Choice Award for Best Fiction. You can find Sarah floating in the ether above Columbus, Ohio, or online at sarahhans.com.

Rob Hartzell

The Hives and the Hive-Nots

(First Publication)

Rob Hartzell is a graduate of the University of Alabama MFA program. He lives and works in Morrow, Ohio, and is presently at work on a story cycle entitled *Pictures of the Floating-Point World*, from which 'The Hives and the Hive-Nots' is taken. Rob is also trying to find a home for his novel *The Virtual Book of the Dead*. His work has most recently appeared, or will appear, at *Milkfist*, *The Black Rabbit* and the *Startling Sci-Fi: New Tales of the Beyond* anthology from New Salon Lit Publications.

Alexis A. Hunter

The Vast Weight of Their Bleeding Hearts

(Originally Published in *Goldfish Grimm's Spicy Fiction Sushi*, 2013

Alexis A. Hunter revels in the endless possibilities of speculative fiction. She frequently writes stories featuring robots, artificial intelligences and synthetic life. Her current inspirations are A. Merc Rustad and Natalia Theodoridou – both of these writers deliver powerful tales, gorgeously rendered with depths Alexis hopes to achieve in her own works. Over fifty of Alexis' short stories have appeared recently in *Shimmer*, *Flash Fiction Online*, *Fantastic Stories of the Imagination* and more. To learn more, visit www.alexisahunter.com.

Rachael K. Jones

Makeisha in Time

(Originally Published in *Crossed Genres*, 2014)

Rachael K. Jones is a speculative fiction author living with her husband in Athens, Georgia. A winner of the 'Writers of the Future' contest, her work has appeared or is forthcoming in many venues, including *Shimmer*, *Lightspeed*, *Accessing the Future*, *Strange Horizons*, *Escape Pod*, *Crossed Genres*, *Diabolical Plots*, *InterGalactic Medicine Show*, *Fantastic Stories of the Imagination*, *The Drabblecast* and *Daily Science Fiction*. She is the co-editor of *PodCastle*, is a SFWA member and is also a secret android. Follow her on Twitter @RachaelKJones.

Henry Kuttner

The Ego Machine

(Originally Published in *Space Science Fiction*, 1952)

A friend of H.P. Lovecraft, Henry Kuttner (1915–58) was an American author who contributed a number of stories to the Cthulhu mythos. Kuttner was born in Los Angeles, California, and met his wife C.L. Moore – another prolific science fiction and fantasy writer – through the 'Lovecraft Circle'. The pair often collaborated closely on projects, writing together under a range of pseudonyms, including 'Lewis Padgett'. Kuttner's tales are good examples of Lovecraftian Horror, most famously perhaps being his short story 'The Graveyard Rats'.

Jacob M. Lambert
The Julius Directive
Originally Published in *Encounters Magazine*, 2015)
First place recipient of the Scott and Zelda Fitzgerald short story award, Jacob M. Lambert has published with *Midnight Echo: The Magazine of the Australian Horror Writers Association*, *Siren's Call Publications* and more. He lives in Montgomery, Alabama, where he teaches English Composition and is an editorial assistant for *The Scriblerian and the Kit-Cats*, an academic journal pertaining to English literature of the late seventeenth-and early eighteenth-century. When not writing, he enjoys time with his wife, Stephanie, and daughter, Annabelle.

Jack London
The Shadow and the Flash
(Originally Published in *The Bookman*, 1903)
The American author John Griffith 'Jack' London (1876–1916) was a successful fiction author, journalist and war correspondent. Considered a pioneer in commercial magazine fiction, London was also a social activist and journalist. London was also a member of the radical San Francisco literary group 'The Crowd'. He wrote his first successful stories while in the Klondike, where he was joined the group mining for gold. His short stories are well regarded and contributed to his becoming a literary celebrity during his lifetime.

Adrian Ludens
Metsys
(Originally Published in *Chrome Baby*, 2013)
Adrian Ludens is a dark fiction author who lives with his family in Rapid City, South Dakota. A member of the Horror Writers Association his favorite and recent anthology stories include: *Blood Lite III: Aftertaste* (Pocket Books), *Shadows Over Main Street* (Hazardous Press), *Darker Edge of Desire* (Tempted Romance), *Insidious Assassins* (Smart Rhino Publications), *Surreal Worlds* (Bizarro Pulp Press) and the *Mammoth Book of Jack the Ripper Stories*. Visit him at www.adrianludens.com.

Edward Page Mitchell
The Tachypomp
(Originally Published in *The Sun*, 1874)
Pioneer of the science fiction genre, Edward Page Mitchell (1852–1927) was a short story writer and editor for *The Sun* newspaper in New York. His work featured predominantly in *The Sun*, and most of his stories were published anonymously. 'The Tachypomp' was at first printed without attribution. His story 'The Clock That Went Backward', which is a contender for the first time-travel story and predates H.G. Wells's *The Time Machine*, was also published anonymously in *The Sun* and Mitchell wasn't revealed as the author until forty years after his death.

Mike Morgan
Fishing Expedition
(First Publication)
Mike was born in London, England, but has also lived in Stoke-on-Trent, Japan, Houston and Iowa. He has been writing for many years, but most recently has had work accepted by

Pole-to-Pole Publishing, Uffda Press and Martian Wave. When he's not writing short stories, Mike is a regular contributor of articles about science fiction TV and movies to the website *WhatCulture.com*, where he has accumulated 1.5 million views. You can follow him on Twitter @CultTVMike.

Philip Francis Nowlan
Buck Rogers' First Adventure: Armageddon – 2419 AD
(Originally Published in *Amazing Stories*, 1928)
Born in Philadelphia, Pennsylvania, science fiction author Philip Francis Nowlan (1888–1940) originally worked as a newspaper columnist. He wrote the novella *Armageddon – 2419 A.D.*, which involved the first appearance of the fictional character 'Anthony Rogers', a space explorer who became known as 'Buck Rogers' in the hugely popular comic strip that followed. The character made a lasting imprint on American popular culture, with the comic strip running for over forty years. As a result, Nowlan is most famously associated with Buck Rogers, although he is also remembered for writing fiction that consistently featured strong female characters.

Kate O'Connor
Red
(Originally Published in *Penumbra*, 2012)
Kate O'Connor was born in Virginia in 1982. She graduated with a degree in Aeronautics from Embry-Riddle Aeronautical University, Prescott, and now lives in the New York area. Kate has been writing science fiction and fantasy since 2011. In between telling stories, she flies airplanes, digs up artifacts (as an archaeology field technician) and manages a kennel full of Airedales. Her short fiction has most recently appeared in *Accessing the Future, Intergalactic Medicine Show, Escape Pod*, and *Daily Science Fiction*.

H. Beam Piper
Time and Time Again
(Originally Published in *Astounding Science Fiction*, 1947)
Henry Beam Piper (1904–64) was born in Altoona, Pennsylvania. Piper wrote a great number of short stories and novels throughout his short but memorable career. He took an extreme interest in science and history, and developed into a very well known science fiction writer. He is best known for his *Terro-Human Future History* series, which included the novels *Space Viking* and *The Cosmic Computer*, his *Fuzzy* series that began with *Little Fuzzy*, and his *Kalvan* novel *Lord Kalvan of Otherwhen*, which formed part of his *Paratime* series.

Conor Powers-Smith
Nude Descending an Elevator Shaft
(Originally Published on The Tomorrow Project website, 2013)
Conor Powers-Smith grew up in New Jersey and Ireland. He currently lives on Cape Cod, in Massachusetts, where he works as a reporter. His stories have appeared in *AE, Daily Science Fiction, Nature* and other magazines, as well as several anthologies. He is a big fan of science, especially evolutionary biology and theoretical physics, and wishes he had paid more attention in school. Most of his favourite speculative fiction was written by Wells, Vonnegut, Pratchett, Lovecraft, King, Huxley, Bradbury, or Adams.

Arthur B. Reeve

The Invisible Ray

(Originally Published in *The Poisoned Pen: The Further Adventures of Craig Kennedy*, Dodd, Mead and Company, 1911)

Arthur B. Reeve (1880–1936), one of the first authors to merge an element of science into the mystery genre, was born in Patchogue, New York. After attending New York Law School, he used much of his gained knowledge to write his science fiction and mystery novels. This led to his creation of "The American Sherlock Holmes", the character Professor Craig Kennedy, who featured in many subsequent short stories. Reeve is also known for his newspaper reporting and for co-writing the film script for *The Mastery Mystery*, which went on to star Harry Houdini.

Andy Sawyer

Foreword: Science Fiction Short Stories

Andy Sawyer is the Science Fiction Collections Librarian in the University of Liverpool Library, responsible for the Science Fiction Foundation Collection – the largest resource of SF and material about SF in the UK. Until 2012, he was also Course Director of the University's M.A. in Science Fiction Studies program. As a critic and editor he writes especially on science fiction and fantasy.

Zach Shephard

Sweet Dreams, Glycerine

(First Publication)

Zach Shephard lives in Enumclaw, Washington, where he plays board games, gorges on ice cream and spends the entire summer looking forward to fall. He believes recreational reading is best done at state parks, preferably in close proximity to flowing water. Zach's fiction has appeared in *Intergalactic Medicine Show*, *Weird Tales*, *Daily Science Fiction* and the *Unidentified Funny Objects* anthology series. He's a big fan of Roger Zelazny, and would probably never have started writing if not for the battered copy of *Nine Princes in Amber* on his bookshelf.

David Tallerman

Jenny's Sick

(Originally Published in *Lightspeed Magazine*, 2010)

David Tallerman is the author of the comic fantasy novels *Giant Thief*, *Crown Thief* and *Prince Thief*, the absurdist steampunk graphic novel *Endangered Weapon B: Mechanimal Science* and *The Sign in the Moonlight and Other Stories*, a collection of pulp-styled horror and dark fantasy fiction. His short fantasy, science fiction and horror stories have appeared in around seventy markets, including *Clarkesworld*, *Nightmare*, *Lightspeed* and *Beneath Ceaseless Skies*, and his genre-bending debut novella *Patchwerk* is due from *Tor.com* in early 2016. David can be found online at davidtallerman.co.uk and davidtallerman.blogspot.com.

Brian Trent

Shortcuts

(Originally Published in *COSMOS*, 2014)

Brian Trent is a prolific writer whose fiction appears regularly in *ANALOG*, *Fantasy & Science Fiction*, *Daily Science Fiction*, *Escape Pod*, *COSMOS*, *Galaxy's Edge*, *Nature*, *Crossed Genres* and more. He was a 2013 winner in the 'Writer of the Future' contest and a 2013 winner for Story of the Year from *Apex Magazine*. His literary influences are varied, and his interests include technology, classical history and sociology – particularly the interplay between all three. Brian lives in New England, where he is a novelist, poet and screenwriter.

Patrick Tumblety

A Life As Warm As Death

(First Publication)

Patrick's writing explores psychological horror and its ongoing battle against the human spirit. His work has been described as being able to deliver both 'genuine fear and genuine hope.' (Amy H. Sturgis – Award Winning Author). His first published release was 2012's *Dark Passages*, a collection of original thrillers. Since his debut, his work has been featured in a variety of notable publications, such as Ross E. Lockhart's *Tales of Jack The Ripper* from Word Horde Press, *Miseria's Chorale* by Forgotten Tomb Press and *Fossil Lake* from Sabledrake Enterprises, edited by Christine Morgan. Patrick's work also appears in film, television and photography. He currently lives in Delaware with his wife, Kathleen, and their cat, Dusty.

Mark Twain

Captain Stormfield's Visit to Heaven

(Originally Published in *Harper's Magazine*, 1907)

Mark Twain (1835–1910), whose real name was Samuel Langhorne Clemens, was born in Florida, Missouri, and has become one of America's most famous literary icons. Twain found his love for writing when working for his older brother's newspaper company, and claimed the inspiration for his pen name came from his days as a river pilot on the Mississippi river. Having written 28 books, several humorous short stories and many letters and sketches, his most famous works include *The Adventures of Tom Sawyer* and *The Adventures of Huckleberry Finn*. Also writing in the science fiction genre, he is cherished for his prediction of something akin to the Internet in his 1898 short story called 'From The "London Times" in 1904'.

Donald Jacob Uitvlugt

Butterfly Dreams

(Originally Published in *Crossed Genres*, 2010)

Donald Jacob Uitvlugt lives on neither coast of the United States, but mostly in a haunted memory palace of his own design. His short fiction has appeared in print and online venues such as *Havok Magazine* and AnotherDimensionMag.com, as well as the forthcoming anthology *Mark of the Beast*. He also regularly serves as a judge at the weekly one-on-one writing competition at TheWritersArena.com. Donald strives to write what he calls "haiku fiction": stories small in scope but big in impact. If you enjoyed 'Butterfly Dreams', let him know at his blog haikufiction.blogspot.com or via Twitter @haikufictiondju.

Jules Verne

The Day of an American Journalist in 2889

(Originally Published in *Forum*, 1889)

Jules Verne (1828–1905) was born in Nantes, France. As a novelist, poet and playwright, he wrote adventure novels and had a big impact on the science fiction genre. Along with H.G. Wells, Verne is considered to be one of the founding fathers of science fiction. His most famous adventure novels formed the series *Voyages Extraordinaires*, and include *Journey to the Center of the Earth* and *Twenty Thousand Leagues Under the Sea*. These had a big impact on the Surrealist movement as well as the literary scene, and numerous explorers and scientists would cite his books as inspirational. His works continue to be popular today, and Verne ranks as the most translated science fiction author to date, with his works often reprinted and adapted for film.

Edgar Wallace
Planetoid 127
(Originally Published in *The Mechanical Boy*, 1924)
Described by *The Economist* as a prolific thriller writer of the twentieth century, Richard Horatio Edgar Wallace (1875–1932) was born in Greenwich, London. Recognized as the creator of *King Kong*, Wallace was born in poverty but developed a name for himself as a war correspondent and crime writer, and became one of the most popular authors in the world. He produced an extensive list of novels, short stories, poems, screen and stage plays, as well as his journalistic writings. While more than 160 films have now been made based on Wallace's works, he died before *King Kong* was fully developed for the screen.

M. Darusha Wehm
The Care and Feeding of Mammalian Bipeds, v. 2.1
(Originally Published in *Escape Pod*, 2012)
M. Darusha Wehm is the three-time Parsec Award shortlisted author of the novels *Beautiful Red*, *Self Made*, *Act of Will* and *The Beauty of Our Weapons*. Her most recent novel, *Children of Arkadia* (Bundoran Press), is now available everywhere. Her short fiction has appeared in many venues, including *Andromeda Spaceways Inflight Magazine*, *Toasted Cake* and *Escape Pod*. She is the editor of the crime and mystery magazine *Plan B*. She is originally from Canada but currently lives in Wellington, New Zealand, after spending the past several years traveling at sea on her sailboat. For more information visit darusha.ca.

Stanley G. Weinbaum
The Worlds of If
(Originally Published in *Wonder Stories*, 1935)
Stanley G. Weinbaum (1902–35) was an American science fiction writer born in Louisville, Kentucky. Never graduating from college, he still became a widely influential writer and is especially recognized for his 1934 science fiction story 'A Martian Odyssey'. His short story 'The Adaptive Ultimate' was turned into the famous film *She Devil*, and it has also been adapted into a television series and performed as part of an anthology show. After his tragic death from lung cancer, a crater in Mars was named in his honour.

Nemma Wollenfang
Clockwork Evangeline
(Originally Published on Titan Books online, 2014)
'Clockwork Evangeline' is Nemma's prize-winning story. It won first place in the Steampunk Style Short Story Competition 2014 run by *Steampunk Journal* and was published online by Titan Books. An MSc postgraduate of Vector Biology and Parasitology, she studied at Keele, Salford and Manchester Universities. Her work has been long/shortlisted on several occasions and has appeared or is upcoming in 18 different publications, including: *Come Into the House* (Corazon Books), *A Bleak New World* (Raven International Publishing) and *Calliope Magazine*. Her unpublished novel was also shortlisted for the Writers' Village International Novel Award in 2014. Follow her on twitter: @NemmaW.

FLAME TREE PUBLISHING
Short Story Series
New & Classic Writing

**Flame Tree's Gothic Fantasy books offer a carefully curated series of
new titles, each with combinations of original and classic writing:**

Chilling Horror Short Stories
Chilling Ghost Short Stories
Science Fiction Short Stories
Murder Mayhem Short Stories
Crime & Mystery Short Stories
Swords & Steam Short Stories
Dystopia Utopia Short Stories
Supernatural Horror Short Stories
Lost Worlds Short Stories
Time Travel Short Stories
Heroic Fantasy Short Stories
Pirates & Ghosts Short Stories
Agents & Spies Short Stories
Endless Apocalypse Short Stories
Alien Invasion Short Stories

**as well as new companion titles which offer rich collections of
classic fiction and legendary tales:**

H.G. Wells Short Stories • *Lovecraft Short Stories*
Sherlock Holmes Collection • *Edgar Allan Poe Collection*
Bram Stoker Horror Stories • *Celtic Myths & Tales*
Norse Myths & Tales • *Greek Myths & Tales*
King Arthur & The Knights of the Round Table

Available from all good bookstores, worldwide, and online at
flametreepublishing.com

...and coming soon:

FLAME TREE PRESS | FICTION WITHOUT FRONTIERS
New and original writing in Horror, Crime, SF and Fantasy